Not Fade Away

Also by
Jim Dodge

FUP
STONE JUNCTION

NOT FADE AWAY

JIM DODGE

GROVE PRESS
NEW YORK

DISCLAIMER

This is a work of fiction. Some of the animating facts have been altered to protect the privacy of individuals and communities.

FIRST GROVE PRESS PAPERBACK EDITION

Published simultaneously in Canada
Printed in the United States of America

Library of Congress Cataloging-in-Publication Data
Dodge, Jim.
  Not fade away.
  I. Title.
PS3554.0335N6   1987   813'.54   87-1859
ISBN 0-8021-3584-6

Design by Laura Hammond Hough

Grove Press
841 Broadway
New York, NY 10003

98 99 00 01 10 9 8 7 6 5 4 3 2 1

This one's going out for Mom, brother Bob, and Victoria (that's right: dedicated to the one I love); for Jacoba, Leonard, and Lynn; for Sylvia, Boney Maroni, and Peggy Sue; for Jeremiah, Jerry, and Jack; Freeman and Nina; Gary, Allen, Lew, and John; for Boots, Annie, Dick, Joe, and all the cats and kitties down at the Tastee-Freeze on a hot summer night; for all the players and dancers and pilgrims of the faith; in memory of Ed O'Conner and Darrell Gray; and to the great spirits of Buddy Holly, Ritchie Valens, and the Big Bopper, R.I.P.

ACKNOWLEDGMENTS

I wish to thank the following people for their gracious assistance in the preparation of this manuscript:

Charles Walk, now publisher of the *Helena Independent Record*, who was the first reporter at the scene of the February 3, 1959, plane crash, and whose story was picked up by the major wire services;

Jean Wallace of the Beaumont Library for her unstinting professional aid and encouragement in the course of my laggardly research;

Eric Gerber of the *Houston Post* for little details that were a big help;

Dr. Alfonso Rodriguez Lopez for medical care and understanding;

Gary Snyder, for background and foreground and a lot of ground in between;

a number of friends whose early readings of the manuscript were uniformly marked by acumen and uncommon tact—Leonard Charles, Richard Cortez Day, Morgan Entrekin, Bob Funt, Jeremiah Gorsline, Michael Helm, Jack Hitt, Freeman House and Nina, Jerry Martien, Lynn Milliman, and Victoria Stockley;

Anne Rumsey, for coordinating permissions and envelopes within envelopes;

Gary Fisketjon, for his sweet heart and sharp pencil;

and Melanie Jackson, for keeping together what tends to fly apart.
My gratitude.

"... music, sweet music ..."
—*Martha and the Vandellas,*
"Dancing in the Street"

PROLOGUE

"To the understanding of such days and events this additional narrative becomes necessary, like a real figure to walk beside a ghost."

—Haniel Long,
Interlinear to Cabeza de Vaca

The day didn't begin well. I woke up at first light with a throbbing brain-core headache, fever and chills, dull pains in all bodily tissues, gagging flashes of nausea, a taste in my mouth like I'd eaten a pound of potato bugs, aching eye sockets, and a general feeling of basic despair. This deepened with the realization that I had to get out of bed, drive a long way on bad roads, negotiate a firewood deal, and then drive back home to the ranch, where I still had my own winter's wood to get in. If I'd had a phone I would've instantly canceled the meeting, but since the ranch was too far out in the hills for the phone company to bother with, and because it had taken me a week to set up the meeting with Jack Strauss, who was driving all the way over from Napa, there was no choice. Besides, Strauss was going to front me $1000 on twenty-five cords, which was $993 more than I had, but about $4000 short of what would've satisfied my creditors. At the mere thought of my finances, despair collapsed into doom. Compelled by circumstance, I arose, dressed, stepped outside, and greeted the day by lurching over behind the empty woodshed and throwing up.

The dawning sky was black with roiling nimbus, wind gusting from the south: rain any minute. I let out the chickens, threw them some scratch, split kindling, and moaned through the rest of the morning chores. Back in the house, I started a fire in the woodstove and put on the tea kettle, then scrabbled through a cupboard till I found my first-aid kit, in which, against all temptation, I'd stashed a single Percodan. Though it looked small and forlorn in the bottom of the vial, I swallowed it with gratitude. I was sending a sowbug against Godzilla, but anything would be an improvement.

I hurt. Since I had taken neither drink nor drug for a week—another depressing realization—I assumed I'd fallen victim to the virus sweeping our rural community. People were calling this one the Smorgasbord Flu, because that's how the bug regarded the body; in some cases the feast had gone on for weeks. The thought of weeks made my stomach start to twist again, but I bore down, fighting it back. To lose the Percodan would've killed me.

Feeling slightly more in command after my show of will, I choked down some tea and dry toast, damped the stove, and then oozed out to my '66 Ford pick-up to begin the long drive to the meeting with Strauss in Monte Rio.

The truck wouldn't start.

I took the long-bladed screwdriver off the dash and got out. Hunched down under the left fender-well, I beat on the electric fuel pump till it began clicking.

The truck started at the same moment as the rain. I switched on the wipers. They didn't work. I got out again and pried up the hood and used the screwdriver to beat on the wiper motor till the blades jerked into motion like the wings of a pelican goosed into flight. I was on my way.

My way, I should explain, is always long. I live deep in the coastal hills of Sonoma County, out where the hoot owls court the chickens, on a nine-hundred-acre ranch that's been in the family for five generations. The house was built in 1859 and still lacks all those new-fangled modern amenities like indoor plumbing and electricity. You can reach the ranch on eight miles of mean dirt road that runs along the ridgetop, or by a two-hour pack from the coast on a steep, overgrown trail. The nearest neighbor is seven miles away. Where the dirt road hits the county road, it's another six miles of twisty one-lane blacktop to the mailbox, and nine more to the nearest store. I live in the country because I like it, but bouncing down the dirt road that morning, my brain shrieking at every jolt, I would have rented a townhouse condo in a hot second, faster if it was near a hospital.

To distract myself from misery, I tuned in a San Francisco station and listened to the early morning traffic report—already snarled up on the Bay Bridge, a stalled car blocking the Army Street on-ramp—but for once it didn't console me. The Percodan, however, was getting there, or at least the pain seemed to be moving away.

By the time I hit the paved county road just past the Chuckstons' place, I was feeling like I might make it. The rain continued, a determined drizzle. Lulled by the smoothness of pavement, mesmerized by the metronomic slap of the wipers, perhaps a bit lost in my appreciation of the Percodan, I didn't see the deer until I was almost on top of him, a big three-point buck with a rut-swollen neck. He leapt clear in a burst of terrified grace as I simultaneously hit the brakes and a slick spot on the road, snapped sideways, fishtailed once, twice, and slammed into a redwood stump on the righthand shoulder. My head smacked off the steering wheel and recoiled backwards just in time to meet my .20-gauge flying off the gunrack. The twin blows knocked me goofier than a woodrat on ether. I dimly remember feeling lost in some pulsating forest, looking for my mind, tormented by the knowledge I needed my mind to find my mind and that's why nothing seemed to make the tiniest bit of sense. Then a blessed rush of adrenalin burned the murk away. I opened the truck door and slid out, jelly legged but standing, hurting but still alive.

The drizzle on my face was refreshing. I paused a moment, then started walking toward town, holding my thumb out even though there was no sign of a car in either direction. I'd gone a half-mile before I realized my best move was to walk back to the Chuckstons' place. They had a CB I could use to call for help. I needed help.

The rain thickened from drizzle to drops. As I walked, I absently kept touching my head, thinking the rainwater was blood, brain leakage, or something equally vital seeping from my skull.

I stopped when I got back to my truck. I hadn't checked for damage, and was suddenly taken by the wild hope it might be driveable, a hope horribly dashed by a closer look: the right-front fender, mashed against the wheel; the tie-rod badly bent; steering knuckle broken. I trudged on.

Nobody was home at the Chuckstons' place—they'd probably left early to gather sheep—but the spare key was still where it had been when I'd taken care of their house the summer before. I wiped my muddy boots on the welcome mat and let myself in. I turned on the CB and tried to think who to call, somebody with both a CB and a phone.

Donnie. Donnie Schatzburg. He came right back like he'd been waiting for me all morning.

I explained what had happened, gave him the location of the truck, and asked him to call Itchman's Garage in Guerneville to send out a tow—if not Itchman's, Bailey's on the coast.

Donnie was back in five minutes with ugly news: both of Itchman's trucks were already out and had calls backed up, so it was liable to be a couple of hours at best and there was no answer at Bailey's.

Donnie kept asking if I was all right, and offering to come over and lend a hand, but I assured him I was broken but unbent, which was much more jaunty than I felt now that the adrenalin was wearing off. I asked him if he'd call the Kozy Korner Kitchen in Monte Rio and leave a message for Jack Strauss that I'd crashed and would call him at home as soon as possible. Donnie said he'd be glad to, and I signed off with heartfelt thanks.

I walked back to my wreck to wait for the tow truck. Why I didn't arrange to wait at the house I still lack the wit to explain. The rain had turned hard and relentless, a three-day storm settling in. I hunched up in the damp cab and considered my situation. In the brightest light I could imagine, it was bleak. I wondered if I could possibly risk using my Visa card. I was pretty certain I'd violated my credit limit long ago, and was sure I hadn't paid them in five months, but this was an emergency. I could ride into Guerneville with the tow truck, rent a car, go to a motel, call Strauss for new arrangements, sleep, meet him the next day and pick up the $1000 in front, buy flu drugs, drive the renter home, stay in bed recovering till the truck was fixed, cut wood like a maniac, sweat profusely, spend most of the money I'd make just to pay for the truck repairs, but without the truck I couldn't cut wood, and no wood, no money. Money. I checked my wallet. One piece of bad plastic and seven bucks in cash. I leaned my head against the steering wheel and whimpered. I wanted my mommy.

That's when I heard the roar. My head snapped up, instantly alert, senses flared. Through the rain-blurred windshield a grey hulk took form, grew larger, denser, the roar taking on a mass of its own, all of it coming right at my face. Without thinking I hit the door and rolled across the road. I came up on all fours in the drainage ditch, poised to flee, fight, shit, or go blind.

A large truck was hurtling down the straight stretch of road. I threw myself against the embankment, pressing myself into the root-clotted clay. At the moment I moved, the truck's rear end locked up; it shimmied for a heartbeat, then the rear end came around in a slow arc, 180°, rubber squealing on the wet pavement, water squeegee'd into a thin roostertail. The whole mass of the truck shuddered against the brakes and slid to a smooth stop, direction reversed, its back end no more than two feet from the twisted front bumper of my truck. I stared, flash-frozen in the moment. It was a tow truck, a big tow truck, all painted a pearly metal-flake grey. Within a thin-line oval on the driver's door, written in a flowing ivory script, it read: THE GHOST.

I felt like I was filling with helium, hovering at the threshold between gravity and ascent. I heard voices chanting in the rain, women's voices, but no words came clear.

There was vague movement behind the fogged side-window of the tow truck, then the door flew open and a ghost leaped out.

I died.

Death laughed and sent me back.

I felt rain on my eyelids. It didn't feel baptismal, holy, or otherwise spiritually endowed; just wet. I felt a warm hand clamped firmly to my wrist. Another touched my cheek. I opened my eyes. Instead of a ghost, it was the tow truck driver, his face and form obscured in a hooded, wind-billowed poncho, the grey oilcloth lustred with rain.

"Well, well: life goes on." That was the first thing George Gastin said to me. He seemed genuinely pleased.

I groaned.

"Yes indeed," he continued, "it *does* go on, don't it now, moment to moment and breath to breath. Looks like Death shot at you and missed and shit at you and didn't, but you'll likely live. Your pulse is outstanding and your color's coming back. Just take it slow and easy. You're in the good hands of the Ghost and the situation is under control . . . or as much control as usual, which—truth be told—is hardly at all, just barely any, one wet thread. But it's certainly enough for our purposes this glorious morning, so hang on here and we'll see if your feet still reach the ground."

He eased me to my feet, a steadying hand on my shoulder. I was soaked, shivering, weak, confused. Everything but his voice and touch seemed blurred. I took a deep, trembling breath. "I'm sick," I told him. "Flu. Wasn't hurt in the wreck."

"That lump on your forehead? That the flu, or just your third eye coming out for a peek?"

"I've seen enough," I said.

He chuckled and patted me on the back, a gesture at once consoling and oddly jovial. "That's the spirit," he said. "You're a mess now, but you'll be laughing about it in fifty years."

"I'll make it," I said bravely. I actually did feel better with my feet back under me.

"Yup," George agreed, "nothing stronger than the will to live. We'll get that truck hooked on and hauled down the line, but let's get you fixed up first." And in a voice calm, direct, and decisive, the shapeless figure swept me gladly into his command. "Start off, we get your ass dry from flopping around in mud puddles." He measured me with a glance. "I pack spare duds, but you look a little on the stubby side of my frame. 'Course this ain't Wilkes-Bashford either, so fuck fashion in the face of need, and fuck it anyway just on good general principles."

He opened a tool bay on the side of his truck and took out a small duffel bag, then reached back inside and removed what looked like a floppy green plastic envelope. "Okay, listen up: strip outside and throw your wet clothes in the bag"—he gave the green envelope a shake and it billowed into a large plastic trash sack—"and leave it outside for me to take care of. When you're stripped down, climb in the cab there where I got the heater humming and put on some dry clothes from the duffel. Should be a towel in there, too. While you're making yourself presentable, I'll survey the damage here."

I appreciated his crisp, step-by-step instructions. I needed them. I was not thinking in an orderly fashion. However, as I stripped off my soggy clothes and stuffed them in the plastic sack as instructed, the cold rain pelting my goose-pimpled flesh seemed to draw me together and steady my wobbling attention.

The cab was a rush of warmth, and strong odors of orange peel and coffee, and a more subtle fragrance, faintly rank, like rotting seaweed or old axle grease. I unzipped the duffel bag. The towel was neatly folded on top. I unfurled it: a huge beach towel, fluffy white, HOTEL HAVANA in maroon block letters emblazoned down the center. I dried off, then wrestled myself into the clothes. The legs of the black Can't-Bust-'Ems and the sleeves of the green-plaid flannel shirt were a little long, but not bad. The grey down vest and sheepskin slippers fit perfectly.

I leaned back, letting the warmth soak toward my bones. Chains rattled behind me, followed by the clank and clunk of couplings, a hydraulic hiss. The truck shuddered slightly as the cable wound up. I turned and watched through the rear window as the mangled front end of my truck rose into view. This wasn't something I wanted to look at, so I turned around and shut my eyes. In a minute or so we'd be on our way. In a couple of hours I'd be asleep in a motel room. Tomorrow there might be money to pay for all of it. The chickens would have to look out for themselves. I wondered if there was a doctor in Geurneville who would prescribe Percodan for the flu.

I was drifting away when a tool bay opened and then slammed shut along the driver's side. George, quick, smooth, slid in behind the wheel, his poncho gone. He glanced at me and recoiled, feigning surprise: "My God, it *was* human. What say we haul in that mess you made—I'd guess you're looking at six bills in fix-it-up."

No ghost at all. Flesh and blood. He was maybe 5'10", 165, angular and lean, but a shade too compact to qualify as gangly. His poncho gone, I saw we were dressed almost exactly alike, except his pants were so faded the grease spots were darker than the fabric, and his grey down vest was scabbed with patches of silver duct tape. The only true difference was our footwear: he was wearing a pair of black high-top Converse All-Stars, a classic I hadn't seen since my last high school gym class.

When I didn't speak, he gave me a frank, appraising look—the first time I'd really noticed his eyes. They were a remarkable blue, the color of the sky on a scorching summer afternoon, almost translucent; and when they took on a sweet, maniacal glitter, a wild flash that faded to reappear as a slow, delighted grin, his eyes for a moment were colorless.

"How's the noggin? Want to swing by a sawbones to check for any extra brain damage?"

"No, really," I blurted, "it's this damn flu. The Smorgasbord Flu. Hope you don't catch it."

"Sure it ain't the Water Buffalo flu?"

"What's that?" I should've known by the gleam in his eyes.

"Feels like you been gang-stomped by a herd of water buffalo."

"Naw, that's just one of the symptoms."

"Sweet Jesus," he laughed, "that does sound bad. But if you don't want to see a doc, how about some medicinal relief? Simple pain is a job for drugs."

I heartily concurred, but tentatively said, "It's a long way to a pharmacy."

"Glovebox." He nodded in its direction. "I think there's some codeine in the first-aid kit. Number fours. Don't know what the four means, but help yourself."

I was. The first-aid kit was already open on my lap, and that despite a conscious effort to mask my eagerness. "The four," I explained, "means you're supposed to take four at a time, otherwise they don't reach the right level of chemical effectiveness."

"Hey, I never thought of that," George said. "I tell ya, that's one of the great things about getting out and meeting the public—get all sorts of new angles and information."

He reached under the seat. Since I was grossly munching the codeine, I thought he'd just turned away to be polite. But when he straightened back up I saw he was holding a black baseball cap, which he slapped on his head and adjusted down over his eyes. In white letters fanned across the crown it read: *Gay Nazis for Jesus*.

"Kwide a had," my powder-thickened tongue managed, even though my brain had stopped. Suddenly it was crowded in the cab.

"Last guy I towed gave it to me. Name was Wayne. Took him from Anchor Bay up to Albion. He said it was a real conversation starter."

"Grabbed me," I admitted, slipping the first-aid kit back into the glovebox.

George tapped the gas impatiently.

"I want to thank you for the dry clothes and the codeine," I told him. "Sure improved a shitty day."

"Been there myself," George said. He tapped the gas again. "So my man, what's the plan? Where to and how soon?"

I leaned back in the seat, overcome by weariness. Sleep, bad plastic, firewood, sweat, loss, cash—somewhere along the line I'd made a plan, but could only remember the pieces. "Take me to Itchman's in Guerneville. If I'm still alive in the morning, I'll figure the rest out then."

"You're on your way," he said, reaching for the emergency brake.

Despite my effort to contain it, my conscience broke through. He'd been kind to me, thoughtful, humane, and I had to pay him in bad plastic. Not even my desperation could justify fucking him over. "Wait a minute," I sighed. "Let me tell you how it is. All I've got to pay you with is a Visa card the bank demanded I return about three months ago. I was on my way into town to pick up a thousand-dollar front on a firewood order. I think I can get it tomorrow, and I could leave the cash with Itchman. How much do you figure it'll be?"

He reached in a vest pocket and handed me what I assumed was a rate card. In a way, it was:

TOWED BY THE GHOST
One of the few free rides in life

George Gastin
No Phone
No Fixed Address

"What are the other free rides?" I asked.

He gave me a sharp look, surprised, appreciative, then an odd little bow of his head. "To tell the truth, I don't know. First love, maybe, though I've heard some hard arguments the other way. I was just allowing for my ignorance, changes, and the possibilities of imagination."

I was suddenly very curious about George Gastin, tow-truck driver. He wasn't with Itchman's or Bailey's "Where you from?" I said. "You sure seemed to get here fast."

"Twenty-one minutes," George said. "I was just turning up Sea View when I picked up the call from Itchman's. His boys were stacked up, so I got on the horn and told 'em I was damn near on your bumper, and they gave me the go. They couldn't get to you for a couple of hours soonest, and Bailey over on the coast is down with a busted crank. Itchman don't give a shit. Best money is in short tows, and his garage is getting the work, anyway, as it turns out."

"So what are you doing driving around at dawn in this neck of the woods?"

"My good sir," George huffed with mock offense, "a gentleman never tells." That maniacal glitter; the slow, delighted grin.

"So you love around here, but don't live around here, right?"

He shrugged. "Sometimes. I bum around the Northwest. Visit friends. Do some fishing. Look around. Mostly I live out of this truck here. Got a tent and a propane stove and a whole shitload of gear stashed in the tool bays. I had the truck built to my own specs by Roger Armature over in Redding. And in my travels, if I can be of help to folks, I'm glad to do it. Always interesting to meet new people, hear their stories, shoot the shit. No reason to hurry."

"And you tow these people for free?" I felt unsettled; he sounded reasonable, but something wasn't meshing.

"Yeah, if they need it. Sometimes they're just out of gas or got a flat or are down with some piddly-ass mechanical problem. I'm not too shabby at twisting wrenches."

"And no charge, right?"

"Well, if they turn out to be *outlandish* assholes, I charge them for parts."

"Been in business long?" I thought this was tactful enough, but George started laughing so hard he had to re-set the emergency brake.

His laughter seemed so disproportionate to my unintentional wit that I was disconcerted, my confusion quickly giving way to a space-collapsing sense of claustrophobia. It struck me that maybe even a free ride with the Ghost was no bargain.

"Hey," George recovered, still chuckling, "I'll be in business forever. I'm not *filthy* rich, but I made a few sound investments in my youth and I'm pretty much free to do what pleases me, and this is what it pleases me to do."

A cuckoo, I thought to myself. *I should've known.* Not that I'm prejudiced against strange kicks or weird behavior—often, in fact, I enjoy them myself—but I wasn't in the mood. Why couldn't he be excessively normal, wholly competent, eminently sane? I didn't want an adventure in consciousness or character; I wanted a savior.

George released the emergency brake again, checked the mirrors, eased slowly off the shoulder onto the pavement, then stood on the gas. Slammed back in the seat, I twisted my head around to check my truck, certain it had torn loose and was tumbling down the road behind us. It hadn't yet, but given the way it was whipping around, we wouldn't be attached for long. Just when I thought his transmission would explode, George slammed into second. The big rear duals squealed for an instant, then bit, hurtling us forward. I glanced at the speedometer, convinced we must be doing 50 already, but the needle was resting on zero. I refused to believe it. My eyes frantically scanned the other gauges: tach, oil pressure, fuel, water: nothing, nada, zip. We might as well have been standing still. With an eerie, spine-freezing jolt of pure dread, for a moment I thought we *were* standing still, that reality had somehow inverted and left us stationary while the landscape blurred by. I felt my brain attempting to curl into a fetal position as a scream dug for traction in my lungs.

George nailed third. Expending my last bit of control, I squelched the scream and gathered my voice. I knew I'd sound foolish, but I didn't care: "Excuse me, but are we standing still?"

George's eyes never left the road. "Nope," he replied matter-of-factly, "we're doing about forty-seven miles per." He flicked it into fourth. "About fifty-two now."

I pointed out as casually as I could manage—no point in alarming him—that none of the dash gauges appeared to be functioning.

"You got that right," he nodded. "Disconnected them. Too distracting. I listen to the engine, feel the road. Been doing it about thirty years. You get dialed-in after a bit, know what I mean? I can damn near calculate the fuel down to the last wisp of fumes and read the oil pressure with my fingertips. Not suggesting I'm *perfect*, understand, but when it comes to whipping it down the road I'm right up there with the best. Never been in a wreck that wasn't on purpose, and I've probably made more long-distance runs in my life than you've whacked-off in yours."

"I doubt that," I said in all sincerity, remembering that unappeasable ache that had wracked me at puberty. The memory deflected whatever my point could've been, and I ended up half-blurting, "I thought you said you refused to live life in a hurry?"

He glanced over at me, smiling. "This ain't in a hurry. This is my normal cruising groove."

I got earnest. "Listen George, I'm amazed and impressed with your abilities, but I drive these roads *all the time*, and seventy miles an hour is about forty too fast. *Slow down.*" I'd hoped to make it sound like a calm, well-reasoned request, but too much pleading quavered into my voice.

"Well," George said, "what you got to understand is that you probably drive like Lawrence Welk, and I drive like John Coltrane. Don't mean that as a put-down at all. I was born with it, had it on the natch; and I've had time to refine it. You can probably lay a tree down a foot either way from where you want it, while I'd be bucking it up in someone's living room. Or maybe you got that nice green touch in the garden. I sure don't. What I'm trying to tell you is *relax*. Just ease back, shake your cares, let it roll. I've been turning wheels since my feet could reach the pedals and I've always brought it in with the shiny side up and the dirty side down. So don't give it a piss-ant worry. The Ghost'll get you there." *His* tone was completely reasonable, without a trace of pleading or terror.

Streaks of ochre and crimson, the maples along Tolan Flat ripped past. George's assurance actually seemed to relax me, or perhaps it was the exhaustion of the day in combination with the four #4's, sweet little 16, coming on strong about then. He *did* seem to hit every gear slick and clean, held the road like a shadow, and generally displayed consummate skill. I gave it a moment of dull contemplation and took the best philosophical position available: *Fuck it. Whatever.*

"How old are you anyway?" George interrupted my metaphysical reverie, "Twenty-seven, twenty-eight?"

I had to think about it a minute. "I'll be twenty-eight a month from today."

George nodded as if the information confirmed some inner conviction. "Yup, that's about how old I was when I went crazy and made *my* pilgrimage."

Pilgrimage. The word wouldn't grab hold on my smooth brain. Caravans across the relentless Sahara. Dust and deprivation. Maybe he really was some twisted religious zealot. *It doesn't matter,* I told myself, truly beginning to relax. If I was going crazy, I was so far gone that all I could really do in my weakened condition was wave goodbye. Even the suicidal speed at which we were hurtling took on a strange comfort—if he wrapped it up, at least we wouldn't suffer. Everything was beyond control. I was fading fast, functioning on my autonomic nervous system and a piece of brain about the size of well-chewed Chiclet. I was no longer capable of the intricacies of conversation, the immense effort necessary to assemble and speak words. All I truly wanted to do was vanish into a warm oblivion and come back at some other time, when everything was better. So I asked him about his pilgrimage, and then slumped back and closed my eyes to listen.

PART ONE

FLOORBOARD GEORGE: COAST TO COAST & GONE AGAIN

"It is good to know
that glasses are to drink from.
The bad thing is not knowing
what thirst is for."

—Antonio Machado

I'm glad you want to hear about my pilgrimage, but I should warn you it's a real ear-bender. Thing is, it doesn't make much sense unless you understand what got me crazy enough to make it, and even then I'm not sure it'll make any sense to you. I'm not sure—what is it now, twenty years later?—that it makes that much sense to me. But let me play you some background and we'll see where we go.

I was born and raised in Florida, near Miami, the youngest of three kids and the only boy. My sisters were married by the time I was eight so we were never really close. My dad was a long-haul trucker, mainly citrus to the Midwest. He was a union man all the way, solid as they come. Driving big rigs was just a job to him, a skill—no romance. What he really loved were his roses. He and Mom grew these miniature roses, and every hour he wasn't on the road he was in the rose garden. By the time he made retirement, the garden was a nursery. He died out in his rose garden one bright summer afternoon about two years after he retired. A stroke. Mom still tends the garden—got a couple of young girls to help her because she's in her late seventies now and getting slowed down a bit, but the nursery actually makes pretty good money. People will pay serious bucks for fine roses.

When I was a kid I'd ride with my dad when school was out in summer. I loved every minute of it. The power of the diesels. Roaring through the night, imagining all the people asleep in their houses and dreaming all those dreams as the moon burned across the sky. Iowa sweltering in August and the little fan on the dash of the Kenworth barely drying the sweat. Guys waving howdy in the truck-stop cafes and kidding me whether I'd finally taken over for the old man or was still riding shotgun. Free ice cream from the waitresses and that hard-edged wiggle they used to move through the men, laughing and kidding and yelling orders to the cook.

I started learning to drive when my feet could reach the pedals at the same time my eyes cleared the wheel. I was driving relief for dad when I was sixteen, and by eighteen I was on my own. I wasn't like dad. I had a bad case of the romance, sitting way up there above the road balling it down the pike, eaten up with white line fever. Bad enough to have the romance, but I was good at the work. Natural hand-eye coordination. The other truckers started calling me Floorboard George, 'cause that's where I kept my right foot. Say what you want about good sense, one thing was for certain: I could cover ground. I took great pride in the fact the only tickets I ever got were *moving* violations, and that's only when they could catch me. Unfortunately, they caught me over thirty times in twenty months, and when the judges in three states have jerked your license, work is hard to find. When you're hauling perishables, it ain't easy to justify driving *around* a state just because they'll bust you for driving through it; trucking companies like you to take the shortest route, even if I could drive around Georgia and still make reasonable time.

Besides, early on I got into the methamphetamine version of speed. The heat wasn't on then, and you could buy a handful of pharmaceutically pure benzedrine from any truck-stop waitress between Tallahassee and L.A. That's why truck-stop waitresses were so good humored and sassy back then: they had a lock on the bennie concession. Just about all the drivers used them, and I sure held up my end. For two years there I thought White Cross was the trucker's health plan. Dad never used them, though, said they'd rot your reflexes and make you try to do things you couldn't do. What I found out was even worse: they helped me do things I shouldn't have.

What Dad used was coffee—one-gallon stainless-steel thermos—and he'd put maybe three shots of peach brandy in it. Hardly taste the brandy. And Dad knew how to sleep. He'd sleep four and drive twenty. Thing was, he *slept* those four hours. Shut his eyes and straight to deep sleep without a quiver. And four hours later, right to the tock, no alarm, he was fresh and ready to roll. He claimed he never dreamed on the road, or no dreams he remembered. Me, I dreamed all the time. But I never slept.

Dad dreamed at home, though. I heard him down in the kitchen one morning telling Mom he'd dreamed his brain had turned into a huge white rose. Mom just burst right out crying. Dad was saying, "Hey, hold on, it was a *great* dream—I loved it." And Mom, really sobbing then, said, "Yes. Yes it is, Harry. I know it is." Dad says, "So why the waterworks?" And I could hear Mom sniffling, trying to gather herself, saying, "No, it's a *fine* dream," and then they must've been holding each other because all I could hear was their muffled voices and the coffee glubbing in the percolator. But I understood why Mom was crying: some dreams are just too beautiful to have.

That's probably part of the reason I was hitting those ol' white cross benzedrines so hard—sometimes twenty a day. They fed my natural inclination to go fast, which I'm sure was also partly the baffled frenzy of being eighteen years old and suddenly cut loose of school. Jamming like a cannonball cross-country, riding it as fast as you could make it go, getting paid to eat the horizon was a magnificent feeling, but pretty soon it got so I didn't want to stop. I was young, restless, and dumb, but I somehow knew deep down in my gut that when it gets so you don't ever want to stop, that's when you *have* to stop, or you're gonna be long gone for good. I'd lost my license in two more states, had a nasty bennie habit, and was spending far too much time getting fried in the short-order hearts of truck-stop waitresses. The life was collapsing on me and I knew I had to make a move. So in October of '56 I headed to San Francisco, mainly because hitchhikers I'd been picking up agreed it was about the only place in the country with a pulse. It's odd, looking back: 1956, and I wanted *off* the road. And I really, truly, cross-my-heart wanted to get away from those little white pills that made you go fast and feel good. Well, to be honest, I didn't *want* to, but I understood that I was going to make a bad and unhappy mess out of myself if I didn't. Even if I wasn't exactly sure what I wanted to be, I knew it wasn't a shit-heap wreck. Maybe the bare minimum, but I had *some* sense.

Soon as I hit Frisco, things started running my way. I found a sweet little apartment, clean and cheap, above an Italian bakery in North Beach, and took a job driving tow truck at Cravetti's garage. After a tough month, I'd cut the bennies back to two a day, which for me, you understand, was virtual abstinence.

Towing was different back then. Any call, whether a bad wreck or just somebody parked in a red zone, went out on an open line to every towing service in the city, and the first truck there got the job. Hell, after 18-wheelers, driving a tow truck was like driving a Maserati. I snagged a lot of work. It took me a while to learn the streets and the best routes, but it never took me long to get there.

The competition was intense. I remember the first call I took. Mainly because I didn't know the turf and innocently went the wrong way up a one-way street, I aced in about three seconds in front of this insane fool, Johnny Strafe, who drove for Pardoo Brothers. I was chortling as I hooked up, but when I got back in the cab and hit the ignition, damn engine wouldn't grab. Like it wasn't getting spark. I look up puzzled, and there's Johnny Strafe holding my plug wires like some greasy bouquet at a marriage of rubber freaks, and before I can even scream he starts stuffing them down the grating on a corner storm drain. I'd have gone after him if the cops hadn't been on the scene. I complained to them, but they had other problems. Finally this older sergeant took me aside and told me, "Hey, if you can't tow him, the other guy gets to. It's called 'eat shit, rookie,' and that's how it is. We've got enough to do without dealing with you crazy assholes. You're new, okay, you didn't know. But don't bother us again."

So I developed a few chops of my own. Turnip up the tailpipe, that's one I introduced. One time around the Fourth of July I slipped under Bill Frobisher's rig and taped a box of sparklers to his manifold. When the heat set 'em off, you should've seen Bill hit the pavement running. I got Johnny Strafe back, too—squirted Charcoal-Lite all over his front seat and set it off. He was hooking on at the time and didn't even notice the flames, but fortunately I'd brought the biggest damn fire extinguisher from Cravetti's shop and I filled his cab up with foam till it was running out both windows and the radio was gurgling like a drowning rat. The second one was even better: I took a can of quick-dry aluminum spray paint and did his windshield.

Anyway, there I was, just a nudge short of twenty, driving tow like a werewolf at top dollar for my trade and generally enjoying myself. I was still holding the bennies steady at two a day—one *after* breakfast and one for lunch, and that was it. It helped that I was living fairly regular, clocking 8 to 5 on the day shift, weekends free, two squares a day, and logging six hours of solid Z's most nights. Health—nothing like it.

The job was great, even if it was work, but the true joy was living in North Beach. The place was alive. This is the late '50's I'm talking about, and the Beats were going strong. Lots of people will tell you the best time was '54, '55, before all the publicity hit, but for a wet-eared kid who'd been stringing his nerves between Miami and St. Lou, this looked like a good time to me. The Beats were the people I'd been looking for. They had a passionate willingness to be moved. It was a little artsy-fartsy, sure, lots of bad pretenders, but it was a whole helluva lot better than Sunday School, which is what the 50's were generally like—a national Sunday School for the soul, smug with dull virtues, mean with smothered desires. But the thing is, you can't live in fear of life. You do and you're dead in the water.

The Beats at least had the courage of their appetites and visions. They *wanted* to be moved by love, truth, beauty, freedom—what my poet friend John Seasons called "the four great illusions"—while my passion, at the time, was the firing stroke in a large-bored internal combustion engine transmitting its power through the drive-train and out to the wheels—four small illusions. Because of the explosive qualities inherent in the liquified remains of dinosaurs, I could roar through the day and the dark at speeds no one even marginally sane could consider reasonable. And if I happened to mention what that felt like in any North Beach bar, more than likely the woman on my left had just written a poem that tried to capture that same abandoned moment and the guy on my right had finished that very afternoon a painting he hoped touched the same soaring spirit, and we'd be yakking drunk and laughing till the bar closed at two in the morning and I was walking down Broadway in the fog, shivering and elated. That was North Beach. An eruption of people hungry for their souls. And for all the poses and silliness, it was splendid.

I did my share of posing, I must admit, most of it prompted by raw teenaged insecurity and a sense of intellectual inadequacy. This I hid with the usual ration of brass and bravado, but bald ignorance is a lot harder to cover. Since I could authentically claim—as few others could—an honest working-class life, I hid at first behind a fairly nasty anti-intellectualism. Fuck big words, I drive a truck. Fortunately, most people were gracious enough to ignore my bullshit, and generous enough to include me in conversations and lend me books. You could pick up a couple of Liberal Arts degrees just sitting in the bars and listening. Gradually I changed from an anti-intellectual to an unbearably eager one. I wanted to know everything—an appetite I've had many subsequent occasions to regret.

It's usually the happy case that you learn best from your friends. My tightest buddy in the early years was this huge horn player everybody called Big Red Loco, a mulatto cat with rusty red hair. He was about 6'7", and every inch of him was music. I heard him play with all the best, and he cut them into fish bait. Big Red could go out there and bring it back alive. Everybody and their aunt wanted to record him, but he'd had this vision when he was seven years old that his gift was for the moment alone, and that if his music was ever recorded, ever duplicated in time outside memory, he would lose his gift. At least this is what he told me, and I don't doubt it at all.

Lou Jones—Loose Lou, they called him—adored Big Red's sound so much that one night he crawled under the bandstand before a gig and hooked up a tape machine through the microphone. He was still shaking when he told me about it the next day: every instrument came through clean on the tape, except Big Red's sax. Not a trace. I never mentioned it to Big Red. No reason to mess with a man's music.

Except for his music, Big Red hardly ever spoke. Ten sentences a day left him hoarse. And when he did say something, it wasn't much. "Let's grab a beer," or "Can you lay a five on me till the weekend?" If you asked him a direct question, he'd just nod, shake his head, or shrug—or, maybe two percent of the time, he'd answer with a few words. It drove me ape-shit when I first knew him, so finally I asked him point-blank why he never said diddley. He shrugged and said, "I'd rather listen."

With all that practice he was an incredible listener. He ate at the

Jackson Cafe because he liked the *sound* of their dishes, if you can feature that. I remember one time we were eating lunch and this busboy came by with a big clattering cart of dirty dishes and Big Red slipped right out of the booth, dropped to all fours, and followed it right into the kitchen, ears locked, listening. However strange, it was fortunate for our friendship that he was such a listener, since it's plain I'm a rapper.

Hanging out with Big Red meant making the local jazz scene. Up till then I'd never given much of an ear to anything besides the singing of tires on asphalt and the throb of a big diesel drilling the dark, but jazz, heard live and close and smoky, with the taste of whiskey in your mouth and a high-stepping woman in the corner of your eye, just took me away. Lifted me right out of myself. I don't know anything about art, but I do know when I'm gone.

It might've been Big Red's influence—he never owned a record— but I only really loved jazz live, right *now,* straight to the spine. I bought some records, which I enjoyed and appreciated and all that, but they weren't the same. I guess I'm one of those people who can't really grasp something if it's more than a foot from the source. I mention this as a way of explaining I really didn't know anything about rock-and-roll, even though it was coming on strong at the time. Blasting from about every jukebox in every bar, it was there in the background, but it never made it through my ears to grab hold of my brain. Besides, people on the jazz scene were constantly putting it down as bubblegum for the soul. But it was interesting that Big Red didn't bad-mouth it. "It's all music," he said. "The rest is taste, culture, style, times." For Big Red, that was a speech. A lot later, about the time the Beatles were taking off, I remember sitting in Gino and Carlo's with John Seasons and Big Red, and John saying, more with sadness than disgust, "The Beatles are the end of North Beach." Big Red, unsolicited, said, "You're right. You can hear it."

John Seasons was, in a strange way, more mentor than friend, and we really didn't get close till late '63, early '64. John was a poet, and through him I met Snyder, Ginsberg, Whalen, Corso, Kerouac, Cassady, and the rest of that crew—though I don't think they were ever all around at once. John was *always* there, it seemed. He'd been living in

North Beach before it was hip, and was still there after the fashion had passed. He was a devoted poet with an aversion to the limelight—certainly a notable trait at the time—and a strong academic background. On his living room walls were about two dozen honorary doctorates in about half that many fields—I remember one from Harvard in physics, another from the Sorbonne in linguistics. They were all excellent forgeries. As John was fond of pointing out, he supported his poetry, which he claimed was a true attempt to forge the real, by creating facsimiles of the fraudulently real. John could find absolutely no good reason why people needed documents and licenses to partake of American culture, and it especially pissed him off that you had to *pay* to obtain them. John wasn't one to favor undue social regulation in the human community. Art, sports, and the Laws of Nature, he argued, were all the regulation necessary for an enjoyable life. As an advocate of personal authority, he thought it was stupid to award *real* power to abstractions like nations, senators, and Departments of Motor Vehicles.

John had a darkroom, two printing presses, a complete assortment of paper stocks, and a collection of official seals that would have shamed the Smithsonian. John was also gay, and it helped that he seemed to prefer highly placed civil servants for lovers. John felt that if your sexual preferences were going to brand you a security risk, you might as well risk some security, and he was convincing enough that his boyfriends helped him expand his collection of official seals, often providing the authentic forms on which to affix them. For John, a bogus California driver's license was little more than a snapshot and a short typing assignment. He claimed he could fake anything on paper except money and a good poem, and that he could do the money with the right plates and proper stock.

So, after about eighteen months in North Beach, closing in on twenty-one and legal American adulthood, I had a job I enjoyed by day and high friends and wild company at night; and through reading, and by talking to people who knew what they were talking about, I was accumulating enough good information to make a run at knowledge. I was beginning to know my own mind, or at least understand I had a mind to know. Or so I thought.

It was February 1, 1959, two days before my twenty-first birthday, when I came in off-shift and Freddie Cravetti—old man Cravetti's son, the swing-shift garage manager—motioned me over and introduced me to this runty guy sporting a blue seersucker suit so filthy you could have cleaned it with dog shit. Freddie introduced him as Scumball Johnson, then discreetly remembered some paperwork. When I shook Scumball's hand, it was like lifting a decayed lamprey out of a slough. He spoke in a low monotone mumble, head down, eyes constantly moving. I made him immediately as an ex-con.

I only liked one thing about Scumball Johnson: the money. Two hundred cash, back when a dollar bought dinner; and that was only the half in front. There was another two yards on delivery. All I had to do was wreck a car without wrecking myself—total it and walk away. Since I'd been making a living either by avoiding wrecks or picking them up, it sounded interesting. First, however, I had to *steal* the car, which reduced my interest considerably until Scumball explained that the car's owner *wanted* it stolen and wrecked so he could collect the insurance. I was completely covered, Scumball assured me. I'd be given a key, a handwritten note from the owner explaining I was checking out the transmission or something, the owner would stay by the phone in case anyone checked, and he wouldn't report it stolen till I'd called in safe and clear. Scumball said I could use a tail to watch my back and pick me up, but I'd have to pay for that out of my cut. Scumball didn't care how or where the car was wrecked as long as it was totaled for insurance purposes. If I got myself hurt or didn't phone within eight hours, I was on my own and nobody knew me. And if I even so much as murmured his name to the law, I would likely be visited by large men who'd had twisted childhoods and would undoubtedly take great delight in tearing off my fingers and feeding them to me.

A sleazy proposition, sure, but not without some provocative attractions, especially if you're young, restless, bored, and stupid. Looking back, I'm more astounded than ashamed that I agreed to the deal, though I must admit the $400 pay-off didn't improve my judgment.

Scumball Johnson. I'll tell you where he was at: he *liked* his name. "That's me all right," he'd chuckle, "a real scumball." As if it confirmed his essence. Those are the people I can't understand: cold rotten to the fucking quick, and quick to brag about it. Maybe that acceptance is close to enlightenment, but to enjoy it so much seems slimy. I can still see his grin. And here's the weird thing: Scumball was a walking compost heap, but his teeth were perfect—strong, straight, brushed to an immaculate luster. And since he showed them only when someone called him Scumball or otherwise confirmed his sleaziness, the grin always carried this shy, pleased, strangely *intimate* acknowledgment, as if you were praising him, or he was trying to seduce your loathing.

From what I gathered, Scumball was running a fairly complex scam. If I was cutting $400, you could bet Scumball was clearing *at least* a grand, with the rest going to the owner. But that arrangement begged an obvious question: if the owner needed the bucks, why didn't he simply *sell* the car and pocket *all* the money? I figured either the insurance value was tremendously inflated—maybe an agent in cahoots—or there was something funny about the cars.

Now I don't know this for a dead mortal cinch, but I'd bet the cars were stolen out of state and probably bought at quarter-price by Scumball, who in turn did a plate and paper job on them, let people use them for six months or so for the cost of full insurance coverage, and then Scumball collected close to full value when they were wrecked. Maybe the "owner" got a small piece of the action, but a guy like Scumball doesn't like to see the pie sliced up too much. I don't know what Scumball did with his loot, but he sure as hell didn't piss it away on clothes.

I trashed my first car for him the very next night, February 2, and I'll admit I had more than a few whiskeys in me when I turned the key on the new Merc conveniently parked just off Folsom. I'd also awarded myself three bonus bennies for bad behavior, preferring a little extra focus for the tight work.

Big Red was my tail and pick-up man, and perfect for the job. He had his own car, an anonymous '54 Chevy sedan, and had proven himself invariably reliable in the hundred small favors of friendship. Plus he needed the money. I'd cut him in for $100, probably too much, but I had a steady job going in and could write it off as a contribution to the arts if I ever paid taxes. Big Red also offered his imposing height, that wild tangle of copper-colored hair, and a nose that looked like it had been broken twice in each direction. Should anyone object to your behavior, he was a good man to have on your side.

Nobody objected as I let the Merc idle while the defroster cleared the glass. The car was close to mint condition, just over 9000 on the odometer, and no visible dings. When the glass cleared I pulled out onto Folsom, Big Red swinging in behind me, and headed for the Golden Gate.

I'd only had a day to think it over, but I'd come up with what seemed a solid plan. I'd go out Highway 1 up above Jenner where the road hugs the ocean bluffs, find a likely turnout, and shove it over into the Pacific. I'd brought along a bag full of empty beer cans and couple of dead pints of cheap vodka to scatter around the interior—make it look like a snorting herd of adolescent males, frenzied on some giant squirt of young warrior hormones, had swiped the short for a joyride and crashed it for fun.

I cruised north on 101 at a legal 65, took 116 through Sebastopol to Guerneville, then followed the Russian River to its mouth at Jenner, where I caught Highway 1. There was hardly any traffic. I checked the rearview to make sure Big Red made the turn, and saw the bobbing lights of his Chevy about a quarter-mile behind.

I found a good spot about twenty minutes up the coast, a wide turnout along the edge of a high cliff. I pulled over to check it out. The ocean air was powerful, a cauldron broth of salty protein and tidal decay. There were no guardrails, so it was an easy roll over the edge and a long way down to the waves bashing the rocks. I looked carefully for lights along the beach, any flashlights or campfires. I didn't want to drop two tons of metal on a couple of lovers fucking their romantic brains out on the narrow beach below. No reason to encourage absurdity. Of course, on the other hand, nobody with a brain more complex than a mollusc's would consider mating on a rocky, wave-wracked beach on a raw winter night, so I might've been doing evolution a favor.

Still wearing the gloves I'd put on before touching the car, I scattered the empties over the floorboards while Big Red wheeled his

Chevy around to screen the Merc. I put the Merc in Neutral and cramped the wheels to the left. Big Red and I put our shoulders to it, a few good grunts at first, and then she was rolling on her own weight. When the front tires dropped over the edge, the back end flipped up, but rather than nosing straight down it dragged on the frame and tilted sideways slow enough for us to hear all the cans sluicing toward the driver's side, and then she cleared the edge and was gone. The earth suddenly seemed lighter. It was silent so long I figured we hadn't heard it hit, that the sound of impact had been muffled by the surge and batter of the waves below, and I was just about to peer over the edge when it smashed on the rocks KAAABBBBLLLAAAAAAM.

Big Red stood there, rooted, eyes closed and head thrown back, swaying slightly from side to side. He was obviously lost in something, but, though I hated to interrupt, it didn't seem wise to hang around appreciating the sonic clarity of a new Mercury meeting ancient stone in the middle of a felony.

I touched his arm. "Let's hit it."

"You drive," Big Red replied; a command, not a request.

Silent, eyes closed, Big Red didn't twitch from his reverie until we were coming back across the Golden Gate. I was half-depressed with spoiled adrenalin, half-pissed that he'd withdrawn when I felt like yammering, so when he finally opened his eyes and asked "Did you hear it," I was a little cross. "Hear what? The waves? The wind? The wreck?"

"No man, the *silence*. The gravitational *mass* of that silence. And *then* that great, brief, twisted cry of metal."

"That sound isn't high on my hit parade, Red. I *like* cars, trucks, four-bys, six-bys, eight-bys, and them great big motherfuckers that bend in the middle and go shooooooosh shoooooosh when you pump the brakes. It'd be like throwing your horn off the cliff."

"Yes!" He grabbed my shoulder, *"Exactly!"*

He was so pleased that it seemed cruel to admit my understanding was the accidental result of petulant exaggeration, if not outright deceit. In fact, only one thing had bothered me about wrecking the Merc: it was too easy.

I reminded Big Red that we still had to check in with the man, and soon as we hit Lombard I called Scumball from a Shell station pay phone. He answered on the third ring. After that first night, I had occasion to call him lots of times, and he *always* answered on the third ring. We used a simple code. I'd say, "The chrome's on the road," and he'd reply, nasty, "Who is this?" Then I'd hang up.

When I slipped back behind the wheel of Big Red's Chevy, Red wasn't interested in what Scumball had said. He wanted to explore that silence. "Let's fall by my place and pick up my horn and see who's out jamming."

North Beach. Where else at 3:00 A.M. could you find some small club that was supposed to be closed and jam and yak and drink because the people who owned it understood better than the law that you can get lonely and thirsty and in need of music at all hours, especially the late hours of the night?

Right before dawn Big Red took the bandstand alone and announced he was going to play a new composition he called "Mercury Falling," and that he wanted to dedicate it to me on my birthday. I'd forgotten that at midnight I'd officially turned twenty-one, but Big Red hadn't, and I felt like a shithook for my impatience with him earlier. But as soon as Big Red's breath shaped that first note, my little puff of shame was blown away.

For the twenty minutes Big Red played, there wasn't a heartbeat in that room. Cigarets went out. Ice melted in drinks. I know it's hopeless to try to describe music, but he *played* that silence he'd heard, heard so clearly, brought every note *through* it and *to* it, pushed them over the edge into the massive suck of gravity, hung them in the wind and hurled them gladly to the surging bash and wash of water wearing down stone, and every note smashing on the claim of silence was a newborn crying at the light. When he finished there wasn't a sound and there wasn't a silence and we all took our first breath together.

Big Red nodded shyly and walked offstage. Applause wasn't necessary. Everyone just sat there breathing again, feeling air curling into lungs, afraid to break the spell, the room silent except for the shifting of weight in chairs, the scuff of shoes on the littered floor. Finally a woman sitting alone at a corner table stood up, and that snapped it. A black bass player named Bottom sitting next to me at the bar groaned, "*Yeeess.* Yes, yes, yes," and then reached over, put his skinny arm around my shoulder, and hugged me, whispering with sweet citric breath, "Happy birthday, man—you got yoself a present there you can unwrap for the rest of yo life."

Then everyone was nodding, smiling; a sweet, low babble filled the room. Everyone except the woman who'd stood up. She was taking off her clothes. Her back was to me, so I hadn't realized what she was doing till the green knit dress slipped from her bare shoulders. She wasn't wearing anything underneath. Tall, lean, with long hair the color of half-weathered pine, she stepped out of the dress around her ankles and made her way, composed and magnificent, between the crowded tables toward the back door. Everyone stopped breathing again. I was in love. She closed the door softly behind her without looking back. "Sweet Leaping God o' Mercy," Bottom moaned beside me, his arm dropping from my shoulders.

I caught up with her at the end of the alley. Thick fog swirling in the first pale light of morning; cold; the odor of garbage. She heard me and turned around. I was trembling too wildly to speak. She brushed her hair back from her face, her fine blue eyes, fierce and amused, looking right into mine.

"Let me walk you home," I said in what can be kindly described as a blurt.

She tilted her head, a playful flicker of a smile, waiting. I immediately understood and began shedding my clothes, hopping around on one foot to take off the opposite shoe—taking forever, it seemed to me, while she stood and waited, hip shot, arms folded across her breasts, watching me frantically trying to pretend I wasn't frantic. And then, somehow, I was standing naked in front of her, my cock hard as a jack handle, shivering, foolish, hopeful. She laughed and took me in her arms. I started laughing, too, relaxing against her fine, long warmth. And then, hand in hand, as natural as night and day, we strolled the seven blocks to my apartment. There was some early morning traffic, first stirrings of the city, but we were invisible in our splendor.

Her name was Katherine Celeste Jonasrad, Kacy Jones to those who loved her, and there were many, definitely including me. When I met her she'd just turned nineteen and, to the relentless dismay of her parents, had recently dropped out of Smith to see what the West Coast had to offer in the way of an education. Her father owned the largest medical supply company in Pennsylvania, and her mother was a frustrated novelist who seemingly regretted her every act and omission since her own graduation from Smith. Kacy phoned them one night from my place—her father's birthday—and I remember her eyes flashing as she repeated her mother's question: " 'What am I going to do?' Well, I'm going to *do* whatever I feel like, whatever I need, whatever it takes, and whatever else I can get away with." That was Kacy in her uncontainable essence: a free force, a true spirit on earth. She did fairly much as she pleased, and if she wasn't sure what pleased her, she was never afraid to go find out.

That birthday morning when we walked naked through the early morning streets to my apartment, she turned to me as the door closed and said, "I'm not interested in a performance. The quality of the permissions, that's what I'm after." I must have shown my confusion because she put it more plainly: "I don't want to be fucked; I want us to feel something."

"I'll try," was all I could think to say.

She slipped her arms around my bare waist and drew me to her. "Let's try together."

I've never known a woman with the range and originality of Kacy's erotic imagination. I don't mean positions and all that sexual gymnastics, or the wilder fantasies and obsessions—those were just the entrances to other realms of possibility. Kacy was interested in the *feelings*, their clarity and nuance and depth, what could be shared and what couldn't. With Kacy there was no casual sex. I told her that much later. With that tone of playful cynicism people use to keep their dreams honest, Kacy said, "Well, a sweet quickie now and then sure never hurt anything."

I don't want to bog you down in the voluptuous details, so suffice it to say that on that birthday morning with Kacy I shoot through Heaven on my way to the Realm of Unimaginable Pleasure Indefinitely

Prolonged. We tried together, heart and soul, and there is nothing like those first permissions to make you believe in magic, and without that belief in magic there's no heart for the rest. In the late afternoon, when Kacy went out for supplies, I just laid there grinning like a fool. She was back in half an hour with a whole bag of groceries. Sourdough bread from the bakery downstairs, a carton of antipasto from the deli around the corner, two cold quarts of steam beer, a jar of pepperocini, a half-pound of dry jack cheese, candles, a Sara Lee chocolate cake, and the afternoon *Examiner.* That was one thing about Kacy: she loved to pull surprises from the bag. According to Kacy, there were only seven things human beings required for a happy life on this planet: food, water, shelter, love, truth, surprises, and secrets. Sounded good to me.

I remember how happy she looked as she unpacked our feast, explaining that there were only eight candles in a package but if I wasn't *too* traditional we could just make the figure of 21 instead of actually using that many candles. Suddenly she stopped in midsentence, obviously arrested, staring down at the table.

I sat up in bed. "Kacy, what's the matter?"

Without turning, she made an impatient gesture with her hand as she looked down at the front page of the newspaper. I saw her shoulders rise as she took a deep breath, then fall; when they remained slumped I knew the news was bad. She turned around, tears in her eyes, and lay down on the bed beside me. "Buddy Holly, Ritchie Valens, and the Big Bopper were all killed in a plane crash last night. That's a *lot* of music to lose all at once."

I held her without saying anything. Fact was, I wasn't really sure who Buddy Holly, Ritchie Valens, and the Big Bopper were, an ignorance I was afraid would only make her sadder. You need the same knowledge to share another's grief, but not to comfort it. I held her till the tears were dry, then we ate my birthday feast and, later that night, opened some more presents.

The party actually lasted another four years. I can't truly say I lived with her those four years, since she came and went as she pleased. Kacy would not be possessed. On Valentine's Day, about a week and a half after we'd met, I came home after work to find a giant red heart pinned to my door, the words BE MINE in great white letters printed across it, the word MINE neatly crossed out. Her life belonged to her; mine to me. Where they touched, the terms were mutual regard, honor, and love without possession, dependency, or greed. I tried to explain it to John Seasons one night after Kacy had been gone a couple of weeks, and I was trying hard to convince myself that that was fine. John said, "Sounds like one of them modern relationships to me." He finished his Johnny Walker and looked at the bottom of the glass. "Actually," he continued, his voice suddenly serious, a bitter trace to his tone, "it sounds like Saint Augustine's definition of love: 'I want you to be.' I've always liked that notion of love, but I've sure as hell never come close to making it real."

I found it difficult myself. Doubt, jealousy, particularly the anxious stabs of inadequacy, all jerked me around at one time or another. Kacy lived out of a battered backpack, and when she left—sometimes for a few days, sometimes for weeks—she took everything with her except the promise she'd be back. When she returned, she'd always call to ask if I was in the mood for company. I always was, but once I said no just to see what she'd say. "Fine," she said. "I'll call again." After a couple years my doubts and dreads fell away, for finally they only compromised the pleasure of her company. Besides, when she was there, she was *really* there, and that's all I could fairly ask if I wanted to love her, not own her.

I don't want to give the impression that all we did was screw ourselves stupid while gazing deeply into each other's eyes. When we were together we were like any other couple. We'd hit the bars and coffeehouses and jazz clubs, visit friends, go to the movies . . . the usual. Kacy loved good food and enjoyed cooking, and was appalled to discover I was a can opener—a can of chili, another of corn, and a six-pack of beer was my idea of an eight-course dinner. Kacy taught me to cook some simple dishes, like pasta and stir-fry. Bought me a wok on *her* birthday. She also introduced me to backpacking. In the time we were together we took eight or nine long trips in the Sierras. Kacy loved high mountain lakes, and after the first trip I shared her appreciation. Air, water, granite, the campfire—Kacy liked the elemental.

She was also partial to marijuana, peyote, the natural highs—"real drugs," she called them. Speed was the only thing she ever ragged me about, and she was remarkably free of judgments. She claimed speed tore holes in the soul. So, ready to give it up anyway, I finally kicked, though I did allow myself a couple when I had a car to wreck for Scumball. I smoked weed with her now and then, but never developed her fondness for it; it softened the focus, distracted concentration, seemed to make my brain mushy. Peyote was more interesting—legal then, too—but I got the bad pukes every time, and that takes the fun out of anything.

Baseball was one thing Kacy and I did hold delightedly in common. For years her father had been part owner of a Class A team in Philly, and Kacy grew up going to every home game they played. We both liked baseball the way we liked jazz, live and close up. Since this was before the Giants moved to San Francisco, that left us the Triple A Seals, though as long as it was baseball, we hardly cared if it was the majors or minors. I always thought it was a sad indictment of the North Beach crowd that you couldn't lure them near anything as American as a baseball game even if you bought them season tickets and sprung for the beer. The only exception was John Seasons, who actually had a season ticket and was honestly offended when I jokingly suggested he print up a couple of extras for me and Kacy.

The three of us truly had a ball at the ballpark. John and Kacy were always drooling over some first-baseman's forearms or the center-fielder's butt, but they enjoyed the drama and strategy as much as the physical grace. And nobody ever rode an umpire like John Seasons. John was sort of gangly and diffident looking, but he had a voice like a meat cleaver. "May you be buggered by a caveful of Corsican thugs! May Zeus fill your loins with curdled goat's milk! May Poe's raven pluck your infirm eyeballs and every being in Rilke's angelic order piss in the empty sockets!" John really worked out.

If it sounds like I was having a good time, a life of high spirit and the pedal pretty much to the metal, I was indeed. Maybe too much so. Because when you're running with a remarkable woman and large-hearted friends, bathing in the fountain of fresh possibilities, pulling forty hours a week gets tremendously boring, even when it's work you like. There just wasn't that much left to learn about tow-truck driving, and nothing's more heartless than mastery without challenge. When you start losing satisfaction with your work, that's the first sign of slippage at the center.

Despite the outlaw thrill, wrecking the occasional car for Scumball was also becoming routine. Maybe, if there'd been one or two jobs a month instead of one every three months, I might've hung it up at Cravetti's. Granted, coming up with new ways to wreck cars without establishing a pattern stretched the imagination. But the fact is, it doesn't take much to total a car for insurance purposes—only has to be more expensive to repair than the car is worth. Your granny could do it in an easy two minutes with an eight-ounce hammer and a handful of sand.

Anyway, this was boring enough that Big Red and I started getting fancy in our destructions. He found a place up on Mount Tam where there was a loose boulder above the road, and after we got everything lined up good we used a couple of pry bars to roll that stone straight down on a new '61 Impala, bullseye. We torched a Chrysler out by Stinson Beach, but the most fun we had destroying a car was probably this Olds 88 we took way the hell and gone up Fort Ross Road, pretending we were deranged service-station attendants. Big Red had bought a couple of red stars at the five-and-dime to give us that official look. We pinned them on and got right to it, humming "You can trust your car, to the man that sports a star," as we bent to the task.

"Fill it up this evening, sir? Would you like mortar mix or regular cement?"

"I'll get that windshield, George," Big Red called cheerfully, putting an eight-pound sledge right through it. "Clean, huh? Just like the glass wasn't there." Red liked this so much he was damn near babbling with enthusiasm.

"Hey, Red! While I'm checking things out here under the hood, why don't you grab that pair of sidecutters and snip off them valve stems and make sure air comes out of those tires. Look overinflated to me."

"You got it, Chief. How's it look under the hood?"

"No damn good: bad oil leak from the valve cover. Toss me that number-eight sledge and I'll see if I can get that gasket *flat*. Maybe reseat the valves a little deeper while I'm at it."

By that time I was really *enjoying* the gig—and remember, I was a long-time faithful at the altar of internal combustion. Another sign that things were coming apart. Of course, I didn't see it then, or not clearly. But what difference does it make to understand you're hungry when there is nothing to eat?

I might not have known the cause, but I could feel something was wrong. I had a good woman, honest work, fine friends, and some illicit thrills to keep me sharp, but I wasn't happy. Had no idea why, and I'm still not dead certain. John's diagnosis was a severe case of late-adolescent spiritual endema, the strange disease of drowning in your own juices. His prescription was to let the affliction run its torpid course, hopefully washing away the more negligible parts of the psyche in the purging process.

Big Red Loco thought it was the air. He didn't elaborate except to add, upon my harshest questioning, "You know, man: the *air.*" He even provided a visual aid by sweeping his hand vaguely above his head.

And Kacy, sweet Kacy, I never found out what she thought, because she was suddenly gone, off to Mexico and eventually South America with two gay Jungian psychologists, brothers named Orville and Lydell Wight. The purpose of the trip was to investigate first-hand the shamanistic use of various drugs employed by native tribes. They had a new Chevy van, some independent financing, and no time limit, although Kacy was talking about at least two years, or about twenty-two months longer than I had in mind.

But what I wanted was at odds with what I knew was going to be. This was an adventure she couldn't pass up and remain true to herself, so against my true sadness and wounded sulking I mustered the dubious grace to let go of what I couldn't hold anyway.

Our last night together is committed to cellular memory. I don't think I've ever held anyone as tightly. In the morning, wishing her off, I had no regrets. None at all. But that didn't stop it from tearing me up.

A month later, the same day I received Kacy's first letter, I heard that Scumball had gotten busted. Young Cravetti let me know it had nothing to do with me, that the arrest was for loan-sharking and conspiracy to commit assault. Evidently Scumball had employed some agents from the Contusion Collection Service, a company of goons who stood completely behind their motto, "Pay or Hurt." The wife of a damaged debtor had gone to the cops, who probably would've filed it in the wastebasket if she and the Police Commissioner's wife hadn't been cheerleaders together in high school. I was out a steady chunk of fun money, but felt worse for Big Red. He'd come to depend on this income, and now had to go back to work for Mort Abberman who, when he was sober enough to pour the molds, had a little cottage industry making latex dildoes in his basement.

According to Kacy's letter they were in Mexico, near Tepic, going to a language school for a crash course in both Spanish and Indian dialects. Orville and Lydell were great company, loose and intelligent and serious scholars, and once they had enough language to proceed, they planned to stop in Mexico City for research before leaving for Peru. She missed me, she said, and thought of me often and fondly, but even as I read the letter I felt her slipping away.

North Beach itself was no longer a consolation. Grey Line had scheduled tours to look at the Beatniks, even though the germinal core were long gone to other parts, leaving young and awkward heirs who seemed more enchanted by the style than the substance, and leaving behind as well the low-life despoilers and cut-and-suck criminals who seem to thrive on exploiting freedoms they're incapable of creating. Jazz clubs closed to become topless joints, silicon tits swinging on the same stages that had once featured music so amazingly real you didn't want it ever to stop. Now you just wanted to leave.

When Scumball finally came to trial in late September, leaving seemed like a good idea—just in case he was more nervous than I was and started talking deals with the D.A. I decided to take a month's vacation, maybe wander down Mexico way. There was no hassle with work; I had plenty of vacation time coming. Old man Cravetti understood my anxiety, but he assured me not to burden my trip with worry since Scumball, though not without his faults, was a stand-up guy, and moved in circles where snitches were often sent on long walks off short piers, usually in cement shoes. Since I'd been introduced to Scumball through the Cravettis, where I usually picked up my delivery money, I understood the garage was involved—maybe some of the mechanics did I.D. changes—but I'd never asked, figuring it was wiser not to know. If they weren't worried, maybe I was overdoing it, though a month in Mexico City was still an attractive idea.

I hardly remember the vacation, most of which I spent pretending I wasn't looking for Kacy. No regrets, like I said, but many, many second thoughts, most of them washed down with tequila. On Gary Snyder's sage advice that it was the most likely place to find the face I sought, and that there was much else of interest and beauty to look at in case she didn't show, I haunted the Museum of Anthropology, maybe the best in the world. I saw wonder upon wonder, but the only glimpse I got of Kacy was in the lines of a gold jaguar, Mayan, seventh century. A letter from Kacy, postmarked Oaxaca, was waiting when I returned to San Francisco, explaining they'd decided to skip Mexico City and head straight for Peru.

A week later, Kennedy was assassinated. I was cleaning up a fender-bender on Gough when a cop came over and said in that stunned, vacant voice you heard all day, "They shot the President. They fucking *shot* the goddamn *President.*" The immediate understanding that it was a conspiracy even if Oswald had acted alone joined the forces of shock, chaos, pain, and grief in that single moment of national violation.

A lot has been made of Kennedy's assassination as some turning point in the 60's, the beginning of a profound disillusionment. And it was, in the sense that it cracked some illusions, but in a strange way. You've got to remember that we were the most privileged children in history, and probably among the most brainwashed. We had been taught history as the inevitable triumph of American ideals: those wonderful, powerful ideals of equality, freedom, justice, and dedication to the God-fearing truth. We believed. And we knew, because we were endlessly told so from kindergarten through high school, that to achieve those ideals required the unstinting application of celebrated American virtues like hard work, gumption, enterprise, courage, sacrifice, and faith. Our teachers pointed to postwar America, the mightiest, most affluent nation on the planet, as inarguable proof of the pudding.

We believed so deeply that Kennedy's death, rather than shattering our ideals served, as only a martyrdom can, to refresh them. We believed those ideals because they were beautiful, spirited, and true. If the realities didn't always agree, realities could be changed—were *made* to be changed—both by the collective will of the people and a single heroic leader with grit and stick-to-itiveness. If Negroes were being denied the right to vote—the *right*—we would go register them. If people in India were starving, we would sustain them with our surplus while we taught them how to farm. If the wretched rose up in a desperate rage of dignity and took arms against their oppressors, they could count on our freedom-loving support. And the more we tried to bring those ideals to reality, the more we understood how deeply the corruption reached. We believed so profoundly that even when we finally realized what hopeless, deluding, bullshit rhetoric those ideals had become, what a seething of maggots they masked, we *still* believed.

Once the shock of Kennedy's assassination was absorbed, you could feel a new energy on the street, a strangely exhilarated seriousness, like that first pull of the current before you hear the whitewater roaring downriver. This quickening seemed most apparent in people my age and younger, the war babies, victims more of the victory than the pain of the effort. The older generation seemed to take Kennedy's death as a defeat, a shocked return to the vulnerability and chaos World War II and Korea were supposed to end. They seemed tired with the knowledge that bad times weren't going to end. But not my generation, reared on the notion that you had to dare to dream, and dream large. But we were never truthfully warned that dreams die hard.

I say "we," my generation, but I don't know how much I can honestly include myself. As things quickened, I was beginning a slow fade into myself. I'd lost some essential connection. I logged my forty a week driving tow, which still retained some pleasure, but no sustaining joy. Nights and weekends I hit the streets, hungry for that old excitement, but for me it was gone.

My friends were sweet and understanding. John Seasons pronounced it a classical case of ennui and recommended a change of life as soon as I could gather my forces. Until then, he suggested strong drink and great poetry, offering to buy me one and lend me the other.

Big Red Loco just shook his head. He was feeling it too, as it turned out, finding less and less that moved him to pick up his horn. Spiders were nesting in the bell, he said, and I knew what he meant. They were nesting in my head. When I finally started boring myself, I went on a brain-cracking rampage. Got shit-faced crazy drunk every night for about a month straight and abused enough drugs to singlehandedly raise the standard of living in Guadalajara. I screwed everything that moved, or at least those who held still for it. The binge ended when I made a desperate play for John, who shocked me with the cold anger of his refusal: "I don't want anything to do with you. You're just thrashing around, and you don't have enough forgiveness in your soul to expiate me if I take advantage of it. This would destroy the true feelings we have for each other, and I won't risk that. Slow down for once, George." I ended up crying on his shoulder right beside the Golden Rocket pinball machine in Gino and Carlo's.

In response to John's admonition and the obvious fact that I was stuck in the mud right up to my frame, I changed my ways—perhaps the most decisively conscious change I'd ever made. I became austere. Not monkish, mind you, but seriously determined to eliminate the reckless waste. No booze, no drugs, no heartless sex. If I was mired in my own mud, there was no reason to blow up the engine in frustration.

Austerity is a good way to fight those bad blues, the ones that turn your soul into sewage. For one thing, *you* assume control, though it is, in all likelihood, sheer delusion. But if nothing else, it helps minimize the damage, if not so much to yourself, at least to others.

In a way, I actually enjoyed myself. I spent a lot of time reading, mainly poetry (taking John's advice) and history, a subject that hadn't much interested me before. I also took long walks around the city, looking at it without the insulation of a moving vehicle. Besides opening my eyes to a wealth of cultural diversity, the sheer exercise helped burn off that free-floating energy that comes of restless boredom. I did my job at Cravetti's diligently, alertly, with a new eye to the fine details. That's yet another benefit of the strict approach: you're forced outside into the whip and welter, which in turn forces you to take refuge in the moment, which is perhaps the only refuge anyway.

Once in a while I went out just to keep in touch with friends, John and Big Red in particular. John, who claimed I'd inspired him, had cleaned up his own act and was doing more writing than drinking. Big Red, however, had all but quit playing horn, and that depressed him.

The letters from Kacy began tapering off. In nine months I heard from her four times: a postcard from Guatemala, a long letter from Lima saying they were about to head into the mountains to live with an Indian tribe, then two more from Lima. The first reported that they'd all come down with hepatitis and were thinking of returning to the States, but in the last letter, two months later, they had recovered and decided to go on. Kacy sounded weary but determined. She missed me, she said, and hoped I was keeping myself pure for her return. Though she was only teasing, this struck me as being uncomfortably close to what I was doing, and perhaps it was her distant tweak that provided the first crack in my regimen.

The trouble with disciplined austerity is that it requires deep resolve, and I'm prone to back-sliding at the slightest nudge. I'd hung tough for almost nine months, damn good for a beginner. What got me really rolling downhill was a seventeen-year-old folksinger named Sharon Cross—emerald eyed, red of mane, and a body that made you sit back on your haunches and howl. She was young, innocent, and warmhearted, three attributes that taken separately are charming, but in Sharon combined to produce the one thing I didn't like about her: she was relentlessly, painfully liberal. But she was also lots of fun and sweet company, just what I needed to wean myself from austerity.

I tried to put some heart into the relationship. Sharon did too, of course—there's hardly a woman who doesn't. But we were both aware it wasn't love. I think she was lightly enchanted by my hip working-class cachet while I was enamored of sipping some nectar from the bud. Sharon intuitively understood she had a whole lot of life ahead of her, rich with possibilities, and I was only a place to start. For my part, I felt a lot of my life chasing me, the possibilities dwindling. We were smart enough to keep it easy and not live together.

About the same time I was getting close to Sharon, late June of '64, the Fourth Wiseman appeared in front of City Lights bookstore. He looked old, maybe in his fifties, but was so burned out on speed you couldn't be sure. He might've been a hard thirty. He always wore the same clothes, a brown sport coat with matching slacks, grubby but not tattered, and a white shirt yellowed with speed-sweats, frayed at the cuffs and collar but always neatly tucked in. The Fourth Wiseman stood in front of City Lights from 10:00 A.M. sharp till exactly 5:00 P.M. every day, twirling a green yo-yo and endlessly repeating the one thing that had survived the amphetamine holocaust in his brain, the one ember his breath kept alive. It was a short poem, or mantra, that he mumbled to himself about once a minute: "The Fourth Wiseman delivered his gift and slipped away." The whole time pacing restlessly back and forth on the sidewalk, snapping the yo-yo down, letting it hang spinning for a couple of heartbeats, retrieving it with a flick of his wrist—no tricks, no variations, none of that baby-in-the-cradle or walking-the-dog. Just spinning at the end of the string. An austerity of sorts. He ignored any efforts to engage him in conversation or otherwise distract him from his work.

"Delivered his gift and slipped away." That phrase, and the idea of a phantom Fourth Wiseman, haunted me. Or perhaps, in combination with the spinning yo-yo—a brilliant blue-green, the color of wet algae—I'd been literally hypnotized. I'd drive by almost every day to see how he was doing, and he was always doing the same. Early on I tried to slip him a sawbuck. He was so startled he took it, but when he saw what it was he shook his head as if I'd completely misunderstood and flipped the bill out into the street. A '57 Ford coupe ran over the bill, which fluttered along in its wake, riding the draft. A wino darted out and snagged it about half a block down. The Fourth Wiseman didn't notice any of this, having already returned to his work, yo-yo singing on the waxed twine as he recited his spare testament.

The Fourth Wiseman disturbed Sharon. One of the troubles with the liberal mind is it can't deal with things too far gone to cure with good intentions. She thought he was sad and tragic, a victim, and she wanted to do something about it. She thought a benefit for him—a hootenany—would be wonderful, something for a real suffering human being in the community rather than some abstract cause. I thought it was presumptuous, pretentious, and perhaps a little bit precious to assume he was suffering when, in fact, he seemed satisfied with his mission, or witness, or whatever it was, and that my offer of money had only seemed to confuse and offend him. I told her so. We argued, but that was nothing new.

It was about six months later, Christmas of '64, that things really started falling apart. I remember walking over to Sharon's on Christmas morning and taking a detour past City Lights. There he was, yo-yo blurring in the winter light, reciting his poem with a beatific fervor that brought tears to my eyes. I blurted the question I'd been burning to ask him: "What was the Fourth Wiseman's gift?"

The yo-yo spun in suspension. When he finally spoke, he said, "The Fourth Wiseman delivered his gift and slipped away."

My impulse, hardly Christian on that most Christian of days, was to strangle him, to take him down on the sidewalk and choke the answer out of him, to hiss in his ear, "Tell me. Tell me *anything,* any truth or lie, that the gift was love or a steaming goat turd or sunlight on our bodies: tell me *anything:* but fucker, you *better tell me something!*"

Maybe he sensed I was about to flip, because when he repeated it again it seemed slightly altered, a shadow change, a glancing inflection: "The Fourth Wiseman delivered *his* gift and slipped away."

I walked away, confounded by the slight shift in emphasis, saying to myself, *"His* gift. Delivered *his* gift. *His."* Confused because I still didn't know what his gift was, or mine, nor, if I even had one, whether I could deliver it or not.

Then came some hard losses. The first was Bottom, the bass player who'd sat beside me on my birthday when Big Red had played "Mercury Falling," whose arm had been around my shoulder the moment I first saw Kacy walking naked toward the door. Bottom was a long-time junkie, so his overdose was less a surprise than a raw sadness. They found him in his one-room apartment on New Year's Eve. He'd been dead five days. That we were playing for keepsies was a hard recognition, another rank whiff of the cold mortal facts. Big Red took it particularly hard. When asked to play at the funeral, he simply said, "I can't." By then he wasn't playing at all, and after Bottom's death he damn near didn't talk for a month. I sensed that silence, once his element, was beginning to corrode him, and felt helpless to watch.

About a month later, a week or so after my birthday, Sharon and I had a bitter fight about music. About the Beatles, of all people, who were just getting hot. Sharon loved them. I thought it was just bubblegum bullshit, yeah yeah yeah. This was their early stuff we were arguing about, which to my ear was weak. I thought they were a cultural phenomenon, not so much for their music as their long hair and brash cuteness, an exotic British import. As far as I understood it (not very), rock-and-roll had ended in '59. Not just the death of Buddy Holly, Ritchie Valens, and the Big Bopper in that plane crash on my birthday, but also Chuck Berry getting busted on a trumped-up Mann Act violation, and the payola scandals, and good ol' Jerry Lee Lewis marrying his thirteen-year-old cousin. Little Richard had returned to the Church, but because he was wearing lipstick and eye shadow the Church wasn't sure what to do with him. Rock-and-roll had gotten too weird, nasty, and corrupt for the four-square American sensibilities of the early 60's. Besides, the King had abdicated: Elvis came out of the Army and turned his back on rock-and-roll; went in a shit-kicker and came out with schlock. An entertainer. The King made about twenty movies; the first two or three were outright stupid, and after that they rapidly declined. The way I saw it, rock had been taken over by white teen idols, the guys you'd feel safe letting your daughter date—Fabian, Frankie Avalon, Ricky Nelson. But that's marketing, not music. They were the last sanitized gasp of the 50's, and after they vanished into their own vacuity came the Twist and other dance crazes, denatured "pop," and then folk music. I figured the Beatles were just a new wrinkle on the old teen-idol number, packaged as a group and imported as an invasion. The odd thing was, due to cultural lag, the Beatles' musical roots were in 50's rock-and-roll.

Anyway, this argument with Sharon was as pointless as most, but that didn't keep it from turning nasty, too bitterly revealing for comfort, and afterwards Sharon and I sort of cooled the relationship. We still saw each other occasionally and even less occasionally slept together, but our fading trust could bear no more permissions.

Sharon left abruptly in the early summer of '65. She came by to tell me she'd decided to take her music to Mississippi and help register Negro voters (they were still Negroes then, though you could tell *that* shit was about to hit the fan). I thought she was doing the right thing for herself and told her I admired her conviction and courage. I didn't tell her I felt a crass glee that her innocence was about to get rolled in some reality, but despite that spot of malice I truly wished her well.

After she left, I drooped around for about a month with a hollow melancholy composed of a self-canceling combination of genuine sadness and deep relief. Women couldn't leave me fast enough, it seemed, sailing off on their spiritual adventures while I stayed behind to move the wreckage around.

Then Big Red left for India. If I hadn't been so wrapped up in my own blues I might've seen he was hurting worse than me. He tried to explain it to John and me our last night together. I mean, Big Red *talked:* a speech, given his usual brevity; a virtual filibuster to forestall his demons. Ironically, he could have said it in four words: the gift was gone. Lost. And for no reason he could understand. It had been given him to hear life's music, to reshape it with his breath, to blow it through our hearts renewed and thereby keep it real. *Keep* it, he insisted, not *make* it. "You can't create what's already there," was how he put it, but that, I thought, was picking the artistic fly shit out of the aesthetic pepper, because it didn't change the pain of his loss. From that vision when he was seven, Big Red had understood his gift and had worked hard to sustain it, to deserve it, practiced till his lips were numb and his lungs ached, listened, listened as deeply as he could, listened and connected and listened again, and never dishonored it with frivolity, ego, or greed. And now he couldn't bear the taste of the mouthpiece; it tasted like rancid milk. And all he could hear was noise.

So he was leaving for India. Why India, he wasn't sure, but it felt right. You had to step over corpses on the way to the temples. A beggar's face clotted with flies. Shiva, who created and destroyed. Buddha, who sowed his breath for the harvest of wind. India for no particular reason or belief, except that people he knew who'd been there just shook their heads, and Big Red felt like he needed his head shaken.

John and I drove him to the airport the next morning. I gave Big Red a $1000 severance bonus for years of faithful and felonious service in the auto-dismantling business and John gave him what he called "a small grant for musical research" as well as a letter-perfect passport, a sheaf of references, and other papers designed to facilitate travel abroad. As we parted at the boarding gate, Red bent to embrace each of us. Direct and simple, that was Big Red's way. No mawkish sentiment about the past, no false and hearty promises to the future. Goodbye and gone.

I'd already decided to take the rest of the day off, so when John suggested we stop by Gino and Carlo's on our way back from the airport, have a drink to honor our departed friend, I was ready. We started drinking around noon and finished a couple of days later when John collapsed in the men's room in some bar. I'd discovered early on in the binge that John had lost his grip on the wagon a week before and by now was rolling from the fall. His new work, a long serial poem about the shapes of water and air, was, he claimed, "an utter piece of shit," and he'd taken a serene pleasure in composting it along with "the rest of the offal, refuse, and garbage I seem doomed to produce." That night, after I'd taken John to the emergency ward, I was lying in bed too exhausted to sleep and no longer drunk enough to pass out when it came to me that the whole problem was with gifts. Big Red had lost his. John couldn't deliver his. And me, I didn't seem to have one at all, no gift to deliver. With that recognition things turned to shit, pure and simple.

After considering this a few days in the grey light of recovered sobriety, I decided I needed a heart-to-heart with the Fourth Wiseman. Since I hadn't been able to crack his mania on the job, I thought I'd follow him home, buttonhole him off-duty as it were, and ask him politely how you could deliver a gift if you didn't have one, or at least didn't know what it was. If he wouldn't talk, I'd cajole, angle, reason, bribe, beg, and, if all else failed, follow my impulse of the previous Christmas and strangle it out of him. But I'd taken too long to gather my resolve into action. July 4, 1965, one year to the tock after he'd first appeared, the Fourth Wiseman vanished—how or where or why, nobody had a clue. I was a day late and a whole lot short.

Scumball's return was another loss in what was quickly becoming a streak, one bad beat after another. He was waiting for me in Cravetti's office. A year and a half in the slammer hadn't changed him much, except the mumble was lower and a little more slurred and his get-out suit hadn't had time to properly scuz. The smile was still an immaculate dazzle and the proposition hadn't substantially changed: "Georgie, you ready to go for some rides?"

"Scumball," I sighed, "you hitting the ground running?"

The mention of his name elicited the full display of teeth. "Well, Georgie my boy, there's a *lot* of ground to cover, know what I mean? I'm sort of an independent contractor, like you, and like you I'm a stand-up guy. I go down, nobody goes down with me; people like that. I paid my debt to society, now you might say I have a little credit, maybe run up a tab. Did some thinking in slam, and some people I work with like the new wrinkles. For you it's still basically the same number, but the bread, the bread, Georgie, is *lots* better. Say five hundred in front, ditto on delivery. There'll be keys and cover, same as before."

"Sure," I said, "why not?" My incentive wasn't the money, though a grand was a hell of a payday. I suppose it was the promise of action, something to snatch me from the morass, a change that might ring more changes—for the better, I hoped, because if I got much lower I'd be under the bottom.

I didn't notice anything special about the '63 Vette till I cranked it over. The engine had belly, and it was dialed to the dot. This was obviously a street racer, stock to the eye but pure blur under the hood, with a drive-train and suspension beefed to take the load. You just couldn't help yourself. I made another entry in the loss column: I lost my mind.

It was 3:00 A.M. and Army Street was straight and empty as far as the eye could see. However, it couldn't see up the side alleys, and that's where the black-and-white was idling, waiting for an idiot just like me. He must've heard me, because I was going too fast to clock. Whoever had put that Vette together understood in his fingertips the balance between power and stability. The cop's red light started as a pulsing speck in the rearview mirror, but about two seconds after I hit high gear and tromped it on down, the light had disappeared. From the mirror, you understand, not my spine.

I had a lot of things going for me, even if brains wasn't one of them. I had a good jump, haul-ass wheels, an equal or better knowledge of the streets, and a raging desire to keep my sweet self out of jail. What pulled me through, though, was luck—but it was ably assisted, I was pleased to note, by a show of excellent instincts and, believe it or not, enough common sense to understand that while it was indeed exhilarating to be sitting in a machine that could blow the doors off anything the cops had on the street, it couldn't outrun their radios.

To *know* what to do without hesitation carries a bottomless sense of serenity, and I got a nice taste of it as I braked and geared down, gauging beyond conscious thought the variables of speed, distance, angle, force, stress, car-body composition, and the survival possibilities of my own mortal, maimable flesh. I took it sideways in a rubber-shredding, scrotum-cinching arc, hit the concrete streetlight stanchion dead center on the right headlight, simultaneously cramping the wheel to whip the rear end around to crash into the side of the bank on the corner. In one fluid movement I yanked the key and hit the concrete running, first down Mission a block, then sprinting up a side street and then cutting down an alley and then, slowing, a plan taking shape as I got my bearings and breath, over to Dolores. The old oak I'd remembered admiring on one of my walks hadn't moved. I celebrated the steadfastness of trees as I went up it. Some neighborhood kids had lashed a few planks together for a low-rent treehouse high in the boughs. By leaning back against a limb I was able to stretch out. I made myself comfortable while I slowly ate the cover note. It was signed "Jason Browne," and while chewing I wondered why Jason Browne would wreck such a beautiful machine. I wondered if he was more desperate than me, then decided it was impossible to know anything like that. I flexed my throbbing left elbow; I must've whacked it in the wreck, but it seemed to work. Everything still functioned, more or less. There was grace in the world. A couple of cop cars cruised by slow, their spotlights stabbing between buildings, but they weren't looking very hard. I waited till dawn collecting such small consolations, then returned to earth.

I called Scumball from a pay phone on 24th and gave him the chrome-on-the-road riff. When he replied, "Who is this?" he sounded truly indignant, so maybe he'd already heard I'd cut it close. Nothing I could do about that. I used another dime to call in sick at Cravetti's, then caught a bus home to North Beach. After a long, hot bath I opened a bottle of brandy and stretched out on the bed and had a long talk with myself.

You might've wondered where my back-up was. For that matter, why hadn't I pulled over at the first pulse of the cop's light, produced the cover letter, and taken the ticket and ton of horseshit you buy when the heat nabs you clocking double the posted limit and still in second gear? Why indeed, except for the natural aversion to scrutiny in such a vulnerable situation. Was I begging for a fall? Provocative question. Did I want to live? Jeez, I thought so, but my behavior wasn't reassuring. I was beginning to doubt myself, that terrible doubt that's like an obsession without an object. Fact was, though, I'd pulled it off, and I was sure that counted for something; but exactly what, I didn't know. I'd been lucky, I supposed, but despite the gambler's truth that it's always better to be lucky than good, luck is subject to sudden change, and I realized that in my condition I couldn't afford even a drop of bad luck. In retrospect it was a poignantly worthless realization, because I was about to drown in it.

But first, to encourage it, I got roaring drunk. That was a week later, during one of those rare September heat waves when the fog doesn't form on the bay and the city stifles. I must say I was hugely and happily drunk, a welcome change from melancholia-in-the-cups. The happiness was born of some spontaneous eruption without discernible cause, a raw, joyous overflow from the fountain within, a definite sign of life. I decided that rather than swelter in my room I'd sleep out in nature. I considered one of the nearby parks, but there were too many people hanging out on the edges who'd turn you into junk sculpture for your loose change. Then I had a great, happy, drunken idea—that old tree-fort oak over on Dolores, my sanctuary from hot pursuit. I hoofed it on over and climbed into its open arms. It was lovely stretched out on the planks, the stars blurring with heat shimmers as the city cooled.

I slept so well I didn't twitch till the morning traffic began to thicken. I checked for approaching pedestrians through the leaves and shinnied down. As soon as my feet hit the ground, I was dizzy. I leaned against the rough, heavy trunk, waiting a few minutes for my head to clear, and a few more to make sure it would stay that way. When I felt stable and lucid, or as much as my hangover allowed, I headed toward the bus stop over on Mission. I was due at Cravetti's by 8:00.

There is no sanctuary. Down the block I saw a woman starting down her front stairs with a large bag in her arms and a heavy purse swinging from her shoulder. I didn't pay any particular attention till she stopped halfway down and yelled something back toward the house. I couldn't make out the words, but her tone was pissed off. A lovers' quarrel, maybe; back to the world. When she yelled again, her voice strident, I was close enough to make it out: "The kitchen table, Eddie. *Kitchen* table! Now goddamn it, would you *please* hurry? We're going to be late." She shook her head angrily.

I was about forty yards from the steps when she shrieked, "Close the door, Eddie!" A door banged shut and a small brown-haired boy about five years old came bounding down the steps, his arms cradled under a bright yellow lunchpail on top of which were a couple of books and some big sheets of paper; he had his head scrunched down so his chin held the papers in place. He went right through his mother's grasp, giggling, mimicking, "Come *on*, we're *late.*" His mother, haggard, started after him.

I was about thirty feet away when he tripped near the bottom stair. I thought he was going to fall but somehow he kept his balance. In doing so, however, he lifted his chin from the papers and an errant breeze lifted off the one on top, which fluttered toward the curb. He almost snagged it, but just as his small hand reached out the paper skirred again, skittered sideways up the block, then, lifting, sailed waist-high toward the street.

I saw it coming and dove for him as he dashed intently between two parked cars and his mother screamed his name. The fingertips of my left hand brushed the leg of his brown corduroy pants. It was that close.

The old guy driving the blue '59 Merc didn't have a chance. The kid was dead before he hit the brakes. When I heard the sound of the car hitting that little boy, a wet smack like a side of beef thrown from the back of a semi onto a loading dock, it was like something reached down into my chest and ripped out my heart. The street was a chaos of brakes and screams. I lay there on the sidewalk, numb except for the burning in my fingertips where they'd grazed his trousers.

When his mother ran into the street, I jumped up to catch her before she could see his body—then realized she *should* go to him, touch him, kneel and hold him, whatever she needed to do.

But she didn't go to his body. She stopped short and pointed a wild, accusing finger at the blood running steadily toward the gutter, floating cigarette butts and a Juicy Fruit wrapper where it pooled against the curb. Her pointed finger shaking, she began a shrill, monotone chant: *"This . . .* is *not . . . right.* No. *No,* this is *not right. It is not right.* No. *Not right."* Long after the cops and neighbors had tried to calm her, comfort her, she persisted in the same stunned, determined accusation, until they led her gently back into the house, assuring her everything would be all right.

The cop who took my statement had as much trouble controlling his voice as I did. When I told him about the paper blowing into the street, he unfastened from his clipboard a crayon drawing on cheap tablet paper. A giant sun hovered over a landscape containing a large red flower, three animals that were either horses or deer, and a long green car with shiny black wheels. The sun dominated the upper center of the picture, high noon, solid gold, its light and warmth flooding the scene.

After the cop recorded my story, he rechecked my name and address and told me I was free to go. I'd seen the old man in the Merc being taken downtown in the back of a black-and-white, so I repeated my conviction that it wasn't his fault, that Eddie had bolted blindly between two parked cars and there was nothing in God's green world the man could've done to stop in time. "Gotcha," he said. "They just took him down to get a statement. Routine under the circumstances. The guy was shook, and it doesn't hurt to get him away from the scene."

An ambulance had taken the body away, and the crowd had thinned to a few gawkers. A couple of cops were measuring skidmarks. A guy with a backpump was flushing away the blood.

"I didn't want to see it," I told the cop. "Didn't want to, didn't need to."

"Me neither, pal."

"How's the mother?"

"Torn up, like you'd expect, but she'll be all right. Or as all right as you can get after something like this."

"You know, I just *barely* missed him." I held up my left hand for the cop to see. "I touched his pants, that's how fucking close it was. One second closer out of all the time in the world, *one* second, *one* goddamn *heartbeat*, and that guy wouldn't be hosing down the street."

"You did what you could," the cop grunted, "that's what matters."

The grunt annoyed me. "Are you *sure?* Are you *really, truly, deep-down positive* about that?" I started yelling. "Fucking utterly *convinced,* are you?"

"Hey pal," he bristled, "don't lay it on me. I gotta see this shit every day, so don't get on *my* ass. Listen, my third month on the street, green-ass rookie, we get a guy out on a ledge fifteen floors up and he's hot to jump. I'm leaning out the window telling him 'Don't.' I'm telling him every reason in the world to live, and I'm telling him straight from my heart, straight as it comes, how it's *worth* it, *life is worth it,* life is *sweet,* come back inside, give it another shot. And I see he's pressing himself back against the wall, I can see the fingernails on his left hand turn *white* he's digging so hard for a grip, and he's inching his way over to me and starting to cry. And when he's almost where I can reach him, he says in a real soft voice, 'You don't know what you're talking about,' and he pushes off. Fifteen stories, straight down. Strawberry jam. But even before he hit the ground I knew it wasn't my fault. I'd done my best, and I figure that's all you can ask, all you can ask of anybody, all you can ask of yourself." His eyes challenged me. "Unless you want to ask more than that."

"No," I said, slumping, "that sounds like plenty."

"Okay. You grabbed, you missed, you'll never know if it could've been any different. Don't get down on yourself. Go home, take a long hot bath, crack a couple of cold ones, watch the tube, forget it. Life goes on."

And that's what I did, all except forgetting. I was weak enough going in, and seeing a happy bouncing kid struck suddenly dead shattered me, just ate me up. Since I didn't know Eddie, you'd think it wouldn't have been so bad, but in a way it was worse, a reminder of the random daily slaughter beyond the tiny circle of my life. Besides, I knew Eddie. I'd touched him.

I took the five weeks of vacation I had coming, bought about three cases of canned stuff—hash, peaches, chili, stew—and about twelve cases of beer, and locked myself in my apartment. I didn't want to see anybody or anything. I took three or four hot baths a day, slept as much as my nightmares allowed, and the rest of the time drank beer and stared at the walls. I didn't know if I was going over the edge or if the edge was going over me. After a week I started pacing back and forth in my small apartment, looking at the floor, every once in a while bursting into tears. I couldn't find anything to hang onto until I remembered the sound of Big Red playing "Mercury Falling," and felt the necessity for music. Since I was afraid to leave the apartment, I switched on the radio.

I couldn't find much jazz on the box and what there was seemed too cool and complex. That's when I discovered rock-and-roll. It was the right time. If it was moribund six years earlier, in '65 the stone was rolled away, and that summer there was a revival, if not a resurrection. The Rolling Stones came out with "Satisfaction," as in can't get no, sounding as if they might get nasty if some didn't show up soon. Same month, Dylan went electric, bringing the power of the troubadour tradition to the power of electrical amplification, the music driving the meaning like a hammer driving a nail, and he sure wasn't singing about holding hands down at the Dairy Queen:

> How does it *feeeeeel*
> To be all *alloooone*
> Like a complete *unknooowwwwnn*
> Like a *roooooollllling STONE!*

With the Stones and Dylan, the airwaves suddenly seemed a long way from pretty-boy idols and teenybop dance fads. The mean gutter blues the Stones drew from, Dylan's electric barbed-wire Madonnas, the raw surrealism of the San Francisco bands that were beginning to break out of garages and lofts—all at once there was a mean and restless bite to the music, a hunger and defiance. Yet around the same time, the Loving Spoonful released "Do You Believe in Magic" and the Beatles' film *Help!* came out in all its grand and whacky foolishness. That sense of lightheartedness cracked the paralyzing fear of being thought uncool, different, weird—and that dread of appearing foolish is one of the biggest locks on the human cage. So all at once, along with a roots-first resurgence of black music into the mainstream, there was a new eruption of possibilities and permissions, a musical profusion of amazing range and open horizons, from the harshest doubts and indictments and a blatant sexual nitty-gritty unthinkable the year before to a sweetly playful and strangely fearless faith. The stone was rolling, and you couldn't mistake the excitement.

It would be silly to say the music saved or healed me, but in my daily routine of hot baths, of opening cans of beer and food, what I held onto was the music. Not for salvation—nothing can do that for you—but for the consolation of its promise, its spark of life, its wild, powerful synaptic arc across spirit, mind, and meat.

By the end of my five-week vacation I was functional, if barely, and aware that life, even by dragging itself wounded down the path, did go on. When I returned to work, however, I felt like I was coated about two inches thick with cold oatmeal. With the help of time and music I'd hauled myself up from a feeling of gutted doom to one of impenetrable depression. My flesh was bloated, my blood gone rancid, my spirit sour. Partly this was physical—I'd gone to hell from sitting on my ass drinking beer and eating out of cans. I could think of only one thing that might sharpen my reflexes, cheer me up, help me shed some flab—those little white pills with crosses on them.

I'd vowed with every fiber of purpose that I wouldn't do it again, fought temptation like a rabid bear, hung on through the shit-mush and doldrums, and I was so determined to scourge that weakness I decided

I'd only buy fifty hits for a last hurrah. In the twisted psychology of collapsed resolve, I figured this lapse was allowable on two unassailable points: first, amphetamines depress the appetite, leading to weight loss, so it was justifiable on medical grounds; and secondly, I was celebrating coming through slaughter, and what's a celebration without treats?

Perked me right up, too, and I needed some enthusiasm to fight back the gloom. Once I got riding that fifty-hit party I knew that what I really needed was to leave, move, split, follow Kacy or Red or any of the others who'd gotten out from under themselves. That I had nowhere to go except somewhere else made me tremendously sad.

I finished the fifty in about a week. Got my nervous system tuned up and my blubber trimmed back, but best of all I didn't try to score more when I ran out. The come-down wasn't that bad—the usual frazzle and funk—or else I was used to misery. My display of pluck was an inspiration. It isn't hard to make the right choices, but sometimes it's hell to stick to them.

In that hopeful mood I met with Scumball on the twentieth of October. He'd left a message for me at Cravetti's to meet him at Bob's Billiards. Scumball hadn't been particularly pleased by the job I'd done on the Corvette. I'd only heard from him once since then, a job in Oakland, but he'd canceled the next day, explaining only that the set-up had fallen through. I figured I'd been scratched from his list of reliable idiots, but then again I'd been out of action for five weeks.

The pool hall was a local hangout where you could shoot more than snooker if you had the inclination and the price. At Scumball's suggestion we went for a walk and were just out the door when he gave me a fraternal pat on the back and said something innocuous like, "How's my man been?" For some reason, and for the first time, I resented his assumption that we were partners, brothers, buddies, pals. Scumball played the small-time edges, mealy-cheap and tight; there was no hunger or grandeur to his imagination. I almost wheeled around to slap his hand off my back when it struck me what really was eating my ass. We *were* alike, literally partners-in-crime, and for all the soaring grandeur of my majestic and altogether superior imagination, I didn't seem to be doing much. Petty as he was, Scumball did have a

certain gift for scamming, and in fact I worked *for* him. I held my
tongue and listened.

It was an interesting earful. Scumball was playing a variation on his
new theme, and this time a story went with it. The car he had in mind
was a mint '59 Cadillac. According to Scumball, it had been purchased
by a whacked-out sixty-year-old spinster named Harriet Gildner as a
present to some hotshot rock star. The old lady was "covered up with
money," to quote Scumball, an heiress to a fortune in steel and rubber.
The Caddy was all crated to ship when the rock star died in a plane
wreck. Since she didn't need the money or the car, and could afford to
indulge her sentimentality, she'd stored it in one of her warehouses on
the docks. She had a nephew, guy named Cory Bingham, who wanted
the Caddy so bad he was wading in his own drool, but the old lady
wouldn't let go. She was a major loony, Scumball claimed, and her
psychic adviser, one Madam Bella, told her to hang on to it, its time
would come.

But Harriet Gildner's time had come first: she fell down the stairs
of her Nob Hill mansion and broke her neck, evidently so loaded that
the autopsy report indicated traces of blood in the drugs. There was
some quiet conjecture that Madam Bella or maybe Cory had given her
a helpful nudge to get her rolling, but it was ruled an accidental death.
That was in early '62, but her will, while legit, was an homage to
surrealism that every relative down to seventh-cousin twice-removed had
contested. The legal dust had finally cleared a few months back. The
nephew received the Cadillac he'd coveted, but that was all. Scumball
didn't remember exactly, but the stipulation in her will, to give you an
idea, went something like "Cory gets the car he panted for, provided
he's become a knight worthy of the steed, but he gets nothing else, never
ever, and if he ever sells the car he has to pay the estate double the sale
price, and if his worthiness is in question the Book of Lamentations
should be consulted if the ghosts see fit to reveal it."

So Cory got the Caddy, others got odd bits and pieces, Madam
Bella (her psychic adviser and, Scumball claimed, drug connection) was
well provided for, and the rest of the estate was divided equally between
the Brompton Society for the Promotion of Painless Death and the

Kinsey Institute. I laughed when Scumball told me that, but he shot me a scornful look. "Fucking dame. Makes me *puke* how it's always her kind that wind up with the big loot and never lifted a finger to earn it, never had to scuffle for one fucking penny."

Cory didn't care much about the car when he finally got it, an attitude evidently influenced by the fact he fancied himself a poker player, an expensive fancy that had placed him in pressing debt and serious disfavor with collection agencies not listed in the Yellow Pages. Although he didn't say so directly, it was easy to guess that Scumball was affiliated with the people who wanted to be paid. Since the Caddy was the only asset, I gathered Scumball had advised Cory that a mint Cadillac—even one only six years old—was a precious collector's item that should be insured to the hilt, and if anything unfortunate should happen to it—well, the insurance money might cover his IOUs and thereby guarantee him the continued use of his arms, legs, and sexual organs. Cory, quick to recognize wisdom when it threatened to club him, had agreed. The Caddy had been uncrated at a storage garage Cory had rented on 7th Street. A mechanic had checked it out, replacing seals and rubber as needed, and fired it up. It was all set: gassed, registered, ready to roll. Fully insured, of course.

But there was an irritating problem. I'd have to break into the garage to steal it. This wasn't a major difficulty, since Scumball had a duplicate key for the garage lock, but I'd have to make it *look* like B&E to keep the heat off Cory, who was nervous about being implicated, though evidently even more worried about being maimed. I told Scumball that Cory was liable to get looked at hard, considering the recent insurance purchase, and that I wasn't particularly interested in the job since he was liable to crumble like a soggy cookie. Scumball assured me that Cory's alibi would be airtight, that a lawyer specializing in such claims would represent him in all transactions with the insurance people, that he knew for a fact that the agent who'd sold Cory the policy was sympathetic, and that Cory himself completely understood that if he so much as squeaked his body was shark bait.

"Forget it," I told Scumball. "The whole thing's got too much wobble."

Scumball was deeply understanding. He appreciated that Breaking & Entering, even if faked, was a companion felony to Grand Theft Auto, and that working without cover substantially increased the risks. That's why I would get two grand in front and another deuce on delivery.

I'd like to think it wasn't the money that swayed me, but rather some profoundly instinctive understanding that the door was opening on a journey I couldn't deny. I've thought about it since, of course, without concluding much except that somewhere in the welter of possibilities I might've felt a way out. The money, for instance, would support a long vacation to check out other places, new ideas; maybe something would click. I was still miserable, though a notch up from the gutted numbness of the month before.

Scumball smiled with pearly pleasure when I agreed to the deal. He gave me another fraternal pat on the shoulder as he slipped me an envelope with a hundred $20 bills inside. I resented the pat, welcomed the money, and wasn't sure how I felt about the rest.

The job was set for late on the twenty-fourth, giving me a couple of days to prepare. The storage garage on 7th was within walking distance of my place, so I hoofed over that evening to check it out. The lock was a heavy-duty Schlage and the door was steel. Getting in, of course, was no problem—I had the duplicate key—but I had to fake my break-in.

What I did was fairly simple. I bought another Schlage lock, same model as the one on the door, and late that night I went over and switched the new one for the original. I took the original to Cravetti's with me the next morning and used a portable oxy-acetylene torch to cut through the shackle just enough that it would slide out of the staple. I saved the metal drippings, putting them in a film cannister when they'd cooled. I fried the duplicate key beyond recognition and tossed it into the scrap bucket. I worked with a concentration and precision I hadn't felt in a couple of months, and let me tell you it felt good. Felt *alive*, like I was finally rolling with the river.

Then I hit a snag. I couldn't find a back-up driver. All my old outlaw cronies were gone except John Seasons, and he wasn't remotely interested. Neal Cassady was supposed to be around, but I couldn't locate him; he was already turning into a rumor. There was an old friend named Laura Dolteca, but her mother was in town for the week in a last-ditch effort to change her daughter's delightfully wild ways. I couldn't think of anyone else I trusted. Three people, when five years before there had been thirty. It was time to move on. Big Sur. Santa Fe. Maybe across town to the Haight—I'd heard rumblings of some high craziness over there. With the four grand from the Caddy job and another two at home in a sock, I could afford to roam around and see what connected, what pieces fit.

But first the business at hand. When I came off-shift at 5:00 I went straight to my apartment, soaked for an hour in a hot bath, and cooked myself a steak dinner. I ate with gusto for the first time in a couple of months, then did the dishes. At 9:00 I checked and packed my tools: the torched original lock and metal drippings, key to the new lock on the garage, flashlight, gloves, and a few odds and ends like sidecutters and jumper wires. Once everything was all set I stretched out on the bed and dialed up some rock on the box and, riding the anticipation, methodically considered the pile of possibilities and contingencies.

The only three crucial problems I hadn't resolved were where and how to wreck the Caddy and how to get away. I say I hadn't decided, but I had—subject to tough review. I applied all the hard-headed logic I could muster, weighing, balancing, trying to enforce an intelligent objectivity, but I finally approved my original inclinations, which were based on pure sentimentality and an aesthetic disposition for the symmetrical: I'd put it over the same cliff out on the Pacific where Big Red and I had dumped that first car, the Mercury falling into silence. Of course this would leave me on foot about a hundred miles from home, but I saw a pleasing way around that. I'd hide out in one of the rugged coastal ravines for a day devoted to contemplating what to do with my life, then hitch back the next evening. That left a minor hang-up, which I solved immediately with a phone call to Cravetti's, telling them that a buddy of mine had been badly hurt in a logging accident near Gualala and I was on my way up to see him for a couple of days.

I lay there listening to the music till almost 1:30 in the morning, then gathered my crime kit and headed for the door. My hand was on the knob before I realized I'd left the radio on, and just as I reached to snap it off the deejay dropped the needle on James Brown's "Pappa's Got a Brand New Bag." I could never figure out whether the new bag was smack, a recharged scrotum, or a new direction in life, but you could sure as shit dance to it. And that's just what I did, bopping around my apartment, little shimmy and slide, touch of Afro-Cuban shuffle here, four beats of off-the-wall flamenco gypsy twist there, a bit of straight-on ass shaking to smooth it out, and ending with a flourished twirl that Mr. Brown himself, King of Flash Cool, would've applauded. Yea, if the heart's beating the blood's gotta move. Flushed with dancing, nearly giddy, I clicked off the tunes and lights and hit the street.

The bars were just beginning to empty as I headed up Columbus toward Kearny. Lots of sailor boys fresh from the tit shows and a handful of new fuzz-beard beatniks who looked like they were wondering where they might score a lid of the good stuff. A black-and-white cruised by and I kept on walking as cool as you can get until it turned the corner, then, irrepressible me, I broke into a full-tilt boogie step and took it right over the top into my newly discovered James Brown whoop-da-twirl, a double this time.

The double whoop-da-twirl was actually a one-and-a-half, and I landed facing a young couple that I hadn't noticed behind me on the sidewalk, scaring the holy bejeesus out of them. "Love each other or die!" I commanded, a line John Seasons was fond of screaming unexpectedly when he was at the peak of a binge. And I'll be go to hell if they both didn't simultaneously blurt, *"Yes, sir!"* They were scared, and that certainly wasn't what I'd intended, nor what I wanted. I could see them flagging down the next cop car with a babbling raw-panic story about some guy who'd spun around and threatened to kill them, so I said, "Hey, relax. I was just quoting a line from a poem. You know, poetry? And that wild old twirl was straight from unbearable exuberance. Sorry if I startled you, but I didn't hear you coming up behind me." I bowed to the woman and offered my hand to the young man as I introduced myself: "My name's Jack Kerouac."

"I thought you were taller," the woman said. I could've kissed her.

"You wrote *On the Road*," the guy announced. "I dug it."

We chatted a few minutes as I basked in their reverence, and then I told them I had to go find Snyder because we were taking off in the morning to climb Mount Shasta. Once we reached the peak we'd each say one word to the wind and then give up speech for a year. Bless their hearts, they wanted to go along.

I was turning to go when the woman stopped me with a touch on the shoulder. She reached in her pocket and handed me a small foil-wrapped package. "LSD," she murmured. "Only take one at a time."

"Thank you," I said politely. I'd been hearing about LSD but hadn't been interested enough to score. I had enough trouble with peyote. I realized it wasn't exceptionally bright to add drug possession to a list of imminent felonies, but there was no way to gracefully refuse.

"Take it in a beautiful place," she advised. "It'll really open things up."

Well, after all, I *was* interested in opening things up, so why not? Keep the spirit of adventure alive. "Wish I had something I could offer in return," I said—*except lies*, my conscience reminded me.

"There's something I'd like to know," she said shyly.

I braced myself. "Name it and I'll try."

"I'd like to know what word you're going to say on top of Mount Shasta."

"I can't tell you because I don't know," I said, relaxing. "I'm just going to say whatever comes to me, whatever I feel. Spontaneous bop of the moment's revelation, you understand. Sorry I can't tell you or I sure would."

"Just a minute," she said, rummaging in her buckskin purse till she found a card and a pen. She talked as she scribbled under the streetlight. "It's a stamped postcard. I'll address it to myself. My name's Natalie. After you come down from the mountain, write what word you said and mail it to me—but *only* if you *feel* like it. No obligation. And I promise not to tell anybody."

"That's fair. Assuming I make the top and have something to say." I pocketed the card.

"Can she tell me?" her boyfriend asked.

"Sure, if you still love each other and haven't died."

They both giggled.

"Don't die," I admonished them, and then I was gone up Columbus to Kearny, strolling up the mountain toward the wild wind and the mighty clouds of joy, letting fly with a bit of the double-shuffle be-bop buck-and-wing as the spirit moved me. From the instrument room of my psyche, a voice as dry as my conscience's but with a more sardonic edge announced, *You're asking for it.* And I answered under my breath, "That's right, I'm asking for it. Hell, I'm begging for it." And I bopped on down the street.

I was more subdued by the time I reached the garage on 7th, but still full of juice. I felt alert, confident, inevitable, and I hadn't felt any of that in a long time. I walked up to the garage door like I owned the place, used the key, and swung the double doors open. I stepped inside, shutting the doors behind me, slipped the flashlight out of my crime kit, and stood still in the darkness, senses straining. The air seemed warmer inside. There was a musky odor of gear oil, sharp tang of solvent. I switched on the flashlight.

The garage was full of Cadillac. The car looked about seventy feet long. Where it wasn't chrome, it was pure white, including the sidewalls on the tires. Six years is a long time for rubber not to roll, and though Scumball had assured me there were new tires all around, I wanted to be sure. There were. I checked the plates: current. Despite my attention to safety items as I made my inspection, it was impossible to miss the extravagance of the styling: swept fins that seemed as high as the roofline, each sporting twin bullet taillights; a front grille divided by a thick horizontal chrome bar and studded with small chrome bullets, a pattern repeated on the rear dummy grille that ran across the lower back panel above the bumper; fenderskirts on the rear wells; tinted wrap-around windows front and back; chrome gleaming everywhere. It was an Eldorado, and if memory serves that meant 390 cubes, 345 horses, fed by three two-barrel carbs. You'd need that kind of thrust to move such a chunk of metal.

I opened the door to check the key and registration and was hit by the odor of new leather upholstery and, over that, a fragrance I knew in my loins and reeled to remember: Shalimar. Kacy's favorite perfume. I inhaled deeply, and again, but still wasn't really sure I still smelled it. The uncertainty spooked me. I kept sniffing, starting to tremble, then willed myself back to the job at hand before I snapped my concentration. Forcing myself to relax and slow down, I slipped the registration from the visor and went over it carefully. Clean as a whistle.

The key was under the front seat where it was supposed to be, and slipped smoothly into the ignition. The engine caught on the first stroke and settled into a purr. I gave the gauges a glance; everything looked good. The tank was full. That just left the tricky part, the point of maximum vulnerability. I had to open the garage doors, drive out, stop, close the garage door, reattach the duplicate lock, scatter some metal drippings under the hasp, toss the cut lock out where it wouldn't be obvious but where it could be found without a struggle, then get back into the Eldorado and cruise away. I figured five minutes at the outside if nothing screwed up; two if it all jammed together smooth. What I didn't need was a cop cruising by or some good neighbor with insomnia who collected the Dick Tracy Crimestopper Notes out of the Sunday funnies.

ABCDEFG. Plans. Pure delusions. How can you ever accommodate the imponderables, the variables, the voluptuous teeming of possibilities, the random assertions of chance, the inflexible dictates of fate? You jump out of a tree and walk down the street and a little boy is slaughtered in front of your eyes. The music ends and a woman stands up and takes off her clothes and you fall in love. I was turning the key when I heard a car swing around the corner and come down the street. Then another right behind it, radio blasting rock-and-roll. Both passed without slowing. Then another cruised by from up the block. Far too much traffic for 2:30 in the morning. Maybe there was a party in the neighborhood, a card game, whorehouse, drug deal, who knows. I figured I'd give it a few minutes to settle out.

I decided there were a couple of useful things I could do while waiting, like get the lock and metal drippings out and ready, and then stash the rest of my kit in the glovebox. When I leaned over and opened the glovebox, the powerful scent of Shalimar carried me back into Kacy's arms.

I came back to reality fast, greatly aided by another memory—that I was in the middle of multiple felonies—and by the fact that Kacy wasn't likely to be curled up in the glovebox awaiting my amorous designs. Shalimar is hardly a rare perfume. Maybe Cory Bingham had a girlfriend who used it, or maybe he liked to splash a little on himself and prance around. I shined the flashlight in the glovebox, expecting to find a leaky perfume bottle or a scented scarf, but the only thing in the glovebox was a crumpled piece of paper which on closer inspection turned out to be an envelope. I lifted it to my nose: absolutely Shalimar, not overwhelming but distinct. Of course, logical, always an explanation—a perfumed letter, addressed in a fine, precise script to Mr. Big Bopper. That was all, just the name. No stamps or postmark. I turned it over in the flashlight's beam and saw the jagged tear where it had been ripped open. The letter inside was typewritten, single-spaced. I took it out and smoothed it on the steering wheel.

I read the letter seven times straight through right then, another seven later that night, and maybe seven hundred times altogether, but after the first time through I knew without doubt or hesitation what I was going to do.

I can recite the letter by heart. The letterhead was embossed in a rich burgundy ink: Miss Harriet Annalee Gildner. Under her name, exactly centered, the date was typed, February 1, 1959.

Dear Mr. Bopper,

I am a 57-year-old virgin. I've never had sex with a man because none has ever moved me. Don't mistake me, please. I'm neither vain in my virtue, nor ashamed. Life is rich with passions and pleasures, and sex is undoubtedly one. I haven't denied myself; I simply haven't found the man and the moment, and see no reason to fake it.

I hope you won't mistake me as a hopeless kook, but one of my deepest interests is the invisible world.

Over the years I've employed some of the most sensitive psychics, shamans, and mediums to provide access to that realm of being which defies the rational circuits of knowledge our culture enforces as reality. I've sought those realms out of a desire to know, not a need to believe. I'll spare you the techniques and metaphysics; since they are much closer to music than "thought," I assume you'll understand.

To the point then: About a week ago, while I was in my office perusing my broker's report and enjoying a pipe of opium, I was visited by formless spirits bearing a large book. It was bound in the horn of a white rhinoceros with the title stamped in gold: THE BOOK OF LAMENTATIONS.

I asked the spirits to open the book.

"One page, one page," voices chanted together in reply, then held the book out to me.

It opened at my touch. The page revealed was in a language I'd never encountered before, but somehow I understood clearly as I read that it was a lament of virgins, both men and women, who, by whatever cause or reason, had never known (I quote the text) "the sweet obliterations of sexual love." The text continued, a chronicle of regrets, but the page faded as I read. In foolish desperation I tried to grab the book. It vanished with the spirits. But immediately a single spirit (they are invisible, but overwhelmingly present) returned. I could feel it waiting.

"Why was I allowed this visit?" I asked.

There was a giggle, a 17-year-old's nervous glee, and a young woman's voice replied, "Trust yourself, not us."

"How will I know?" I asked her.

She giggled again. "You just *do*. And you'll probably be wrong."

"Are *you* a virgin?" I asked.

"Are you kidding?" She vanished into her laughter, leaving me confused and, I must admit, distraught.

I didn't fall asleep until late that night, but I slept deeply. When I woke the next morning, shrouded in the membranes of dreams I couldn't remember, I reached over to my nightstand to turn on the radio to a classical station I frequently listen to. Or such was my attempt. I somehow turned the tuning dial rather than the on-off switch. I realized my mistake and turned the right knob, forgetting the station would be at random.

And there you were: "Helllooo bay-beeee, this is the Big Bopper." And I was moved. Men that have made sexual advances toward me in the past have always made it seem such an awkward, harrowing pursuit. When I heard the playfulness in your voice, the happy, loose lechery, I knew. And maybe—*probably*—I'm wrong, but that doesn't alter the conviction.

I want you to understand this car is a gift, yours without strings or conditions. It is a gift to acknowledge your music, the desire that spins the planets, and the power it portends. So it is very much a gift to the possibilities of friendship, communion, and love. You owe me nothing. I can afford it because I'm ridiculously wealthy.

If you're ever in San Francisco, please give me a call or drop by my house. I would like very much to meet you.

Sincerely yours,

Harriet Gildner

I sat there in the Shalimar-scented darkness, a man without a gift inside a gift undelivered, a heartfelt crazy gift meant to celebrate music and the possibilities of human love. I would deliver it, all right.

Then a couple of pieces fell together. Scumball had said it was a present to some rock star who'd up and died, but the Big Bopper's name hung on the threshold of memory for a moment before it arced across. "That's a lot of music to lose," Kacy had said. Buddy Holly, Ritchie Valens, and the Big Bopper. And now this jerkoff expected *me* to wreck the Bopper's Cadillac, his aunt's gift, to pay off his stupidity at the poker table? Nope. No way was it going to happen. The car didn't belong to him. It belonged to the ghosts of Harriet and the Big Bopper, to love and music. I, too, was probably wrong, but fuck it. You move as you're moved, and what I felt moved to do was drive it to the Big Bopper's grave, stand on the hood and read Harriet's letter, and then set it all ablaze, a monument of fire. I was going to climb the mountain and say my word; deliver my gift and slip away.

I knew this was going to be more difficult than it sounded. Besides a whole pile of luck, I needed a couple of other things I could think of offhand: solid cover and a little information. I figured the cover shouldn't be too difficult. John Seasons and his many official seals could probably handle it as long as I didn't come under hard scrutiny. The only information that seemed crucial was the location of the Big Bopper's grave, and I figured I could find that out on the way.

I carefully refolded the letter and returned it to the envelope, pissed that someone—most likely that asshole Cory—had ripped it open and then crumpled it. The letter was a noble document, a little strange maybe, but that's no reason to treat it like a used Kleenex.

The occasional car still passed on the street, but I felt charmed in my elated conviction of doing right—or at least doing *something*—and if you're going to throw your ass up for grabs, that's a good time.

I didn't hurry. I cranked the Caddy over again and let it idle while I opened the garage doors. I pulled out into the driveway, put it in neutral, and set the brake. That damn Caddy was so long half of it was in the street. I closed the doors, snapped on the duplicate lock, sprinkled the container of melted drippings around, side-armed the torch-cut original into the space between the garage and the building next door, climbed back in the Caddy, snugged up my gloves, took off the brake, and my ass was gone.

John Seasons answered the door with a distant grin. It was 3:30 in the morning and he'd just finished a poem he thought was worthy. He understood before I spoke that something was up, and fixed me with a cocked gaze. "My, you're looking *awfully* lively this morning."

I ran it down for him as quickly and as clearly as I could. "I bow to the romance of the gesture," he said, and actually gave me a formal little bow. That he liked the idea made it seem even better.

I explained my need for cover. I told him the Caddy was legally registered to Cory Bingham, so what I needed was either new registration or a damn good reason for being in the car.

John had an innate understanding of such things. "Do you have any leverage on Bingham?"

"Since I'm off and running, and know the scam, he should be reasonable. I wouldn't say I had him by the nuts, but I could sure yank on some short hairs."

"It would probably be best for all concerned if the guy took a vacation where he couldn't be reached for a few days. Then he wouldn't have to lie."

"I was thinking along the same lines," I said. "No need to pull on a wet noodle."

John said, "All I need from you is a photograph for a new driver's license, and the rest is easy. And I will need the current registration and that letter from the woman . . . Harriet Gildner, was it? Think I met her once at the Magic Workshop. Definitely out there."

I had the registration and letter with me. John was impressed. "Why, George, you're becoming lucidly thorough in your foolishness."

"I'll take that as a compliment."

John shrugged. "Well, at least it's *grand* foolishness."

"I hate to hurry an artist at work," I said, "but do you think you could have the paperwork finished in four or five hours?"

"By dawn's early light."

"Well, shit, if you have time to kill, how about putting some of your legendary scholarship to work and see what you can find out about the Big Bopper for me? Especially where he's buried."

"Really, George, that's not my field. Prosody, history, the graphic arts, baseball—those I might be able to help you with. But I lack the proper references for the burial sites of rock-and-roll musicians. However, I recently met a darling young boy who happens to be a janitor at the library. He should be there now, and maybe he can help us out."

70

"I just want to get rolling in the right direction."

"I understand," John said. "What's a pilgrimage without a destination?"

My immediate destination was my apartment. I parked around back and climbed the stairs. I stood in the center of the room and thought about what I'd need, and decided to go as light as possible. I threw together a duffle of clothes and my shaving kit, then withdrew my life savings from the First Bank of the Innersprings. I counted it on the kitchen table—$4170, including the $2000 Scumball had fronted me.

That reminded me I had to call. I dialed the new number he'd given me. As always, he answered on the third ring.

"Complications," I said.

There was short silence, then a displeased question: "Yes?"

"Of the heart."

The pause was longer, but I waited him out. "Well?" he said, not happy.

"Don't worry. The job'll get done. It's just going to take some time."

"I hope we're talking minutes."

"Maybe three or four days. Could be a week."

"No."

"Fuck you," I said.

"I don't know what your problem is," Scumball hissed, "but if you got a dumb urge to play games or mention names I got something for *you* to remember, wise-ass. There's over two hundred bones in the body, and I have friends who'd enjoy breaking them for you, one by one, slowly. When they got done, you'd be a fucking *puddle,* savvy?"

"Fuck your friends, too, and the Sheriff, and the whole posse. If you want your ass covered, tell your shithead friend to be gone for a week. Might do his slimy soul some good to take a long hike in the Sierras. I'll take care of my end. I don't need any premature mention about missing machinery. That might make it tough on everybody concerned. You can keep what I have coming, make up for your inconvenience, but this one gets played my way. I'm going to deliver it where it rightfully belongs."

"You're gonna eat shit, is what you're gonna do. Save some money for doctor bills. This is gonna make a *lot* of people unhappy."

"Not for long. And they'll get over it. But you know what? It's going to make *me* very happy. Ecstatic, I hope. I'm going to send it roaring upward in the flames. What do you think of that?"

"I think it'd be nice you went with it."

"Listen, it's *not* a rip-off, you understand? It's going to go down, like all the rest. A few days' extra time ought to be worth the balance due. Goes in *your* grubby pocket. I'm not jerking you around. It's just something that I need to do, and you can't do shit about it, so why not squeeze a little grace out of that fucking mustard seed you call a heart?"

"Die," he snarled, and hung up, depriving me of the chance to urge him to improve his imagination.

Given Scumball's nasty mood I figured it wouldn't be wise to hang around my apartment too long—nor the city, for that matter—so I locked up and loaded my stuff in the Caddy's trunk, then cruised over to the all-night Doggie Diner for two large coffees and a double burger, which I ate on my way over to John's.

My traveling papers were ready. At John's insistence, we sat down at the kitchen table to go over them. He flipped through and explained each one. A new California driver's license in the name of George Teo Gass (John's sense of humor), a Social Security card, draft card, and other I.D. featuring my new name. In addition, a very official looking DMV Certificate of Interstate Transport, a document I didn't even know existed, and I'm not sure John did either. There was a notarized letter from Cory Bingham attesting to the fact that Mr. Gass was authorized to transport the vehicle for display at a memorial tribute to the Big Bopper. Cory's letter was accompanied by a sheaf of papers on letterhead from the law offices of Dewey, Scrum, and Howe, which covered the terms and liabilities of the car's display at the memorial. John said that if I got stopped, I should be sure to explain I'd been hired through an agent for the lawyers and had never personally met Mr. Bingham or the lawyers, though the agent had told me there was a kind of legal hassle going on between Cory Bingham and the Big Bopper's estate. He even had a card from the agent, one Odysseus Jones.

Poetry or forgery, John Seasons knew what to do with paper and ink. He wouldn't take a penny for it, either. I told him I had a wad of money to cover travel expenses and that proper documentation was foremost in the budget, but John, with the exaggerated professorial tone he used to mock himself, said, "Ah, but my dear young man, the object of price is to measure value, and the highest value is blessings. One easily infers from the works of Lao-Tze, Dogen, and other Masters of the Path that blessed most deeply is he who helps a pilgrim on the way."

I was about to insist on a token $50 to at least cover wear and tear on the seals when there was a loud pounding on the door. I spun around, the ruby neon flight-light pulsing in my brain stem, certain one of Scumball's goons had spotted the Caddy down the block. John grabbed my arm. "Easy," he said softly. "Too late for fear." He went to the door and asked, "May I inquire who has come to call at this ungodly hour?"

Myron and Messerschmidt, as it happened, both wired to the tits, just hitting town after a forty-hour nonstop run to Mexico and back. They came in babbling, each bearing a large, rattling shopping bag full of drugs available only by prescription in this country, while in Mexico, with its less formal notions of restriction, they were available in bulk over-the-counter, especially at the more enlightened border *farmacias*. The first item out of Myron's bag was a 1000-tablet bottle of benzedrine, factory sealed. They wanted $150, and got it on the spot. John clucked his tongue but I ignored him. I was already tired, and it might be a long drive. Besides, I was bold, imaginative, and decisive; such virtues wither without reward.

While Myron and Messerschmidt rummaged through the portable pharmacy for John's order of Percodan—I clucked at *him*—he accompanied me to the door. "Any info on the Big Bopper," I asked.

"Ah, yes. I called my young friend at the library and he went through the newspaper files. The Big Bopper's real name was Jiles Perry Richardson, born and raised in Sabine Pass, Texas. If my spotty geography serves, that's right on the Louisiana border, near the mouth of the Red River. He was working as a disc jockey in Beaumont when he 'hit the charts,' as they say. My friend said there was no information on his burial site in the papers, but I would assume he was interred in Sabine

Pass, or possibly Beaumont. If I were you, I'd head out yonder to East Texas—Beaumont's not far from Sabine Pass—but it would be smart indeed to do a little library research along the way. Shouldn't be difficult to find out where he's buried. But I'd find out before you get too far, because you're going to feel like a dumb shit if you're parked in Sabine Pass and find out his bones found their rest in L.A."

I blessed him for his help and gave him a big hug, putting some feeling into it. He returned it, then held me at arms' length and looked in my eyes. "So," he said approvingly, "the Pilgrim Ghost."

"Hey, I'm no ghost yet," I objected, slightly unnerved. But I'd misunderstood.

"No, no," John laughed. "Goest. *Go-est.* Like, 'The pilgrim goest forth, the journey his prayer.' "

"More like it," I said, relieved.

"Well, give my best to the dragons and wizards, and pledge my honor to the maidens fair. And the pages, if you see any cute ones. And George, seriously: fare well."

The stars were fading in the dawnlight as I left, forged papers under one arm and a 1000-hit bottle of bennies tucked inside my jacket. The Caddy was waiting where I'd left it, pure white and heavily chromed, blast-off styling and power everything, a cross between a rocketship and Leviathan, an excessive manifestation of garish excellence, a twisted notion of the American dreamboat.

I slipped inside and turned it over. While it warmed up I put the papers in the glovebox and clipped the registration back on the visor. I lined up three bennies on my tongue like miniature communion wafers, swallowed, and stashed the bottle under the seat. I sat there tapping the gas, wondering if I was forgetting anything. But I'd reached that point where anything I was forgetting was forgotten. The clutch plate kissed the power and I came down on the juice. By the time I hit the end of the block I was long gone.

MESOLOGUE

Just as George was taking off on his pilgrimage in '65, we arrived in the present, the tow truck bucking as he geared down for the Monte Rio stop sign.

"Monte Rio," I announced. Given my nearly comatose condition resulting from the tangled combination of the doom flu, many milligrams of codeine, the paralysis of speed-induced terror, and the hypnotic lull of George's voice, I was as impressed by my perspicacity as my ability to articulate it. "Monte Rio," I repeated, enthralled by its existential certainty.

"Yes indeed," George confirmed. "Five miles to Guerneville now; got it by the dick on a downhill pull and tomorrow will be a different world." He hung a left on 12 and took it up through the gears. "How you feeling? Hanging in there? Ears bleeding?"

I thought about it but I couldn't find the words. I'd shot my wad on "Monte Rio."

"Better?" George prompted. "Same? Worse?"

I nodded.

"All of the above?"

I nodded.

He nodded back. I couldn't tell if he was sympathetically acknowledging my inability to construct and utter words or simply confirming some inner judgment of his own—about what, I didn't know and didn't care. I sank into that luxurious indifference like a high-plains cowboy sliding down into his first bath after five weeks of merciless heat and horse sweat on the trail. The words to "Red River Valley" were floating through the remnants of my brain. ". . . hasten to bid me adieu . . ." *Adieu?* What sort of horseshit was "adieu." Cowboys didn't go around talking French.

George was giving me a look of pure appraisal, friendly but frank.

"Might be smart to stop by the Redwood Health Clinic for a quick check-up. I think you're fine, but opinions ain't diplomas."

"Bed!" I sobbed, distantly astonished that I'd spoken. It was the voice of my involuntary nervous system seizing control from a cowboy-consciousness now bidding adieu to the home of buffalo roaming. Bed. A bed. A physical demand, the need of it pure, unsullied by lengthy evaluation, careful consideration, or thoughtful judgment. Rest, sleep, surcease. The last round-up.

George was passing a log truck like it was frozen in time. Deft, decisive—no question the man could drive. As the log truck faded in the side mirror, he said, "You're the boss. The first order of business, then, is to get you to bed. When you're squared away I'll haul your rig over to Itchman's."

My head nodded itself.

"If you got no place particular in mind," George said, "how about the Rio del Rio? Bill and Dorie Carpenter run it. Good folks. Towed in their '54 Hudson when they snapped an axle up near Skagg Springs. They'd been out bird watching. The Rio del Rio isn't fancy-ass, but what it lacks in glitz it more than makes up for in comfort. Very quiet. Always clean."

"Faster," I said.

George, laughing at my regrettably invincible wit, gladly obliged. Though all the windows were cranked up tight, I could feel the wind roaring against my face. It felt good. It felt even better to be a mile out of Guerneville and closing fast.

The Rio del Rio was on the west side of town, set back in a grove of second-growth redwood on a plateau above the Russian River flood-plain. There were nine cabins, counting the office, all painted dark green with white trim, the green the same shade as the moss tufted between the cracks of the redwood-shake roofs.

George flicked the floorshift into neutral and set the brake. I hadn't realized we'd stopped. "I'll check in with Bill and Dorie and see what's what," he said. "Hang tight. Back in a flash."

The rain had relented into a swirling mist. Through the wet wind-shield, George seemed to blur as he approached the office. I heard a loud knock, followed in a few seconds by a delighted female whoop, immediately sharpening into a mock scold: "You crazy ol' ghost, we see you about as often as we do a pileated woodpecker." My brain refused the comparison as impossibly complex.

I glanced down at my hands folded rather primly on my lap. They seemed far away and unconcerned. I wondered if they could open the glovebox for more codeine. The index finger of my right hand twitched. Where there's communication, there's hope. I was sure George wouldn't mind; there seemed to be plenty, and I might need some later in case I hemorrhaged or something. Might save my life, a life, it was not lost on me, that seemed remarkably free of moral or ethical restraint. Why did generosity seem to inspire my rapacity?

I was still pondering this when I heard the slish-slap of someone running toward the truck. The driver's door flew open and George dumped an armful of paper and kindling on the front seat and swung himself in as he cheerfully announced, "Okay, pardner, you're all set." He held up a key, dangling it like bait. "Lucky seven. You have it as long as you need it, pay when you can. Doric says there's a special winter basket-case rate of three-fifty a day. *Told* you these were people with soul. Allow me to chauffeur you to your quarters."

In the middle of a time warp, this was way too much information for me to process. Ten seconds to the cabin. Hours to climb down out of the truck and get inside while George jabbered encouragement, comments, commands. "Easy does it now. . . . Watch those flagstones— slick as snot on a doorknob. . . . Now take a dead bead on the bed there, and I'll put some flames in the fireplace. Little warmth and a couple of days' sleep appeal to you any? You make a conked-out zombie look like a fucking speedfreak, but hey, lookee here, you made it to the land of your dreams! Just peel off those duds and crawl right in. Yes! Curl up like a baby and let it all go so far away your toes will have to shoot off flares to get your mind's attention. That's right. Now I'll go prove I deserved my Fire-Building Merit Badge while you snuggle down solid and sing for the Sandman. Nothing like wood heat to get the warmth to the bones . . ." His voice trailed off as he disappeared through the door.

It was complicated, especially the buttons on the shirt, but I got undressed, slipped shivering between the cold sheets, and pulled the quilt up to my ears. George was back with the paper and wood, saying something I couldn't hear over the crackle of the kindling catching in the riverstone fireplace. He came over and grinned down at me in bed and said something about my wet clothes and picking them up at the office and I could leave his there or keep them if I needed a more diverse wardrobe with a working-class cut to properly woo the Guerneville women, but I was already gliding away, his words lost in the sound of fire and the rainy redwoods dripping on the roof.

"Dreamers awake," a voice murmured. "Soup's on." George held a steaming cup in his hand. "Hate to wake you, but even if you had a sword stuck through your heart I wouldn't let you miss this soup. This is Dorie's justly famous Cosmic Cure-All Root Broth. Over thirty different roots simmered down slow. And by slow, I'm talking a couple of weeks, you understand? Sloooow. Extracting essences. It'll put some lead in your pencil or I've never been out of first gear."

I feebly accepted the cup. The broth was almost translucent, with a faint greenish-brown tint. Every swallow had a different taste: carrot, hickory, ginseng, licorice; now ginger, burdock, parsnip, garlic. It felt wonderful in my gut, a calm radiance soaking outward from the center. "More," I asked hopefully.

"Whole thermos on the nightstand here," George said, reaching to pour me another cup. "Comes compliments of the house with best wishes for a speedy recovery. But it's all there is, they ain't no more—this was the last container from the freezer. You can only make it once a year. Best fresh, Dorie claims, but it doesn't lose a hell of a lot in aging if you ask me. Incredible stuff. Cures flu and the bad blues, gout, malaria, shingles, impotence, schizophrenia, serum and viral hepatitis, terminal morbidity, most moral quandaries, senility, bad karma, and even that dreaded Hawaiian killer, lackanookie."

I drank greedily while my reviving brain analyzed corporeal input. My joints ached like decayed teeth, the fever (or perhaps the codeine) had turned my skull rubbery, but the piercing headache seemed blunted and the gastrointestinal maelstrom had definitely abated.

"You getting on top of it," George asked solicitously.

"Leg up," I mumbled. It was still a long way from my brain to my mouth.

"Thought so. You got some shine back in your eyes."

"This soup's good. Thank Dorie."

"I'll do it for sure." George smiled and turned toward the door.

It took a great effort but I managed: "And thank *you*, George. Most of all. Your kindness is enough to make me—"

George turned around, a gleam in his eye, the grin following. "Wasn't leaving just yet. You're not getting off *that* easy. Just wanted to grab myself a chair here so I could make myself comfortable while I finished my story. You should know how it turned out."

I was confused for an instant, then embarrassed. The story. Oh, shit. I felt like I'd insulted him, and tried to recover. "George, you're living proof it turned out good."

"Hard to know for sure." He shrugged, sliding the chair over next to the bed.

"I want to hear it, George, but I'm afraid I may nod out on you. Full of flu and codeine. Piss-poor audience." The effort of sustained thought and speech left me weak and breathless.

"Whatever." George waved a hand in dismissal. "I need to hear it more than you, anyway." The hand abruptly reached toward me, as if to touch my face. I flinched slightly, and unnecessarily, for he was just reaching over to snap off the nightstand lamp.

The only light in the room came from the windows, seeping through the redwoods and rolling mist outside. Unless I'd completely lost track of time it was around noon, but the quality of light belonged to dusk. The fire was burning down to a glow across the room, an occasional flare at a pocket of pitch, but its light seemed to reach us only as a change in the density of shadows. I could barely make out George's face.

I stretched out, clenched my muscles, then relaxed and closed my eyes, waiting for him to begin. A minute passed, then another. I could hear him breathing beside me in the dark. After another minute my pathological antipathy for dramatics crawled up my throat like bile. I tried to make it sound light and friendly, but I could feel the sarcasm in my voice: "George, what happened? You lose the key?"

"Naw," he said amiably, "I was trying to remember a feeling. It's important that the feeling is right. You'd think the feeling would be unforgettable—and it *is*—but you never can recall it with the clarity of the original, never whole and present like it was."

"What feeling?" I said.

"Free," he said. That got him started, and he didn't stop till the end.

PART TWO

DOO-WOP TO THE BOPPER'S GRAVE

At the moment I took off in that stolen Eldorado I wasn't contemplating the exquisitely bottomless metaphysical definitions of freedom, you understand, I was *feeling* the wild, crazy joy of actually cutting loose and *doing* it. Blinking in the dawnlight shaping the bridge, the bay, the hills beyond, I felt like I'd just kicked down a wall and stepped through clean. Not a hint of what lay ahead or how it would end, but free to find out.

As I crossed the Bay Bridge and took a right toward Oakland and the 580 connector, I was riding on romance, the grand gesture of delivering the gift not because it was essential or necessary to existence—how much really is?—but in fact because it *wasn't;* there was no reason to risk the hazards except those reasons which were my own.

Sweet Leaping Jesus and Beaming Buddha, I felt *good.* Full of powerful purpose and amazing grace. Solid on the path. I gave a little whoop when I cleared the toll plaza and tromped on the gas, the three deuces sucking the juice down, the pistons compressing it into a dense volatility, the spark unleashing the power, driving the wheels. The Caddy handled like a sick whale, but with all the mass riding on air suspension and eleven feet of wheelbase you could eat road in heavy comfort, truly *cruise,* your mind free to roam through itself, rest, or wail on down the line. She wasn't made to race, she was built to roll, and I was holding at a steady 100 without a sound or shiver.

In my defense I'll say that while lost in the flush of freedom and a bit swept away in the righteousness of my journey, I wasn't completely inattentive. I saw the highway patrol car in my rearview mirror about a quarter of a mile back. Just by the way he was coming on, I knew my ass was wearing the bullseye; I was pulling over before he even hit his party lights.

Heart knocking, I scanned the floors and seats for my usual collection of felonies—open containers, for example, or bennies spilling from under the seat—and was relieved to note that nothing was in plain view. Watching in my side mirror as the trooper's door swung open behind me, I told myself to be cool and take the consequences as they came. If nothing else, I'd learn at the git-go if Scumball or Bingham had squealed, and if the paper held up. Then I prayed to any god who'd listen that the cop wasn't some Nazi jerk who'd just had a shit-screamer fight with his old lady before leaving the house.

Praise the power of heartfelt, blood-sweating prayer, he wasn't.

"Good morning," he greeted me—quite cordially, I thought, considering the circumstances.

"Good morning, officer," I replied, letting the sunshine beam through.

"I've stopped you for exceeding the posted speed limit of sixty-five miles-per-hour. I clocked you at one-oh-two." Very precise, a little ice in his tone. Maybe he appreciated accuracy.

"That's correct, sir," I said.

"Could I see your driver's license and registration please?"

"Of course," I replied, and the dance began.

No trouble with my license—solid as the law itself. He examined the registration long enough that I anticipated his concern and pulled the folder of papers from the glovebox, the lovely odor of Shalimar now worrisomely mixed with that of fresh ink. Following my old friend Mott Stoker's advice that the only two things to do with your mouth in a tight situation are to keep it closed or get it moving, I got it moving, explaining how I was delivering the car to Texas for some sort of memorial tribute . . . didn't really know much about it . . . was hired by an agent for the estate and the lawyers had fixed me up with this wad of papers, you see, affidavits and certificates and such. I dumped the whole folder on him. He opened it and began shuffling.

"I haven't read all the legal stuff myself," I told him. "There was evidently a hassle between the two estates or some damn thing. Only thing I've checked double-solid is the insurance. I won't transport an uninsured car."

He grunted. "Don't blame you, speed you drive."

"Officer," I said, edging in a hint of wounded sincerity, "I've been driving *professionally* for *twelve* years—semis, stock cars, tow trucks, cabs, buses, damn near everything with wheels that turn—and I haven't had a ticket since '53 and never even came *close* to a wreck. Agent who hired me said this car's been in storage for six years while the estate was being settled. Check it out"—I pointed at the odometer—"seventy miles. *You* know cars: store one six years and seals can dry up on you, gaskets crack, oil gets gumballed in the crankcase. I wanted to know early on whether it's running tight or not, 'cause it's a whole bunch easier to fix it here than in the Mojave Desert two o'clock this afternoon." I nodded for emphasis, then pointed vaguely down the road. "And this—light traffic, triple-lane freeway—seemed the safest time and place to check it out. I know I broke the law, no argument there. *But* I didn't do it thoughtlessly or maliciously. Nor recklessly, or not to my mind, since driving's my profession."

He wasn't impressed. "The car is registered to Mr. Cory Bingham, is that correct?"

"Yup, you got it. Though it may be getting transferred to the Richardson estate—he was the Big Bopper, remember him? This car was supposed to be a gift to him. Except both parties died—this was back in '59—and the estate was just settled about six months ago. Or that's what they tell me."

"Just a minute, please." He took the registration with him back to the patrol car. I watched in the rearview mirror as he slipped inside the cruiser and reached for the radio. Flat electric crackle; muffled numbers. I looked down the road in front of me and hoped I'd be able to use it.

Five minutes later—obviously protected by the righteousness of my journey—I was indeed happily on my way, a ticket in the glovebox, a curt lecture on the-law-is-the-law fresh in my ears if not in my heart, and the bottle of bennies clamped between my thighs. I cracked the lid and ate three to celebrate.

Keeping it down to a sane 75 mph, I cruised south past San Leandro and took 580 toward the valley. I figured I'd take 99 down to Bakersfield, avoid the L.A. snarl by grabbing 58 to Barstow, then 247 down to Yucca

Valley, a short blast on 62 to the junction with Interstate 10, and then hang a big left for Texas. Might've been quicker through L.A., but I'd rather run than crawl.

Again it struck me that although I knew I was going to the Big Bopper's grave, I didn't know where it was. One of my major problems with amphetamines is they give me a rage for order, a craving for the voluptuous convolutions of routes, schedules, and plans; and at the same time they wire me to the white lines so tight I don't even want to stop for fuel. John had suggested hitting a library to research the Bopper, sensible advice for someone who felt like taking the time to stop, but I figured I could stop in Texas and look it up there. But maybe he wasn't buried in Texas. Or buried at all, come to think of it—he might've been cremated. After fifty miles I was already obsessively enmeshed in the complexity of possibilities, and needed another fifty to decide I should know what was what and where it exactly was. Otherwise I was likely to go on going till the speed ran out, and with 1000 hits at my disposal that might take awhile. This was essentially an aesthetic question. I wanted to make the trip clean and clear, with elegance, dispatch, and grace. I didn't want to end up pinballing blindly from coast to coast babbling to myself. I wanted to deliver the gift and slip away, not get caught in the slop.

Bolstered by this direct, no-bullshit appraisal of my true desires, I decided that knowledge and self-control were critical. I'd stop at the next town, go to the library, run down the info I needed, figure out what I was going to do, and do it.

The other imperative was to dump the speed, feed it to the asphalt. Or perhaps dump all but fifty and ration them with my iron willpower; use *them*, not let them use me. If the drugs got on top I wouldn't feel that *I'd* done it, and I sensed that might prove a sadness to last the rest of my life.

I pulled over a couple of a miles past Modesto and dug the bottle out from under the seat. I hit the button for the power window and, while it hummed down, unscrewed the cap, sighed, shut my eyes, then poured the contents out the window. Shook the bottle upside-down to be sure.

DOO-WOP TO THE BOPPER'S GRAVE

Then I got out and picked them all up. Fast. Lots of traffic was ripping by, and some of the bennies were blowing around in the draft. All I needed was for some Highway Patrolman to get wind of a frantic motorist gathering white pills off the blacktop out on 99 and have him stop by to give me a hand.

The thing was, as I was shaking the last bean from the bottle I realized—in one of those magnetic reversals of rationality—this was cheating. To dump the speed wasn't resolve; or if so, the weakest sort. This was actually an act of cowardice—instead of facing temptation, merely removing it. Virtue is empty without temptation. I'd never had any trouble resisting drugs when I didn't have any; only when they were in my hand did the trouble start. I finished picking up the bennies— maybe a hundred short—and screwed the lid down tight. I stashed them back under the seat and promised myself I wouldn't touch them till the delivery was made. Save 'em for the celebration, as it were.

The next stop on my itinerary was a library. I figured a city was a better shot than a small town for the info I wanted, so I waited till I hit Fresno. I stopped at a Union station for fuel and got directions to the library from the young kid working the pumps. "Gonna do a little reading, huh?" He smirked.

"Actually," I smiled back, "I heard Fresno has the only illustrated copy of *Tantric Sexual Secrets*. Stuff on proper breathing and arcane positions that'll keep it up for *weeks*. That's no problem for you young guys, but you get to be my age, all wore down, you need all the help you can get."

When I pulled out, he was still repeating the title to himself. I felt good about my contribution to scholarly pursuits as I followed his directions into town.

The library was quiet and cool inside. I checked the subject catalogue under *B* for both Big and Bopper, then *R* for Richardson, J.P. Nothing. Since I had the *R*'s open, I looked under Rock-and-Roll. Paydirt. I jotted down the call numbers of everything that sounded useful, then hit the stacks. Nothing. Zero. Not one. Probably a popular subject, but it seemed odd they'd all be out. I checked at the Reference Desk. According to the tall, sharp-boned librarian, they *were* out all right—for good. "The kids steal them faster than we can put them on the shelves," she explained.

"*Steal* them? *Why?*"

She lowered her voice to provide me with a model of appropriate volume: "For the pictures, I suppose."

"*What* pictures?" I hissed, an attempted whisper.

"Of the stars, I guess. We had a policy meeting yesterday and decided that all the rock books from now on will be in the closed stacks."

I felt baffled, deflected, so I plunged on to my purpose: "Do you know where the Big Bopper's buried?"

"I'm sorry?" she said, tilting her head as if she hadn't heard me, a nervous flutter of eyelids.

"The Big Bopper. I need to know where he's buried."

"I'm sorry," she repeated, "but who is—or *was*—the Big Bopper?"

"A rock star. He died in a plane crash in 1959. February third."

She spent half an hour searching for information, but found nothing I didn't already have. Real name Jiles Perry Richardson. Died at age twenty-seven. Born in Sabine Pass and worked as a disc jockey. Hit single with "Chantilly Lace." Nothing in any of the papers regarding the funeral arrangements.

I thanked the librarian for her help and walked out into the bright autumn sunlight. The swept-fin Caddy spacemobile was stretched along the curb like an abandoned prop from a Flash Gordon movie. I wondered about Harriet's taste in automotive styling for a moment, then shook my head. Who's to say what sort of wheels a Texas rocker might tumble to? And maybe Harriet had a sense of humor.

Fresno to Bakerfield was straight double-lane freeway. I kept the needle steady on 90, smiling with the knowledge that every time the wheels turned I was farther away from Scumball's clutches and closer to my destination, as vague as that was. Even though I'd come up empty, the library stop had fulfilled my scholarly obligation. I could enjoy the road, roaring along with the speed coming on solid in my brain, and I figured my itinerary would sort itself out along the way. When you're feeling good, there's no hurry—and what's a pilgrim without faith?

The Caddy needed gas again, so I stopped at a station in Bakersfield, a Texaco on the corner of a shopping mall. While the rocket guzzled Super Chief I hit the men's room and washed my face with cold water. Already I felt road-wired and gritty, and the usual amphetamine dry-mouth had left me parched, so when the Caddy was gassed I drove to the supermarket in the center of the mall and bought an ice chest, a couple of bags of cubes, and a cold case of Bud. I downed two fast, cracked a third for immediate use, and iced a dozen in the cooler, which I stashed in the trunk. The front seat would've been my first choice, but good sense prevailed. The trunk meant I'd have to stop every time my thirst caught up, but it was a lot less likely I'd find myself performing silly exercises for law enforcement officials.

Between Bakersfield and Barstow it was hot and windy. For one of those reasons of odd association, I remembered telling Natalie and her boyfriend that I was Jack Kerouac and on my way to climb Mount Shasta to whisper a word to the wind, and started to feel rotten about the lies. Granted, I'd been covering myself, but other evasions, less sleazy, leapt to mind. Squirm as I might, the truth was that even in my exuberance I'd resented their awed innocence, their eagerness to believe. The cold fact was that I'd wronged them, cheap and cruel. The postcard Natalie had given me was still in my pocket, and I decided to send her a much deserved apology. All the way to Barstow my speed-soaked brain entertained itself by composing and revising appropriate expressions of regret.

It was after dark when I pulled into the Barstow Gas-N-Go and topped off the Caddy for $8, which back then was a hefty cut for fuel. The attendant, a chubby red-haired kid who had to count on his fingers to make change, was absolutely slack-jaw *awed* by the Caddy—washed all the windows and polished the chrome just to stay near it, touching. Handing me my change, he smiled bashfully and said, "My daddy says a man that can afford a Cadillac sure ain't gonna worry 'bout paying its gas. Guess that's close to right, huh?"

"I wouldn't know," I told him. "I can't afford one. I'm just delivering it to the Big Bopper."

"What's that?"

"An old rock-and-roller. A singer."

"Here in Barstow?" He looked dubious.

"Nope. Texas is where I'm headed."

"He's *paying* you to drive this car? Goddamn, I'd love a job like that."

"No money involved. I'm doing it sort of as a favor."

"Yeah, hell," he said, "I would too. Damn *right.*"

I had an impulse to invite him along but thought better of it. He was too enthralled by the machinery. But when he shuffled along after me as I headed back to the car, his eyes caressing the Eldorado's lines, I invited him to take a slow cruise around town.

"Mister, *goddamn* you don't know how much I'd like that, but I can't. I'm the only one here till Bobby comes on at midnight, and Mr. Hoffer—he's the owner—he'd fire me sure as anything if I took off. Almost fired me last week 'cause these two guys from L.A. came in and did this trick on me about makin' change and the cash box come up thirty-seven bucks short. Mr. Hoffer said when I messed up next I was gone. I was already fired from two jobs this summer and Daddy said just once more and he'd kick my ass so hard I'd have to take my hat off to shit. I can't do 'er, much as I'd like to."

"Well," I offered, "how about a spin around the block?"

He shook his head doggedly. "Nope, better not."

"Okay, how's this: I'll watch the station—I've pumped lots of gas in my time—and *you* take it for a short ride." I was *determined.* "Lock up the cash box if you want. I'll make change out of my own pocket."

As he considered this, I could feel how much he wanted to do it, but finally he said, "Naw, I just can't risk it—getting fired by Mr. Hoffer, beat on by Daddy. But much obliged for offering. Honest."

"Tell you what," I persisted, now maniacal. "Why don't you drive me around to the men's room. I've never been chauffeured to the pisser before, and at least you'll get a taste of this fine piece of automotion."

"Yeah," he grinned, "I could do that. Sure. Great!"

He was so happy I felt like giving him the damn thing and taking the Greyhound back home. I've never seen anyone more delighted by a fifty-foot drive in my life. I took my time pissing, and when I came out he was sitting behind the wheel running the power windows up and down. I almost had to use a tire-iron to pry him out.

I wasn't hungry—they don't call bennies diet pills for nothing—but I knew from my days of high-balling speed that if you run your gut on empty too long it'll start eating itself, so I stopped at a drive-in joint down the road and dutifully choked down a 30¢ Deluxe Burger and an order of fries that tasted like greased cardboard.

The whole time I was eating I thought about the bottle of benzedrine under the seat. When I drove long-haul it was my habit to reward myself for eating food by eating a handful of speed for dessert, and the old pleasure center never forgets a pattern. I wanted some and told myself no. Instead I cracked another beer and congratulated myself on steadfastness in the face of temptation while I rinsed down the grease and thought some more about the young woman in North Beach.

When I reached in my jacket pocket for her self-addressed postcard, my fingertips brushed the crinkled ball of tinfoil I'd forgotten about—her tender gift, the LSD. Inside were three sugar cubes, their edges crumbled. I remembered her advice about taking one at a time in a beautiful place. Bradley's Burger Pit in Barstow didn't seem like a beautiful place, and I still owed Natalie Hurley of 322 Bryant Street a deserved apology. Using the dash for a desk, I printed in small, firm letters:

Dear Natalie,

I lied to you and your friend. I'm not Jack Kerouac. My motives for such deceit were complex—joy, fear, meanness, and self-protection. I regret my thoughtlessness and disrespect to both of you and hope you'll accept my sincere apologies.

Sincerely,

The Big Bopper

I shook my head at this perversity and diligently inked the Bopper's name into a thick black rectangle. Underneath I managed to cramp in "Love, George."

It was a clear night, moonless, the temperature warm but cooling fast. Mirage shimmers of rising heat off the desert made the horizon appear to be under water. The highway was as straight as the shortest distance between two points and flat as a grade-setter's vision of heaven. I powered down all the windows, locked the needle on 100, and took it south.

An hour or so later I hit the junction of 62 around Yucca Valley and ripped on down to Interstate 10, stopping in Indio for gas. From Barstow on, my brain had been cruising entranced, but the Indio pit stop had broken the spell. Back on the road, the twitters, skreeks, and jangles of speed-comedown rapidly became unbearable. A brackish exhaustion now stained my attention, my eyes felt like dried pudding, and I grew increasingly distracted, restless, and bored bored bored. I'd been up for a couple of days, one of them chemically aided, and it was catching up hard.

To resist temptation once you've already eliminated it is always easy, but to resist it when it's within easy reach under the front seat is difficult—especially when you've passed the soft flirtations of desire and are down to raw need and can hear those little go-fast pills squealing "Eat me, eat me." Difficult, yes, but not impossible, not if you're strong. I resisted the magnetic siren song of benzedrine by fumbling the tinfoil package from my pocket and letting a sugar cube dissolve on my tongue—a sweet, cloying trickle sliding down my throat.

Nothing happened. I should've known better. You can't expect the young to provide reliable drugs. But I was careful. I didn't know anything about LSD except what I'd heard, and most of what I'd heard had come from people like Allen Pound, a kid who drove graveyard at Cravetti's. He'd taken some with a psychiatrist in Berkeley, he said, and it turned him every way but loose. A bookcase became a brickwall. When he rested his forehead against a window, half his head went through without disturbing the glass; he'd felt the cold air outside stinging his eyes while, back in the room, his ears were burning. Always curious, I'd sidled into the conversation and asked him if LSD was like peyote. He smiled one of those cool, knowing smiles that afflict the terminally hip and replied, "Is a Harley like a Cushman?"

So, even though I suspected Allen Pound of self-inflating bullshit,

I was careful. I waited almost seventy miles worth of crumbling nerves before I ate the second cube. Either this had something in it or the stars, like tiny volcanoes, began erupting on their own, spewing molten tendrils of color until the night sky was an entangling net of jewels.

Nothing is more tedious than someone else's acid trip, so I'll spare you the cosmic insights—except for the real obvious stuff, like *it's all one* (more or less), composed wholly of holy parts, the sum of which is no greater or less than the individual gifts of possibility, all wrapped up pretty in the bright ribbon of past and future, the ribbon of moonlit highway, the spiral ribbons of amino acids twining into the quick and the dead, the ribbon of sound unwinding its endless music through breath and horn, the silver dancer with ribbons in her hair. Oh man, I was out there marching to Peoria, aeons out, all fucked up.

I made two intelligent moves, both making up in smarts what they so obviously lacked in grace. First I got off the road. Simply cranked the wheel hard right and drove into the desert, slewing between cactus plants till the exploding Godzilla eyes of on-coming traffic disappeared. Then, once the Caddy stopped, I tumbled out the door and jammed a finger down my throat. Maybe it wasn't too late to puke up the second hit. Of course, maybe I *hadn't* double-dosed, maybe the first was just a blank. But then again, maybe the shit came on slow. I didn't care; I just wanted to get as much of it as possible out of my system before my brain became a bowl of onion dip at a Rotarian no-host cocktail party. I managed to gag up the sour remains of the gristle burger and cardboard fries in a slurry of beer. My mind was vomit on the alkaline sand, as indifferently illuminated by the starlight as anything else of matter made.

I rolled onto my back and watched the stars pulse till I could get my breath. Watched them erupt, swirl, and dissolve like so many specks of sugar in the belly of the universe, only to re-precipitate, glittering. I felt what I always feel when I really look at the stars and remember they are enormous furnaces of light, when I look past them and imagine how many billions more exist beyond vision because their light hasn't yet reached us or they're obscured behind the curve of space, only now I felt this with an unbearable clarity, the impossible magnitude of it all, my own self barely a twitch of existence, a speck of sugar dissolving in the gut, fuel for the furnace, food for us fools. I forced myself to quit looking (otherwise I'd *die*) and curled up, trembling, on the hot desert sand. Eyes clamped shut, I sat on the bank and watched the river burn. Felt my empty body lifted on a wave, lifted on the wind, hurled into the darkness to be lifted again.

I have no idea how many eternities I required to regather myself and re-open my eyes. The stars were stars again, but possibly they wouldn't stay that way if I kept looking, so I cautiously peered sideways across the cactus-studded plain. I don't know what kind of cactus these were, but they vaguely resembled stick figures, legs together in a single line, arms curving up from each side in an ambiguous gesture of either jubilation or surrender. They looked like sentries—not so much guardians, though, as passive observers, witnesses for some unfathomable conscience. Nonetheless I was trying to fathom it when one of the arms moved. I started crawling pronto for the white shimmer of the Eldorado. I reached up to seize the door handle and put my hand right through the starlight mirage of metal. In a panicked glance over my shoulder I saw more cactus limbs move, but, daring a longer look, saw they were staying put, not advancing, and my fear began fading into a very careful curiosity. It took me a few baffled moments to comprehend that the cactuses were dancing to a music I could neither hear nor imagine. I knew that if I wanted to know their music, I would have to join their dance and feel it in the movement of my mortal meat, within time and space, outside in.

I know I danced, but remember neither the movements nor the music. Or anything else until I came to in the front seat of the Cadillac with sweat in my eyes. The sun was up with a passion. I checked the dash clock—9:30. I felt like scorched jelly. *Need sleep,* my brain was flashing; I hadn't begun to scrape myself from the floor of exhaustion. But the Caddy threw the thickest shade around, and even with all the windows down it was an oven. I *had* to move. I sat up and turned the key, so wasted that for the pain to reach my brain took about ten seconds. I yelped, hands recoiling to my chest. I examined them dully. They were pin-cushioned with cactus spines. Sweat-blinded and on the verge of screaming, I yanked the spines with my teeth and spit them out the window, thinking distantly to myself that if someone were watching they'd probably say, "Now, *he's* fucked-up: got enough money to afford a fancy car, then parks in the desert and eats his hands for breakfast."

Even with the spines removed, my hands were almost unbearably tender. I examined them carefully to make sure I'd removed all the needles, then tenderly reached under the front seat for the bottle of bennies. I wasn't tempted. Can you say a drowning man is *tempted* by a life-preserver? Temptation was crushed by necessity. Besides, it's all one, ceaselessly changing to sustain the dynamic equilibrium that maintains itself through change. And that dynamic equilibrium requires human effort. We each have to do what we can. I did seven.

Tuned me right up, too—had those acid-warped synapses firing at top dead center in no time. For example, I remembered the beer in the trunk. The ice was all melted but the water was still cool. I drank two quickly, tasted the next two, and savored another as I lumbered the Caddy back onto the highway.

The next sixty miles were devoted to severe self-questioning of the round-and-round variety. In retrospect I'd been foolish, first of all, to take the LSD, and then to take more. On the other hand, as that old saying has it, when you're up to your ass in alligators it's hard to remember you only wanted to drain the swamp. And what's an adventure without risk, danger, daring? Excitement was the whole point, in a way. Or was I secretly afraid of accepting the responsibility of delivering the gift, that deep down I knew it was an insignificant gesture, a spasm of fake affirmation in an indifferent universe? I didn't have a fucking clue.

And from this speed-lashed tautological self-analysis, only vaguely slowed by beer, out of a puddle of confusion I created a whirlpool of doubt; despite the energetic rush of amphetamine confidence, I felt myself sucked down toward depression. There's no drug stronger than reality, John Seasons once told me, because reality, despite our arrogant, terrified, hopeful insistence, doesn't require our perceptions, merely our helpless presence. I debated the truth of this all the way to the Arizona border. Finally I pulled over and banged my head against the steering wheel to make myself stop thinking.

I started with a light, rhythmic tapping, but that only seemed to increase the babble in my brain and I did it harder, hard enough to hurt. Then I slumped back in the seat, gasping, eyes tightly closed, and immediately had a vision: a tiny orange man, maybe three inches tall, naked, was carrying what appeared to be a piece of glossy black plywood as big as he was across a thin black line suspended in space. He was walking anxiously back and forth on the line, intently peering down. The plywood was cut roughly in the shape of an artist's palette, but lacked a thumbhole. The shape strongly reminded me of something personal, but was obscured in a shroud of associations. Finally it came to me: chicken pox, seven years old, an image of Hopalong Cassidy astride his horse. That was it, a jigsaw puzzle, a piece of Hoppy's black shirt.

The tiny orange man, the color of a neon tangerine, was still aimlessly walking back and forth along the line, his eyes shifting between the line and the plywood. It wasn't until he turned and walked away from me for a moment that I realized the black line was the edge of a surface, and looking more closely I saw it was a thin slab of crystal suspended in the air; it was exactly at eye level, and without the black line on its upper margin, I might've missed it completely. I tried to stretch myself up to see over its edge, get a better view of the surface the little orange man was stalking, but I couldn't break the angle of sight.

I watched, fascinated, as he roamed back and forth, looking all around, occasionally setting the piece of plywood down and sliding it around with his toe, then picking it up to continue what was evidently a search. I strained again to see the surface, but my gaze was locked dead level with the crystal edge and the parallel black line above it, a shadow laminated to translucence. At last I grasped the obvious: the little orange man *was* working on some crazy fucking jigsaw puzzle.

By the way he moved, lugging the puzzle piece as big as he was, it was plain he had no idea where it fit and, judging from his tight jaw, was becoming increasingly frustrated. I desperately wanted to scan the puzzle, to see what was done so far and what the emerging image might suggest, but despite one last effort of fierce concentration I couldn't see beyond the edge—a barrier I couldn't break. I wanted to offer the little orange man my help, add my vision to his, but there wasn't much I could do. I decided, though, that I could at least encourage him, and had just opened my mouth to speak when all hell broke loose.

I guess I should say all *heaven* broke loose, because the sky opened and poured rain, rivers and tidal waves of it, a deluge. The little man lifted the piece of puzzle above his head for what meager shelter it offered. I was sure he'd be washed away. But as abruptly as it'd started, the rain stopped, and he immediately returned to his work, even more intently, as if the torrential downpour had washed the image clean. Then the hail began, chunks of ice the size of tennis balls. Again the orange man took cover by lifting the puzzle piece above his head, staggering under the hammerstroke force of the blows, grimacing at the deafening roar, his tiny penis flopping against his thigh as he struggled to stay upright. The moment the ice-storm abated, the wind came up in huge gusts that sent him reeling almost to the edge before he was able to hunker down behind his piece of the puzzle, the power of the wind bending it over him like a shell. No sooner had the wind eased than lightning fractured the sky, fat blue-white bolts sizzling toward his head. He lifted the puzzle piece to deflect the stunning power of the bolts, spun by the brain-wrenching blasts of thunder that instantly followed, and I was already laughing by the time the tomatoes started splatting down, followed by a literal shit-storm of raw sewage, then writhing clumps of maggots, large gobs of spit, and decayed fruit. Once the fusillade of cream pies ended, I was tear blind and gasping for breath, doubled up on the front seat of the Caddy. I swear by all that's holy that I was laughing *with* him, not *at* him; laughing in true sympathy for all of us caught, tiny and naked and nearly helpless, in the maelstrom of forces we can't control. This was the laughter of honest commiseration, of true celebration for the splendid and foolish tenacity that keeps us hanging on despite the blows.

When I finally managed to look again, the little orange man was still standing there, resolutely holding the battered piece of the puzzle above his head even though the sky was clear. He was looking directly at me, glaring. His lips moved, but there was no sound—he looked like a goldfish pressed against the aquarium's glass, working water through his gills. It took a couple of heartbeats for his voice to reach the interior of the Caddy, to break with a deafening boom that rocked the car on its springs and flattened my lungs. He vanished with the sonic blast, but when my hearing returned a few moments later his words were waiting for me, not shrill or angry or bitter or even very loud, but absolutely corrosive with disdain: "That's right, you idiot—*laugh.*"

"Fuck you!" I screamed back, enraged by the injustice of his flagrant misunderstanding. "You don't know *shit!*" There was no reply.

Seething, I fired up the Eldorado and aimed it down the road, yelling still. "How could you *say* that? I was laughing *with* you. *Completely* with you." But even righteously wronged, I heard the false note in "completely." I *was* laughing with him, at least 80 percent, and another 10 percent from relief that it wasn't me, and another 10 percent just because it was funny. So even if my claim wasn't *completely* true, it was true enough, and I didn't deserve his contempt. "You mean little orange shithead!" I railed. "Jerk! Who are you to judge my laughter? You know I would've helped you if I could. That black piece shaped like a palette—it's part of Hopalong Cassidy's shirt. I put that one together when I was *seven*, you asshole."

By then I was tapering off to mutters, the dull throb in my skull reminding me I'd been beating my head against the steering wheel, and I twisted the rearview mirror around to check for damage. Fear hit me like a hell-bound freight. It wasn't the small lump or little smear of blood that jolted me. It was my eyes. They were crazy.

I pulled over immediately. At the rate I was going, I'd be lucky to make Texas by Christmas—if I made it at all. I was insane. Out of my mind. Why kid myself? I'd been beating my head on the steering wheel, watching a naked little orange man running around working on jigsaw puzzles. Worse, I'd talked to him. The night before I'd died in a whirl of starlight and danced with a cactus to music I couldn't remember. The night before that I'd stolen a car and crossed a man who was at that very moment probably rounding up a posse of well-paid goons who would be grossly pleased to turn me into a shopping bag full of charred meat and bone chips. By any objective standard of sanity, I wasn't. Not even within hailing distance, not if facts were faced and no bullshit allowed. But even granting that I was totally flipped out, maybe this was only a temporary condition, the result of drugs, exhaustion, stress, dislocation, and a weak psychic constitution going in. Maybe I didn't even know what crazy was, in its deeply twisted forms and dark forces. Maybe I *wanted* to be crazy so I wouldn't have to go through the normal rationalizations and self-justifications of unfettered indulgence. And thus my speed-racing mind babbled on until I finally gave up and pulled back onto the road. If it really got bad, I could always pound my head on the wheel and try another vision. That I'd seen the little orange man secretly cheered me; vision belonged to pilgrimage, and despite all my romantic notions, I'm a classicist at heart. I was disappointed, however, in the *quality* of the vision—neither heavenly nor beatific, more on the order of grotesque slapstick. Maybe I should've pounded my brain with something heavier. I wondered what sort of vision a solid whack from a ball peen hammer might produce, or what undreamable cosmic insight might accompany the blow from a wrecking ball. I wondered how much it cost to rent a crane for thirty seconds. I wondered if the orange man had been a real pilgrim's vision, or just a leftover from last night's acid feast, the deluded projection of spiritual hunger. I wondered what spirit was. I wondered what I actually wanted out of all this. I wanted to get there, wherever *there* was. I wanted to deliver the gift. I wanted to lie naked against Kacy and have her turn sleepily and snuggle as I ran my hand along her fine warm flank. I wondered where she was and what she was thinking, then I wondered why I was delivering Harriet's gift to the Big Bopper when both were dead, gone, and done with. Was it because I couldn't deliver my own gift to the living? Babble babble babble on into Arizona. When I looked in the rearview mirror again my eyes didn't look so crazy, just tired and confused. I needed a break.

I got it on a long stretch of empty highway about five miles out of Quartzsite, Arizona, when I saw a figure walking east on the shoulder of the road, back turned toward me. True, I was tired of listening to myself and felt a sudden desire for company, but there was something in the walk, in the slope of the shoulders, the sense of weight, the trudge, the isolation against the landscape, something indefinite but definitely wrong that made me come off the gas. When I was fifty yards away, down to a roll, I saw it was a woman. She wasn't hitching. She didn't even glance up as I passed.

It's always tricky when it's a woman alone in a lonely place and you're a man; no matter how noble your intentions, you have to be considered a threat—there's just too much ugly proof you are. I pulled off about seventy yards past her and got out. She walked closer and then stopped. She was short, chubby, in her early thirties by my guess, with messed auburn hair cut short, wearing faded jeans and a wrinkled grey blouse clinging where sweat had soaked through. At that distance I couldn't see her eyes, but her face looked dull and puffy. It wasn't something wrong that I'd noticed, but that something was missing: no purse. Five miles from the nearest town, no broken-down cars left on the shoulder, and no purse. I felt a sickening conviction that she'd been raped or mugged. I couldn't think of anything to say, so I waved, smiled, and leaned against the Caddy's left-rear fin, waiting for her to offer some sign, but she stopped and stood still, watching me. I didn't feel fear from her, no wariness at all; just fatigue.

"You all right?" I tried to put into my voice the truth of my concern, but it sounded clumsy even to me.

Her chin lifted half an inch. "I don't know," she said. It sounded like the truth.

So I told her the truth, too. "Well, I was asking myself the same question about forty miles back down the road, and I didn't know if I'm all right either. But I *am* headed for Texas, and I'd be glad to give you a ride anywhere between here and Sabine Pass, with no come-on, no hassle. If you'd prefer, I'd be glad to call you a cab in the next town to pick you up—even pay the fare if you're short—or call a friend to come pick you up. But if you'd rather just walk on along, say the word and I'm gone. Or if there's some other way I can help, I'll see what I can do." This had turned out to be a speech, but I was having trouble keeping the truth simple.

She walked five steps toward me. "I'd appreciate a ride into town.

Thank you." She said this with a sad formality, as if manners were all that remained of her dignity.

I went around to the passenger's side. "Do you want to sit up front with the idiots or would you rather sit in the back and be chauffeured like a princess on her way to the casino for an afternoon of baccarat and dashing young men?"

She smiled thinly to show she appreciated my attempt. She had lovely eyes, the dark, lustrous brown of raw chocolate. I wasn't an expert, but I was sure she'd been crying. "The front will be fine," she said, "with the idiots."

I ushered her into the front seat and said, "I know where you're going, but where are you coming from?"

"Same place. Quartzsite. That's where I live."

"Well then," I asked, irrepressible, "where've you been?"

"Changing my mind," she answered, her voice husky.

"Yes indeed, I know what you mean. When I'm not changing mine, it's changing me. We'll have to discuss the importance of change in sustaining equilibrium as well as its relation to timing, knowledge, spirit, and the meaning of life. And what love and music have to do with the purpose of being. When we get those figured out, we can tackle the tough ones."

She looked at me sharply, a flash of irritation, a hint of contempt. "I have two young kids. Boys. Allard's seven; Danny's almost six."

Her name was Donna Walsh. Besides the two boys, she had a husband, Warren, who'd lost his job in the Oklahoma oil fields and finally joined the Air Force in desperation. He was learning aircraft mechanics so he'd have a trade when he got out. He was overseas, Germany, and she and the boys were staying in his uncle's trailer in Quartzsite.

She'd fallen in love with Warren her last year of high school and slept with him the night after the senior prom because she was tired of making him stop when she didn't want him to. She got pregnant, and in Oklahoma if you got pregnant, you got married.

Warren had left for Germany six months ago, in April. This was only a year's assignment, then he'd have another year of service in the States, and after his discharge he'd get a job with one of the big airlines as a jet mechanic. Warren could do just about anything with machines, she claimed, especially engines. She wished he was home to fix the '55 Ford pick-up, which had leaked so much oil the engine burned out. Repairs would run $200 to fix it, but Johnny Palmer at the Texaco said it wasn't worth fixing. Not that it mattered, really, since Warren could only send $150 a month, and that had to cover everything. Tech Sergeants didn't make much, but like Warren said, learning jet mechanics was an investment in the future.

Warren was basically a good person, Donna said, but it was a lot of responsibility and pressure to get married so young, with two babies right away. And when he got laid off in the oil fields, he'd started drinking too much, and he only hit her when he was drunk. Not that he beat on her much—she didn't want to give that impression. It had only been three or four times tops, and once she'd asked for it by nagging him about finding a job, and he really had been trying.

Another time it was just one of those things: she was cooking dinner and little Danny was three and he wouldn't quit crying and it was hot that evening, over a 100° easy, and Danny just wouldn't stop and Warren had drunk way too much beer and started screaming at him to shut up, which only made Allard start in crying too; and Warren had slapped Danny so hard it sent him flying against the dinette, and when he did that Donna didn't even think, just swung on him with what she happened to have in her hand, a frozen package of Bel-Air corn, and it opened Warren's left eyebrow along its whole length—he still had the scar—but he didn't make a peep, even with the blood running all over his face, he just stood up real slow, pushed her against the fridge and started hitting her in the body with his fists, hitting her hard in the stomach and ribs and breasts until she passed out.

He didn't come back for a week after that, a week in which it sometimes hurt her so bad to breathe she'd hold her breath till she got dizzy, a week when it was all she could do to make peanut butter and jelly sandwiches for the boys. She'd called around to Warren's family and friends, but nobody had seen him. When he came back he was pale and both his eyes were black-and-blue; he'd needed nine stitches to close the cut. He was sober when he came back, and he was sorry. It was the only time she'd ever seen him cry. She made him promise never to hit the boys like that again.

That was the last time he'd beat on her till just before he'd finally given up job-hunting and enlisted. She was asleep when she heard him stagger against the table, then lurch toward the pull-out sofa bed they shared in the front room. He loomed over her. She was lying on her back looking up at him, but there was enough glare from the porch light shining through the uncurtained window behind him that his face was hidden in shadows. She could smell the whiskey.

"It's all your fault," he said quietly.

Donna saw the blow coming but couldn't move. He hit her in the belly, doubling her up. She couldn't breathe or scream or kick. Paralyzed, terrified, she watched his fist ball up again tighter and tighter till she thought the knuckles were going to pop out of the skin. She thought she was going to die. She heard what a scream sounds like when you don't have the breath to scream. But he didn't hit her again. He hit himself square in the stomach, right where he'd hit her, and began to methodically beat on his own face. Gasping, she inched across the bed until she could throw out an arm and reach him. He stopped at her touch. His fist opened and he reached down and touched her hair, lightly, and then down to the base of her neck, gently massaging as she choked for air. Still rubbing her neck, he pulled the sheet back slowly and lay down beside her and took her in his arms. She was naked; he was fully clothed. They held each other tightly, silently, for a long time. Donna said it was the most intimate she'd ever felt with him, and was aroused even as she cried. She pressed her thighs along his legs and wiggled in closer, but he had fallen asleep or passed out.

Warren always sent the money every month with the same short letter. "Hi. How are you? I'm working on B-52s. Keeps me busy. You boys mind your momma." He'd called on the Fourth of July. Mostly he'd talked to the boys, who were so thrilled they just jabbered away about everything. When she got the phone back, she couldn't think of anything to say, so she just said they all missed him. She wanted to tell him how much she missed him, and how, but the boys were yammering and tugging at her and he was too far away. She'd written him every week till that phone call. Now it was about every two weeks. It was so hard to say what you felt when you couldn't look at each other.

She told me all this as we sat beside the road and, after a while, drove the five miles to town. She spoke in a husky monotone, staring down the highway as if she were trying to describe a picture she'd seen as a child. She needed to talk. If you can't believe she'd open up to a total stranger—a man at that—well, it stunned me, too. Stunned me. I sat there with speed racing in my blood and didn't say a word; just listened. Sometimes it's easier to be honest with a stranger, someone you know you'll never see again. Safer. No obligation but the blind trust opening the moment.

As we pulled into Quartzsite I told her I was starved and offered to buy her a late lunch if she wasn't in a hurry. She said she had to be at the trailer by 4:30, when the boys got home from school. Usually they were home by 3:00, but today the lower grades were putting up Halloween decorations.

We stopped at Joe's Burger Palace and ate in the car. We picked at our burgers in silence for a few minutes, a comfortable silence, then made small talk about life in Quartzsite. But small talk seemed to diminish whatever had passed between us, and after a few meaningless exchanges she shifted around on the seat to face me and told me, without introduction, what had happened that morning. As she spoke, her voice gathered force, but it barely escaped the undertow of weariness in her tone.

"I got up at six like always, then woke up the boys and got them dressed. Danny couldn't find his blue socks. They're his favorites. He couldn't remember where he'd left them. I told him it wasn't going to hurt him to wear his brown ones for a day, and he started crying. Kids can get *so* strange about clothes, like they're little pieces of their lives. So I hunted for his socks and finally found them under his pillow. *Under* his pillow, can you believe that? They were so filthy I think I found them by smell. It reminded me everything was dirty, and I *had* to do the laundry.

106

"I got Danny's sock on him and then made their oatmeal and poured their milk. Allard was telling Danny all about skeletons and ghosts and how ghosts can just *wooooosshh* at you out of nowhere, and when he was woooosshhhing his hand to show what he meant he knocked over his milk. I wiped off the table and was about to get what had dripped on the floor when I smelled something burning: I'd put the oatmeal pan back on the burner but hadn't turned it off like I thought. The oatmeal was charred to the pan. I filled the pan with water and some baking soda to soak, but the smell of burnt oatmeal had filled up the trailer. By then the boys were going to be late for school, so I got them all gathered up and figured I'd take care of the mess when I got back.

"I walked the boys to school, which is about eight blocks, but when I got back to the trailer I couldn't open the door. I don't mean it was stuck or I'd forgotten the key—I just *could not open it* and go back inside to the smell of burnt oatmeal and spilled milk and dirty laundry. *Physically* couldn't. So I turned around and started walking.

"At first I thought I'd go to Curry's market a couple of streets down, but I walked right past it—just as well, 'cause my purse was in the trailer. Then I thought I'd go by the old Baptist church, but when I saw it, with all the stained glass and heavy doors, I didn't want to go in. I walked on past the church and just kept *going*, know what I mean? Not thinking about anything in particular except how good it felt to be moving in the clear air. Just walking. When I reached the highway and saw the broken white lines going on so far in the distance that they seemed to turn solid, I felt happy. I kept walking. Two or three cars stopped but I shook my head. I wanted to keep going.

"I know I'm a little overweight but as I walked along I started feeling lighter and lighter and lighter, like the wind could pick me up and fly me away, the way I felt it could when I was a little girl. Then it all collapsed in me and I started crying."

Donna blinked rapidly as she remembered that moment, jaw quivering, but there were no tears. She shook her head. "But you know how it ended. Here I am. But I walked a long way down the highway thinking how every promise gets broken one way or another, how every hope you have is hoped for so hard and so long it's almost like praying, praying

107

so you can believe in *something,* but it never turns out that way. I'll tell you what really got me blubbering, was that I *knew* I was going to turn around, cross that damn road, and come back. *Knew* I couldn't leave. I'm ashamed to admit it, but there's been a few nights when I felt like the best thing to do was get the butcher knife out of the kitchen and go stab the boys in their sleep, kill them before they found out what happens to dreams. Is that *sick?* But you can't do that any more than you could let them come home to an empty house with Daddy in Germany and Momma run away crazy. They're too real to hurt like that, too real to escape. So I'm coming back because I don't *really* have a choice. I didn't understand it, but I made a choice with Allard and Danny. I'm going back and opening that goddamn door of that trailer and walk into the smoked-in smell of scorched oatmeal and curdled milk and filthy socks. Now that's *grim.*"

"I admire your courage," I told her.

Donna shook her head. "If I could walk away and be happy, I'd still be going. But something *that* wrong gnawing on my heart, I could never be happy. Not that I'm happy now, with no break from the boys and the walls pressing in and a husband I don't know about, but this way there's a *chance* things'll work out. Maybe not, but I have to do what I think's right and hope it is, I guess."

"I hope so, too," I said, "and I think it is. But if Warren ever hits you again, I'd get out from under. No maybes. Just leave."

"Yeah," she said, "I told myself that."

"Promise yourself."

"What about you?" Donna asked. "You coming or going?" She was deflecting the pressure of the question, not begging it, and she'd had enough pressure for the day. So, still sitting in the Caddy, our half-eaten burgers long cold, I told Donna what I was up to, my own mess and now this journey. I didn't mention Eddie getting run over—it wasn't necessary—nor that the car was stolen. I did tell her about dancing with a cactus and the little orange man and the upwelling babble in my brain. In the course of explaining, I was taken with a strong intuition that she'd appreciate Harriet's letter, so I asked. She thought about it a moment and said she would. I dug it out of the glovebox and handed it over.

Donna sniffed the envelope. "Ooo-laa-laa." She giggled. "Miss Harriet was serious."

She read the letter slowly, nodding, shaking her head, smiling. When she finished she folded it neatly, returned it to the envelope, and began to weep. *So much for my deep intuitions,* I said to myself, but then she reached for me across the front seat and we held each other.

As it turned out, however, my intuition was better than it seemed at first. It wasn't the letter that got to her, she said, as it was remembering that Ritchie Valens had died in the same plane crash. Ritchie Valens, it turned out, was one of the reasons she'd slept with Warren that first night, the night she got pregnant with Allard. Not Ritchie Valens personally, but a song of his called "Donna," Donna the heartbreaker, a lament for his lost love. The school she went to in Oklahoma was too small to afford a band for the senior prom, so they'd used records. And when Ritchie Valens sang her name that night in the dimly lit gym—Donna in her gown with her hair done up and an orchid on her wrist, her stockinged feet sliding on the waxed floor as she danced slow and close with Warren—she wanted to grow up into the woman she felt in herself.

When I admitted I didn't recall the song, Donna looked at me with deep suspicion, like a border guard confronted with dubious credentials, but then she shook her head, smiling, and said, "Well, it doesn't make much sense without the song." And in a high, clear voice with just a touch of a whiskey edge and a power and clarity that left me breathless, she sang:

> *I had a girl*
> *Dooonnaa was her name*
> *And though I loved her*
> *She left me just the same*
> *Oohhhhh Donnnaaa*
> *Ooohhhhh Doonnnaaaaa . . .*

And I was thinking she'd break my heart when she abruptly stopped and said, "That's why I'm crying about the letter. And because it's sad that they never had the chance to meet. And because it's really a sweet thing you're doing—a little crazy, but sweet."

"Then allow me to deliver this gift in your name, too—as a tribute to Ritchie Valens, music, and the possibilities of friendship, communion, and love."

She cocked her head and gave me a smile that was in odd but happy contrast to the tears on her cheeks. "That would be nice," she said.

"Well I'm a nice, sweet guy and it's a very romantic journey—some might even call it foolish, or pointless. You wouldn't happen to know where the Big Bopper's buried, would you?"

"No," she said, "but I just thought of a good gift for you." She sounded excited. "It's in a big box under the bed, lugged all the way from Oklahoma: a battery-powered record player and a young girl's collection of forty-fives to play on it."

"You're kidding. Old forty-fives? Are they mainly from the Fifties?"

"I was seventeen in '59. Your record player was all there was in Braxton, Oklahoma."

"Mainly rock-and-roll?"

"What else was there?"

"Well, listen, that's what I'm supposed to do on my way *back* from delivering the Caddy—look around for Fifties record collections. I've got this friend in 'Frisco named Scumball Johnson, a used car salesman, and he collects Fifties rock the way some people collect baseball cards. Kind of a hobby, but he's real passionate about it. When he heard I was making this trip, he gave me a thousand bucks to buy with, and out of that I can cover my travel expenses home. I told him I didn't know diddley about the music but he said that was no big problem—if in doubt, buy everything. He buys 'em, sells 'em, trades 'em, reads these obscure little collectors' magazines with circulations of half a dozen— you know, just a nut. So, since you've got the records and I've got the money and we're both in the same place, I could buy some now."

"No, I want it to be a gift," Donna said firmly.

I was ready for this. "If you insist, I'd be honored to accept the record player as a gift. Scumball doesn't collect record players. The records, those I have to pay for. That's business. Of course they've got to be in good shape. Not scratched or warped, labels intact, things like that."

She eyed me with open doubt, and I wasn't sure whether she was considering the offer's intrinsic value or its clumsiness. Frankly, I thought I was pretty slick. Finally she said, "Okay, but the record player's a gift—as long as that's understood."

"Understood and gratefully accepted." I bowed as much as I could in the front seat. "I'd like to take a look at the records, but I'm not sure what your situation is. I'd be glad to drive you to your trailer if you think your neighbors wouldn't take it wrong. And I wouldn't mind at all if you'd rather have me call you a cab and meet you somewhere else with the records—*and* the record player. What do you think?"

She fixed me with those lustrous brown eyes and a smile. "I think you're a very thoughtful man. And for all your supposed craziness, very, very careful. We can go to the trailer. None of the neighbors thinks anything about me as far as I know. About the only person I ever talk to is Warren's uncle when he comes around the first of the month to collect the rent and try to feel my ass." Her nose wrinkled with disgust. "The kids'll be home in a couple of hours. I can move the mess around while you check out the records."

The trailer, closed all day in the heat, reeked of burned oatmeal, curdled milk, and dirty socks, just as Donna had said. She stopped in the doorway, took a deep breath, and let it out slowly in a murmuring sigh. "Ah, home sweet home. You're welcome to it. See if you can find a place to sit down." She left the outside door open and went into a tiny room at the back of the trailer. She didn't have far to go: the trailer seemed about seven feet long. I hadn't spent that much time around kids, but even if they sat stone-still that place would've been cramped.

Donna was back in a couple of minutes with two large plastic cases, each half again as big as a portable typewriter case. One was turquoise with yellow flecks, the other light green. The latter contained the record player. It was a bit dusty and the batteries were long dead, but the turntable spun smoothly and the needle looked sharp.

Sounding upset, Donna said it worked fine the last time she'd played it. I assured her of my utter confidence that new batteries would do the trick and, if not, that I was an ace mechanic, but she insisted on searching for the four-cell flashlight so we could use its batteries to test the machine. She couldn't find the flashlight and grew increasingly distracted. "The boys were using it last night to play flashlight tag. How can they lose *everything* they touch? I mean," she spread her arms, "how can you lose *anything* in a place this size? Damn flashlight's bigger than the table."

She was still looking for the flashlight when I opened a small compartment on the side of the case and found a cord for a 12-volt connection; you could plug it right into the cigarette lighter. I held it up. "Forget the flashlight. Lookee here at the miracles of modern technology—I can run it straight off the car's system."

The turquoise case was full of records. There were three tightly slotted rows, all but a dozen in paper slip jackets. Most looked like they might've been pressed the day before. "You sure kept your record collection immaculate. Hardly a speck of dust. No reason you shouldn't get top dollar."

"You'd never know to look at this place that I used to be a tidy young lady, would you?"

"I bet two rambunctious young boys really sharpen your personal sense of order."

"Ain't that a fact," she said ruefully. "Listen, I'm going to attack the dishes. Take your time going through the records. And take anything you want; they're all for sale."

I went through the records quickly. A fairly comprehensive collection, to my limited knowledge. I found the Big Bopper's "Chantilly Lace" right off, a bunch of Elvis, Jerry Lee Lewis, Fats Domino, Bill Haley & the Comets, Chuck Berry, Buddy Holly galore, five or six of Little Richard's wailings, the Everly Brothers, some folk and calypso, and a whole bunch of groups and people I'd never heard of. Ritchie Valens's "La Bamba" and "Donna" were near the end of the last row. I set "Donna" aside.

She was behind me at the sink, scrubbing dishes. I told her I'd set "Donna" aside and asked if she had any other favorites.

She damn near wheeled on me. "Take 'Donna,' " she said flatly, "that's the one I really want gone."

"No sentimental favorites?"

"Not anymore." She turned back to the sink.

I counted the records and then my money. I was short out-of-pocket and had to go out to the Caddy for the roll in the duffle bag. When I came back in, I counted out the cash on top of the turquoise case. "Okay," I said, "let's get down to business. I get two hundred and seven records at two bucks a pop, makes it four-fourteen, so I'll call it an even four-fifteen if you'll throw in the carrying case."

Donna was shocked. "You're buying *all* the records for two dollars *each?*"

"I know that seems low, but Scumball says it's standard price for good-to-excellent condition. I don't know what the market's like here, but even in 'Frisco he can't get more than three dollars a pop. And I *am* buying them all, remember, not high-grading it for the good stuff."

Donna pointed at the turquoise case. "You're gonna give me over four *hundred* dollars for those records, is that what you're telling me?"

"Four-fifteen," I corrected her. "I'm sorry, but I really can't go higher." I tried to look sorry.

Donna was shaking her head. "You know those records aren't worth nothing much. You're just looking for a way to give me charity. I appreciate it, George, but that ain't right."

The truth was, I didn't have the vaguest idea what used records were going for, but two dollars seemed fair to me and that allowed me to put some honest righteousness in my bluff. "Donna, I'll write down Scumball's number. Call him at work and he'll tell you whether I'm bullshitting or not."

She decided to believe me. "No, there's no need for that. God, I guess not. You'll have to excuse me, but I was figuring a dime at the most, and you're telling me two dollars. Four *hundred!* Hell, if I knew I was sitting on a gold mine, I'd of sold 'em a long time ago."

"Glad you didn't." I grinned. "And I *know* Scumball will be."

Donna insisted on coming out to the Caddy to say goodbye—plus she wanted to make sure the record player worked. I plugged the adapter into the cigarette lighter and hit the switch; the turntable began revolving. I was tempted to play "Donna" and ask the real one to dance a slow one right there in her scuffed yard in front of God and the neighbors, holding her close before I aimed it back down the Interstate. But seeing as how she didn't need the pain, I picked a Buddy Holly at random. It dropped smoothly onto the turntable and the tone arm lifted over and laid the needle in the groove:

> *I'm gonna tell you how it's gonna be:*
> *You're gonna give-a your love to me.*
> *I wanna love you night and day,*
> *You know my love not fade away.*
>
> *Doo-wop: doo-wop: doo-wop-bop.*
>
> *My love is bigger than a Cadillac,*
> *I try to show it and you drive me back.*
> *Your love for me has got to be real*
> *For you to know just how I feel.*
> *A love for real not fade away!*

I hit the freeway full-bore and feeling good, a farewell kiss from Donna still warm on my cheek. Since I had the record player all set up, I figured I might as well listen to "Chantilly Lace," seeing as how I was riding its ripple of consequence into my present madness. I dropped it on the box. There was the sound of a phone jingling, then a low lecherous purr:

> *Hellooooo, bay-bee.*
> *Yeah, this is the Big Bopper speaking.*
> *[a prurient laugh]*
> *Oh, you sweet thang!*

> *Do I* what?
> *Will I* what?
> *Oh bay-beeee, you* know *what I* like:

And *then* he starts singing.

> *Chantilly lace and a pretty face*
> *and a ponytail hangin' down,*
> *a wiggle in her walk*
> *and a giggle in her talk*
> *Lawd, makes the world go 'round 'round 'round . . .*

Listening, I agreed with the Bopper that we all need a little human connection, some critter warmth. It was sad, but in the music was an invincible joy that proved sadness could be balanced, if not beat, and for a while there, rocking toward Phoenix with Donna's record player turned up full blast, so exhausted I could barely blink, I was serene. Mostly it was the music, the captivating power of the beat; I didn't have to think. No wonder the young loved it. Adolescence is excruciating enough without thinking about it; better to fill your head with cleansing energy. I kept filling mine, hoping this feeling of serenity could last forever, but when I started to nod at the wheel it clearly was time for either speed or sleep. Acting upon the sanity serenity inspires, I pulled into the Fat Cactus Motel on the outskirts of Phoenix, signed in semiconscious, and raced the Sandman to Room 17. It was a dead heat.

I woke around noon the next day, reborn. I showered for about forty-five minutes, washing off the road grit and speed grease, then put on clean clothes. I felt fresh, fit, and ready to take on Texas. After filling the Caddy with high-test, I stopped down the street and stretched my shrunken gut with a tall stack at the House of Pancakes.

I said I felt good, and that's a fact, but you can always feel *better*. My nervous system, after the cleansing flush of sleep, was beginning to twitter for its amphetamine, asserting a need that was undoubtedly sharpened by the knowledge that the means of satisfaction was near at hand. I invoked my recently refreshed sense of purpose and limited myself to three. A man buffeted by general weakness and a tendency toward utter indulgence needs to bolster his resolve with such acts of self-control. Of course, it's not a tremendous consolation to tell yourself you only took three when you could have taken thirty, but Fortune favors those who at least *try.*

Eight miles out of Phoenix, Fortune, quick to pay off, rewarded me with Joshua Springfield, make of him what I might. At first it was difficult to make anything of him, just the shadow of a shape in a blaze of light, but as the angle of vision changed with my approach I saw what was what—apparently, anyway—and pulled over in response to his upraised thumb.

This man is proof of the impossibility of description. He was large and round, easily over two hundred pounds, with short legs, large torso, and a massive head, yet altogether there was a sense of spare grace in the proportions. He was moon faced, so smooth as to seem featureless, or maybe the features were blurred by the power of his dark blue eyes, a color at odds with the short, tightly curled reddish hair that covered his crown like a fungus attacking a pink balloon. He was wearing a lime-green gabardine suit apparently made by a tailor suffering severe impairment of his sensory and motor faculties. The color of his suit clashed with his red shirt, though it matched the body feathers of the parrots printed on it. Joshua was standing on a large rectangular silver box the size of a footlocker, and it was the dazzle of sunlight off the silver box that made him appear, despite his considerable substance, apparitional.

"Good afternoon," he greeted me in a mellow bass. "It is kind of you to stop. I hope you won't mind being burdened with this heavy and rather unwieldy box."

He wasn't lying about that: we both were panting by the time we got it secured on the back seat. Back on the road, still mopping sweat, I said, "Must be the family gold in there to haul it around hitching."

"Ah, if it was gold I assure you I wouldn't be hitching. I would rent a helicopter. But since it isn't gold, and since I've never learned to drive an automobile, I must accept the luck of the road and the kindness of fellow travelers like yourself."

"My pleasure. Do you mind my asking what *is* in the box? I'm always curious about what I've been wrestling."

"Not at all. It's not very spectacular, I assure you. Merely equipment I use in my work—amplifiers, speakers, that sort of thing."

"You an electrician?"

"I dabble. By vocation I'm a chemist, so I suppose it's accurate to say that the electrical is within my field."

"A chemist," I repeated. Visions of sugarplums danced in my head. "What exactly do you do?"

"Oh, the usual. Dissolve and coagulate; join and sunder; generally stir the elemental soup."

"Well, yes . . . but what sort of substances do you make?"

"For the last twenty years I've primarily been interested in medicines, but I've made all sorts of things—metal polish, soap, plastics, paper, cosmetics, dyes, and the rest."

"Have you ever heard of lysergic acid? LSD?"

I listened carefully for a note of caution in his tone, a trace of reserve, but he was direct: "Yes. I ran across it in Hoffman's work on grain molds."

"Have you ever made any?"

"No."

"Taken any?"

"No."

"You weren't curious?"

"I'm curious both by nature and aesthetic disposition, but I've found that psychotropic drugs are like funhouse mirrors—they reveal by distortion."

"And you want a funhouse with honest mirrors?"

Joshua thought for a moment. "Actually, I guess I'm more interested in a funhouse *without* mirrors."

"You think it would still be fun?" I'll admit to a snotty note of the disingenuous in my tone.

"Why else would it interest me?" he replied sharply, lifting his arms in exasperation. One sleeve came to midforearm, the other to his knuckles. When I didn't reply he continued in a softer, but still testy, tone, "There's no need to poke at me like a crab in a hole. If you have a point, come to it; if you have a question, ask."

I lacked a point but had far too many questions, and the three hits of speed were kicking into high, so instead I told him my tale much like I'm telling you, the road and story rolling together, Phoenix to Tucson and on down the hard-rock highway. Joshua listened with complete attention and without comment, which unnerved me at first and made me hurry for fear of boring him. But when I realized he was absorbed, not bored, I relaxed, and that inspired my honesty. I told him the car was stolen, that I'd been taking drugs and might be crazy. This information didn't seem to alarm him; his hands were folded on his lap and he briefly turned them palms up, as if to indicate it was an insignificant matter of fact.

I didn't finish bending his ear until we were passing the Dos Cabezas range. Joshua turned his attention from me to the mountains, then stuck his head out the window and craned his neck to look at the sky. When he sat back and settled himself again in the seat, he said, "There are many possible responses to being lost in the wilds. You can stay put and wait for help. You can build fires and flash mirrors and construct huge S.O.S. signals by piling stones or dead branches. You can pray. You can hurl yourself off a cliff. You can try to find your way out by backtracking, or you can plunge on ahead. Or sideways. Or in circles. Or randomly, willy-nilly. I don't think it probably makes much difference what method you adopt, though it *is* a reflection of character, and certainly an expression of style. The romantic is a dangerous impulse, easily confused with the most pathetic sentimentality, yet so wonderfully capable of a magnificence borne and illuminated not by mere endurance, but by a joy so elemental it will gladly risk the spectacular foolishness of its likely failure."

"So you approve?"

"My approval isn't required. I will confess I'm prey to such gestures myself, though they generally offend me with their excesses. A splash where a stroke would serve. The jelly of adjectives instead of the bread of a noun. Ah, but if the connection is made, the arc completed: what powerful grace! An eruption so marvelous a million spirits are joined!"

"What you're saying basically, if I understand it, is that my ass is up for grabs."

"You're strafing a mouse, but yes, essentially."

"What about your ass, Joshua?" I said. "Is it up for grabs, too?"

He gave me a huge moonbeam smile, the kind we draw as children on the round faces of our imagination, U-shaped, the corners of the mouth nearly touching the eyes. "Of course my ass is up for grabs. It seems to be a perpetual condition of asses."

"You don't seem unduly concerned," I noted.

"I'm not. I don't *care* if it gets grabbed. I might not like it, of course, but I don't care." He gave me a wonderful wink, convivial and conspiratorial, and at that moment, though I wouldn't realize it till later, our journeys were joined. I'm sure Joshua had already recognized this and was acknowledging it with the wink—but then he was a chemist, and finally it was a matter of chemistry, of congruence and charge.

As we started up Apache Pass, Joshua explained he was on something of a journey himself. As he talked, it became clear that Joshua was one of those eminently functional people who are remarkably crazy, a psychic equilibrium that few can sustain, and which may well constitute a profound form of sanity. Or may not.

"I'm on an experimental field trip," he explained. "As a chemist it is one of my duties to stir the soup. Not to season it necessarily, but to keep it from sticking to the bottom and, not incidentally, to see what precipitates or dissolves. Perhaps I flatter myself in thinking I'm an agent of the possible, but we all suffer our vanities. Like your little orange man protecting himself with a piece of the puzzle. Classically it's the catalytic burden, but why snivel or shrivel at the load when the trees can bear the wind with such grace, and the mountains bear the sky? 'Don't matter if the mule's blind, just keep loading the wagon.' In that silver box burdening the back seat is a self-contained amplification system, from turntable to two powerful speakers. There is also a microphone hook-up. Primitive, really: twelve-volt D.C., nickel-cadmium battery. Electrical amplification is a new force in the world and it needs to be assessed. Can clarity be made clearer by amplification? Is sound meant to be carried beyond the natural range of its source? Or are we about to start worshipping another overpowering technological distortion as some degraded puritanical form of magic?

"My experiment is crude, but not without certain possibilities of elegant resonance. I intend to go to San Picante, a small village of perhaps ten thousand souls; it's in New Mexico, out of Lordsburg and up through Silver City, in the Mimbres mountains. No trains have ever passed within ninety-four miles of San Picante. At approximately four o'clock tonight—or, more precisely, tomorrow morning—I will set up my amplification equipment and put on a recording of an approaching train—at full volume. I've tested it, of course, and the effect is *quite* impressive. I'm planning to do this in a residential area, and if a crowd gathers, I may hook up the microphone and make a few remarks."

"If I was you," I told him, "I'd make tracks. Some folks might be a little upset about getting the ever-loving shit scared out of them just so they can lose two or three hours' sleep before they have to go to work."

Joshua inclined his massive head an eighth of an inch in acknowledgment. "I concur; that's highly probable. But without that probability, how can we court the marvelous exception? Speaking as a *true* scientist—as opposed to those who line up to lick the tight ass of Logos, if you'll forgive my justified vulgarity—I maintain a *reluctant* objectivity that I'm willing to abandon at any hint of the marvelous. In my first science class in college, we each looked at a drop of our own blood under the microscope. I saw a million women naked, singing as they ascended the mountain in the rain. Who's to say what can happen when literally *anything* can happen? These people tonight may hear the train and walk radiantly from their houses, jolted into the reality of their being. But if their reactions confirm your grim predictions, you are a capable driver. Even excellent."

I noted my inclusion in his "experiment" and took it as a shy invitation rather than an arrogant presumption. I was about to respond when Joshua pointed down the highway. "Look at that lovely live-oak. That is an outstanding tree. You look at it and immediately know it couldn't be anywhere else. That tree could *not* be on television. That's a good sign, don't you think?"

I didn't know what to think, so I smiled and said, "Joshua, you're crazier than I am."

He leaned his head back on the seat and shut his eyes as if preparing for sleep, but immediately leaned forward and looked at me. "George, my friend, when I was seven years old, living with my family in Wyoming, one day I was sitting in a mountain meadow examining the patterns the wind was making in the grass when a raven flew over my head and asked in one hoarse syllable, *'Ark?'* Having been a Sunday School regular, I was convinced this was the very raven Noah had sent out centuries before to seek out land—the raven that preceded the dove, remember, never to return?—and now, after what an unimaginably mysterious and exhausting journey, had found land but lost the Ark. I could feel its joyous message dying in its throat. So I set to work building an Ark in our backyard, using scrap lumber from a nearby construction site. It wasn't much of an Ark, more of a pointed raft, but I worked on it with singleminded concentration and completed it within a week. Then I climbed aboard and waited for the raven to return. After three weeks of my absolute intransigence, my parents had me committed.

"The doctors told me I had misunderstood. They said all ravens uttered a harsh croaking sound that could be easily mistaken for the word *Ark*. That, I thought, was fairly obvious. But they hadn't been in the meadow with me; they hadn't *heard* it. I understood their doubt, but not their adamant refusal to admit even the slightest possibility that they might be wrong. Nor could they offer textual evidence from the Bible of the raven's fate, though it was impossible, they said, that this bird could've flown since Noah's time, that it would have died of old age, and so forth. Despite this they claimed to believe in God. And yet they could not see, or refused to see, that if God could create the earth, and sky, and water, and stars, He could surely keep a poor lost raven aloft. Theirs was a disgusting violation of logic and an insult to intelligent inquiry. That's why it's a relief and a pleasure to meet people like you, people who understand—"

"Joshua," I interrupted, not wanting him to think I was dense, "I notice you seem to have included me in your plans for tonight as the getaway driver, and I just want to keep things clear and plain. That's sort of one of my rules for the trip: no bullshit."

"That's rather bold," he said, blinking. "But I meant as a cohort and friend, not just as a chauffeur."

"I accept the honor of being your accomplice."

He broke into a smile I'll never forget, that still shines on me sometimes with unexpected blessing. That smile was what I was agreeing to.

"And," I added, "I hope you'll accept *my* offer to continue on with me and make this delivery to the Big Bopper's grave. I would welcome your company."

Joshua sighed. "There are lessons not even the wisest counsel can prevent us from learning. Nor should it. Each raindrop is different unto the river and equally waters the trees. After two years of pale green walls and apostate doctors I knew the raven wouldn't come to me, so I went looking for it. I found it in the trees, in the sky, in the water, the flames, and in myself. I have built many arks for many ravens, burned many empty nests. I have some experience in these matters, George, believe me. I am no more a teacher than you are a student. But it's best for both of us if I don't accompany you. Yours is the journey of a young man. I'm nearly fifty. What help I might offer would merely obstruct you; my company would prove a distraction. Trust me when I say that you are much more essential to me than I am to you." He reached across the front seat and patted my shoulder. "You do understand?"

"Of course not," I said, stung at his refusal. "I don't understand anything these days. I guess I do understand that you can't drive and I can—which, if I understand it right, is what makes me necessary."

Calmly, patiently, Joshua said, "That's a beginning." Then added, with a pointedness his patience couldn't restrain, "It was an *invitation*, George, and can be declined."

I wasn't sure if he meant his or mine, and decided it didn't matter. "I thought I made it clear I'd be glad to help."

Joshua leaned closer. "Well then," he whispered, "let's conspire."

It wasn't much of a conspiracy. We'd pull into San Picante well after dark, find an appropriate neighborhood, Joshua would set up his equipment, we'd send a train screaming through the residents' peaceful slumbers, Joshua would deliver his remarks, and then we'd split—and be prepared to do so triple-lickety in case of enraged pursuit. I had a few quibbles, questions, and doubts. About my fear that the Caddy was far too conspicuous for the job, Joshua argued that, on the contrary, it possessed "the perverse invisibility of insane proportion." As for its being stolen, he claimed this would make it harder to trace to us and, moreover, that the legal status of automobiles was an unnecessary burden on minds about to undertake an important scientific experiment. He did agree that I should smear mud on the license plates to "confound identification," though he personally felt we had nothing to hide and shouldn't behave as if we did.

I wasn't particularly hungry myself but, playing the thoughtful host, asked Joshua if he was. He said he wouldn't mind a milkshake, so we stopped at a Dairy-Freeze in Lordsburg and grabbed four shakes to go—vanilla for me; raspberry, butterscotch, and chocolate-chip for Joshua. I washed down four hits of speed with mine, seeing as how I'd be up late doing some tight work. Joshua declined my offer of the open speed bottle, claiming the milkshakes were sufficient. He drank alternately from the three cups, consuming them at an equal rate and with obvious pleasure.

I pulled in at the local U-Save for ice, potato chips, and Dolley Madison donuts, then gassed the Caddy to the gunwales. As we headed into the mountains, I asked Joshua what he planned to say, assuming there was time for a speech. He said he had nothing in particular in mind; perhaps just a few general comments on the nature of reality and the meaning of life—nothing beyond what the moment might offer. Sounded an awful lot like me lying to Natalie and her friend about the word I'd whisper on the peak of Mount Shasta.

On roads that narrowed as they climbed through the night, we talked about moments and what they might offer. We were an hour early in San Picante—a result, according to Joshua, of my driving faster than his calculations—but the town was already long asleep. Even Dottie's All-Nite Diner was closed, a fact that for some reason irritated me and amused Joshua immensely. We cruised the small residential areas off the the main drag until Joshua found exactly what he wanted, "a pure-product middle-class tract subdivision, sumptuous with stunted dreams, ripe for the river." He said he could feel it, and I, more nervous by the minute, hoped he knew what he was doing.

I parked in the shadow-deepened darkness of a large tree. Joshua took about fifteen heart-thudding minutes, nine hundred long moments, to get the sound system hooked up in the back seat. The battery, turntable, and amplifier stayed in the silver box; the speakers, which had some sort of adjustable metal tabs, were fitted into the open rear windows. Joshua hummed the sprightly "Wabash Cannonball" as he worked. For my part, I worried, studying the county map I'd bought in Silver City while gassing up, and by the time Joshua had his instruments set up I'd memorized every possible escape route, from major roads to obscure hiking trails. I was looking for feasible cross-country routes when Joshua slung the microphone over into the front seat and then crawled over himself. "Are you ready for a ride in the patently unreal," he asked cheerfully.

"I guess," I said.

Joshua looked out the window. "I'm afraid this tree may cause some distortion in the sonic configuration from the right speaker. Can you back up about fifty feet?"

In the interest of clarity, I kissed our cover goodbye and backed up as requested. As soon as I cut the engine, Joshua reached over into the back seat and hit the start switch on the turntable. I heard the record drop, then a whisper of static as the needle touched down.

Joshua touched my arm in the darkness and whispered, "Isn't this an amazing moment? Not the vaguest idea what will happen." Beside me, I could feel him swelling with happiness.

You could hear the train coming far down the tracks, wailing on fast and hard and louder than I ever imagined it would be, mounting to a crescendo that was everywhere and right on top of you at once, its air horn blasting you out through the roof of your skull. I'm telling you, the fucking street *shook*. The Caddy started flopping like a gaffed fish, bucking so bad I instinctively jumped on the brakes. I *knew* that train was a fake, an utter hoax, and it *still* scared me shitless. I cringed to imagine the havoc inside those sleepy houses, houses never rattled by the roar and rumble of the railroad. I glanced over at Joshua. His eyes were mild, lips parted, but as the silence gathered mass in the wake of the ghost train's shattering passage, before the muffled screams and curses issued from the houses and lights flicked on randomly down the street, a tiny smile lifted toward his cheekbones as he bent his head to the microphone like a man about to pray.

Directly across the street I saw a grimacing face flash behind a parted curtain, then heard more shouts and shrieks. Imagined many trembling fingers dialing numbers that are found in the front of phone-books under *In Case of Emergency*. I hoped Joshua wouldn't *literally* wait for a crowd to gather. A front door two houses down flew open and a huge man in rumpled pajamas lurched out onto the front lawn brandishing a baseball bat. He didn't seem radiantly transformed to me; on the contrary, he appeared monstrously pissed. I was reaching for the ignition when Joshua's voice, amplified to a deafening roar, stunned the night: "REALITY IS FINAL!" He paused, then added softly, "But it is not complete.

"How *could* it be complete without a Mystery Train hurtling through our dreams? How could it possibly be complete without imagining that together we have all dreamt it up, to *make* it real, so that at this moment, right *now*, our entire lives could come to this? A rather provocative state of affairs, don't you think?

"The train we dreamt of was the *Celestial Express*. I don't know about you, but my arms are tired from trying to flag down the *Celestial Express*. The train we dreamt of was an old freight hauling grain, refrigerators, newsprint, tractor parts, munitions, salt. The train we dreamt of was the *Dawn Death Zephyr*, burning human breath and broken dreams for fuel. The train we dreamt up was the raw possibility of any real train we want to ride.

"All aboard! All aboard that train!

"But of course we're already all aboard. That is the practicality of the joke. A joke, I promise you, that wasn't intended to demean you as fools or scare you witless, but rather to illuminate your own face in the rain and hear the thousand songs in your blood. To perhaps touch your mother's breast the way you did, a week old in a magical world—her clean mammal warmth most magical of all. To refresh the magic. The real magic of holding each other in our real arms.

"We hurt each other. We help each other. We kill each other and love each other and generally seem to suffer the slaughter of bored failure in between. We treat others—people, plants, animals, earth—with contempt, deceit, unbound venality, slobbering greed. What faith we muster is often blind with self-righteousness or merely a garbage can lid to keep the flies from making maggots, the dogs from scattering our trash on the front lawn, our dirty little secrets and decaying shame there displayed for all to see. And then a small child cuts a crooked cherry limb for a sword, lifts the garbage can lid for a shield, and sallies forth to vanquish the real dragons guarding the real grails, the empty grails depicting in precious stone the marriage of the sun and moon."

Joshua paused a long moment, the echo of his last words rolling down the valley, then continued with a boom: "I'm not talking about *religion*. I'm not trying to sell you a ticket on the train. I'm neither owner nor conductor; I'm a passenger just like you. Maybe some seats on the train are better than others, but all religions are basically the same. After that, the churches and temples fill with accountants, warriors, and delusion—and, quite frankly, I would have them fill with rivers, with ravens, with real wishes.

"Reality is final, but not complete. We will fade into the rain, the river, the restless and infinitely suggestive wishes that spawn our faces. A raven will appear or not. All we have is what is real. What we can comprehend, replenish, sustain, create. And if the possibilities are beyond our comprehension, they are not beyond our choice or, by that same choice, our faith. The *is* is the real-right-now it all gets down to, and I assure you I know how really and truly hearts are mangled, how the weight of our loneliness collapses on us, the way doubt and ignorance leach our salts. We don't know if we're solid, gas, or liquid; light or space; deranged angels or the devil's fools; all or none or some of the time; or who, what, where, how, or why-oh-why the is *is*—except as we make it so, affirm it so, and live it as our own witness.

"But here we are. Here we are tonight, alive. We live by life. And we are bound by being, by being life, to make and accept our choices as the truths of ourselves and not excuses wrenched from the impossibility of choosing. All I truly want to say is that I know the choices aren't easy, that there's a wilderness between intention and consequence, that if you've never been lost you have no way to understand how lucky you are. I address you out of commiseration, not instruction, hoping to remind you that we can hurt each other or help each other, fester or flower, freeze or leap.

"*Leap.*"

He'd barely uttered the word when I caught the muzzle flash in the corner of my eye, and in the same instant the left-rear speaker was wrenched from the window and Joshua sagged against the door, hand to his head, blood seeping between his fingers. I leapt across the front seat and pulled his hand away. Expecting the worst, I was elated to see a shallow scratch instead of the brain-dripping hole I feared. I decided it must've been a fragment from the speaker or the bullet. I also decided that an explanation for the oddity of the wound could wait, which is about the same instant I was deciding we should get the fuck out of there. I made another leap—back behind the wheel—and was twisting the key when a hand seized mine. Joshua's.

"*No.*" He meant it.

"They're shooting at us," I said reasonably.

He shrugged. "It wasn't a very inspired speech." He idly wiped at the trickle of blood tangling in his left eyebrow. "One has to accept criticism."

"You're bleeding," I told him.

"It's nothing. A wood fragment from the speaker, I think." He picked up the microphone and handed it to me. "You try."

By now people in bathrobes or half-dressed were pouring outside, the name Henry being screamed. I sat with the microphone in my hand, my mind—so recently and incessantly possessed of babble—a blank. I waited about fifteen seconds for the next bullet; then, unable to bear the suspense, I jerked the mike to my mouth and bellowed, "You've got three minutes to kill us! That's all my nerves can stand!" My voice sounded weird to me, fractured, hollow. "If you haven't killed us in three minutes, I'm going to respond to my friend's statement. I'll be brief. Then we'll leave." *Why three minutes?* I thought to myself. Why indeed? Why not?

Joshua was climbing into the backseat. "Forsaking me in my time of need, huh?"

"On the contrary, George," he grunted as he squeezed on over, "I'm checking on the damage to the speaker. There's tremendous distortion somewhere. You sound like a frog chewing ping-pong balls."

"It's the fear and madness," I explained.

"Nonsense. They've shot a speaker. You *do* understand they were shooting at the speaker, not us?"

"Whew," I said, letting the sarcasm drip, "that's a relief." I glanced at my watch, suffering a moment's panic when I realized I hadn't marked the beginning of three minutes. At least a minute had gone by, it seemed to me, so I called it two, wondering if anybody was actually keeping track.

Outside, a woman yelled, "Eddie, get back in here."

From up the block, a man shouted, "Goddamn it, Henry, that's enough shooting. You're crazier than they are. There's no reason to kill them." I hoped that sentiment was sweeping the neighborhood.

"Ah-ha," Joshua said behind me. "The bullet hit the edge of the speaker; a wire pulled loose when it fell. Just what I thought." He started humming "Zippity-doo-dah" as he commenced the repairs. He had remarkable grace under pressure, or else a serious mental defect.

In clock time, every second is of equal duration, but our experience proves this simply isn't true. The duration between tick and tock stretches, compresses, and, to judge from this occasion, sometimes stops. I stared at the second hand until I was sure it was moving again, figuring I'd lost half a minute minimum during my watch's malfunction. That would make it three minutes, maybe more. I switched on the microphone.

"Time's up," I announced. "Thank you, folks. We meant you no harm at all and hoped you'd feel the same way." Evidently Joshua had reconnected the wire because my voice was loud and clear. Which was a waste of a good sound system and speedy repairs, since I had nothing more to say; and even if I did, my mouth was suddenly too dry to speak. I flipped off the mike and dropped it on the front seat. Then, with a desperation disguised as bravado, I opened the door and slowly got out of the car, careful to keep my open hands in plain view. I walked around to the front of the car, then climbed up on the warm hood, and then onto the roof. There I stood in the clear-night mountain air, looking at every face I could see, people standing in protective clusters, faces at windows, families jamming doorways or half-hidden on darkened porches, and then I began to applaud, steadily, sincerely, and painfully, for my hands were still tender from the cactus waltz.

"Get your worthless asses outa here!" a voice snarled from the shadows.

"Yeah, before you get 'em kicked," the guy with the baseball bat added.

I continued my applause.

"You people're crazy and shouldn't be loose." It was an old woman's voice, sharp with a judgment born of experience, cranky with the fuss caused by fools.

I clapped madly.

The shouts stopped and I could hear my applause echoing down the street. I don't know the sound of one hand clapping, but I can tell you for sure what two sound like. My hands hurt, but I continued my ovation.

And finally a person I couldn't see—just a shadow on a porch at the end of the block, not a clue if it was man, woman, or child—joined my applause. *Only* one, true, but that was enough. Besides, nobody booed. I stopped clapping.

"Thank you for your patience," I said, and jumped to the pavement, opened the door to Joshua's honoring nod, cranked the Caddy over, and we made away in the night—a departure, in my view, not without a certain touch of panache.

Within two miles the graceful dignity of our exit was fouled by a flashing red light, and what had been a cool slipaway became a for-real, rootin'-tootin', flat-out, ass-haulin' and bawlin'-for-momma getaway.

As the red light hammered on behind us, I turned to Joshua for instructions. He was holding the microphone by its cord, swinging it like a pendulum to the pulse of the red light, his other hand pressing a chartreuse handkerchief to his forehead. He was lost in either thought or shock.

I prodded him: "I believe some sort of law enforcement official is signaling us to pull over."

"Ignore him."

"He won't go away."

"That's sheer conjecture on your part, George," he replied, still swinging the microphone. He stopped abruptly when the sheriff hit his siren. "That siren is certainly obnoxious, isn't it?"

"Unless you're deaf," I agreed.

"Ignore it if you can," Joshua advised.

I kept it just above the speed limit, the sheriff on our tail like glue. About a mile on, as we entered a long straightaway, he swung out and pulled even with the left-rear window. I decided I'd treat him like any other motorist, hitting my highbeams to indicate it was clear to pass.

The sheriff killed the siren and pulled up even with the Caddy. He used the roof-mounted bullhorn to issue a crisp, professional request: "Pull over, cocksuckers!"

"Must we also endure slurs on our sexuality," I asked Joshua, who was reaching over into the backseat.

"Yes," he grunted.

"Sticks and stones, huh?"

"Within reason."

"PULL OVER AND STOP OR I'LL SHOOT!" the sheriff commanded.

"What about bullets," I asked Joshua.

"We should display compassion for his crabbed and envious mind," he replied mildly, turning back around in the seat and gazing thoughtfully down the road as he fiddled with the microphone in his hand.

"*NOW*, MOTHERFUCKERS!" the bullhorn boomed.

The next thing I heard was Joshua's voice, still mild, but at a decibel level far beyond the capabilities of the sheriff's puny bullhorn:

"Sir, we don't recognize your authority to detain scientists at work or pilgrims on their appointed way."

I glanced over to see how the officer was responding to this modest objection just in time to see him lift an ugly sawed-off .12-gauge from the floor rack. There was a burst of static or sputtering over the bullhorn, followed by a rage-gored bellow: "RIGHT *NOW*, FUCKERS!"

"*EAT SHIT!*" Joshua screamed.

I don't know who was more shocked, me or the sheriff. As if blown apart by the sonic blast from Joshua's souped-up system, the Caddy and his Dodge swerved away from each other. I recovered and he didn't. However, he did manage to slow it down enough that when he twirled off the shoulder and took out thirty yards of barbed-wire fence he didn't roll it.

"Stop," Joshua recommended.

I pulled over and we looked back. The red light was still flashing, but erratically. The interior light came on and we could see the sheriff jump out and immediately go down screaming, tangled in barbed wire.

"He's fine," Joshua said, "merely rendered inept by his rage and our magic. Let's leave him here, preferably with haste." He clicked the mike switch on and murmured cheerfully, "Good night, officer."

I pulled back onto the road and put my foot in it, romping it up into triple digits within fifteen seconds.

After a minute Joshua asked, "How fast are we traveling?"

"About a hundred and ten."

"Is that necessary?"

I thought about it for a moment. "Not really. But you said 'with haste' and, given the likelihood of pursuit, I find speed comforting."

"Then by all means enjoy it. And should it contribute to our safety, all the better."

"Speaking of escape, Joshua, it might not be a bad idea to get rid of the silver box and its contents—that's the sort of evidence that could really nail our sacks to a wall. Unless you don't want to dump it. Sentimental attachment, investment, whatever."

Joshua smiled. "I'd already decided to give it to you in appreciation for your help. A gift to the giver, as it were. It's yours to dispose of as you will."

"Joshua, did anyone ever tell you you're a sneaky ol' fart?"

"I always thought generosity the simplest of virtues."

"Thanks," I said, nodding my acknowledgment.

Joshua nodded in return. "Good. Enjoy it. I've spent months refining it."

"Will it handle a forty-five R.P.M.?"

"Yes. The train recording is a forty-five."

"Would you mind if I played some records from a friend's collection on my new machine? As loud as possible?"

"Rock-and-roll, I assume?" He didn't sound enthusiastic.

"That's right," I said.

"Am I being punished, or is this an attempt at persuasion?"

"Neither," I said. "In celebration."

"George," Joshua muttered, "it isn't sporting to flog a man with his own rhetoric; our mouths too often prove larger than our hearts."

"Tough," I said.

We started with Chuck Berry's "Maybelline," followed by Jerry Lee Lewis's "Shake, Rattle, and Roll," which we were doing, and that followed by four hits of speed for me and one for Joshua, bless his heart, who decided he at least owed it to the music to hear it in its proper context. I even saw him tap his foot a few times as he stared straight down the road, lost in what marvelous eruptions of mind I couldn't imagine, or couldn't imagine except as my own.

At Joshua's suggestion, we drove around at random till well after dawn. His theory held that we could confuse any pursuit by confusing ourselves; to lose them by getting lost. Getting lost, however, turned out to be difficult. Usually we hit a dead end and had to turn around, so more than once we had the vague feeling of having been there before. Joshua would say, "Let's take the next right and then drive for nine minutes and take the next seven lefts." Almost always we wound up at a gate or dead end. Besides, there were frequent road signs telling you where you were and how far it was to the next place. But it worked. We saw a few cops, but none who seemed to notice us.

132

Joshua and I parted company in Truth or Consequences, New Mexico, a town he selected from a highway mileage sign as appropriate to our farewell. I let him off just inside the city limits, within easy milkshake distance of a Dairy Queen that was about to open for the morning. He thanked me for the ride and a memorable night. I thanked him for the silver music box and for making me feel possible. I was sad to see him go.

I took 25 South toward Las Cruces and the intersection with 10. I looked for some company but there wasn't a thumb on the road. I missed Joshua's bent but somehow reassuring presence, and that, along with feeling bone weary and emotionally drained from the night's adrenalin hits, left me blue. It's common cultural knowledge that the best cure for the blues is music, so I turned Little Richard up full volume and listened to him rave about a woman named Lucille.

No doubt about it, the music helped keep the blues at bay, but what helped even more was a quiet afternoon spent on the banks of the Rio Grande, watching the wide dirty water roll by. I'd stopped to take a quick piss, but by the time my bladder was empty I was caught in the soothing pull of the river. I decided to rest for half an hour and ended up sitting there damn near till dark. Drowsing off on occasion, I watched the water move, calmed by its broad, sullied, inevitable force. When I finally fired up the Caddy, I felt like I'd had a good night's sleep. Nothing was left of the blues but the shadow that's almost always there.

I stopped in El Paso to gas up for the West Texas run. I fueled myself with two tacos from Juan's Taco Take-Out Shack, of which I ate one and two bites of the second, followed by benzedrine, of which I ate five. Thus fortified and clear of mind, I put the Diamonds' "Little Darlin'" on the box and began the slow curve east into the hill country.

I even had myself something of a plan. I'd haul down to Houston, grab a motel, sleep till I woke up, chow down, then hit the library or do whatever else was required to find out *exactly* where the Bopper's bones had found their repose. I felt sure he was buried in his hometown, or else in Beaumont, but it was time to know for sure. Past time. I'd been sloppy, a truth I calmly acknowledged and calmly vowed to change. Yup, no doubt about it: time to gather everything tight and true. I felt a surge of purpose and knew I was going to pull it off. I was closing on the end, about to deliver.

Clint, Torillo, Finlay, up the Quitman Range as the moon rose, past Sierra Blanca and down to Eagle Flat and on through Allamore, Van Horne, Plateau, I took West Texas at full gallop, whipping it down the highway behind the cut-loose combo of drugs and rock-and-roll. "Pow! Pow! Shoot 'em up now . . . ah-hoooo, my baby loves 'em Western Movies." Blues dusted, even the shadow blown away. I didn't need Joshua or Kacy or sleep. I remember saying over and over for miles, lyrics to my own music, "Myself, this moment, this journey." Seriously.

I pitted for gas at the 10-20 Junction Texaco Truck Stop. A scrawny young guy buttonholed me outside the men's room and asked for a ride to Dallas. His eyes alone constituted probable cause, and his breath was so cheap-wine sour it would've straightened out a sidewinder. I told him I was taking the other fork, to Houston, and that I didn't feel like company anyway, that for the first time in too long I was enjoying being alone.

I pulled back on 10 with Little Richard wailing "Tutti Frutti" up my spine. With a quickness and accuracy that would shame your average computer, I plotted time and distance, assessed my neural system for evidence of fatigue, considered a snarl of intangible intrinsic needs, and determined seven bennies was the optimum dose. I washed them down with a cold beer. The run to Houston was going to be long and empty— exactly what I wanted. I leaned back in the Caddy's plush seat, powered down a window for fresh air, flexed my fingers on the wheel, and screwed the juice to it till the stars blurred. I was a white rocket in a wall of sound; pure, powerful, ready to tighten down and deliver the gift, kiss the Caddy's grille against the Bopper's stone, soak down the backseat with gasoline, then set Harriet's letter ablaze and toss it in, a little torch to spark off a magnificent fireball, love's monument and proof. Yes, mama, yes. Wild into the wilderness. Wop-bop-a-lu-bop. Flower and root.

And there, right there, precisely at the diamond point of affirmed purpose, riding that bridge-burning music and wholly committed to my unknown end, I caught the shadowy semblance of Double-Gone Johnson in the headlights' halo and got myself turned around. Not *completely* around, or not immediately, but a definite hard left, 90°, due north.

Later I wondered why, given my mood, I even thought to stop, but the fact is I was stopping *before* I thought. Neural impulse, social reflex, whatever: I snapped to him. Whether this was wise or stupid, lucky or fucked, are judgments I leave to you. But before leaping to a conclusion, let me describe the man as I saw him—the raw impressions in the headlights as I slowed, the finer details as he eased himself in—and ask you to consider what you would've done in similar mood and circumstance, in that same span of three skipping heartbeats I had to decide.

The color of his stingy-brim hat might've stopped me by itself: a screaming flamingo pink, about three decibels short of glowing in the dark, and hardly muted by a satin band of neon lavender. The hat might not stop you, but not because you didn't see it.

He was tall, six-one or -two.

Not hitching, or no sign of an upraised thumb or flagging arm. Standing tall and straight.

Holding a squarish, shiny, mottled-white object, which on closer examination was a King James Bible bound in the hide of some South American lizard.

Slender, but without any sense of being skinny.

Black. That alone would've stopped me for sure, a black man hitching on a Texas freeway at 2 A.M. in 1965, because he was either fearless, magical, desperate, or seriously dumb—and which, or what braid of those strands, is the kind of question I find intriguing.

I suspected it was fearlessness, the sort that springs from a deep personal sense of heavenly protection, for he was dressed as a clergyman, and though Double-Gone Johnson was indeed a minister of the faith, he was also, as his vestments revealed, a man of the cloth in the sartorial as well as the ecclesiastical sense. A frockcoat of black velvet, its severe cut gracefully tailored into sleekness. Black velvet pants, modestly pegged and impeccably fit. Black alpaca sweater. A clerical collar, but with a color variation: instead of a starched white square at the throat, a patch of glowing lavender satin cut from the same electric bolt as his hatband. To the ecclesiastical basics he added a black velvet opera cape lined in a silk the dyer's hand had tortured into the same shade as his hat. A pair of snakeskin cowboy boots completed his wardrobe.

I rolled to a stop and reached across to open the passenger door. "Houston bound or anywhere in between."

Double-Gone stooped to look me over with his dark brown eyes—not wary or nervous, but languidly alert. He had wide, fleshy lips and, when he smiled, an expanse of stong white teeth. He reached in and gently placed his lizard-bound Bible on the front seat, but he didn't get in himself. "One moment please," he requested in a caramel baritone, holding up a long finger.

I thought he was gathering luggage I hadn't seen or was going to take a leak, but instead he circled the Eldorado, touching the hood and front grille, running his hands along the chrome and the roof line, over the twin-bullet taillights, nodding rapidly, crooning to himself as he made the circuit, "Yes. *Solid.* My, my. You long and sweet. Oooh baby, *yes.* Fo' real and fo' sure. Much, much, much, far and away truly *too much.*" All the way around and back to the open passenger's door. He slid himself in, picked up his Bible, gently shut the door, and bestowed onto me a full-force smile. "The Holy Spirit must love yo' act to lay it on sooo *thick.*"

"Actually," I confessed, "I stole it."

"Well all right, yes," he blinked, "sometimes yo' forced to gather the Heavenly Bounty with yo' own two hands, I dig that, but it makes fo' a *bad* situation, catch my riff? Means the Law be looking fo' it. Means they find it, they gonna find *me in it,* and that's a hard five in the slammer if yo' black and in Texas, both of which I am, and those are conditions that don't allow for much innocence and *no* justice. And since I *do* truthfully enjoy fresh air and wide open spaces and woman's sweet flesh and *all* the Holy Manifestations of the Almighty Light, I do not have the time fo' the time, you dig it? So bless ya fo' offerin' a pilgrim soul a boost along the way, but man, y'all best be getting on without me, sad to say."

"Good enough," I said, and waited for him to get out.

Instead, he sank back in the seat, rolled his eyes heavenward for guidance, then closed them as he sighed to himself, "Double-Gone, you be *long gone* if honky Law comes down on yo' ass; jus the nigger to make their night. White man and a black man in a stolen cherry Cadillac with California plates, *who* they gonna believe stole it? Man, even if this righteous white cat next to you confesses all the way to the fucking Supreme Court, yo' ass is down fo' five. Count on it."

"Stolen," I interrupted his reverie, "may be too harsh. Legally, I have a pile of illegal documents that explain I'm merely transporting this car to a memorial service. I've been stopped once already, just out of Frisco, and the paper stood up. And—."

"Yes," Double-Gone swung in eagerly, "talk that talk."

"And morally, I'm actually delivering it as a gift of love from a spinster woman who was awakened by the music."

"Oooeeeee! More!" Double-Gone clapped his hands. "Pile it on!"

"But it's only straight to tell you that early this morning a sheriff in hot pursuit of a car *real close* to matching the description of this one ran off the road, though he might feel he was forced off."

"Thas *ugly* news. Kind of thing might be misunderstood as attempted murder or some such bad shit."

"However," I went on, "that was in the mountains of New Mexico, and like I say it was early this morning, and time *is* distance."

Double-Gone nodded, but without conviction.

"And you'll notice in the backseat a box of about two hundred rock-and-roll records and a funny-looking sound system so powerful it'll cave in your skull."

Double-Gone brightened. "Thas better, yes, now we're back in the groove; thas the kinda music I *like* to hear."

"And—"

"Do it to me!" Double-Gone urged.

I did. *"And* in the glovebox is a bottle of maybe nine hundred amphetamine tablets, factory fresh."

"Great Lawd God o' Mercy!" Double-Gone shouted, palms raised heavenward in jubilant surrender. "We best eat 'em up 'fo the Law seizes 'em as evidence."

This struck me as enlightened strategy. Houston was still somewhere over the horizon, and I could feel exhaustion creeping in. Besides, as Double-Gone had astutely noted, there's no call to leave incriminating evidence lying around. We both took a small handful, though Double-Gone had big hands.

I lifted the box of records off the backseat and handed them over. "You're the deejay."

"Awright! I dig it! And now get ready fo' KRZY brain-blasting radio, the Reverend Double-Gone Johnson keeping the beat and whipping some o' that sweet gospel on yo' ears."

"Well, Reverend Double-Gone," I said, swinging the Caddy back onto the road, "you're riding with Irreverent George: glad to have you aboard."

"Five," he laughed, extending his hand.

I took it. "Now maybe between cuts you might explain your religious affiliations and the exact nature of your ministry, because I've never in my life seen such downtown vestments, nor a clergyman who gobbled bennies for communion. It's always been my understanding, and certainly my experience, that amphetamines are the Devil's work."

Double-Gone snorted. "Lord made the Devil to play with. *Made* it all, every thing and every being; *is* it *all;* and *will be* long past that blast on the clarion horn that lifts us up into the Unending Light. What you gotta dig from the jump is there ain't no salvation lackin' some sin to salvage yo' ass from. Otherwise, we all be bored shitless and I'm outa work."

"I'm ripe for conversion. What's the name of your church?"

Double-Gone groaned—at the forlorn hopelessness of my spiritual state, I thought at first. "Man," he sighed heavily, "my whole life been a trouble with names."

He elaborated as we ripped down the road, his baritone beating back whatever song was blaring from the speakers as I jammed the white lines together, thinning them into a shimmering string, still happily unaware that it led into the labyrinth, not out.

Double-Gone was going home to Houston after nine years of scuffling in L.A. He'd taken off at fifteen, when his parents split up; Momma could no longer abide Daddy's drinking, and Daddy couldn't stand his nighttime janitor's job at the Texaco building without some lush.

Double-Gone was the youngest child by six years; three older sisters were married and gone by the time his folks called it quits. "No reason to hang anybody up," he explained, "Momma, Daddy, or me."

Double-Gone wasn't his given name. " 'Clement Avrial' is what they hung on me—after my granddaddy—but with all due respect fo' tradition, *Clem* jus don't make it. Sounds like yo' 'bout half a jump ahead of a dirt clod, with an I.Q. 'round room temperature. So when I cut for the coast I changed my name to Onyx . . . and dig, man, I was fifteen, wanted a little *flash* in my life. No sooner make L.A. than I latch up with this white hooker chick grabs her own kicks from tender young black boys like me. Right after we make it—and this is my first piece we talking about; my *cherry,* right?—and I'm still collapsed there on top, fuck-stunned and gaspin', she start up giggling like girls do and her giggling jus keeps growing till it's some *crazy* laughing. Ask her what it is, she laughs so hard it takes her a minute to strangle it out. 'Onyx,' she howls, and that *really* cracks her up. So there I am, can't figure my toes from my nose, my dick from a popsicle stick, but I do got one thing covered fo' sure, and that's that I don' want *no* name that's a joke I don't get. So I slid on out, got dressed, and found my way to the door. She's *still* laughing. Ah, women is a wonderful grief. Learned early on jus to love 'em and not worry on figuring 'em out. Different species. But how it is, you see, is the Lord don't make mistakes, just mysteries—and man, he made one fo' sure when he made women.

"Anyway, what I done was have *no* name. Hacked it back to plain Johnson. Decided if I couldn't dazzle 'em with bullshit, I'd hit 'em with mystery. Worked, too—snagged a bunch—'course it mighta had more to do with my natural good looks and smooth moves. Tried to put a coupla girls to work, but L.A. is tight turf and mean streets, you under-stand? I stepped on some big toes inside hundred-dollar shoes and got my sixteen-year-old ass thumped good . . . or good enough to spend a few weeks in L.A. General eating through a straw. No *fun,* but it sorta opened my eyes by swelling 'em shut, you might say.

"When I limp outa General, I decide I be doin' it the American way. Got on at Denny's washing dishes graveyard. Rented me a room was so small you couldn't spring a decent boner without getting pressed up against a wall. Bagged enough plate scraping to keep my guts from greasing my backbone. Start at the bottom and work my way up—that's the plan, man. Read them Help Wanteds like a map to the City of Gold, and I took me a smile an' shoeshine to every interview, but they don't call it nigger work because there's a bunch o' white folks lining up to do it, I know yo' hep to that. I worked my way *sideways*, one shit job after another, till I looked in my wallet on my twentieth birthday and didn't have the jack for a free blowjob and a bottle o' Ripple both. Life's a groove, and thas the truth; but man, the bullshit can break ya down.

"So I start workin' the street again, *real careful* this time, penny-ante hustling. You know the gig: weed by the matchbox, numbers and nowhere cons, fencing stuff so hot it's third-degree burns jus lookin' at it. And when yo' margin's ten percent of alley discount, yo' lucky to get high fo' a night on what you clear on a diamond ring. I was being *bad*. Small-time bad. *Loser* bad. I was goin' down like one of them dinosaurs in the tar pit. Started lushing and joy-popping and sleeping where I fell. Couldn't get my soul up off the ground.

"But the evening of January seventh, jus last year, 'bout as down drunk as a man can be, I get lost going 'round the corner to the liquor store and end up right in front of this concrete building with a bitty purple neon cross 'bove this slab-oak door with a sign says BESSIE HAR-MON'S CHURCH OF ENDLESS JOY. I turn right around to make me a fast getaway from *that* shit but my lush feet get all tangled up and I go lurching 'gainst the door. And man, that door's *pulsating*. I press my ear on it and what I hear but a hundred human voices rocking high up in the gospel. Push open the door into a room musky with rapture and full of shiny black faces all lifted heavenward in song, eyes closed, singing fo' all they worth, and right now, *wham!* the singing stops and Bessie Harmon grab the pulpit and cries out in that raw crystal trumpet voice, 'Do you want to *feeeeelllllll* the *mighty, endless joy?*'

"A hundred hearts shout *yeah* with a single voice—a hundred *and one*, 'cause I figured it wouldn't hurt me none to feel a little myself, seeing as how I'd been short some lately.

"Bessie let the silence work a second, then say soft, matter o' fact, 'Well, it's easy.' Then she leans out over the pulpit, her sweet face shining like a black moon, and whispers, 'All ya gotta do is *open* your *heart.*'

"I do like she said, opened up my ol' raggedy-ass heart, and the Light came *pouring* in, flooding me so full I overflowed on the spot. When the singing started again I was right up there with 'em, and I was dancin' in the aisle like a man who'd never be empty again.

"I went home with Miss Bessie herself that evening fo' some of her *personal* ministry, and she laid it on me as I laid her down: 'I seen 'em gone on the light and gone on the music, but yo' *double-gone*, Johnson, and I can't wait to get next to ya.' I didn't hang her up, ya dig? And when she moaned out 'O Lawd, Lawd, Lawd!' in that deep springwater voice, you *knew* He heard our human prayers, loud and clear.

"Bessie brought me into the Church and kept me at her place to continue her personal ministry. She started me reading the Bible and learning the hymns and jumpin' her bones when the spirit moved her— and she was a woman *full* of spirit, my-oh-fucking-my. You ever get a chance to hear that Bessie woman sing 'Amazing Grace' lying naked on silk sheets, yo' liable to have yo'self a religious experience that whups the shit outa talking to angels.

"Bessie got me going on the preaching gig. Jus seemed to come to me on the natch, like it was waiting there all my life, lying low in the weeds. Bessie taught me high and godly preaching's one-part Bible, one-part style, and ninety-eight-parts heart and soul. I hear what she laying down. In five months she made me Assistant Minister of True Witness and cut me ten percent of the plate.

"End of the year we're packing 'em to the rafters. My job was warm-up . . . get the hellfire lickin' at their heels. I'd bring that power-ful need down like a hammer, smash the lid open on all their sin and sickness, get 'em squirming with guilt and failure, and then Mama Bessie'd come on and vault they po' souls into heavenly bliss. But man, even though we *raking* in the bucks, I can't stand making 'em *sweat* like that, playing the heavy. *I* wanted to lift 'em up, but Bessie wasn't hearin' none of it. *I* wanted to add some electric guitar, a little bass, a taste of drums to the hymn singing. Bessie say no way and never happen. Plus she being a restless woman, she laying the hot-eye on this pretty-boy mulatto. I come home the other night, she says why don' I make myself *triple* gone fo' the evening, she had some emergency salvation work to do on Sammy—this mulatto cat, dig?—who was having some spiritual crisis in his pants. Now I'm a man who knows that when it's got to the point where yo' just standing in the way, it's time fo' *somebody* to make a move, so I hit the petty cash box on my way to the door.

"So here I am in downtown L.A., old threads on my frame, nothing but this Bible Bessie gave me on my twenty-first birthday and three hundred and change to get me clear, standing on some nowhere corner at midnight with the bad blues in my heart and no clue what to do, when the Lord tells me plain as I'm telling you, 'Go *home*, Double-Gone; go *home* and flourish.' Now when the Lord speaketh, you *heedeth*—and pronto, my man. I'm choosing between a used car and some new threads, and I figured I couldn't get much of a short for three bills but I could boss up my wardrobe good, so I go for the clothes—Lord likes his evangels to be lookin' sharp, not like some low-rent Yankee philosopher or some such shit.

"So now *here* I am, almost *there*. What I got in mind fo' my old hometown of Houston is the world's first rock-and-roll church. Bring the Light down strong on the young so they *know* their bodies and souls are one, and joy ain't no sin, or not in *my* gospel. Should rack me some healthy in-come once we get rollin'. Maybe branch out with a couple of rib joints. Lord put me on it, so you know it's got to be good. Got that can't-miss feeling. I mean, there's three things *at least* that black folks do better than you whiteys ever dreamed of, and that'd be sing the blues, do ribs up right, and go to church.

"Which brings me smack-back to my troubles with names. 'Double-Gone' got my personal handle covered, but now I need a name fo' my church. Something says *what it is*—you dig it?—and hooks 'em solid. Something wild, but cool too. Been twirling some around in my skull between rides. Let me whip out a couple, see what ya think. Dig this one: The Holy Writ Church of Awesome Joy. *Too* much, huh? Then let me lay down something else: The First Church of the Monster Rapture Hits. 'Monster' too *down*, ya think? Scare the kiddies? Well, here's something more quiet and smooth: The Full Soul Church of Pure Joy. How 'bout Soulful Church of Rocking Joy? The Rocking Joy Church of Atomic Gospel? You know, something *modern.*"

I stepped in with a suggestion. "Why not keep it simple? Something like The Church of Faith?"

Double-Gone was offended. "Thas too tight-ass white. No *pop* to it, man. You Unitarian or something?"

"All right, how about The Rock Faith Church of the Wild Shaking Light and Wall-Blowing Glory?"

"Now yo' at least *breathin'.*"

That encouraged me. "Okay now, hang on: The Whirlpool Church of Undreamable Felicity."

"Hey now! Whoa up, mule! What's this 'Felicity'? That the same chick I knew in Watts with them tight pink shorts spray-painted on an ass guaranteed to make yo' heart stand still?"

"Just another word for happiness," I explained.

" 'Deed she was, but I don't want no congregation where you gotta put a motherfuckin' dictionary in the hymnal."

"Well," I said, "you should look for a name in what *you* actually feel. It's your church, right? Something like The Open-Heart Church of the Flooding Light."

"Thought of that," Double-Gone said, "but 'open-heart'? 'Floodlight?' Sounds like serious surgery. But I dig yo' drift. Now check this out: The Gospel Wallop Church of Eternal Bliss."

We went on and on, riffing back and forth, a playful speed-rave ring-shout, trading solos over whatever tune he'd dropped on the box. Nothing stuck, but we had fun.

The sun was trying to come up when we stopped for fuel and donuts at a Gas Mart outside Austin. Frost sparkled on the oil-stained cement of the pump bays. The donuts were stale the week before, so we ate some more speed to cut the grease. I was beginning to feel gone and gritty. The pale dawnlight scratched my raw eyes, and my neck and shoulder muscles felt torqued down tighter than the nut on the Caddy's flywheel. I needed a long hot bath and a good day's sleep. I was looking forward to Houston.

Double-Gone was shuffling records as we fishtailed off the frost-slick on-ramp back onto the highway and I took it up to cruising speed, the needle locked solid between the nine and the zero.

"This indeed be the Lord's bounty," Double-Gone chuckled, tipping a record to read the label in the strengthening light. "Yes, oh yes! Head full o' volts and some good boogie fo' the box and a short so boss it could be the Lord's chariot driving to the Pearly Gates. I catch what yo' doing besides some widow's memorial gift or some such?"

"The memorial is the paper cover. And she was a spinster, not a widow. I'm delivering it to the man who moved her. You're holding him in your hands there someplace: the Big Bopper."

"The Bopper?" Double-Gone looked dubious. "Thought the Bopper went down with Holly and that Valens cat."

"Exactly. He died just before she was going to ship this Caddy here off to him. Had it all crated up and ready to go. Put it in a warehouse when she got the sad news."

"Man, that is *sad.*" Double-Gone patted the dash consolingly. "Machine like you all caged up in some dark corner."

"Then when *she* died," I continued, "her jerk-off nephew scored it from the estate."

"Yo' breaking my heart."

"The nephew's up to his nuts in gambling debts. He and this low-life by the name of Scumball—he's the brains—insured it at top value as a mint collector's item or cultural artifact or some damn thing, and I was supposed to make it look like Grand Theft Auto before I totaled it."

"You *wreck,* they *co-*lect—that the gig?"

"That *was* the gig. I stole it and kept going. And here we are."

"I'm digging it." Double-Gone nodded. "And speaking as a humble servant of the Lord, my heart tells me it's righteous in His eyes."

"Glad you and the Lord agree."

" 'Course I don't feature the Law's gonna pump yo' paw and give you a good-ol'-boy slap on the back and cut you loose, 'cause there be good reasons that lady holding the scales got a blindfold over her eyes. And those two cats back home prob'ly ain't over*whelmed* with joy

. . . 'fact, maybe they dialing the number gets answered by the kinda people like to hear bones snap."

"Yup, that's the kind of noise they made when I told them how it was, but I got the goods to take 'em down with me, and I made *real sure* they understood how it was."

"That is: *if* yo' alive. But say these goons wreck you *and* this lovely chunk of automotion? *They* collect and *yo'* be wrecked."

"First they have to find me, then they have to catch me."

"And they don't know where yo' going to, right?"

Oh, fuck! Harriet's letter. Cory Bingham had read it, and I told Scumball I was taking the Caddy where it belonged. How specific had I been? But the sudden dark lash of dread-squeezed adrenalin had locked the memory vault.

"Yo' looking ill," Double-Gone pointed out.

"Well, they *might* figure it out, but I'd call it long odds on short money."

"These cats connected?"

"Connected to what?"

"I mean," Double-Gone said patiently, "do they have friends, family, or business associates here in the Lone Star state that Ma Bell could put 'em onto faster than even you can drive?"

"I don't know. One of them, maybe. But hey, they're looking to take in forty or fifty grand at the outside, and that's an expensive effort you're talking about."

Double-Gone was shaking his head. "I know some cats whose souls so twisted they'd snuff you for a six-pack and the giggle. Cats like that everywhere. Then you got those jus out to make a name or impress the Man. It ain't *always* the money; the Man's got to save face an' set good examples fo' the boys."

"Reverend, you're not lifting my spirits."

"First yo' spirit gotta understand *what is.* We ain't jus talking 'bout yo' ass, dig? What about the Bopper's people? You give 'em this fine automobile, you might be givin' 'em the gift o' grief."

"Wait a second," I said, sensing the misunderstanding, "I'm taking it to the Bopper himself."

Double-Gone blinked. "Say what?"

"The Big Bopper. I'm delivering this car to *him*, with love from Harriet, ashes to ashes and dust to dust."

"The Bopper *dead*, man, crashed and burned."

"I'm hip."

Maybe my tone was a little sharp, because Double-Gone's response was icy on the edges. "Well now, you *hip* that the dead *can't drive?*"

I laughed with relief. "Listen, I forgot you don't have the whole picture, and damn near forgot I do. See, what I'm up to is this: I deliver the Eldorado here to the Bopper's *grave*, soak it down with a gallon of high-test, stand on the hood while I read Harriet's letter—kind of a eulogy—and then it's up in flames."

Double-Gone pinned me with a bulge-eyed stare: "Yo' *sick*, man."

"Ah," I replied, "but wait: I not only deliver this lost gift of love, and honor the power of music to move us and complete another connection in the Holy Circuit, but my two scuzzy friends also collect their insurance money."

"I'm hearing you, but *they* don't know that. Far as they know, you got it parked on Sunset and Vine with a FOR SALE sign taped up in the window."

"Wrong," I said. "They *do* know it. I told them I'd wreck it, but it was going to take a little longer than usual."

"Why sure," Double-Gone took on a look of feigned innocence, "they ain't saying to themselves, 'Well here's a speed-cranking daddy with a two-monkey habit running loose with our fifty-G pay-off machine, our income fo' sure on the line and, should the Law come down, maybe our asses, but George say *be cool, don't worry,* and you know ol' George wouldn't think of anything like a paint-and-plate job or a side-street discount or even keeping it stashed somewhere fo' a steady blackmail income. Naw, shit man: we trust ol' George. Sure, we'll do like he say and hang here cool and make no whatsoever effort to bust his fucking chops.' "

"Double-Gone, I got the perfect name for your church: The Come-Down Tabernacle of the Grim View."

"Lord give us eyes so we could dig it *all*, not jus what we *want* to see. Besides, man, it breaks my po' heart to picture this fine, high-styled piece of fast machinery wasted in flames. And it would be double-sadder, a true burden o' sorrow, if you happened to be sacked up in the trunk."

"Wasn't that long ago you said what I'm doing is righteous in the eyes of the Lord."

"No doubt about it, but being righteous ain't no excuse fo' bein' dumb."

"You think I'm being dumb?"

Double-Gone nodded once solemnly. " 'Fraid I'd have to cop to that."

"Well, man, looking at it through the Lord's eyes, tell me a smarter way."

Double-Gone grinned. "Now George, you *know* I never claimed to that. Only total fools think they looking through the Lord's eyes. Ain't you never dug the Book of Job?" He slapped the Bible on the seat between us. I felt the sermon coming.

"Now ol' Job was a truly righteous cat with all this wide-flung real estate and livestock and a loving wife, not to mention seven boss sons and three daughters so good lookin' make yo' teeth chatter.

"But Satan hanging around the scene, strutting to and fro in the earth and bopping up and down. Lord spots him and says, 'Hey Satan, dig my servant Job. He loves me like he should and does no evil.'

"Satan says, 'Well sure, no shit and no wonder: you got him *covered up* with goodies. Take *them* away and Job'll spit in yo' eye.'

"Lord knows that's jive, so he tells Satan, 'Do what you want to convince yo'self—just don't touch his flesh.'

"No sooner said than Satan lays it on Job hard: sends these goons to rustle the mules; drops a gob of fireballs on the servants and sheep; blows a horrible wind outa the mountains that flattens the eldest son's house where the sons and daughters partying and they *all* wasted. Now what do you think Job says to all this ruination and heavy grief? He say, 'The Lord *gave*, and the Lord *taketh* away. *Blessed* be the name o' the Lord.'

"The Lord's loving it. He tells Satan, 'Hey, I told you my man was cool.'

"But Satan comes back with the big scoff: 'Well fuck, why not? Didn't hurt *him* none. You put some pain on Job's own frame, he'll curse yo' name as a ratprick bastard; can count on it.'

"The Lord tells Satan, 'Go ahead; his ass is yours—jus spare his life is all.'

"Now Satan's got it tight when it comes to putting the serious torment on folks, and he smotes Job with horrible pus-bubbling boils from wig to toes. It's an agony so hard makes piss dribble down yo' leg. Job's wife flips out when she digs the pain he's in. She tells him, 'Job, curse the Lord and die. This ain't making it.'

"But Job don't budge. Tells her to hush her fool mouth. Tells her, 'Shall we receive good at the hand o' God, and shall we not receive evil?'

"Then a bunch of Job's buddies shows up to comfort him. Job's all naked and pus-runny and covered with ashes, and when they clock how monstrous his hurt be, none of 'em can speak fo' seven *days*. But Job's boils eatin' him up something fierce, and he commences to snivel and bad mouth ever being born, and generally lays it down that he's a righteous cat that never crossed the Lord and can't believe he's done *anything* to deserve such bad action. But dig this close: he don't ask the Lord to *end* the suffering. *No.* All he prays for is the *strength* to endure it. *That's* righteous.

"But his buddies be getting in his shit, saying stuff like, 'Job, my man, you *musta* sinned else the Lord wouldn't be on yo' case. 'Or like, 'You getting worked over for thinkin' Job mo' righteous than the Lord.'

"Job calls 'em what you been calling me: 'miserable comforters.' But he won't cop to being a sinner 'cause it ain't the truthful fact. His buddies all whipping on him hard, telling him to repent and trust the Lord and Job's jawing right back at Elihu and Eliphaz and Bildad and them other cats to bug off, he ain't got nothin' to repent for, always trusted and obeyed the Lord, and near as he can dig he's getting fucked over fo' no reason.

"Then all of a sudden—*bam!*—the Lord's voice comes roaring out the whirlwind, and He gets *down*. What he lays on Job and his buddies runs like this: 'Maybe yo' getting fucked over—but hey, you mine to fuck. *I am the Lord!* You get whatever it is you get and what you get is yours, high times or bad blues, good luck or tough shit. I gotta maintain a harmony so far beyond yo' experience that it's fucking *pathetic.'*

"But jus to make sure, the Lord lays it down in all His beautiful sweetness and light, puts it right in their faces: 'Do *you* know the treasures of the snow? Do *you* make the tender buds open in bloom? Is it *you* that feeds the baby lions? *You* that makes sure the ravens have food or divide the waters so them big ol' hippos have rivers to loll in? Can *you* bind the sweet influences of the Pleiades, or loose the bands of Orion?' Ooowheeeee, I love that one—he's talking *stars,* man. And the Lord goes wailing on: 'Is it *you* that lets the heart understand? Did you give yo'*self* life? Do you *really* think you knowing better than me what's what and what ain't? That you got more than a few pitiful clues what it's all about? What *I am?* Well, get hip: no fuckin' way.'

"Now when a man lays it down, liable as not it'll bounce back up in his face. But when the *Lord* lays it down, it *stays* down—and Job, he copped on the spot, saying 'I was blind, but now mine eyes doth see. Do what Thou wilt. I can dig it.'

"So the Lord healed his boils *like that* and no scars neither, and gave Job back *double* all his camels and she-asses and other livestock, plus ten *more* children—seven boys so tall and strong they coulda whupped ass on the Celtics, and three daughters *so fine* you immediately jump to hard. And if that wasn't fair enough, He let Job live another hundred and forty years so he could play with all his grandchildren and *their* children and on and on like that fo' many sweet and swinging generations till Job cashed out, being old and full o' days."

I spoke right up: "How does that make me dumb? You didn't hear me claiming I saw through the Lord's eyes either, did you?"

"See?" Double-Gone sounded exasperated. "Yo' taking it *personal.* Yo' putting yo'self in the way. Point is, don't even *try* to understand the Lord's will; jus' follow."

"I'm hearing you," I said—a little testily, I suppose—"and I'm *all* for it. I guess *I* don't know what His will happens to be."

"Finest thing that Bessie woman ever preached me was 'quit trying and stop denying.' *Feel* it. Feel it like you feel music. Like you feel sunlight on yo' skin. Like it feel when you lie down with a sweet-lovin' woman. I swear, you white folks damn near a lost cause."

"Not much I can do about the color of my soul," I said, jaws tight.

"You know why the Lord gave black folks so much soul?" Double-Gone asked, his tone suddenly playful.

I wasn't feeling playful. "No. Why?"

"To make up fo' what he did to our hair." His dazzling smile, combined with the pink flash of his hat, almost made my raw eyes water. " 'Course," Double-Gone continued, "it ain't really the color o' the soul that matters, though having some cultural heritage is a mighty help when it comes to feeling the spirit move."

What I was feeling again was the babble rising in my brain so bad I wanted to scream. But I took a deep breath. "You still haven't told me how I'm being dumb."

"George," Double-Gone said quietly, "yo' being dumb because you getting in yo' own way. You dumb because you got the man and the music confused. You dumb because you got so high an' mighty on yo' own righteousness that you didn't cover yo' ass—them others be foolish dumb, but that's *dangerous* dumb, getting so sucked up in yo' own wild wonderfulness that you don't take care of business. The Bopper buried in Houston?"

The question, erupting in the litany of my idiocies, caught me by embarrassed surprise. "Well, you know, actually I'm not sure where he's buried," I hemmed, then hawed, "I assume Sabine Pass—that's his hometown—or maybe Beaumont."

"But you don't know for sure." This wasn't a question.

"I've been moving fast lately."

"Not knowing where you going—tell me that ain't dumb. Lazy dumb. You think jus 'cause you on the journey that the Lord gonna do *all* the work?"

"No," I agreed. "I was calling it 'sloppy dumb' to myself right before I saw you standing beside the road, that hat of yours warming the night."

"Hope to shout. Be a little awkward turns out the Bopper's sixed in San Jose. But I'd imagine those two cats you cut on know jus where to send them flowers. People like that pay some mind to details; them that don't, they pay the dues."

"Gotcha, man, loud and clear. But you're telling me what I already know, which maybe isn't much for a dummy like me. Tell me a smarter way. I'm all ears."

Double-Gone shifted his weight slightly and leaned toward me. "I was you, *no way* I'd get near the Bopper's grave. I dig *high,* and I groove on *risk,* but when I see 'em together, like in *high risk,* I stop for a close look, and what I be looking fo' is a way around it."

"Not much glory in that," I said. This sounded poor, but it usually does when you're defending your ignorance.

"George," Double-Gone said sadly, "even money says goons be waiting at the grave to hand you yo' ass on a platter and bring yo' little romance to an ugly end. You go on ahead and you liable to join the Bopper, and on yo' stone they'll chisel, 'This man *looked* to suffer.'"

I felt the first brush of a hustle. "And what are *you* looking for?" I asked as pointedly as possible.

"Man," Double-Gone huffed, "don't shine the light on me when I'm sneaking up. Breaks my rhythm."

"Even money says it has something to do with confusing the man and the music."

"You on the beat, George. You do dig I don't got my heart in it to *push* the point—I don't like bad-mouthing the dead, 'specially if they was so wild alive—but I don't think the Bopper's yo' man. Got my reasons. Number one is like I say: if they gonna hit ya, his grave's the place. Number two, I ain't convinced the Bopper deserves it. That's cold, I know, but there it is. He only made it once, and that was some diddley novelty number with fun and joy, but nothing *deep.* Here, let me drop it on the box and you can hear—"

"No need," I cut in. "I heard it already and I'm hearing you. But I'm not delivering it to the Bopper as a reward for musical excellence or a pack-train of hits; I'm delivering it because it was *meant* for him, Harriet to the Bopper, soul to soul, the way love's supposed to be."

"Now you jus *got* to know that ain't true." Double-Gone was adamant. "That spinster woman never laid eyes on the cat. He sneak up and do her doggie-style in the dark, she wouldn't even know it was the Bopper's bop."

"She was moved by his music. That's good enough for me."

"Hallelujah brother, I'm hearing *that.* But you got to ask yo'self jus where that music coming from."

"Says on the label he's singing it and playing it and that he wrote it, so I'd say it's his."

"You mistaking the flower fo' the root," Double-Gone gently chided. "Where you think rock-and-roll come from?"

I was getting annoyed. "Hey, I never claimed to know jackshit about music."

"That a fact?" Double-Gone was polite. "Well, you remember me playing Elvis doing 'Don't Be Cruel,' right?"

"Yeah," I said, wary.

"And Elvis doing 'All Shook Up'?"

"Yeah."

"Jerry Lee working out on 'Great Balls of Fire'?"

"Yeah."

"Any idea who wrote those numbers?"

"No."

"Black cat name o' Otis Blackwell."

"Otis does good work." I was getting the point.

"Remember 'Hound Dog,' monster hit fo' Elvis? Black woman named Mama Thornton did that song early on, long 'fore Elvis's pouty face and cute wiggle came on TV and got so many teenybop panties damp that America's daddies was scared shitless their daughters was gonna crawl out in the yard and howl at the moon."

I smiled at the image, but I wasn't talking—mainly because this was obviously time to listen.

Double-Gone continued, "You ever heard of T-Bone Walker? Joe Turner? Sonny Boy Williamson? Big Bill Broonzy? Mississippi John Hurt?"

"Can't say I have."

"They were playing the rock-on blues and paying some nasty dues when Elvis was still a gleam in his daddy's eye."

"Double-Gone," I said, growing tired, "I told you out front I don't know shit about music. I spent my youth turning wheels and chasing truck-stop waitresses. Didn't even have a fucking radio in any of my rigs."

"But what you don't know *either,*" Double-Gone said with surprising vehemence, "is when the *need* could arise. Little knowledge maybe give you some angle on the action, help you see yo' way clear of mean trouble, spare yo' heart some grief. That's why I'm hipping you to the straight fact that if you follow rock music back down the tracks, yo' traveling through rhythm an' blues, plain ol' dirt blues, jazz music, back-porch jugband, field-hollers, an' right on to the heart of 'em all, music born in the simple joy and hurt of living, and thas *gospel* music. You travel back to them raw human voices lifted up in praise an' pain, yo' gonna see a *trillion* black faces never been on no TV, never heard no big concert crowd go crazy, never rode in no fine cars, didn't never see fucking *penny one* fo' pouring their souls empty, and never broke faith when their music was stole."

"Double-Gone," I said, "that's a righteous claim, delivered with honest passion and high eloquence, but you're not getting this Cadillac."

"But man"—he smiled hugely—"I'd look so *gooood* cruising the street—that'd be after I arranged for some changes in paint and I.D. numbers, new plates and paper."

"You did it to yourself. If you hadn't got me so paranoid about Scumball running me down, I wouldn't feel so responsible." That much was true, but the unspoken reason was even simpler, and one I'm sure he both understood and appreciated: it was mine to deliver, not his.

Double-Gone was all sympathy. "Responsibility is a heavy burden, brother. Let me take this load off yo' hands."

"It isn't gonna happen," I told him. "You know that."

"George, you jus jumpin' on my little joke there about copping it fo' my *personal* use. Not so. Far too hot fo' a new cat in town. I was gonna pass it on to Chuck Berry or Otis Blackwell or Mama Thornton or somebody nobody ever heard of singing his heart out in the choir."

"Nope. That'd just transfer the grief you're so certain is coming my way. Hate to see Chuck Berry or any of them busted up over this sweet Eldorado."

"I wasn't jivin' on that, George. I think they'll be looking fo' *you,* and if they do some *finding,* you liable to get messed around."

"And I know you weren't jiving about the music," I said in an attempt at graciousness. "The music belongs to its makers."

"Yeah, thas true, but the thing is I didn't take it far enough. See now, gospel music don't *belong* to black folks. We jus hear it best. Gospel music, rock music, Beethoven music, country music, *all* that music rightfully belong to the Holy Ghost. That Harriet woman, she feel her love *through* the music. Jus happened to be the Bopper's, may his high soul rock on fo'ever, but when you get down to the nitty-gritty, it belong to the Holy Ghost. You want some burnt offering, light a candle fo' love on the stone altar, thas fine. But if it's crowded at the Bopper's grave—you hearing me?—you can always deliver it right to the Holy Ghost. He'll see the Bopper gets it."

I started to reply when Double-Gone suddenly held up a palm for silence. His hand was trembling. *"Got it!"* he rejoiced. "The Lord— bless Him!—just spoke it aloud smack-dab in the center of my brain. Now get a good grip on the wheel there, George, 'cause here it is: THE ROCK SOLID GOSPEL LIGHT CHURCH OF THE HOLY RELEASE!"

"I love it," I said, glad to share his joy, and no sooner had I spoken than a voice—though it sounded like my own—spoke in my addled brain, saying, *If not to his grave, to the place he died,* and a whole new possibility opened: the enlargement of the gesture to include Ritchie Valens for Donna and Buddy Holly for the millions who loved him and, yes, for the Holy Ghost, too. Considering Double-Gone's warning that Scumball might have some rotten friends waiting for me at the Bopper's grave, it made better sense to deliver the Caddy to the site of the plane crash itself, let the gift honor them all and at the same time cut the risk.

I told Double-Gone. *"Yes!"* he shouted. "Thas fox-solid smart. Didn't I tell yo' disbelieving ass the Lord got us covered? *Didn't* I jus finish preaching the Book o' Job to open yo' ears to His whirlwind voice? O mercy, mercy, and hallelujah to the Holy Ghost, you jus got the Lord's

Word plain as fucking day, jammed up and jelly-tight, jus like He spoke the name of my church in my ear."

"Hold on," I cautioned. "I don't mean to doubt, but I'd have to say I didn't hear the voice real clear. Might've been me babbling to myself."

"George," Double-Gone warned, "take His blessings as they flow."

"I'm just not sure it *was* the Lord."

"Had to be. I know, 'cause he jus got done talkin' to me, whippin' that fine name on my brain. Figured long as He was on the scene, help you out too—Lord don't waste a move, dig, and the way we haulin' ass He didn't want to run us down twice." I must've looked as dubious as I felt, because Double-Gone kept on. "You making a mistake here, George my man. Don't mess yo'self around heaping doubt on what comes down. You hear what I'm saying? Do you?"

"Count your blessings." It seemed clear enough.

"Not count 'em like nickels, no. Take 'em in *deep. Dig* 'em. *Use* 'em. *Ride* 'em over the mountain. And most of all, the *very most* of all, give something *back.* Keep that juice movin' down the wire. Keep that voice raised in prayer and praise. Reflect the Holy Spirit's bounteous generosity, make His abundance yo' own. Reach down in yo' soul's bankroll and peel off what you think's *right.* "

"When I heard that sweet name of your church, Reverend, I knew nothing was going to make me happier than offering a small donation toward making it real . . . call it an investment in the faith."

"Now what's *this?* I didn't see no collection plate passing by."

"Only because you can't afford one yet. You'll need a collection plate and rough-hewn wood for a cross and maybe a month's rent on a storefront where you can gather your flock."

"You don't mind me prying," Double-Gone asked, "what was yo' piece of this car wreck action?"

"Four grand, half up front, which is the only half I'll ever see."

"If my math'matics ain't failing me, thas two thousand."

"Minus expenses," I reminded him. "The paper was free from a friend, but bennies, gas, food, and motel rooms add up, plus I bought this record collection from a woman in Arizona for four hundred."

Double-Gone jackknifed like he'd been kicked in the guts. "Ooooo, it *hurts* to hear that sum went down fo' this pile o' vinyl. Got its moments fo' sure, but I damn near come to gagging seen it all cluttered up with this Pat Boone and Fabian and Frankie Avalon." He chuckled. "That woman musta done you right . . . right up one side and down the other."

"She needed it. Tap City, with two kids."

"Uh-huh. So you down to twelve bills or thereabouts?"

"Thereabouts."

"Well, half would seem about right. Spirit ain't cheap, you dig that, I know."

"Is it tax deductible?"

"Now what's this shit? Spirit don't charge no taxes, man—just dues."

I had an impulse. "Way I understand it, standard tithe is ten percent, but since you're double-full of the spirit, I'll double it up. So let's say two and a half. *But,* you got to throw in your hat."

"Man," Double-Gone grimaced, "you *hard.* From six bills to two-fifty, plus my lid. And what you want it fo'? Just pale you out worse than you already are."

"I like it," I said.

"Me *too,* man—thas why I *bought* it."

"Two hundred, then. I'll use the fifty bucks to buy my own. Should be able to get one *easy* for fifty."

"George my man, why you want to do me like this? I put my best preachin' on ya. Practical *salvation.* You be headed right to Goon City if I hadn't put you straight. And do you *deep down* think the Lord be talkin' to you if he wasn't already on His way down to lay The Rock Solid Gospel Light Church of Holy Release on his faithful servant here?"

"That's why it's two-fifty *and* the hat."

Double-Gone glared down the road, muttering, making a show of it—then, with a big double groan, took off his hat and handed it over. I put it on. He watched me, shaking his head as I admired it in the rearview mirror. "Don't make it, George. Not an inch."

"What I *really* dig is the color," I said. "Looks like a flamingo getting hit with a million volts."

"Ruint my color coordination," Double-Gone grumbled. "Feel *de*frocked. I jus' don't think I can abide this, George; takes away from the man I *am,* dig? Man's got to feel good about himself. Now it might make me feel better—fact, I *know* it would—if you throw in some of them go-fast pills."

"Leave me a hundred. And Double-Gone? No more sniveling."

"You right. You did me. It's down, done, gone, and forgotten." He gave a forlorn little wave in the direction of my head. "Bye, you boss top. Wear him well. And now, 'bout that charitable contribution . . ."

We jammed on down ·the line as Double-Gone counted out 100 hits of speed for me and the rest for him, which he stashed with the money in a secret pocket in his cape. Then he leaned back, smiling. "You a strange cat, George; good, but strange. Just can't figure where the fuck you at."

"Twenty miles out of Houston, closing fast."

"You know that ol' truth, you can run but you can't hide? I'd pay some mind to that."

"Get thee behind me, Satan." I smiled when I said it.

"George," Double-Gone said tenderly, "I'm behind you all the way. Thas why I'd like to see you make it."

"Faith, Reverend."

"There it is." Double-Gone grinned.

We parted company a half-hour later at the steps of the Houston Public Library where, taking Double-Gone's advice to heart, I intended to do my research. In farewell I told him, "You preach that solid rock gospel light, Reverend Double-Gone. I hope you and your flock flourish till you're all so fat with blessings you curl up and die of happiness, old and full of days."

Double-Gone graced me with a stylish benediction, though it was difficult to tell if it was the sign of the cross or a Z hacked in the air by some bebop, speed-gobbling Zorro. "George, I want you to get it done, my man. Now you get *on* the beat and *stay* on it, hear?"

I waved and started up the steps when his baritone, calling my name, turned me around. He pointed his right index finger straight at my head. "And George: hang onto yo' hat."

I wasn't sure whether to take his words as a stern injunction to guard his recent and rightful property or as a graceful acknowledgment that he was letting it go. Either way, I decided, was fine. Later I realized both readings were wrong. The Good Reverend was neither admonishing nor releasing; it was pure, rock-solid gospel-light prophecy.

A heavy-tongued church bell began to toll, its resonance muffled in the rev and honk of downtown morning traffic. I hit the library right on the beat—a short, lean black man in work khakis was just unlocking the door. He held it open for me as I entered, his sharp brown eyes flicking upward to check out my stingy-brim.

I stopped and turned around. "Good morning, sir," I said. "I'm a wondering scholar just wandering through and have found myself with an urgent need for some reliable information about a plane crash that sadly claimed the lives of some notable musicians on the third day of February, 1959."

"Reference Desk be to yo' right, sir." He pointed mechanically.

I leaned in close and lowered my voice: "What do you think?"

"Beg yo' pardon, sir?" he asked nervously.

"I noticed you checking out my new hat." I tugged the brim down a notch. "What do you think?"

He shrugged his bony shoulders, his eyes looking steadily past me. "Don't think nothin' in particular. Brightly colorful, fo' sure. But that's jus looking, not thinking."

"Do you think it possesses that elusive quality known as *soul?*"

"None that jumps right on me . . . but then that's rightfully something fo' you to be thinking on."

"That's interesting," I said. "I bought it because it was *beyond* thought. And also for the practical reason that I need something to reinforce my skull in case my brain blows."

He looked in my eyes and said in a forceful whisper, "You either messed up on drugs or natch'ly crazy—not sure which, don't care—but you fo' sure looking trashed and sour, so you might think about wandering *on*, 'cause you don't be *cool*, you gonna *lose*. This library don't tol'rate no misbehaving. You be covered with *po*lice yo' first wrong move. Got that?"

"Got it. I want information, not trouble," I assured him, disconcerted that my playfulness had obviously hit him wrong.

He slipped the key from the door lock and, as he turned to face me, snapped it back on his belt. " 'Nother thing: *fuck* yo' hat."

"Hold on. I apologize for crowding you. I only meant to be friendly, but I guess I'm just a little too giddy and excited and exhausted. Been a wild ride."

"I jus bet it has. Now if you'll 'scuse me, I got work to do."

"That's why I'm here, too." I smiled. "So let's get on with it."

"Mind yo'self," he called over his shoulder.

I did, being absolutely sweet and professional with the reference librarian, a middle-aged brunette who went out of her way to be helpful. I went through everything she dug up, mostly newspaper clips with the same wire-service stories, plus a couple of record industry journals and a few paragraphs in music histories. Subtracting the duplications, there wasn't much, but the one thing I *had* to know—the location of the crash—I found right away. However, I stayed with it like a serious pilgrim, and my diligence was rewarded by the discovery of what I'd wanted to know for a couple of thousand miles: the Big Bopper was buried in Beaumont. I'd been on the track all the way.

When I left the library two hours later, I was a bunch less dumb but also twice as depressed, sorely pissed, more determined, strangely fearful, and—still in seeming accord with the Lord's will—completely confused, especially about what my next move should be. I slid behind the Caddy's wheel and turned the key. Then I decided *Nope, no more wasted motion*, and shut it down. I leaned back in the seat and shut my eyes, took seven deep breaths, slid my stingy-brim down to cover my face, and considered the general mess.

For openers, I was better informed, and that was to my favor. I knew within a few square miles where I was going—certainly an improvement—and I had a fairly solid idea of the events surrounding the crash.

The chartered plane had left the Mason City airport at 1:00 A.M. headed for Fargo, South Dakota. It was snowing and cold, but nowhere near a blizzard. The plane evidently crashed shortly after take-off, for when the flight was overdue in Fargo the owner of the charter service took another plane up to search and spotted the wreckage northwest of the Mason City airport in a snow-crusted field of corn stubble. Around 11:30 that morning the coroner arrived to confirm what the extent of the wreckage made obvious, that the four people aboard were dead: Buddy Holly, 22; Ritchie Valens, 17; J. P. Richardson (aka the Big Bopper), 27; and the pilot, Roger Petersen, 21. According to the wire service reporter, the plane was no longer recognizable as such, and the victims' identities were impossible to determine without extensive lab work.

I was depressed as much by my morbid imagination as by the bare sadness of their deaths. Sitting there in the bright, warm library, everything neatly organized, I'd felt for a horrible moment the gut-wrenching fear as the plane plunged, heard the begging, blurted prayers as the earth whirled up to meet them, all possible future of their music lost in the instant of impact, from life to death in the span of a heartbeat, just like Eddie.

They shouldn't have been flying to Fargo, in a plane they'd chartered themselves, but they didn't have much choice. For six days they'd been living on piece-of-shit buses without adequate heaters during a mean Midwestern winter. The tour, in fact, was billed as the Winter Dance Party. Six days on a cold, slow bus. Six days, six gigs, and drive away whipped. Trying to sleep sitting up half-frozen in the seats; kidneys punished by shocks that had turned to jello 30,000 miles before; sick from exhaust leaks; wearing clothes that hadn't been laundered since who could remember when. The Big Bopper, nursing a bad cold, broke down and bought a sleeping bag to keep warm. Finally Buddy Holly decided to charter a plane along with two of his band members, Waylon Jennings and Tommy Allsup, and fly ahead to Fargo, get everyone's stage clothes laundered, and log a night of true sleep in a hotel room with the heater turned up high. The Big Bopper, whose frame matched his name, found the cramped seats particularly unbearable and persuaded his buddy Waylon to give up his seat on the flight. At the last moment, Ritchie Valens wanted to go, and pestered Tommy Allsup into flipping a coin to decide who would get the last seat. Allsup reluctantly agreed, but only if he got to use the Bopper's sleeping bag if he lost. Ritchie called heads, and heads it was.

The promoters of the Winter Dance Party, Super Enterprises and General Artists Corporation, evidently believed good business is best defined—as it so often is in this country—by fat black ink on the bottom line. You want to fatten the take, you cut frills like heaters in the tour bus, laundry, or an occasional open date for rest somewhere among those all-night bus rides between Milwaukee, Kenosha, Eau Claire, Duluth, Green Bay, and all the other exhausting points along the way. Fair profit from able dealing is one thing; exploitive greed, that gluttony of heart and ego, starves everything near it as it buries its face in the trough. When you wrong the people who make the music, you wrong the music; and if Double-Gone had it right, if the music does belong to the Holy Spirit, you wrong the Holy Spirit, too. You fuck-over the Spirit, you deserve what you finally get.

My cold, vengeful anger and the freshened sadness at their deaths inspired me to honor their lives and music, and I was glad Buddy Holly and Ritchie Valens were now included. Mine was a tooth-sunk, jaw-locked, bulldog determination, the kind that makes you die trying. But I feared that determination, not only because I was afraid of dying, trying or otherwise, but also because I didn't really understand my deepened resolve. I wanted to deliver the gift and slip away. There was no need for the further entanglement of these interior motives. Just as we can disguise greed as ambition, we can dress obsession as necessity. I was afraid of not knowing which was which, afraid of losing the thread of my purpose. I was afraid I would be equally destroyed by certainty and doubt.

I sat there with my hat over my face, trying in vain to think my way through this new confusion. At last I decided motion was best, that I'd take three beans and I-35 up through Dallas and on past Oklahoma City to Posthole Joe's Truck Stop Cafe, where I'd see if Joe still made the best chicken-fried steak on the twenty-four thousand miles of Interstate that used to be my home. I'd be hungry by then if I laid off the speed, and I intended to do just that. I was already out on the fried, jittery edge, just asking for it, and I didn't want to waste myself on what amounted to crazed recreation. I had to get tougher.

A plan took shape. After Posthole's chicken-fried steak with biscuits and gravy, I'd maybe take four more—but *no* more—hits of speed for dessert, and then ride on up to Kansas City, Kansas City here I come. From K.C. to Des Moines was only about a 2½ hour run, and I could do that with my eyes closed if I had to. But I didn't have to, I reminded myself. I'd sleep if I got tired. But it was mighty tempting to think that if I kept at it I could be soaking in a hot bath by midnight. After that, a solid eight hours of shut-eye, a good breakfast, then an hour's drive up to Mason City and the crash site, rested and sharp for the ceremony.

I cranked up the Eldorado and got rolling, my eyes literally peeled for that elusive sign that would read 35 NORTH: DALLAS, POSTHOLE JOE'S, K.C., DES MOINES, MASON CITY, CRASH SITE, DELIVERY, AND MAMA ON DOWN THE LINE, a sign made even more elusive by the design of downtown Houston, yet another city where the traffic engineers evidently take their professional inspiration from barbecue sauce dribbled across a local map. To find a fast lane pointing north took me ten minutes, so I put my foot in it to make up for lost time.

The day was clear and bright, but the temperature seemed to plummet as the sun climbed. From Dallas to Oklahoma City is a flat, straight shot, with nothing much to entertain the eye except the oil rigs looming like huge skeletal birds, each mechanically dripping and rising as if locked in a tug-of-war with a cable-fleshed worm, slowly pulling it out only to have it recoil into the earth, yanking the bird's head down with it.

North of Gainesville I crossed the Red River, the Tex/Okie border in the north, the Tex/Louisiana boundary to the east. I remembered the Big Bopper was born near the mouth of the Red River, and doffed my hat in respectful salute. I also remembered a record I'd seen while going through Donna's collection, "Red River Rock" by Johnny and the Hurricanes; I dug it out and put it on the box, though by then I was fifteen miles into Oklahoma. Still, it seemed an appropriate gesture. The water bearing my blessing would eventually get there.

My eyes felt like they might start bleeding if there wasn't a total eclipse of the sun within minutes. I tried pulling my hat down for shade, but they're not called stingy-brims for nothing. My mouth was drier than a three-year drought and my stomach had shrunk to the size of a walnut. I'd gassed up just out of Houston and again before leaving Dallas, but twenty miles across the Oklahoma line I stopped again. The place was called Max and Maxine's Maxi-Gas Stop, and the paint-flaked sign promised HOT GAS, COLD BEER, & ALL SORTS OF NOTIONS. I told the young pump jockey to top it with ethyl and walked into the store. To my hollowed senses it seemed I was walking through pudding that hadn't quite set.

I bought a case of Bud, a bag of crushed ice, a bottle of eyedrops, and one of the two pairs of sunglasses left on the rack, preferring the wrap-arounds with the glossy yellow frames over the green up-swept cat-eyes studded with rhinestones. The lenses of both were caked with dust.

I restocked the cooler in the trunk, holding out a couple of bottles for immediate consumption. By the time I had the others properly iced, my fingertips were so numb I could barely pinch a twenty from my wallet to pay the attendant. It was a pleasure to slip back inside the warm Caddy. I drank a beer, then treated my eyes to some drops; they stung like hell at first, but gradually soothed. Still blinking, dabbing at the dribbles of eyewash on my cheeks, I angled back onto the freeway. Once I was up to cruising speed, I looked around for something to wipe the dust from my new pair of Foster Grants and, when I automatically glanced up to check traffic, a sheet of white paper came swirling across the road from the right shoulder and I stood on the brakes, a scream gathering in my guts as I waited for the sickening thud of flesh against metal.

But there was no thud, no Eddie, no child ruined against the blinding chrome; only the shriek of rubber and the brake shoes smoking on the drums as I fought to keep the rear end from whipping around— but when I heard another wheel-locked scream behind me and caught a flash of a pick-up in the rearview mirror bearing down on my ass, I cranked the wheel hard right, whipping the rear end around as the pick-up, bucking against its clamped brakes, cleared me by half a hair. I came to a stop way off on the right-hand shoulder, turned around 180°, looking straight back at where I'd just come from as adrenalin swamped my blood. I could hear myself panting. Hear my heartbeat and the barely audible throb of arteries in my neck. Hear the pounding slap of heavy boots running on pavement, growing louder as they approached: the guy in the pick-up.

He almost tore off my door, an act I considered understandable given *his* adrenalin surge, his rage at my sudden and inexplicable braking, and his size. He looked like he could go bear hunting with a pocketknife and come home with meat for the table. He was wearing grungy Levis, a heavy plaid flannel shirt, a blue down vest with one pocket half ripped off, and a scuffed yellow hard hat with a Gulf Oil logo.

"What the *fuck* do you think you're *fucking* doing, you *fuckhead?*"

This wasn't a particularly civil question—not really a question at all, in fact—but was fair enough, under the strained circumstances, to deserve a prompt and truthful answer. "A week ago in San Francisco I was walking down the street and a little boy five years old came running down some stairs and one of the drawings he was carrying blew out in the street and Eddie—that was his name, Eddie—went right after it without a thought. I saw it coming and dove out full length to try to stop him but my fingertips just barely grazed his pants as he scooted off the curb between two parked cars and got splattered by a '59 Merc before your heart could skip a beat. I don't know if you saw it, but a piece of paper blew out on the road right in front of me back there and I locked 'em up on gut reflex because I never, ever-again want to see a little five-year-old mangled on the pavement, dead in his own blood."

"Yeah, okay," the guy said. He shut the door softly, turned, and walked away.

Sometimes there's nothing more devastating than understanding. I burst into tears. I didn't try to fight it. I slumped over the wheel and wept for Eddie, for the kind understanding that confirms one's pain and changes nothing, for every shocked soul forced to bear helpless witness to random mayhem, and, with a self-pity I couldn't escape, for myself.

When I began to notice cars slowing to check out this Cadillac pointing ass-backwards to the flow of traffic, I snuffled my nose clear and got out and made a cursory, tear-blurred check of the car to see if I'd bent or broken anything in that high-stress 180° onto the shoulder. As I squatted to check out the front end, I saw the piece of paper plastered against the grille. It was a mimeographed note, the ink sun-bleached to a faint violet shadow. My eyes hurt to read it, but I finally made it out:

Dear Parents of Second Graders

The second grade is having a classroom Halloween Party on the afternoon of October 31. Students are encouraged to wear their costumes to the party. The Halloween Party will be held during the last two hours of class time. Students will be dismissed at the regular time unless Rainy Day Session applies. Buses will run on normal schedule.

I wish you all a scary (but safe!) Halloween.

Sincerely,

Judy Gollawin
Second Grade Teacher

The note really tore me up. One happily mindless mistake and the party's over, kid. A single misstep and you break through the crust. I got back in the car and slumped against the wheel and let the tears roll. Not sniveling, or not to my sense of it. Crying because it hurt.

You might be able to grieve forever, but you can't weep that long, so after a while I wiped away the tears, folded up the note and put it in the glovebox with Harriet's letter, and got myself turned around and back on the road, taking it up till the needle quivered between the double zeros of 100. This might've been terrifying if I'd stopped to think, the slowest mind in the west going that fast, hellbent for glory, goddamn it, no matter if I had to stop and weep at every scrap of paper that blew across my path, every sweet kid skipping off to school, every splash of blood on the highway.

Within twenty miles I was overtaken by an undreamable feeling of peace, no doubt a combination of raw exhaustion and emotional release, but I didn't try to figure it out. I realized, to my baffled delight, that I'd blundered into a wobbling balance, a vagrant equilibrium, a fragile poise between water and moon, and I was riding the resolution of a wave.

It was a short ride, about an hour and a half between the last tear and Posthole Joe's, and it felt so good I slowed down to savor it. As I passed Oklahoma City there was still an hour before sunset, but under a sky grown so leaden through the afternoon that it was almost dark, only a faint pinkish light, the ghost color of my florid hat, was holding at the horizon.

My peace deepened when I pulled into the lot at Posthole Joe's. The long, flat-roofed diner was the same dingy white with tired red trim, the light inside still softened to an inviting glow by the exhaust-grimed glass of the windows. Two Kenworths and a White Freightliner idled in the lot. This was a memory exactly as I remembered it, familiar and sure, a reference solidly retained, and it gladdened me that something had prevailed against change. As I walked toward the door my peaceful happiness began expanding into a sense of elation I could neither understand nor contain, only welcome. When I stepped into the warmth and rich tangle of odors inside and saw Kacy standing just to my left—tall loose blond, lovelier than I could've hoped to remember, wearing the white rayon dress and brown apron that Posthole's waitresses have worn forever, just standing there out of nowhere taking the orders of two drivers in a booth against the wall—my elation vaulted into joy, and I yelled her name and took her in my arms.

The deepest memories are the claims of the flesh, and as soon as my arms brought her close I knew I'd made a mistake. She wasn't Kacy, but that information was caught in the joy-jammed circuits of my brain, arriving just a helpless instant before her knee flattened my testicles.

"Sorry," I gasped on my way to the floor. "Honest. Mistake." I barely managed to wheeze out "mistake" before I curled up on the scuffed beige linoleum and abandoned apology to agony. I could no longer speak, but for some reason I could hear with an amazing clarity.

"Well, *shit!*" Kacy's double shouted down at me.

"Man oughta look before he lunges," one of the guys in the booth offered as a judgment or general truth. His buddy snickered.

The waitress knelt and touched my shoulder. "You all right?"

From my new point of view it was obvious she wasn't Kacy's twin, or even a sister, but the resemblance was close enough to fool the desperate or hopeful. I couldn't answer her question, though.

She gently squeezed my shoulder. "I'm sorry. You scared the hell out of me, grabbing ahold like that. You want to stretch out in a booth or something?"

I shook my head. "My . . . fault."

She snapped at the two men in the booth, "You boys done hee-hawing, maybe you could give him a hand. Christ, *I* don't know what you're supposed to do for that."

The philosopher in the booth said, "Shot you gave him, Ellie, ain't a hand he needs, it's a search party—to go looking for his gonads. Reckon first place I'd check is up around his collarbones." His buddy thought this was even funnier.

I reached around and patted her hand resting on my left shoulder.

"You gonna make it?" she said tenderly.

I nodded once, patted her hand again to express my thanks, then flopped over on knees and forearms, ass in the air, and started crawling for the door. I'd lost my appetite and my happiness.

"Tommy! Wes!" she barked. "God*damn* it, help him up!"

They both started to slide from the booth, the witty one whining back, "Don't go chewing on *our* asses. Wasn't us copping feels. Man deserves what he gets."

I stopped and rolled over onto a hip, raising a palm to stop them. After a few breaths I'd gathered enough surplus air to form the words into half-gagged croaks. "What you get . . . belongs to you . . . yours." I nodded vigorously for the emphasis my voice couldn't supply, then added, "I'll crawl."

I negotiated the yard to the door, pulled myself to my knees, then used the doorknob to leverage myself upright. I wasn't standing tall, but I was on my feet. I touched my head to make sure I hadn't lost my hat. The waitress and truckers were watching me, a guy at the counter I hadn't noticed before had turned around to stare, a pair of heads were craning from another booth, and a cook I didn't recognize was peering from the kitchen. "Sorry," I told them, "for disturbance. Good night." I tipped my flaming flamingo hat politely, thinking its color was about three shades lighter than my nuts felt, then eased out the door. The Caddy was gleaming across the lot, and I headed toward it with a mincing, bow-legged shuffle, slow and easy.

I didn't realize till I opened the Caddy's door and was trying to figure out how to slide in without adding to my pain that the waitress had followed me outside and was standing in front of the diner, her arms wrapped around herself against the cold. She'd wanted to make sure I made it, or so I assumed. I wished fleetingly that her arms were wrapped around *me,* but in my condition that would've been cruel for the both of us, so I simply waved. She waved in return and slipped back inside.

Using the car door and steering wheel for support, I eased myself onto the seat, my groans and whimpers amplified in the Caddy's voluminous interior. To keep my pelvis elevated, I braced my shoulders against the seatback and my feet against the floorboards. But you can't drive all stretched out like that, so I held my breath and assumed the standard position; the pain wasn't any worse, and at least I could drive. I pulled back onto the highway, running it up through the gears as fast as I could so I wouldn't have to think about moving my legs again.

I couldn't help thinking about Kacy, though. The mistaken moment in the waitress's arms was a cruel reminder of how much I missed her, how much I wanted to hold her real and right now. The feeling triggered a rush of memories, each sweet particular sad with loss. If I had a shred of sense, I thought, I'd hang a U for South America, and go get her. If the gift is love, why wasn't I delivering my own, face to face, belly to belly, heart to beating heart? But that good sense met the stronger conviction that Kacy couldn't be hounded into love. She might appreciate the gesture, but not the pressure. To chase her was to lose her. I could dangle my throbbing balls in the ice chest to numb that ache, or pull in to the closest emergency room, or knock over a pharmacy for every narcotic in the locker, but there was nothing I could do about the pain of wanting Kacy, nothing except forget her, and her memory was all I had.

There's a shock-trance that mercifully accompanies trauma, shutting the brain down to dumb function and removing you far enough to withstand the pain. Even more fortunately, it renders you incapable of convoluted metaphysical thought and prolonged self-analysis, truly subtracting insult from injury and properly placing the anguish of inquiry far beyond the immediate agony of the flesh. When the dam breaks there's no need to examine it for cracks or to discuss the intricacies of hydraulic engineering; you best head for higher ground. The body knows what *it*'s doing.

As the shock gradually faded, my balls settled into a tender, throbbing ache and my mind added primitive consideration to mere perception: I was exhausted. Given that exhaustion—so sorely compounded by my recent testicular trauma—I wondered whether I should stop in Wichita for food and a good night's rest, or just pop the four bennies I had coming for dessert and bore on for K.C. and Des Moines. I wondered briefly if the problem was with *my* plans or plans in general, and why I seemed to keep falling into traps I didn't know I'd set, but I caught myself short of that metaphysical deadfall and stepped instead into the snare of compromise: I ate the four bennies on the spot and an hour later, when I stopped in Wichita for gas, after examining myself for damage in the men's room stall and finding them both tender but without obvious need of medical attention, I walked gingerly across the street to Grissom's Liquors and Deli, where I got a fatty ham sandwich on Wonder Bread and a half-pint carton of limp slaw.

I ate in the car, distracting my palate with a perfunctory reconsideration of whether to grab a room for the night right there or make a run at Des Moines, four hundred miles upstream. It was 7:13 P.M. by the station's Hire's Root Beer clock: I could make Des Moines by midnight easy, which meant I could still soak an hour in a hot bath, get a solid

eight hours of snooze, dally over breakfast, and hit Mason City by high
noon. This sounded so much like a plan that I summarily abandoned it.
I'd play it on the move—it always seemed to come to that anyway. In
the unlikely event that none of the billions of unforeseen complications
occurred, I could always fall back on the plan.

I headed 'em out for Kansas City feeling refreshingly realistic—
getting nailed in the nuts will do that to you—and also, to my surprise,
feeling playful enough to slap Jerry Lee Lewis on the box, keeping time
with my fingers on the steering wheel because it proved too painful to
tap my foot:

> *You broke my will,*
> *What a thrill!*
> *Goodness, gracious,*
> *Great Balls o' Fire!*

I made the selection as an arrogantly humble acknowledgment that I
could take a joke, accompanied by a silent prayer that the gods had a
sense of humor.

Sailing along the Interstate somewhere between Wichita and Kansas City, I suddenly found myself deep in the drunken memory of a
North Beach midnight where somebody was yelling to me through time,
"You show me *one place* in the Bible where God the Father or Jesus
Christ His Son *laughs,* and I'll convert to Christianity. Otherwise, fuck
it." Whose voice was it? One of the Buddhist poets, it sounded like,
maybe Welch or Snyder, but whoever said it was two tables away in the
wine-blurred babble and clatter of Vesuvio's, where I was enthralled by
the sight of a voluptuous redhead named Irene throwing back a shot of
Jack Daniels at the end of the bar. That was its own joke, being an
adolescent American male, because if it didn't get me high, have a pussy,
or hit 65 in second gear, it wasn't of compelling concern. Who cares
about the place of humor in the cosmic order when you're nineteen years
old and never had a blowjob? When there's drugs to take and tracks to
make and music that carries you away? I hadn't sinned enough to need
salvation, and hadn't lost enough to truly laugh.

But what a thrill!
Goooodd-ness, Graaaa-shuuus;
Greaaaaaaaaat Balls o' Fire!!!

Indeed. And if neither the Father or that lucky ol' son had the required sense of humor, perhaps it resided in the Holy Spirit, in speed and music and fucking your brains out, in roaming the mountains and roaring through the night, the bare wire, the straight shot. That might be funny.

It was altogether too fitting that my little reverie on the possibilities of divine humor was obliterated by the pulsing flash of a red light in my rearview mirror. Since I was going close to 100, it wasn't gaining much, which gave me time to die a thousand deaths before I instinctively punched it and instantly changed my mind. I came off the gas and pulled slowly into the right-hand lane, hoping with all my heart that it wasn't a cop, and if it was, that he had someone other than me in mind.

It was a fire engine, a big red fire engine. I pulled over to hug the shoulder as it wailed by. I was just about to put my foot back down on the pedal when another red light came streaking up, and then another: a state trooper followed by an ambulance. Wreck ahead, probably a bad one. I told myself that if I saw another mangled five-year-old kid I'd *drink* that bottle of speed, bash the Bopper's Cadillac through the Heavenly Gates, and grab God by the throat and demand a justification, an explanation, and some satisfaction. A dead kid isn't funny.

It was two miles up the road, and I was the fourth or fifth car on the scene. The cops had blocked both northbound lanes about two hundred yards from the wreck. I couldn't see much in the distracting light of flares and whirling red flashers, but it didn't look like the fire crew was necessary—they were standing around jawing as the flames died down. The charred hulk of an upside-down car was lying diagonally in the right lane, nose just touching the shoulder, rear end jutting out on the road. The air reeked of burnt rubber and scorched grease. It looked bad, so bad I didn't want to look again; in ten years of driving and towing I hadn't seen many much worse.

I powered down my window and yelled to a nearby trooper, asking if they needed any help.

171

"Nope, no thanks," he called back. "It's not as bad as it looks. Tow truck lost it—clevis snapped. Nobody inside. We'll have a lane open in about ten minutes."

Wonderful news all around. I had to strain to see the tow truck another hundred yards down, its flashers barely visible in the oily haze. Probably take a squadron of troopers to write up the citations on the driver. Never lost one myself, but there's lots of good drivers that have. The trooper didn't mention the safety chain, but I fraternally hoped it had failed and hadn't been forgotten.

They opened the left lane about fifteen minutes later. By then traffic was backed up a quarter-mile, but I was right in front. I was so gleefully anticipating some open road to run on while half the night shift of Oklahoma law enforcement was otherwise engaged that I was almost past the smoldering hulk before I recognized it was a '59 Cadillac— impossible to tell the model, but even crashed, burned, and upside-down you couldn't mistake the space-shot styling.

I didn't know if this wreck in my path was supposed to be funny or not. I didn't laugh, but I smiled—grimly, I admit—because if I took it as something beyond indifferent coincidence or random connection, then I had to think of it as a sign or omen, and to decide whether it augured well or ill: well if it foreshadowed accomplishment, the gift aflame, delivered, nobody inside, nobody hurt; ill if it portended some pitiful failure, a weak connection snapping, an opportunity squandered to ignorance, negligence, delusion—merely lost instead of released. I wasn't sure what it meant—nothing new there—but I didn't like it.

However, I liked the open road a lot and put everything else behind me in no time flat, including endless speculation about unclear omens. This seemed an ideal time to put KRZY back on the air, and since 110 mph requires most of your attention, I just grabbed a handful and stacked them on the spindle, announcing to the night, "This is KRZY coming on to darkness, Floorboard George flopping the sides and bab-bling in your ear. What you hear is what you get, and it sounds like what we got is Jerry Lee and 'A Whole Lot of Shaking Going On.' Won't be doing much shaking myself, you understand, having received a bad blow to the go-daddies earlier this evening, but you guys go right ahead and strut yo' stuff."

Less than halfway through the stack, the program was interrupted by the greatest traveling salesman in the world. Clad only in dark pants and a white undershirt, bouncing up and down barefoot alongside the road in 35° weather, I might've guessed he was the craziest fucker within a thousand miles, or the best Human Pogo Stick act west of the Mississippi, but it never even crossed my mind that he might be the greatest traveling salesman in the world until he was in the Caddy and shaking my hand, introducing himself as Phillip Lewis Kerr, "please call me Lew," and handing me a silver card with deeply embossed blue print that read:

PHILLIP LEWIS KERR

Greatest Traveling Salesman in the
World
(212) 698-7000

He was an old guy, easily in his early sixties, belly slumping over his waistband, but not at all sloppy—in fact, his general bearing, the close-cropped grey beard and neatly trimmed mustache, the small blue eyes forcefully alert and mildly amused, the directness of his manner and speech, all combined to imbue him with the calm dignity of a man who knows what he's about, even if he's hitchhiking half-naked on a freezing night.

I introduced myself as he stowed a battered leather attaché case under the front seat. His feet were broad, gnarly toed, and blue with cold; I don't know whether I shivered in sympathy or at the icy blast pouring in through the open door. Suddenly I was freezing.

"Hey, Lew," I hissed, jaw clamped to keep from chattering. "Unless you got more gear to load, how 'bout putting some door in that hole."

He looked at me, startled. "Oh! I *am* sorry." He swung the door shut, killing the domelight. In the darkness his voice was disembodied. "That was thoughtless of me, George, inexcusably thoughtless. The warmth was so welcome I didn't imagine you could be cold. And it *is* cold outside, I assure you." I felt the seat tremble as he shivered beside me.

I put the Caddy back on the asphalt and eased it up through the gears, still very much aware of the tenderness in my loins. Reminded by my own discomfort, I asked Lew if he'd like the heat turned up.

"Oh no, not at all. It's better to thaw slowly. At my age the cell walls can't tolerate rapid changes; they rupture."

"Never considered that," I said truthfully. Everything he was saying seemed forthright and direct as it entered my ear, but seemed to make oblique jumps in my brain. We weren't connecting. I was willing to grant that the problem was in the receiver. However, I didn't want him to get going on his cell walls the way old folks sometimes do, elaborating their ills with lurid physiological details of how the flesh fails—I had a couple of aching examples of my own—so I changed the subject by asking him if he was going to Kansas City.

"I'll be going there, yes. Yourself?"

"Des Moines—and I'm running late. I may just drop you off at the closest warm place to an off-ramp."

"Well," he began, pausing so long I thought he was through, "you must have left *awfully* late, because at this speed you would *have* to be early." He smiled tentatively.

I smiled in kind. "Lew, you mind if I ask if you always dress like this for freezing weather?"

"My goodness, no," he said. "I sold my coat, shirt, tie, socks, and shoes to a young fellow that works in the oil fields. He had a date with a young lady this evening, but he'd stopped with his friends after work for a few drinks and didn't have time to drop by a haberdashery."

Again, this didn't sound right to me. "Didn't he want the pants, too? He'd look strange wearing crusty old Levis with a coat and tie."

"Oh, he inquired about the trousers, but I couldn't risk the possibility of being incarcerated for indecent exposure."

"Rather die of regular exposure," I asked lightly.

"I figured someone would come along shortly. And besides, the trousers were too small."

"I'm glad you explained things, because I'd have to wonder why the world's greatest salesman couldn't afford to put some fabric between his flesh and a nasty night. That your usual line, men's clothes?"

"I sell anything and everything. I've found that in the long run diversity is stability."

"Looks like you're about sold out."

"Indeed I am. It's been an interesting trip."

I figured out what was bothering me. "You know, Lew, I've wanted to ask you a question ever since you handed me your business card here, but I can't see a way to ask it without sounding offensive, like I was challenging your credentials, and that's not what I mean to do."

"George," he said, "I'm a salesman. I started with a lemonade stand in Sweetwater, Indiana, when I was five years old. I learned very early that it was expensive to take offense. It deflects you from your purpose."

I wanted to ask what his purpose was—profit? the transaction itself? the necessary appeasement of demons and dreams?—but didn't want to lose my original question. "All right, since you won't take offense, I was wondering about what it says on your card, that you're the greatest salesman in the world."

He interrupted softly, "Actually, the greatest *traveling* salesman."

"Right. But it was 'greatest' that grabbed me. I mean, how do you *know* you're the greatest in the world, traveling or standing still? Is there some measure, an objective standard, a committee of judges, a general consensus, or do you just step out and claim the title?"

"George, you're a remarkable man, the one out of a thousand whose first reaction doesn't concern farmers' daughters." Evidently sensing my puzzlement, he added helpfully, "You know, the traveling salesman and the farmer's daughter—there's a tradition of jokes. I'm sure you've heard some."

"Yeh, sure, but I can't remember any offhand." In fact I was trying hard to remember one—an act, considering my mental state, akin to fishing in a parking lot—when I realized that he'd evaded my question with a little flourish of distracting flattery. But I was too tired and too wired to play whatever game I sensed was going on, so I rammed straight ahead—not *heedlessly*, for I did understand *something* was going on, but with a wariness recklessly short of giving a rat's ass. "Lew, I asked the question because I wanted your answer."

"Mr. Gastin," he said, his voice soft as a cotton swab, "I thought I'd lost you there for a minute. Perhaps you should disregard your tardiness and rest in Kansas City. And though obviously less capable, I would be glad to drive."

The abuse of amphetamine is notorious for producing bad paranoia, and I got a sudden, deep stab: old Lew was a hit man hired by Scumball to murder me and wreck the car. I had to be cool, keep a sense of craziness in the air, keep my control—I doubted if he'd make his move while I had the wheel in my hands, especially at 110. "Appreciate your concern, Lew." I giggled. "I admit that my mental health is not all it should be. Not at all. Lately I've been having these recurring losses of thought, and frankly I'm alarmed by their increasing frequency. Only thing that seems to stop them temporarily is a hard knee in the balls. But again I think you've squirmed the question. It's a fair question. Why don't you answer it?"

"If you insist," he said evenly, "though it's pointless."

"Not to me."

"But George, you would have absolutely no way of knowing whether I was lying or not."

"That's exactly my point," I said and, not having the slightest idea what my point was, jumped: "You see, it doesn't matter if I can know the truth of what you tell me; the point is, I trust you to tell the truth, exactly as you trust my belief. And if the truth is boring or embarrassing, then tell me an illuminating lie. We've got to have faith in each other. I get a little incoherent when I'm this far gone, especially considering I'm pretty fucked-up to start with, so let me put it as bluntly as I can: Answer or get out."

He said it quietly, as if to himself, "No." I then understood that he wasn't a hit man, but I'd already committed myself. I was lifting my foot from the gas and angling for the shoulder when he said, only slightly louder, "No, Mr. Gastin, I will not converse under duress. And certainly if trust is your point, duress betrays it. If you'll withdraw your ill-considered threat, I'll answer the question gladly, as I intended. After all, I did invite it. And it *is* a fair question."

That coercion denies trust is obvious. I was properly chastened, both for my glaring lack of logic and my paranoid delusion. "You're welcome to the ride," I said, "whether you answer or not."

"Thank you." There wasn't a trace of triumph or mockery in his voice.

I was about to burst into tears again, felt my throat tighten and my eyes begin to burn. I turned and screamed. *"Fuck this song and dance! You wandering half-naked and coming on so calm and coy, who the fuck knows what your game is? Who knows whose . . . whose . . ."* but I'd lost it, and in frustrated rage slammed my open palm against the dash, the slap sharp as a gunshot.

Lewis Kerr flinched badly, recoiling toward the door. But he spoke in the same tone of imperturbable sympathy. "George, if you'll permit a candid observation, you're in bad shape."

"No shit!" I howled in agreement. "Would you sell your soul?" I hurled it at him, more demand than question, and without immediate reference except my bad shape.

He looked confused for a moment, then said, "Don't be silly."

"Do you *have* a soul to sell?"

"Yes, I make that assumption."

I wanted to nail his slippery ass down. "Why," I asked him, my throat tight, "are you being so fucking *careful?*"

"Because you're *not,*" he shot back, some heat in his voice for the first time.

"Why should I be?"

"Because you're terrified, and terror inspires disastrous stupidity, and stupidity is slavery. Because, George, you're not a slave."

If you've ever been inside a slaughterhouse and seen a big, prime steer crumple and splay at the stun-hammer's blow, that's close to what

I felt like—both steer and observer. I was floating out of myself. I couldn't think in words. I couldn't tell if I was breathing or not, if my tongue was still in my mouth, if it was the car or the road moving, or the night moving through us both. My normally narrow field of awareness was suddenly constricted to a single sensation of terror. Not the profound cellular fear of death, or of time's star-jeweled movement and stone gears grinding on, or the gangrenous dread that I was among those randomly picked to be randomly destroyed, any time now, without warning. No, it was an embarrassing terror, like you were lost in your own house.

Though it had been a long silence, Lew continued as if he'd only paused. "Or I *assume* you're not a slave, much in the way I assume a soul."

I didn't say anything. A person driving 110 mph down a road whose existence he questions should neither be required to think nor allowed to.

"But," Lew continued, "enough of my assumptions; you'll accuse me of evading the question while I was merely framing a reply."

He paused as he shifted his weight on the seat, then continued, "I'm a proud man. It's a pride based on accomplishment, not on arrogant assumption—or so I like to think. Pride is a powerful strength, and therefore a dangerous weakness. I try to temper it with honest humility. I don't brag. I don't gloat. I don't flaunt my achievements. I sell. In the fifty-nine years since I sold that first glass of lemonade on the muggy streets of Sweetwater, I have devoted myself to the mastery of selling. I've sold four *billion* dollars worth of products. I've made millions in profit and commissions. When I was nineteen years old I sold a hundred and sixty-eight used cars off one lot in Akron, Ohio, during a twenty-four-hour period—that's seven cars an hour, one every eight and a half minutes—though of course I wasn't handling the paperwork. I sold out a semi-truck full of vacuum cleaners in Santa Rosa, California, in two days. Before I was thirty years old I went to Labrador and sold refrigerators to Eskimos. They had no electricity and lots of ice, but I had the ability to see possible applications for the product where others saw only the superficial absurdity of the venture:

refrigerators, being insulated, are much like a thermos—they can keep, say, fish from freezing in a frozen climate, as long as they're not plugged in. Further, if properly drilled and vented, a refrigerator also makes an excellent smokehouse, thereby preserving with heat in a structure designed to preserve with cold. I sold the motors separately to the Air Force and used the money to buy electric heaters, which I sold to Indians in the Amazon Basin. They understood both the intrinsic beauty of the coils and their decorative possibilities. The electrical cords were similarly used for adornment, and for binding. The dismantled sheet metal frames proved to have a thousand applications, including arrow points.

"Through my thirties and forties I traveled the world selling every commodity you can imagine, including cinnamon in Ceylon and tea in China, the whole time refining my abilities and distilling the principles of the craft. The principles, I discovered, were surprisingly simple: listen well and tell the truth."

Abruptly he leaned down and picked up his attaché case. He set it on the seat between us and snapped it open for my inspection. It was crammed with neatly stacked piles of money, twenties being the smallest visible denomination. "That's a lot of money," I said, no doubt hoping to impress him with my firm grasp of the obvious.

"I don't even count it anymore. My accountant handles all that. I have no wife, no children, no expensive tastes. I've found it's wise to keep one's pleasures simple and that in my case, even the simple pleasures are ruined by indulgence. I enjoy the constant anonymity of motel rooms, the neutrality of passing through. I relish the stimulus of travel and contact. I'm still compelled by the possibilities of my work—each knock on the door, the face revealed as it opens—but beyond my work I need very little and want even less. So to me this money is relatively meaningless, even as a measure. Rather than make the excruciating and impossible decisions about who might best benefit from my surplus, it all goes to buy land to be held undeveloped in various land trusts for perpetuity."

"You're a very romantic salesman," I said. While I believed the money in the attaché, I wasn't sure I believed the explanation.

"Romantic?" he repeated. "Well, I do believe there's a connection between ability and possibility."

"Maybe you have a romantic heart and a classical mind. I'm just the opposite, I think. It gives me fits. Does it bother you much?"

"I think I mentioned," he said dryly, "that my pleasures can't bear indulgence."

"Mine seem to encourage it."

Lew shrugged. "You're young. The price increases."

"You know," I said, "you probably *are* the greatest traveling salesman in the world. I just have this feeling you are, know what I mean? I believe you."

"Oh, well, perhaps—but it's certainly not a claim I'd make for myself."

I didn't get it. "But it's there on *your* card, right?"

Lew said primly, "Perhaps it's not a claim I'm making, but a title I'm accepting."

"So there *is* a body of judges, or a committee, or something like that?"

"Yes, something like that."

I was pleased, having figured out enough to feel functionally recovered. "So, who says you're the best in the world?"

"The gods."

No, I thought to myself, *why the fuck don't you learn?* What I managed to say was, "Gods? Plural?"

"Yes. Plural."

"How did they tell you you were the greatest in the world? Divine revelation? A plaque?"

"They called my answering service in New York."

"Lew, you've *got* to be shitting me. Be careful; my mind's extremely frail these days."

"So I noticed. That's why I *have* been careful. But it's the truth nonetheless. The gods left a message with my answering service . . . a number, no name. I returned the call. A woman answered—a secretary, I assumed from her manner—and put me on hold for a moment. There was a rapid clicking sound on the line, and then suddenly a very aggressive male voice demanded, 'Would you sell a rat's asshole to a blind man and tell him it was a diamond ring?' I didn't have time to think, of course, so I replied from principle. 'Only if I charged him at the fair market value for rat rectums and was utterly convinced the blind man had the imagination to appreciate the brilliance of the stone."

" 'Excellent, Lew,' the voice replied. 'We'll get back to you.' The connection went dead. I immediately dialed the number again but received a recording that informed me the number was no longer in service.

"Three days later, again through my answering service, I returned a call to a nameless number. This time it was a deep male voice that answered. 'Yes?' he said. I gave my name and noted I was returning a call.

" 'Kerr? Kerr?' he muttered, and I could hear papers rustling. 'Oh yes, here we have it. Mr. Kerr, we're the gods. We consider you the greatest traveling salesman in the world and would like to employ your talents.'

"I thought it was a joke, of course, so I said, 'Suppose I'm not available?'

" 'Then neither are we,' he said, and what impressed me wasn't so much the implied threat as the tone in which he said it—an indifferent statement of finality.

"So I asked, 'What would I be selling?'

"After a thoughtful pause, he answered, 'Well, you wouldn't really be *selling* anything. You would be returning lost goods and collecting the delivery charges.'

" 'What sort of lost goods?'

" 'Ghosts,' he said matter-of-factly, as if we were discussing light bulbs or paper towels.

"I was incredulous, naturally, but just as naturally I was intrigued by the inherent possibilities, so I asked, 'Will the people know their ghosts have been returned, or even that they were lost in the first place?'

" 'No,' he said, 'or not unless you tell them.'

"Now that piece of information made it infinitely intriguing . . . essentially selling an invisible product that a person wouldn't even be sure they'd bought. I had another question: 'Suppose these people refuse to pay the delivery charges?'

" 'Then you're not a great salesman. But,' he added, after just the right length pause to let the challenge stir me, 'we wouldn't have solicited your talents if we weren't confident of our choice.' "

I couldn't help myself, and interrupted, "And you fell for it, Lew? Hell, you're not the greatest salesman in the world—*he* is. Or they are. Tell me, where do you send the money?"

"That was exactly my next question to him."

"Well," I prodded, "*where* do you send it?"

"That's what truly confounded me. He said, 'Keep the money. We can't use money. We're gods.' "

"No. You're kidding."

"Yes. And no, I'm not kidding you. Provocative, isn't it? It's either the gods or the product of a highly unusual human mind. Or minds, perhaps. Can you comprehend the effort and expense required to perpetrate a hoax of that magnitude without any return on the investment except your own amusement?"

He had a point: it was awfully elaborate for a practical joke. But it seemed to me some important points hadn't been covered. "Where do you pick up these lost ghosts you're supposed to return?"

"I don't," Lew said benignly, "they evidently pick me up."

Holy shit, I hope he doesn't mean me. The thought streaked through my buckling brain; my heart had grown legs and was running up my throat.

Lew must've sensed my fear because he immediately explained, "I don't mean they pick me up hitchhiking. Ghosts don't drive, or not that I'm aware of. The ghosts find me, I gather, along the way. Invisibly attach themselves. I don't even know they're with me until I hear their names spoken, which is the same name as the person who lost the ghost. That sounds garbled. Let me try to be more exact. I return calls left with my answering service. I usually get a woman's voice, and she gives me a list of names, usually seven to nine. I transcribe the names in my notebook and then go on about my normal travels. Without any search or intention on my part, I invariably end up meeting those people whose names are on the list. Sometimes it takes two or three months to exhaust the list; the shortest was five days for seven names. Do you understand my point now? No one could endure the incredible expense or egomania necessary to sustain that godlike illusion. They would have to place me under constant surveillance, and I've hired the best private investigators available—who assure me there are no tails or bugs or any sort of monitoring devices. You see, whoever it is would have to employ people to run into me, people whose names are on the list they give me, and that means they would have to know my moves in advance—and I assure you I've made it a point lately to act randomly. My only conclusion, George, is that it *is* the gods, whoever *they* may be. Here, let me show you." He fumbled around for a moment, and finally produced a small leatherbound notebook slimmer than a wallet. He flipped through it quickly, then stopped and turned back the page. He offered it over for my inspection. I eased off the gas and then took a look. He was pointing to a page with a list of seven names. "See?" he said. "Right here. Number four. George Gastin."

I wished for a long time that I could've thought of something witty to say, something like, "Lew, perhaps these 'gods' of yours are simply deranged angels," but lately I've come to believe that my response had a certain eloquence. I looked at my name there on the list and said, "*Arrrggggghhh.*"

"My sentiments exactly." Lew nodded, watching me intently. "But what I'd like to know, George, the question you might trustingly and truthfully answer for me: if *not* the gods, *who* paid you to do this? And why is he, or she, or they, going to such great trouble to drive me crazy?"

Hook, line, sinker, and the rod and reel, too. He was good. I sighed. "What are the delivery charges?" Why start fighting after you've already landed yourself?

"So you deny any knowledge of what's going on?"

"Lew," I raised my right hand, "I swear that the following is the most complete and accurate and honest truth I have ever uttered in my life: I don't have the barest fucking inkling what's going on. Not at all. Not any."

"Well, George, that makes two of us, a virtual unanimity at this particular juncture of time and space."

"I don't think so," I disagreed affably. "One of us is a great salesman; one of us is kind of a lost soul. The great salesman is not merely great, he's the best in the world, so accomplished that he alone is capable of inventing challenges for himself, because he knows if he quits exploring and extending his talents, polishing his brilliance, he won't have anything to justify his pride. But that's his problem. The lost soul's problem is terminal confusion, and it doesn't help that he's a romantic sucker for truth, beauty, love, hope, trust, honor, faith, justice, and all those big *gleaming* abstractions that his spirit constantly fails—or so he secretly believes. Plus he's suffering from exhaustion, sexual injury, and drug abuse. The salesman, being a keen observer, notes this, but since he has no goods to sell in a situation of outstanding sales potential, he brilliantly contrives to do exactly that: sell nothing. Which he proceeds to do, flawlessly, after a bit of sleight-of-hand jotting in the dark. Both the conception and execution are, in fact, so flawless that the lost soul sees it clearly and *still* has no choice but to buy his ghost—which he can neither see nor feel—because even if he's almost positive it's bullshit, he—being lost, romantic, and generally fucked-up—can't risk the slim chance that it *is* the truth. And if it *is* the truth, if the gods think it important enough to return lost ghosts—though he doesn't remember either having one or losing it—he'd be a fool not to accept delivery and pay the charges. So: Bravo, Mr. Kerr. You are indeed the greatest traveling salesman in the world. How much do I owe you?"

"That's the beauty of it, isn't it, George? And that's why I'm beginning to believe it really is the gods: there are so many possibilities for disbelief, so much beyond proof. It's perfect."

"And the price of this perfection?" I sourly reminded him.

"George," he sounded pained, "if *the gods* don't take payment for returning your ghost, how could *I* possibly ask any reward beyond the privilege of delivering it?" He tapped the leather attaché case. "I certainly don't need the money."

"You can afford to do it for kicks."

"You *could* believe me, George, even though I'm not sure I believe this myself. *Trust,* remember? You keep missing your own point, so it's no wonder you're confused."

"So what you're saying is there's no charge? I get my wayward ghost back for free?"

"Not exactly for free. The gods have no use for money and I personally take no commission, but there *is* a fee for the transaction, sort of an emblematic tax on the thermal exchange—call it a donation to cover charges on the cosmic freight. It's a dollar ninety-eight. Symbolic, like I said, but the gods insist on it."

"What happens if I just flat-ass refuse to pay? Do you repossess my ghost?"

"I don't know. Nobody's ever refused."

"Who gets the money?"

"I've been including it in my land trust purchases. So far I've collected one hundred fifty dollars and forty-eight cents. The gods said they didn't care what I did with it as long as it was collected. This figure is obviously capricious; the gods didn't say so, but I gather it's meant as a symbolic reminder that there are things beyond the normal considerations of price and value."

"Would they accept *symbolic* payment?"

Lew cocked his head. "I don't know. It's never come up. But speaking as their ignorant agent, I don't see why not."

Without slowing down I reached over into the backseat and snagged my secondhand Salvation Army jacket. I tossed it to him. "A symbolic payment to keep you warm in a universe getting colder all the time. I'm going to let you out here because my brain's near death, and I want it to die in peace."

"I understand," said Lew as he put on the jacket. "It's interesting, you know: invariably when I return a ghost the person suddenly wants to be alone."

"Or together with his ghost. Sort of a second honeymoon."

Lew looked at me sternly. "I'd be particularly wary of irony, George; it mutilates what it's helpless to transform."

"Now how can I be careful of irony when I didn't even know I'd lost my ghost?"

"That's a point," Lew said, zipping up the jacket.

"You don't happen to know where I lost my ghost, do you? Or when? Or how? Or why?"

Lew picked up his attaché case. "No, I don't."

"What do the gods say about these lost ghosts?"

"Nothing."

"Did you press them?"

"Of course. I'm a curious man myself."

I had my neck bowed. "So, what did they say when you pressed them?"

"They told me not to worry about it. The gods don't seemed disposed to idle chatter. I'm just given a list of names. It's all very crisp and distant."

"And you're sure it's gods, plural?"

"Positive. I wouldn't make a mistake on something like that."

"Last guy I gave a ride to was the pastor of the Rock Solid Gospel Light Church of the Holy Release. The Lord speaks to him. One god. *Mono* theism, right? And you're telling me gods. At least more than one. Voices out of the blue and out of whirlwinds and over the phone— evidently the spirits are just babbling away out there. Not that I've personally heard them. They haven't said diddley-shit to me. Well, maybe a whisper once or twice, but nothing I could be sure of."

"You know what frightens me?" Lew said. "I'm afraid I'm going to get the gods on the phone one of these days and be sitting there writing down names of lost ghosts to return and my name is going to be on the list."

"Just drop your buck ninety-eight in the pot like everyone else."

"I guess so," he said uneasily, "but for me I don't think it would be that simple. They say the only mark you can't beat is the mark inside. I'd probably try to sell it back to them."

"They'd probably buy it." I slowed to let him off. "I really am sorry to put you out like this. I don't know what's going on, but I guess I should thank you for your help in keeping it going."

"My pleasure," Lew said. "I know you'll ignore me, but George, you shouldn't go on much farther without some rest. It's not helping."

"Three more hours and I'm soaking in a hot bath." I pulled over onto the shoulder and stopped. "I'm tempted to kidnap you for company and counsel, but I need to be alone for a while to think, to make up my mind."

"Make up a good one," the greatest traveling salesman in the world advised me as he offered a little wave in farewell.

As I nosed back onto the blacktop I caught a glimpse of him in the rearview mirror as he sprinted across the freeway to the southbound lanes and stuck his thumb up for a ride back the way he'd come. Something else to think about.

But I don't remember thinking about that or anything else on the drive into Des Moines. I don't remember the drive, either. The only evidence that I actually did is that I woke up in a Des Moines motel the next morning. Between dropping off Lewis Kerr and waking up is pretty much a hole; there are a few clinging fragments, and if they were the high points I can understand why the rest are forgotten. Perhaps my strongest memory is a feeling of frustrated rage that I'd been cheated out of Paradise. I remember a huge green figure that seemed to beckon to me. I recall giving money to a sallow young man with a prominent Adam's apple who—except for a bright green blazer—looked like an apprentice embalmer. There was one sliver of pleasure, the immense relief I felt as I slid into a steaming bath, but the next memory is of screaming awake in cold, grease-slicked water, terrified I'd drowned my ghost. I remember clawing and sloshing my way out of the tub, the freezing linoleum, and—most vividly—the explosive bitterness in my mouth as I scrabbled on hands and knees to puke in the toilet. I remember passing the wall heater as I crawled toward the bed and stopping to crank it up full blast before I died of exposure. Still dripping wet, I heaved myself up on the bed and wriggled under the covers. The last memory-shard of that night is so faint it may have been a dream: uncontrollable shivers that became convulsions; praying they would stop before my skeleton flew apart; begging the mercy of every god I could remember, from Allah to Zeus. After that, nothing.

Memory did not resume gently. I woke the next morning convulsed by a heart-stopping shock that was like getting hit with a souped-up cattle prod. *Phone!* my brain screeched. *Nightstand. To your right.* I saw it. A green and yellow plastic phone that resembled an ear of corn. "Please don't!" I blurted just as it rang again. I reached to pick it up and make it quit when an alarm went off in my brain stem—*who knows you're here? who knows you're here?*—and the crank of adrenalin turned my mind over; it was idling rough, but it was running. The phone rang again. *Nobody knows I'm here, wherever it is.* The phone rang again. Maybe it was the gods returning my call. It rang again. Whoever invented the telephone's alleged "bell" should have his skull drilled with a dull bit until it's a gossamer of bone. I snatched up the receiver, lifted it to my ear, but didn't speak.

"*Good* morning!" a scratchy recording of a pert female voice began brightly, "this is your wake-up call as requested." I didn't remember requesting one, but then again I didn't remember much of anything. I relaxed as the voice continued, "Thank you for staying with us at the Jolly Green Giant Motel. If you're hungry, may we suggest Pancake Paradise, conveniently located next to the motel. And please keep in mind that any prolonged irregularity in your bowel habits or the presence of blood in the stool are both warning signs of rectal cancer and you should see a doctor immediately. It's been our pleasure to serve you. We hope you've enjoyed your stay. If you'll be journeying on today, have a safe and successful trip, and do stop and see us if you get back this way again."

Rectal cancer? Blood? Stool? My brain denied it. I kept the phone to my ear. "*Good* morning!" she began again, and I listened intently through "signs of rectal cancer," then decisively hung up. The room was gorged with rank humidity. I was sweating and shivering. The bed looked like I'd been cavorting with a school of mermaids all night. I was simultaneously numb-dumb and jangled with an unfocused frenzy. Muscles in my body twitched randomly. I wasn't feeling well. In fact, objectively, I was a wretched mess. Subjectively, however, all I needed was a dozen hits of speed. Soon. Otherwise I was going to turn into a big clot of algae.

The speed was in . . . where? The bottle. The bottle of speed. Now I was getting somewhere. Under the seat of the car, right. Car? Where's the car? Parked where? Keys? Pants? To think and crave at the same time is extremely difficult, particularly when you're handicapped by the loss of recent memory.

If you think I bolted bare-ass from the room, keys clutched in a sweaty palm, and careened around the parking lot looking for something large and white with swept fins sporting dual bullet taillights and a bottle of amphetamine under the seat, you've forgotten—as I had until that moment—my purpose in subjecting myself to exhaustion, amnesia, drug withdrawals, the dangers of the road, and rectal cancer in wake-up calls. It was delivery day, arrival, the point of completion, and I'd damn near forgotten. "You pathetic piece of shit," I said aloud. "Must really be important, a deeply serious matter of love, music, spirit. But first get that speed. Don't stand there jerking yourself off with this gift-of-love horse-shit. You can go get the speed or you can get serious."

I got serious. It wasn't what I felt like doing—what I felt like doing was a tall stack of crank—but when Saint George came galloping in on his ethereal white charger, I submitted to what I wanted to be rather than what I was.

Following Saint George's command, I marched to the bathroom. The undrained water in the tub was slicked with grey congealed oils, but it was an enchanted lake with lily pads compared to the toilet, which I understandably, if unfortunately, hadn't flushed after vomiting. "Take a good look in the mirror," Saint George ordered. I obeyed. Not as bad as the toilet bowl, but if the blood in my eyes had been in my stool I would've been fanning the Yellow Pages under *Physicians*.

"This is what you've come to," Saint George sneered. "But you don't have to live your life like this. You don't have to die with pee-stains on your underwear in a scabby motel room reeking of disinfectant, holding your broken dreams in your arms like some ghostly lover whose every touch you failed. This bathroom is the image of your soul. Clean it up."

I cleaned the bathroom till it sparkled, then started on myself. First a hot shower, then a cold one, followed by a shave and a clean change of clothes. That my duffle bag and shaving kit were already in the room was proof I'd at least retained some mental functions the night before.

Though I was trying to be playful about it, I was distressed by the black-out. My last coherent memory was of Lewis Kerr selling me my ghost, and that was hardly encouraging. I hoped my ghost wasn't as fucked-up as I was. "You fight with what you have," Saint George rebuked me, his formidable white charger trembling for action. "Go eat, and then let's do it."

When you're bullwhipping yourself with self-loathing, there's a tendency to want to spread the pain. I made a point of returning the key to the office instead of leaving it in the room, hoping that the sallow young man was on duty; a few lashes might get his blood moving. That I was disappointed to find a freckle-faced woman in her midtwenties in the office was evidence of my mean mood. She was pleasantly chubby, with a cute nose and bright hazel eyes, wearing more make-up than she needed—the milky farmer's daughter of a traveling salesman's wettest dreams. I was disconcerted by her healthy glow, but any inclination to spare the lash vanished at her cheerful chirp of a greeting: *"Good morning, Dr. Gass."* Hers was the same perky voice I'd heard on the wake-up call.

"Wrong." I slapped the room key on the counter. "It might've been a bearable morning had it not been besmirched by the malignant anus of your wake-up call."

The weight of her collapsing smile bowed her head. I felt like I'd run over a puppy. "I like words," I told her. "I read the dictionary with breakfast. I'm secretly vain about my abilities to express myself in all sorts of situations, and in company ranging from scumballs to poets. Perhaps it's because I've been sick with the flu this week, but I find I can't even *begin* to express my disgust at the utter tastelessness of including the warning signs of rectal cancer in a wake-up call."

She lifted her face, tears trembling in the corners of her eyes. "Try 'putrid.' Or 'hideous.' 'A grossly thoughtless insult to human sensibility and the hope of a new day.' That's the best one so far. 'Sick' and 'disgusting' are the most common." She paused to knuckle the brimming tears. "I get ten complaints every morning." She sniffled, sniffled again, then tried to smile.

I wasn't moved. "If you get complaints every morning," I said icily, "why do you persist in including it? Why not remove it?"

"I *want* to," she pleaded, "but Mr. Hilderbrand won't let me."

"*Who* is Mr. Hilderbrand?" He was going to pay double, for my pain and hers.

"He's the owner."

"Is he here?"

She shook her head. "Excuse me a moment, please." She went into an adjoining room, out of view. I could hear her blowing her nose.

I was waiting like a moray eel when she returned. "Will Mr. Hilderbrand be in soon?"

"Not till this evening." Her voice was a bit tight and breathless, but steady.

"Do you have his home number? I see no purpose in haranguing you if you're only doing it at his insistence."

"He's at the hospital most of the day."

"A mental hospital, I assume." Spare the rod, spoil the child. Too blind to see.

"Oh no, of course not. His wife is dying of cancer. Rectal cancer. I mean, don't you *see?* That's *why.* Harriet—that's his wife—knew something was wrong but she was too embarrassed to go to the doctor or even tell Mr. Hilderbrand until it was too late. It's so *sad.* Embarrassed by a thing like that. They've been married *twenty-nine years.*"

"Do they love each other?" It was a foolish question, but far less foolish than I felt.

She appeared baffled by the question. "I suppose so. Twenty-nine years is a lot, and he spends all his time with her at the hospital."

I couldn't think of anything to say, foolish or not, so nodded my head as if I understood.

She continued, "For a while I told him about the complaints, but he wouldn't budge. He said people have to face what's real. That it needs to be reinforced or they'll ignore it."

"I agree. But why make *you* say it? Why make you suffer the consequences?"

"Well, to tell the truth"—a flicker of a smile—"Mr. Hilderbrand has a squeaky voice, and it's worse on tape. And every day for the last six weeks he's been at the hospital with his wife—that's suffering enough without the complaints. So I try to handle them and not bother him."

"What's your name?"

"Carol."

"Carol, you have a fine heart."

"That's nice of you to say." Her eyes glistened with tears. She gave a funny little shrug of her shoulders, swiped at the tears with a tissue crumpled in her hand, then managed an awkward smile.

"Could I borrow a paper and pen? I'd like to leave Mr. Hilderbrand a note."

"Of course." She was glad to have something to do besides fight back tears in front of a stranger.

I explained. "I'm going to suggest to Mr. Hilderbrand that instead of enforcing reality on the wake-up call he instead have *all* the warning signs of cancer printed on a piece of paper and placed in every room as a bookmark for the Gideon Bibles . . . sort of diagnosis and consolation at the same time. Slip them right in there at the Book of Job."

Carol hesitantly slid a ballpoint pen and a livid green sheet of paper across the counter. I didn't understand the hesitation till she said, "But Dr. Gass, we don't place Bibles in the rooms. Mr. Hilderbrand won't allow it. He says it's presumptuous . . . not everybody is a Christian."

"But it's *not* presumptuous to wake up guests, whatever their religious preferences, with graphic descriptions of the warning signs of rectal cancer?" I felt sense disintegrating.

"I guess Mr. Hilderbrand doesn't think so." I noted a new, noncommittal coolness in her tone. She was tired of dealing with me.

I picked up the pen and briskly began, *Dear Mr. Hilderbrand* . . . but then couldn't think of anything to say. The last hour I'd been riding that combination of self-loathing and false power that accompanies the fervor of renewal, the righteousness released by fresh conviction, but it was fading fast. The pen trembled in my hand, and I put it down. "I don't know what the hell to say," I confessed to Carol. "I can't *think* with this damn flu." I suddenly wanted to bury my face in her bosom and weep.

"Ralph—he's the night manager—he said you didn't look well."

"I was a zombie."

"Well, I hope you feel better soon, Dr. Gass. And I hope you won't hold the wake-up call against us." This was a reasonable facsimile of her perky self, but not the real item. She'd receded.

So had I. "Thanks. I hope I feel better, too. And now I understand how you knew my name—the night manager told you."

"Ralph was concerned. He said if you stayed past checkout to look in on you . . . that sounds bad, like it was the money, but it was to make sure you were all right."

"What did he say? 'Look for a guy I can practice my embalming on?' "

Carol tittered. "No, he just said you looked sick and tired. And that you were wearing a colorful hat."

"He liked the hat, did he?" I reached up and gave the narrow brim a tug.

"He said you asked him if he *understood* your hat."

"Well, I was extremely ill last night. The fever was peaking. I suppose I was babbling. To tell the truth, I don't even remember talking to him."

"Dr. Gass, do you *really* wear that hat so the gods can spot you more easily?"

"Did I say that?"

"That's what Ralph *said* you told him. I don't think Ralph realized how sick you were. *He* thought you might be a little loony-tunes."

"I can certainly understand why," I chuckled nervously, "going around saying things like that. Or it may be that Ralph doesn't *personally* feel the gods are watching. And maybe he's right."

"Oh," Carol said. Now we both were nervous. "Do you mind my asking what sort of doctor you are? Ralph didn't think you were a medical doctor, but I said you could be a professor."

"Bless you, but you're both wrong—though *you're* closer. I'm a

Doctor of Divinity. I'm doing missionary work for the Rock Solid Gospel Light Church of the Holy Release."

"It's pretty much Methodists around here," Carol said.

"It's a new church," I explained, "greater ecclesiastical emphasis on the role of the Holy Spirit as manifested in love and music. Which reminds me that I must be on my missionary way. It was a pleasure to meet you, Carol. I hope our paths cross again. Good day." I was out the door, feeling I'd handled the explanations and my exit with dignity and aplomb.

Out in the parking lot, the dignity and aplomb quickly withered: I couldn't find the Eldorado. I felt the keys in my pocket; all I lacked was the car. I went around back. No Caddy. I circled the entire motel, shivering with cold and impending collapse. Nothing. As gone as any memory of where I might've parked it.

Trying to fight down the panic, I returned to the office. Carol seemed startled to see me.

"I can't seem to locate my car," I told her, my attempted smile more like a twitch.

She put her hand to her mouth. "Oh, I'm *sorry*. I was supposed to remind you—Ralph asked me to . . . but I got involved talking and . . . oh, I'm *really* sorry. It's parked in front of the restaurant . . . the pancake house next to us." She pointed helpfully.

"I don't remember parking it there," I said, excruciatingly aware as soon as the feeble words left my mouth that that was obvious.

"Well, according to Ralph you were very upset."

"Did he say why?" I wasn't sure I wanted to know.

"Because the neon letters were the same color as your hat," Carol said.

I shouldn't have asked. "The fever." I shook my head sadly. "I must've been delirious."

"I don't know if it's true, but Ralph said they almost called the police."

"Oh?"

"You were threatening to tear the sign down with your bare hands."

"I was? I *like* the color."

"But it wasn't Paradise."

"*What* wasn't?" I demanded. I needed speed just to keep up with the conversation.

Carol shied at my tone. "I only know what Ralph told me."

"Yes?" I urged.

"You were upset because the pancake house wasn't Paradise. The sign said it was, but it wasn't. And if it wasn't, you said they shouldn't use an honest color like your hat's for false advertising."

"Sounds like my sort of logic. Wish I could've been there."

"It *is* kind of funny." Carol grinned, glee flashing in her lovely hazel eyes. "I always thought Pancake Paradise was a really stupid name. Mr. Hilderbrand's ex-partner owns it, a Mr. Granger. They bought the motel and restaurant together, but they couldn't get along—mainly because Mr. Granger is such a jerk—so they split it up. The restaurant isn't doing so good now that Mr. Granger has it. He's never there. He's more interested in chasing women. He thinks he's *so* neat. He's always coming over and asking me to go out and have a drink with him, and he's *married.*"

"Do they make good pancakes over there?"

"Urp." She giggled.

I liked her giggle. "Well, if it isn't Paradise and they serve urpy food and Mr. Granger is an adulterous jerk, why don't you and me go over there and tear the sign down together right now. Strike a blow for truth, justice, beauty, and good eats. Then, soon as I take care of a little business, we can run away to Brazil."

She wasn't shocked or offended. She just looked at me and shook her head.

"You can say no."

"Dr. Gass, I *have* to say no."

"No you don't."

"I *work* here. I *live* here. I don't *know* you."

I lost heart against that three-gun salvo of logic. "You're right. You have to say no, I guess, and I have to wonder if that's the reason I asked you. I mean that respectfully, as a compliment. So maybe in the future, under the influence of different circumstances, different signs." Graceful exits were becoming my specialty.

"Don't do it," Carol warned me. "They'll call the cops for sure this time and put you in jail."

"The Paradise sign?" I waved my hand in dismissal. "I'm too weak to do it without your help. But I wasn't really intending to anyway. I'm not *that* dumb. Or that smart, maybe. Besides, I've got plenty of other foolishness to keep me busy today, and though it's proving difficult to release myself from your captivating company, I best get on to it. Call farewell to your rejected suitor as he rides into the desert."

She shook her head. "You *are* loony-tunes."

My first step out the office door I saw the Caddy's bullet taillights jutting between two pick-ups. I decided the best tactic was to stroll over casually, jump in, and make tracks. Everything with an easy quickness. The place could still be simmering with animosity. I was about halfway across to the Caddy when I heard Carol's maiden voice, a bellnote cutting the cold air: "Fare-thee-well!"

I turned around and cupped my hands: "I'll never stop loving you!"

That sent her jumping back inside the office door. I'd forgotten for a moment she worked there, lived there, had to say no. So had she.

The Cadillac, praise my autonomic nervous system, was securely locked. I opened the driver's door and slid in, relocking it immediately. It seemed to me there were a lot of faces peering through the windows of Pancake Paradise. I squirmed on the freezing front seat; no wonder Preparation H, Doan's pills, and amphetamines are a trucker's best friends. I shouldn't have thought of amphetamine, but instead of reaching under the front seat, I reached up and turned the key. The engine cranked slowly, not enough juice in the cold, but then it caught—ragged at first, but warming toward a purr.

I was so intent on the engine sounds that it took me a moment to notice, right next to my door, the two huge men dressed identically in blue bib-overalls and white T-shirts. They looked like twins, except the one standing to the rear had a silly, glazed smile on his face and a very distant look in his pale blue eyes, while the one rapping on my window with knuckles the size of unshelled walnuts had a very close look in his

196

eyes and no smile at all. I figured that together they could rip the door off the Caddy faster than I could slam it into reverse and pop the clutch, so I powered the window down a short inch and pleasantly said, "Good morning, gentlemen."

The one with the close look and no smile didn't believe in such idle pleasantries. "Wha'chu out there in the parkin' lot bellerin' about?"

"Love," I said, nudging the stick into reverse.

He hunkered down and grinned hugely against the glass. "Yup," he rumbled, "ain't love a bitch?"

"Glad to see you're a man of understanding," I told him, glad indeed. It was nice to see him smiling.

He pointed to his massive chest. "I'm Harvey." He pointed at the other young giant. "That there's Bubba. He's my brother."

"George, here." I nodded to Harvey, then raised my voice so his brother could hear me: "Ho there, Bubba. I'm George. Glad to meet you."

Bubba rotated his head slightly to look at me, a movement that elicited the uneasy feeling that someone I couldn't see was running him by remote control. His mouth began to work for words, a labor that didn't change his happy, vacant expression.

"What's happening, Bubba?" I encouraged him.

"Bubba like head," he announced.

"Don't we all. But love's a bitch, Bubba. You listen to your brother Harvey here."

"We're looking for a whorehouse," Harvey confided. "Promised Bubba we'd get us some pussy once the crops was all in. One we been to last year and year before got closed up. You know where one is?"

I looked them over carefully, then lowered my voice. "Not a whore-*house*, but I know where you can get you a couple of *fine* women that'll party you boys till you beg for mercy."

"Tell me slow so I can remember," Harvey said.

I pointed at the door to Pancake Paradise. "Right inside."

Harvey shook his head. "Been inside. Didn't see none. Just waitress ladies in there."

"Whoa down now, Harvey. The *women* aren't in there, but their *pimp* is. Name's Granger. *Granger.* He owns the place. Don't talk to anyone else. Just Mr. Granger. He'll pretend he doesn't know what you're talking about and tell you to leave and generally act mad—that's what he did with me at first—so what you have to do is tell him you're going to come out here in the parking lot, you and Bubba, and you're going to tear down his fucking lying Paradise sign with your bare hands unless he sets you up with Mandy and Ramona."

"Mandy and Ramona," Harvey repeated.

"They're my recommendation. You boys might want bigger girls to romp with, but I'll tell you, I spent last night with Mandy and Ramona, and look at *me.*"

Harvey leaned close against the glass and gave me a long look. "Whoooooweeeeee," he clapped his hands, beaming.

"Now the thing about Mandy and Ramona is they're both about five-foot-ten, and Mandy's got an ass like a valentine and Ramona can suck the knots out of an oak. And let me tell you true, they're both big where it really matters, you know what I mean?"

"Sure *do.*"

"That's right, Harvey, they've got the biggest hearts that ever poured selfless love out on a lucky man. You don't just *come* with these two, you *arrive.*"

Harvey looked puzzled but agreeable.

Bubba joined the conversation. "Bubba like head."

"Well then," Harvey said decisively, grinning at his brother as he stood up, "let's go get us some from that Mr. Grange in there."

"Wait, wait, wait," I cautioned. "Mr. Grang*er* might not be in. If he's not, get his home address. Tell whoever has it that you want to sell Mr. Granger some buckwheat flour. Be *really* polite to everybody. None of them knows Mr. Granger runs the wildest call-girl operation in the county. And remember: he doesn't like dealing with strangers, which is why you'll probably have to threaten to tear down this Paradise sign here—shit, I actually had to start rocking on it before he called the girls. And be sure to tell him that if he even *thinks* about calling the cops, you'll run his ass through your harvester and chop him up for silage."

"That'd be *murder!*" Harvey was shocked.

"Well Good Christ, don't do it! Just *threaten*. Now the sign, of course, you *can* tear down. You see, you got to show pimps a little muscle or they'll just ignore you. Personally, I don't hold with hurting people."

"Me neither," Harvey said. "I go to church come Sundays. Bubba don't like church much."

"Yeah, but he likes head, and that's just as good."

"Come *on*, Harv," Bubba whined, tugging at his brother's arm.

"Now another thing," I said as I slipped the clutch, "whatever you do, stay away from the motel over there. It's *swarming* with undercover cops. You'll be in jail before your overalls hit your ankles." The clutch engaged and I started to move. "You boys have yourself a *good* time. Give Mandy and Ramona my best."

They waved gratefully as I pulled away.

Siccing Harvey and Bubba on Granger and his false Paradise was mean, dangerous, and stupid, but it was not without wit, and there was the intriguing possibility of justice. Besides, I felt so rotten I wanted it to spread. Benzedrine withdrawal is not conducive to exquisite moral judgments, especially when there's a bottle of relief as close as the floor, a whole bunch of tiny white prisoners bearing the sign of the cross, each pounding on the glass and begging, "George! Please save me. Swallow me now. Help! Please!"

I couldn't bear their pitiful wails, so I pulled over just before the Clear Lake/Mason City on-ramp, took the bottle out from under the seat, and, holding my breath, leaped out of the car and dashed around back and locked them in the trunk inside the cooler, plucking out two cans of beer to make room. I noticed the ice had hardly melted. Colder days and colder nights. I thought about dumping the ice to lighten my load, but that meant opening the trunk and resisting the temptation of that bottle of go-fast again, and once had been tempting enough. Let the ice melt in the blaze, sizzle through liquidity as it leaped from solid to gas. Let the cooler melt and the beer explode. Fuck yes, let it all roar upward in the cleansing flames. Ready or not, I was on my way, the last run. Even if I was crazy, it didn't matter now.

PART THREE

THE PILGRIM GHOST

"The self-seeker finds nothing."
—Goethe

Right foot nailed to the juice, needle jammed in triple digits, running full bore and pointblank, I made Mason City in about forty minutes. Given my punky reflexes, to justify flying like that was difficult, but it was a question of paying attention either to haul-ass driving or the wharf rats chewing on my nerves. I was, however, hanging on—like an old toothless hound with a gum-lock on a grizzly's ass, perhaps, but hanging on nonetheless. Two cold beers helped, the alcohol numbing the rawer edges while the liquid replenished my parched cells. I would've downed two more if I thought I could've opened the coolor without jumping the bottle of speed; yet another obstacle of my own devising, almost enough to make me curl up on the floorboards and weep. But that I was standing fast against the howling neural need for chemical refreshment made me believe I had a chance—slim, for sure, but gaining weight.

I didn't have a plan, though, which was just as well, since I lacked the sustained coherence to carry one out. However, in a typical burst of perversity I recalled all the recent stern injunctions to be careful, attend to details, assess the full range of possibilities, and generally keep in mind that fortune favors preparation—though it seemed to me that both mind and fortune were drunk monkeys in the tiger's eye. Startled by the Mason City city limits sign, I decided to at least take a lunge at the basics, so I made a jangled survey of the essential steps: eat; fill the Caddy with high-test; buy some white gas; and find out as exactly as possible where the plane had gone down. I did briefly consider how to get myself and my gear back from the crash site after burning my ride, but I figured a phone call to Yellow Cab could cover that. The first thing was to deliver the gift; then I'd worry about slipping away.

My first stop was the Blue Moon Cafe for an order of bacon, eggs, a short stack of buckwheat cakes, and some information. They had everything but the information, but one waitress conferred with the other, the other waitress queried the cook, and then the three together quizzed the other four patrons. The consensus was that Tommy Jorgenson was the person most likely to know exactly where the plane hit ground, and that I could probably find him at his Standard station eight blocks down on the left.

I finished what I could of my breakfast, left a $10 tip, and humped back out to the Caddy through the stinging cold. I'd overheard a ruddy-faced guy in a John Deere cap trying to sucker the Blue Moon's cook into betting that it wouldn't snow before dark, and as I fired up the Caddy I wished the cook had jumped on the wager. Not that I would've—you could feel snow gathering in the air. I just hoped it held off for a couple of hours. I didn't need to get sideways on a snow-slick road and wrap the Caddy around a power pole a few miles short of my destination. I'd come too long and too hard for that kind of cruel irony. Once the Caddy was warmed up, I drove downtown to the Standard station at nary a quiver over the posted 25 mph.

Tommy Jorgenson surprised me. I suppose his name had made me expect a tall, slowly thoughtful Scandinavian instead of what I got, a short wiry guy with spring-coiled black hair and intense brown eyes that never quit moving even when he was looking straight at me—one of those restlessly kinetic people who wash their ceilings every week just to burn off the energy. Until you get to know them, you suspect they're secretly banging speed. But they don't need it. They run off their own systems, D.C.; they're just naturally wrapped tight.

I told Tommy to fill 'er up, then got out and followed him around as he put the nozzle in the tank and started on checking the oil and cleaning glass. I introduced myself as a reporter for *Life* magazine and told him I'd been on vacation visiting my sister in Des Moines when I'd gotten this wild idea about doing a major feature on the three musicians who'd been killed in the plane wreck—sort of a retrospective memorial piece—and that I was interested in visiting the crash site.

Tommy shot me a glance as he wiped the dipstick. "Isn't there no more." He dropped the dipstick back into the hole.

"What do you mean," I chattered, "it's *not* there? It *has* to be there. It's a place, a site, a point in fact—even if it's been paved over for a parking lot, it's still *there.*" The cold was numbing.

Tommy pulled out the dipstick and held it up for my inspection. It was a hair under full. I nodded rapidly, as much to move some blood to my brain as to indicate that the oil level was fine.

Tommy said a bit sharply, "Of *course* nobody's *moved* the place. I meant there's nothing left to see. They had the wreck cleaned up right away and the field was plowed and planted the next spring."

"Now we're talking." I grinned.

"You still want to check it out?" Tommy replaced the dipstick and dropped the hood.

"You bet."

"Why?"

"Good question." I stalled, thinking to myself, *Fuck good questions. What I need are good, precise, unequivocal answers.* "I have lots of reasons, all complicated. I guess the main reason is simply to pay my respects. Another's more practical. I've got this idea for a lead running around in my head. Something like: 'On a snow-swirling night in early February, 1959, a small Beechcraft left the Mason City airport and shortly thereafter crashed in an Iowa cornfield. Along with the pilot, three young musicians were killed: the Big Bopper, Buddy Holly, and Ritchie Valens. As I stand here at the precise point of impact on a late October afternoon six years later, there is no visible evidence of the wreckage. For six springs this field has been plowed and sown; for six autumns the harvest reaped. The earth and the music heal quickly. The heart takes longer.' " I paused for whatever effect a pause might have. "I know, it's rough as hell, but you get the angle. I suppose the best way to put it is that I'm hoping to draw some inspiration from the place."

"I'll draw you a map," Tommy said.

Music to my ears, the last piece clicking into place. I was starting to like the little dynamo. Maybe the reason Tommy throbbed with energy was that he didn't waste any. I felt like grabbing a pair of jumper cables and hooking us up, brain to brain—boost some of his juice. The cold was draining mine through the corroded terminals. "I take it," I said, "you've been out to the crash site."

"Yup."

"Recently?"

"Nope. Last time was early '62, over three years ago."

"You see it after it happened?"

"My old man's a deputy sheriff. I heard the call come in on the box at home. I'd been there the night before, at the Surf Ballroom, where they played that night. That was over in Clear Lake. Almost every kid from around these parts was there; we don't draw much top-line entertainment in these parts. It was a good show, but not great. They looked tired and beat. 'Course I was shit-faced on vodka. What we called a Cat Screwdriver—half a pint of Royal Gate, half a pint of Nehi orange soda. So when the call came in, even though I was hung over down to my ankles, I had to go out and see if it was true. Had no idea how true it was. Turned me inside out. Must've puked for an hour."

My stomach churned in empathy. Breakfast wasn't setting well. The bellyful of cold beer had congealed the bacon grease into a solid, sinking chunk; if it kept falling, it was sure to come back up. It's hard to grit your teeth when they're chattering, and it was my turn to ask why: "But you went back in '62, right?"

Tommy's sigh plumed in the air. "Yeah. Actually, I went out there a couple of times a month for a while. Don't know why. Nothing to see but the corn growing. I had a chopped '51 Ford coupe at the time, metal-flake green, dropped a T-Bird engine in it. All souped-up and nowhere to go. Or nowhere better. One thing, it was real peaceful just sitting there watching the breeze move the cornstalks. So, I'd tool out there fairly often—ain't far, and there's a long straight stretch where you can run flat out, coming and going. But after I blew the transmission, I went out less and less. Last time was February third, '62. The anniversary. Don't know why, though. Never thought about it. Just did."

Before I could ask my next question, he turned and was moving back along the Caddy. By the time I caught up he was topping off the tank. "Don't mean to pester a man on the job, but I wonder if you know who owns the land where the plane crashed? Figure I should get permission before I go trespassing around in somebody's corn patch."

"Corn's in," Tommy noted, withdrawing the nozzle and shutting down the pump.

"That's just less cover for my ass."

Tommy smiled. "Bert Julhal used to own it, but I heard Gladys Nogardam bought it from him a couple of years ago. I'm not sure about that, wouldn't bet on it anyway, but I'm pretty sure ol' Gladys bought it. She must be a hundred years old now and people say she's still sharp as a tack."

"What's her story?" Information is ammunition, and I had a bad feeling I'd best load up. A woman that old and still lucid would undoubtedly know her own mind, which would make changing it more difficult in case she didn't dig my romantic gesture. I hadn't been around a lot of old women lately, and the few I knew no longer seemed inclined to suffer what they found disagreeable.

Tommy was shaking his head. "Never met the woman myself, but I've heard a lot about her. She lived over in Clear Lake for about twenty years, married to Duster Nogardam. Duster was this big Swede dentist, but what he was famous for was skeet shooting. He was on the '34 Olympic team, came in fifth or ninth or something like that. Anyway, sometime after that—don't remember exactly—he went out pheasant hunting over on the Lindstrom place and just vanished. Car parked right beside the road. Never seen or heard from since. She finally inherited his estate. She got a little weird, I gather—wandered around at night, stuff like that. She bought the Julhal place because she said she was too old for city life and needed some fresh air. That's what she told Lottie Williams, anyway. I heard it from my mom. You know how small towns are—live in each other's pockets. Old lady Nogardam don't work the place, of course. Leases it to the Potts brothers is what I heard."

"Wait a minute. Let's take that back. Her husband just *vanished?* Poof? No trace?" For some reason I wasn't liking that at all.

I liked it three times less when Tommy said, "Same thing happened to her first two husbands, too. That's the *strange* thing."

"Three husbands and they *all* disappeared?"

"Yup."

"*Who* says? I mean, are we talking rumor, fact, or what?"

"My old man's a deputy, right? He read the police reports."

"How'd she *explain* it? They must've grilled the ever-loving shit out of her—three husbands vanishing is damn near impossible. Hell, *two*'s impossible."

"According to Dad, she said she couldn't explain it. She said explaining it was their job."

"And they couldn't, right?"

"Like Dad said, 'Coincidence isn't evidence.' "

"I assume her husbands all had hefty estates. Or some heavy insurance."

"Nope," Tommy shook his head, "that's the kicker. Duster had a few bucks, and the second one—I think he had a ranch in Arizona—was barely making ends meet, but the first one was hocked to his armpits. He was a linoleum distributor in Chicago. They'd only been married a couple of years. She and Duster had been together for twenty or thereabouts; ten with the guy in Arizona, I think."

"And she had alibis and all that?"

"Airtight, ironclad, not a crack. For all of them, not just Duster. Or that's what my dad said."

"I don't get it," I said, flapping my arms for warmth.

"Don't feel like the Lone Ranger."

"What do *you* think? She hire it out, they just get called to their Maker, take a walk, spaceships come down and spirit them away, what?"

"Spaceships," Tommy said.

I couldn't tell if he was kidding or not, and suddenly I didn't care. I was freezing, and in a rotten mood to start with. Spaceships, sure—made as much fucking sense as anything. I reached for my wallet. "How much do I owe you?"

He glanced at the pump. "Six eighty-five ought to get it."

"You carry white gas?"

"Gallon cans. Nothing in bulk."

"Gallon's perfect. I've got a little single-burner Coleman in the trunk to brew up coffee—put a little antifreeze in my system."

"Might try a jacket along with it," Tommy observed.

"No shit." I chuckled, handing him a twenty. "I gave mine to some poor bastard I picked up hitching last night. All he had on was an undershirt."

"You meet some nuts, all right," Tommy said as he took the bill. He headed for the office, calling over his shoulder, "I'll bring you the map and the white gas with your change. Might be a few minutes with the map."

"Hey, no problem," I called after him. "And you keep the change. Good information's more valuable than gas. And that map: I would really appreciate it if you make it as precise as possible . . . you know, 'X marks the spot.' "

Tommy stopped to protest the tip but I waved him on. "The magazine pays for it. Legit expense. Hell, I'd give you a hundred if they'd hold still for it."

I waited in the Caddy, letting it idle with the heater on full blast. I made a mental note to buy a heavy jacket before I left town, chastising myself for giving mine to Lewis Kerr when I remembered the foil-wrapped cube of LSD that was still in the pocket. This added another dimension of possibilities to last night's transactions. I hoped the acid somehow managed to get into his bloodstream—not that the world was ready for a hallucinating Lewis Kerr, though the notion pleased me immensely.

I wasn't happy about Granny Nogardam and her missing husbands, so I gave this a few minutes of serious worry, cursing my luck. Why couldn't it *ever* be simple? Why wasn't the landowner some crop-failed farmer who'd be overjoyed to let me do any damn fool thing I wanted for twenty bucks and a six-pack, and throw in a ride back to town? But what the hell, maybe she would, too. No way to know till I asked. And I'd be doing that soon enough. I felt a tiny, voluptuous tremor of anticipation surge through me then, a little premonitory quiver of impending completion, and it thrilled me. I closed my eyes to savor the feeling and saw the Caddy parked in the middle of an ivory desolation, gleaming white-on-white. No sound. No movement. Then a flat, muffled WHUMP! as the white gas ignited and then a blinding roar as the gas tank exploded. Yes, yes, yes. Signed with love; sealed with a kiss. The gift delivered. I was dreaming on the verge of occurrence. I felt its inevitability in my bones. It was *meant* to happen. *Had* to be. No question.

When Tommy came hustling across the slab a few minutes later with the map and white gas, I was ready to make the last move, set the last piece in place. I was wasted but drawing strength from the promise of imminent release, about to lay that burden down.

The map, as I expected, was deft and precise. Tommy went over it with me quickly, and unnecessarily since the route was so simple— maybe ten miles of straight roads with only three turns to remember. In the field in back of the house marked NOGARDAM was a large *X*, carefully circled. I thanked Tommy for his help and insisted he keep the change, my sincerity not the least compromised by the fact I'd solicited his help under false pretenses.

Heading out of town, I remembered I should buy a warm jacket and generally get my shit together . . . have things organized in case Granny Nogardam proved intractable and I was forced to hit and run. I was all set to let it rip, but as Joshua and Double-Gone had cautioned me, that wasn't sufficient justification for the wholesale violation of common sense.

As if in reward for my display of mature judgment, I immediately spotted a J.C. Penney's and was about to hang a left when to my right I saw a hand-lettered sign propped against a sawhorse next to a Phillips station:

CAR WASH $1
BENEFIT METHODIST CHOIR

I hung the right on impulse, figuring the least I could do was send the Caddy to its sacrifice clean.

The Methodist Choir Car Wash crew seemed to be composed entirely of ruddy-cheeked, blue-eyed, vestal eighteen-year-old girls, all of whom, unfortunately, were bundled against the cold. I wondered who sang bass. They were swabbing away on a '63 Chrysler, with an old

Jimmy pick-up next in line. They were singing "What a Fortress Is My Lord" as they worked. The young lady who bounced over to greet me said it would be fifteen or twenty minutes if I didn't mind waiting. I told her that would be fine as long as they'd keep an eye on the car and hold my place while I trotted across the road.

I was back in fifteen sporting a new red-and-green plaid wool jacket and carrying a bag with insulated longjohns and a pair of pink mohair earmuffs that almost matched my hat. The girls were still rinsing pig shit off the Jimmy, so I used the Phillips men's room to slip into my longjohns. By the time I was properly dressed for the weather, the choir was ready to baptise the Caddy. Before I pulled it up I took my duffle bag from the trunk, using their witness to curb any temptation to hit the cooler for crank.

While they scrubbed off three thousand miles of road grime and sang "Rock of Ages," I sat in the Caddy getting my gear together and cleaning up beer cans and donut wrappers off the floor. I divided my possessions into three categories: immediate getaway essentials, basically the clothes on my back and the balance of my funds, which looked considerably depleted; the second category was walkaway, namely my duffle bag and everything I could fit into it; the third category was breezeaway, and included the first two plus everything else I felt like taking, notably Joshua's sound system and the record collection. I figured the cooler was dispensable, but I'd take the speed. I deserved it.

I finished arranging my gear at about the same time that the Methodist Choir was wringing out their chamois. I powered down the window to pay and learned that the price included vacuuming the inside, and for another 50¢ they'd do the interior glass. Sounded like a deal to me, so I got out and wandered over to a phone booth while four of them, Windex squirting and vacuum humming, swarmed inside.

Just for fun I decided to give Scumball a jingle and tell him the deal was about to go down: time to relax. I dialed the last number he'd given me. On the third ring a recording informed me the number was no longer in service.

The girls were still working so, hoping to hear a friendly voice, I tried John Seasons's number. Nobody home. I hoped he wasn't out drinking, then recalled the remark about a physician first healing himself.

I thought about calling Gladys Nogardam, but decided against it. Let us both be surprised.

The Caddy looked so good I tipped the gospel ladies a five-spot, much to their wowed delight. They wanted to ask me about the car and California and the strange record player in the back seat, but I told them I was running late for a religious duty of my own and departed with a gallant tip of my hat.

Going slow and easy, I rolled out to the crossroads noted on Tommy's map and took the left. Thinking it would be an appropriate touch, I put some music on the box, first the Bopper with "Chantilly Lace," then Ritchie Valens's "Donna." I took a right on Elbert Road, and two miles later a left. Feeling serious, confident, ceremonially formal, I put on Buddy Holly's "Not Fade Away," drumming my fingers on the steering wheel rim as I checked the mailboxes against the map: Altman, Potts, Peligro, and there it was—Nogardam.

A white farmhouse with dark green trim, freshly painted, it was set back from the road and fronted a large fenced field of corn stubble. Next to the house was a garage or some sort of storage building, but no car or other sign of occupancy. I turned down the gravelled drive just as Buddy belted out the last line, "Love that's love not fade away." I clicked it off on the last note and shut down the Caddy. *Wop: doo-wop: doo-wop-bop.* On the beat, right on time; there, ready, and arrived. I took a deep breath and stepped out to ask Mrs. Nogardam's permission—not that I was going to need it, just that it would make things easier. As I walked toward the enclosed porch I found myself repeating her name to myself like a charm: *Nogardam; No-gard-am; No-guard-em.* I certainly hoped so.

She caught me badly off guard. The porch was damn near dark and I'd already given the heavy screendoor frame two strong, confident raps before I realized the front door was open behind the screen and she was already standing there. "Oh," I said in a burst of wit, "I didn't see you."

"Obviously." Her voice was raspy but plenty forceful. In the interior shadows of the darkened house, further obscured by the screen, I could barely make her out. There was enough light to see she was hardly a withered crone—in fact, though indeed stooped with age, she was just a bit shorter than me, which must've put her over six feet in her prime. She was wearing a dark grey dress of some coarse material, her shoulders draped in a black shawl. Her hair, pulled severely back, was the silver color of leached ashes. Her face was deeply wrinkled, and the lines drew inward toward her eyes, eyes the color of dark beer held up to the light, a gold at once clear and obscure, eyes that were watching me unblinking, waiting.

"Mrs. Nogardam?" I inquired tentatively, trying to recover my equilibrium.

"Yes."

I tipped my hat, hoping to make it look boyishly charming.

"That's a ridiculous hat," she declared, her voice like a file hitting a nail.

"Yes, ma'am," I said benignly, buying time while frantically considering an angle of approach. That she wasn't going to invite me in for a glass of warm milk and a plate of cookies was plain, nor would she likely yield to stuttering good intentions and scuff-toed boyish charm. Her unflinching gaze made up my mind. I touched my hat brim again, a gesture I hoped looked absently wounded, and said, "Sure it's ridiculous, but that's altogether appropriate to the rather strange journey that brings me to your door. I call it 'strange,' but it has also become urgent and compelling, important enough that I would call it 'essential,' at least to me, and a journey that's impossible to complete without your kind permission, Mrs. Nogardam."

"Whistles and flutes," she said.

"No ma'am," I assured her, "even worse: I'm going to tell you the truth."

That got her interest. She cocked her head slightly and folded her arms across her bosom. Encouraged by her attention, I laid it on her, the whole truth and nothing but, the condensed version, about ten minutes straight as she listened without comment, shift of weight, change of expression, or any indication of judgment. Told her how I came to have the car; quoted Harriet's letter; explained Eddie, Kacy, Big

Red, John, Scumball; the Big Bopper, Buddy Holly, and Ritchie Valens, and their music; mentioned Joshua, Double-Gone, Donna, and the rest. I told her as directly and forcefully as I could and, considering the duress of necessity, did an amazing job, damn near eloquent. I finished by telling her exactly what I wanted to do—to let it all roar upwards in an offering to the ghosts, the living spirits, the enduring possibilities of friendship, communion, and love. I concluded with a flourish: "It is all grandly romantic, yes; ridiculous, of course; surely melodramatic; indubitably flawed; rightfully suspect—but it is as real to me as hunger and thirst, as crucial as food and water. I've told you my truth, such as it is. I've done everything I have the wit and spirit to do. This is the end of my journey. Now it's up to you, Mrs. Nogardam. Please permit me to complete it."

She uncrossed her arms. "You're a fool," she said flatly.

"Yes ma'am, I believe I've conceded that point."

"I'm ninety-seven years old."

I didn't see the relevance of that, but murmured politely, "People in town said you were over a hundred."

"People in town talk too much for people who have little to say. In that they're like you, Mr. Gastin."

"Be that as it may, Mrs. Nogardam," I said, trying to keep a nasty edge from my tone, "what do *you* say?"

"I already said it: you're a fool. And one of the few blessings of my age is that I don't have to suffer fools—either gladly or at all."

I felt like tearing down the screendoor and strangling the old witch, but instead took a deep, shuddering lungful of air. "Then don't. Just tell me yes or no."

"That's why you're a fool," she snapped. "You want to be told. You think you've earned the right simply because you have an idea that you've allowed to bloat into a need. Because you're paralyzed with confusion. Because you've driven a few thousand miles on drugs and good intentions and a fool's hope. Phooeey. Does believing you're in love make you capable of love? Are you a priest simply because you're willing to perform the sacrifice? What rights have you *earned* in these matters? Mr. Gastin, there's no permission I can give you; only folly I can prevent. If you want to make this grand offering of yours, this homage you've concocted as some secret proof of your worthiness, this testament to a faith you so obviously suspect, don't saddle *me* with the responsibility of judgment. It isn't a question of my yes or no."

"You mean it's up to me?" I didn't follow at all. She was full of judgments, it seemed to me.

"Of course it's up to you, since you won't accept anything other than certainty. Very well, then: if you can go out in that field and find exactly where that plane crashed, you'll have earned the right to deliver your gift, as you call it; and you'll not only have my permission to set it ablaze or any other fool thing you choose, but I'll gladly come out and dance around the fire with you, and pay to have the remains hauled away. But if you *can't* discover the precise point of impact, you must give me your word that you'll go on your way without bothering me further."

"With due respect, Mrs. Nogardam, I've come a long way, I'm very tired, and I'm not in the mood for proofs of my worthiness, or yours."

"Then leave."

"The fact that it's your property by purchase doesn't grant you the privileges of the heart. People own a lot of things that don't belong to them."

In the dim light I saw her bony fingers flutter at her throat. "Well, dear me. I must say, Mr. Gastin, that that's pretty high-falutin' from someone whose property is literally theft, whose gift is stolen. But you *are* right, and I do agree. The fact of it is that I walked out in that field and felt exactly where those young men died. *Felt it,* do you understand? I am able or allowed to do so. And *that,* not ownership, is my claim to privilege. If you can do the same, you'll have as much right in the matter as I do. But any shenanigans or tomfoolery, and I'll stop you."

"You will?" I wasn't challenging her, merely curious about the means.

"I'll certainly try. And if *I* can't, there's neighbors or the sheriff."

I softened my tone and played the ace she'd dealt me: "I told you the truth because I want to do this without deception on my part or objection on yours. I didn't have to tell you the car was stolen; I could've said it was mine, or a friend's, or thousands of other lies. But I want this to be *right*. That's why it's a point of honor with me to tell you I *already* know where the plane crashed." I took Tommy's map from my jacket pocket and unfolded it, spreading it flat against the screen for her to look at. "There it is."

Her attention locked on the map. After a minute of hard scrutiny, she stabbed with a crooked finger and asked, "Here? The *X?*"

"Yes, ma'am. The man who drew that map for me saw the wreckage before it was cleared, and came back many times afterwards."

"The map's wrong."

I hadn't even considered that possibility and was momentarily confounded. "Well, now," I began with feigned reluctance, "*you* say it's wrong. *He* claims it's right. He was *here* and you *weren't*. You say you *felt* it. He *saw* it. It seems awfully relative to—"

"If you want to discuss philosophy," she bluntly interrupted, "I suggest you try the university—they've made an institution out of mistaking the map for the journey."

"I'm not trying to be offensive, Mrs. Nogardam. All I'm saying is you *could* be wrong. That's all. That it *is* possible you're mistaken."

"Then go look for yourself. You have till dark. No tricks." She shut the door.

The door was white, and shutting it had the bizarre effect of making the porch seem brighter. I stared at it, all at once pissed off, crushed, set to explode, dejected, gutted, wrecked, enraged, and lost. I headed back to the Caddy in a dazed stomp, mumbling aloud, "Why, why, why, why, why, why did it have to be some batshit old lady culled from the geriatric ward, some vestal guardian of corn stubble? *Fuck her*, goddamn it anyway . . . just get in the Caddy and crank it up till the head glows and turn it loose right through the motherfucking fence out into the field and grab your shit and touch it off and run like hell . . ." mumble grumble till I was standing next to the Caddy. The air seemed to have thickened. I gazed out into the field toward the general area of the *X* on Tommy's map. " 'Go look for yourself.' What the holy shit does she *think* I've been doing?" I opened the Caddy's door, slid in, and slammed it behind me.

As the sound of the slamming door carried across the harvested field, as if precipitated by the sonic disturbance big fat flakes of snow began to fall. Just what I needed. Was it meant to cover the clues I was supposed to seek, or was it supposed to cloak my getaway? Or was it a shroud to conveniently cover that old witch's body should I follow my deepest impulse and beat her to death with a ball peen hammer? Did it in fact signify anything other than what it was? It was snowing.

I was getting all wound up for another bout of metaphysical babble. The snow was swirling thick, silent, peaceful. I leaned forward, my chin resting on my hands on the wheel, and gradually relaxed as I watched snow swaddle the field; mound on the fenceposts; settle then melt on the Caddy's hood, still warm from engine heat; stick to the windshield for a heartbeat, the intricate crystals dissolving into slow rivulets sliding down. Within fifteen minutes, about the time the snowflakes began sticking on the cooled windshield to obliterate my view, a weary calm came over me. I decided to try it her way first, maybe I'd learn something. I zipped my jacket all the way up and slapped on my new earmuffs.

I must've spent a couple of hours in that field searching for physical evidence that was perhaps being obliterated as I sought it, and for some sort of metaphysical evidence that I wasn't sure I'd recognize even if I were capable of sensing it. Wild, dense, relentless, the snow fell, cutting visibility to the length of a stride. I tried to approach the task methodically, crossing back and forth between the east-west fences, trying to maintain roughly parallel lines, but when the tracks of your last pass are buried before you can start back, when you can't see the fences till you twang into them, when you're essentially following your frozen face, that method is doomed. I had no idea whether I was constructing a crisp, evenly proportioned grid or merely lurching back and forth in the same groove. But I *did know* that I was rapidly losing feeling in my extremities in absolute direct proportion to the feeling of immense futility swelling in my heart. By the time I floundered back to the Caddy I couldn't even feel the cold anymore, just a powerful desire to lie down on the front seat and sleep. Maybe even die. It was all the same.

But first I had to get into the car, and to get the door open took a good jerk, and then another to free my bare hand from the frozen handle. It was almost as cold inside the Caddy as in that forsaken field. After considerable crude fumbling with the key, the Caddy turned over torpidly, then caught. I used my elbow to turn the heater up to cook and spread my hands in front of the vent.

My fingers resembled some mad confectioner's display of blueberry popsicles. As they thawed toward tingling, I thought about energy and its wondrous, manifold, interpenetrating forms: thermal, kinetic, moral, hydraulic, metabolic, all of it. The energy required to warm you, maintain you, move you. Ergs—that basic grunt unit—in waves, calorie, current: x ergs required for each step on the journey, each turn of the wheels, each prayer uttered, answered, acted upon. The energy captured, transformed, released. The energy just to drive the welter of transactions. This was a melancholy contemplation, because while the world plainly vibrated with energy, personally I was just about out, the flesh sorely overdrawn and the soul about to be foreclosed. What remained to me as possible energy, the power I would need to act on the intractable Mrs. Nogardam and answer her psychic pop quiz, was energy that I, with sad realism, understood was *false:* money, amphetamines, and madness. But I'd said I'd give it everything I had.

Once my fingers were again semifunctional, the tips alive with a burning ache, I dug out my bankroll and counted out $2000 in a hundred $20 bills. I folded and wadded it in my jacket pocket, flexed my fingers a few times, and headed back to Mrs. Nogardam's lair to talk business. I left the Caddy running in case the negotiations dragged on; I didn't want to come home to a cold house. Besides, I had plenty of gas and nowhere left to go.

She'd seen me coming and had the door open, her gold eyes boring into me through the screen, only this time I saw her, too, and didn't knock. Instead, the hand I raised contained $2000. Fanning the bills like a deck of cards, I pressed them against the screen for her authentication. "What you see, ma'am, is what you get. That's two grand, a considerable dent in my cash assets—leaves me enough for a half-dozen grilled cheese sandwiches and a Greyhound ticket home. And it's all yours, right now, *if* you let me honor the dead." I tapped the money lightly against the screen. "So what do you say we cut the horseshit here and both make ourselves happy?"

"You can't buy it," she said, her voice flat as Iowa. The door closed.

I kicked the aluminum-framed bottom of the screendoor, screaming in frustration, "Be reasonable, you old cunt!"

The door flew back open. "You mind your foul mouth, Mr. Gastin, or your time will be up right now. Do you understand?"

The fire in her eyes had the paradoxical effect of forming ice in my scrotum. I flapped the money weakly, then tucked my hand into my jacket pocket as I nodded my meek understanding.

She continued, "I made the conditions clear. It is almost three o'clock. By five it's dark."

"But ma'am," I pleaded, "it's a snow storm out there."

Her eyes didn't leave me. "So it is." The door closed.

I trudged back to the Caddy through snow up to midcalf, though it seemed to have slackened a bit. Before getting back in my snow-bound landrocket I scraped the crust off the windshield with my coat sleeve. Softened by the heat from inside, it wiped right off.

I leaned back behind the wheel, a clear view through the windshield now, and watched the snow fall like cold confetti on my stalled parade. I felt utterly, dismally deflated. To try and buy it had been stupid. I closed my eyes and tried to concentrate on the options, but either my concentration was shot or there weren't many options. I could leave, try to find Tommy, and bring him back with me, though he'd probably come on-shift at 6:00 and was gone for the day. Besides, I'd have to convince him to drive out and tangle assholes with Granny, and there was no guarantee the old hag would acknowledge Tommy's memory of the crash. Nope, I decided, it was pretty much down to satisfying her or running her over, and I didn't have the energy for either job.

Well, not *on* me. The trunk, however, wasn't that far away. After all, it had taken me this far, and I sure didn't seem to be getting anywhere without the help. I would take three—no more—to freshen up. I promised myself that if I took them, I'd try her way one more time before resorting to mine. I reached down and turned off the engine and was withdrawing the key when I noticed that in the course of my brief reverie it had stopped snowing. The sky was still leaden, but the scene to my eye was silent, pristine, clear. Looked like a sign.

When I opened the cooler in the trunk and seized the bottle of crank like an osprey nailing a fish, I perceived a small problem. Instead of a bottle of small, neatly cross-hatched white tablets, I had a bottle about a quarter full of a pale white liquid: I hadn't screwed the lid down tight and water from the cooler had trickled in, dissolving the tablets into a thin slurry. Well, as long as only the form and not the substance had been altered, I'd merely have to make a careful guess at the proper dosage. Recalling from high-school chemistry that alcohol lowered the freezing point, I fished a six-pack out of the cooler while I was at it, and then closed the trunk.

I ended up having a wonderful wake in the front seat: three sips of speed, four beers, and a solid hour of Golden Oldies turned up so loud they blew the snow off the Caddy and loosened the siding on Granny Nogardam's house. I listened to everything I had of the Bopper, Buddy, and Ritchie, hoping the sound of their music would stir their lingering spirits to help me.

A love for real not fade away!!!

"Not!" I screamed. "Not! *Not!*" I hoped Granny was listening.

I stumbled from the Caddy and headed out to the field in the long-shadowed dusk. I hadn't left myself much time. As I went over the fence I yelled, "Bopper, my man! Buddy Holly! Ritchie! Talk to me. Tell me where to deliver this load of a gift. Got love and prayers for you. Got 'em from Harriet. Got 'em from Donna, Ritchie—she's sending her best. She's sort of fucked-up in Arizona right now, but she's trying, man. Everybody's trying, you guys hear me? Double-Gone, Joshua, Kacy, John—they all send their love. The real kind that doesn't fade away. So even if it doesn't matter to you guys now, don't mean shit to your gone spirits, it matters to me, to us. So talk to me. Guide me. Tell me where you want this monument to love and music burned, where you want the dark lit up."

The snow started falling again, lightly, a few drifting flakes. No voices answered, inside or out, but I felt a faint tug of direction and began walking, starting around the fence-line and then spiraling inward, closing as the snow fell faster, thicker, until I could hardly see my own feet, till I felt like I was vanishing, and then my left foot came down on something solid. I knelt and searched with both hands in the snow until I touched it, slick and cold, and lifted it close to my face for a look. I bit back a scream when I realized it was a bone; then laughed with crazy relief when I recognized it as an antler, a deer's shed horn, a thick main beam forked into two long tines, weathered a faint moss-green, nicked here and there with sharp, double-incised grooves where rodents had chewed it for minerals. I couldn't stop laughing. "Great. Just what I needed. A fucking deer horn. Don't you guys understand I already got enough pieces for the puzzle? Probably got more fucking pieces than there *is* puzzle. Come on, now: help me out, don't mess me around." I brandished the horn to emphasize my point. It slipped out of my numb hand, burying itself base down in the snow, tines spread upright like the forks of a river joining to plunge straight down into the earth. And there it was, by sheer accident, right in front of my face: a divining rod, a witcher's forked stick, a wand to dowse the spot where their ghosts broke free of their broken bodies. The key, or at least a tool to pick the lock.

With snow mounding on my flamingo hat, piling across the plaid shoulders of my jacket, my hands, feet, and face frozen beyond feeling, I worked the field with the bone wand held steadily poised in front of me, my whole being condensed to the receptive tip, waiting for its plunge. I spiraled slowly out from the center of the field, wired to the slightest stirring, faintest sense, a pulse, a trembling, anything. And I didn't feel the slightest quiver of response—nothing; zilch; zero. It was solid dark when I gave up.

The porchlight was the only sign of life at the house. I expected her to be waiting behind the screen, but the door was closed. I knocked. Coming back defeated across the field, I'd tried to compose a new plea, but it no longer seemed to matter. When she opened the door I didn't even look up.

"Well?" she demanded, friendly as ever.

I felt the tears coming and, afraid my voice would crack, shook my head without speaking.

"You'd better go now," she said, and for the first time, I sensed a hint of sympathy in her voice.

Not much, but it encouraged me to give it a try. "I'd guess somewhere near the center of the field. It's the only place I felt anything. I found a deer horn there, close to where the X is on the map. But you already said that was wrong."

"It is."

"You couldn't be mistaken?"

"It's unlikely."

"Would you tell me where the spot is?"

"No. You agreed to the conditions. You didn't fulfill them. Now kindly leave."

"I want to come back tomorrow and try again."

She didn't answer or give any indication she'd heard.

I'd tried everything except begging, so I figured I'd give that a shot: "Please, Mrs. Nogardam. *Please?*"

"I told you *no*, Mr. Gastin. Now I want you to leave."

I slammed my fist against the screendoor frame, jolting it open for an instant before the spring whipped it shut again. *"Damn* your cold ass," I wept. "How can you possibly judge what I'm all about, what this means to me, how much . . ." but I stopped because she hadn't even flinched, not a blink, a start, a step back, nothing. Just watching me with those dark gold eyes.

I wiped at the tears with my sleeve, some clinging snow from my stingy-brim plopping to the porch floor. "Why can't I make you see how much this matters? And not just to me, either. Donna, Joshua, Double-Gone, my friends in San Francisco—what do I tell *them?*"

"Tell them you failed. Tell them pity is a polite form of loathing. Tell them I didn't pity you."

"What fucking *right*—" I started to rage but she suddenly lifted an arm and pointed past me into the darkness. I stopped cold.

"Mr. Gastin, if you want to work off your anger and confusion there's a snow shovel leaning against the back of the porch. You'll need it to clear a path to get out. Good night." She shut the door.

I picked up the shovel on my way back to the Eldorado. I started the car to let it warm up, took a little gulp of speed to lubricate my muscles, then started shoveling. There was about 200 feet of driveway out to the main road and I dug right in, not a thought in my raving mind except moving snow, and without thought there was no confusion, just the scrape of shovel against the gravel roadway, the grunt of breath as I lifted, pitched, and took another bite. In about twenty minutes I finished, walked back down the cleared drive, and replaced the shovel, figuring that I was, if nothing else, a success as a human snowplow.

Back across the drifted yard, I used my forearm to wipe snow from the corners of the windshield, then wiped the same forearm across my sweaty face. I was so warm, in fact, that when I slipped behind the wheel, I had to turn down the heater. I took another gritty swig of speed to replace lost fluids, turned on the wipers to clear the slush from the windshield, clicked the lights to highbeams, dropped it into reverse, and came off the clutch. The drive wheels spun for a second, then gripped. Aiming between the bullet taillights, staying light and steady on the gas, I backed out to the road.

When I felt the rear wheels on the pavement I stopped, slammed it into low, and screaming "Oh *baaay-beeee,* you *know* what I *like!*" I stood on the gas. There was a shuddering second before the rubber fastened the power to the road and then I was smoking back down the driveway like a silver bullet, a dead bead on the fence, hoping I'd have enough speed to crash through into the field.

I never found out. Just as I nailed it into second and felt the Caddy leap forward in a spray of gravel and snow, a blast of flame exploded from near the porch and the Caddy's right front end collapsed, the momentum snapping the rear end around so hard I felt it wanting to flip, but I squared it away as best I could and whipped around through a full 360°, showering snow. Then, I cut the lights and engine and bailed out, still uncertain what had happened.

Mrs. Nogardam was standing in front of me in a white parka, hood drawn tight about her face, the shotgun in her hands pointed at my throat. "I asked you to leave," she said with a mean, even patience.

"Ma'am, that's what I was doing." I couldn't keep the pounding of my heart out of my voice.

"No, you were just being foolish."

"I stand corrected," I said, beginning to relax—she wasn't going to shoot. "And it looks like I might be standing here corrected for a while longer, because I think you just shot my way out. Where were you aiming?"

"Where I hit: the right-front tire." She lowered the gun slightly. "If you've got a spare, change it. If not, it looks like you'll have to use some of that money on a tow truck."

The possibility of that irony made me reckless.

"Ma'am," I asked mildly, "is that by any chance a Remington twenty-gauge pump?"

"It is."

"I had one just like it when I was a kid growing up in Florida. Used it on quail. You use yours on your husbands?"

Reckless, but it got to her: her eyes flashed and the gun barrel came back up to lock on my throat. Her voice was tight. "I find it difficult to believe you grew up, Mr. Gastin. I find about as much evidence for your maturity as the police found for my involvement in my husbands' disappearances. None. Because there was none."

"You realize, of course," I said softly, "you'll have to kill me. I'm not giving up. This is something I *have* to do."

"No you don't," she said. "But you probably will. That does not mean you're going to do it here. I was calling the sheriff about the time you were putting the shovel back. I told him I thought there was a prowler. I doubt if he'll hurry—I'm not popular with local law enforcement—but he should make it in twenty minutes or so, and then you can discuss rights and wrongs with him. Or you can hurry and change your tire. Or you can try to take this gun away. I won't kill you—believe me or not, I've never killed anything in my life. But you might live the rest of yours without a knee, or the ability to reproduce."

"I was wrong," I told her. "You didn't shoot your husbands—you froze 'em to death. Or froze 'em out so bad they were glad to vanish."

Though she didn't reply, her shoulders seemed to slump. I think I could've gotten to her in half an hour, but I didn't have the time. If she was bluffing about the sheriff, she was bluffing with the best hand. "I have a spare in the trunk," I told her, hoping a new tire was all I'd need.

She held the shotgun on me as I fumbled the spare tire and tools from the trunk, and kept it on me till I was down on my belly digging out a place for the jack. While I can usually change a tire in five minutes on dry ground, I didn't know how long it would take in the snow, so I ignored her to concentrate on my work. There was no reason to slow things down with more nasty exchanges. We were done talking. I'd be back. She had to sleep sometime.

I set the jack solid under the axle and then crawled out to spin off the lug nuts. I glanced in her direction to see how close I was covered, and for a strange, splintering instant I thought she'd disappeared. But she was there, all right, sitting cross-legged in the snow, gun cradled across her left arm, her head bowed against the snowfall—a few flakes blowing from the storm's edge, a handful of stars glittering where the sky had cleared—and she looked for all the world like an old buffalo hunter hunkered down to wait out the weather.

I went back to work. The tire was shredded. There were pellet dents in the hubcap and a few concave dings in the fender, bare steel glinting through the chipped white paint and primer. I slipped the lug wrench over the first nut and twisted, leaning into it. The nut broke loose with a tiny shriek. I spun it off and dropped it clattering into the hubcap.

The sound had barely faded before she began to speak. I was stunned by the change in her voice, that hard edge turned to a delicate keening. "I loved them all, you know. Kenneth was the first. We were young, two years married. He had a lot of debts, a lot of doubts about himself, and we had some troubles—but when it was there for us, it was really there. I thought he'd just walked away from it. Snapped one moment and just kept going. Men can do that. I never tried to look for him. I was six months pregnant and somehow believed the baby would bring him back. The baby was stillborn. The minister and I were the only ones at the funeral, and the minister was there because he got paid. I used to visit the grave every day, hoping I'd find Kenneth waiting. I ' never did.

"Joe, my second husband, disappeared out rounding up strays on the Arizona-Mexico border. The sheriff thought he might have been killed by drug smugglers. Stumbled on them by mistake and tried to stop them. Joe would have: he was big and rough, not a drop of sentiment in him, but he was so decent he was almost fragile. I *knew* he hadn't just kept riding.

"I remember pacing in the ranch house as it got later and later. Praying on the flagstone floor that he was all right. Beating on it with my fists.

"I looked for Joe. Months after the posse had given up I was still out there every day. People said I was crazy, hysterical, a ghost-chaser. I looked in every baranca, arroyo, draw, and canyon, behind every tree and boulder for thirty miles. I never found a trace. But after a while out there alone in the mountains, looking so hard, so devoutly, I got so I could ride up a gully and *feel* the presence of death—tendrils, subtle odors, a particular stillness—and after three years of looking I could feel death where only a hair remained, or a fleck of dried blood, and soon I could feel it when there was nothing at all. You called me a hard woman; well, it's a hard knowledge."

"Ma'am—" I started to defend myself, but she sliced right through it, the old flint in her voice, "You listen while you change that tire. If you want to talk, talk to the sheriff."

That shut me up. I spun off another lug nut as she continued. "I might still be riding that border if Duster hadn't come along. His wife had died of cancer six months before and he was traveling around hunting and fishing, trying to let go. He stopped by the ranch house asking for permission to hunt doves down by the pond. We talked a bit, and the next day he came to hunt again and asked me out to dinner. I warned him about my husbands disappearing but he took it the same way he took my heart, with a kind of crazy, carefree seriousness. Duster was a rare man. He knew who he was, so he loved you for who *you* were, not something he wanted you to be.

"Twenty-one years Duster and I were together, most of them around here. And one day he went out pheasant hunting over at the Lindstroms' place and disappeared. I can't tell you how hard that was. The police kept after me for months. I couldn't blame them. But what could I tell them? I didn't know what to tell myself. But I made up my mind I'd find Duster, and when the hullabaloo died down I started looking. I looked every night for seven years. Every single night.

"You see, Mr. Gastin, that's how I learned to sense the dead, to feel the earth reveal the spirits it's claimed, to sense the presence, read the signs. I learned it by looking for those dearly lost to me."

I had the spare on the axle and was finishing the lug nuts. "Did you find him," I asked.

"Mr. Gastin, I'm sorry I have to be so stern with you. You *are* foolish, yet I admire your spunk."

"Then give me another chance at it when it's not snowing. You had years of practice."

"No," she said, "not here."

"Then where?" I asked, cinching down the last lug nut.

"I don't know. You can always try to get back to the beginning, but I'm sure you understand how difficult that is, and dangerous. Take it where you find it—that's my advice."

"I'm not sure I understand," I told her politely, "but that's hardly a new state of affairs." I worked the jack out and stood up. She stood up with me, the gun barrel pointed down at the snow, but she watched closely as I put the blasted tire and the tools back in the trunk, then back around and into the car. As I closed the door she stepped around to the driver's side. When the gears meshed, as simple and smooth as that I understood what she was guarding in the field. I powered down the window. "Maybe I haven't earned the right to deliver the gift," I said, "but I do think I've earned the right to ask you what you're protecting here. I just can't believe it's the ghosts of three rock musicians."

"I'm protecting my ignorance," she said.

That wasn't what I'd expected. "I thought ignorance was my affliction."

"You're hardly alone."

"What is it you don't understand?"

Her head turned slightly to gaze out across the field. "I told you I looked for the spot where Duster vanished, looked for seven years, and this is where I found him. I was sure of it. In the center, near where you found the antler. Of course, the antler wasn't there then. This place is about nine miles from the Lindstroms', in the opposite direction from where we lived at the time, but the feeling was powerful and clear. I thought maybe he'd been murdered and his body buried here." She closed her eyes, then immediately opened them. "The truth is, I *hoped* he'd been murdered . . . I wanted a *reason*, you see—"

"I see," I said. "I *thought* it was your husband you were protecting. Now it makes sense."

"Don't be so sure," she said sadly. "When I dug down that night, yes, there it was, a human skull. But it was the skull on an *infant*, Mr. Gastin, a baby less than a year old, and it had been there long before my husband or your musicians died. There were no other bones. Just the skull. You could almost hold it in the palm of your hand. So you understand why I couldn't let you drive this car out there and set it on fire? There are forces here beyond my understanding, so I had to insist that you prove yours."

I felt my skull shining in the moonlight. I finally managed to say, "I'm not sure I wanted to know that."

Mrs. Nogardam leaned her hooded head to the open window and gave me a quick, dry smile. "Neither did I. It only added to the confusion. But if we don't want to know, why do we seek?" She smiled again, almost girlishly, then stepped back from the car, the shotgun swinging up level with the grille to remind me to act intelligently.

I backed out to the paved road, swung to the left, and got on it as fast as the snow allowed. For someone with nowhere to go I sure found myself in a hurry to get there, although on reflection there was a place I wanted with an overwhelming desire to reach, and that was *far away* from all the madness, the ghost salesman and ghost guardian and the moonlit skulls of children and a gift that didn't seem to want delivery— but most of all I wanted away from my continual inability to make sense out of any of it, and my tumorous fear that there was no sense to make.

When I met a sheriff's car at the first crossroads—had she actually called, or was this a routine patrol?—I came very close to turning myself in. I stifled a powerful impulse to put a broadslide block on his cruiser and jump out jabbering, "Officer, this Caddy's so hot the paint's runny and that bottle of white stuff on the front seat is pure Hong Kong heroin I sell to schoolchildren and the papers in the glovebox still have wet ink and the baby's corpse in the trunk is missing its head and my goodness is that an open container in my hand, you child-molesting Nazi cocksucker. Oh, pretty please: lock me up! Yes! I *need* custody."

But I didn't. We eased past each other on the snow-slick road. I watched his taillights in the rearview mirror as they disappeared into where I'd been, the point from which I was unraveling. Where next, and why? *Drive*, I said to myself, *for Christsake find out where you're going.* Yet even that pure injunction was stymied: because of the snow, the roads were so treacherous I had to doodle when I wanted to jam. I couldn't even get it up past the posted till I hit I35, freshly plowed and sanded. I took it south, back toward Des Moines, mainly because there were more stars in that direction.

I don't want to give the impression I was flying apart. In fact, I was fairly stable, paralyzed as I was by the triangulated suck of stark confusion, dread, and depression. It was just as Gladys Nogardam had so coldly put it: I'd failed. If I was smart, I told myself, I'd simply shoulder my duffle bag and walk away from the whole fucked-up mess. Quit while I was only behind. I'd entered that state of mind where flight is spurred by the vulnerable belief and poignant hope that what's chasing you is worse than what's waiting ahead. But if I wasn't smart enough to cut my losses, at least I was bright enough to stop and catch my breath.

After knowing Joshua Springfield, how could I possibly have resisted the Raven's Haven Motel on the north edge of Des Moines? The office reeked of the liver-and-onions frying in the manager's adjacent apartment. On a small table opposite the business counter was a stuffed, ratty-feathered raven mounted on a jack-o-lantern. The manager kept eyeing me nervously as I signed in, then examined the registration card closely as I dug in my pocket for money.

"Ah, under occupation here, Dr. Gass . . . what sort of pharmaceutical testing do you do?"

"Freelance," I explained. "But right now I'm working for the Feds. Some of them damn beatniks are putting ground-up marijuana in Saint Joseph's Baby Aspirin. Found a batch up in Fargo this morning. Company says it was a split shipment, Fargo and Des Moines, so I'm down here to check it out. I'll try to run it down in the morning. Haven't slept in two days, that's why I'd appreciate it if I wasn't disturbed. I get disturbed easily. And whatever you do, don't tell anybody—no need to start a panic. They might not even be on the shelves yet. But just between you and me, don't give your kids Saint Joseph's."

"I thought marijuana was green. That should make them easy to spot."

"It *is* green, pal, in its natural state—and I'm glad to see an alert citizen—but they're bleaching it with mescaline tritripinate."

"Somebody ought to shoot the lousy bastards," he said with disgust.

"Tell you what: we break the case, I'll give you the names of the jerks as soon as I get them. Maybe try to work something out with the Feds to take their time, know what I mean? You can close the case before the shithooks even have a *chance* to call their fancy New York lawyers. You got a card with a number where I can reach you on short notice? You should be ready to move on it in a hurry."

He gave me his card along with the room key, though he didn't seem particularly eager to give me either.

"Citizen involvement," I told him as I headed for the door, "that's what separates the sheep from the goats." I turned around at the door. "Another thing: you on city water?"

"Yes," he said uncertainly.

"A word to the wise: get bottled. A retarded baboon could dump a vial of chemicals in the water supply any time he took the notion. Lysergic acid, hashish extract, opium crystals—a pound of any of that shit in the water supply could take out Des Moines for a week. You have a cup of coffee one morning and ten minutes later you're up on the roof here trying to plug your dick into the neon sign. Don't think I'm kidding."

"Bottled water," he repeated.

"You got it. In this day and age, you can't be too sure. Hard to be sure at all, in fact."

I fetched my duffle, a six-pack, and the bottle of crank from the trunk and then started looking for #14. I wondered about my perverse delight in jacking around the Harveys and Bubbas and Walter Mittys of the world. To beat up on the defenseless didn't show much character, nor much heart. No wonder I failed or fucked-up at every opportunity.

But the self-flagellation, meant to raise the welts of self-pity, stopped the moment I stepped into my room—not that it was breathtakingly spacious or tastefully appointed. Standard issue down to the smoke-yellowed floral wallpaper, a linty-green Sear's close-out carpet, Magnavox fifteen-inch black-and-white T.V. bolted to the desk, and a lumpy double bed that had probably known more sexual joy and despair in a month than I had in twenty years—but #14 offered the welcome sanctuary of transient neutrality, space without claims.

I locked and bolted the door, set my bag on the luggage rack, opened a beer, and moseyed into the bathroom hoping to find a spacious tub. The tub wasn't luxurious, but it was adequate. I wiggled the bead-chained plug in tight and opened the hot water all the way. As the steam curled, I stripped off my grungy clothes and pawed through my duffle looking for something I hadn't worn recently. Making a mental note to do laundry in the morning, I grinned at my display of confidence. But indeed, this was the trick—to carry on as if everything was normal. I needed rest, especially rest from thinking, but had to make some decisions about what to do now that I'd failed the delivery and lost my way.

In the time it took me to shut off the hot water, I decided I believed Gladys Nogardam or else was scared shitless of her, either of which was sufficient reason not to attempt a midnight run on the crash site, a notion I hadn't realized I was still seriously considering. Nope, I was in over my head with Mrs. Nogardam. But the point she'd made about returning to the beginning made more and more sense. In the spiritual inflation of enlarging the gesture—abetted by the baseless paranoia inspired by Double-Gone that Scumball's goons might be awaiting me—I'd lost my original purpose and therefore my way, the simple, uncomplicated point of delivering it to the Bopper's grave and then quietly slipping away.

According to the information I'd found at the Houston Public Library, the Bopper, as I'd assumed, was buried in Beaumont. The obvious move was to drive down and make delivery, and that's what I decided I'd do after a good night's sleep. While this amounted to a two thousand-mile detour, I could chalk it up as a learning experience. That was the ticket: get up early and back on track, rested, refreshed, and wiser. And no picking up any hitchhikers along the way or talking to anyone who might possibly deflect me from that simple task. I was too suggestible, too vulnerable to my own doubts. And another decision: if I didn't pull it off this time, I'd just forget it and walk away. Abandon the journey as a fair try that failed, a victim of my own fuck-ups and fate. Sad, but no cause for shame.

I went in to check the bathwater and jerked my hand right back out—I wanted to soak myself, not cook lobsters. I was reaching for the cold water handle when it crossed my mind that I didn't know which Beaumont cemetery had won the Bopper's bones. It was about 8:00 and I was fairly sure Texas and Iowa were in the same time zone. With any luck the Beaumont Library was still open.

If the bathwater had been 20° cooler, I wouldn't have phoned the library before it closed and my story might've ended up in a different place altogether. The temperature of water—such a simple thing. Everything intimately and ultimately involved, millions of convoluted contingencies, none of them meaningless, any one potentially critical, and potential itself subject to the infinite dimensional intersections of time, space, and luck. Obviously a mind is not enough.

I sat my bare ass down on the desk chair, put the beer within easy reach, then dialed information through the motel office. The number in Beaumont was busy, so I asked the operator to try Houston. The call went through smoothly, answered by a woman on the second ring: "Houston Public Library, may I help you?"

"Could I have the Reference Desk, please?"

"This is the Reference Desk."

I put some honey in my tone. "Well now, ma'am. I have an unusual request, but so far in my research I've found that the world would get pig-ignorant mighty quick if it wasn't for the patience and dedication of you librarians, so I'll just blunder ahead here and trust you to sort it out. What I'm doing is some research on early rock-and-roll musicians and I'm having trouble with some background on a Beaumont musician known as the Big Bopper. That was his stage name; his given name was Richardson, J. P., Jiles Perry. Now the thing—"

"I bet y'all want to know where he's buried."

That snapped me to attention. "Now, *how* did *you* know *that?* You librarians telepathic?"

"No sir, y'all just the *third* person today wanted to know where this Bopper's buried, and a man in yesterday wanted the same information. That Bopper's sure been popular around here the last few days."

"Myself, I'm doing an article for *Life* magazine. I don't know if these other folks are reporters, scholars, or just interested citizens."

"I don't know either. They didn't say. But I can tell without going to the clippings that Mr. Richardson died in a plane crash on February the third, 1959, up around Mason City—that's in Iowa—and he's buried over in Beaumont at Forest Lawn. Is that what y'all wanted?"

As I inched forward on the chair, my bare ass squeaked on the vinyl. I shared the sentiment. "The burial place, yes ma'am, that's what I wanted. I'm not interested in the crash site. Is that what the other researchers are covering, the crash site?"

"Truth be told," she lowered her voice confidentially, "the two men that were here today seemed more interested in the man that was in yesterday than they did in Mr. Richardson. They didn't come right out and say so, but I gather this other fellow, he'd taken some research notes from them? They asked Helen—she works the early shift—what he looked like, what sort of car he was driving, what he wanted, that sort of thing. They talked to Peebles, too—he's the morning custodian."

"Sounds like the usual research rivalry to me. You wouldn't believe how some of these scholars carry on."

"Lee—that's the janitor, Leland Peebles—he didn't think so."

"No?"

"No sir. He said he talked to the young one with the crazy hat yesterday when he first came in—he was wearing this bright pink hat, but I didn't see him. I don't come on until noon. Anyway, Peebles said the young one was either crazy or on drugs, and he thinks the other two are after him for stealing their car or some money."

"I don't see what that has to do with the Big Bopper."

"I don't either, but it must have *something* to do with it—this Mr. Richardson's the one they all asked after."

"Well, I want to thank you for your help with this. It's appreciated, believe me. And you sure got my curiosity going about those other three guys; hope we're not all covering the same ground."

"Glad to help y'all. 'Night, now."

No, I said to myself as I frantically redialed Houston Information for a number for Leland Peebles. *Just help me. I'm the good guy.*

Mr. Peebles recognized my voice before I got seven words into my awkward ploy. "Mister, there's no way I wanna be even *re-mote-ly* involved in this shit. *None* fo' me, thanks jus the same. I don't know you an' I don't know them, but I tell ya what I *do* know, and that's that them men lookin' fo' you is *ex*actly the sort you don' want to be *findin'*. Big and nasty sort, you understand? I got my own burden of griefs, don't need yours *or* theirs. Hullo an' goodbye." He hung up.

"Hold on!" I shouted. When there was only that empty hum in response, I fell apart. Paranoia started playing my brain like a pinball machine, racking up seventeen free games by the time I got the phone back in the cradle. Lights and rollovers were flashing and popping, flares exploding in the darkness, livid yellows and lurid reds. I saw the two goons in the motel office, *right that minute,* showing my picture to our helpful manager. "Yeah, sure, the guy in fourteen, that's him. The one works for the Feds." I saw myself tied to the chair I was sitting on, a guy about twice Bubba's size gagging me with a ping-pong ball and a swatch of wide adhesive tape while the smaller one fished his tools from a black doctor's satchel.

One shoe in my hand, an arm up a pantleg, I was scrambling around for clothes, knocking over the beer on the desk as I thrashed around on hands and knees groping for my other shoe as the cold beer dribbled off the edge of the desk onto the small of my back and down the crack of my ass, my brain screaming *HEMORRHAGE!* when a dry voice spoke to me with neither disgust nor loathing, just calm amusement. "George, not only is the mind not enough, it is evidently too much."

And that voice snapped my panic, pulled the plug. It was me, of course, unless I'd locked someone in the room with me, but the voice seemed to come from outside that elusive entity I generally considered my self. I reached back and gingerly touched the wetness along my ass, then examined my fingers. Beer. I cringed with humiliation: I'd blown apart under pressure like a cheap transmission scattering down the stretch. I wondered abjectly what sort of quivering puddle of shit I'd turn into if Scumball's specialists ever caught up.

I mustered a sort of fatal dignity and went into the bathroom, glad the mirror was so fogged with steam I couldn't see my face. With a towel from the rack I sopped up the beer, then gathered the cleanest clothes I could find and laid them out neatly on the bed. So the bad guys were hot on my trail. Would Zorro fall apart? Shit no. Hopalong Cassidy? Are you kidding? Davy Crockett, John Dillinger, Zapata, Errol Flynn—would those guys be scrabbling around on a motel room floor too panicked by the mere *idea* of the crunch coming to pick up their fucking shoes? Surely you jest. I went back in the bathroom and wrung out the towel in the washbowl, then, facing myself, swabbed at the mirror. No dashing Zorro there, no cool-eyed Dillinger; neither swash nor buckle. Just crank-eyed, lip-quivering, day's growth, sweat-gritty, wrinkle-dicked me. I walked over to the tub, lifted myself in, and sank.

I tried not to think, but it was like trying not to breathe. My first thought, oddly enough, was that I should call Gladys Nogardam and warn her she might expect some bad company. On second thought, I figured I should call the Houston Library and leave a warning for the goons, should they consider heading *her* way. That gave me heart. If a ninety-seven-year-old woman could stand her ground, then so could I. If Joshua Springfield could ride his *Celestial Express* into a sleeping town and challenge the prevailing dreamless version of reality and not even flinch when the shooting started, surely I could dream on. After all, Gladys admired my spunk, or so she said, and they'd shot at me as well as Joshua. And Donna trying to wash the stink of sour milk out of that sweltering trailer and feed the kids—if she could go on, what was stopping me? Besides fear, doubt, and no direction known.

What to do, where to go; the same old boring shit. Go to sleep. Go roaring back to Beaumont right into their teeth and touch it off on the Bopper's grave. Or go to the phone, call a taxi for the airport, book a seat on the next flight to Mexico. Fuck the gift and fly away.

Thinking, thinking, stopping only long enough to add more hot water or crack another beer. By two in the morning I was out of beer, my face was raw from the steam, and my body was beginning to pucker and prune pretty seriously, so I stood up, dripping and shriveled, and watched the water spiral down the drain, a circle sucked through itself, disappearing to wherever it went—pipes, sewer, sewer pond, evaporating back to the air, falling again as rain for the roots—and remembered again Gladys Nogardam saying, "You can always try to get back to the beginning."

I spent the next hour pacing the bedroom naked, trying to figure out some sort of beginning to return to, thinking I had to be desperately lost if I was trying to find a beginning just to begin again, assuming I was capable of distinguishing beginnings from endings, assuming they weren't just illusions.

That's how it was in room 14 of the Raven's Haven Motel in Des Moines, Iowa, at 3:00 in the morning, full of failure, dread, doubt, beer, and speed. Pacing, pacing, pacing. I think it was the monotonous rhythm of walking rather than the monotony of thinking that conjured the echo of the beginning I sought. Big Red Loco taking the bandstand to play "Mercury Falling," shaping his breath into the silence we'd heard together as the stolen car flopped over the edge and fell, fell, fell, vanishing then bursting within the roar of waves breaking on the rocks. The same night the small Beechcraft fireballed into an Iowa cornfield. The first night I held Kacy naked in my arms. That was the beginning I wanted returned. Not to recapture the past but to open the present. Not a *re*birth, you understand, but *this* birth. This life. My bewildered love, my fucked-up music, my shaky faith. But even so, it was a love with hope, a music I could still dance to, and a faith suddenly steadied by the feeling I'd finally got it right, that I knew where I was going: full circle, back to that turn-out above Jenner. A familiar plan to me, maybe even the original one, and it made me laugh. My laugh sounded a little unnerved, oddly wild.

I dressed, packed my gear, left $10 on the dresser for the phone calls that probably saved my ass, and went out and started the Caddy. While it patiently idled, gathering warmth against the predawn freeze, I stowed my duffle and celebrated the new beginning of the end with a sip of speed chased with beer, the first of the last six-pack left in the cooler. Either I'd been lost in concentration or he hadn't yet appeared, but it wasn't till I popped the emergency brake that I noticed my ghost. He was sitting on the passenger's side of the front seat, watching. Our eyes met. "You're crazy, you know," he said.

"I know."

"Well, suit yourself."

"Leave me alone unless you're going to help," I said, but he had already vanished.

I swung the white rocket around in the parking lot, eased out onto the empty street, and eight blocks later found the on-ramp I wanted. The freeway was a little slick, and snow from yesterday's storm was plowed up along the shoulders. I took it easy, getting the feel of the road. When I hit the I-80 junction I stopped for gas. I sat staring at the dinosaur on the Sinclair logo while the yawning attendant topped off the tank. I took I-80 West, headed for the California coast. A big Kenworth rumbled past me as I pulled onto the freeway, and I honked and waved. He tooted back. The road was slushy in spots, but generally good. A green mileage sign read OMAHA 130. I put Bill Haley and the Comets on the box, "Rock Around the Clock," and then put some leather to the pedal, some sole on the go. If anybody was chasing me, they were going to be further behind. I was still eighteen hundred miles out, but I was closing fast.

I made Omaha before 6:00 Central, light just beginning to pale the sky. There was a strong cross-wind from the north, but the road was clear. It looked like straight sailing to the coast. I hoped to reach Jenner before the next dawn and figured that if I gained two hours in time changes and averaged around 80 mph, I could make a few stops and still have time on my side. Things were looking good.

A couple of things, however, were nagging at me. One was the gut-shot spare in the trunk. Or non-spare, since it was worthless. The rubber on the right-front was new, but I've never liked running without some extra on board; I can't stand how dumb you feel when you have a flat. And although I have no statistical proof, personal experience has convinced me you're fifty times more likely to have a flat when you don't have a spare.

Then there was my ghost. Not that he'd returned to ride shotgun or anything alarming, but that he'd made an appearance in the first place. I figured he was a hallucination born of psychic distress and physical exhaustion, and I was certainly no stranger to hallucination. It seemed like only yesterday I'd been waltzing with cactus under the melting desert stars, and it *was* yesterday that I'd seen Kacy in an Oklahoma waitress and got my gonads tenderized. I knew a hallucination when I saw one, and I'd driven truck long enough to know what tired, wired eyes could do with a heat mirage, tricks of light and shadow, semblances suggested by blurred or distant shapes, ghost-images dancing down the optic nerves when an oncoming driver neglected to dim his highbeams and left you half-blind and batting your eyes in his wake, all kinds of wild shit out there in the dark. But I'd never seen my ghost before.

Granted, there's a first time for everything, but it nagged me, like I said, particularly since Lewis Kerr had only the night before supposedly returned my errant ghost. I didn't want to consider the possibility it *was* my ghost, for as nearly as I understood it, ghosts were disembodied spirits of the dead, and I wasn't dead, of that I was certain—although, like a clutch plate with an oil leak, that certainty was beginning to experience some slippage. If ghosts were spirits of the dead and I wasn't dead, maybe it was a preview of coming attractions, a warning to watch myself. Or perhaps—and this struck me as so ludicrous I immediately accepted its possibility—I was being haunted by my own ghost.

It *was* mine. I was convinced of that, although recalling its visit I had to admit I hadn't so much seen it as *felt* it, or maybe I'd seen it *because* I'd felt it so clearly. But ghost, hallucination, mirage, psycho-projection, whatever it was, it was *of me.*

And yet I wasn't alarmed. For one thing, I didn't think it was real, at least not *real* in the sense that little Eddie's blood was real, or Red's music, or Kacy's coiled warmth. And real or not, my ghost hadn't seemed threatening. If anything, it apparently wanted to help—it had pointed out I was crazy more as a reminder than a judgment or warning. Maybe I now was crazy enough to have split in two, which was all right with me; I could use a spare mind.

In Lincoln I stopped at another Sinclair station for a fill-up. I was beginning to think of that green dinosaur as a personal good luck charm. I wanted his pressed oils to power my run to the coast. I told the pump jockey to stock it to the top with gravity's wine. When he looked baffled, I pointed to the dinosaur revolving above us atop the stanchion and explained, "Some of that prime, high-test dinosaur juice from the Meso-zoic crush. Gas." He seemed glad to tear himself away from our conver-sation and get pumping. As I opened the trunk to get out the mangled tire, I cautioned myself that Lincoln, Nebraska, at 6:30 A.M. was not a good place to succumb to an attack of the mad jabbers.

The tire was the shredded mess I remembered, but the rim looked fine. I held it up for the attendant's inspection: "You carry my size?"

"Think so, mister," he said, staring at the blasted casing. "Jesus Christ, what did you *do* to it?"

"Misjudged an old woman's determination."

He shook his head. "Boy, I *guess* so."

Although he did have one in stock, he couldn't—or didn't want to—mount it until the number-two man came on at 8:00 to cover the pumps. He looked alarmed when I volunteered to mount it myself, or to watch the pumps while he did it, and mumbled something about insurance problems. Fuck him, I decided. The right-front looked plenty good to get me to Grand Island; in fact the rubber was good enough all the way around to get me to Alaska if I wanted to risk it.

Nebraska is a flat state—the roads so straight they have to put rumble-strips on them to keep you from going into highway trance—but it's great terrain for making time, and I kept it up in the high 90's as

I blew down the pike. The traffic was light, and the hard cross-wind let up not far out of Lincoln.

It was beginning to look like a classic autumn day, crisp and full of color, when I hit Grand Island one hundred fifty miles and ninety minutes later. I'd barely entered the city limits when I saw a sign that read AL HAYLOCK'S TIRE N' TUNE, and damned if the sign didn't feature a picture of a rubber tree. Yes sir, that's the kind of advertising to attract a man looking for the beginning, the raw material, the unrefined source. When the mechanic said he'd need about ten minutes to mount the tire, I told him to change the oil and filter while he was at it, and to give it a quick tune as well. I used his restroom to drain some beer, then went off in search of a donut to throw my growling stomach.

There was a greasy spoon two blocks west, the mechanic said, so I headed in that direction. A long stretch in the fresh morning sunlight felt good after sitting behind a wheel for hours. I was checking for traffic as I crossed a side street when my glance was seized by a huge chartreuse sign on the roof of a building about the size of a large cable car: ELMER'S HOUSE OF A THOUSAND LAUGHS. All the *O*s in the sign were tilted like heads thrown back in laughter, and in fact had faces painted on them, closed eyes and big open mouths out of which emerged, in pale flamingo script, assorted hee-haws, yuks, chortles, snorts, whoops, hyugha-hyughas, and other expressions of amusement and delight.

I was attracted by the oddity of the place, but admonished myself not to court distraction when things were clicking along just fine. Besides, the place looked closed. And just as I made up my mind, someone started waving a white flag in the store window as if signaling my attention or his surrender, or perhaps a meeting under the sign of safe conduct.

As I approached, I saw the waving flag was none of the above, but instead a floppy, butcher-paper sign a woman was taping inside a front window. HALLOWEEN SPECIAL, GET YOUR TRICKS HERE. Who could resist? Especially when I noticed that the woman behind the glass had the dourest face I'd ever seen. She looked like her breakfast had been a bowl of alum and a cup of humorless disgust.

On the door, in small, neat script, was another sign: "A practical joke is one that makes you laugh." Above it was one of those plastic squares with two clock faces commonly used to indicate store hours, but the hands had been removed. On one clock face the sun-leached letters read: "Time flies like an arrow." On the other: "Fruit flies like bananas."

I was having serious second thoughts, but pushed the door open anyway, freezing immediately when I heard a hoarse male voice whisper urgently, "Edna, did you hear that? *Oh Christ,* I think it's your husband."

"It's just one of Elmer's jokes," a weary female voice informed me. "A recording. Breaking the circuit in the door activates it. I tell Elmer it's bad for business but he don't listen to me." The speaker was the dour-faced woman I'd seen in the window. She didn't look any happier in the dingy glow of the two forty-watts lighting the store. She was in her fifties, a few inches over five feet but showing all the signs of shrinking fast. She was dressed entirely in dull black except for a large, round pin on her bosom, a grinning, bright orange pumpkin with the legend KEEP FUN SAFE FOR KIDS. As I looked at her narrow, tight-lipped face, the legend seemed less a plea for the safety of innocence than a personal admission of its loss—her matte-brown eyes had given up on fun long ago.

"No problem." I smiled to show her I could take a joke. My instinct was to cheer her up.

"There's not much stock left," she said, "but go ahead and look around. You need any help I'll be behind the counter."

It was a joke shop: joy buzzers, whoopee cushions that emitted long flatulent squeals when you sat on them, fountain pens designed to leak all over the unsuspecting user, plastic lapel flowers with hidden water-filled squeeze-bulbs to flush the sinuses of sniffers, kaleidoscopes that left the viewer with a black eye—that sort of thing, and more bare shelf than merchandise.

A section of plastics caught my eye. A pile of dogshit that looked so real you could smell it. Below that a display of severed extremities—fingertips to put in somebody's beer, whole fingers to wedge in doors, the entire hand for under the pillow or the lip of the toilet bowl. Not to mention plastic snakes, spiders, bats, scorpions, flies, and hideously bloated sewer rats that I instantly envisioned floating belly-up in suburban swimming pools. Next to the animals were plastic puddles of vomit with realistic chunks of potatoes and half-digested meat. None of them made me laugh, but I'll admit to a smile.

In the next aisle were books of matches that wouldn't light, rolling papers saturated with invisible chemicals guaranteed to gag the smoker, exploding loads for cigarettes and cigars, and boxes of birthday candles that appeared normal but could not be blown out. The last struck me as cruel. If you couldn't blow out your birthday candles, your wish wouldn't come true; not that it did anyway, which was a different sort of cruelty. But if the candles couldn't be blown out, was the birthday eternal, the wish kept alive without a future to grant it, deny it, betray it? The candles didn't make me laugh, but since they provoked me with possibilities I decided to buy a box.

The next aisle was devoted to humor of a chemical nature. A handsomely packaged soap that promised to turn the user's skin a gangrenous green a half hour after application. Something called Uro-Stim, invisible when dissolved in liquid and guaranteed to create in any drinker the frantic need to piss. I immediately thought of a couple of long-winded North Beach poets who could use a few hits in their pre-reading wine. There was also Rainbow P, a little packet of six colorless capsules that would turn your urine a choice of colors. I thought Uro-Stim and Rainbow P might make a devastating combination—send the victim hopping pigeon-toed and grimacing to the pisser only to deliver a stream of bright maroon urine . . . looking down, stunned, and thinking, *It can't be me! Jesus, who was I fucking last night?* I started laughing, clearly getting in the mood.

I skipped a section of playing cards—some shaved or marked for tricks, others obviously for viewing ("52 Different Beauties—No Pose the Same")—and browsed a miscellaneous aisle of Chinese handcuffs, balloons called Lung Busters because you couldn't blow them up with anything lighter than an air compressor, and a cheap-looking fry pan ostensibly coated with a revolutionary stick-proof compound, although the accompanying literature guaranteed this miracle coating would melt into industrial-strength epoxy within two minutes of heating, locking your eggs to the pan.

What sort of mind thinks of such things? I wondered as I shuffled on past the mustache wax that caramelized fifteen minutes after you put it on, a dusty box of Chocolate Creme Surprises (the surprise was either a licorice-tapioca filling or a hidden capsule of raw jalapeno extract), a display of rubber kitchen utensils, and, all alone at the end of a bare shelf, a big magenta tube with a screw top that looked like a Tinker-Toy package except for the gold lettering that identified it as "S.D. Rollo's Divinity Confections, The Finest Sweets This Side of Heaven." No telling what those were. I unscrewed the lid to take a peek and *great fucking Jesus!* a giant spring-coiled snake shot halfway across the store, its flannel skin a blinding yellow with glaring polka-dots of baby blue and a flamingo pink only slightly more muted than my hat, its black button eyes glossy as sin and its tongue of red stiffened velvet ready to lie for pleasure. The shock of the vaulting snake made me drop the box of Uro-Stim, then step on it as I moved to retrieve the snake from over by the whoopee cushions. Blushing brighter than the serpent's scarlet tongue and trying to babble an apology to the sour-puss clerk, who hadn't even *looked up* from what she was doing, I was stumbling in total disarray when a familiar voice called, "Hey, George," and I wheeled around to see my ghost pointing to a stack of small white boxes. "Get me a couple of these, would you?"

"What are they," I asked, but then he was gone.

"I beg your pardon?" called the woman behind the counter.

In my attempt to turn around, I tripped on the damn snake and fell against the shelf of whoopee cushions, instinctively grabbing one to break my fall. Which it did, to the long accompaniment of what we young boys in Jacksonville used to call a "tight-ass screamer," only this one ended more like a siren sinking in bubbling mud.

"My goodness! Are you all right?" She was peering down at me, sounding even wearier than before.

"Fine, no problem," I mumbled, flailing my way up off the floor with the whoopee cushion under one arm and a hand around the snake's throat.

"I tell Elmer he should put a warning on that darn snake, but he thinks there's already too many jokes that are explained. He thinks people can't develop a sense of humor unless they *experience* the joke themselves. Here, let me help you get that snake back in the can."

"No, that's okay; I got him." I was enjoying jamming him back in his container. "And don't worry about that package I stepped on; I was going to buy it anyway." I screwed the lid down on S.D. Rollo's Heavenly Confections with mad delight. "How much is this obnoxious snake anyway?"

"Nineteen ninety-five," she said, sounding dismayed.

"That's a lot." I'd figured it'd be around two bucks.

"The company that made it, Fallaho Novelties, went out of business a couple of years ago. They don't make them with flannel bodies anymore—make them overseas cheaper with plastic now, but the plastic don't hold up. Three or four leaps and the plastic cracks. And the spring's some new alloy, not steel. Elmer wanted to keep it as a collector's item, but he already had eight or nine of them so I insisted it go on the shelf. Elmer just marked the price way up there where he said somebody would have to be crazy to buy it."

"You and Elmer are partners in the store, is that it?" Suddenly I was interested in old Elmer.

"I'm his wife."

"Ma'am, if you tell me Elmer has cancer or has mysteriously disappeared, I'm going to jump through your front window and *sprint* for the Pacific Ocean."

Her lips parted in surprise. "Why would you do that?"

"Because I'm crazy enough to buy this damn snake," I said, smacking the can down on the counter, "plus the whoopee cushion here, and the Uro-Stim and some Rainbow P, and these birthday candles you can't blow out, and a couple of boxes of that stuff over there, whatever it is—my ghost wants some. What is it anyway?"

"Rabi-Tabs. They're little tablets you put under your tongue that work up into a froth. Supposed to make you look like you're foaming at the mouth. Like you have rabies."

"I'll take two." I went over and plucked them off the shelf. "Anything else you want, Ghost?" I said loudly. He didn't reply. I picked up the squashed box of Uro-Stim on my way back to the counter.

"Is that who you're talking to? A ghost?" Dismay and weariness joined forces in her voice.

"Yup. I think so."

"Elmer'd like you."

"Ma'am," I asked gently, knowing better, "where *is* Elmer? What's he up to?"

"He's in the hospital. In Omaha." She said it as if surprised I didn't know.

I felt guilty for having forced the painful information. "I'm sorry to hear that. I hope it's nothing serious."

She looked up at me and said in a flat voice, "I thought everyone knew. It was ten months ago, last Christmas Eve. He went to midnight mass and slipped this new dental dye in the communion wine. Turned everybody's teeth bright purple. People were furious. It was *Christmas.* They knew who did it, of course, and they turned on him. He went running from the church—laughing like crazy, they said—and his feet went out from under him on the icy steps and he cracked his head. He's been in a coma ever since, in the V.A. down there. The doctors say they don't know what's keeping him alive.

"I go over there every weekend. He doesn't recognize me, though. He has this huge, happy smile on his face. It never changes, or not that any of us has ever seen. I tried once to pull the corners of his mouth down—so he'd look more dignified, you know?—but they went right back up. But he never opens his eyes, never looks at me, never says a word. I don't know if he's happy or paralyzed or near dead. I'm selling off all the stuff in the store. I guess I'm just waiting for him to die, and I don't even know why I'm waiting for that."

"I think he's happy," I said. "And I think this weekend he's going to open his eyes and look in yours and say, 'Honey, let's run away to Brazil and start all over.' But if he doesn't, if he dies, I hope you can find it within yourself to sit on his headstone and laugh, really *laugh,* from way down in your guts, for him and for you."

"It's not funny," she said.

"*Some* of it surely is. Why lose that, too?"

"Because you just do," she said sourly, and started ringing up my purchases.

"You should smother your husband," my ghost said, appearing briefly over her shoulder before he faded.

"Did you hear that?" I asked her, though she'd given no indication she had.

"No," she glanced up, "what?"

"My ghost said, 'Mother him.' "

"You're just like Elmer. He loved Halloween."

"My ghost's like Elmer. I'm really like you. Except I'm not waiting. You know why? Because time flies like an arrow."

"I know, I know," she waved a hand, "and fruit flies like rotten fruit." She handed me my bag of purchases. "You and your ghost have a nice Halloween." I wish she could've smiled when she said it.

I went straight back to the tire shop. The Caddy was ready and waiting, chrome flashing with sunlight. I put the bag of tricks on the passenger-side floor, except for the whoopee cushion, which I carefully placed on the passenger seat. If my ghost showed up again, still along for the ride, I wanted to find out if he'd set it off. This might well have been the first fart trap ever designed to detect the physical presence of a ghost. Never too crazy for empirical experiments in reality.

I paid for the tire and tune-up, then wheeled the car around the block a few times to make sure it was running tight. Couldn't have been better. I headed back out for I-80, stopping along the way for dinosaur power at a Sinclair, and then at the Allied Superette for a couple of six-packs of Bud to restock the cooler. By the dash clock it was 9:20. I took a little sip from the crank mix to keep me on track, and a few minutes later I was ripping down the Interstate, California-bound.

Using my benny-quickened brain, I calculated that the Caddy would be introduced to the Pacific in about twenty hours, some twelve hundred minutes. I had roughly two hundred records in the back seat, two sides each, say three minutes a side, six per disc—well how about that? Talk about your celestial clickety-click, that was about twelve hundred minutes of music if I listened to it all, and that was exactly my intention. I could feel myself starting to hit the nerve snap-point of too much speed and not enough sleep, and music soothes the beast. I set aside everything by the Bopper, Buddy Holly, and Ritchie Valens; it seemed only fitting to save them for the last wild-heart run at the sea.

Between watching the road and shuffling records it took me about ten minutes to get set up. The spindle on Joshua's turntable would take a stack of ten, which meant all I had to do was flip them every half-hour and change the stack on the hour. The first tune, Elvis' "Now Or Never," sounded about right to me. I leaned back and cruised as I listened to him croon.

From Grand Island through North Platte and on to the state line, Nebraska—if you can believe it—gets flatter. You don't really have to drive; just put it in boogie and hold it between the lines. It's boring, and I suppose it was boredom that inspired the idea of sailing the records out the window once the whole stack had played. By the time this occurred to me I already had a stockpile of twenty records, so by restricting myself to one toss for every two cuts, I had some physical activity every six minutes. The interim was well occupied with drinking beer, listening to the music blast at cone-wrenching volume, choosing suitable targets, and, best of all, matching titles to their fates. For Brenda Lee's "I'm Sorry," for instance, I just plopped into the slow lane to get run over. The Everly Brothers' "Bird Dog" I sailed out into a cornfield to hunt pheasants. "Teen Angel" I saved till the highway cut in to parallel some railroad tracks, but I undershot it badly into a weedy ditch. Since I had some slack, I saved a few titles for more appropriate places—"Mr. Custer" definitely belonged to Wyoming, while the Drifters' "Save the Last Dance for Me" was obviously meant for a late-night fling.

Those whose titles didn't suggest targets became general ammunition in my war on control, and were gleefully winged at billboards and road signs, and especially at speed limit signs. To sail a record out of a car moving 95 mph and hit anything except the ground is a real trick, and about 98 percent of the time I probably missed. But I tell you, it's a *magnificent* feeling when you connect. Damn near blew my shoes off with joy when I sent "The Duke of Earl" tearing through a Bank of America billboard. And as to the musical question "Who Put the Bomp in the Bomp-Da-Bomp?" I'm not sure, but I know the record itself put one hell of a bomp on a 65 mph sign—folded the fucker almost in half, much to my delight. I celebrated this rare bull's-eye with a toot on the horn and a solid squeeze of the whoopee cushion, happy as a seven-year-old with a slingshot in a glass factory. Shit, even the misses were fun—sailing gracefully out over the fields to drop like miniature spacecraft from Pluto.

I was having so much fun my ghost couldn't resist. I'd just barely missed a Burger Hut billboard with "Theme from a Summer Place" when he appeared in the passenger seat.

"Ah ha!" I pounced, "you're not real: the whoopee cushion didn't go off."

He ignored me in his excitement. "Salvoes," he urged, "fusillades, machine guns, cluster bombs. Shotgun the fuckers! To hell with this johnny-one-note stuff." And he was gone.

I was reluctant but had a few spares, so I picked up five together, waited for a large green road sign announcing "CHEYENNE 37," came within a hundred yards and, allowing for some lead, snapped them backhanded out the passenger window. But something wasn't right—the weight, the throw, the aerodynamics—because one nosed down and the other four fluttered and died way short of the target. I wrote it off as bad advice and told my ghost to forget it. I didn't hear any argument.

If throwing music away like that seems sacrilegious . . . well, maybe it was. But I'd already decided to send the records and sound system down with the ship; they belonged with the Caddy as part of the gift, but rather than do it all at once I was delivering pieces along the way. The Bopper's records, Buddy's, Ritchie's—I still intended to send them over the edge with the blazing Caddy, maybe even stacked on the spindle as a crowning touch. The rest I felt free to fling like seeds across the landscape, scatter like ashes. If they happened to collide with billboards, road signs, and other emblems of oppressive enterprise and gratuitous control, all the better—that seemed altogether congruent with the spirit of the music, doubly fitting considering it was also a lot of fun.

I gassed at a Sinclair station in Cheyenne, tipping my flamingo hat to the dinosaur, then hauled on for Laramie. I was starting up the east slope of the Rockies, where driving required a bit more attention, but there were still plenty of opportunities to cast the music far and wide.

"What's that, Mr. Charles? 'Hit the road, Jack'? No sweat." I reached out the window and fired it straight down; hard to miss when you're right on top of it. No need to tell me not to come back no more, no more, no more, no more.

When Frankie Avalon asked the musical question "Why?" I told him it was just to see how far he could sail into the sagebrush, that's why. And I flung him out there as far as I could.

"And Tom Dooley," I said aloud to myself and my ghost if he was listening, "sweet Jesus, man, you've been hanging your head since the Civil War, poor boy. Let me cut you some slack." And with a sharp backhanded toss I set him free.

Just out of Rawlins, about to crest the Continental Divide, I tired of the game and decided to use the thin air to go for distance—but was going so fast I couldn't keep the longer shots in sight. When I hit the crest I pulled over, scooped up my pile of reserves and, after pissing beer into both watersheds, alternately sailed records east and west, watching them hang majestically and curve away, a few disappearing before I could see where they hit, and I'd bet some of them carried for miles.

I returned to the Caddy refreshed, though my break from rapid motion made me realize I was probably a bit overamped on speed; I made a mental note to lay off for a while or I'd be chewing on the steering wheel by midnight. Generally, however, I felt wonderful. I was on the Pacific side of the country, halfway to the edge with a downhill run, looking good and having fun.

It didn't last long. "Hound Dog" had just finished playing, and either the bennies had sped up my hearing or Elvis was singing slower—something was out of time. The next platter down was the Kingsmen's "Louie, Louie." If you want to hear music for the end of the world try a 45 of "Louie, Louie" played at 33 and progressively fading to about 13:

Looouuuuiiiieeeeee, Looouuuuiiiieeeeeeeeeee,
Ooooooohhhhhhh yeeeaaaaaaaaaaahhhhhhhhhhhhhhhh
Weeeeeeeeeeeeeeeeeeeee
Goooooooooooooooottttttttaaaaaaahhhhhhhhhhhhhhhh
Goooooooooooooooooooooo
Nnnnnnoooooooooooooooowwwwwwwwwwwwwwwwwwwwwwwwww

The battery was dying in Joshua's magic box. "Aaawwwwwwww fuuuuuuuuccccccckkkkk," I said, trying to maintain my sense of humor as I reached back and snapped it off.

"Music!" my ghost demanded, suddenly beside me in the passenger's seat. "Sounds! Give me the *beat!"*

"If you don't like it, leave," I told him, slowing to pull over.

He whined like a five-year-old. "But it's *boring* without music." He disappeared.

"Just take it easy." I wondered if he could still hear me. "Your man's on the job."

I stopped and got out. I could've switched batteries, but Joshua's sounded so low I probably would've had to roll start the car, and I hate running on low power. To dig out Donna's machine and plug it into the lighter socket seemed smarter; this would do till I got to Rock Springs, where I could buy new juice for Joshua's system. In theory this sounded good, but when I lifted Donna's record player from the trunk I noticed the tone arm was jammed down on the turntable, and the needle was broken. Somewhere along the line—probably in Gladys Nogardam's driveway—the cooler must've slid into it. Or maybe I'd thrown the shot-up tire on it. Didn't make any fucking difference *how* at that point—it was useless. I considered trying a needle swap but figured by the time I discovered they weren't interchangeable I could be leaving Rock Springs with a new battery. Till then we'd just have to do without music.

Two silent minutes down the freeway, my ghost reappeared beside me, commenting in that nasal snottiness five-year-olds find so withering, "Well, *my man;* where's the *music?"*

I ignored him. No reason to pamper hallucinations.

"I *need* the beat!" he demanded. "The sound of fucking music!"

"I'll sing for you," I offered sarcastically.

"Why don't you just turn on the radio there?" He pointed. "They're amazing inventions. Magic. You click on the switch and sometimes music jumps right out." He disappeared.

It was embarrassing. Like I said, I don't normally have a radio in a working vehicle. Music is fine, but all the deejay chit-chat and commercials poison your attention. But the fact was I hadn't even thought of the radio.

I was glad my ghost had, though. We picked up KROM out of Boulder, almost solid music and a lot of it what I'd been listening to a couple months earlier holed up in my apartment trying to stay sane. After a steady diet of Donna's collection, it was a nice leap forward to hear what was blooming from those roots. My ghost must've enjoyed it, too; not a peep out of him for fifty miles.

When he reappeared again it wasn't to complain about the music, but to offer an observation. "Jeez, George, maybe *I'm* the paranoid one, but at the speed we're traveling it seems hard to believe that black car behind us is catching up—well, not actually catching up, but sort of *settled* in, if you know what I mean."

Two big mothers in an Olds 88. I use the mirrors on reflex and was sure I'd checked in the last half-minute, so unless I'd missed them or was slipping badly they hadn't been there long. Considering their adverse impact on my pulse rate, I saw no reason for them to be there any longer than necessary. I was doing a smooth 90 at the time, coming off a long downhill stretch, and I had lots of pedal left. I was just stomping on it when I saw another car coming fast down the hill and, unless the dusk light was playing tricks, this one had a bubblegum machine bolted to its roof and generally conveyed the feeling of a state trooper. So rather than punch it, I let the accelerator spring push my foot back up to a more sensible 65 mph.

By coming off the gas suddenly like that, the Olds, if it wanted to stay on my tail, would've had to hit its brakes, thus making its intentions obvious, or at least provide some rational basis for the paranoia playing my heart like a kettle drum. If the Olds passed—the exact move I was

hoping to force—I'd at least get a good look at them, and with any luck
the trooper would nail their ass. I'd get two birds with one stone. Just
call me Slick. Unfortunately the Olds must've spotted the trooper too,
and didn't gain an inch.

The Caddy, Olds, and trooper's Dodge settled into a stately proces-
sion, an extremely nervous one from my vantage, marked by a great deal
of wishing, hoping, and nonchalant concealment of visible felonies, and
not untainted by a certain mean irony as Bob Dylan asked through the
magic of KROM radio,

> *How does it feeeeelll*
> To be on your *ooooownnn*

"Tell you the truth, Bob, not too fucking good right now, sort of
caught between goons and the heat out here on the alkali Wyoming sage
flats with a bad case of dread and my ghost hiding under the front seat,
but I guess that's what makes existence the wonderful adventure it is."

We kept moving in strict formation, me in front, my worries right
behind at hundred-yard intervals. Dylan finished his biting lament and
the KROM deejay was announcing a license plate number for some
promotional contest—if it was yours and you called within ten minutes
you won two tickets to hear Moon Cap and the Car Thieves at the first
annual KROM Goblin Rock-and-Roll Horror Romp at Vet's Hall. I'd
rather have been there than where I was and, worse yet, with a decision
to make: should I take the upcoming Rock Springs turn-off or not? Not,
I decided; I didn't know the turf, a severe disadvantage if I had to run
for it.

The black Olds, however, did take the exit, making me wonder for
a minute whether they were simply a couple of big guys out for a drive.
That left just me and the trooper, me wildly radiating innocence and
the trooper, I hoped to Christ, receiving. Unfortunately, a discreet
glance in the rearview revealed he actually seemed to be sending, since
he was holding the radio mike to his mouth. Maybe a little spot-check
on a five-niner Cadillac Eldorado, California license plate number B as

in busted, O as in Oh-shit, and P as in prison, 3 as in the square root of nine, 3 as in trinity, 3 like the wise men. Such moments have led me to the firm conviction that driving our nation's highways would be a hell of a lot more fun without license plates.

I held my speed at an even 65 for the next few minutes, then held my breath as I saw him coming up quickly behind. But he went on around, giving me a long look as he passed.

He saw a smile. Far better for a paranoid to have them in front instead of behind. Unless they're playing games, as he apparently was, because in less than a mile he began to slow down. *Now what?* I silently shrieked, but ahhh, blink-blink, he was taking the Green River exit.

I continued driving as if he was right behind me, but after a few more miles and no sign of him, I romped on it. On the radio, the Rolling Stones were laying claim to their cloud, a position I shared, though by then it was dark enough that no clouds were visible.

No more than three minutes later, just as I made a mental note to gas at the next available station and pick up a battery, another trooper passed me in the eastbound lane, his brake lights casting an apocalyptic glow in my rearview mirror as he slowed to cross the divider strip. I momentarily lost sight of him as the road, approaching the Green River bridge, swung abruptly.

I snapped off my lights and started looking for somewhere else to go—there's almost always a frontage road along rivers, and I hoped I could make one out in the fast-fading light. And there it was, just on the other side of the bridge; no need to signal or slow down much. Then I started looking for cover, a campground or spur road or anything. I came off the gas, though, going too fast to see, and to slow down seemed smarter than turning on the headlights. I finally spotted an abrupt right that dropped down to the floodplain; it looked like gravel trucks had used this through the summer. Banging bottom and rattling my teeth, I took it at full speed. I whipped the Caddy around so I was facing back up the road, backed in close to some willows, then shut the engine down and started gathering the beer cans and other incriminating evidence. I needed something to carry the empties so I dumped my joke house purchases on the front seat and used the bag. The first thing I heard when I opened the door was the river. It *sounded* green. I wondered if that was the reason for its name, but doubted anything so seductive. Probably it was named for the color of its water, though all I could make out in the heavy dusk was a broad shimmer of light.

I hid the beer cans and benzedrine behind a clump of willows, then strolled down to the river, keeping a sharp eye out for traffic on the road to my right. Far downstream I could see the headlights of cars crossing the I-80 bridge.

At the river's edge, it was cold. As I stood there watching the light fade, three dark shapes winged over, one crying, "Argk! Argk! Argk!"

Ravens. "Argggk," I called back weakly, but they disappeared downstream.

My ghost appeared in front of me, standing on a rock about ten feet out in the river. "You're crazy," he announced. "Barking at the sky."

"They were ravens." I defended myself. "Looking for the ark. Noah's Ark, remember? All the animals two by two. You know, I've always wondered how it was that ravens were able to reproduce if Noah sent one off that never came back. That only left one, right? So how—"

"Please." My ghost stopped me. "Let's listen to the babble of running water; it's so much more soothing than the ravings of your poor mind."

"Hey, you're *my* ghost—you've got to be crazy, too."

"I don't have to be anything," he said, vanishing.

I bent over and scooped up some water and splashed it over my face, trembling as it ran down my neck. It was cold. When I opened my eyes, blinking water from the lashes, I thought I saw a flicker of light upstream. I wiped my eyes and looked again. Still there. I couldn't tell if the light itself was flickering or if something was crossing in front of it. I walked upstream till I could see more clearly. As nearly as I could tell, it was behind a screen of willows. A campfire, I decided. Maybe Smokey was having a wiener roast for his forest friends. I splashed another sobering shot of water on my face to sharpen my focus. Yup, I was sure I saw Bambi's shadow, and then Thumper's. But whose shadow was that, the tall naked woman unfurling her wings? I headed back to the car.

"Where are you going now?" my ghost demanded. I couldn't see him but his voice was clear. "Don't you think it might be wise to wait a few minutes before resuming this fool's errand? I like it here by the river."

"I'm going swimming," I told him.

"The river's this way."

"I'm going to the car first. For a present."

"George," my ghost said with strained patience, "hasn't it ever struck you that you're one of those warriors who, every time he girds up his loins for another reckless leap into the unknown, gets his little pee-pee caught in the buckle?"

"There's always a first time," I said without breaking stride.

"And a last," he reminded me.

On the way back from the car with the can of S.D. Rollo's Divinity Confections in my hand, I cautioned myself over and over *Don't expect it to be Kacy; don't even think of it.* A far-fetched notion, I realized even at the time. I picked the slowest water I could find, a long bellying pool downstream from the flickering firelight. I caught a faint scent of wood-smoke.

I stripped to my shorts and, holding the Divinity Confections aloft, waded in to midthigh, then launched myself gently into the current. The water was so cold that all bodily sensations gasped to a numb stop, and if I hadn't been so full of crank I doubt they'd ever have started again. After two stunned minutes of mechanical exertion I was across, crawling out on the opposite shore like some blue-fleshed proof of unnatural selection.

I flopped around on the sandy beach to reheat my body, then, still shivering badly, picked up the can of Divinity Confections and lurched upstream toward the fire. While the road-side of the river had a wide floodplain, the other side rose into steep, rockface bluffs with only a narrow, willow-choked flat between river and rock. I crashed my way through the willows, muttering and grunting to myself until I realized I probably sounded like a rabid bear. I felt the crosshairs centering on my heart. No need to frighten anybody into such unthinking defensive behavior as shooting me, so I stopped and hollered, "Hello there! Company coming with gifts and good cheer!"

"*Please*, go away," a young woman's voice answered close by, genuine appeal in her tone.

"Nothing to fear," I called back, moving forward a few steps and stumbling into a small clearing. The fire was built against the base of the bluff, set back under a ledge that high water had cut through the centuries. The woman was standing in front of the fire shaking her head vehemently. She wasn't tall, she didn't have wings, and, of course, she wasn't Kacy. She was a couple of inches over five feet, and what I'd taken for wings from across the river was a poncho made of an olive-drab Army blanket.

"Please listen a minute before you send me away," I asked. "I'm probably stone crazy and a fool to boot, but my intentions are wholesome and altogether honorable. I was attracted by the light, and I just swam that icicle of a river because I wanted to bring you a present— whoever you are." I held up the can of Divinity Confections as if it were irrefutable truth.

"That's nice of you," she said evenly, lowering her head, "but I don't want company. I'm not in the mood to entertain."

"Don't worry," I assured her—as if there was assurance to be found in a wild-eyed, sand-blotched fool wearing nothing but his soaked jockey shorts and waving what looked like a large tinker-toy can. "*I'll* entertain *you*. Please? I just want to talk to another human being."

"All right," she said reluctantly.

Her name was Mira Whitman, twenty years old, and she listened to my tale of low adventure and high stupidity as she sat on a log in front of the fire, her shoulders hunched and head down, staring at her fingers entwined on her lap. She had a small, squarish head, brown hair cut short, with a thin, sharp nose at odds with her broad cheekbones. Her face was deeply tanned.

When I finished my narration, bringing her right up to date on my mission and the imminent delivery at the continental edge, she said, still staring at her hands, "I guess you are kind of crazy. But, you know, at least it's a *real* craziness; at least it has a point. And I hope you make it, if that's what you want to do. Wreck that car, I mean."

"That's what I want to do. But I didn't tell you I'm starting to see my ghost lately. He just shows up. He looks just like me only he's not flesh and blood. I talk to him. Do you think that's cause for alarm, or does it matter?"

"I have no idea. You're talking to the wrong person. I mean, I don't really even understand what you've been telling me. Don't you see that? I have *no* understanding. It's all I can do right now to wake up in the morning and see the river. Or a leaf. Or an ant."

"Why's that," I asked gently, quickly adding, "But don't tell me if it has anything to do with a man—one who loves you or doesn't, beats you, adores you, who's died or's dying. I don't want to know. Seems like every woman I've talked to in the last year has man troubles."

She glanced at me, then looked down at her hands. "I thought you were *doing* it for love and music?" But fortunately, before I had to defend the untenable, she went on, "But no, it's not a man. That just hurts. Or infuriates. No, it's *me*. Or not me." She bit her lip and glanced up again. "I got lost." This time she didn't look back down. "Does that make any sense?"

I sighed. "Sounds painfully familiar."

"No." She was adamant. "With you it's meaning. Making it *mean* something."

"And with you?"

She looked past me into the fire, then back to my face. "You're nice, George. And I like what you're trying to do. But it's pointless for me to talk about it. For you the words help carry it, give you something to hold on to, but for me they tear it out of my hands, or turn it mushy." She started to add something, then changed her mind, her gaze moving back to the fire. "I've enjoyed talking to you, George, but the best thing you could do is leave."

"No," I told her, "I won't." That surprised her. Me, too. "I want to know what happened and what you're going to do about it, or what you're trying to do. You sit here and tell me you're lost and imply you have no sense of being real, and I see the real light from this real fire dancing in your real pretty brown eyes, and I *know* you're wrong, me who doesn't know very much at all. Maybe what you lost is a feeling, maybe a feeling I've lost, too; or that we're both trying to create, or fake, or somehow just patch enough together to make it through another day."

"You're so *hungry,*" she said, looking straight at me.

I looked straight back. "Maybe you're not hungry enough?"

"I'm not *like* you," she pleaded, "can't you see that? You with your lost lover and stolen car and wild adventures all over the country. For you—oh, Jesus, this doesn't make any sense—for you it's like you can't blow up a balloon big enough to hold it all, can't find a balloon *large* enough . . . and me, it's like a little balloon I was blowing up every day, and every day the air leaked out until I was emptying faster than I could fill it. Ever since I was twelve, right around junior high, I've just *dwindled.* I'll spare you adolescence in a small town in Colorado. I wasn't pretty. I wasn't popular. I wasn't particularly smart. I didn't have any friends that were the way I thought friends should be, men *or* women. But it was manageable. As soon as I graduated from high school I left and moved to Boulder. The Big City! I had a tiny apartment and I cleaned motel rooms in the morning and worked at Burger Hut in the evening. I liked being on my own, doing what I felt like when I didn't have to work, but I was still shrinking. I could feel it every morning, like I was running away from myself over the hills. Then I got a break: this woman who came into Burger Hut all the time mentioned a job was opening at a radio station down the block, KROM, not as a deejay or anything, just a receptionist, record librarian, general assistant . . . and I got it. The pay was two dollars an hour, but I loved the job. The people were nutty and it was always chaos and it was fun being involved with the music. Music touches people, you know that, and I was part of it, and it had been a long time since I felt like a part of anything.

"Then about three months ago they started this big bumper-sticker promotion. You know: you put a KROM bumper-sticker on your car, and if your license number's announced and you call in, you win some kind of prize—albums, merchandise, tickets to a dance or concert or movie. The license plates are picked by what they called 'The Mystery

Spotter.' That was me, The Mystery Spotter. It sounds pretty important but all it meant was that when I was driving to work, or at lunch, or whatever, I'd pick four or five cars with KROM bumper-stickers and write down the license numbers and then turn them over to the manager. I was fair, too. I tried to be random, and it didn't matter if it was a new car or old one or who was driving.

"But what happened was *none* of the numbers I'd collected *ever* called in. The whole idea of the promotion is to make people listen to the station to hear their number called—plus the advertising from the bumper-stickers themselves. So after three days of no winners, nobody calling in, it got horribly embarrassing because it was like nobody was listening. The deejays started joking on the air that maybe The Mystery Spotter needed glasses. Then the station manager said, 'Hey, bring in ten numbers; we'll go till we get a winner.' And still nobody called. So the manager wanted twenty numbers. He told Evans, the night security guy, to bring in ten and me ten. None of my ten called. Eight of Evans's did.

"You understand what I'm getting at? It's like I wasn't connected. So I started cheating. I'd *tell* people I was The Mystery Spotter and that if they listened at eight o'clock or whenever, their number would be called and they'd win something. And they'd go, 'Oh great! Hey, all right!' But they never called. And these were people who *put* those dumb stickers on their cars. It's like I wasn't real to them. Evans's numbers? At least seventy percent of the time.

"It seems dumb, but it really got to me. The Mystery Spotter who couldn't spot anything. I could stand there telling someone I was the KROM Mystery Spotter and feel my voice go right through them without touching, and they'd smile back right through me, and I'd go back to my apartment and open the door and walk in and wonder who lived there. Go look in her closet and touch her clothes and my hand would pass through them like air.

"You can't live like that, without any substance. I had this dream where I cut my wrists. Took a razor blade and sliced in deep, waiting for the blood to spurt. But there was no blood. I cut deeper and deeper till my hand flopped back and I could look right down into my wrist and there was nothing there—no muscles, no arteries, no blood. I think I would've actually tried to kill myself if I wasn't so terrified nobody was there to die.

"The only thing I could think to do was to get away. I took my sleeping bag, some blankets, borrowed a fishing pole, stole a knife, and eventually ended up here. I like it, but it's getting cold and I don't think I'll stay when the snows come. But maybe I'll try. I'm doing better now, trying to make myself real again. At first I was like a little baby—not learning the *names,* that was just confusing—but touching the water, trying to feel the light on my skin, the texture and color of this stone, that stone, the leaves and the trees, with nothing in the way. Going back to nothing and starting over. And I'm doing all right. It's slow. I'm not ready for people yet is all."

"Mira," I said, resisting the impulse to take her in my arms, "I want you to spot me."

She tilted her head. "What?"

"You're a Mystery Spotter and I desperately need to be spotted. So please spot me. We need each other."

She shook her head. "Maybe you're *too* crazy."

"And you're not? You're crawling around touching things you're afraid to name, licking rocks, going to extraordinary lengths to comprehend the most obvious things, and *you* call *me* nuts? Hey, the crazy have to help each other; nobody else knows how. My license number is BOP three-three-three. Call it in. I'll be listening for it."

She shrugged her shoulders under the poncho. "I can't. There's no phone. I don't even work there anymore."

"You're so *literal,* Mira; that's part of your problem, I think. And maybe mine. Probably the opposite is true. But I don't know." I picked up a small chunk of firewood and handed it to her. "Here's a phone. Or use that rock over there. Use one of those hands you keep staring at—they'll work. Or you can do it in your mind without props, even without words, certainly without reason."

"It'd just make it worse."

There was an abject finality in her tone that freshened my determination, but I took a different tack. "Do you ever see ravens around here?"

"Sure." She looked puzzled.

"That guy I told you about that played the train recording? Joshua Springfield? Well, when Josh was a kid he heard a raven flying over calling 'Ark, Ark' and he was sure it was the raven Noah'd sent out in the flood to look for land, the one that never came back, and Joshua figured it was still looking for the Ark. So you know what Joshua did? He went out in his backyard and built an ark so the raven would have a place to land. Joshua refused to leave his ark, to give up his vigil. Finally his parents had him committed. Does that make it worse?"

"I'm not Joshua," she said, some fire in her voice.

"No, you're not Joshua. I'm not Joshua. Even Joshua knows he's not Joshua. We're ravens. That's why we build arks."

"I guess I'm too dumb to understand. It's just words to me, George."

My ghost appeared beside her, looking down consolingly. "Don't worry," he told her, "he doesn't understand either."

"Did you hear that?" I said sharply.

"No." Mira was startled. "What?"

"My ghost. He's right beside you. He said I didn't understand it either, so not to worry about it."

"George," my ghost said with irritated disgust, "leave this woman alone. She seems to know what her problem is, and what to do about it, which is more than can be said for you, and she undoubtedly has better things to do than listen to your bullshit. She wisely asked you to leave a couple of times already, so why don't you lay off? If you need some miraculous conversion to bolster yourself, preach your madness at me."

I repeated his speech verbatim, and Mira simply nodded—in terror or agreement, I wasn't sure which. My ghost had disappeared, looking sorely annoyed, as I repeated his words. I waited a moment for Mira to comment. When she didn't I went on. "There seems to be a general agreement that this fool should leave, so that's what I'm going to do. I should get on with the night's work anyway. I've enjoyed talking to you, Mira, and I'm inspired by your faith. Excuse my preaching when I should've been listening—it's one of my larger faults. And please"—I smiled warmly—"do accept this small gift I braved the river to bring you, a gift I hope will be the first of two I'll deliver tonight." I picked up the Divinity Confections from where I'd set it down behind the rock and presented it to her with a small bow. "It's candy, for a sweetheart."

She smiled as she accepted it with both hands. "Thank you."

Her smile almost made me cry. "You have a lovely smile, Mira. Under different circumstances it would be easy for me to hang around and fall in love." I pointed at the can. "I hope you like sweets. They make an excellent dessert for twig soup, tossed moss salad, and grubs in willow sauce."

I was embarrassing her, and she looked at the can for something to do. "You know," she said, "this looks like one of those things you buy in joke shops, where something leaps out."

"A practical joke is one that makes you laugh," I quoted. "And no doubt there's both sweetness and nutrition in humor, but it would be in the poorest of taste considering the situation, don't you think?"

Before she could answer I took my leave, thanking her for her warm hospitality on a cold night.

"Good luck, George," she said. "I mean it."

"Ah, you're not *real* enough to mean it."

She smiled again. "Maybe so, but you deserve the effort."

"Then put some effort into spotting me." I waved and walked into the dark thicket of willows. I loved her smile but wanted to hear her laugh.

I was about forty feet from her camp when I heard the springing *whooosh* of the snake uncoiling, and then her quick, piercing shriek. There was a faint, flat *whump!* followed instantly by a flare of light so intense I could make out veins in the willow leaves: the snake had evidently landed in the fire. As the burst of light faded, her laughter began—warm, full-throated, belly-rich laughter that rang against the stone bluffs and swelled down the river canyon.

I turned around and yelled through cupped hands: "That's right, you idiot: *laugh!*"

"You're fucking hopeless, George," my ghost said at my shoulder.

"Oh yeah? I *feel* like I'm *brimming* with hope." I stepped out of the willows at the river's edge. "So you don't think I'm one of the ravens, huh?" There was no answer. Though it was to dark to tell for sure, I assumed he'd vanished. "Well, my ghost, just watch me—I'm going to *fly* across this river here and not wet a pinkie."

I walked downstream till the bank widened. I concentrated fiercely, trying to let Mira's laughter lighten my bones and feather my flesh, and then I ran for the river, flapping for lift, vaulting into the air. I flew seven or eight feet before I belly-flopped into the icy water. I'd flailed halfway across before I managed my first breath. The current was stronger than I remembered, but swimming was easier without the burden of a gift.

When I finally pulled myself up on the opposite shore, hunching out on all fours, panting and shivering like a sick dog, my ghost was waiting for me. "That was a spectacular flight," he said, "maybe a foot, fourteen inches."

I trembled to my feet, jerkily stripped off my water-logged shorts, and swung them at his face. They passed right through it. Gasping, I said, "You haven't seen anything. Foot's a good start. Like seeing a leaf. Mira's inspired me." I turned and flung my jockey shorts out in the river, then scrabbled around in the dark till I found my pile of clothes. I put them on gratefully, topping the outfit with my flamingo hat. I imagined it glowing like a beacon. The gods knew where to find me, if they were looking. As I walked back to the car I looked for a raven's feather to stick in the band. I didn't find any.

I started the Caddy and cranked up the heat, then gathered my bag from the trunk and five or six records that had already played. I stopped and retrieved the bottle of liquid benzedrine, reshouldered my duffle bag, and took it all down to the river.

I threw the records at the stars, missing by a couple jillion miles. I unzipped the duffle, took out my bankroll, added the two grand still wadded in my pocket, peeled off $500 for expenses, and hurled the rest toward the river. The unwieldy wad fluttered apart into rectangular leaves, dropping silently on the water, whirling away. I stuffed several good-sized stones into the duffle bag and zipped it shut. I grabbed a strap, braced myself for an Olympian effort, spun once, twice, thrice, and cut loose. It hit halfway across in a tremendous splash, and sank. I unscrewed the cap on the bottle of crank and sidearmed it across the water like a skipping stone, lifted the bottle in a salute to the night sky, took a couple of farewell glugs, then whipped it out there as far as I could.

I trotted back up to the Eldorado's heat, absently working my tongue around teeth and gums to cleanse the bitter chalk residue of the benzedrine. I smiled as I imagined some fisherman hooking into a trout full of speed, the pole nearly ripped from his hands, line smoking off the reel as he stumbled downstream howling to his buddy, "Holy fuck, Ted!" just as the backing ran out on his reel and his $200 split-bamboo rod shattered in his hands. And Ted yelling back, "Hey, piss on the rod. I'll buy you a new one. I'm wading in twenty-dollar bills here." Even if this wouldn't happen, the possibility made me happy.

My ghost was sitting in the driver's seat when I opened the Caddy's door. "I better drive," he said.

"Move your ass over."

He glared at me; I glared back. "All right," he said. "Why should I care if you continue to wildly overestimate your capabilities and underestimate mine. But if it's going to be like that, let's fucking *do* it. No little lost raven-poo going 'ark, ark, ark.' Burn the goddamn Ark! Let's have some spirit, George. Let's scream through the night like eagles. Let's do it right." And he was gone.

Fuck him and his eagles. I took it extra easy pulling up the embankment back onto the frontage road, not wanting to bottom out. I'd been abusing the Caddy lately, and it was built for cruising, not off-road racing. I approached I-80 with caution, then hung a right. No sign of official forces or black Oldsmobiles. We needed gas pronto, and a new battery for Joshua's solid-drive master blaster. I snapped on the radio, but KROM was gone—must cut back their signal at night, I figured. Or maybe this was some topographical anomaly, because I couldn't seem to find anything at all: just a blur of static from one end of the band to the other. *Or perhaps a little electronic interference*, I thought to myself, *like radar.* I went back through the dial and at 1400, crisp and clear, I heard a man talking to me:

"Awwwwri̇i̇ight, brothers and sisters! If you're twisting one up, keep right on it; but if you're twisting the dial, *stop* right there, 'cause you got KRZE, one billion megawatts of pure blow hammering your skull from our studio *high* atop the Wind River Range. Coming up in tonight's lifetime we got you some tricks and treats, some goblin chuckles and that monster beat, plus tons more good stuff than you'll be able to believe, so dig it like a grave while I whisper some sweet nothings in your ear. That's right, relax. This is Captain Midnight at the controls, if there are any; I want you to enjoy your flight.

"Now did I say treats? You might be worrying where you're gonna find a bag big enough to bring back all your goodies tonight, one that's big enough to truck the whole load home. No sweat, 'cause here's Mr. James Brown and I do believe he's got a bag you can borrow, a brand new one at that."

"Hey ghost," I yelled as James Brown worked out, "how do you like this station?" But ghost wasn't talking.

To save on gas, and because I was still jittery about troopers, I kept it at an even 65. "Papa's Got a Brand New Bag" segued into Bobby "Boris" Pickett and the Crypt Kickers doing "Monster Mash," which in turn slid without pause into Frankie Laine's "Ghost Riders in the Sky."

Then back to Captain Midnight, who was hopping with excitement: *"Did* you *dig* that message? Cowboys you *better* change your ways or it looks like eternity for sure busting ass, chasing them fire-eyed longhorns through the clouds. Yiiiiiippeeee-i-o, that's *hard.* And you little cowgirls better be good, too, or they won't let you ride horsies in Heaven, little britches, and you *know* that's hell on a girl. Hey, but enough cheap Christian morality, *right?* Tonight belongs to the beasties and demons, vamping vampires and the living dead. Yes, it's All Hallow's Eve, and something darkly stalks the land and the furthermost recesses of the human brain, which has always loved recess. But something good stalks it, too, because our Mystery Spotter is out there spotting mysteries left and right, as well as a few well-chosen license plates, and maybe tonight's the night your number comes up. That's right, hot dog: you may already be a wiener. So stay tuned and you might pick up a couple of tickets to the dance. And while you're waiting, we flat *guarantee* we'll have a few other numbers that will both elucidate and amuse. How's that grab your happy ass, fool? You got Captain Midnight in your ear, KRZE, where you find it is where it's at, so *high up* we're underground. Now catch a listen to this monstrosity."

"Purple People Eater" came tooting on, but I'd just spotted a Sinclair station in some strange tourist trap called Miniature America and was already pulling into the pumps. The attendant, a sawed-off geezer in red, white, and blue overalls, was curious about the car and the big silver box in the back seat, not to mention the fried-eyed idiot in the pink hat. Too curious. He craned to watch me through the back window as he topped the tank and I hooked up the new battery. I don't know if it was his oppressive attention, the raw Wyoming cold, or a case of speed-jangles, but my hands were shaking so bad I damn near couldn't get the clamps cinched down.

The battery and gas came to $34. I gave the old geezer two twenties and told him to keep the change. He shook his head in disbelief, then grinned. "Mister, if I had your money I'd throw mine away."

"Throw it away anyway," I advised him. "It feels good."

I rolled back onto I-80 and aimed at Salt Lake City, holding it at a solid 80. If I got stopped I could always argue I'd mistaken the highway number for the speed limit. I listened to the radio instead of records on Joshua's revived system, just in case my license number was called. But first got an earful of Captain Midnight:

"Now you might have thought your soul pilot, Captain Midnight here, was just flapping his lips when he said there was going to be some boss tricks and big treats on tonight's special show. Maybe you've got us pegged as some no-class outfit jiving in the sagebrush, don't know get-along-little-doggie from dactylic hexameter, so dumb we think Grape Nuts Flakes is a venereal disease. Well, how's this for some air-you-fucking-dition: we got America's main expert on poetry, history, and everything else to do us some short spots on the historical-emotional background of trick-or-treat. I mean this guy's got *fifteen*—count 'em— Ph.Ds on his wall. We're talking words like *foremost* and *intellectual* and *anagogic insights into symbolic expressions of metaphorical parallels,* and when you're talking that sort of stuff, only one man rises with the cream: that's the poet John Seasons. He works out of Baghdad-by-the-Bay, but his spirit abounds. Hey, when you want the tops you go to the top. So let me introduce John Seasons with Part One of a KRZE exclusive, 'A Social Demonology of the Hollow Weenie.' "

There was a brief pause, then, no doubt about it, John's voice, his fake professorial tone resonant with five scotches: "Good evening, ladies and gentlemen. My name is Christopher Columbus and you're a dead Indian."

That was it.

Captain Midnight jumped back in: "Didn't I *tell you* the man knows his shit? We're gonna hear more from him, just hang on, but first a little paean to his name, and another man you might wisely have for company on this night of wandering zombies and rabid werewolves, ain't that right, Jimmy Dean? Who're we talking about? Who else but 'Big Bad John.' "

I only half-listened to the song. The John I knew was neither big nor bad. Sharp tongued and a bit severe, like most poets, but sweet at heart. If he was self-destructive, it was only because he'd rather hurt himself than someone else. I was perplexed he hadn't mentioned the KRZE gig to me; John's only deep vanity was as an historian. He claimed to be a Metasexual Marxist, a school of historical scholarship where, according to John, one arrived at the dialectical truth by kissing tears from the eyes of victims. Maybe his KRZE series had come up after I left, or he'd neglected to tell me in the frenzy of my departure. But if all went right I'd probably see him in a day or so, and I could tell him he'd kept me company through a wild night. And maybe I could get a line on this weird radio station out of the Wind River Range.

"And speaking of the man," Captain Midnight came in at the end of the song, "here he is with Part Two in our public service series, 'A

Social Demonology of the Ol' Hollow Weenie.' This time we're going to hear from a famous seventeenth-century religious leader, an old-fashioned, honest-to-God, down-home preacher man."

John's voice came on: "The Reverend Cotton Mather at your service. In 1691, one of the female members of my congregation at North Church came to me with the sad admission that she could not open her mouth to pray. I, of course, made every effort to help her. I tried physical manipulation, prayer, admonitions . . . all without success—though, in a noble effort to save her soul, I refused to admit failure. A few nights later I had a dream in which an angel appeared to me and urged me to kiss the unfortunate woman and thereby unlock her mouth to offer her prayers to God for the redemption of her soul. A less experienced theologian might have been fooled. In the past, you see, I had always been visited by angels in my *study*, not my sleeping quarters, and while *awake*, not in the vulnerable state of dreams. It was obviously a false visitation, the devil in the guise of an angel, and a devil plainly manifested through the woman who would not open her mouth to pray. I denounced her as a witch. Following a proper trial, she was burned at the stake, and so completely had Satan inhabited her that even under the scourge of fire she refused to open her mouth except to scream."

"My *oh my*," Captain Midnight cut back in, "Reverend Mather don't seem too kindly disposed toward womenfolk. But don't you get blue behind it, honey. You give the Captain here a jingle on this Satanic night—he'd *like* to bob for your apples, know what I mean? While I'm waiting for the switchboard to light up, let's pin an ear to men of more modern understanding—Sam Cooke, say, with 'Bring It on Home to Me' and Roy Orbison's 'O Pretty Woman.'"

It had been John Seasons for sure. The supercilious, righteous whine, the smug, zealous certainty of the conclusions—I'd heard his Mather imitation many nights in North Beach bars.

"This John Seasons is a good buddy of mine, you know," I told my ghost. Evidently he wasn't impressed.

I honked the horn for the hell of it and bored on deeper into the night. It was all in my imagination, of course, but I could clearly hear the Pacific Ocean breaking on the edge of the continent.

About fifteen minutes later, John came on again, manifesting one of those inexplicable congruencies we call coincidence. At the same instant I saw the highway sign for Fort Bridger, John's voice began:

"Jim Bridger's the name. I trapped beaver in these mountains nigh onto a century ago. Traded the pelts for provisions and possibles, and pretty much went wherever my stick floated. Now what I wanna know, the thing that plagues on me, is what have you ignorant dungheads done with the buffalo? I used to traipse this country all over and it weren't nothing to eyeball thousands of them critters at the same time. Now I don't see hide nor ha'r. You got 'em on reservations like the Injuns?"

All right, John! Maybe needed a little work on the mountain man accent, but it was nice to hear a whack for the natural world. Not that I remember John *personally* caring much for the wilds. I'd once tried to get him to go backpacking with me and Kacy, but he'd declined with the explanation that every time he saw a blade of grass he wanted to jump on the nearest cable car. His heart knew better, though.

I was just outside Evanston, moving right along, when his next lick hit: a lugubrious blackface, the parody of a parody: "Mah name's John. John Henry. Ahm a steel-drivin' man. Whup tha steel. Whup the steel on down, Lawd Lawd. An' now them Southe'n Pacific muthafucks own half the Sierra Nevada."

I couldn't help myself. I had to stop in Evanston and call him, tell him how good it was to hear his voice, let him know there were listeners in the night. I figured the program was taped, so I called him at home from a Standard station. There was no answer but I let it ring; maybe he was in the basement printing.

About the fourteenth buzz someone answered, either out of breath or patience. "My *God*, all right, *who* is it?"

"My name's George Gastin," I said, thinking this was one of his boyfriends and maybe I'd interrupted something. "I'm calling John Seasons. We're old friends."

There was a breathy pause on the other end, then: "Well. I don't *like* bearing bad news, but John's in the hospital."

I sagged. "Is he all right?"

"They *think* so. All the tests are *good*. But for heavenssakes, he's been *unconscious* for *three* days."

"What happened?"

"It's . . . *unclear.*"

"Hey, pal—fuck that shit. I told you he was an old *friend.* I've taken him to the Emergency Room more times than I care to remember."

"Well don't get mad at *me* about it! *I* don't know you."

"Okay. You're right. I'm sorry. But I don't know you either, though you're answering his phone."

"I'm Steven."

Steven? *Steven?* I racked my brain. "You work at the Federal Building, right?"

"Yes, I do."

"I haven't met you, Steven, but I know from John he holds you in high regard. You looking after his place? The manuscripts and presses?"

"Yes. Larry asked if I would."

"I'm sure they're in good hands. Now tell me what happened. He get those Percodans mixed up with some Scotch?"

"Well, that's what the doctors are saying. Or he got drunk and forgot how many pills he was taking."

"Did he try to kill himself, Steven?" I made this as direct as I could.

"No one *really* knows. Larry found him on the kitchen floor unconscious. It could've been a mistake."

"No note?"

"No, nothing like *that.*"

"And this was three days ago, right?"

"Yes."

"And he's in a coma?"

"Yes. But as I said, all the signs are good. The brain waves are absolutely *normal.* The liver function isn't *great,* but with the amount he drinks that's to be expected. The doctors say it isn't really a coma. I ask if he's still in a coma and they say, 'No, he just hasn't regained consciousness yet.' Good Lord, you know how *technical* doctors are."

"What hospital is he in?"

270

"General."

"Well, listen. I'll be there as soon as I can. I'm on my way now, but I'm coming from Wyoming and there's some business first."

"I go by the hospital every morning before work. If he's awake I'll tell him to expect you."

"Did you know he's on the radio here tonight in Wyoming? A special series called 'A Social Demonology of the Hollow Weenie.' "

"*Really?* He never mentioned it to me, and we discuss his work all the time. I think he's a *fabulous* writer, but you know he's so hard on himself. It must be taped, of course, but I just can't believe he wouldn't have mentioned it. Are you sure it's John? The title sounds . . . well, *tacky.*"

"It's his name, it sounds just like him, and he lives in San Francisco."

"How odd."

"Yeah," I agreed, "and getting odder all the time."

"That's *so* true. You should see Haight Street these days."

I wanted to avoid the sociological at all costs. "Steven, listen, my time's up. Thanks, and sorry I jumped on you. I felt I had a right to know."

"I understand," Steven said. "I can appreciate your concern."

When I pulled out of the gas station I was so preoccupied I didn't realize for six blocks that I was heading downtown instead of out to I-80. I hung a U and had just straightened out the wheels when I saw three small skeletons dancing across the street about a block away, their bones shining with a pale green luminescence in the headlights. I wasn't frightened by their appearance—they obviously were kids dressed up in five-and-dime Halloween costumes—but I was terrified by my desire to stomp on the gas and run them down.

I didn't. I didn't even come close, not really. I hit the brakes instead and immediately pulled over and turned off the car, jamming on the emergency brake as hard as I could. I sat there watching the three little skeletons continue their skipping dance across the pavement and then disappear down a cross street, happily unaware that a man with an impulse to murder them sat watching from a car parked down the block.

After Eddie, how could the impulse even have entered my mind? I felt my exhaustion collapsing on its empty center, my point and purpose caving in to an oblivion of regrets I could neither shape nor salvage, an oblivion I was clearly seeking with a twisted vengeance, trying to destroy what I couldn't redeem, the gift I could neither deliver nor accept.

Yet it was also true that I hadn't even come close; I'd smothered the desire the moment it seized me. But would I again? I raised my fists and hammered them down on the steering wheel, hoping the wheel would break or the bones in my hands shatter or both: any reason to get out of that sleek white Cadillac and walk away. But with each blow all I felt was the congealing certainty that the only choice left was forward and my only chance was fast. I understood too late that it was too late to stop. So, with the rush of freedom that is doom's honey spilling in the heart, I got on it.

As I hit the on-ramp my ghost appeared, in the backseat this time, leaning forward to whisper, "George, oooh George, you almost did it back there. You better let me drive. You can't trust yourself anymore."

"Why don't you vanish for good," I said. "You're no help."

He laughed. "Okay, George. Sure thing. You bet." And he was gone, leaving an unnerving silence.

Five minutes and ten miles later, when I thought to turn the radio back on, Captain Midnight was doling out the encouragement: "Yup, the Captain's back from that trip down the voodoo track, and hey!, ain't we got fun? How are *you* doing on this night when the insane rip their chains from the walls and roam the night to play with the dead and plague the innocent? You still getting where you're going? Keeping on *keeping on?* I hope so, friend, 'cause if life ain't right with you, you better get right with life. Whatever *that* is on this ghoul-ridden night. You just tell 'em Captain Midnight, patron deejay of fool dreamers, prays nightly for your soul and twice on Halloween and Easter. *Lapidem esse aquam fontis vivi. Obscurum per obscurius, ignotum per ignotius.* Yes. And may the gods go with you, child.

"And now, because KRZE is dedicated to giving you heart for the path, or some path for the heart, whatever it is you think you need, here's John Seasons again with some more insightful demonology."

"My name's Black Bart. A lot of people asked me why I only robbed Wells Fargo stages . . . if it was something *personal* against Mr. Wells or Mr. Fargo or both. Well, not really. I just sorta figured anybody with that much money should be robbed."

"OW!" Captain Midnight shouted, "now there's a jack-o-lantern with a fuse. But your Captain's forced to concur that large piles of money are dangerous, so send me some if it's piling up on you and save yourself the grief. While you're getting it together, I got to attend to a couple of personal gigs. I could slap on a stack of platters and hope they didn't stick, but since it's Halloween I thought it might be a touch of class to leave you with some dead air. But to make it right by you, I'll bring back goodies that'll make you *drool.* Not just more boss sounds and John Seasons's exclusive demonology, but things you can't even imagine. But go ahead and wonder while yours truly visits the Lizard King and throws a few snowballs at the moon. Back in a flash, Jack—I'll make it up to you, and that's a promise."

The air went dead. I would've turned it off and listened to Donna's collection if it hadn't been for John's social commentaries. I didn't want to miss one. They connected me to someone real, and I was convinced beyond reason that John would live so long as I kept listening. I thought of him drifting in his coma and wondered if, like Elmer, he had a smile on his face.

I slipped into something of a coma myself, my mind blurred as the night blurred with speed, shadows whipping around me like torn sails, waves breaking in my mind, a mind I'd maybe gone out of, long gone, blooey, nobody home on the range, but I was taking it on home anyway. I flew down the west slope of the Rockies into Salt Lake City before I knew I was there. The lights snapped me out of my trance. I started looking for my buddy, the green dinosaur, and, when I didn't see him, felt like I'd lost a piece of magic. I settled for a Conoco next to an interchange. My bladder was a drop from bursting, but I stayed in the car with the windows up tight, cracking mine only a quick inch to tell the pump jockey to fill it with supreme. I was certain if I started talking the way I was thinking I'd be surrounded by squad cars faster than you could say, "Up against the wall, motherfucker." I didn't want to fly apart when my only hope was to fly, to freeze my bead on the Pacific shore and stand on the juice. I gave the kid a twenty for the gas and told him he could keep the change whether he prayed for my doomed ass or not. I came off the on-ramp running.

When you have to piss so bad your tonsils are under water, it's as hard to fly as it is to stand still, so at the beginning of the long desolate run across the saltflats between Salt Lake and Wendover, I cracked my momentum to pull over and piss, doing so with the profound appreciation that much of pleasure is mere relief. The night was so cold that my piss steamed as it soaked into the moonlit salt. There's nothing like a good, basic piss to clear the mind, and by volume I should've become lucid; but perhaps I was just giddy, because I asked my ghost as if he were present, "Are saltflats the ghosts of old oceans? Feel like the seashore? Can we count it as the Pacific if we come up short?"

No ghost. No answers. But I could feel him then, feel him as he waited for his moment, waited with the massive patience of a boulder that knows it will someday be sand for the hourglass. That was his presence, but underneath I felt his essence, and his essence was wind. I stood there with my dick in my hand—suddenly alive in a memory when I was ten and a hurricane had hit out of nowhere and I'd watched, awed, as the wind ripped petals from the rose garden and flung them against the windows, pressing their colors against the quivering glass. The next morning, as he looked at his stripped and ravaged roses, was the only time I'd ever seen my father cry. The memory of it made me start crying, too. "Help me, ghost," I asked, not sure whether I was talking to my father's or my own—both, I decided, since I needed all the help I could get. If ghosts help. No ghosts. No answers. I got back in the Cadillac and burned on down the line.

The best thing about saltflats is the flat: a straight, level shot to the horizon, the meeting of heaven and earth, the limit of sight. If you can go fast enough, you can see over the edge. The road was two-lane blacktop, and I opened it up all the way, straddling the white line unless the rare oncoming car sent me back to my lane.

The silence and distance were eating me up. I was just about to shut off Captain Midnight and spin a few records myself when there was an explosion of static on the radio and my Captain said, "Ah, back alive; proof against the demons so far, and so far, so good. 'But who can tell on this witch's flight/the true darkness from the dancing light?' Them fuckin' demons are tricky. That's why we asked troubadour John Seasons to offer us some insights into the dark. Oh John, *way up* there in your shaman trance, come in please."

"Good evening," John said mildly. "My name, if you don't know it, is J.P. Morgan, and I'm here tonight to reveal the secret to success in American business. I think you'll be surprised how simple it is. First, buy a steel mill. Secondly, buy workers. Buy them for as little as possible, but pay just enough to keep them going. Lastly, buy Congressmen, and pay them to enact tariff laws to keep out foreign steel. Politicians can be purchased cheaply, so buy in quantity. The goal, you see, is stability, and nothing destabilizes like competition. So remember: high prices, low wages, and a lock on the market. Because when you scrape off all the sentiment and rhetoric, spirit is for idiots and poetry for fools. Money is power. And, put bluntly, power rules."

Captain Midnight was right behind him. "Right on, Brother John! Time to get real out there. Get your nose to the stone. Bear down and deliver. You've got to be at least as real as the demons, and that's just to break even, Jack, hold your own ground. You got to get up over it or slide down under it or slip away in between. Think that over if you've got a mind, and in the meanwhile I'll make more than good on my promise to make it right by you for that dead air. You think I'm jiving? Well, eat shit and crawl under a rock, because sitting right beside me live in the studio is that legendary street prophet and avatar of the damaged, the one and only Fourth Wiseman. You've probably heard the mantra he chants every day, all day, for your edification and maybe salvation: 'The Fourth Wiseman delivered his gift and slipped away.' That *one* sentence, that single expression of holy being, is all his priestly vows allow him. But what you might *not* know is that he permits himself to answer *one* question every Halloween eve, and tonight it's my privilege, and yours, to have him here in the studio with us, and I blush with the honor of having been chosen to ask him his question for the year. Welcome to KRZE, sir. He's nodding his head and winging his yo-yo."

"Ask him what the gift was," I begged.

"We understand, sir," Captain Midnight went on, "that you can only answer your one question and not engage in conversational pleasantries, so let me get right to it. Will you tell us, please, *what* was the Fourth Wiseman's gift?"

I cheered.

"No one knows," the Fourth Wiseman said, and hearing his voice I knew this was either the Fourth Wiseman or an exceptional mimic. "Scholars generally recognize three possibilities, for which the evidence is about equal. The three most supportable possibilities for the Fourth Wiseman's gift are a song, a white rose, and a bow—the gesture of acknowledgment and respect, not the bough of a tree. But again, no one really knows."

"And which of the three do you favor," the Captain asked politely.

Silence. I heard my mother crying softly and my father, confused, saying, "Hey, it was a *great* dream: my brain turned into a white rose." I saw the rose petal kaleidoscope of colors smeared against the buckling glass as the wind milked their essence and infused the storm. I needed the names of the roses. I needed their protection.

"I beg your pardon, sir," Captain Midnight apologized. "I see the rules are strict—one question only. Thank you for being with us, you burned-out old speed freak, and please feel welcome to stay."

The Fourth Wiseman said, "The Fourth Wiseman delivered his gift and slipped away."

"Well, slip away if you want, but you listeners out there rocketing through the dark better stay glued to the groove and be ready to move because *here it is,* a lucky license plate number picked by our own Mystery Spotter, plucked from the random churn of things like a speck of gold from the cosmic froth, and if it's *your* number that's up and you call and identify yourself within *fifteen* minutes, you're gonna win two tickets to the dance. *The* dance, you dig what I'm saying?"

I looked down the road into my parents' rose garden and tried to remember the names of all the roses while Captain Midnight paused for a thunderous drumroll before announcing, "Well, well, well, we got a California plate—just goes to show our Mystery Spotter is everywhere you are, and you never know when her wild eyes may fall on you. Could be never. Could be your next heartbeat. Could be, ooooh, couldie be. But tonight's number could only be this one: BOP three-three-three. That's B as in Boo, O as in Overboard; P as in Psalm; three as in treys; three as in blind mice; three as in tri—be it trilogy, trident, trial and error, trick, or just a little bit harder. So okay, BOP three-three-three, California dreamer, whoever you are out there raving in the dark, you got fifteen minutes to call me at Beechwood 4-5789. But hey, Captain Midnight's gonna cut you some slack, Jack—I'm gonna give you twenty minutes to call in. Not only because I'm a righteous fool myself, but because the next side I'm gonna drop on you is so *rare* and so *fine* I don't want it interrupted by some crass promotional gimmick. This side just happens to be twenty minutes long. It's the only recording of this tune in *existence,* and the moment it's over I'm gonna burn it. That's right, you heard it straight: I'm laying on the flame the instant it's finished. So listen well, because the next time you hear it you'll be listening to your memory. And while the Captain isn't one to pass judgment on the musical sensibilities of his listeners, if this don't touch the living spirit in your poor, ragged heart, you best call a mortuary and make an appointment. I'll tell you the name of the man who made this music when it's done and burning."

I didn't have to wait long on the knowledge. The exhausted keening of the opening passage was already etched in my memory: Big Red playing my birthday song, "Mercury Falling."

I felt like everything at once and nothing forever. I felt triumphant my license number had been called, joyous that I'd connected with Mira, who I was sure had spotted me. But I was crushed by the realization that there wasn't a phone within a half-hour in any direction, and moved to tears by the first bars of Big Red's sax calling to the ghosts across the water as we pushed the glossy Merc coupe over the cliffs and stood at the windswept edge waiting for it to hit. I was stunned, confused, possessed, lost, found, confirmed in my faith and strangely bereft.

You can't be moved in that many directions at once without tearing apart.

My ghost was there beside me on the front seat. "You worthless jerk-off, *I want to dance.* You think when he said *the* dance he meant some fucking sock-hop in a crepe-festooned gym smelling of fifty-thousand P.E. classes? No, *you* make sure we're in the middle of absolutely nowhere, a thousand light-years from a phone, so we can't win the tickets. Screw your dumb moral victories. I'm sick of being cooped up in your cloying romance. If we make it to the ocean, you'll probably want to pave it so you don't have to finish and admit your failure. You've gone crazy, George. That's what I'm stuck to, a crazy fuck-up. But we'll just see about that—"

"Shut up!" I bellowed. "I want to listen to the music."

"Well, *I* want to dance. You too proud to dance with your ghost? Afraid people will point and giggle? What do you think they're doing now? Come on, George, if you're not going to do anything with your body but abuse it, give it to me. I could use one. Just don't include your mind in the deal, all right?"

"Shut the fuck up!" I screamed again, "this is my *birthday* song!" I reached over and twisted the volume all the way up.

But you can't drown out your ghost. He began singing, relentlessly off-key:

> *Happy birthday to you,*
> *Happy birthday to you,*
> *Happy birthday, mad George,*
> *Happy birthday toooo youuuu . . .*

Birthday Bow, I remembered. That was a name of one of the roses in the garden. My father was crying in the silence that Big Red had created. I could feel Kacy moving with me like a wave. A small blue rectangular miracle appeared before my eyes, a road sign:

EMERGENCY PHONE
1 MILE

I came off the gas and told my ghost, "Go get your dancing shoes, asshole." He laughed as he vanished.

The light above the phone box was broken so I used one of the birthday candles that couldn't be blown out for light as I carefully dialed BE4-5789.

Be-beep; be-beep; be-beep; be-beep; be-beep. The sound like an auger up my spinal cord. Busy.

I hung up and tried again. Still busy. I figured I had a minute left. I called the operator, hoping she'd believe my claim of emergency and cut in. I couldn't get the operator, not even a ring. Not even a hum. I tried BE4-5789 again and got nothing at all. The line was dead.

My ghost was standing beside me. "Irony eating you up is it, George? I'm afraid you're gonna become mutilated, just like that old con salesman warned you about. But that's *your* problem, buddy. *Me,* I'm going to dance."

"Be home early," I snarled at him as he disappeared.

Back in the Caddy and on the road, I caught the last notes of "Mercury Falling." *"Burn it,"* I urged Captain Midnight, seeing the brilliant red petals in my mind. "Gypsy Fire," I remembered aloud. "Borderflame. My Valentine."

Captain Midnight whispered, "Let's let his ghost go now." I heard him strike a match. "Whooooosh!" He laughed. "Memory."

The room growing darker as the petals clotted against the window. The yellow and orange was Carnival Glass. "Carnival Glass," I said it aloud. The orange and pink was Puppy Love. "Puppy Love, Kacy, isn't that a wonderful name for a rose?"

"Ashes to ashes," Captain Midnight intoned, "dust to dust. Round and round the music goes, here in the majesty of bloom, gone in the voluptuous exhilarations of decay. Purchase for the roots, food for its green flesh, and where it stops nobody knows. But don't you worry. The whole is perfect. It's just never the same. For example, stick an ear on these new kids from England doing good-ol'-boy Buddy Holly's tune from six years back—that's right, brighten up for some truth, grab some stash and hang *on* to your ass, because you got the Rolling Stones and 'Not Fade Away.'"

Tell me it still couldn't come up roses. I joined in on the second chorus, singing it with rock-solid, gospel-light joy,

Love for real not fade away!

And my ghost, suddenly appearing sitting cross-legged on the hood, pressed his face against the windshield and roared,

Doo-wop; doo-wop; doo-wop-bop.

He smiled sweetly and then reached down and tore off the windshield wipers like a baby giant tearing the wings off a fly. I was so shocked it took me a second to realize I couldn't see the road. He'd turned solid. My hands froze the wheel in position as I came down easy on the brakes, craning to see around him, my heart lurching against my ribs.

"Better let me drive now, George," my ghost said. "You're so fucked-up you can't see through me."

"Nova Red!" I yelled in his grinning face. "Warwhoop! Sun Maid! Candleflame! Trinket! Seabreeze!" I was under 50 and still on the road. As I strained to see around him he moved with me, but I caught a glimpse off to the right of a low shoulder and open saltflats beyond, and that was all I needed. I cranked the wheel to the right, bottomed out in the drainage swale, then shot out clear and clean, mashing the gas.

My ghost was still hanging on, still sitting calmly and cross-legged on the hood, grinning madly as foam drooled from his mouth and flecked the windshield. I glanced at the floorboards. Both packages of Rabi-Tabs were gone. It no longer mattered what was possible.

My ghost lifted a hand to his foamy mouth, wiped off a viscous gob, smeared it across the windshield.

"The Hokey-Pokey," I cried, "is raw orange with a yellow center. You put your whole self in and take your whole self out. The Bo Peep is light pink, white compared to my hat." I whipped off my stingy-brim and waved it in front of his foam-blurred face to blind him, then suddenly cranked the wheel hard-left and spun the Caddy through a full

360°, your classic brodie, and then I punched the gas and snapped one off to the right.

To see through the opaque Rabi-Tab film on the glass was difficult, but it looked like I'd thrown him off. My spirit broke with his first jarring stomp on the roof, dancing as he merrily sang:

> The kids in Bristol are as sharp as a pistol
> When they do the Bristol Stomp.

STOMP. STOMP. The headliner rippling as the roof buckled.

> It's really sumpin' when the joint is jumping
> When they do the Bristol Stomp.

STOMP. STOMP. Stomping on the roof.

My eardrums ached as I fishtailed to a stop, slammed it into reverse, punched it, and then did some stomping myself, down hard on the brakes. Nothing could budge him.

"Who am I?" he screamed. "*Who am I?*" He started singing again, to the tune of "Popeye,"

> I'm Ahab the Sailor Man—toot! toot!
> I stay as obsessed as I can—toot! toot!
> When weirdness starts swarming
> It's too late for warning
> Because things have got way out of hand.

"And you, George," he murmured, "you're the innocent heart of the whale."

The tip of a harpoon plunged through the roof, the barbed head burying itself in the seat about a half-inch from my head, so close it nicked the brim of my hat. A harpoon. How can you even think about something like that?

"Let me drive," he demanded. "You're wasted. It's over."

I drove. Rammed it in low, tached it up, popped the clutch. The nose of the Caddy lifted like it was some supercharged, nitro-snorting dragster getting off the mark. My ghost jumped back down on the hood and started tap dancing, stopping abruptly to say, "Let me drive. I *know* what you want; *I* know what you're looking for." And *tappidy-tappidy-dappity-tap* he started dancing again, not even swaying as I hit second and wound it out.

Over the engine scream and my dancing ghost and the blood pounding in my skull, a voice spoke clearly from the radio, a voice I'd only heard once in my life, four words in mimicry of his mother: "Come on . . . we're *late.*" Eddie. I hit the brakes so hard I whacked my head on the steering wheel.

My ghost, unmoved on the hood, was lip-synching with great exaggeration as Eddie's voice explained through the radio, "It was my favorite drawing. The horses are really deer who can pick up signals from ghosts with their horns like they were TV antennas or something. The big red flower can pick up signals from the sun and aim them at the deer. It's just a big red flower, I don't know what kind. The long green car is to go look for the flower and the deers. It needs big, tough wheels because it's a long way and the flower is hidden and the deer can run like the wind. And the sun's just there in the middle, you know, so you can see things. I didn't want to lose it."

I got the Caddy stopped, brought my knees out from under the wheel and up to my chest, and uncoiled a savage two-heeled kick at the radio. A woman screamed as the glass shattered. "It's done, George," my ghost said softly, his voice coming through the radio. I kicked it again and again, and with every blow a woman screamed through the speaker and my ghost told me it was over, to let go. I was reaching for the battery out of Joshua's music box to knock out the radio when I caught the glint off the gallon can of white gas on the backseat floor. In one motion I picked it up, swung it over the seat back, and bashed it against the radio. A woman screamed. I was swinging the can for another blow when I understood she was Kacy. I'd never heard her scream before, but I knew it was her. I dropped the can on the front seat. The blow had cracked a seam in the thin metal. The gas leaked in erratic dribbles, soaking into the seat. My sinuses burned from the fumes, tears spilling down my cheeks. I sagged back against the seat. My ghost grinned down trium-phantly.

"You drive," I said.

I swabbed my jacket sleeve across my face to wipe the tears, and when I blinked them open a moment later I was lying on the Caddy's hood, my face pressed to the windshield, staring into the empty eyes of my ghost.

"George," he said sweetly, "if you want to live you must throw yourself to death like a handful of pennies into a wishing well."

He pivoted from the waist and reached over into the backseat. He was putting a record on the turntable. I knew he was going to mock me by playing "Chantilly Lace," so I was stunned by the sound of an approaching train, its distant wail slicing the dark. For a spin-ning instant I thought we were parked on railroad tracks and would have leaped if I hadn't been hurled against the windshield as my ghost popped the clutch and smoked it through first into second as the train bore down and my brain bloomed with white roses. I shouted their names as he ripped it into high, wind tearing the petals away, flinging them to darkness and salt: "Cinderella! White King, White Madonna, White Feather, White Angel! Misty Dawn! Careless Moment!"

" 'Careless Moment?' " My ghost roared with laughter. He thought it was so funny he turned off the headlights. I was going to die. Meal for the roses, meat for the dream. "It's such a beautiful dream," my mother told me as the garden burned and the train screamed through my skull, obliterating every name I knew. I looked down at my body and only the skeleton remained. Then, taken by an undreamable serenity, I calmly stood up on the hood of the Caddy. I bowed to my ghost and then leapt lightly up on the roof. The wind sang through my bones. I could feel the exact pressure against every bone in my hands as I wrapped them around the jutting shaft of the harpoon and in one concerted movement snapped it off. I jumped back down on the hood, pivoting neatly as I swung the wooden shaft and smashed it through the windshield with all my might.

My ghost smiled up at me. "Took you long enough, George. I thought I was going to have to do it by myself."

I dove through the smashed-out window and went for his throat.

My flesh and blood hands were locked on the wheel where his had been, 130 mph straight ahead into the salt-glittering dark. I could have gone on forever if the engine hadn't blown.

The instant it blew I lost control. I tried to correct as it started sideways; a useless reflex. I was gone, and all I could do was hold on helpless and terrified as the Caddy slewed across the saltflats and finally went over, flipping three times bang-bang-bang, then skidding driver's side down, my cheek pressed against the window, greenish sparks shooting past as if I was being hurled through the stars. Then, violently, the Caddy flipped again, end over end, twisting, then again on its side in a wild twirl, and as it was slowing I felt like I was inside the milk bottle we'd used in our first, nervous game of spin-the-bottle. My first spin stopped on Mary Ann Meyers. I felt her lips touch mine, the jelly-tremor roll through my loins. I felt Kacy's arms slip around me naked in the sunlight. The whirling stopped. It was utterly still.

I took Harriet's letter from the glovebox and kicked out the smashed door. As I slid through the twisted frame I instinctively reached up to protect my hat, deeply pleased to find it still in place.

The cold night air was luxurious. I breathed deeply and looked around me. Not a thing for as far as I could see, just the totaled Eldorado against the salt, gleaming white-on-white. I thought about what I wanted to say as I struck a match to the box of candles you can't blow out, using their steady flame to ignite Harriet's letter, which burned with the scent of Shalimar.

I had run out of grand statements. I kept it so simple I didn't even say it aloud: *To the Big Bopper, Ritchie Valens, Buddy Holly, and the possibilities of love and music. And to the Holy Spirit.* I tossed Harriet's letter through a shattered window. The spilled gas detonated, flames billowing through the twisted metal, white paint bubbling as it charred, then the gas tank blew and it all roared upward. I stood there and watched it burn.

I had no idea where the highway was, so I started walking with the wind. I hadn't gone a mile when I saw a bloodstain spreading across the salt. Eddie's mother appeared before me, pointing at the bloodstain, her voice trembling like her finger: "It's just *not* right," she said. *"It is not right."*

"Yes it is," I told her. I kept walking.

The spreading bloodstain began to contract, rushing back to its center, spiraling downward into itself. As it vanished, a great whirlwind rose in its place. Blinded by flying salt, I knelt into a tight ball and covered my eyes. I awaited my judgment. But there were no words in the wind, no sound but it's own wild howl, nothing but itself. Within minutes it died away.

I'd walked another mile before realizing my hat was gone. I hoped it had blown all the way to Houston and landed on Double-Gone's head in a gospel stroke of glory.

In the distance I saw headlights on I-80 and took the shortest angle to the freeway. I was still a long ways out when I saw Kacy waiting in a cloud of light. I ran up, close enough to touch her, before I understood she was a ghost.

"Oh, George," she said, her voice breaking, "we were on a dirt road in the mountains out of La Paz. It was pouring rain. A huge slide came down and swept the van away. I was in the back. I hardly had time to scream. Nobody knows, George. It happened in late September and nobody even knows we're dead."

"Kacy," I cried, reaching for her, "it's not right; it's just not *right!*" And I held her a moment real in my arms before she disappeared.

EPILOGUE

That was the end of George Gastin's story. If there was more, I heard it in my dreams, because I was asleep— or, more accurately, given the combination of doom flu, car wreck, codeine, the root soup (which I don't think was an entirely innocent brew), and George himself, I lost consciousness at that point in the narrative. But I *was* there, and heard a sense of conclusion in his voice that left little doubt I was free to go.

When I awoke the next morning, I felt much better. Not hale and hearty, but human. The first thing I noticed was that George was gone. I checked out the window for his tow truck, but the lot was empty. I got dressed and walked over to the motel office. A note from Dorie and Bill, tacked on the door, explained they'd gone bird watching and would be back by nightfall; I was welcome to stay as long as I needed, pay when I was able. I decided I might as well take care of business while I could, in case I suffered a relapse.

I walked the four blocks to Itchman's to check on my truck. I caught Gus on his way to lunch.

"Well," he said in greeting, "I heard you've got so goddamned lazy you been trying to breed your truck to a redwood stump, hoping to produce some firewood. Seems to me it might be easier on the equipment to just go out and cut it regular."

"Gus, there's no need to run your lunch hour short just to abuse me. Give me the damages and the date I can pick it up."

"Six bills should cover it and four days ought to get it done. We got to order the steering knuckle out of Oxnard; they'll greydog it up tomorrow. There's terms if you need 'em."

"Six hundred." I sighed. "That's just what George said. Guy seems to know his shit. He bring you a lot of business?"

Gus shrugged. "When he's around and if he's in the mood. George sort of dances to his own music, know what I mean?"

"I know what you mean," I said in full agreement.

Gus smiled. "He bend your ear, did he?"

"Some."

"Yup, George can sling the shit. Did he tell you how he and some congressman's sixteen-year-old nympho daughter aced the CIA out a million-and-a-half in gold down in one of them South American countries, Peru or Bolivia or one of them? How he set it up so the CIA couldn't touch 'em?"

"No, but he said he had some money. He didn't charge me, did he tell you that?"

"Hell, he never charges anybody. But for all I know he lives on Welfare. Different music, like I said."

"Still music."

"Did he tell you about his rose garden? He's trying to produce a black rose."

"No, but that'd make sense. What he told me about was his pilgrimage in the Big Bopper's Cadillac."

"That's one I haven't heard," Gus said.

"He sure did right by me."

"I'm not saying George ain't a good one. I'm just saying he's something else."

"He sure is," I agreed.

And as I walked up the street a few minutes later, passing jack-o-lanterns and paper skeletons in the store windows, I thought to myself, *Yeah, he's something else all right: He's a ghost.*

And two years later I still think he's a ghost. His own, maybe mine, yours in disguise, a random shade. But a ghost for real and in fact, holy or otherwise. The ghost spun from the silver thread the white lines thin to when you're running on the edge. A ghost loosed with the bands of Orion and squeezed from the sweet influences of Pleiades bound. A ghost risen on the river mist or released in the coil of flames. A rogue ghost. Spirit. A white rose. Rain for the flower in the spiraling root of the dream.

I don't know, and make no claims. But he was at least the ghost of what his journey honored: the love and music already made; the love and music yet possible for making. A ghost of a chance. A ghost of the honest gospel light and wild joy shaking our bones. The ghost in all of us who would dance at the wedding of the sun and moon.

Wop-bop-a-loop-bop-a-wham-bam-boom.

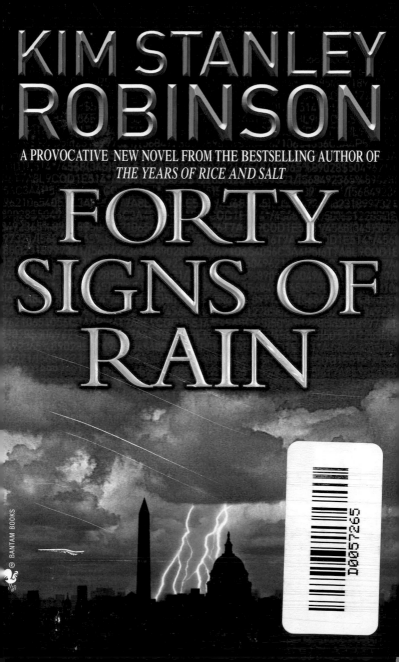

KIM STANLEY ROBINSON

A PROVOCATIVE NEW NOVEL FROM THE BESTSELLING AUTHOR OF
THE YEARS OF RICE AND SALT

FORTY SIGNS OF RAIN

ALSO BY KIM STANLEY ROBINSON

And don't miss

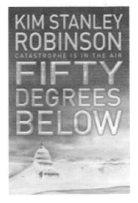

the thrilling follow-up to
FORTY SIGNS OF RAIN
coming in November 2005

Praise for FORTY SIGNS OF RAIN

Chosen as Required Reading by the *New York Post*

"It would be a very good thing if more people with actual influence read Kim Stanley Robinson's *Forty Signs of Rain*. It's a funny, convincing, intelligent book."
—*Independent* (UK)

"Brings together the ideas-driven format of science fiction with a narrative that is rich in closely observed characters and a wonderfully vivid sense of place... *Forty Signs of Rain* depicts a society sleep-walking towards the abyss.... The Washington flood forms the novel's dramatic conclusion and is a sign of worse to come. Robinson has written a slow-moving yet absorbing narrative; it's clear he is pacing himself for the long run of a trilogy. His great achievement here is to bring the practice of science alive—from the supposedly objective peer review process, to the day-to-day work of researchers in the lab—and to place this in an all-too-familiar world of greedy capitalists and unprincipled politicians. Robinson's critique of science is heartfelt: scientists should stop being tools in someone else's endgame. But his message to us all is no less challenging and urgent. Humans have gone from being the smartest animal on the savannah to being 'experts at denial.' He suggests that the storm clouds are gathering on the horizon, but we can no longer read the danger signs."
—*Guardian* (UK)

"Provide[s] an unforgettable demonstration of what can go wrong when an ecological balance is upset."
—*New York Times Book Review*

"Shows us the dysfunctional intersection of science and politics ... Its climactic scene—a giant storm that produces catastrophic flooding and submerges most of Washington—announces a cascade of long-denied consequences, just as the title promised."
—*Washington Post*

"Robinson knows how to juxtapose the quotidian details of urban life with really big, really scary environmental disasters." —*San Francisco Chronicle*

"Absorbing and convincing."
—*Nature*

"A convincing story of weather disasters in the not-too-distant future ... Robinson skips between the domestic, scientific and political spheres without missing a beat and delivers a hot-topic page-turner that leaves the reader gasping and stranded at high tide." —*BookPage*

"Topical and compelling."
—*Booklist*

"Utterly convincing. Robinson clearly cares deeply about our planet's future, and he makes the reader care as well."
—*Publishers Weekly*

"Filled with the suspense and disaster of what global warming may bring ... the second and third installments of the trilogy should be humdingers."
—*Rocky Mountain News*

"A scientifically grounded thriller that should raise eyebrows in Washington." —*St. Louis Post-Dispatch*

"Kim Stanley Robinson presents the warning signs of environmental disaster in a warm, gentle novel of family life. He makes heroes of scientific bureaucrats who still remember why they became scientists.... Continuously engaging." —*Denver Post*

"Robinson giv[es] voice to scientific, ecological and well-thought-out musings about near-future paybacks from Mother Nature. And you know what they say about paybacks." —*Kansas City Star*

"Kim Stanley Robinson is science fiction's answer to Martin Luther King Jr. and Louis Farrakhan."
—*Washington City Paper*

"A fascinating depiction of the workings of science and politics, and an urgent call for us to pull our heads from the sand and confront the threat of climate change. We should listen." —*F&SF*

"The first part of *The Day After Tomorrow,* but with good science and a more realistic time frame...Robinson's books are an interesting combination of character and exposition. He creates...a cast of engaging folks and sets them about their daily lives, then slowly moves the stage around them. As a result, there's not a lot of what you might call plot, but it really doesn't matter. You're hooked and you want to watch the scientific soap opera for just one more episode before you put it down, and hey, all that climate stuff is pretty darn interesting too. The first book takes us up to the edge of the climactic precipice, and the world in it looks pretty much like the one we're used to.... The next two books, due to come out at one-year intervals, will show a more dramatically changed world. I can't wait."
—*SFRevu*

"A glorious stew of disparate elements, from displaced Tibetans and their white tigers, to UCSD bioscience types, to National Science Foundation administrators and lusty triathletes. Warming weather and geopolitical considerations are the broth in which characters float.... The novel's concerns range from local to global, from anthropology and politics to gene therapy, abstruse mathematics, and surfers losing and maybe finding love. Even as the Potomac floods, Robinson tosses in a scene that made me whoop with joyous relief, before piling on the tensions again. Yep, it is the start of a trilogy, and, appropriately enough, ends with a...cliffhanger."
—*San Diego Union-Tribune*

PRAISE FOR *THE YEARS OF RICE AND SALT*

"This vast, magisterial novel is Robinson's most ambitious effort at alternate history...refracted by the ensorcelled lens of a wizard with a doctorate in history and a wicked sense of humor.... Brilliantly conceived...this book will probably place high on the list of Robinson's best work."
—*Booklist*

"Exceptional and engrossing." —*New York Post*

"Ambitious...ingenious." —*Newsday*

"A thoughtful, magisterial alternate history from one of science fiction's most important writers."
—*New York Times Book Review*

BOOKS BY
KIM STANLEY ROBINSON

Fiction

The Mars Trilogy
Red Mars
Green Mars
Blue Mars

Three Californias
The Wild Shore
The Gold Coast
Pacific Edge

Escape from Kathmandu
A Short, Sharp Shock
Green Mars (novella)
The Blind Geometer
The Memory of Whiteness
Icehenge
The Planet on the Table
Remaking History
Antarctica
The Martians
The Years of Rice and Salt

Nonfiction
The Novels of Philip K. Dick

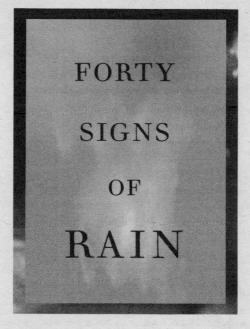

FORTY

SIGNS

OF

RAIN

Kim Stanley Robinson

BANTAM BOOKS

FORTY SIGNS OF RAIN

A Bantam Book

PUBLISHING HISTORY

Bantam hardcover edition published June 2004
Bantam mass market edition / August 2005

Published by
Bantam Dell
A Division of Random House, Inc.
New York, New York

Library of Congress Catalog Card Number: 2003063683

Bantam Books and the rooster colophon are registered trademarks of
Random House, Inc.

ISBN 0-553-58580-0

Printed in the United States of America
Published simultaneously in Canada

www.bantamdell.com

OPM 10 9 8 7 6 5 4 3 2 1

TABLE OF CONTENTS

FORTY

SIGNS

OF

RAIN

I

THE

BUDDHA

ARRIVES

The Earth is bathed in a flood of sunlight. A fierce inundation of photons—on average, 342 joules per second per square meter. 4185 joules (one Calorie) will raise the temperature of one kilogram of water by one degree Celsius. If all this energy were captured by the Earth's atmosphere, its temperature would rise by ten degrees Celsius in one day.

Luckily much of it radiates back to space. How much depends on albedo and the chemical composition of the atmosphere, both of which vary over time.

A good portion of Earth's albedo, or reflectivity, is created by its polar ice caps. If polar ice and snow were to shrink significantly, more solar energy would stay on Earth. Sunlight would penetrate oceans previously covered by ice, and warm the water. This would add heat and melt more ice, in a positive feedback loop.

The Arctic Ocean ice pack reflects back out to space a few percent of the total annual solar energy budget. When the Arctic ice pack was first measured by nuclear submarines in the 1950's, it averaged thirty feet thick in midwinter. By the end of the century it was down to fifteen. Then one August the ice broke up into large tabular bergs, drifting on the currents, colliding and separating, leaving broad lanes of water open to the continuous po-

lar summer sunlight. The next year the breakup started in July, and at times more than half the surface of the Arctic Ocean was open water. The third year, the breakup began in May.

That was last year.

WEEKDAYS ALWAYS begin the same. The alarm goes off and you are startled out of dreams that you immediately forget. Predawn light in a dim room. Stagger into a hot shower and try to wake up all the way. Feel the scalding hot water on the back of your neck, ah, the best part of the day, already passing with the inexorable clock. Fragment of a dream, you were deep in some problem set now escaping you, just as you tried to escape it in the dream. Duck down the halls of memory—gone. Dreams don't want to be remembered.

Evaluate the night's sleep. Anna Quibler decided the previous night had not been so good. She was exhausted already. Joe had cried twice, and though it was Charlie who had gotten up to reassure him, as part of their behavioral conditioning plan which was intended to convey to Joe that he would never again get Mom to visit him at night, Anna had of course woken up too, and vaguely heard Charlie's reassurances: "Hey. Joe. What's up. Go back to sleep, buddy, it's the middle of the night here. Nothing gets to happen until morning, so you might as well. This is pointless this wailing, why do you do this, good night damn it."

A brusque bedside manner at best, but that was part of the plan. After that she had tossed and turned for long minutes, trying heroically not to think of work. In years past she had recited in her head Edgar Allan Poe's poem "The Raven," which she had memorized in high school and which had a nice soporific effect, but then one night she had thought to herself, "Quoth the raven, 'Livermore,'" because of work troubles she was having with some people out at Lawrence Livermore. After that the poem was ruined as a sleep aid because the moment she even thought of "The Raven" she thought about work. In general Anna's thoughts had a tropism toward work issues.

Shower over, alas. She dried and dressed in three minutes. Downstairs she filled a lunch box for her older boy. Nick liked and indeed insisted that his lunch be exactly the same every day, so it was no great trouble to assemble it. Peanut butter sandwich, five carrots, apple, chocolate milk, yogurt, roll of lunch meat, cheese stick, cookie. Two minutes for that, then throw in a freeze pack to keep it chilled. As she got the coldpacks out of the freezer she saw the neat rows of plastic bottles full of her frozen milk, there for Charlie to thaw and feed to Joe during the day when she was gone. That reminded her, not that she would have forgotten much longer given how full her breasts felt, that she had to nurse the bairn before she left. She clumped back upstairs and lifted Joe out of his crib, sat on the couch beside it. "Hey love, time for some sleepy nurses."

Joe was used to this, and glommed onto her while still almost entirely asleep. With his eyes closed he looked like an angel. He was getting bigger but she could still cradle him in her arms and watch him curl into her like a new infant. Closer to two than one now, and a regular bruiser, a wild man who wearied her; but not now. The warm sensation of being suckled put her body back to sleep, but a part of her mind was already at work, and so she detached him and shifted him around to the other breast for four more minutes. In his first months she had had to pinch his nostrils together to get him to come off, but now a tap on the nose would do it, for the first breast at least. On the second one he was more recalcitrant. She watched the second hand on the big clock in his room sweep up and around. When they were done he would go back to sleep and snooze happily until about nine, Charlie said.

She hefted him back into his crib, buttoned up and kissed all her boys lightly on the head. Charlie mumbled "Call me, be careful." Then she was down the stairs and out the door, her big work bag over her shoulder.

The cool air on her face and wet hair woke her fully for the first time that day. It was May now and the late spring mornings had only a little bit of chill left to them, a delicious sensation given the humid heat that was to come. Fat gray clouds rolled just over the buildings lining Wisconsin Avenue. Truck traffic roared south. Splashes of dawn sunlight struck the metallic blue sheen of the windows on the skyscrapers up at Bethesda Metro, and as Anna walked briskly along it occurred to her, not for the first time, that this was one of the high points of her day. There were some disturbing implications in that fact, but she banished those and enjoyed the feel of the air and the tumble of the clouds over the city.

She passed the Metro elevator kiosk to extend her walk by fifty yards, then turned and clumped down the little stairs to the bus stop. Then down the big stairs of the escalator, into the dimness of the great tube of ribbed concrete that was the underground station. Card into the turnstile, *thwack* as the triangular barriers disappeared into the unit, pull her card out and through to the escalator down to the tracks. No train there, none coming immediately (you could hear them and feel their wind long before the lights set into the platform began to flash) so there was no need to hurry. She sat on a concrete bench that positioned her such that she could walk straight into the car that would let her out at Metro Center directly in the place closest to the escalators down to the Orange Line East.

At this hour she was probably going to find an open seat on the train when it arrived, so she opened her laptop and began to study one of the jackets, as they still called them: the grant proposals that the National Science Foundation received at a rate of fifty thousand a year. "Mathematical and Algorithmic Analysis of Palindromic Codons as Predictors of a Gene's Protein Expression." The project hoped to develop an algorithm that had shown some success in predicting which proteins any given gene sequence in human DNA would express. As genes expressed a huge variety of proteins, by unknown ways and with variations that were not understood, this kind of predicting operation would be a very useful thing if it could be done. Anna was dubious, but genomics was not her field. It would be one to give to Frank Vanderwal. She noted it as such and queued it in a forward to him, then opened the next jacket.

The arrival of a train, the getting on and finding of a seat, the change of trains at Metro Center, the getting off at the Ballston stop in Arlington, Virginia: all were actions accomplished without conscious thought, as she read or pondered the proposals she had in her laptop. The first one still struck her as the most interesting of the morning's bunch. She would be interested to hear what Frank made of it.

Coming up out of a Metro station is about the same everywhere: up a long escalator, toward an oval of gray sky and the heat of the day. Emerge abruptly into a busy urban scene.

The Ballston stop's distinction was that the escalator topped out in a big vestibule leading to the multiple glass doors of a building. Anna entered this building without glancing around, went to the nice little open-walled shop selling better-than-usual pastries and packaged sandwiches, and bought a lunch to eat at her desk. Then she went back outside to make her usual stop at the Starbucks facing the street.

This particular Starbucks was graced by a staff maniacally devoted to speed and precision; they went at their work like a drum and bugle corps. Anna loved to see it. She liked efficiency anywhere she found it, and more so as she grew older. That a group of young people could turn what was potentially a very boring job into a kind of strenuous athletic performance struck her as admirable and heartening. Now it cheered her once again to move rapidly forward in the long queue, and see the woman at the computer look up at her when she was still two back in line and call out to her teammates, "Tall latte half-caf, nonfat, no foam!" and then, when Anna got to the front of the line, ask her if she wanted anything else today. It was easy to smile as she shook her head.

Then outside again, doubled paper coffee cup in hand, to the NSF building's west entrance. Inside she showed her badge to security in the hall, then crossed the atrium to get to the south elevators.

Anna liked the NSF building's interior. The structure was hollow, featuring a gigantic central atrium, an octagonal space that extended from the floor to the skylight, twelve stories above. This empty space, as big as some buildings all by itself, was walled by the interior windows of all the NSF offices. Its upper part was occupied by a large hanging mobile, made of metal curved bars painted in primary colors. The ground floor was occupied by various small businesses facing the atrium—pizza place, hair stylist, travel agency, bank outlet.

A disturbance caught Anna's eye. At the far door to the atrium there was a flurry of maroon, a flash of brass, and then suddenly a resonant low chord sounded, filling the big space with a vibrating *blaaa,* as if the atrium itself were a kind of huge horn.

A bunch of Tibetans, it looked like, were now marching into the atrium: men and women wearing belted maroon robes and yellow winged conical caps. Some played long straight antique horns, others thumped drums or swung censers around, dispensing clouds of sandalwood. It was as if a parade entry had wandered in from the street by mistake. They crossed the atrium chanting, skip-stepping, swirling, all in majestic slow motion.

They headed for the travel agency, and for a second Anna wondered if they had come in to book a flight home. But then she saw that the travel agency's windows were empty.

This gave her a momentary pang, because these windows had always been filled by bright posters of tropical beaches and European castles, changing monthly like calendar photos, and Anna had often stood before them while eating her lunch, traveling mentally within them as a kind of replacement for the real travel that she and Charlie had given up when Nick was born. Sometimes it had occurred to her that given the kinds of political and bacterial violence that were often behind the scenes in those photos, mental travel was perhaps the best kind.

But now the windows were empty, the small room behind them likewise. In the doorway the Tibetanesque performers were now massing, in a crescendo of chant and brassy brass, the incredibly low notes vibrating the air almost visibly, like the cartoon soundtrack bassoon in *Fantasia*.

Anna moved closer, dismissing her small regret for the loss of the travel agency. New occupants, fogging the air with incense, chanting or blowing their hearts out: it was interesting.

In the midst of the celebrants stood an old man, his brown face a maze of deep wrinkles. He smiled, and Anna saw that the wrinkles mapped a lifetime of smiling that smile. He raised his right hand, and the music came to a ragged end in a hyperbass note that fluttered Anna's stomach.

The old man stepped free of the group and bowed to the four walls of the atrium, his hands held together before him. He dipped his chin and sang, his chant as low as any of the horns, and split into two notes, with a resonant head tone distinctly audible over the deep clear bass, all very surprising coming out of such a slight man. Singing thus, he walked to the doorway of the travel agency and there touched the doorjambs on each side, exclaiming something sharp each time.

"Rig yal ba! Chos min gon pa!"

The others all exclaimed *"Jetsun Gyatso!"*

The old man bowed to them.

And then they all cried *"Om!"* and filed into the little office space, the brassmen angling their long horns to make it in the door.

A young monk came back out. He took a small rectangular card from the loose sleeve of his robe, pulled some protective backing from sticky strips on the back of the card, and affixed it carefully to the window next to the door. Then he retreated inside.

Anna approached the window. The little sign said

EMBASSY OF KHEMBALUNG

An embassy! And a country she had never heard of, not that that was particularly surprising, new countries were popping up all the time, they were one of the UN's favorite dispute-settlement strategies. Perhaps a deal had been cut in some troubled part of Asia, and this Khembalung created as a result.

But no matter where they were from, this was a strange place for an embassy. It was very far from Massachusetts Avenue's ambassadorial stretch of unlikely architecture, unfamiliar flags, and expensive landscaping; far from Georgetown, Dupont Circle, Adams-Morgan, Foggy Bottom, East Capitol Hill, or any of the other likely haunts for locating a respectable embassy. Not just Arlington, but the NSF building no less!

Maybe it was a scientific country.

Pleased at the thought, pleased to have something new in the building, Anna approached closer still. She tried to read some small print she saw at the bottom of the new sign.

The young man who had put out the sign reappeared. He had a round face, a shaved head, and a quick little mouth, like Betty Boop's. His expressive black eyes met hers directly.

"Can I help you?" he said, in what sounded to her like an Indian accent.

"Yes," Anna said. "I saw your arrival ceremony, and I was just curious. I was wondering where you all come from."

"Thank you for your interest," the youth said politely, ducking his head and smiling. "We are from Khembalung."

"Yes, I saw that, but..."

"Ah. Our country is an island nation. We are living in the Bay of Bengal, near the mouth of the Ganges."

"I see," Anna said, surprised; she had thought they

would be from somewhere in the Himalayas. "I hadn't heard of it."

"It is not a big island. Nation status has been a recent development, you could say. Only now are we establishing a representation."

"Good idea. Although, to tell the truth, I'm surprised to see an embassy in here. I didn't think of this as being the right kind of space."

"We chose it very carefully," the young monk said.

They regarded each other.

"Well," Anna said, "very interesting. Good luck moving in. I'm glad you're here."

"Thank you." Again he nodded.

Anna did the same and took her leave.

But as she turned to go, something caused her to look back. The young monk still stood there in the doorway, looking across at the pizza place, his face marked by a tiny grimace of distress.

Anna recognized the expression at once. When her older son Nick was born she had stayed home with him, and those first several months of his life were a kind of blur to her. She had missed her work, and doing it from home had not been possible. By the time maternity leave was over they had clearly needed her at the office, and so she had started working again, sharing the care of Nick with Charlie and some baby-sitters, and eventually a day-care center in a building in Bethesda, near the Metro stop. At first Nick had cried furiously whenever she left for any reason, which she found excruciating; but then he had seemed to get used to it. And so did she, adjusting as everyone must to the small pains of the daily departure. It was just the way it was.

Then one day she had taken Nick down to the day-care center—it was the routine by then—and he didn't cry when she said good-bye, didn't even seem to care or to notice.

But for some reason she had paused to look back into the window of the place, and there on his face she saw a look of unhappy, stoical determination—determination not to cry, determination to get through another long lonely boring day—a look which on the face of a toddler was simply heartbreaking. It had pierced her like an arrow. She had cried out involuntarily, even started to rush back inside to take him in her arms and comfort him. Then she reconsidered how another good-bye would affect him, and with a horrible wrenching feeling, a sort of despair at all the world, she had left.

Now here was that very same look again, on the face of this young man. Anna stopped in her tracks, feeling again that stab from five years before. Who knew what had caused these people to come halfway around the world? Who knew what they had left behind?

She walked back over to him.

He saw her coming, composed his features. "Yes?"

"If you want," she said, "later on, when it's convenient, I could show you some of the good lunch spots in this neighborhood. I've worked here a long time."

"Why, thank you," he said. "That would be most kind."

"Is there a particular day that would be good?"

"Well—we will be getting hungry today," he said, and smiled. He had a sweet smile, not unlike Nick's.

She smiled too, feeling pleased. "I'll come back down at one o'clock and take you to a good one then, if you like."

"That would be most welcome. Very kind."

She nodded. "At one, then," already recalibrating her work schedule for the day. The boxed sandwich could be stored in her office's little refrigerator.

Anna completed her journey to the south elevators. Waiting there she was joined by Frank Vanderwal. They greeted each other, and she said, "Hey I've got an interesting jacket for you."

He mock-rolled his eyes. "Is there any such thing for a burnt-out case like me?"

"Oh I think so." She gestured back at the atrium. "Did you see our new neighbor? We lost the travel agency but gained an embassy, from a little country in Asia."

"An embassy, here?"

"I'm not sure they know much about Washington."

"I see." Frank grinned his crooked grin, a completely different thing than the young monk's sweet smile, sardonic and knowing. "Ambassadors from Shangri-La, eh?" One of the UP arrows lit, and the elevator door next to it opened. "Well, we can use them."

PRIMATES IN elevators. People stood in silence looking up at the lit numbers on the display console, as per custom.

Again the experience caused Frank Vanderwal to contemplate the nature of their species, in his usual sociobiologist's mode. They were mammals, social primates: a kind of hairless chimp. Their bodies, brains, minds, and societies had grown to their current state in East Africa over a period of about two million years, while the climate was shifting in such a way that forest cover was giving way to open savannah.

Much was explained by this. Naturally they were distressed to be trapped in a small moving box. No savannah experience could be compared to it. The closest analog might have been crawling into a cave, no doubt behind a shaman carrying a torch, everyone filled with great awe and very possibly under the influence of psychotropic drugs and religious rituals. An earthquake during such a visit to the underworld would be about all the savannah mind could contrive as an explanation for a modern trip in an elevator car. No wonder an uneasy silence reigned; they were in the presence of the sacred. And the last five thousand years of civilization had not been anywhere near enough time for any evolutionary adaptations to alter these mental reactions. They were still only good at the things they had been good at on the savannah.

Anna Quibler broke the taboo on speech, as people would when all the fellow passengers were cohorts. She said to Frank, continuing her story, "I went over and introduced myself. They're from an island country in the Bay of Bengal."

"Did they say why they rented the space here?"

"They said they had picked it very carefully."

"Using what criteria?"

"I didn't ask. On the face of it, you'd have to say proximity to NSF, wouldn't you?"

Frank snorted. "That's like the joke about the starlet and the Hollywood writer, isn't it?"

Anna wrinkled her nose at this, surprising Frank; although she was proper, she was not prudish. Then he got it: her disapproval was not at the joke, but at the idea that these new arrivals would be that hapless. She said, "I think they're more together than that. I think they'll be interesting to have here."

Homo sapiens is a species that exhibits sexual dimorphism. And it's more than a matter of bodies; the archaeological record seemed to Frank to support the notion that the social roles of the two sexes had deviated early on. These differing roles could have led to differing thought processes, such that it would be possible to characterize plausibly the existence of unlike approaches even to ostensibly non-gender-differentiated activities, such as science. So that there could be a male practice of science and a female practice of science, in other words, and these could be substantially different activities.

These thoughts flitted through Frank's mind as their elevator ride ended and he and Anna walked down the hall around to their offices. Anna was as tall as he was, with a nice figure, but the dimorphism differentiating them extended to their habits of mind and their scientific practice, and that might explain why he was a bit uncomfortable with her. Not that this was a full characterization of his attitude. But she did science in a way that he found annoying. It was not a matter of her being warm and fuzzy, as you might expect from the usual characterizations of feminine thought—on the contrary, Anna's scientific work (she still often coauthored papers in statistics, despite her bureaucratic load) often displayed a finicky perfectionism that made her a very meticulous scientist, a first-rate statistician— smart, quick, competent in a range of fields and really excellent in more than one. As good a scientist as one could find for the rather odd job of running the Bioinformatics Division at NSF, good almost to the point of exaggeration—too precise, too interrogatory—it kept her from pursuing a course of action with drive. Then again, at NSF maybe that was an advantage.

In any case she was so intense about it. A kind of Puritan of science, rational to an extreme. And yet of course at the same time that was all such a front, as with the early Puritans; the hyperrational coexisted in her with all the emotional openness, intensity, and variability that was the American female interactional paradigm and social role. Every female scientist was therefore potentially a kind of Mr. Spock, the rational side foregrounded and emphasized while the emotional side was denied, and the two coexisting at odds with one another.

On the other hand, judged on that basis, Frank had to admit that Anna seemed less split-natured than many women scientists he had known. Pretty well integrated, really. He had spent many hours of the past year working

with her, engaged in interesting discussions in the pursuit
of their shared work. No, he liked her. The discomfort
came not from any of her irritating habits, not even the nit-
picking or hairsplitting that made her so strikingly eponymous (though no one dared joke about that to her), habits
that she couldn't seem to help and didn't seem to notice—
no—it was more the way her hyperscientific attitude combined with her passionate female expressiveness to suggest
a complete science, or even a complete humanity. It reminded Frank of himself.

Not of the social self that he allowed others to see, admittedly; but of his internal life as he alone experienced it.
He too was stuffed with extreme aspects of both rationality and emotionality. This was what made him uncomfortable: Anna was too much like him. She reminded him of
things about himself he did not want to think about. But
he was helpless to stop his trains of thought. That was one
of his problems.

Halfway around the circumference of the sixth floor,
they came to their offices. Frank's was one of a number of
cubicles carving up a larger space; Anna's was a true office
right across from his cubicle, a room of her own, with a
foyer for her secretary Aleesha. Both their spaces, and all
the others in the maze of crannies and rooms, were filled
with the computers, tables, file cabinets, and crammed
bookshelves that one found in scientific offices everywhere. The decor was standard degree-zero beige for
everything, indicating the purity of science.

In this case it was all rendered human, and even handsome, by the omnipresent big windows on the interior
sides of the rooms, allowing everyone to look across the
central atrium and into all the other offices. This combination of open space and the sight of fifty to a hundred other
humans made each office a slice or echo of the savannah.
The occupants were correspondingly more comfortable at

the primate level. Frank did not suffer the illusion that anyone had consciously planned this effect, but he admired the instinctive grasp on the architect's part of what would get the best work out of the building's occupants.

He sat down at his desk. He had angled his computer screen away from the window so that when necessary he could focus on it, but now he sat in his chair and gazed out across the atrium. He was near the end of his yearlong stay at NSF, and the workload, while never receding, was simply becoming less and less important to him. Piles of articles and hard-copy jackets lay in stacks on every horizontal surface, arranged in Frank's complex throughput system. He had a lot of work to do. Instead he looked out the window.

The colorful mobile filling the upper half of the atrium was a painfully simple thing, basic shapes in primary colors, very like a kindergartner's scribble. Frank's many activities included rock climbing, and often he had occupied his mind by imagining the moves he would need to make to climb the mobile. There were some hard sections, but it would make for a fun route.

Past the mobile, he could see into one hundred and eight other rooms (he had counted). In them people typed at screens, talked in couples or on the phone, read, or sat in seminar rooms around paper-strewn tables, looking at slide shows, or talking. Mostly talking. If the interior of the National Science Foundation were all you had to go on, you would have to conclude that doing science consisted mostly of sitting around in rooms talking.

This was not even close to true, and it was one of the reasons Frank was bored. The real action of science took place in laboratories, and anywhere else experiments were being conducted. What happened here was different, a kind of metascience, one might say, which coordinated scientific activities, or connected them to other human action, or funded them. Something like that; he was having trouble characterizing it, actually.

The smell of Anna's Starbucks latte wafted in from her office next door, and he could hear her on the phone already. She too did a lot of talking on the phone. "I don't know, I have no idea what the other sample sizes are like. . . . No, not statistically insignificant, that would mean the numbers were smaller than the margin of error. What you're talking about is just statistically meaningless. Sure, ask him, good idea."

Meanwhile Aleesha, her assistant, was on her phone as well, patiently explaining something in her rich D.C. contralto. Unraveling some misunderstanding. It was an obvious if seldom acknowledged fact that much of NSF's daily business was accomplished by a cadre of African-American women from the local area, women who often seemed decidedly unconvinced of the earth-shattering importance that their mostly Caucasian employers attributed to the work. Aleesha, for instance, displayed the most skeptical politeness Frank had ever seen; he often tried to emulate it, but without, he feared, much success.

Anna appeared in the doorway, tapping on the door-jamb as she always did, to pretend that his space was an office. "Frank, I forwarded a jacket to you, one about an algorithm."

"Let's see if it arrived." He hit CHECK MAIL, and up came a new one from *aquibler@nsf.gov.* He loved that address. "It's here, I'll take a look at it."

"Thanks." She turned, then stopped. "Hey listen, when are you due to go back to UCSD?"

"End of July or end of August."

"Well, I'll be sorry to see you go. I know it's nice out there, but we'd love it if you'd consider putting in a second year, or even think about staying permanently, if you like it. Of course you must have a lot of irons in the fire."

"Yes," Frank said noncommittally. Staying longer than his one-year stint was completely out of the question. "That's nice of you to ask. I've enjoyed it, but I should probably get back home. I'll think about it, though."

"Thanks. It would be good to have you here."

Much of the work at NSF was done by visiting scientists, who came on leave from their home institutions to run NSF programs in their area of expertise for periods of a year or two. The grant proposals came pouring in by the thousands, and program directors like Frank read them, sorted them, convened panels of outside experts, and ran the meetings in which these experts rated batches of proposals in particular fields. This was a major manifestation of the peer-review process, a process Frank thoroughly approved of—in principle. But a year of it was enough.

Anna had been watching him, and now she said, "I suppose it is a bit of a rat race."

"Well, no more than anywhere else. In fact if I were home it'd probably be worse."

They laughed.

"And you have your journal work too."

"That's right." Frank waved at the piles of typescripts: three stacks for *Review of Bioinformatics,* two for *The Journal of Sociobiology.* "Always behind. Luckily the other editors are better at keeping up."

Anna nodded. Editing a journal was a privilege and an honor, even though usually unpaid—indeed, one often had to continue to subscribe to a journal just to get copies of what one had edited. It was another of science's many noncompensated activities, part of its extensive economy of social credit.

"Okay," Anna said. "I just wanted to see if we could tempt you. That's how we do it, you know. When visitors come through who are particularly good, we try to hold on to them."

"Yes, of course." Frank nodded uncomfortably. Touched despite himself; he valued her opinion. He rolled his chair toward his screen as if to get to work, and she turned and left.

He clicked to the jacket Anna had forwarded. Immediately he recognized one of the investigators' names.

"Hey Anna?" he called out.

"Yes?" She reappeared in the doorway.

"I know one of the guys on this jacket. The P.I. is a guy from Caltech, but the real work is by one of his students."

"Yes?" This was a typical situation, a younger scientist using the prestige of his or her advisor to advance a project.

"Well, I know the student. I was the outside member on his dissertation committee, a few years ago."

"That wouldn't be enough to be a conflict."

Frank nodded as he read on. "But he's also been working on a temporary contract at Torrey Pines Generique, which is a company in San Diego that I helped start."

"Ah. Do you still have any financial stake in it?"

"No. Well, my stocks are in a blind trust for the year I'm here, so I can't be positive, but I don't think so."

"But you're not on the board, or a consultant?"

"No no. And it looks like his contract there was due to be over about now anyway."

"That's fine, then. Go for it."

No part of the scientific community could afford to be *too* picky about conflicts of interest. If they were, they'd never find anyone free to peer-review anything; hyperspecialization made every field so small that within them, everyone seemed to know everyone. Because of that, so long as there were no current financial or institutional ties with a person, it was considered okay to proceed to evaluate their work in the various peer-review systems.

But Frank had wanted to make sure. Yann Pierzinski

had been a very sharp young biomathematician—he was one of those doctoral students whom one watched with the near certainty that one would hear from them again later in their career. Now here he was, with something Frank was particularly interested in.

"Okay," he said now to Anna. "I'll put it in the hopper." He closed the file and turned as if to check out something else.

After Anna was gone, he pulled the jacket back up. "Mathematical and Algorithmic Analysis of Palindromic Codons as Predictors of a Gene's Protein Expression." A proposal to fund continuing work on an algorithm for predicting which proteins any given gene would express.

Very interesting. This was an assault on one of the fundamental mysteries, an unknown step in biology that presented a considerable blockage to any robust biotechnology. The three billion base pairs of the human genome encoded along their way some hundred thousand genes; and most of these genes contained instructions for the assembly of one or more proteins, the basic building blocks of organic chemistry and life itself. But which genes expressed which proteins, and how exactly they did it, and why certain genes would create more than one protein, or different proteins in different circumstances—all these matters were very poorly understood, or completely mysterious. This ignorance made much of biotechnology an endless and very expensive matter of trial and error. A key to any part of the mystery could be very valuable.

Frank scrolled down the pages of the application with practiced speed. Yann Pierzinski, Ph.D. in biomath, Caltech. Still doing postdoc work with his thesis advisor there, a man Frank had come to consider a bit of a credit hog, if not worse. It was interesting, then, that Pierzinski had gone down to Torrey Pines to work on a temporary contract, for a bioinformatics researcher whom Frank didn't know. Perhaps that had been a bid to escape the advisor. But now he was back.

Frank dug into the substantive part of the proposal. The algorithm set was one Pierzinski had been working on even back in his dissertation. Chemical mechanics of protein creation as a sort of natural algorithm, in effect. Frank considered the idea, operation by operation. This was his real expertise; this was what had interested him from childhood, when the puzzles solved had been simple ciphers. He had always loved this work, and now perhaps more than ever, offering as it did a complete escape from consciousness of himself. Why he might want to make that escape remained moot; howsoever it might be, when he came back he felt refreshed, as if finally he had been in a good place.

He also liked to see patterns emerge from the apparent randomness of the world. This was why he had recently taken such an interest in sociobiology; he had hoped there might be algorithms to be found there which would crack the code of human behavior. So far that quest had not been very satisfactory, mostly because so little in human behavior was susceptible to a controlled experiment, so no theory could even be tested. That was a shame. He badly wanted some clarification in that realm.

At the level of the four chemicals of the genome, however—in the long dance of cytosine, adenine, guanine, and thymine—much more seemed to be amenable to mathematical explanation and experiment, with results that could be conveyed to other scientists, and put to use. One could test Pierzinski's ideas, in other words, and find out if they worked.

He came out of this trance of thought hungry, and with a full bladder. He felt quite sure there was some real potential in the work. And that was giving him some ideas.

He got up stiffly, went to the bathroom, came back. It was midafternoon already. If he left soon he would be able to hack through the traffic to his apartment, eat quickly, then go out to Great Falls. By then the day's blanching heat would have started to subside, and the river's gorge walls would be nearly empty of climbers. He could climb until well past sunset, and do some more thinking about this algorithm, out where he thought best these days, on the hard old schist walls of the only place in the Washington D.C. area where a scrap of nature had survived.

II

IN

THE

HYPERPOWER

Mathematics sometimes seems like a universe of its own. But it comes to us as part of the brain's engagement with the world, and appears to be part of the world, its structure or recipe.

Over historical time humanity has explored farther and farther into the various realms of mathematics, in a cumulative and collective process, an ongoing conversation between the species and reality. The discovery of the calculus. The invention of formal arithmetic and symbolic logic, both mathematicizing the instinctive strategies of human reason, making them as distinct and solid as geometric proofs. The attempt to make the entire system contained and self-consistent. The invention of set theory, and the finessing of the various paradoxes engendered by considering sets as members of themselves. The discovery of the incompletability of all systems. The step-by-step mechanics of programming new calculating machines. All this resulted in an amalgam of math and logic, the symbols and methods drawn from both realms, combining in the often long and complicated operations that we call algorithms.

In the time of the development of the algorithm, we also made discoveries in the real world: the double helix within our cells. DNA. Within half a century the whole genome was read, base pair by base pair. Three billion base pairs, parts of which are called genes, and serve as instruction packets for protein creation.

But despite the fully explicated genome, the details of its expression and growth are still very mysterious. Spiraling pairs of cytosine, guanine, adenine, and thymine: we know these are instructions for growth, for the development of life, all coded in sequences of paired elements. We know the elements; we see the organisms. The code between them remains to be learned.

Mathematics continues to develop under the momentum of its own internal logic, seemingly independent of everything else. But several times in the past, purely mathematical developments have later proved to be powerfully descriptive of operations in nature that were either unknown or unexplainable at the time the math was being developed. This is a strange fact, calling into question all that we think we know about the relationship between math and reality, the mind and the cosmos.

Perhaps no explanation of this mysterious adherence of nature to mathematics of great subtlety will ever be forthcoming. Meanwhile, the operations called algorithms become ever more convoluted and interesting to those devising them. Are they making portraits, recipes, magic spells? Does reality use algorithms, do genes use algorithms? The mathematicians can't say, and many of them don't seem to care. They like the work, whatever it is.

LEO MULHOUSE kissed his wife Roxanne and left their bedroom. In the living room the light was half-way between night and dawn. He went out onto their balcony: screeching gulls, the rumble of the surf against the cliff below. The vast gray plate of the Pacific Ocean.

Leo had married into this spectacular house, so to speak; Roxanne had inherited it from her mother. Its view from the edge of the sea cliff in Leucadia, California, was something Leo loved, but the little grass yard below the second-story porch was only about fifteen feet wide, and beyond it was an open gulf of air and the gray foaming ocean, eighty feet below. And not that stable a cliff. He wished that the house had been placed a little farther back on its lot.

Back inside, fill his travel coffee cup, down to the car. Down Europa, past the Pannikin, hang a right and head to work.

The Pacific Coast Highway in San Diego County was a beautiful drive at dawn. In any kind of weather it was handsome: in new sun with all the pale blues lifting out of the sea, in scattered cloud when shards and rays of horizontal sunlight broke through, or on rainy or foggy mornings when the narrow but rich palette of grays filled the eye with the subtlest of gradations. The gray dawns were by far the most frequent, as the region's climate settled into what appeared to be a permanent El Niño—the Hyperniño, as people called it. The whole idea of a Mediterranean climate leaving the world, even in the Mediterranean, people said. Here coastal residents were getting sunlight deficiency disorders, and taking vitamin D and antidepressants to counteract the effects, even though ten miles inland it was a cloudless baking desert all the year round. The June Gloom had come home to roost.

Leo Mulhouse took the coast highway to work every morning. He liked seeing the ocean, and feeling the slight roller-coaster effect of dropping down to cross the lagoons, then motoring back up little rises to Cardiff, Solano Beach, and Del Mar. These towns looked best at this hour, deserted and as if washed for the new day. Hiss of tires on wet road, wet squeak of windshield wipers, distant boom of the waves breaking—it all combined to make a kind of aquatic experience, the drive like surfing, up and down the same bowls every time, riding the perpetual wave of land about to break into the sea.

Up the big hill onto Torrey Pines, past the golf course, quick right into Torrey Pines Generique. Down into its parking garage, descending into the belly of work. Into the biotech beast.

Meaning a complete security exam, just to get in. If they didn't know what you came in with, they wouldn't be able to judge what you went out with. So, metal detector, inspection by the bored security team with their huge coffee cups, computer turned on, hardware and software check by experts, sniff-over by Clyde the morning dog, trained to detect signature molecules: all standard in biotech now, after some famous incidents of industrial espionage. The stakes were too high to trust anybody.

Then Leo was inside the compound, walking down long white hallways. He put his coffee on his desk, turned on his desktop computer, went out to check the experiments in progress. The most important current one was reaching an endpoint, and Leo was particularly interested in the results. They had been using high-throughput screening of some of the many thousands of proteins listed in the Protein Data Bank at UCSD, trying to identify some that would activate certain cells in a way that would make these cells express more high-density lipoprotein than they would normally—perhaps ten times as much. Ten times as much HDL, the "good cholesterol," would be a lifesaver for people suffering from any number of ailments—atherosclerosis, obesity, diabetes, even Alzheimer's. Any one of these ailments mitigated (or cured!) would be worth billions; a therapy that helped all of them would be—well. It explained the high-alert security enclosing the compound, that was for sure.

The experiment was proceeding but not yet done, so Leo went back to his office and drank his coffee and read *Bioworld Today* on-screen. Higher throughput screening robotics, analysis protocols for artificial hormones, proteomic analyses—every article could have described something that was going on at Torrey Pines Generique. The whole industry was looking for ways to improve the hunt for therapeutic proteins, and for ways to get those proteins into living people. Half the day's articles were devoted to one of these problems or the other, as in any other issue of the newszine. They were the recalcitrant outstanding problems, standing between "biotechnology" as an idea and medicine as it actually existed. If they didn't solve these problems, the idea and the industry based on it could go the way of nuclear power, and turn into something that somehow did not work out. If they did solve them, then it would turn into something more like the computer industry in terms of financial returns—not to mention the impacts on health of course!

When Leo next checked the lab, two of his assistants, Marta and Brian, were standing at the bench, both wearing lab coats and rubber gloves, working the pipettes on a bank of flasks filling a countertop.

"Good morning guys."

"Hey Leo." Marta aimed her pipette like a Power-Point cursor at the small window on a long low refrigerator. "Ready to check it out?"

"Sure am. Can you help?"

"In just a sec." She moved down the bench.

Brian said, "This better work, because Derek just told the press that it was the most promising self-healing therapy of the decade."

Leo was startled to hear this. "No. You're kidding."

"I'm not kidding."

"Oh not really. Not really."

"Really."

"How *could* he?"

"Press release. Also calls to his favorite reporters, and on his webpage. The chat room is already talking about the ramifications. They're betting one of the big pharms will buy us within the month."

"Please Bri, don't be saying these things."

"Sorry, but you know Derek." Brian gestured at one of the computer screens glowing on the bench across the way. "It's all over."

Leo squinted at a screen. "It wasn't on *Bioworld Today*."

"It will be tomorrow."

The company website's BREAKING NEWS box was blinking. Leo leaned over and jabbed it. Yep—lead story. HDL factory, potential for obesity, diabetes, Alzheimer's, heart disease...

"Oh my God," Leo muttered as he read. "Oh my God." His face was flushed. "Why does he *do* this?"

"He wants it to be true."

"So *what*? We don't *know* yet."

With her sly grin Marta said, "He wants you to make it happen, Leo. He's like the Road Runner and you're Wile E. Coyote. He gets you to run off the edge of a cliff, and then you have to build the bridge back to the cliff before you fall."

"But it never works! He always falls!"

Marta laughed at him. She liked him, but she was tough. "Come on," she said. "This time we'll do it."

Leo nodded, tried to calm down. He appreciated Marta's spirit, and liked to be at least as positive as the most positive person in any given situation. That was getting tough these days, but he smiled the best he could and said, "Yeah, right, you're good," and started to put on rubber gloves.

"Remember the time he announced that we had hemophilia A whipped?" Brian said.

"Please."

"Remember the time he put out a press release saying he had decapitated mice at a thousand rpm to show how well our therapy worked?"

"The guillotine turntable experiment?"

"Please," Leo begged. "No more."

He picked up a pipette and tried to focus on the work. Withdraw, inject, withdraw, inject—alas, most of the work in this stage was automated, leaving people free to think, whether they wanted to or not. After a while Leo left them to it and went back to his office to check his e-mail, then helplessly to read what portion of Derek's press release he could stomach. "Why does he *do* this, why why why?"

It was a rhetorical question, but Marta and Brian were

now standing in the doorway, and Marta was implacable: "I tell you—he thinks he can *make* us do it."

"It's not *us* doing it," Leo protested, "it's the gene. We can't do a thing if the altered gene doesn't get into the cell we're trying to target."

"You'll just have to think of something that will work."

"You mean like, build it and they will come?"

"Yeah. Say it and they will make it."

Out in the lab a timer beeped, sounding uncannily like the Road Runner. *Meep-meep! Meep-meep!* They went to the incubator and read the graph paper as it rolled out of the machine, like a receipt out of an automated teller—like money out of an automated teller, in fact, if the results were good. One very big wad of twenties rolling out into the world from nowhere, if the numbers were good.

And they were. They were very good. They would have to plot it to be sure, but they had been doing this series of experiments for so long that they knew what the raw data would look like. The data were good. So now they *were* like Wile E. Coyote, standing in midair staring amazed at the viewers, because a bridge from the cliff had magically extended out and saved them. Saved them from the long plunge of a retraction in the press and subsequent NASDAQ free fall.

Except that Wile E. Coyote was invariably premature in his sense of relief. The Road Runner always had another devastating move to make. Leo's hand was shaking.

"Shit," he said. "I would be totally celebrating right now if it weren't for Derek. Look at this"—pointing—"it's even better than before."

"See, Derek knew it would turn out like this."

"The fuck he did."

"Pretty good numbers," Brian said with a grin. "Paper's almost written too. It's just plug these in and do a conclusion."

Marta said, "Conclusions will be simple, if we tell the truth."

Leo nodded. "Only problem is, the truth would have to admit that even though this part works, we still don't have a therapy, because we haven't got targeted delivery. We can make it but we can't get it into living bodies where it needs to be."

"You didn't read the whole website," Marta told him, smiling angrily again.

"What do you mean?" Leo was in no mood for teasing. His stomach had already shrunk to the size of a walnut.

Marta laughed, which was her way of showing sympathy without admitting to any. "He's going to buy Urtech."

"What's Urtech?"

"They have a targeted delivery method that works."

"What do you mean, what would that be?"

"It's new. They just got awarded the patent on it."

"Oh no."

"Oh yes."

"Oh my God. It hasn't been validated?"

"Except by the patent, and Derek's offer to buy it, no."

"Oh my *God*. Why does he *do* this kind of stuff?"

"Because he intends to be the CEO of the biggest pharmaceutical of all time. Like he told *People* magazine."

"Yeah right."

Torrey Pines Generique, like most biotech start-ups, was undercapitalized, and could only afford a few rolls of the dice. One of them had to look promising enough to attract the capital that would allow it to grow further. That was what they had been trying to accomplish for the five years of the company's existence, and the effort was just beginning to show results with these experiments. What they needed now was to be able to insert their successfully tailored gene into the patient's own cells, so that afterward it would be the patient's own body producing increased amounts of the needed proteins. If that worked, there would be no immune response from the body's immune system, and with the protein being produced in therapeutic amounts, the patient would be not just helped, but cured.

Amazing.

But (and it was getting to be a big but) the problem of getting the altered DNA into living patients' cells hadn't been solved. Leo and his people were not physiologists, and they hadn't been able to do it. No one had. Immune systems existed precisely to keep these sorts of intrusions from happening. Indeed, one method of inserting the altered DNA into the body was to put it into a virus and give the patient a viral infection, benign in its ultimate effects because the altered DNA reached its target. But since the body fought viral infections, it was not a good solution. You didn't want to compromise further the immune systems of people who were already sick.

So, for a long time now they had been in the same boat as everyone else, chasing the Holy Grail of gene therapy, a "targeted nonviral delivery system." Any company that came up with such a system, and patented it, would immediately have the method licensed for scores of procedures, and very likely one of the big pharmaceuticals would buy the company, making everyone in it rich, and often still employed. Over time the pharmaceutical might dismantle the acquisition, keeping only the method, but at that point the start-up's employees would be wealthy enough to laugh that off—retire and go surfing, or start up another start-up and try to hit the jackpot again. At that point it would be more of a philanthropic hobby than the cutthroat struggle to make a living that it often seemed before the big success arrived.

So the hunt for a targeted nonviral delivery system was most definitely on, in hundreds of labs around the world. And now Derek had bought one of these labs. Leo stared at the new announcement on the company website. Derek had to have bought it on spec, because if the method had been well-proven, there was no way Derek would have been able to afford it. Some biotech firm even smaller than Torrey Pines—Urtech, based in Bethesda, Maryland (Leo had never heard of it)—had convinced Derek that they had found a way to deliver altered DNA into humans. Derek had made the purchase without consulting Leo, his chief research scientist. His scientific advice had to have come from his vice president, Dr. Sam Houston, an old friend and early partner. A man who had not done lab work in a decade.

So. It was true.

Leo sat at his desk, trying to relax his stomach. They would have to assimilate this new company, learn their technique, test it. It *had* been patented, Leo noted, which meant they had it exclusively at this point, as a kind of trade secret—a concept many working scientists had trouble accepting. A secret scientific method? Was that not a contradiction in terms? Of course a patent was a matter of public record, and eventually it would enter the public domain. So it wasn't a trade secret in literal fact. But at this stage it was secret enough. And it could not be a sure thing. There wasn't much published about it, as far as Leo could tell. Some papers in preparation, some papers submitted, one paper accepted—he would have to check that one out as soon as possible—and a patent. Sometimes they awarded them so early. One or two papers were all that supported the whole approach.

Secret science. "God *damn* it," Leo said to his room. Derek had bought a pig in a poke. And Leo was going to have to open the poke and poke around.

There was a hesitant knock on his opened door, and he looked up.

"Oh hi, Yann, how are you?"

"I'm good Leo, thanks. I'm just coming by to say good-bye. I'm back to Pasadena now, my job here is finished."

"Too bad. I bet you could have helped us figure out this pig in a poke we just bought."

"Really?"

Yann's face brightened like a child's. He was a true mathematician, and had what Leo considered to be the standard mathematician personality: smart, spacy, enthusiastic, full of notions. All these qualities were a bit under the surface, until you really got him going. As Marta had remarked, not unkindly (for her), if it weren't for the head tilt and the speed-talking, he wouldn't have seemed like a mathematician at all. Whatever; Leo liked him, and his work on protein identification had been really interesting, and potentially very helpful.

"Actually, I don't know what we've got yet," Leo admitted. "It's likely to be a biology problem, but who knows? You sure have been helpful with our selection protocols."

"Thanks, I appreciate that. I may be back anyway, I've got a project going with Sam's math team that might pan out. If it does they'll try to hire me on another temporary contract, he says."

"That's good to hear. Well, have fun in Pasadena in the meantime."

"Oh I will. See you soon."

And their best biomath guy slipped out the door.

CHARLIE QUIBLER had barely woken when Anna left for work. He got up an hour later to his own alarm, woke up Nick with difficulty, got him to dress and eat, put the still-sleeping Joe in his car seat while Nick climbed in the other side of the car. "Have you got your backpack *and* your lunch?"—this not always being the case—and off to Nick's school. They dropped him off, returned home to fall asleep again on the couch, Joe never waking during the entire process. An hour or so later he would rouse them both with his hungry cries, and then the day would really begin, the earlier interval like a problem dream that always played out the same.

"Joey and Daddy!" Charlie would say then, or "Joe and Dad at home, here we go!" or "How about breakfast? Here—how about you get into your playpen for a second, and I'll go warm up some of *Mom's milk.*"

This had always worked like a charm with Nick, and sometimes Charlie forgot and put Joe down in the old blue plastic playpen in the living room, but if he did Joe would let out a scandalized howl the moment he saw where he was. Joe refused to associate with baby things; even getting him into the car seat or the baby backpack or the stroller was a matter of very strict invariability. Where choices were known to be possible, Joe rejected the baby stuff as an affront to his dignity.

So now Charlie had Joe there with him in the kitchen, crawling underfoot or investigating the gate that blocked the steep stairs to the cellar. Careening around like a human pinball. Anna had taped bubblewrap to all the corners; it looked like the kitchen had just recently arrived and not yet been completely unpacked.

"Okay watch out now, don't. Don't! Your bottle will be ready in a second."

"Ba!"

"Yes, bottle."

This was satisfactory, and Joe plopped on his butt directly under Charlie's feet. Charlie worked over him, taking some of Anna's frozen milk out of the freezer and putting it in a pot of warming water on the back burner. Anna had her milk stored in precise quantities of either four or ten ounces, in tall or short permanent plastic cylinders that were filled with disposable plastic bags, capped by brown rubber nipples that Charlie had pricked many times with a needle, and topped by snap-on plastic tops to protect the nipples from contamination in the freezer. Contamination in the freezer? Charlie had wanted to ask Anna, but he hadn't. There was a lab book on the kitchen counter for Charlie to fill out the times and amounts of Joe's feedings. Anna liked to know these things, she said, to determine how much milk to pump at work. So Charlie logged in while the water started to bubble, thinking as he always did that the main purpose here was to fulfill Anna's pleasure in making quantified records of any kind.

He was testing the temperature of the thawed milk by

taking a quick suck on the nipple when his phone rang. He whipped on a headset and answered.

"Hi Charlie, it's Roy."

"Oh hi Roy, what's up."

"Well I've got your latest draft here and I'm about to read it, and I thought I'd check first to see what I should be looking for, how you solved the IPCC stuff."

"Oh yeah. The new stuff that matters is all in the third section." The bill as Charlie had drafted it for Phil would require the U.S. to act on certain recommendations of the Intergovernmental Panel on Climate Change.

"Did you kind of bury the part about us conforming to IPCC findings?"

"I don't think there's earth deep enough to bury that one. I tried to put it in a context that made it look inevitable. International body that we are part of, climate change clearly real, the UN the best body to work through global issues, support for them pretty much mandatory for us or else the whole world cooks in our juices, that sort of thing."

"Well, but that's never worked before, has it? Come on, Charlie, this is Phil's big pre-election bill and you're his climate guy, if he can't get this bill out of committee then we're in big trouble."

"Yeah I know. Wait just a second."

Charlie took another test pull from the bottle. Now it was at body temperature, or almost.

"A bit early to be hitting the bottle, Charlie, what you drinking there?"

"Well, I'm drinking my wife's breast milk, if you must know."

"Say what?"

"I'm testing the temperature of one of Joe's bottles. They have to be thawed to a very exact temperature or else he gets annoyed."

"So you're drinking your wife's breast milk out of a baby bottle?"

"Yes I am."

"How is it?"

"It's good. Thin but sweet. A potent mix of protein, fat, and sugar. No doubt the perfect food."

"I bet." Roy cackled. "Do you ever get it straight from the source?"

"Well I try, sure, who doesn't, but Anna doesn't like it. She says it's a mixed message and if I don't watch out she'll wean me when she weans Joe."

"Ah ha. So you have to take the long-term view."

"Yes. Although actually I tried it one time when Joe fell asleep nursing, so she couldn't move without waking him. She was hissing at me and I was trying to get it to work but apparently you have to suck much harder than, you know, one usually would, there's a trick to it, and I still hadn't gotten any when Joe woke up and saw me. Anna and I froze, expecting him to freak out, but he just reached out and patted me on the head."

"He understood!"

"Yeah. It was like he was saying I know how you feel, Dad, and I will share with you this amazing bounty. Didn't you Joe?" he said, handing him the warmed bottle. He watched with a smile as Joe took it one-handed and tilted it back, elbow thrown out like Popeye with a can of spinach. Because of all the pinpricks Charlie had made in the rubber nipples, Joe could choke down a bottle in a few minutes, and he seemed to take great satisfaction in doing so. No doubt a sugar rush.

"Okay, well, you are a kinky guy my friend and obviously deep in the world of domestic bliss, but we're still relying on you here and this may be the most important bill Phil introduces in this session."

"Come on it's a lot more than that, young man, it's one

of the few chances we have left to avoid complete global disaster, I mean—"

"Preaching to the converted! Preaching to the converted!"

"I certainly hope so."

"Sure sure. Okay, I'll read this draft and get back to you ASAP. I want to move on with this, and the committee discussion is now scheduled for Tuesday."

"That's fine, I'll have my phone with me all day."

"Sounds good, I'll be in touch, but meanwhile be thinking about how to slip the IPCC thing in even deeper."

"Yeah okay but see what I did already."

"Sure bye."

"Bye."

Charlie pulled off the headset and turned off the stove. Joe finished his bottle, inspected it, tossed it casually aside.

"Man, you are fast," Charlie said as he always did. One of the mutual satisfactions of their days together was doing the same things over and over again, and saying the same things about them. Joe was not as insistent on pattern as Nick had been, in fact he liked a kind of structured variability, as Charlie thought of it, but the pleasure in repetition was still there.

There was no denying his boys were very different. When Nick had been Joe's age, Charlie had still found it necessary to hold him cradled in his arm, head wedged in the nook of his elbow to make him take the bottle, because Nick had had a curious moment of aversion, even when he was hungry. He would whine and refuse the nipple, perhaps because it was not the real thing, perhaps because it had taken Charlie months to learn to puncture the bottle nipples with lots of extra holes. In any case he would refuse and twist away, head whipping from side to side, and the hungrier he was the more he would do it, until with a rush like a fish to a lure he would strike, latching on and sucking desperately. It was a fairly frustrating routine, part of the larger Shock of Lost Adult Freedom that had hammered Charlie so hard that first time around, though he could hardly now remember why. A perfect image for all the compromised joys and irritations of Mr. Momhood, those hundreds of sessions with reluctant Nick and his bottle.

With Joe life was in some ways much easier. Charlie was more used to it, for one thing, and Joe, though difficult in his own ways, would certainly never refuse a bottle.

Now he decided he would try again to climb the baby gate and dive down the cellar stairs, but Charlie moved quickly to detach him, then shooed him out into the dining room while cleaning up the counter, ignoring the loud cries of complaint.

"Okay okay! Quiet! Hey let's go for a walk! Let's go walk!"

"No!"

"Ah come on. Oh wait, it's your day for Gymboree, and then we'll go to the park and have lunch, and then go for a walk!"

"NO!"

But that was just Joe's way of saying yes.

Charlie wrestled him into the baby backpack, which was mostly a matter of controlling his legs, not an easy thing. Joe was strong, a compact animal with bulging thigh muscles, and though not as loud a screamer as Nick had been, a tough guy to overpower. "Gymboree, Joe! You love it! Then a *walk,* guy, a walk to the *park*!"

Off they went.

First to Gymboree, located in a big building just off Wisconsin. Gymboree was a chance to get infants together when they did not have some other day care to do it. It was an hour-long class, and always a bit depressing, Charlie felt, to be paying to get his kid into a play situation with other kids but there it was; without Gymboree they all would have been on their own.

Joe disappeared into the tunnels of a big plastic jungle gym. It may have been a commercial replacement for real community, but Joe didn't know that; all he saw was that it had lots of stuff to play with and climb on, and so he scampered around the colorful structures, crawling through tubes and climbing up things, ignoring the other kids to the point of treating them as movable parts of the apparatus, which could cause problems. "Oops, say you're sorry, Joe. Sorry!"

Off he shot again, evading Charlie. He didn't want to waste any time. Once again the contrast with Nick could not have been more acute. Nick had seldom moved at Gymboree. One time he had found a giant red ball and stood embracing the thing for the full hour of the class. All the moms had stared sympathetically (or not), and the instructor, Ally, had done her best to help Charlie get him interested in something else; but Nick would not budge from his mystical red ball.

Embarrassing. But Charlie was used to that. The problem was not just Nick's immobility or Joe's hyperactivity, but the fact that Charlie was always the only dad there. Without him it would have been a complete momspace, and comfortable as such. He knew that his presence wrecked that comfort. It happened in all kinds of infant-toddler contexts. As far as Charlie could tell, there was not a single other man inside the Beltway who ever spent the business hours of a weekday with preschool children. It just wasn't done. That wasn't why people moved to D.C. It wasn't why Charlie had moved there either, for that matter, but he and Anna had talked it over before Nick was born, and they had come to the realization that Charlie could do his job (on a part-time basis anyway) and their infant care at the same time, by using phone and e-mail to keep in contact with Senator Chase's office. Phil Chase himself had perfected the method of working at a distance back when he had been the World's Senator, always on the road; and being the good guy he was, he had thoroughly approved of Charlie's plan. While on the other hand Anna's job absolutely required her to be at work at least fifty hours a week, and often more. So Charlie had happily volunteered to be the stay-at-home parent. It would be an adventure.

And an adventure it had been, there was no denying that. But first time's a charm; and now he had been doing it for over a year with kid number two, and what had been shocking and all-absorbing with kid number one was now simply routine. The repetitions were beginning to get to him. Joe was beginning to get to him.

So now Charlie sat there in Gymboree, hanging with the moms and the nannies. A nice situation in theory, but in practice a diplomatic challenge of the highest order. No one wanted to be misunderstood. No one would regard it as a coincidence if he happened to end up talking to one of the more attractive women there, or to anyone in particular on a regular basis. That was fine with Charlie, but with Joe doing his thing, he could not completely control the situation. There was Joe now, doing it again—going after a black-haired little girl who had the perfect features of a model. Charlie was obliged to go over and make sure Joe didn't mug her, as he had a wont to do with girls he liked, and yes, the little girl had an attractive mom, or in this case a nanny—a young blonde au pair from Germany whom Charlie had spoken to before. Charlie could feel the eyes of the other women on him; not a single adult in that room believed in his innocence.

"Hi Asta."

"Hello Charlie."

He even began to doubt it himself. Asta was one of those lively European women of twenty or so who gave the impression of being a decade ahead of their American contemporaries in terms of adult experiences—not easy, given the way American teens were these days. Charlie felt a little surge of protest: It's not me who goes after the babes, he wanted to shout, it's my son! My son the hyperactive girl-chasing mugger! But of course he couldn't do that, and now even Asta regarded him warily, perhaps because the first time they had chatted over their kids he had made some remark complimenting her on her child's nice hair. He felt himself begin to blush again, remembering the look of amused surprise she had given him as she corrected him.

Sing-along saved him from the moment. It was designed to calm the kids down a bit before the session ended and they had to be lassoed back into their car seats for the ride home. Joe took Ally's announcement as his cue to dive into the depths of the tube structure, where it was impossible to follow him or to coax him out. He would only emerge when Ally started singing "Ring Around the Rosie," which he enjoyed. Round in circles they all went, Charlie avoiding anyone's eye but Joe's. Ally, who was from New Jersey, belted out the lead, and so all the kids and moms joined her loudly in the final chorus:

"Eshes, eshes, we all, fall, DOWN!"

And down they all fell.

Then it was off to the park.

Their park was a small one, located just west of Wisconsin Avenue, a few blocks south of their home. A narrow grassy area held a square sandpit, which contained play structures for young kids. Tennis courts lined the south edge of the park. Against Wisconsin stood a fire station, and to the west a field extended out to one of the many little creeks that still cut through the grid of streets.

Midday the sandpit and the benches flanking it were almost always occupied by a few infants and toddlers, moms and nannies. Many more nannies than moms here, most of them West Indian, to judge by their appearance and voices. They sat on the benches together, resting in the steamy heat, talking. The kids wandered on their own, absorbed or bored.

Joe kept Charlie on his toes. Nick had been content to sit in one spot for long periods of time, and when playing he had been pathologically cautious; on a low wooden bouncy bridge his little fists had gone white on the chain railing. Joe however had quickly located the spot on the bridge that would launch him the highest—not the middle, but about halfway down to it. He would stand right there and jump up and down in time to the wooden oscillation until he was catching big air, his unhappy expression utterly different from Nick's, in that it was caused by his dissatisfaction that he could not get higher. This was part of his general habit of using his body as an experimental object, including walking in front of kids on swings, etc. Countless times Charlie had been forced to jerk him out of dangerous situations, and they had become less frequent only because Joe didn't like how loud Charlie yelled afterward. "Give me a break!" Charlie would shout. "What do you think, you're made of steel?"

Now Joe was flying up and down on the bouncy bridge's sweet spot. The sad little girl whose nanny talked on the phone for hours at a time wandered in slow circles around the merry-go-round. Charlie avoided meeting her eager eye, staring instead at the nanny and thinking it might be a good idea to stuff a note into the girl's clothes: *Your daughter wanders the Earth bored and lonely at age two—SHAME!*

Whereas he was virtuous. That would have been the point of such a note, and so he never wrote it. He was virtuous, but bored. No that wasn't really true. That was a disagreeable stereotype. He therefore tried to focus and play with his second-born. It was truly unfair how much less parental attention the second child got. With the first, although admittedly there was the huge Shock of Lost Adult Freedom to recover from, there was also the deep absorption of watching one's own offspring—a living human being whose genes were a fifty-fifty mix of one's own and one's partner's. It was frankly hard to believe that any such process could actually work, but there the kid was, out walking the world in the temporary guise of a kind of pet, a wordless little animal of surpassing fascination.

Whereas with the second one it was as they all said: just try to make sure they don't eat out of the cat's dish. Not always successful in Joe's case. But not to worry. They would survive. They might even prosper. Meanwhile there was the newspaper to read.

But now here they were at the park, Joe and Dad, so might as well make the best of it. And it was true that Joe was more fun to play with than Nick had been at that age. He would chase Charlie for hours, ask to be chased, wrestle, fight, go down the slide and up the steps again like a perpetuum mobile. All this in the middle of a D.C. May day, the air going for a triple-triple, the sun smashing down through the wet air and diffusing until its light exploded out of a huge patch of the zenith. Sweaty gasping play, yes, but never a moment spent coaxing. Never a dull moment.

After another such runaround they sprawled on the grass to eat lunch. Both of them liked this part. Fruit juices, various baby foods carefully spooned out and inserted into Joe's baby-bird mouth, applesauce likewise, a cheerio or two that he could choke down by himself. He was still mostly a breast-milk guy.

When they were done Joe struggled up to play again.

"Oh God Joe can't we rest a bit."

"No!"

Ballasted by his meal, however, he staggered as if drunk. Naptime, as sudden as a blow to the head, would soon fell him.

Charlie's phone beeped. He slipped in an earplug and let the cord dangle under his face, clicked it on. "Hello."

"Hi Charlie, where are you?"

"Hey Roy, I'm at the park like always. What's up?"

"Well, I've read your latest draft, and I was wondering if you could discuss some things in it now, because we need to get it over to Senator Winston's office so they can see what's coming."

"Is that a good idea?"

"Phil thinks we have to do it."

"Okay, what do you want to discuss."

There was a pause while Roy found a place in the draft. "Here we go. Quote, 'The Congress, being deeply concerned that the lack of speed in America's conversion from a hydrocarbon to a carbohydrate fuel economy is rapidly leading to chaotic climate changes with a profoundly negative impact on the U.S. economy,' unquote, we've been told that Ellington is only concerned, not deeply concerned. Should we change that?"

"No, we're deeply concerned. He is too, he just doesn't know it."

"Okay, then down in the third paragraph, in the operative clauses, quote, 'The United States will peg hydrocarbon fuel reductions in a two-to-one ratio to such reductions by China and India, and will provide matching funds for all tidal and wind power plants built in those countries and in all countries that fall under a five in the UN's prospering countries index, these plants to be operated by a joint-powers agency that will include the United States as a permanent member; four, these provisions will combine with the climate-neutral power production—'"

"Wait, call that 'power generation.'"

" 'Power generation,' okay, 'such that any savings in environmental mitigation in participating countries as determined by IPCC ratings will be credited equally to the U.S. rating, and not less than fifty million dollars per year in savings is to be earmarked specifically for the construction of more such climate-neutral power plants; and not less than fifty million dollars per year in savings is to be earmarked specifically for the construction of so-called "carbon sinks," meaning any environmental engineering project designed to capture and sequester atmospheric carbon dioxide safely, in forests, peat beds, oceans, or other locations—' "

"Yeah, hey you know carbon sinks are *so* crucial, scrubbing CO_2 out of the air may eventually turn out to be our only option, so maybe we should reverse those two clauses. Make carbon sinks come first and the climate-neutral power plants second in that paragraph."

"You think?"

"Yes. Definitely. Carbon sinks could be the only way that our kids, and about a thousand years' worth of kids actually, can save themselves from living in Swamp World. From living their whole lives on Venus."

"Or should we say Washington, D.C."

"Please."

"Okay, those are flip-flopped then. So that's that paragraph, now, hmm, that's it for text. I guess the next question is, what can we offer Winston and his gang to get them to accept this version."

"Get Winston's people to give you their list of riders, and then pick the two least offensive ones and tell them they're the most we could get Phil to accept, but only if they accept our changes first."

"But will they go for that?"

"No, but—wait—Joe?"

Charlie didn't see Joe anywhere. He ducked to be able

to see under the climbing structure to the other side. No Joe.

"Hey Roy let me call you back okay? I gotta find Joe he's wandered off."

"Okay, give me a buzz."

Charlie clicked off and yanked the earplug out of his ear, jammed it in his pocket.

"JOE!"

He looked around at the West Indian nannies—none of them were watching, none of them would meet his eye. No help there. He jogged south to be able to see farther around the back of the fire station. Ah ha! There was Joe, trundling full speed for Wisconsin Avenue.

"JOE! STOP!"

That was as loud as Charlie could shout. He saw that Joe had indeed heard him, and had redoubled the speed of his diaper-waddle toward the busy street.

Charlie took off in a sprint after him. "JOE!" he shouted as he pelted over the grass. "STOP! JOE! STOP RIGHT THERE!" He didn't believe that Joe would stop, but possibly he would try to go even faster, and fall.

No such luck. Joe was in stride now, running like a duck trying to escape something without taking flight. He was on the sidewalk next to the fire station, and had a clear shot at Wisconsin, where trucks and cars zipped by as always.

Charlie closed in, cleared the fire station, saw big trucks bearing down. By the time he caught up to Joe he was so close to the edge that Charlie had to grab him by the back of his shirt and lift him off his feet, whirling him around in a broad circle through the air, back onto Charlie as they both fell in a heap on the sidewalk.

"Ow!" Joe howled.

"WHAT ARE YOU DOING!" Charlie shouted in his face. "WHAT ARE YOU DOING? DON'T EVER DO THAT AGAIN!"

Joe, amazed, stopped howling for a moment. He stared at his father, face crimson. Then he recommenced howling.

Charlie shifted into a cross-legged position, hefted the crying boy into his lap. He was shaking, his heart was pounding; he could feel it tripping away madly in his hands and chest. In an old reflex he put his thumb to the other wrist and watched the seconds pass on his watch for fifteen seconds. Multiply by four. Impossible. One hundred and eighty beats a minute. Surely that was impossible. Sweat was pouring out of all his skin at once. He was gasping.

The parade of trucks and cars continued to roar by, inches away. Wisconsin Avenue was a major truck route from the Beltway into the city. Most of the trucks entirely filled the right lane, from curb to lane line; and most were moving at about forty miles an hour.

"Why do you *do* that," Charlie whispered into his boy's hair. Suddenly he was filled with fear, and some kind of dread or despair. "It's just crazy."

"Ow," Joe said.

Big shuddering sighs racked them both.

Charlie's phone rang. He clicked it on and held an earplug to his ear.

"Hello?"

"Hi love."

"Oh hi hon!"

"What's wrong?"

"Oh nothing, nothing. I've just been chasing Joe around. We're at the park."

"Wow, you must be cooking. Isn't it the hottest part of the day?"

"Yeah it is, almost, but we've been having fun so we stayed. We're about to head back now."

"Okay, I won't keep you. I just wanted to check if we had any plans for next weekend."

"None that I know of."

"Okay, good. Because I had an interesting thing happen this morning, I met a bunch of people downstairs, new to the building. They're like Tibetans, I think, only they live on an island. They've taken the office space downstairs that the travel agency used to have."

"That's nice dear."

"Yes. I'm going to have lunch with them, and if it seems like a good idea I might ask them over for dinner sometime, if you don't mind."

"No, that's fine snooks. Whatever you like. It sounds interesting."

"Great, okay. I'm going to go meet them soon, I'll tell you about it."

"Okay good."

"Okay bye dove."

"Bye love, talk to you."

Charlie clicked off.

After ten giant breaths he stood, lifting Joe in his arms. Joe buried his face in Charlie's neck. Shakily Charlie retraced their course. It was somewhere between fifty and a hundred yards. Rivulets of sweat ran down his ribs, and off his forehead into his eyes. He wiped them against Joe's shirt. Joe was sweaty too. When he reached their stuff Charlie swung Joe around, down into his backpack. For once Joe did not resist. "Sowy Da," he said, and fell asleep as Charlie swung him onto his back.

Charlie took off walking. Joe's head rested against his neck, a sensation that had always pleased him before. Sometimes the child would even suckle the tendon there. Now it was like the touch of some meaning so great that he couldn't bear it, a huge cloudy aura of danger and love. He started to cry, wiped his eyes and shook it off as if shaking away a nightmare. Hostages to fortune, he thought. You get married, have kids, you give up such hostages to fortune. No avoiding it, no help for it. It's just the price you pay for such love. His son was a complete maniac and it only made him love him more.

He walked hard for most of an hour, through all the neighborhoods he had come to know so well in his years of lonely Mr. Momhood. The vestiges of an older way of life lay under the trees like a network of ley lines: rail beds, canal systems, Indian trails, even deer trails, all could be discerned. Charlie walked them sightlessly. The ductile world drooped around him in the heat. Sweat lubricated his every move.

Slowly he regained his sense of normalcy. Just an ordinary day with Joe and Da.

The residential streets of Bethesda and Chevy Chase were in many ways quite beautiful. It had mostly to do with the immense trees, and the grass underfoot. Green everywhere. On a weekday afternoon like this, there was almost no one to be seen. The slight hilliness was just right for walking. Tall old hardwoods gave some relief from the heat; above them the sky was an incandescent white. The trees were undoubtedly second or even third growth, there couldn't be many old growth hardwoods anywhere east of the Mississippi. Still they were old trees, and tall. Charlie had never shifted out of his California consciousness, in which open landscapes were the norm and the desire, so that on the one hand he found the omnipresent forest claustrophobic—he pined for a pineless view—while on the other hand it remained always exotic and compelling, even slightly ominous or spooky. The dapple of leaves at every level, from the ground to the highest canopy, was a perpetual revelation to him; nothing in his home ground or in his bookish sense of forests had prepared him for this vast and delicate venation of the air. On the other hand he longed for a view of distant mountains as if for oxygen itself. On this day especially he felt stifled and gasping.

His phone beeped again, and he pulled the earplug out of his pocket and stuck it in his ear, clicked the set on.

"Hello."

"Hey Charlie I don't want to bug you, but are you and Joe okay?"

"Oh yeah, thanks Roy. Thanks for checking back in, I forgot to call you."

"So you found him."

"Yeah I found him, but I had to stop him from running into traffic, and he was upset and I forgot to call back."

"Hey that's okay. It's just that I was wondering, you know, if you could finish off this draft with me."

"I guess." Charlie sighed. "To tell the truth, Roy boy, I'm not so sure how well this work-at-home thing is going for me these days."

"Oh you're doing fine. You're Phil's gold standard. But look, if now isn't a good time…"

"No no, Joe's asleep on my back. It's fine. I'm still just kind of freaked out."

"Sure, I can imagine. Listen we can do it later, although I must say we do need to get this thing staffed out soon or else Phil might get caught short. Dr. Strangelove"—this was their name for the President's science advisor—"has been asking to see our draft too."

"I know, okay talk to me. I can tell you what I think anyway."

So for a while as he walked he listened to Roy read sentences from his draft, and then discussed with him the whys and wherefores, and possible revisions. Roy had been Phil's chief of staff ever since Wade Norton hit the road and became an advisor in absentia, and after his years of staffing for the House Resources Committee (called the Environment Committee until the Gingrich Congress renamed it), he was deeply knowledgeable, and sharp too; one of Charlie's favorite people. And Charlie himself was so steeped now in the climate bill that he could see it all in his head, indeed it helped him now just to hear it, without the print before him to distract him. As if someone were telling him a bedtime story.

Eventually, however, some question of Roy's couldn't be resolved without the text before him. "Sorry. I'll call you back when I get home."

"Okay but don't forget, we need to get this finished."

"I won't."

They clicked off.

His walk home took him south, down the west edge of the Bethesda Metro district, an urban neighborhood of restaurants and apartment blocks, all ringing the hole in the ground out of which people and money fountained so prodigiously, changing everything: streets rerouted, neighborhoods redeveloped, a whole clutch of skyscrapers bursting up through the canopy and establishing another purely urban zone in the endless hardwood forest.

He stopped in at Second Story Books, the biggest and best of the area's several used bookstores. It was a matter of habit only; he had visited it so often with Joe asleep on his back that he had memorized the stock, and was reduced to checking the hidden books in the inner rows, or alphabetizing sections that he liked. No one in the supremely arrogant and slovenly shop cared what he did there. It was soothing in that sense.

Finally he gave up trying to pretend he felt normal, and walked past the auto dealer and home. There it was a tough call whether to take the baby backpack off and hope not to wake Joe prematurely, or just to keep him on his back and work from the bench he had put by his desk for this very purpose. The discomfort of Joe's weight was more than compensated for by the quiet, and so as usual he kept Joe snoozing on his back.

When he had his material open, and had read up on

tidal power generation cost/benefit figures from the UN study on same, he called Roy back, and they got the job finished. The revised draft was ready for Phil to review, and in a pinch could be shown to Senator Winston or Dr. Strangelove.

"Thanks Charlie. That looks good."

"I like it too. It'll be interesting to see what Phil says about it. I wonder if we're hanging him too far out there."

"I think he'll be okay, but I wonder what Winston's staff will say."

"They'll have a cow."

"It's true. They're worse than Winston himself. A bunch of Sir Humphreys if I ever saw one."

"I don't know, I think they're just fundamentalist know-nothings."

"True, but we'll show them."

"I hope."

"Charles my man, you're sounding tired. I suppose the Joe is about to wake up."

"Yeah."

"Unrelenting eh?"

"Yeah."

"But you are the man, you are the greatest Mr. Mom inside the Beltway!"

Charlie laughed. "And all that competition."

Roy laughed too, pleased to be able to cheer Charlie up. "Well it's an accomplishment anyway."

"That's nice of you to say. Most people don't notice. It's just something weird that I do."

"Well that's true too. But people don't know what it entails."

"No they don't. The only ones who know are real moms, but they don't think I count."

"You'd think they'd be the ones who would."

"Well, in a way they're right. There's no reason me doing it should be anything special. It may just be me wanting some strokes. It's turned out to be harder than I thought it would be. A real psychic shock."

"Because..."

"Well, I was thirty-eight when Nick arrived, and I had been doing exactly what I wanted ever since I was eighteen. Twenty years of white male American freedom, just like what you have, young man, and then Nick arrived and suddenly I was at the command of a speechless mad tyrant. I mean, think about it. Tonight you can go wherever you want to, go out and have some fun, right?"

"That's right, I'm going to go to a party for some new folks at Brookings, supposed to be wild."

"All right, don't rub it in. Because I'm going to be in the same room I've been in every night for the past seven years, more or less."

"So by now you're used to it, right?"

"Well, yes. That's true. It was harder with Nick, when I could remember what freedom was."

"You have morphed into momhood."

"Yeah. But morphing hurts, baby, just like in *X-Men*. I remember the first Mother's Day after Nick was born, I was most deep into the shock of it, and Anna had to be away that day, maybe to visit her mom, I can't remember, and I was trying to get Nick to take a bottle and he was refusing it as usual. And I suddenly realized I would never be free again for the whole rest of my life, but that as a non-mom I was never going to get a day to honor *my* efforts, because Father's Day is not what this stuff is about, and Nick was whipping his head around even though he was in desperate need of a bottle, and I freaked out, Roy. I freaked out and threw that bottle down."

"You threw it?"

"Yeah I slung it down and it hit at the wrong angle or something and just *exploded*. The baggie broke and the milk shot up and sprayed all over the room. I couldn't believe one bottle could hold that much. Even now when I'm cleaning the living room I come across little white dots of dried milk here and there, like on the mantelpiece or the windowsill. Another little reminder of my Mother's Day freak-out."

"Ha. The morph moment. Well Charlie you are indeed a pathetic specimen of American manhood, yearning for your own Mother's Day card, but just hang in there—only seventeen more years and you'll be free again!"

"Oh fuckyouverymuch! By then I won't want to be."

"Even now you don't wanna be. You love it, you know you do. But listen I gotta go Phil's here bye."

"Bye."

AFTER TALKING with Charlie, Anna got absorbed in work in her usual manner, and might well have forgotten her lunch date with the people from Khembalung; but because this was a perpetual problem of hers, she had set her watch alarm for one o'clock, and when it beeped she saved and went downstairs. She could see through the front window that the new embassy's staff was still unpacking, releasing visible clouds of dust or incense smoke into the air. The young monk she had spoken to and his most elderly companion sat on the floor inspecting a box containing necklaces and the like.

They noticed her and looked up curiously, then the younger one nodded, remembering her from the morning conversation after their ceremony.

"Still interested in some pizza?" Anna asked. "If pizza is okay?"

"Oh yes," the young one said. The two men got to their feet, the old man in several distinct moves; one leg was stiff. "We love pizza." The old man nodded politely, glancing at his young assistant, who said something to him rapidly, in a language that while not guttural did seem mostly to be generated at the back of the mouth.

As they crossed the atrium to Pizzeria Uno Anna said uncertainly, "Do you eat pizza where you come from?"

The younger man smiled. "No. But in Nepal I have eaten pizza in teahouses."

"Are you vegetarian?"

"No. Tibetan Buddhism has never been vegetarian. There were not enough vegetables."

"So you are Tibetans! But I thought you said you were an island nation?"

"We are. But originally we came from Tibet. The old ones, like Rudra Cakrin here, left when the Chinese took over. The rest of us were born in India, or on Khembalung itself."

"I see."

They entered the restaurant, where big booths were walled by high wooden partitions. The three of them sat in one, Anna across from the two men.

"I am Drepung," the young man said, "and the rimpoche here, our ambassador to America, is Gyatso Sonam Rudra Cakrin."

"I'm Anna Quibler," Anna said, and shook hands with each of them. The men's hands were heavily callused.

Their waitress appeared. She did not appear to notice the unusual garb of the men, but took their orders with sublime indifference. After a quick muttered consultation, Drepung asked Anna for suggestions, and in the end they ordered a combination pizza with everything on it.

Anna sipped her water. "Tell me more about Khembalung, and about your new embassy."

Drepung nodded. "I wish Rudra Cakrin himself could tell you, but he is still taking his English lessons, I'm afraid. Apparently they are going very badly. In any case, you know that China invaded Tibet in 1950, and that the Dalai Lama escaped to India in 1959?"

"Yes, that sounds familiar."

"Yes. And during those years, and ever since then too, many Tibetans have moved to India to get away from the Chinese, and closer to the Dalai Lama. India took us in very hospitably, but when the Chinese and Indian governments had their disagreement over their border in 1960, the situation became very awkward for India. They were already in a bad way with Pakistan, and a serious controversy with China would have been..." He searched for the word, waggling a hand.

"Too much?" Anna suggested.

"Yes. Much too much. So, the support India had been giving to the Tibetans in exile—"

Rudra Cakrin made a little hiss.

"Small to begin with, although very helpful nevertheless," Drepung added, "shrank even further. It was requested that the Tibetan community in Dharamsala make itself as small and inconspicuous as possible. The Dalai Lama and his government did their best, and many Tibetans were relocated to other places in India, mostly in the far south. But elsewhere as well. Then some more years passed, and there were some, how shall I say, arguments or splits within the Tibetan exile community, too complicated to go into, I assure you. I can hardly understand them myself. But in the end a group called the Yellow Hat School took the offer of this island of ours, and moved there. This was just before the India-Pakistan war of 1970, unfortunately, so the timing was bad, and everything was on the hush-hush for a time. But the island was ours from that point, as a kind of protectorate of India, like Sikkim, only not so formally arranged."

"Is Khembalung the island's original name?"

"No. I do not think it had a name before. Most of

our sect lived at one time or another in the valley of Khembalung. So that name was kept, and we have shifted away from the Dalai Lama's government in Dharamsala, to a certain extent."

At the sound of the words "Dalai Lama" the old monk made a face and said something in Tibetan.

"The Dalai Lama is still number one with us," Drepung clarified. "It is a matter of some religious controversies with his associates. A matter of how best to support him."

Anna said, "I thought the mouth of the Ganges was in Bangladesh?"

"Much of it is. But you must know that it is a very big delta, and the west side of it is in India. Part of Bengal. Many islands. The Sundarbans? You have not heard?"

Their pizza arrived, and Drepung began talking between big bites. "Lightly populated islands, the Sundarbans. Some of them anyway. Ours was uninhabited."

"Did you say uninhabitable?"

"No no. Inhabitable, obviously."

Another noise from Rudra Cakrin.

"People with lots of choices might say they were uninhabitable," Drepung went on. "And they may yet become so. They are best for tigers. But we have done well there. We have become like tigers. Over the years we have built a nice town. A little seaside potala for Gyatso Rudra and the other lamas. Schools, houses—hospital. All that. And sea walls. The whole island has been ringed by dikes. Lots of work. Hard labor." He nodded as if personally acquainted with this work. "Dutch advisors helped us. Very nice. Our home, you know? Khembalung has moved from age to age. But now…" He waggled a hand again, took another slice of pizza, bit into it.

"Global warming?" Anna ventured.

He nodded, swallowed. "Our Dutch friends suggested

that we establish an embassy here, to join their campaign to influence American policy in these matters."

Anna quickly bit into her pizza so that she would not reveal the thought that had struck her, that the Dutch must be desperate indeed if they had been reduced to help like this. She thought things over as she chewed. "So here you are," she said. "Have you been to America before?"

Drepung shook his head. "None of us have."

"It must be pretty overwhelming."

He frowned at this word. "I have been to Calcutta."

"Oh I see."

"This is very different, of course."

"Yes, I'm sure."

She liked him: his musical Indian English, his round face and big liquid eyes, his ready smile. The two men made quite a contrast: Drepung young and tall, round-faced, with a kind of baby-fat look; Rudra Cakrin old, small and wizened, his face lined with a million wrinkles, his cheekbones and narrow jaw prominent in an angular, nearly fleshless face.

The wrinkles were laugh lines, however, combined with the lines of a wide-eyed expression of surprise that bunched up his forehead. Despite his noises and muttering under Drepung's account, he still seemed cheerful enough. He certainly attacked his pizza with the same enthusiasm as his young assistant. With their shaved heads they shared a certain family resemblance.

She said, "I suppose going from Tibet to a tropical island must have been a bigger shock than coming from the island to here."

"I suppose. I was born in Khembalung myself, so I don't know for sure. But the old ones like Rudra here, who made that very move, seem to have adjusted quite well. Just to have any kind of home is a blessing, I think you will find."

Anna nodded. The two of them did project a certain calm. They sat in the booth as if there was no hurry to go anywhere else. Anna couldn't imagine any such state of mind. She was always in a tearing hurry. She tried to match their air of being at ease. At ease in Arlington, Virginia, after a lifetime on an island in the Ganges. Well, the climate would be familiar. But everything else had to have changed quite stupendously.

And, on closer examination, there was a certain guardedness to them. Drepung glanced surreptitiously at their waitress; he looked at the pedestrians passing by; he watched Anna herself, all with a slightly cautious look, reminding her of the pained expression she had seen earlier in the day.

"How is it that you came to rent a space in this particular building?"

Drepung paused and considered this question for a suprisingly long time. Rudra Cakrin asked him something and he replied, and Rudra said something more.

"We had some advice there also," Drepung said. "The Pew Center on Global Climate Change has been helping us, and their office is located on Wilson Boulevard, nearby."

"I didn't know that. They've helped you to meet people?"

"Yes, with the Dutch, and with some island nations, like Fiji and Tuvalu."

"Tuvalu?"

"A very small country in the Pacific. They have perhaps been less than helpful to the cause, telling people that sea level has risen in their area of the Pacific but not elsewhere, and asking for financial compensation for this from Australia and other countries."

"In their area of the Pacific only?"

"Measurements have not confirmed the claim." Drepung smiled. "But I can assure you, if you are on a storm track and spring tides are upon you, it can seem like sea level has risen quite a great deal."

"I'm sure."

Anna thought it over while she ate. It was good to know that they hadn't just rented the first office they found vacant. Nevertheless, their effort in Washington looked to her to be underpowered at this point. "You should meet my husband," she said. "He works for a senator, one who is up on all these things, a very helpful guy, the chair of the Foreign Relations Committee."

"Ah—Senator Chase?"

"Yes. You know about him?"

"He has visited Khembalung."

"Has he? Well, I'm not surprised, he's been every— He's been a lot of places. Anyway, my husband Charlie works for him as an environmental policy advisor. It would be good for you to talk to Charlie and get his perspective on your situation. He'll be full of suggestions for things you could do."

"That would be an honor."

"I don't know if I'd go that far. But useful."

"Useful, yes. Perhaps we could have you to dinner at our residence."

"Thank you, that would be nice. But we have two small boys and we've lost all our baby-sitters, so to tell the truth it would be easier if you and some of your colleagues came to our place. In fact I've already talked to Charlie about this, and he's looking forward to meeting you. We live in Bethesda, just across the border from the District. It's not far."

"Red Line."

"Yes, very good. Red Line, Bethesda stop. I can give you directions from there."

She got out her calendar, checked the coming weeks.

Very full, as always. "How about a week from Friday? On a Friday we'll be able to relax a little."

"Thank you," Drepung said, ducking his head. He and Rudra Cakrin had an exchange in Tibetan. "That would be very kind. And on the full moon too."

"Is it? I'm afraid I don't keep track."

"We do. The tides, you see."

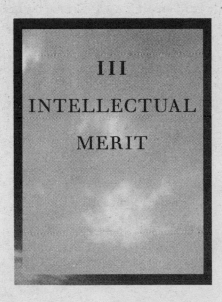

III

INTELLECTUAL

MERIT

Water flows through the oceans in steady recycling patterns, determined by the Coriolis force and the particular positions of the continents in our time. Surface currents can move in the opposite direction to bottom currents below them, and often do, forming systems like giant conveyor belts of water. The largest one is already famous, at least in part: the Gulf Stream is a segment of a warm surface current that flows north up the entire length of the Atlantic, all the way to Norway and Greenland. There the water cools and sinks, and begins a long journey south on the Atlantic Ocean floor, to the Cape of Good Hope and then east toward Australia, and even into the Pacific, where the water upwells and rejoins the surface flow, west to the Atlantic for the long haul north again. The round trip for any given water molecule takes about a thousand years.

Cooling salty water sinks more easily than cooling fresh water. Trade winds sweep clouds generated in the Gulf of Mexico west over Central America to dump their rain in the Pacific, leaving the remaining water in the Atlantic that much saltier. So the cooling water in the North Atlantic sinks well, aiding the power of the Gulf Stream. If the surface of the North Atlantic were to become rapidly fresher, it would not sink so well when it cooled, and that could stall the conveyor belt. The Gulf Stream would have nowhere to go, and would slow down, and sink farther south. Weather everywhere would change, becoming windier and drier in the Northern Hemisphere, and colder in places, especially in Europe.

The sudden desalination of the North Atlantic might seem an unlikely occurrence, but it has happened before. At the end of the last Ice Age, for instance, vast shallow lakes were created by the melting of the polar ice cap. Eventually these lakes broke through their ice dams and poured off into the oceans. The Canadian shield still sports the scars from three or four of these cataclysmic floods; one flowed down the Mississippi, one the Hudson, one the St. Lawrence.

These flows apparently stalled the world ocean conveyor belt current, and the climate of the whole world changed as a result, sometimes in as little as three years.

Now, would the Arctic sea ice, breaking into bergs and flowing south past Greenland, dump enough fresh water into the North Atlantic to stall the Gulf Stream again?

FRANK VANDERWAL kept track of climate news as a sort of morbid hobby. His friend Kenzo Hayakawa, an old climbing partner and grad school housemate, had spent time at NOAA before coming to NSF to work with the weather crowd on the ninth floor, and so Frank occasionally checked in with him to say hi and find out the latest. Things were getting wild out there; extreme weather events were touching down all over the world, the violent, short-term ones almost daily, the chronic problem situations piling one on the next, so that never were they entirely clear of one or another of them. The Hyperniño, severe drought in India and Peru, perpetual lightning fires in Malaysia; then on the daily scale, a typhoon destroying most of Mindanao, a snap freeze killing crops and breaking pipes all over Texas, and so on. Something every day.

Like a lot of climatologists and other weather people Frank had met, Kenzo presented all this news with a faintly proprietary air, as if he were curating the weather. He liked the wild stuff, and enjoyed sharing news of it, especially if it seemed to support his contention that the heat added anthropogenically to the atmosphere had been enough to change the Indian Ocean monsoon patterns for good, triggering global repercussions; this meant, in practice, almost everything that happened. This week for instance it was tornadoes, previously confined almost entirely to North America, as a kind of freak of that continent's topography and latitude, but now appearing in East Africa and in Central Asia. Last week it had been the weakening of the Great World Ocean Current in the Indian Ocean rather than the Atlantic.

"Unbelievable," Frank would say.

"I know. Isn't it great?"

Before leaving for home at the end of the day, Frank often passed by another source of news, the little room filled with file cabinets and copy machines, informally called "The Department of Unfortunate Statistics." Someone had started to tape on the beige walls of this room extra copies of pages that held interesting statistics or other bits of recent quantitative information. No one knew who had started the tradition, but now it was clearly a communal thing.

The oldest ones were headlines, things like:

WORLD BANK PRESIDENT SAYS FOUR BILLION LIVE ON LESS THAN TWO DOLLARS A DAY

or

AMERICA: FIVE PERCENT OF WORLD POPULATION, FIFTY PERCENT OF CORPORATE OWNERSHIP

Later pages were charts or tables of figures out of journal articles, or short articles of a quantitative nature out of the scientific literature.

When Frank went by on this day, Edgardo was in there

at the coffee machine, as he so often was, looking at the latest. It was another headline:

352 RICHEST PEOPLE OWN AS MUCH AS THE
POOREST TWO BILLION, SAYS CANADIAN FOOD
PROJECT

"I don't think this can be right," Edgardo declared.

"How so?" Frank said.

"Because the poorest two billion have nothing, whereas the richest three hundred and fifty-two have a big percentage of the world's total capital. I suspect it would take the poorest four billion at least to match the top three hundred and fifty."

Anna came in as he was saying this, and wrinkled her nose as she went to the copying machine. She didn't like this kind of conversation, Frank knew. It seemed to be a matter of distaste for belaboring the obvious. Or distrust in the data. Maybe she was the one who had taped up the brief quote: *72.8% of all statistics are made up on the spot.*

Frank, wanting to bug her, said, "What do you think, Anna?"

"About what?"

Edgardo pointed to the headline and explained his objection.

Anna said, "I don't know. Maybe if you add two billion small households up, it matches the richest three hundred."

"Not this top three hundred. Have you seen the latest *Forbes 500* reports?"

Anna shook her head impatiently, as if to say, Of course not, why would I waste my time? But Edgardo was an inveterate student of the stock market and the financial world in general. He tapped another taped-up page. "The average surplus value created by American workers is thirty-three dollars an hour."

Anna said, "I wonder how they define surplus value."

"Profit," Frank said.

Edgardo shook his head. "You can cook the books and get rid of profit, but the surplus value, the value created beyond the pay for the labor, is still there."

Anna said, "There was a page in here that said the average American worker puts in 1,950 hours a year. I thought that was questionable too, that's forty hours a week for about forty-nine weeks."

"Three weeks of vacation a year," Frank pointed out. "Pretty normal."

"Yeah, but that's the average? What about all the part-time workers?"

"There must be an equivalent number of people who work overtime."

"Can that be true? I thought overtime was a thing of the past."

"You work overtime."

"Yeah but I don't get *paid* for it."

The men laughed at her.

"They should have used the median," she said. "The average is a skewed measure of central tendency. Anyway, that's..." Anna could do calculations in her head. "Sixty-four thousand three hundred and fifty dollars a year, generated by the average worker in surplus value. If you can believe these figures."

"What's the average income?" Edgardo asked. "Thirty thousand?"

"Maybe less," Frank said.

"We don't have any idea," Anna objected.

"Call it thirty, and what's the average taxes paid?"

"About ten? Or is it less?"

Edgardo said, "Call it ten. So let's see. You work every day of the year, except for three lousy weeks. You make around a hundred thousand dollars. Your boss takes two thirds, and gives you one third, and you give a third of that to the government. Your government uses what it takes to build all the roads and schools and police and pensions, and your boss takes his share and buys a mansion on an island somewhere. So naturally you complain about your bloated inefficient Big Brother of a government, and you always vote for the pro-owner party." He grinned at Frank and Anna. "How stupid is that?"

Anna shook her head. "People don't see it that way."

"But here are the statistics!"

"People don't usually put them together like that. Besides, you made half of them up."

"They're close enough for people to get the idea! But they are not taught to think! In fact they're taught *not* to think. And they are stupid to begin with."

Even Frank was not willing to go this far. "It's a matter of what you can see," he suggested. "You see your boss, you see your paycheck, it's given to you. You have it. Then you're forced to give some of it to the government. You never know about the surplus value you've created, because it was disappeared in the first place. Cooked in the books."

"But the rich are all over the news! Everyone can see they have more than they have earned, because no one *earns* that much."

"The only things people understand are sensory," Frank insisted. "We're hard-wired to understand life on the savannah. Someone gives you meat, they're your friend. Someone takes your meat, they're your enemy. Abstract concepts like surplus value, or statistics on the value of a year's work, these just aren't as real as what you see and touch. People are only good at what they can think out in terms of their senses. That's just the way we evolved."

"That's what I'm saying," Edgardo said cheerfully. "We are stupid!"

"I've got to get back to it," Anna said, and left. It really wasn't her kind of conversation.

Frank followed her out, and finally headed home. He drove his little fuel-cell Honda out Old Dominion Parkway, already jammed; over the Beltway, and then up to a condo complex called Swink's New Mill, where he had rented a condominium for his year at NSF.

He parked in the complex's cellar garage and took the elevator up to the fourteenth floor. His apartment looked out toward the Potomac—a long view and a nice apartment, rented out for the year by a young State Department guy who was doing a stint in Brasilia. It was furnished in a stripped-down style that suggested the man did not live there very often. But a nice kitchen, functional spaces, everything easy, and most of the time Frank was home he was asleep anyway, so he didn't care what it was like.

He had picked up one of the free papers back at work, and now as he spooned down some cottage cheese he looked again at the Personals section, a regrettable habit he had had for years, fascinated as he was by the glimpse these pages gave of a subworld of radically efflorescing sexual diversity—a subculture that had understood the implications of the removal of biological constraints in the techno-urban landscape, and were therefore able and willing to create a kind of polymorphous panmixia. Were these people really out there, or was this merely the collective fantasy life of a bunch of lonely souls like himself? He had never contacted any of the people putting in the ads to try to find out. He suspected the worst, and would rather be lonely. Although the sections devoted to people looking for LTRs, meaning "long-term relationships," went far beyond the sexual fantasies, and sometimes struck him with force. ISO LTR: "in search of long-term relation-

ship." The species had long ago evolved toward monogamous relationships, they were wired into the brain's structure, every culture manifesting the same overwhelming
tendency toward pair-bonding. Not a cultural imposition
but a biological instinct. They might as well be storks in
that regard.

And so he read the ads, but never replied. He was only
here for a year; San Diego was his home. It made no sense
to take any action on this particular front, no matter what
he felt or read.

The ads themselves also tended to stop him.

Husband hunting, SWF, licensed nurse, seeks a
hardworking, handsome SWM for LTR. Must be a
dedicated Jehovah's Witness

SBM, 5' 5", shy, quiet, a little bit serious, seeking
Woman, age open. Not good-looking or wealthy but
Nice Guy. Enjoy foreign movies, opera, theater, mu-
sic, books, quiet evenings

These entries were not going to get a lot of responses.
But they, like all the rest, were as clear as could be on the
fundamental primate needs they were asking for. Frank
could have written the urtext underneath them all, and one
time he had, and had even sent it in to a paper, as a joke of
course, for all those reading these confessions with the
same analytical slant he had—it would make them laugh.
Although of course if any woman reading it liked the joke
well enough to call, well, that would have been a sign.

Male *Homo sapiens* desires company of female *Homo
sapiens* for mutual talk and grooming behaviors, possibly mating and reproduction. Must be happy, run
fast.

But no one had replied.

He went out onto the bas-relief balcony, into the sultry late afternoon. Another two months and he would be going home, back to resume his real life. He was looking forward to it. He wanted to float in the Pacific. He wanted to walk around beautiful UCSD in its cool warmth, eat lunch with old colleagues among the eucalyptus trees.

Thinking about that reminded him of the grant application from Yann Pierzinski. He went inside to his laptop and Googled him to try to learn more about what he had been up to. Then he reopened his application, and found the section on the part of the algorithm to be developed. Primitive recursion at the boundary limit...it was interesting.

After some more thought, he called up Derek Gaspar at Torrey Pines Generique.

"What's up?" Derek said after the preliminaries.

"Well, I just got a grant proposal from one of your people, and I'm wondering if you can tell me anything about it."

"From one of mine, what do you mean?"

"A Yann Pierzinski, do you know him?"

"No, never heard of him. He works here you say?"

"He was there on a temporary contract, working with Simpson. He's a post-doc from Caltech."

"Ah yeah, here we go. Mathematician, got a paper in *Biomathematics* on algorithms."

"Yeah that comes up first on my Google too."

"Well sure. I can't be expected to know everyone who ever worked with us here, that's hundreds of people, you know that."

"Sure sure."

"So what's his proposal about? Are you going to give him a grant?"

"Not up to me, you know that. We'll see what the panel says. But meanwhile, maybe you should check it out."

"Oh you like it then."

"I think it may be interesting, it's hard to tell at this stage. Just don't drop him."

"Well, our records show him as already gone back up to Pasadena, to finish his work up there I presume. Like you said, his gig here was temporary."

"Ah ha. Man, your research groups have been gutted."

"Not gutted, Frank, we're down to the bare bones in some areas, but we've kept what we need to. There have been some hard choices to make. Kenton wanted his note repaid, and the timing couldn't have been worse. Coming after that stage two in India it's been tough, really tough. That's one of the reasons I'll be happy when you're back out here."

"I don't work for Torrey Pines anymore."

"No I know, but maybe you could rejoin us when you move back here."

"Maybe. If you get new financing."

"I'm trying, believe me. That's why I'd like to have you back on board."

"We'll see. Let's talk about it when I'm out there. Meanwhile, don't cut any more of your other research efforts. They might be what draws the new financing."

"I hope so. I'm doing what I can, believe me. We're trying to hold on til something comes through."

"Yeah. Hang in there then. I'll be out looking for a place to live in a couple of weeks, I'll come see you then."

"Good, make an appointment with Susan."

Frank clicked off his phone, sat back in his chair thinking it over. Derek was like a lot of first-generation CEOs of biotech start-ups. He had come out of the biology department at UCSD, and his business acumen had been gained on the job. Some people managed to do this successfully, others didn't, but all tended to fall behind on the actual science being done, and had to take on faith what was really possible in the labs. Certainly Derek could use some help in guiding policy at Torrey Pines Generique.

Frank went back to studying the grant proposal. There were elements of the algorithm missing, as was typical. That was what the grant was for, to pay for the work that would finish the project. And some people made a habit of describing crucial aspects of their work in general terms when at the prepub stage, a matter of being cautious. So he could not be sure about it, but he could see the potential for a very powerful method there. Earlier in the day he had thought he saw a way to plug one of the gaps that Pierzinski had left, and if that worked as he thought it might…

"Hmmmm," he said to the empty room.

If the situation was still fluid when he went out to San Diego, he could perhaps set things up quite nicely. There were some potential problems, of course. NSF's guidelines stated explicitly that although any copyrights, patents, or project income belonged to the grant holder, NSF always kept a public-right use for all grant-subsidized work. That would keep any big gains from being made by an individual or company on a project like this, if it was awarded a grant. Purely private control could only be maintained if there had not been any public money granted.

Also, the P.I. on the proposal was Pierzinski's advisor at Caltech, battening off the work of his students in the usual way. Of course it was an exchange—the advisor gave the student credibility, a sort of license to apply for a grant, by contributing his name and prestige to the project. The student provided the work, sometimes all of it, sometimes just a portion of it. In this case, it looked to Frank like all of it.

Anyway, the grant proposal came from Caltech. Caltech

and the P.I. would hold the rights to anything the project made, along with NSF itself, even if Pierzinski moved afterward. So, if for instance an effort was going to be made to bring Pierzinski to Torrey Pines Generique, it would be best if this particular proposal were to fail. And if the algorithm worked and became patentable, then again, keeping control of what it made would only be possible if the proposal were to fail.

That line of thought made him feel jumpy. In fact he was on his feet, pacing out to the minibalcony and back in again. Then he remembered he had been planning to go out to Great Falls anyway. He quickly finished his cottage cheese, pulled his climbing kit out of the closet, changed clothes, and went back down to his car.

The Great Falls of the Potomac was a complicated thing, a long tumble of whitewater falling down past a few islands. The complexity of the falls was its main visual appeal, as it was no very great thing in terms of total height, or even volume of water. Its roar was the biggest thing about it.

The spray it threw up seemed to consolidate and knock down the humidity, so that paradoxically it was less humid here than elsewhere, although wet and mossy underfoot. Frank walked downstream along the edge of the gorge. Below the falls the river re-collected itself and ran through a defile called Mather Gorge, a ravine with a south wall so steep that climbers were drawn to it. One section called Carter Rock was Frank's favorite. It was a simple matter to tie a rope to a top belay, usually a stout tree trunk near the cliff's edge, and then rappel down the rope to the bottom and either free-climb up, or clip onto the rope with an ascender and go through the hassles of self-belay.

One could climb in teams too, of course, and many did, but there were about as many singletons like Frank here as there were duets. Some even free-soloed the wall, dispensing with all protection. Frank liked to play it just a little safer than that, but he had climbed here so many times now that sometimes he rappelled down and free-climbed next to his rope, pretending to himself that he could grab it if he fell. The few routes available were all chalked and greasy from repeated use. He decided this time to clip onto the rope with the ascender.

The river and its gorge created a band of open sky that was unusually big for the metropolitan area. This as much as anything else gave Frank the feeling that he was in a good place: on a wall route, near water, and open to the sky. Out of the claustrophobia of the great hardwood forest, one of the things about the East Coast that Frank hated the most. There were times he would have given a finger for the sight of open land.

Now, as he rappelled down to the small tumble of big boulders at the foot of the cliff, chalked his hands, and began to climb the fine-grained old schist of the route, he cheered up. He focused on his immediate surroundings to a degree unimaginable when he was not climbing. It was like the math work, only then he wasn't anywhere at all. Here, he was right on these very particular rocks.

This route he had climbed before many times. About a 5.8 or 5.9 at its crux, much easier elsewhere. Hard to find really hard pitches here, but that didn't matter. Even climbing up out of a ravine, rather than up onto a peak, didn't matter. The constant roar, the spray, those didn't matter. Only the climbing itself mattered.

His legs did most of the work. Find the footholds, fit his rock-climbing shoes into cracks or onto knobs, then look for handholds; and up, and up again, using his hands only for balance, and a kind of tactile reassurance that he was seeing what he was seeing, that the footholds he was expecting to use would be enough. Climbing was the bliss of perfect attention, a kind of devotion, or prayer. Or simply a retreat into the supreme competencies of the primate cerebellum. A lot was conserved.

By now it was evening. A sultry summer evening, sunset near, the air itself going yellow. He topped out and sat on the rim, feeling the sweat on his face fail to evaporate.

There was a kayaker, below in the river. A woman, he thought, though she wore a helmet and was broad-shouldered and flat-chested—he would have been hard-pressed to say exactly how he knew, and yet he was sure. This was another savannah competency, and indeed some anthropologists postulated that this kind of rapid identification of reproductive possibility was what the enlarged neocortex had grown to do. The brain growing with such evolutionary speed, specifically to get along with the other sex. A depressing thought given the results so far.

This woman was paddling smoothly upstream, into the hissing water that only around her seemed to be re-collecting itself as a liquid. Upstream it was a steep rapids, leading to the white smash at the bottom of the falls proper.

The kayaker pushed up into this wilder section, paddling harder upstream, then held her position against the flow while she studied the falls ahead. Then she took off hard, attacking a white smooth flow in the lowest section, a kind of ramp through the smash, up to a terrace in the whitewater. When she reached the little flat she could rest again, in another slightly more strenuous maintenance paddle, gathering her strength for the next salmonlike climb.

Abruptly leaving the strange refuge of that flat spot, she attacked another ramp that led up to a bigger plateau of flat black water, a pool that had an eddy in it, apparently, rolling backward and allowing her to rest in place. There was no room there to gain any speed for another leap up, so that she appeared to be stuck; but maybe she was only studying her way, or waiting for a moment of reduced flow, because all of a sudden she attacked the water with a fierce flurry of paddle strokes, and seemingly willed her craft up the next pouring ramp. Five or seven desperate seconds later she leveled out again, on a tiny little bench of a refuge that did not have a pushback eddy, judging by the intensity of her maintenance paddling there. After only a few seconds she had to try a ramp to her right or get pushed back off her perch, and so she took off and fought upstream, fists moving fast as a boxer's, the kayak at an impossible angle, looking like a miracle—until all of a sudden it was swept back down, and she had to make a quick turn and then take a wild ride, bouncing down the falls by a different and steeper route than the one she had ascended, losing in a few swift seconds the height that she had taken a minute or two's hard labor to gain.

"Wow," Frank said, smitten.

She was already almost down to the hissing tapestry of flat river right below him, and he felt an urge to wave to her, or stand and applaud. He restrained himself, not wanting to impose upon another athlete obviously deep in her own space. But he did whip out his cell phone and try out a GPS-oriented directory search, figuring that if she had a cell phone with a transponder in the kayak, it had to be very close to his own phone's position. He checked his position, entered thirty meters north of that; got nothing. Same with the position twenty meters farther east.

"Ah well," he said, and stood to go. It was sunset now, and the smooth stretches of the river had turned a pale orange. Time to go home and try to fall asleep.

"In search of kayaker gal, seen going upstream at Great Falls. Great ride, I love you, please respond."

He would not send that in to the free papers, but only spoke it as a kind of prayer to the sunset. Down below the kayaker was turning to start upstream again.

IT COULD be said that science is boring, or even that science wants to be boring, in that it wants to be beyond all dispute. It wants to understand the phenomena of the world in ways that everyone can agree on and share; it wants to make assertions from a position that is not any particular subject's position, assertions that if tested for accuracy by any sentient being would cause that being to agree with the assertion. Complete agreement; the world put under a description—stated that way, it begins to sound interesting.

And indeed it is. Nothing human is boring. Nevertheless, the minute details of the everyday grind involved in any particular bit of scientific practice can be tedious even to the practitioners. A lot of it, as with most work in this world, involves wasted time, false leads, dead ends, faulty equipment, dubious techniques, bad data, and a huge amount of detail work. Only when it is written up in a paper does it tell a tale of things going right, step-by-step, in meticulous and replicable detail, like a proof in Euclid.

That stage is a highly artificial result of a long process of grinding.

In the case of Leo and his lab, and the matter of the new targeted nonviral delivery system from Maryland, several hundred hours of human labor and many more of computer time were devoted to an attempted repetition of an experiment described in the crucial paper, "In Vivo Insertion of cDNA 1568rr into CBA/H, BALB/c, and C57BL/6 Mice."

At the end of this process, Leo had confirmed the theory he had formulated the very moment he had read the paper describing the experiment.

"It's a goddamned artifact."

Marta and Brian sat there staring at the printouts. Marta had killed a couple hundred of the Jackson labs' finest mice in the course of confirming this theory of Leo's, and now she was looking more murderous than ever. You didn't want to mess with Marta on the days when she had to sacrifice some mice, nor even talk to her.

Brian sighed.

Leo said, "It only works if you pump the mice full of the stuff til they just about explode. I mean look at them. They look like hamsters. Or guinea pigs. Their little eyes are about to pop out of their heads."

"No wonder," Brian said. "There's only two milliliters of blood in a mouse, and we're injecting them with one."

Leo shook his head. "How the hell did they get away with that?"

"The CBAs are kind of round and furry."

"What are you saying, they're bred to hide artifacts?"

"No."

"It's an artifact!"

"Well, it's useless, anyway."

An artifact was what they called an experimental result that was specific to the methodology of the experiment, but not illustrating anything beyond that. A kind of accident or false result, and in a few celebrated cases, part of a deliberate hoax.

So Brian was trying to be careful using the word. It was possible that it was no worse than a real result that happened to be generated in a way that made it useless for their particular purposes. Trying to turn things that people have learned about biological processes into medicines led to that sort of result. It happened all the time, and all those experimental results were not necessarily artifacts. They just weren't useful facts.

Not yet, anyway. That's why there were so many experiments, and so many stages to the human trials that had to be so carefully conducted; so many double blind studies, held with as many patients as possible, to get good statistical data. Hundreds of Swedish nurses, all with the same habits, studied for half a century—but these kinds of powerful long-term studies were very rarely possible. Never, when the substances being tested were brand-new—literally, in the sense that they were still under patent and had brand names different from their scientific appellations.

So all the little baby biotechs, and all the start-up pharmaceuticals, paid for the best stage-one studies they could afford. They scoured the literature, and ran experiments on computers and lab samples, and then on mice or other lab animals, hunting for data that could be put through a reliable analysis that would tell them something about how a potential new medicine worked in people. Then the human trials.

It was usually a matter of two to ten years of work, costing anywhere up to five hundred million dollars, though naturally cheaper was better. Longer and more expensive than that, and the new drug or method would almost certainly be abandoned; the money would run out, and the scientists involved would by necessity move on to something else.

In this case, however, where Leo was dealing with a method that Derek Gaspar had bought for fifty-one million dollars, there could be no stage-one human trials. They would be impossible. "No one's gonna let themselves be blown up like a balloon! Blown up like a goddamn bike tire! Your kidneys would get swamped or some kind of edema would kill you."

"We're going to have to tell Derek the bad news."

"Derek is not going to like it."

"Not going to like it! Fifty-one million dollars? He's going to hate it!"

"Think about blowing that much money. What an idiot he is."

"Is it worse to have a scientist who is a bad businessman as your CEO, or a businessman who is a bad scientist?"

"What about when they're both?"

They sat around the bench looking at the mice cages and the rolls of data sheets. A Dilbert cartoon mocked them as it peeled away from the end of the counter. It was a sign of something deep that this lab had Dilberts taped to the walls rather than Far Sides.

"An in-person meeting for this particular communication is contraindicated," said Brian.

"No shit," Leo said.

Marta snorted. "You can't get a meeting with him anyway."

"Ha ha." But Leo was far enough out on the periphery of Torrey Pines Generique's power structure that getting a meeting with Derek was indeed difficult.

"It's true," Marta insisted. "You might as well be trying to schedule a doctor's appointment."

"Which is stupid," Brian pointed out. "The company is totally dependent on what happens in this lab."

"Not totally," Leo said.

"Yes it is! But that's not what the business schools teach these guys. The lab is just another place of production. Management tells production what to produce, and the place of production produces it. Input from the agency of production would be wrong."

"Like the assembly line choosing what to make," Marta said.

"Right. Thus the idiocy of business management theory in our time."

"I'll send him an e-mail," Leo decided.

So Leo sent Derek an e-mail concerning what Brian and Marta persisted in calling the exploding mice problem. Derek (according to reports they heard later) swelled up like one of their experimental subjects. It appeared he had been IVed with two quarts of genetically engineered righteous indignation.

"It's in the literature!" he was reported to have shouted at Dr. Sam Houston, his vice president in charge of research and development. "It was in *The Journal of Immunology*, there were two papers that were peer-reviewed, they *got a patent for it*! I went out there to Maryland and checked it all out myself! It worked there, damn it. So *make it work here*."

" 'Make it work'?" Marta said when she heard this story. "You see what I mean?"

"Well, you know," Leo said grimly. "That's the tech in biotech, right?"

"Hmmm," Brian said, interested despite himself.

After all, the manipulations of gene and cell that they made were hardly ever done "just to find things out," though they did that too. They were done to accomplish certain things inside the cell, and hopefully later, inside a living body. Biotechnology, *bio techno logos;* the word on how to put the tool into the living organism. Genetic engineering meant designing and building something new inside a body's DNA, to effect something in the metabolism.

They had done the genetics; now it was time for the engineering.

So Leo and Brian and Marta, and the rest of Leo's lab, and some people from labs elsewhere in the building, began to work on this problem. Sometimes at the end of a day, when the sun was breaking sideways through gaps in the clouds out to sea, shining weakly in the tinted windows and illuminating their faces as they sat around two desks covered by reprints and offprints, they would talk over the issues involved, and compare their most recent results, and try to make sense of the problem. Sometimes one of them would stand up and use the whiteboard to sketch out some diagram illustrating his or her conception of what was going on, down there forever below the level of their physical senses. The rest would comment, and drink coffee, and think it over.

For a while they considered assumptions the original experimenters had made:

"Maybe the flushing dose doesn't have to be that high."

"Maybe the solution could be stronger, they seem to have topped out kind of low."

"But that's because of what happens to the..."

"See, the group at UW found that out when they were working on..."

"Yeah that's right. Shit."

"The thing is, it does work, when you do everything they did. I mean the transference will happen in vitro, and in mice."

"What about drawing blood, treating it and then putting it back in?"

"Or hepatocytes?"

"Uptake is in blood."

"What we need is to package the inserts with a ligand that is really specific for the target cells. If we could find that specificity, out of all the possible proteins, without going through all the rigamarole of trial and error..."

"Too bad we don't still have Pierzinski here. He could run the array of possibilities through his operation set."

"Well, we could call him up and ask him to give it a try."

"Sure, but who's got time for that kind of thing?"

"He's still working on a paper with Eleanor over on campus," Marta said, meaning UCSD. "I'll ask him when he comes down."

Brian said, almost as if joking, "Maybe you could try to make the insertion in a limb, away from the organs. Tourniquet a lower leg or a forearm, blow it up with the full dose, wait for it to permeate the endothelial cells lining the veins and arteries in the limb, then release the tourniquet. They'd pee off the extra water, and still have a certain number of altered cells. It wouldn't be any worse than chugging a few beers, would it?"

"Your hand would hurt."

"Big fucking deal."

"You might get phlebitis if it was your leg. Isn't that how it happens?"

"Well use the hand then."

"Interesting," Leo said. "Heck, let's try it at least. The other options look worse to me. Although we should probably try the mice on the various limits on volume and dosage in the original experiment, just to be sure."

So the meeting petered out, and they wandered off to go home, or back to their desks and benches, thinking over plans for more experiments. Getting the mice, getting the time on the machines, sequencing genes, sequencing schedules; when you were doing science the hours flew by, and the days, and the weeks. This was the main feeling: there was never enough time to do it all. Was this different from other kinds of work? Papers almost written were rewritten, checked, rewritten again—finally sent off. Papers with their problems papered over. Lots of times the lab was like some old-fashioned newspaper office with a deadline approaching, all the starving journalists churning out the next day's fishwrap. Except people would not wrap fish with these papers; they would save them, file them by category, test all their assertions, cite them—and report any errors to the authorities.

Leo's THINGS TO DO list grew and shrank, grew and shrank, grew and then refused to shrink. He spent much less time than he wanted to at home in Leucadia with Roxanne. Roxanne understood, but it bothered him, even if it didn't bother her.

He called the Jackson labs and ordered new and different strains of mice, each strain with its own number and bar code and genome. He got his lab's machines scheduled, and assigned the techs to use them, moving some things to the front burner, others to the back, all to accommodate this project's urgency.

On certain days, he went into the lab where the mouse cages were kept, and opened a cage door. He took out a mouse, small and white, wriggling and sniffing the way they did, checking things out with its whiskers. Quickly he shifted it so that he was holding it at the neck with the forefingers and thumbs of both hands. A quick hard twist and the neck broke. Very soon after that the mouse was dead.

This was not unusual. During this round of experiments, he and Brian and Marta and the rest of them tourniqueted and injected about three hundred mice, drew their blood, then killed and rendered and analyzed them. That was an aspect of the process they didn't talk about, not even Brian. Marta in particular went black with disgust;

it was worse than when she was premenstrual, as Brian
joked (once). Her headphones stayed on her head all day
long, the music turned up so loud that even the other people in the lab could hear it. Terrible, ultraprofane hip-hop
rap whatever. If she can't hear she can't feel, Brian joked
right next to her, Marta oblivious and trembling with rage,
or something like it.

But it was no joke, even though the mice existed to be
killed, even though they were killed mercifully, and usually
only some few months before they would have died naturally. There was no real reason to have qualms, and yet still
there was no joking about it. Maybe Brian would joke
about Marta (if she couldn't hear him), but he wouldn't
joke about that. In fact, he insisted on using the word "kill"
rather than "sacrifice," even in write-ups and papers, to
keep it clear what they were doing. Usually they had to
break their necks right behind the head; you couldn't inject
them to "put them to sleep," because their tissue samples
had to be clear of all contaminants. So it was a matter of
breaking necks, as if they were tigers pouncing on prey.
Marta was as blank as a mask as she did it, and very deftly
too. If done properly it paralyzed them so that it was quick
and painless—or at least quick. No feeling below the head,
no breathing, immediate loss of mouse consciousness, one
hoped. Leaving only the killers to think it over. The victims
were dead, and their bodies had been donated to science
for many generations on end. The lab had the pedigrees to
prove it. The scientists involved went home and thought
about other things, most of the time. Usually the mice
deaths occurred in the mornings, so they could get to work
on the samples. By the time the scientists got home the
experience was somewhat forgotten, its effects muted.
But people like Marta went home and dosed themselves
with drugs on those days—she said she did—and played
the most hostile music they could find, 110 decibels of

forgetting. Or went out surfing. They didn't talk about it to anyone, at least most of them didn't—this was what made Marta so obvious, she would talk about it—but most of them didn't, because it would sound both silly and vaguely shameful at the same time. If it bothered them so much, why did they keep doing it? Why did they stay in that line of business?

But—that line of business was doing science. It was doing biology, it was studying life, improving life, increasing life! And in most labs the mouse-killing was done only by the lowliest of techs, so that it was only a temporary bad job that one had to get through on the way to the good jobs.

Someone's got to do it, they thought.

In the meantime, while they were working on this problem, their good results with the HDL "factory cells" had been plugged into the paper they had written about the process, and sent upstairs to Torrey Pines' legal department, where it had gotten hung up. Repeated queries from Leo got the same e-mailed response: still reviewing—do not publish yet.

"They want to find out what they can patent in it," Brian said.

"They won't let us publish until we have a delivery method and a patent," Marta predicted.

"But that may never happen!" Leo cried. "It's good work, it's interesting! It could help make a big breakthrough!"

"That's what they don't want," Brian said.

"They don't want a big breakthrough unless it's our big breakthrough."

"Shit."

This had happened before, but Leo had never gotten

used to it. Sitting on results, doing private science, secret science—it went against the grain. It wasn't science as he understood it, which was a matter of finding out things and publishing them for all to see and test, critique, put to use.

But it was getting to be standard operating procedure. Security in the building remained intense; even e-mails out had to be checked for approval, not to mention laptops, briefcases, and boxes leaving the building. "You have to check in your brain when you leave," as Brian put it.

"Fine by me," Marta said.

"I just want to publish," Leo insisted grimly.

"You'd better find a targeted delivery method if you want to publish that particular paper, Leo."

So they continued to work on the Urtech method. The new experiments slowly yielded their results. The volumes and dosages had sharp parameters on all sides. The "tourniquet injection" method did not actually insert very many copy DNAs into the subject animals' endothelial cells, and a lot of what was inserted was damaged by the process, and later flushed out of the body.

In short, the Maryland method was still an artifact.

By now, however, enough time had passed that Derek could pretend that the whole thing had never happened. It was a new financial quarter; there were other fish to fry, and for now the pretense could be plausibly maintained that it was a work in progress rather than a total bust. It wasn't as if anyone else had solved the targeted nonviral delivery problem, after all. It was a hard problem. Or so Derek could say, in all truth, and did so whenever anyone was inconsiderate enough to bring the matter up. Whiners on the company's website chat room could be ignored as always.

Analysts on Wall Street, however, and in the big pharmaceuticals, and in relevant venture capital firms, could not be ignored. And while they weren't saying anything directly, investment money started to go elsewhere. Torrey Pines' stock fell, and because it was falling it fell some more, and then more again. Biotechs were fluky, and so far Torrey Pines had not generated any potential cash cows. They remained a start-up. Fifty-one million dollars was being swept under the rug, but the big lump in the rug gave it away to anyone who remembered what it was.

No. Torrey Pines Generique was in trouble.

In Leo's lab they had done what they could. Their job had been to get certain cell lines to become unnaturally prolific protein factories, and they had done that. Delivery wasn't their part of the deal, and they weren't physiologists, and now they didn't have the wherewithal to do that part of the job. Torrey Pines needed a whole different wing for that, a whole different field of science. It was not an expertise that could be bought for fifty-one million dollars. Or maybe it could have been, but Derek had bought defective expertise. And because of that, a multibillion-dollar cash-cow method was stalled right on the brink; and the whole company might go under.

Nothing Leo could do about it. He couldn't even publish his results.

THE QUIBLERS' small house was located at the end of a street of similar houses. All of them stood blankly, blinds drawn, no clues given as to who lived inside. They could have been empty for all an outsider could tell: no cars in the driveways, no kids in the yards, no yard or porch activity of any kind. They could have been walled compounds in Saudi Arabia, hiding their life from the desert outside.

Walking these streets with Joe on his back, Charlie assumed as he always did that these houses were mostly owned by people who worked in the District, people who were always either working or on vacation. Their homes were places to sleep. Charlie had been that way himself before the boys had arrived. That was how people lived in Bethesda, west of Wisconsin Avenue—west all the way to the Pacific, Charlie didn't know. But he didn't think so; he tended to put it on Bethesda specifically.

So he walked to the grocery store shaking his head as he always did. "It's like a ghost town, Joe, it's like some *Twilight*

Zone episode in which we're the only two people left on Earth."

Then they rounded the corner, and all thought of ghost towns was rendered ridiculous. Shopping center. They walked through the automatic glass doors into a giant Giant grocery store. Joe, excited by the place as always, stood up in his baby backpack, his knees on Charlie's shoulders, and whacked Charlie on the ears as if he were directing an elephant. Charlie reached up, lifted him around and stuffed him into the baby seat of the grocery cart, strapped him down with the cart's little red seat belt. A very useful feature, that.

Okay. Buddhists coming to dinner, Asians from the mouth of the Ganges. He had no idea what to cook. He assumed they were vegetarians. It was not unusual for Anna to invite people from NSF over to dinner and then be somewhat at a loss in the matter of the meal itself. But Charlie liked that. He enjoyed cooking, though he was not good at it, and had gotten worse in the years since the boys had arrived. Time had grown short, and he and Anna had both cooked and recooked their repertoire of recipes until they were sick of them, and yet hadn't learned anything new. So now they often did takeout, or ate as plainly as Nick; or Charlie tried something new and botched it. Dinner guests were a chance to do that again.

Now he decided to resuscitate an old recipe from their student years, pasta with an olive and basil sauce that a friend had first cooked for them in Italy. He wandered the familiar aisles of the store, looking for the ingredients. He should have made a list. On a typical trip he would go home having forgotten something crucial, and today he wanted to avoid that, but he was also thinking of other things, and making comments aloud from time to time. Joe's presence disguised his tendency to talk to himself in public spaces. "Okay, whole peeled tomatoes, pitted kala-

```
            NORTHTOWN BOOKS
             957 H STREET
       ARCATA, CALIFORNIA 95521
            (707) 822-2834

A              10659 08/16/05 15:56

   11   1 MAGAZINE(S)        5.95      5.95
 4257   1 FORTY SIGNS OF RA 7.99      7.99

        2      Subtotal:              13.94
               Tax:                    1.01
               Total due:            14.95
               Cash                  14.95

        Bono vinci satius est quam
       malo more iniuriam vincere
```

matas, olive oil extra virgin first cold press—it's the first press that really matters," slipping into their friend's Italian accent, "now vat I am forgetting, hm, hm, oh, ze pasta! But you must never keel ze pasta, my God! Oh and bread. And wine, but not more than we can carry home, huh Joe."

Groceries tucked into the backpack pocket under Joe's butt, and slung in plastic bags from both hands, Charlie walked Joe back along the empty street to their house, singing "I Can't Give You Anything but Love," one of Joe's favorites. Then they were up the steps and home.

Their street dead-ended in a little triangle of trees next to Woodson Ave, a feeder road that poured its load of cars onto Wisconsin south. It was a nice location, within sight of Wisconsin and yet peaceful. An old four-story apartment block wrapped around their backyard like a huge brick sound barrier, its stacked windows like a hundred live webcasts streaming all at once, daily lives that were much too partial and mundane to be interesting. No *Rear Window* here, and thank God for that. The wall of apartments was like a dull screensaver, and might as well have been trees, though trees would have been nicer. The world outside was irrelevant. Each nuclear family in its domicile is inside its own pocket universe, and for the time it is together it exists inside a kind of event horizon: no one sees it and it sees no one. Millions of pocket universes, scattered across the surface of the planet like the dots of light in nighttime satellite photos.

On this night, however, the bubble containing the Quiblers was breached. Visitors from afar, aliens! When the doorbell rang they almost didn't recognize the sound.

Anna was occupied with Joe and a diaper upstairs, so Charlie left the kitchen and hurried through the house to answer the door. Four men in off-white cotton pants and shirts stood on the stoop, like visitors from Calcutta; only their vests were the maroon color Charlie associated with

Tibetan monks. Joe had run to the top of the stairs, and he grabbed a banister to keep his balance, agog at the sight of them. In the living room Nick was struck shy, his nose quickly back into his book, but he was glancing over the top of it frequently as the strangers were ushered in and made comfortable around him. Charlie offered them drinks, and they accepted beers, and when he came back with those, Anna and Joe were downstairs and had joined the fun. Two of their visitors sat on the living room floor, laughing off Anna's offer of the little couches, and they all put their beer bottles on the coffee table.

The oldest monk and the youngest one leaned back against the radiator, down at Joe's level, and soon they were engaged with his vast collection of blocks—a heaping mound of plain or painted cubes, rhomboids, cylinders and other polygons, which they quickly assembled into walls and towers, working with and around Joe's Godzilla-like interventions.

The young one, Drepung, answered Anna's questions directly, and also translated for the oldest one, named Rudra Cakrin. Rudra was the official ambassador of Khembalung, but while he was without English, apparently, his two middle-aged associates, Sucandra and Padma Sambhava, spoke it pretty well—not as well as Drepung, but adequately.

These two followed Charlie back out into the kitchen and stood there, beer bottles in hand, talking to him as he cooked. They stirred the unkilled pasta to keep the pot from boiling over, checked out the spices in the spice rack, and stuck their noses deep into the saucepot, sniffing with great interest and appreciation. Charlie found them surprisingly easy to talk to. They were about his age. Both had been born in Tibet, and both had spent years, they did not say how many, imprisoned by the Chinese, like so many other Tibetan Buddhist monks. They had met in prison, and after their release they had crossed the Himalayas and escaped Tibet together, afterward making their way gradually to Khembalung.

"Amazing," Charlie kept saying to their stories. He could not help but compare these to his own relatively straightforward and serene passage through the years. "And now, after all that, you're getting flooded?"

"Many times," they said in unison. Padma, still sniffing Charlie's sauce as if it were the perfect ambrosia, elaborated. "Used to happen only every eighteen years or about, moon tides, you know. We could plan it happening, and be prepared. But now, whenever the monsoon hits hard."

"Also every month at moon tide," Sucandra added. "Certainly three, four times a year. No one can live that way for long. If it gets worse, then the island will no longer be habitable. So we came here."

Charlie shook his head, tried to joke: "This place may be lower in elevation than your island."

They laughed politely. Not the funniest joke. Charlie said, "Listen, speaking of elevation, have you talked to the other low-lying countries?"

Padma said, "Oh yes, we are part of the League of Drowning Nations, of course. Charter member."

"Headquarters in The Hague, near the World Court."

"Very appropriate," Charlie said. "And now you are establishing an embassy here...."

"To argue our case, yes."

Sucandra said, "We must speak to the hyperpower."

The two men smiled cheerily.

"Well. That's very interesting." Charlie tested the pasta to see if it was ready. "I've been working on climate issues myself, for Senator Chase. I'll have to get you in there to talk to him. And you need to hire a good firm of lobbyists too."

"Yes?" They regarded him with interest. Padma said, "You think it best?"

"Yes. Definitely. You're here to lobby the U.S. government, that's what it comes down to. And there are pros in town to help foreign governments do that. I used to do it myself, and I've still got a good friend working for one of the better firms. I'll put you in touch with him and you can see what he tells you."

Charlie slipped on potholders and lifted the pasta pot over to the sink, tipped it into the colander until it was overflowing. Always a problem with their little colander, which he never thought to replace except at moments like this. "I think my friend's firm already represents the Dutch on these issues—oops—so it's a perfect match. They'll be knowledgeable about your suite of problems, you'll fit right in there."

"Do they lobby for Tibet?"

"That I don't know. Separate issues, I should think. But they have a lot of client countries. You'll see how they fit your needs when you talk to them."

They nodded. "Thank you for that. We will enjoy that."

They took the food into the little dining room, which was a kind of corner in the passageway between kitchen and living room, and with a great deal of to-and-froing, all of them just managed to fit around the dining room table. Joe consented to a booster seat to get his head up to the level of the table, where he shoveled baby food industriously into his mouth or onto the floor as the case might be, narrating the process all the while in his own tongue. Sucandra and Rudra Cakrin had seated themselves on either side of him, and they watched his performance with pleasure. Both attended to him as if they thought he was speaking a real language. They ate in a style that was not that dissimilar to his, Charlie thought—absorbed, happy, shoveling it in. The sauce was a hit with everyone but Nick, who ate his pasta plain. Joe tossed a roll across the table at Nick, who batted it aside expertly, and all the Khembalis laughed.

Charlie got up and followed Anna out to the kitchen when she went to get the salad. He said to her under his breath, "I bet the old man speaks English too."

"What?"

"It's like in that Ang Lee movie, remember? The old man pretends not to understand English, but really he does? It's like that I bet."

Anna shook her head. "Why would he do that? It's a hassle, all that translating. It doesn't give him any advantage."

"You don't know that! Watch his eyes, see how he's getting it all."

"He's just paying attention. Don't be silly."

"You'll see." Charlie leaned into her conspiratorially: "Maybe he learned English in an earlier incarnation. Just be aware of that when you're talking around him."

"Quit it," she said, laughing her low laugh. "*You* be aware. *You* learn to pay attention like that."

"Oh and then you'll believe I understand English?"

"That's right yeah."

They returned to the dining room, laughing, and found Joe holding forth in a language anyone could understand, a language of imperious gesture and commanding eye, and the assumption of authority in the world. Which worked like a charm over them all, even though he was babbling.

After salad, and seconds on the pasta, they returned to the living room and settled around the coffee table again. Anna brought out tea and cookies. "We'll have to have Tibetan tea next time," she said.

The Khembalis nodded uncertainly.

"An acquired taste," Drepung suggested. "Not actually tea as you know it."

"Bitter," Padma said appreciatively.

"You can use as blood coagulant," Sucandra said.

Drepung added, "Also we add yak butter to it, aged until a bit rancid."

"The butter has to be rancid?" Charlie said.

"Traditional."

"Think fermentation," Sucandra explained.

"Well, let's have that for sure. Nick will love it."

A scrunch-faced pretend-scowl from Nick: Yeah right Dad.

Rudra Cakrin sat again with Joe on the floor. He stacked blocks into elaborate towers. Whenever they began to sway, Joe leaned in and chopped them to the floor. Tumbling *clack* of colored wood, instant catastrophe: the two of them cast their heads back and laughed in exactly the same way. Kindred souls.

The others watched. From the couch Drepung observed the old man, smiling fondly, although Charlie thought he also saw traces of the look that Anna had tried to describe to him when explaining why she had invited them to lunch in the first place: a kind of concern that came perhaps from an intensity of love. Charlie knew that feeling. It had been a good idea to invite them over. He had groaned when Anna told him about it, life was simply Too Busy for more to be added. Or so it had seemed; though at the same time he was somewhat starved for adult company. Now he was enjoying himself, watching Rudra Cakrin and Joe play on the floor as if there were no tomorrow.

Anna was deep in conversation with Sucandra. Charlie heard Sucandra say to her, "We give patients quantities, very small, keep records, of course, and judge results. There is a personal element to all medicine, as you know. People talking about how they feel. You can average numbers, I know you do that, but the subjective feeling remains."

Anna nodded, but Charlie knew she thought this aspect of medicine was unscientific, and it annoyed her as such. She kept to the quantitative as much as she could in her work, as far as he could tell, precisely to avoid this kind of subjective residual in the facts.

Now she said, "But you do support attempts to make objective studies of such matters?"

"Of course," Sucandra replied. "Buddhist science is much like Western science in that regard."

Anna nodded, brow furrowed like a hawk. Her definition of science was extremely narrow. "Reproducible studies?"

"Yes, that is Buddhism precisely."

Now Anna's eyebrows met in a deep vertical furrow that split the horizontal ones higher on her brow. "I thought Buddhism was a kind of feeling, you know—meditation, compassion?"

"This is to speak of the goal. What the investigation is for. Same for you, yes? Why do you pursue the sciences?"

"Well—to understand things better, I guess."

This was not the kind of thing Anna thought about. It was like asking her why she breathed.

"And why?" Sucandra persisted, watching her.

"Well—just because."

"A matter of curiosity."

"Yes, I suppose so."

"But what if curiosity is a luxury?"

"How so?"

"In that first you must have a full belly. Good health, a certain amount of leisure time, a certain amount of serenity. Absence of pain. Only then can one be curious."

Anna nodded, thinking it over.

Sucandra saw this and continued. "So, if curiosity is a value—a quality to be treasured—a form of contemplation, or prayer—then you must reduce suffering to reach that state. So, in Buddhism, understanding works to reduce suffering, and by reduction of suffering gains more knowledge. Just like science."

Anna frowned. Charlie watched her, fascinated. This was a basic part of her self, this stuff, but largely unconsidered. Self-definition by function. She was a scientist. And science was science, unlike anything else.

Rudra Cakrin leaned forward to say something to Sucandra, who listened to him, then asked him a question in Tibetan. Rudra answered, gesturing at Anna.

Charlie shot a quick look at her—see, he was following things! Evidence!

Rudra Cakrin insisted on something to Sucandra, who then said to Anna, "Rudra wants to say, 'What do you believe in?'"

"Me?"

"Yes. 'What do you believe in?' he says."

"*I* don't know," she said, surprised. "I believe in the double blind study."

Charlie laughed, he couldn't help it. Anna blushed and beat on his arm, crying "Stop it! It's *true*."

"I *know* it is," Charlie said, laughing harder, until she started laughing too, along with everyone else, the Khembalis looking delighted—everyone so amused that Joe got mad and stomped his foot to make them stop. But this only made them laugh more. In the end they had to stop so he would not throw a fit.

Rudra Cakrin restored his mood by diving back into the blocks. Soon he and Joe sat half-buried in them, absorbed in their play. Stack them up, knock them down. They certainly spoke the same language.

The others watched them, sipping tea and offering particular blocks to them at certain moments in the construction process. Sucandra and Padma and Anna and Charlie and Nick sat on the couches, talking about Khembalung and Washington D.C. and how much they were alike.

Then one tower of cubes and beams stood longer than the others had. Rudra Cakrin had constructed it with care, and the repetition of basic colors was pretty: blue, red, yellow, green, blue, yellow, red, green, blue, red, green, red. It was tall enough that ordinarily Joe would have already knocked it over, but he seemed to like this one. He stared at it, mouth hanging open in a less-than-brilliant expression. Rudra Cakrin looked over at Sucandra, said something. Sucandra replied quickly, sounding displeased, which surprised Charlie. Drepung and Padma were suddenly paying attention. Rudra Cakrin picked out a yellow cube, showed it to Sucandra and said something more. He put it on the top of the tower.

"Oooh," Joe said. He tilted his head to one side, then the other, observing it.

"He likes that one," Charlie noted.

At first no one answered. Then Drepung said, "It's an old Tibetan pattern. You see it in mandalas." He looked to Sucandra, who said something sharp in Tibetan. Rudra Cakrin replied easily, shifted so that his knee knocked a long blue cylinder into the tower, collapsing it. Joe shuddered as if startled by a noise on the street.

"Ah ga," he declared.

The Tibetans resumed the conversation. Nick was now explaining to Padma the distinction between whales and dolphins. Sucandra went out and helped Charlie a bit with the cleanup in the kitchen; finally Charlie shooed him out, feeling embarrassed that their pots were going to end up substantially cleaner after this visit than they had been before; Sucandra had been expertly scrubbing their bottoms with a wire pad found under the sink.

Around nine-thirty they took their leave. Anna offered to call a cab, but they said the Metro was fine. They did not need guidance back to the station: "Very easy. Interesting too. There are many fine carpets in the windows of this part of town."

Charlie was about to explain that this was the work of Iranians who had come to Washington after the fall of the Shah, but then he thought better of it. Not a happy precedent: the Iranians had never left.

Instead he said to Sucandra, "I'll give my friend Sridar a call and ask him to meet with you. He'll be very helpful, even if you don't end up hiring his firm."

"I'm sure. Many thanks." And they were off into the balmy night.

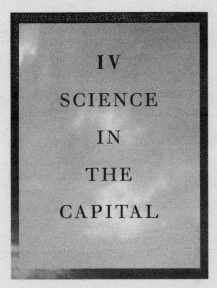

IV

SCIENCE

IN

THE

CAPITAL

What's New From the Department of Unfortunate Statistics?

Extinction Rate in Oceans Now Faster Than on Land. Coral Reef Collapses Leading to Mass Extinctions; Thirty Percent of Warm-water Species Estimated Gone. Fishing Stocks Depleted, UN Declares Scaleback Necessary or Commercial Species Will Crash.

Topsoil Loss Nears a Million Acres a Year. Deforestation now faster in temperate than tropical forests. Only 35% of tropical forests left.

The average Indian consumes 200 kilograms of grain a year; the average American, 800 kilograms; the average Italian, 400 kilograms. The Italian diet was rated best in the world for heart disease.

300 Tons of Weapons-grade Uranium and Plutonium Unaccounted For. High Mutation Rate of Microorganisms Near Radioactive Waste-treatment Sites. Antibiotics in Animal Feed Reduce Medical Effectiveness of Antibiotics for Humans. Environmental estrogens suspected in lowest-ever human sperm counts.

Two Billion Tons of Carbon Added to the Atmosphere This Year. One of the five hottest years on record. The Fed Hopes U.S. Economy Will Grow by Four Percent in the Final Quarter.

ANNA QUIBLER was in her office getting pumped. Her door was closed, the drapes (installed for her) were drawn. The pump was whirring in its triple sequence: low sigh, wheeze, clunk. The big suction cup made its vacuum pull during the wheeze, tugging her distended left breast outward and causing drips of white milk to fall off the end of her nipple. The milk then ran down a clear tube into the little clear bag in a plastic protective tube, which she would fill to the ten ounce mark.

It was an unconscious activity by now, and she was working on her computer while it happened. She only had to remember not to overfill the bottle, and to switch breasts. Her right breast produced more than the left even though they were the same size, a mystery that she had given up solving. She had long since explored the biological and engineering details of this process, and had gotten not exactly bored, but as far as she could go with it, and used to the sameness of it all. There was nothing new to investigate, so she was on to other things. What Anna liked was to study new things. This was what kept her coauthoring papers with her sometime-collaborators at Duke, and kept her on the editorial board of *The Journal of Statistical Biology,* despite the fact that her job at NSF as director of the Bioinformatics Division might be said to be occupying her more than full-time already; but much of that job was administrative, and like the milk pumping, fully explored. It was in her other projects where she could still learn new things.

Right now her new thing was a little search investigating the NSF's ability to help Khembalung. She navigated her way through the on-line network of scientific institutions with an ease born of long practice, click by click.

Among NSF's array of departments was an Office of International Science and Engineering, which Anna was impressed to find had managed to garner ten percent of the total NSF budget. It ran an International Biological Program, which sponsored a project called TOGA—"Tropical Oceans, Global Atmosphere." TOGA funded study programs, many including an infrastructure-dispersion element, in which the scientific infrastructure built for the work was given to the host institution at the end of the study period.

Anna had already been tracking NSF's infrastructure-dispersion programs for another project, so she added this one to that list too. Projects like these were why people joked about the mobile hanging in the atrium being meant to represent a hammer and sickle, deconstructed so that outsiders would not recognize the socialistic nature of NSF's tendency to give away capital and to act as if everyone owned the world equally. Anna liked these tendencies and the projects that resulted, though she did not think of them in political terms. She just liked the way NSF focused on work rather than theory or talk. That was her preference too. She liked quantitative solutions to quantified problems.

In this case, the problem was the Khembalis' little island (fifty-two square kilometers, their website said), which was clearly in all-too-good a location to contribute to on-going studies of Gangean flooding and tidal storms in the Indian Ocean. Anna tapped at her keyboard, bookmark-ing for an e-mail to Drepung, cc-ing also the Khembalung Institute for Higher Studies, which he had told her about. This institute's website indicated it was devoted to me-dicinal and religious studies (whatever those were, she didn't want to know) but that would be all right—if the Khembalis could get a good proposal together, the need for a wider range of fields among their researchers could become part of its "broader impacts" element, and thus an advantage.

She searched the web further. USGCRP, the "U.S. Global Change Research Program," two billion dollars a year; the South Asian START Regional Research Centre (SAS-RRC), based at the National Physical Laboratory in New Delhi, stations in Bangladesh, Nepal, and Mauritius... China and Thailand, aerosol study... INDOEX, the Indian Ocean Experiment, also concerned with aerosols, as was its offspring, Project Asian Brown Cloud. These studied the ever-thickening haze covering South Asia and making the monsoon irregular, with disastrous results. Certainly Khembalung was well-situated to join that study. Also ALGAS, the "Asia Least Cost Greenhouse Gas Abatement Strategy"; and LOICZ, "Land Ocean Interaction in the Coastal Zones." That one had to be right on the money. Sri Lanka was the leader there, lots of estuarine modeling—Khembalung would make a perfect study site. Training, networking, bio-geo-chemical cycle budgeting, socioeco-nomic modeling, impacts on the coastal systems of South Asia. Bookmark the site, add to the e-mail. A research facil-ity in the mouth of the Ganges would be a very useful thing for all concerned.

"Ah shit."

She had overflowed the milk bottle. Not the first time for that mistake. She turned off the pump, poured off some of the milk from the full bottle into a four-ounce sack. She always filled quite a few four-ouncers, for use as snacks or supplements when Joe was feeling extra hungry; she had never told Charlie that most of these were the result of her inattention. Since Joe often was extra hungry, Charlie said, they were useful.

As for herself, she was starving. It was always that way after pumping sessions. Each twenty ounces of milk she gave was the result of some thousand calories burned by her in the previous day, as far as she had been able to calculate; the analyses she had found had been pretty rough. In any case, she could with a clear conscience (and great pleasure) run down to the pizza place and eat till she was stuffed. Indeed she needed to eat or she would get light-headed.

But first she had to pump the other breast at least a little, because let-down happened in both when she pumped, and she would end up uncomfortable if she didn't. So she put the ten-ouncer in the little refrigerator, then got the other side going into the four-ouncer, while printing out a list of all the sites she had visited, so that over her lunch she could write notes on them before she forgot what she had learned.

She called Drepung, who answered his cell phone number.

"Drepung, can you meet for lunch? I've got some ideas for how you might get some science support there in Khembalung. Some of it's from NSF, some from elsewhere."

"Yes, of course Anna, thanks very much. I'll meet you at the Food Factory in twenty minutes, if that's all right, I'm just trying to buy some shoes for Rudra down the street here."

"Perfect. What kind are you getting him?"

"Running shoes. He'll love them."

On her way out she ran into Frank, also headed for the elevator.

"What you got?" he asked, gesturing at her list.

"Some stuff for the Khembalis," she said. "Various programs we run or take part in that might help them out."

"So they can study how to adapt to higher sea levels?"

She frowned. "No, it's more than that. We can get them a lot of infrastructural help if it's configured right."

"Good. But, you know. In the end they're going to need more than studies. And NSF doesn't do remediation. It just serves its clients. Pays for their studies."

Frank's comment bugged Anna, and after a nice lunch with Drepung she went up to her office and called Sophie Harper, NSF's liaison to Congress.

"Sophie, does NSF ever do requests for proposals?"

"Not for a long time. In general it's been policy to make the program proposal-driven."

"So is there any way that NSF can, you know, set the agenda so to speak?"

"I don't know what you mean. We ask Congress for funding in very specific ways, and they earmark the money they give us for very specific purposes."

"So we might be able to ask for funds for various things?"

"Yes, we do that. I think the way to think of it is that science sets its own agenda. To tell the truth, that's why the appropriations committees don't like us very much."

"Why?"

"Because they hold the purse strings, honey. And they're very jealous of that power. I've had senators who believe the Earth is flat say to me, 'Are you trying to tell me that *you* know what's good for science better than *I* do?' And of course that's exactly what I'm trying to tell them, because it's true, but what can you say? That's the kind of person we sometimes have to deal with. Even with the best of committees, there's a basic dislike for science's autonomy."

"But we're only free to study things."

"I don't know what you mean."

Anna sighed. "I don't either. Listen Sophie, thanks for that. I'll get back to you when I have a better idea what I'm trying to ask."

"Always here. Check out NSF's history pages on the website, you'll learn some things you didn't know."

Anna hung up, and then did that very thing.

She had never gone to the website's history pages before; she was not much for looking back. But she valued Sophie's advice, and as she read, she realized Sophie had been right; because she had worked there for so long, unconsciously she had felt that she knew the Foundation's story. But it wasn't true.

Basically it was a story of science struggling to extend its reach in the world, with mixed success. After World War Two, Vannevar Bush, head of the wartime Office of Science and Technology, advocated a permanent federal agency to support basic scientific research. He argued that it was their basic scientific research that had won the war (radar, penicillin, the bomb), and Congress had been convinced, and had passed a bill bringing the NSF into being.

After that it was one battle after another, with both Congress and the President, contesting how much say scientists would have in setting national policy. President Truman forcing a presidentially selected board of directors on the Foundation in the beginning. President Nixon abolishing the Office of Science and Technology, which NSF had in effect staffed, replacing it with a single "scientific advisor." The Gingrich Congress abolishing its Office of Technology Assessment. The Bush administrations zeroing out major science programs in every single budget. On it went.

Only occasionally in this political battle did science rally and win a few. After Sputnik, scientists were begged to take over again; NSF's budget had ballooned. Then in the 1960's, when everyone was an activist, NSF had created a program called "Interdisciplinary Research Relevant to Problems of Our Society." What a name from its time that was!

Although, come to think of it, the phrase described very well what Anna had had in mind when querying Sophie in the first place. Interdisciplinary research, relevant to problems of our society—was that really such a sixties joke of an idea?

Back then, IRRPOS had morphed into RANN, "Research Applied to National Needs." RANN had then gotten killed for being too applied; President Nixon had not liked its objections to his antiballistic missile defense. At the same time he preemptively established the EPA so that it would be under him rather than Congress.

The battle for control of science went on. Many administrations and Congresses hadn't wanted technology or the environment assessed at all, as far as Anna could see. It might get in the way of business. They didn't want to know.

For Anna there could be no greater intellectual crime. It was incomprehensible to her: *they didn't want to know.* And yet they did want to call the shots. To Anna this was clearly crazy. Even Joe's logic was stronger. How could such people exist, what could they be thinking? On what basis did they build such an incoherent mix of desires, to want to stay ignorant and to be powerful as well? Were these two parts of the same insanity?

She abandoned that train of thought, and read on to the end of the piece. "No agency operates in a vacuum," it said. That was one way to put it! The NSF had been buffeted, grown, stagnated, adapted—done the best it could. Throughout all, its basic purposes and methods had held fast: to support basic research; to award grants rather than purchase contracts; to decide things by peer-review rather than bureaucratic fiat; to hire skilled scientists for permanent staff; to hire temporary staff from the expert cutting edges in every field.

Anna believed in all these, and she believed they had done demonstrable good. Fifty thousand proposals a year, eighty thousand people peer-reviewing them, ten thousand new proposals funded, twenty thousand grants continuing to be supported. All functioning to expand scientific knowledge, and the influence of science in human affairs.

She sat back in her chair, thinking it over. All that basic research, all that good work; and yet—thinking over the state of the world—somehow it had not been enough. Possibly they would have to consider doing something more.

PRIMATES IN the driver's seat. It looked like they should all be dead. Multicar accidents, bloody incidents of road rage. Cars should have been ramming one another in huge demolition derbies, a global auto-da-fé.

But they were primates, they were social creatures. The brain had ballooned to its current size precisely to enable it to make the calculations necessary to get along in groups. These were the parts of the brain engaged when people drove in crowded traffic. Thus along with all the jockeying and frustration came the almost subliminal satisfactions of winning a competition, or the grudging solidarities of cooperating to mutual advantage. Let that poor idiot merge before his on-ramp lane disappeared; it would pay off in the overall speed of traffic. Thus the little primate buzz.

When things went well. But so often what one saw were people playing badly. It was like a giant game of prisoners' dilemma, the classic game in which two prisoners are separated and asked to tell tales on the other one, with release offered to them if they do. The standard computer model scoring system had it that if the prisoners cooperate with each other by staying silent, they each get three points; if both defect against the other, they each get one point; and if one defects and the other doesn't, the defector gets five points and the sap gets zero points. Using this scoring system to play the game time after time, there is a first iteration which says, it is best always to defect. That's the strategy that will gain the most points over the long haul, the computer simulations said—if you are only playing strangers once, and never seeing them again. And of course traffic looked as if it were that situation.

But the shadow of the future made all the difference. Day in and day out you drove into the same traffic jam, with the same basic population of players. If you therefore played the game as if playing with the same opponent every time, which in a sense you were, with you learning them and them learning you, then more elaborate strategies would gain more points than always defect. The first version of the more successful strategy was called tit for tat, in which you did to your opponent what they last did to you. This out-competed always defect, which in a way was a rather encouraging finding. But tit for tat was not the perfect strategy, because it could spiral in either direction, good or bad, and the bad was an endless feud. Thus further trials had found successful variously revised versions of tit for tat, like generous tit for tat, in which you gave opponents one defection before turning on them, or always generous, which in certain limited conditions worked well. Or, the most powerful strategy Frank knew of, an irregularly generous tit for tat, where you forgave defecting opponents once before turning on them, but only about a third of the time, and unpredictably, so you were not regularly taken advantage of by one of the less cooperative strategies, but could still pull out of a death spiral of tit-for-tat feuding if one should arise. Various versions of these firm but fair irregular strategies appeared to be best if you were dealing with the same opponent over and over.

In traffic, at work, in relationships of every kind—social life was nothing but a series of prisoners' dilemmas. Compete or cooperate? Be selfish or generous? It would be best if you could always trust other players to cooperate, and safely practice always generous; but in real life people did not turn out to earn that trust. That was one of the great shocks of adolescence, perhaps, that realization; which alas came to many at an even younger age. And after that you had to work things out case by case, your strategy a matter of your history, or your personality, who could say.

Traffic was not a good place to try to decide. Stop and go, stop and go, at a speed just faster than Frank could have walked. He wondered how it was that certain turn-signal indicators managed to express a great desperation to change lanes, while others seemed patient and dignified. The speed of blinking, perhaps, or how close the car hugged the lane line it wanted to cross. Although rapid blinking did look insistent and whiny, while slow blinking bespoke a determined inertia.

It had been a bad mistake to get on the Beltway in the first place. By and large Beltway drivers were defectors. In general, drivers on the East Coast were less generous than Californians, Frank found. On the West Coast they played tit for tat, or even firm but fair, because it moved things along faster. Maybe this only meant Californians had lived through that many more freeway traffic jams. People had learned the game from birth, sitting in their baby seats, and so in California cars in two merging lanes would alternate like the halves of a zipper, at considerable speed, everyone trusting everyone else to know the game and play it right. Even young males cooperated. In that sense if none other, California was indeed the edge of history, the evolutionary edge of *Homo automobilicus*.

Here on the Beltway, on the other hand, it was always defect. That was what all the SUVs were about, everyone girding up to get one point in a crash. Every SUV was a defection. Then there were the little cars that always gave way, the saps. A terrible combination. It was so slow, so unnecessarily, unobservantly slow. It made you want to scream.

And from time to time, Frank did scream. This was a different primate satisfaction of traffic: you could loudly curse people from ten feet away and they did not hear you. There was no way the primate brain could explain this, so it was like witnessing magic, the "technological sublime" people spoke of, which was the emotion experienced when the primate mind could not find a natural explanation for what it saw.

And it was indeed sublime to lose all restraint and just *curse* someone ferociously, from a few feet away, and yet have no ramifications to such a grave social transgression. It was not much compared to the satisfactions of cooperation, but perhaps rarer. It was something, anyway.

He crept forward in his car, cursing. He should not have gotten onto the Beltway. It was often badly overloaded at this hour. Stop and go, inch along. Curse defectors and saps. Inch along.

It stayed so bad that Frank realized he was going to be late to work. And this was the morning when his bioinformatics panel was to begin! He needed to get there for the panel to start on time; there was no slack in the schedule. The panel members were all in town, having spent a boring night the night before, probably. And the Holiday Inn in the Ballston complex often did not have enough hot water to supply everyone showering at that hour of the morning, so some of the panelists would be grumpy about that. Some would be gathering at this very moment in their third floor conference room, ready to go and feeling that there wasn't enough time to judge all the proposals on the docket. Frank had crowded it on purpose, and they had flights home late the next day that they could not miss. To arrive late in this situation would be bad form indeed, no matter traffic on the Beltway. There would be looks, or perhaps a joke or two from Pritchard or Lee; he would have to explain himself, make excuses. It could interfere with his plan. He cursed the driver of a car cutting uselessly in front of him.

Then he was coming on Route 66, and impulsively he decided to get on it going east, even though at this hour it was restricted to High Occupancy Vehicles only. Normally Frank obeyed this rule, but feeling a little desperate, he took the turn and curved onto 66, where traffic was indeed moving faster. Every vehicle was occupied by at least two people, of course, and Frank stayed in the right lane and drove as unobtrusively as possible, counting on the generally inward attention of multiply occupied vehicles to keep too many people from noticing his transgression. Of course there were highway patrol cars on the lookout for lawbreakers like Frank, so he was taking a risk that he didn't like to take, but it seemed to him a lower risk than staying on the Beltway as far as arriving late was concerned.

He drove in great suspense, therefore, until finally he could signal to get off at Fairfax. Then as he approached he saw a police car parked beside the exit, its officers walking back toward their car after dealing with another miscreant. They might easily look up and see him.

A big old pickup truck was slowing down to exit before him, and again without pausing to consider his actions, Frank floored the accelerator, swerved around the truck on its left side, using it to block the policemen's view, then cut back across in front of the truck, accelerating so as not to bother it. Room to spare and no one the wiser. He curved to the right down the exit lane, slowing for the light around the turn.

Suddenly there was loud honking from behind, and his rearview mirror had been entirely filled by the front grille of the pickup truck, its headlights at about the same height as the roof of his car. Frank speeded up. Then, closing on the car in front of him, he had to slow down. Suddenly the truck was now passing him on the left, as he had passed it earlier, even though this took the truck up onto the exit lane's tilted shoulder. Frank looked and glimpsed the infuriated face of the driver, leaning over to shout down at him. Long stringy hair, mustache, red skin, furious anger.

Frank looked over again and shrugged, making a face and gesture that said *What?* He slowed down so that the truck could cut in front of him, a good thing as it slammed into the lane so hard it missed Frank's left headlight by an inch. He would have struck Frank for sure if Frank hadn't slowed down. What a jerk!

Then the guy hit his brakes so hard that Frank nearly rear-ended him, which could have been a disaster given how high the truck was jacked up: Frank would have hit windshield first.

"What the *fuck*!" Frank said, shocked. "Fuck you! I didn't come anywhere near you!"

The truck came to a full stop, right there on the exit.

"Jesus, you fucking idiot!" Frank shouted.

Maybe Frank had cut closer to this guy than he thought he had. Or maybe the guy was hounding him for driving solo on 66, even though he had been doing the same thing himself. Now his door flew open and out he jumped, swaggering back toward Frank. He caught sight of Frank still shouting, stopped and pointed a quivering finger, reached into the bed of his truck and pulled out a crowbar.

Frank reversed gear, backed up and braked, shifted into drive and spun his steering wheel as he accelerated around the pickup truck's right side. People behind them were honking, but they didn't know the half of it. Frank zoomed down the now empty exit lane, shouting triumphant abuse at the crazy guy.

Unfortunately the traffic light at the end of the exit ramp was red and there was a car stopped there, waiting for it to change. Frank had to stop. Instantly there was a *thunk* and he jerked forward. The pickup truck had rear-ended him, tapping him hard from behind.

"YOU FUCKER!" Frank shouted, now frightened; he had tangled with a madman! The truck was backing up, presumably to ram him again, so he put his little Honda in reverse and shot back into the truck, like hitting a wall, then shifted again and shot off into the narrow gap to the right of the car waiting at the light, turning right and accelerating into a gap between the cars zipping by, which caused more angry honks. He checked his rearview mirror and saw the light had changed and the pickup truck was turning to follow him, and not far behind. "Shit!"

Frank accelerated, saw an opening in traffic coming the other way, and took a sharp left across all lanes onto Glebe, even though it was the wrong direction for NSF. Then he floored it and began weaving desperately through cars he was rapidly overtaking, checking the rearview mirror when he could. The pickup appeared in the distance, squealing onto Glebe after him. Frank cursed in dismay.

He decided to drive directly to a fire station he recalled seeing on Lee Highway. He took a left on Lee and accelerated as hard as the little fuel-cell car could to the fire station, squealing into its parking lot and then jumping out and hurrying toward the building, looking back down Lee toward Glebe.

But the madman never appeared. Gone. Lost the trail, or lost interest. Off to harass someone else.

Cursing still, Frank checked his car's rear. No visible damage, amazingly. He got back in and drove south to the NSF building, involuntarily reliving the experience. He had no clear idea why it had happened. He had driven around the guy but he had not really cut him off, and though it was true he had been poaching on 66, so had the guy. It was inexplicable. And it occurred to him that in the face of such behavior modeling devices like prisoners' dilemma were useless. People did not make rational judgments. Especially, perhaps, the people driving too-large pickup trucks, this one of the dirty-and-dinged variety rather than the factory-fresh steroidal battleships that the area's carpenters drove. Possibly then it had been some kind of class thing, the resentment of an unemployed gas-guzzler against a white-collar type in a fuel-cell car. The past attacking the future, reactionary attacking progressive, poor attacking affluent. A beta male in an alpha machine, enraged that an alpha male thought he was so alpha he could zip around in a beta machine and get away with it.

Something like that. Some kind of asshole jerk-off loser, already drunk and disorderly at seven A.M.

Despite all that, Frank found himself driving into the NSF building's basement parking with just enough time to get to the elevators and up to the third floor at the last possible on-time moment. He hurried to the men's room, splashed water on his face. He had to clear his mind of the ugly incident immediately, and it had been so strange and unpleasant that this was not particularly difficult. Incongruent awfulness without consequence is easily dismissed from the mind. So he pulled himself together, went out to do his job. Time to concentrate on the day's work. His plan for the panel was locked in by the people he had convened for it. The scare on the road only hardened his resolve, chilled his blood.

He entered the conference room assigned to their panel. Its big inner window gave everyone the standard view of the rest of NSF, and the panelists who hadn't been there before looked up into the beehive of offices making the usual comments about *Rear Window* and the like. "A kind of ersatz collegiality," one of them said, must have been Nigel Pritchard.

"Keeps people working."

On the savannah a view like this would have come from a high outcrop, where the troop would be resting in relative safety, surveying everything important in their lives. In the realm of grooming, of chatter, of dominance conflicts. Perfect, in other words, for a grant proposal evaluation panel, which in essence was one of the most ancient of discussions: whom do we let in, whom do we kick out? A basic troop economy, of social credit, of access to food and mates—everything measured and exchanged in deeds good and bad—yes—it was another game of prisoners' dilemma. They never ended.

Frank liked this one. It was very nuanced compared to most of them, and one of the few still outside the world of money. Anonymous peer-review—unpaid labor—a scandal!

But science didn't work like capitalism. That was the rub, that was one of the rubs in the general dysfunction of the world. Capitalism ruled, but money was too simplistic and inadequate a measure of the wealth that science generated. In science, one built up over the course of a career a fund of "scientific credit," by giving work to the system in a way that could seem altruistic. People remembered what you gave, and later on there were various forms of return on the gift—jobs, labs. In that sense a good investment for the individual, but in the form of a gift to the group. It was the non zero-sum game that prisoners' dilemma could become if everyone played by the strategies of always generous, or, better, firm but fair. That was one of the things science was—a place that one entered by agreeing to hold

to the strategies of cooperation, to maximize the total return of the game.

In theory that was true. It was also the usual troop of
primates. There was a lot of tit for tat. Defections happened. Everyone was jockeying for a lab of their own, or
any project of their own. As long as that was generating
enough income for a comfortable physical existence for
oneself and one's family, then one had reached the optimal
human state. Having money beyond that was unnecessary,
and usually involved a descent into the world of hassle and
stupidity. That was what greed got you. So there was in science a sufficiency of means, and an achievable limit to
one's goals, that kept it tightly aligned with the brain's deepest savannah values. A scientist wanted the same things out
of life as an *Australopithecus;* and here they were.

Thus Frank surveyed the panelists milling about the
room with a rare degree of happiness. "Let's get started."

They sat down, putting laptops and coffee cups beside the
computer consoles built into the tabletop. These allowed
the panelists to see a spreadsheet page for each proposal in
turn, displaying their grades and comments. This particular
group all knew the drill. Some of them had met before,
more had read one another's work.

There were eight of them sitting around the long cluttered conference table.

Dr. Frank Vanderwal, moderator, NSF (on leave from
University of California, San Diego, Department of
Bioinformatics).

Dr. Nigel Pritchard, Georgia Institute of Technology,
Computer Sciences.

Dr. Alice Freundlich, Harvard University, Department
of Biochemistry.

Dr. Habib Ndina, University of Virginia Medical School.

Dr. Stuart Thornton, University of Maryland, College Park, Genomics Department.

Dr. Francesca Taolini, Massachusetts Institute of Technology, Center for Biocomputational Studies.

Dr. Jerome Frenkel, University of Pennsylvania, Department of Genomics.

Dr. Yao Lee, Cambridge University (visiting GWU's Department of Microbiology).

Frank made his usual introductory remarks and then said, "We've got a lot of them to go through this time. I'm sorry it's so many, but that's what we've received. I'm sure we'll hack our way through them all if we keep on track. Let's start with the fifteen-minutes-per-jacket drill, and see if we can get twelve or even fourteen done before lunch. Sound good?"

Everyone nodded and tapped away, calling up the first one.

"Oh, and before we start, let's have everyone give me their conflict-of-interest forms, please. I have to remind you that as referees here, you have a conflict if you're the applying principal investigator's thesis advisor or advisee, an employee of the same institution as the P.I. or a co-P.I., a collaborator within the last four years of the P.I. or a co-P.I., an applicant for employment in any department at the submitting institution, a recipient of an honorarium or other pay from the submitting institution within the last year, someone with a close personal relationship to the P.I. or a co-P.I., a shareholder in a company participating in the proposal, or someone who would otherwise gain or lose financially if the proposal were awarded or declined.

"Everybody got that? Okay, hand those forms down to me, then. We'll have a couple of people step outside for some of the proposals today, but mostly we're clear as far as I know, is that right?"

"I'll be leaving for the Esterhaus proposal, as I told you," Stuart Thornton said.

Then they started the group evaluations. This was the heart of their task for that day and the next—also the heart of NSF's method, indeed of science more generally. Peer-review; a jury of fellow experts. Frank clicked the first proposal's page onto his screen. "Seven reviewers, forty-four jackets. Let's start with EIA-02 18599, 'Electromagnetic and Informational Processes in Molecular Polymers.' Habib, you're the lead on this?"

Habib Ndina nodded and opened with a description of the proposal. "They want to immobilize cytoskeletal networks on biochips, and explore whether tubulin can be used as bits in protein logic gates. They intend to do this by measuring the electric dipole moment, and what the P.I. calls the predicted kink-solitonic electric dipole moment flip waves."

"Predicted by whom?"

"By the P.I." Habib smiled. "He also states that this will be a method to test out the theories of the so-called quantum brain."

"Hmm." People read past the abstract.

"What are you thinking?" Frank said after a while. "I see Habib has given it a 'Good,' Stuart a 'Fair,' and Alice a 'Very Good.'"

This represented the middle range of their scale, which ran Poor, Fair, Good, Very Good, and Excellent.

Habib replied first. "I'm not so sure that you can get these biochips to array in neural nets. I saw Inouye try something like that at MIT, and they got stuck at the level of chip viability."

"Hmm."

The others chimed in with questions and opinions. At

the end of fifteen minutes, Frank stopped the discussion and asked them to mark their final judgments in the two categories they used: *intellectual merit* and *broader impacts*.

Frank summed up the responses. "Four 'Goods,' two 'Very Goods' and a 'Fair.' Okay, let's move on. But tell you what, I'm going to start the big board right now."

He had a whiteboard in the corner next to him, and a pile of Post-it pads on the table. He drew three zones on the whiteboard with marker, and wrote at the top "Fund," "Fund If Possible," and "Don't Fund."

"I'll put this one in the 'Fund If Possible' column for now, although naturally it may get bumped." He stuck the proposal's Post-it in the middle zone. "We'll move these around as the day progresses and we get a sense of the range."

Then they began the next one. "Okay. 'Efficient Decoherence Control Algorithms for Computing Genome Construction.'"

This jacket Frank had assigned to Stuart Thornton.

Thornton started by shaking his head. "This one's gotten two 'Goods' and two 'Fairs,' and it wasn't very impressive to me either. It may be a candidate for limited discussion. It doesn't really exhibit a grasp of the difficulties involved with codon tampering, and I think it replicates the work being done in Seattle by Johnson's lab. The applicant seems to have been too busy with the broader impacts component to fully acquaint himself with the literature. Besides which, it won't work."

People laughed shortly at this extra measure of disdain, which was palpable, and to those who didn't know Thornton, a little surprising. But Frank had seen Stuart Thornton on panels before. He was the kind of scientist who habitually displayed an ultrapure devotion to the scientific method, in the form of a relentless skepticism about everything. No study was designed tightly enough, no data were clean enough. To Frank it seemed obvious that it was really a kind of insecurity, part of the gestural set of a beta male convincing the group he was tough enough to be an alpha male, and maybe already was.

The problem with these gestures was that in science one's intellectual power was like the muscle mass of an *Australopithecus*—there for all to see. You couldn't fake it. No matter how much you ruffed your fur or exposed your teeth, in the end your intellectual strength was discernible in what you said and how insightful it was. Mere skepticism was like baring teeth; anyone could do it. For that reason Thornton was a bad choice for a panel, because while people could see his attitude and try to discount it, he set a tone that was hard to shake off. If there was an always defector in the group, one had to be less generous oneself in order not to become a sap.

That was why Frank had invited him.

Thornton went on, "The basic problem is at the level of their understanding of an algorithm. An algorithm is not just a simple sequence of mathematical operations that can each be performed in turn. It's a matter of designing a grammar that will adjust the operations at each stage, depending on what the results are from the stage before. There's a very specific encoding math that makes that work. They don't have that here, as far as I can tell."

The others nodded and tapped in notes at their consoles. Soon enough they were on to the next proposal, with the previous one posted under "Don't Fund."

Now Frank could predict with some confidence how the rest of the day would go. A depressed norm had been set, and even though the third reporter, Alice Freundlich from Harvard, subtly rebuked Thornton by talking about how well-designed her first jacket was, she did so in a less generous context, and was not overly enthusiastic. "They think that the evolutionary processes of gene conservation can be mapped by cascade studies, and they want to model it with big computer array simulations. They claim they'll be able to identify genes prone to mutation."

Habib Ndina shook his head. He too was a habitual skeptic, although from a much deeper well of intelligence than Thornton's; he wasn't just making a display, he was thinking. "Isn't the genome's past pretty much mapped by now?" he complained. "Do we really need more about evolutionary history?"

"Well, maybe not. Broader impacts might suffer there."

And so the day proceeded, and, with some subliminal prompting from Frank ("Are you sure they have the lab space?" "Do you think that's really true, though?" "How would that work?" "How could that work?"), the full Shooting Gallery Syndrome slowly emerged. The panelists very slightly lost contact with their sense of the proposals as human efforts performed under a deadline, and started to compare them to some perfect model of scientific practice. In that light, of course, all the candidates were wanting. They all had feet of clay and their proposals all became clay pigeons, cast into the air for the group to take potshots at. New jacket tossed up: *bang! bang! bang!*

"This one's toast," someone said at one point.

Of course a few people in such a situation would stay anchored, and begin to shake their heads or wrinkle their noses, or even protest the mood, humorously or otherwise. But Frank had avoided inviting any of the real stalwarts he knew, and Alice Freundlich did no more than keep things pleasant. The impulse in a group toward piling on was so strong that it often took on extraordinary momentum. On the savannah it would have meant an expulsion and a hungry night out. Or some poor guy torn limb from limb.

Frank didn't need to tip things that far. Nothing explicit, nothing heavy. He was only the facilitator. He did not express an obvious opinion on the substance of the proposals at any point. He watched the clock, ran down the list, asked if everybody had said what they wanted to say when there were three minutes left out of the fifteen; made sure everyone got their scores into the system at the end of the discussion period. "That's an 'Excellent' and five 'Very Goods.' Alice do you have your scores on this one?"

Meanwhile the discussions got tougher and tougher.

"I don't know what she could have been thinking with this one, it's absurd!"

"Let me start by suggesting limited discussion."

Frank began subtly to apply the brakes. He didn't want them to think he was a bad panel manager.

Nevertheless, the attack mood gained momentum. Baboons descending on wounded prey; it was almost Pavlovian, a food-rewarded joy in destruction that did not bode well for the species. The pleasure taken in wrecking anything meticulous. Frank had seen it many times: a carpenter doing demolition with a sledgehammer, a vet who went duck-hunting on weekends...It was unfortunate, given their current overextended moment in planetary history, but nevertheless real. As a species they were therefore probably doomed. And so the only real adaptive strategy, for the individual, was to do one's best to secure one's own position. And sometimes that meant a little strategic defection.

Near the end of the day it was Thornton's turn again. Finally they had come to the proposal from Yann Pierzinski. People were getting tired.

Frank said, "Okay, almost done here. Let's finish them off, shall we? Two more to go. Stu, we're to you again, on 'Mathematical and Algorithmic Analysis of Palindromic Codons as Predictors of a Gene's Protein Expression.' Mandel and Pierzinski, Caltech."

Thornton shook his head wearily. "I see it's got a couple of 'Very Goods' from people, but I give it a 'Fair.' It's a nice thought, but it seems to be promising too much. I mean, predicting the proteome from the genome would be enough in itself, but then understanding how the genome evolved, building error-tolerant biocomputers—it's like a list of the big unsolved problems."

Francesca Taolini asked him what he thought of the algorithm that the proposal hoped to develop.

"It's too sketchy to be sure! That's really what he's hoping to find, as far as I can tell. There would be a final toolbox with a software environment and language, then a gene grammar to make sense of palindromes in particular, he seems to think those are important, but I think they're just redundancy and repair sequences, that's why the palindromic structure. They're like the reinforcement at the bottom of a zipper. To think that he could use this to predict all the proteins that a particular gene would produce!"

"But if you could, you would see what proteins you would get without needing to do microassays and use crystallography to see what came up," Francesca pointed out. "That would be very useful. I thought the line he was following had potential, myself. I know people working on something like this, and it would be good to have more people on it, it's a broad front. That's why I gave it a 'Very Good,' and I'd still recommend we fund it." She kept her eyes on her screen.

"Well yeah," Thornton said crossly, "but where would he get the biosensors that would tell him if he was right or not? There's no controls."

"That would be someone else's problem. If the predictions were turning out good you wouldn't have to test all of them, that would be the point."

Frank waited a beat. "Anyone else?" he said in a neutral tone.

Pritchard and Yao Lee joined in. Lee obviously thought it was a good idea, in theory. He started describing it as a kind of cookbook with evolving recipes, and Frank ventured to say, "How would that work?"

"Well, by successive iterations of the operation, you know. It would be to get you started, suggest directions to try."

"Look," Francesca interjected, "eventually we're going to have to tackle this issue, because until we do, the mechanics of gene expression are just a black box. It's a very valid line of inquiry."

"Habib?" Frank asked.

"It would be nice, I guess, if he could make it work. It's not so easy. It would be like a roll of the dice to support it."

Before Francesca could collect herself and start again, Frank said, "Well, we could go round and round on that, but we're out of time on this one, and it's late. Those of you who haven't done it yet, write down your scores, and let's finish with one more from Alice before we go to dinner."

Hunger made them nod and tap away at their consoles, and then they were on to the last one for the day, "Ribozymes as Molecular Logic Gates." When they were done with that, Frank stuck its Post-it on the whiteboard with the rest. Each little square of paper had its proposal's averaged scores written on it. It was a tight scale; the difference between 4.63 and 4.70 could matter a great deal. They had already put three proposals in the "Fund" column, two in the "Fund If Possible," and six in the "Do Not Fund." The rest were stuck to the bottom of the board, waiting to be sorted out the following day. Pierzinski's was among those.

That evening the group went out for dinner at Tara, a good nearby Thai restaurant with a wall-sized fish tank. The conversation was animated and wide-ranging, the mood getting better as the meal wore on. Afterward a few of them went to the hotel bar; the rest retreated to their rooms. At eight the next morning they were back in the conference room doing everything over again, working their way through the proposals with an increasing efficiency. Thornton recused himself for a discussion of a proposal from someone at his university, and the mood in the room noticeably lightened; even when he returned they held to this. They were learning each other's predilections, and sometimes jetted off into discussions of theory that were very interesting even though they were only a few minutes long. Some of the proposals brought up interesting problems, and several strong ones in a row made them aware of just how amazing contemporary work in bioinformatics was, and what some of the potential benefits for human health might be, if all this were to come together and make a robust biotechnology. The shadow of a good future drove the group toward more generous strategies. The second day went better. The scores were, on average, higher.

"My Lord," Alice said at one point, looking at the whiteboard. "There are going to be some very good proposals that we're not going to be able to fund."

Everyone nodded. It was a common feeling at the end of a panel.

"I sometimes wonder what would happen if we could fund about ninety percent of all the applications. You know, only reject the limited-discussions. Fund everything else."

"It might speed things up."

"Might cause a revolution."

"Now back to reality," Frank suggested. "Last jacket here."

When they had all tapped in their grading of the forty-fourth jacket, Frank quickly crunched the numbers on his general spreadsheet, sorting the applicants into a hierarchy from one to forty-four, with a lot of ties.

He printed out the results, including the funding each proposal was asking for, then called the group back to order. They started moving the unsorted Post-its up into one or another of the three columns.

Pierzinski's proposal had ended up ranked fourteenth out of the forty-four. It wouldn't have been that high if it weren't for Francesca. Now she urged them to fund it; but because it was in fourteenth place, the group decided it should be put in "Fund If Possible," with a bullet.

Frank moved its Post-it on the whiteboard up into the "Fund If Possible" column, keeping his face perfectly blank. There were eight in "Fund If Possible," six in "Fund," twelve in "Do Not Fund." Eighteen to go, therefore, but the arithmetic of the situation would doom most of these to the "Do Not Fund" column, with a few stuck into the "Fund If Possible" as faint hopes.

Later it would be Frank's job to fill out a Form Seven for every proposal, summarizing the key aspects of the discussion, acknowledging outlier reviews that were more than one full place off the average, and explaining any "Excellents" awarded to nonfunded reviews; this was part of keeping the process transparent to the applicants, and making sure that nothing untoward happened. The panel was advisory only, NSF had the right to overrule it, but in the great majority of cases the panel's judgments would stand—that was the whole point—that was scientific objectivity, at least in this part of the process.

In a way it was funny. Solicit seven intensely subjective and sometimes contradictory opinions; quantify them; average them; and that was objectivity. A numerical grading that you could point to on a graph. Ridiculous, of course. But it was the best they could do. Indeed, what other choice did they have? No algorithm could make these kinds of decisions. The only computer powerful enough to do it was one made up of a networked array of human brains—that is to say, a panel. Beyond that they could not reach.

So they discussed the proposals one last time, their scientific potential and also their educational and benefit-to-society aspects, the "broader impacts" rubric, usually spelled out rather vaguely in the proposals, and unpopular with research purists. But as Frank put it now, "NSF isn't here just to *do* science but also to *promote* science, and that means all these other criteria. What it will add to society." What Anna will do with it, he almost said.

And speak of the devil, Anna came in to thank the panelists for their efforts, slightly flushed and formal in her remarks. When she left, Frank said, "Thanks from me too. It's been exhausting as usual, but good work was done. I hope to see all of you here again at some point, but I won't bother you too soon either. I know some of you have planes to catch, so let's quit now, and if any of you have anything else you want to add, tell me individually. Okay, we're done."

Frank printed out a final copy of the spreadsheet. The money numbers suggested they would end up funding about ten of the forty-four proposals. There were seven in the "Fund" column already, and six of those in the "Fund If Possible" column had been ranked slightly higher than Yann Pierzinski's proposal. If Frank, as NSF's representative, did not exercise any of his discretionary power to find a way to fund it, that proposal would be declined.

ANOTHER DAY for Charlie and Joe. A late spring morning, temperatures already in the high nineties and rising, humidity likewise.

They stayed in the house for the balm of the air-conditioning, falling out of the ceiling vents like spills of clear syrup. They wrestled, they cleaned house, they ate breakfast and elevenses. Charlie read some of the *Post* while Joe devastated dinosaurs. Something in the *Post* about India's drought reminded Charlie of the Khembalis, and he put in his earphone and gave his friend Sridar a call.

"Hey Sridar, it's Charlie."

"Charlie, good to hear from you! I got your message."

"Oh good, I was hoping you had. How's the lobbying business going?"

"We're keeping at it. We've got some interesting clients, if you know what I mean."

"Yes I do."

Charlie and Sridar had worked together for a lobbying firm several years before. Now Sridar worked for Branson and Ananda, a small but prestigious firm representing several foreign governments in their dealings with the American government. Some of these governments had customs at home that made representing them to Congress a challenge.

"So you said something about a new country? I'm glad you're keeping an eye out for new clients for me."

"Well it was through Anna, like I said." Charlie explained how they had met. "When I was talking to them I thought they could use your help."

"Oh dear, how nice."

"Yeah well, you need some challenges."

"Right, like I have no challenges. What's this new country, then?"

"Have you heard of Khembalung?"

"I think so. One of the League of Drowning Nations?"

"Yeah that's right."

"You're asking me to take on a sinking island nation?"

"Actually they're not sinking, it's the ocean that's rising."

"Even worse. I mean what are we going to be able to do about that, stop global warming?"

"Well, yeah. That's the idea. But you know. There'll be all sorts of other countries working on the same thing. You'd have lots of allies."

"Uh-huh."

"Anyway they could use your help, and they're good guys. Interesting. I think you'd enjoy them. You should at least meet with them and see."

"Yeah okay. My plate is kinda full right now, but I could do that. No harm in meeting."

"Oh good. Thanks Sridar, I appreciate that."

"No problem. Hey can I have Krakatoa too?"

"Bye."

"Bye."

After that Charlie was in the mood to talk, but he had no real reason to call anybody. He and Joe played again.

Bored, Charlie even resorted to turning on the TV. A pundit show came on and helplessly he watched. "They are such *lapdogs,*" he complained to Joe. "See, that whole studio is a kind of pet's bed, and these guys sit in their places like pets in the palm of a giant, speaking what the giant wants to hear. My God how can they stand it! They know *perfectly well* what they're up to, you can see the way they parade their little hobbies to try to distract us, see that one copies definitions out of the dictionary, and that one there has memorized all the rules of *pinochle* for Christ's sake, all to disguise the fact that they have not a single principle in their heads except to defend the rich. Disgusting."

"BOOM!" Joe concurred, catching Charlie's mood and flinging a tyrannosaurus into the radiator with a clang.

"That's right," Charlie said. "Good job."

He changed the channel to ESPN 5, which showed classic women's volleyball doubles all day along. Retired guys at home must be a big demographic. And so tall muscular women in bathing suits jumped around and dove in the sand; they were amazingly skillful. Charlie particularly liked the exploits of the Brazilian Jackie Silva, who always won even though she was not the best hitter, server, passer, blocker, or looker. But she was always in the right place doing the best thing, making miraculous saves and accidental winners.

"I'm going to be the Jackie Silva of Senate staffers," Charlie told Joe.

But Joe had had enough of being in the house. "Go!" he said imperiously, hammering the front door with a diplodocus. "Go! Go! Go!"

"All right all right."

His point was undeniable. They couldn't stay in this house all day. "Let's see. What shall we do. I'm tired of the park. Let's go down to the Mall, we haven't done that for a

while. The Mall, Joe! But you have to get in your backpack."

Joe nodded and tried to climb into his baby backpack
immediately, a very tippy business. He was ready to party.

"Wait, let's change your diaper first."

"NO!"

"Ah come on Joe. Yes."

"NO!"

"But yes."

They fought like maniacs through a diaper change, each
ruthless and determined, each shouting, beating, pinching.
Charlie followed Jackie Silva's lead and did the necessary
things.

Red-faced and sweating, finally they were ready to
emerge from the house into the steambath of the city. Out
they went. Down to the Metro, down into that dim cool
underground world.

It would have been good if the Metro pacified Joe as it
once had Nick, but in fact it usually energized him. Charlie
could not understand that; he himself found the dimness
and coolness a powerful soporific. But Joe wanted to play
around just above the drop to the power rail, he was naturally attracted to that enormous source of energy. The
hundred-thousand-watt child. Charlie ran around keeping
Joe from the edge, like Jackie Silva keeping the ball off the
sand.

Finally a train came. Joe liked the Metro cars. He stood
on the seat next to Charlie and stared at the concrete walls
sliding by outside the tinted windows of the car, then at
the bright orange or pink seats, the ads, the people in their
car, the brief views of the underground stations they
stopped in.

A young black man got on carrying a helium-filled
birthday balloon. He sat down across the car from Charlie
and Joe. Joe stared at the balloon, boggled by it. Clearly it

was for him a kind of miraculous object. The youth pulled down on its string and let the balloon jump back up to its full extension. Joe jerked, then burst out laughing. His giggle was like his mom's, a low gorgeous burbling. People in the car grinned to hear it. The young man pulled the balloon down again, let it go again. Joe laughed so hard he had to sit down. People began to laugh with him, they couldn't help it. The young man was smiling shyly. He did the trick again and now the whole car followed Joe into paroxysms of laughter. They laughed all the way to Metro Center.

Charlie got out, grinning, and carried Joe to the Blue/Orange level. He marveled at the infectiousness of moods in a group. Strangers who would never meet again, unified suddenly by a youth and a toddler playing a game. By laughter. Maybe the real oddity was how much one's fellow citizens were usually like furniture in one's life.

Joe bounced in Charlie's arms. He liked Metro Center's crisscrossing mysterious vastness. The incident of the balloon was already forgotten. It had been unremarkable to him; he was still in that stage of life where all the evidence supported the idea that he was the center of the universe, and miracles happened. Kind of like a U.S. Senator.

Luckily Phil Chase was not like that. Certainly Phil enjoyed his life and his public role, it reminded Charlie of what he had read about FDR's attitude toward the presidency. But that was mostly a matter of being the star of one's own movie; thus, just like everyone else. No, Phil was very good to work for, Charlie thought, which was one of the ultimate tests of a person.

Their next Metro car reached the Smithsonian station, and Charlie put Joe into the backpack and on his back, and rode the escalator up and out, into the kiln blaze of the Mall.

The sky was milky white everywhere. It felt like the inside of a sauna. Charlie fought his way through the heat to an open patch of grass in the shade of the Washington Monument. He sat them down and got out some food. The big views up to the Capitol and down to the Lincoln Memorial pleased him. Out from under the great forest. It was like escaping Mirkwood. This in Charlie's opinion accounted for the great popularity of the Mall; the monuments and the big Smithsonian buildings were nice but supplementary, it was really a matter of getting out into the open. The ordinary reality of the American West was like a glimpse of heaven here in the green depths of the swamp.

Charlie knew and cherished the old story: how the first thirteen states had needed a capital, and so someone had to give up some land for it, or else one particular state would nab the honor; and Virginia and the other southern states were particularly concerned it would go to Philadelphia or New York. And so they had bickered, you give up some land, no you give it. No bureaucracy ever wanted to give up sovereignty over anything whatsoever, be it the smallest patch of sand in the sea; and so finally Virginia had said to Maryland, look, where the Potomac meets the Anacostia there's a big nasty swamp. It's worthless, dreadful, pestilent land. You'll never be able to make anything out of a festering pit like that.

True, Maryland had said, you're right. Okay, we'll give that land to the nation for its capital. But not too much! Just a section of the worst part. And good luck draining it!

And so here they were. Charlie sat on grass, drowsing. Joe gamboled about him like a bumblebee, investigating things. The diffuse midday light lay on them like asthma. Big white clouds mushroomed to the west, and the scene turned glossy, bulging with internal light, like a computer photo with more pixels than the human eye could process. The ductile world, everything bursting with light. He really had to try to remember to bring his sunglasses on these trips.

To get a good long nap from Joe, he needed to tank him up. Charlie fought his own sleep, got the food bag out of the backpack's undercarriage pocket, waved it so Joe could see it. Joe trundled over, eyelids at half-mast; there was no time to lose. He settled into Charlie's lap and Charlie popped a bottle of Anna's milk into his mouth just as his head was snapping to the side.

They were like zombies together: Joe sucked himself unconscious while Charlie slumped over him, chin on chest, comatose. Snuggling an infant in mind-numbing heat, what could be cozier.

Clouds over the White House were billowing up like the spirit of the building's feisty inhabitant, round, dense, shiny white. In the other direction, over the Supreme Court's neighborhood, stood a black nine-lobed cloud, dangerously laden with incipient lightning. Yes, the powers of Washington were casting up thermals and forming clouds over themselves, clouds that filled out precisely the shapes and colors of their spirits. Charlie saw that each cumulobureaucracy transcended the individuals who temporarily performed its functions in the world. These transhuman spirits all had inborn characters, and biographies, and abilities and desires and habits all their own; and in the sky over the city they contested their fates with one another. Humans were like cells in their bodies. Probably one's cells also thought their lives were important and under their individual control. But the great bodies knew better.

Thus Charlie now saw that the White House was a great white thunderhead of a spirit, like an old emperor or a small-town sheriff, dominating the landscape and the other players. The Supreme Court on the other hand was dangerously dark and low, like a multiheaded minotaur, brooding and powerful. Over the white dome of the Capitol, the air shimmered; Congress was a roaring thermal so hot that no cloud could form in it.

Oh yes—there were big spirits above this low city, hammering one another like Zeus and his crowd, or Odin, or Krishna, or all of them at once. To make one's way in a world like that one had to blow like the North Wind.

He had fallen into a slumber as deep as Joe's when his phone rang. He answered it before waking, his head snapping dangerously on his neck.

"Wha."

"Charlie? Charlie, where are you? We need you down here right now."

"I'm already down here."

"Really? That's great. Charlie?"

"Yes, Roy?"

"Look, Charlie, sorry to bother you, but Phil is out of town and I've got to meet with Senator Ellington in twenty minutes, and we just got a call from the White House saying that Dr. Strangelove wants to meet with us to talk about Phil's climate bill. It sounds like they're ready to listen, maybe ready to talk too, or even to deal. We need someone to get over there."

"Now?"

"Now. You've got to get over there."

"I'm already over there, but look, I can't. I've got Joe here with me. Where is Phil again?"

"San Francisco."

"Wasn't Wade supposed to get back?"

"No he's still in Antarctica. Listen Charlie, there's no one here who can do this right but you."

"What about Andrea?" Andrea Palmer was Phil's legislative director, the person in charge of all his bills.

"She's in New York today. Besides you're the point man on this, it's your bill more than anyone else's and you know it inside and out."

"But I've got Joe!"

"Maybe you can take Joe along."

"Yeah right."

"Hey, why not? Won't he be taking a nap soon?"

"He is right now."

Charlie could see the trees backing the White House, there on the other side of the Ellipse. He could walk over there in ten minutes. Theoretically Joe would stay asleep a couple of hours. And certainly they should seize the moment on this, because so far the President and his people had shown no interest whatsoever in dealing on this issue.

"Listen," Roy cajoled, "I've had entire lunches with you where Joe is asleep on your back, and believe me, no one can tell the difference. I mean you hold yourself upright like you've got the weight of the world on your shoulders, but you did that *before* you had Joe, so now he just fills up that space and makes you look more normal, I swear to God. You've voted with him on your back, you've shopped, you've *showered,* hey once you even *made love with your wife* while Joe was on your back, didn't you tell me that?"

"What!"

"You told me that, Charlie."

"I must have been drunk to tell you that, and it wasn't really sex anyway. I couldn't even move."

Roy laughed his raucous laugh. "Since when does that make it not sex? You had sex with Joe in a backpack asleep on your back, so you sure as hell can talk to the President's science advisor that way. Doctor Strangelove isn't going to care."

"He's a jerk."

"So? They're all jerks over there but the President, and he is too but he's a nice guy. And he's the *family* President, right? He would approve on principle, you can tell Strengloft that. You can say that if the President were there he would love it. He would autograph Joe's head like a base-ball."

"Yeah right."

"Charlie, this is your bill!"

"Okay okay okay!" It was true. "I'll go give it a try."

So, by the time Charlie got Joe back on his back (the child was twice as heavy when asleep) and walked across the Mall and the Ellipse, Roy had made the calls and they were expecting him at the west entry to the White House. Joe was passed through security with a light-fingered shake-down that was especially squeamish around his diaper. Then they were through, and quickly escorted into a con-ference room.

The room was brightly lit, and empty. Charlie had never been in it before, though he had visited the White House several times. Joe weighed on his shoulders.

Dr. Zacharius Strengloft, the President's science advi-sor, entered the room. He and Charlie had sparred by proxy several times before, Charlie whispering killer ques-tions into Phil's ear while Strengloft testified before Phil's committee, but the two of them had never spoken one-on-one. Now they shook hands, Strengloft peering curiously over Charlie's shoulder. Charlie explained Joe's presence as briefly as he could, and Strengloft received the explanation with precisely the kind of frosty faux benevolence that Charlie had been expecting. Strengloft in Charlie's opinion was a pompous ex-academic of the worst kind, hauled out of the depths of a second-rate conservative think tank when the administration's first science advisor had been sent packing for saying that global warming might be real and not only that, amenable to human mitigations. That went too far for this administration. Their line was that no one knew for sure and it would be much too expensive to

do anything about even if they were certain it was coming—everything would have to change, the power generation system, cars, a shift from hydrocarbons to helium or
something, they didn't know, and they didn't own patents
or already existing infrastructure for that kind of new
thing, so they were going to punt and let the next generation solve their own problems in their own time. In other
words, the hell with them. Easier to destroy the world than
to change capitalism even one little bit.

All this had become quite blatant since Strengloft's appointment. He had taken over the candidate lists for most
of the federal government's science-advisory panels, and
very quickly candidates were being routinely asked who
they had voted for in the last election, and what they
thought of stem-cell research and abortion and evolution.
This had recently culminated in a lead industry defense
witness being appointed to the panel for setting safety
standards for lead in children's blood, and immediately declaring that seventy micrograms per deciliter would be
harmless to children, though the EPA's maximum was ten.
When his views were publicized and criticized, Strengloft
had commented, "You need a diversity of opinions to get
good advice." Mentioning his name was enough to make
Anna hiss.

Be that as it may, here he was standing before Charlie;
he had to be dealt with, and in the flesh he seemed friendly.

They had just gotten through their introductory pleasantries when the President himself entered the room.
Strengloft nodded complacently, as if he were often joined
in his crucial work by the happy man.

"Oh, hello Mr. President," Charlie said helplessly.

"Hello, Charles," the President said, and came over and
shook his hand.

This was bad. Not unprecedented, or even terribly surprising; the President had become known for wandering

into meetings like this, apparently by accident but perhaps not. It had become part of his legendarily informal style.

Now he saw Joe sacked out on Charlie's back, and stepped around Charlie to get a better view. "What's this, Charles, you got your kid with you?"

"Yes sir, I was called in on short notice when Dr. Strengloft asked for a meeting with Phil and Wade, they're both out of town."

The President found this amusing. "Ha! Well, good for you. That's sweet. Find me a marker pen and I'll sign his little head." This was another signature move, so to speak. "Is he a boy or a girl?"

"A boy. Joe Quibler."

"Well that's great. Saving the world before bedtime, that's your story, eh Charles?" He smiled to himself and moved restlessly over to the chair at the window end of the table. One of his people was standing in the door, watching them without expression.

The President's face was smaller than it appeared on TV, Charlie found. The size of an ordinary human face, no doubt, looking small precisely because of all the TV images. On the other hand it had a tremendous solidity and three-dimensionality to it. It gleamed with reality.

His eyes were slightly close-set, as was often remarked, but apart from that he looked like an aging movie star or catalog model. A successful businessman who had retired to get into public service. His features, as many observers had observed, mixed qualities of several recent presidents into one blandly familiar and reassuring face, with a little dash of Ross Perot to give him a piquant antiquity and edgy charm.

Now his amused look was like that of everyone's favorite uncle. "So they reeled you in for this on the fly." Then, holding a hand up to stop all of them, he nearly whispered: "Sorry—should I whisper?"

"No sir, no need for that," Charlie assured him in his ordinary speaking voice. "He's out for the duration. Pay no attention to that man behind the shoulder."

The President smiled. "Got a wizard on your back, eh?"

Charlie nodded, smiling quickly to conceal his surprise. It was a pastime in some circles to judge just how much of a dimwit the President was, how much of a performing puppet for the people manipulating him; but facing him in person, Charlie felt instantly confirmed in his minority position that the man had such a huge amount of low cunning that it amounted to a kind of genius. The President was no fool. And hip to at least the most obvious of movie trivia. Charlie couldn't help feeling a bit reassured.

Now the President said, "That's nice, Charles, let's get to it then, shall we? I heard from Dr. S. here about the meeting this morning, and I wanted to check in on it in person, because I like Phil Chase. And I understand that Phil now wants us to join in with the actions of the Intergovernmental Panel on Climate Change, to the point of introducing a bill mandating our participation in whatever action they recommend, no matter what it is. And this is a UN panel."

"Well," Charlie said, shifting gears into ultradiplomatic mode, not just for the President but for the absent Phil, who was going to be upset with him no matter what he said, since only Phil should actually be talking to the President about this stuff. "That isn't exactly how I would put it, Mr. President. You know the Senate Foreign Relations Committee held a number of hearings this year, and Phil's conclusion after all that testimony was that the global climate situation is quite real. And serious to the point of being already almost too late."

The President shot a glance at Strengloft. "Would you agree with that, Dr. S.?"

"We've agreed that there is general agreement that the observed warming is real."

The President looked to Charlie, who said, "That's good as far as it goes, certainly. It's what follows from that that matters—you know, in the sense of us trying to do something about it."

Charlie swiftly rehearsed the situation, known to all: average temperatures up by six degrees Fahrenheit already, CO_2 levels in the atmosphere topping four hundred and forty parts per million, from a start before the industrial revolution of 280, and predicted to hit six hundred ppm within a decade, which would be higher than it had been at any time in the past seventy million years. Two and a half billion metric tons of CO_2 added to the atmosphere by American industry every year, some 150 percent more than the Kyoto agreement would have allowed if they had signed it, and rising fast. Also long-term persistence of greenhouse gases, on the order of thousands of years.

Charlie also spoke briefly of the death of all coral reefs, which would lead to even more severe consequences for oceanic ecosystems. "The thing is, Mr. President, the world's climate can shift very rapidly. There are scenarios in which the general warming causes parts of the Northern Hemisphere to get quite cold, especially in Europe. If that were to happen, Europe could become something like the Yukon of Asia."

"Really!" the President said. "Are we sure that would be a bad thing? Just kidding of course."

"Of course sir, ha ha."

The President fixed him with a look of mock displeasure. "Well, Charles, all that may be true, but we don't know for sure if any of that is the result of human activity. Isn't that a fact?"

"Depends on what you mean by 'know for sure,' "

Charlie said doggedly. "Two and a half billion tons of carbon per year, that's got to make a difference, it's just plain physics. You could say it isn't for sure that the sun will come up tomorrow morning, and in a limited sense you'd be right, but I'll bet you the sun will come up."

"Don't be tempting me to gamble now."

"And besides, Mr. President, there's also what they call the precautionary principle, meaning you don't delay acting on crucial matters when you have a disaster that might happen, just because you can't be one hundred percent sure that it will happen. Because you can never be one hundred percent sure of anything, and some of these matters are too important to wait on."

The President frowned at this, and Strengloft interjected, "Charlie, you know the precautionary principle is an imitation of actuarial insurance that has no real resemblance to it, because the risk and the premium paid can't be calculated. That's why we refused to hear any precautionary principle language in the discussions we attended at the UN. We said we wouldn't even attend if they talked about precautionary principles or ecological footprints, and we had very good reasons for those exclusions, because those concepts are not good science."

The President nodded his "So That Is That" nod, familiar to Charlie from many a press conference. He added, "I always thought a footprint was kind of a simplistic measurement for something this complex anyway."

Charlie countered, "It's just a name for a good economic index, Mr. President, calculating use of resources in terms of how much land it would take to provide them. It's pretty educational, really," and he launched into a quick description of the way it worked. "It's a good thing to know, like balancing your checkbook, and what it shows is that America is consuming the resources of ten times the acreage it actually occupies. So that if everyone on Earth tried to live as we do, given the greater population densities in much of the world, it would take fourteen Earths to support us all."

"Come on, Charlie," Dr. Strengloft objected. "Next you'll be wanting us to use Bhutan's Gross Domestic Happiness, for goodness' sake. But we can't use little countries' indexes, they don't do the job. We're the hyperpower. And really, the anticarbon-dioxide crowd is a special interest lobby in itself. You've fallen prey to their arguments, but it's not like CO_2 is some toxic pollutant. It's a gas that is natural in our air, and it's essential for plants, even good for them. The last time there was a significant rise in atmospheric carbon dioxide, human agricultural productivity boomed. The Norse settled Greenland during that period, and there were generally rising lifespans."

"The end of the Black Death might account for that," Charlie pointed out.

"Well, maybe rising CO_2 levels ended the Black Death."

Charlie felt his jaw gape.

"It's the bubbly in my club soda," the President told him gently.

"Yes." Charlie rallied. "But a greenhouse gas nevertheless. It holds in heat that would otherwise escape back into space. And we're putting more than two billion tons of it into the atmosphere every year. It's like putting a plug in your exhaust pipe, sir. The car is bound to warm up. There's general agreement from the scientific community that it causes *really significant warming*."

"Our models show the recent temperature changes to be within the range of natural fluctuation," Dr. Strengloft replied. "In fact, temperatures in the stratosphere have gone down. It's complex, and we're studying it, and we're going to make the best and most cost-effective response to it, because we're taking the time to do that. Meanwhile, we're already taking effective precautions. The President has asked American businesses to keep to a new national goal of limiting the growth of carbon dioxide emissions to one-third of the economy's rate of growth."

"But that's the same ratio of emissions to growth that we have already."

"Yes, but the President has gone further, by asking American businesses to try to reduce that ratio over the next decade by eighteen percent. It's a growth-based approach that will accelerate new technologies, and the partnerships that we'll need with the developing world on climate change."

As the President looked to Charlie to see what he would reply to this errant nonsense, Charlie felt Joe stir on his back. This was unfortunate, as things were already complicated enough. The President and his science advisor were not only ignoring the specifics of Phil's bill, they were actively attacking its underlying concepts. Any hope Charlie had had that the President had come to throw his weight behind some real dickering was gone.

And Joe was definitely stirring. His face was burrowed sideways into the back of Charlie's neck, as usual, and now he began doing something that he sometimes did when napping: he latched onto the right tendon at the back of Charlie's neck and began sucking it rhythmically, like a pacifier. Always before Charlie had found this a sweet thing, one of the most momlike moments of his Mr. Momhood. Now he had to steel himself to it and forge on.

The President said, "I think we have to be very careful what kind of science we use in matters like these."

Joe sucked a ticklish spot and Charlie smiled reflexively and then grimaced, not wanting to appear amused by this double-edged pronouncement.

"Naturally that's true, Mr. President. But the arguments for taking vigorous action are coming from a broad range of scientific organizations, also governments, the UN,

NGOs, universities, about ninety-seven percent of all the scientists who have ever declared on the issue," everyone but the very far right end of the think tank and pundit pool, he wanted to add, everyone but hack pseudoscientists who would say anything for money, like Dr. Strengloft here—but he bit his tongue and tried to shift track. "Think of the world as a balloon, Mr. President. And the atmosphere as the skin of the balloon. Now, if you wanted the thickness of the skin of a balloon to correctly represent the thickness of our atmosphere in relation to Earth, the balloon would have to be about as big as a basketball."

This barely made sense even to Charlie, although it was a good analogy if you could enunciate it clearly. "What I mean is that the atmosphere is really, really thin, sir. It's well within our power to alter it greatly."

"No one contests that, Charles. But look, didn't you say the amount of CO_2 in the atmosphere was six hundred parts per million? So if that CO_2 were to be the skin of your balloon, and the rest of the atmosphere was the air inside it, then that balloon would have to be a lot bigger than a basketball, right? About the size of the moon or something?"

Strengloft snorted happily at this thought, and went to a computer console on a desk in the corner, no doubt to compute the exact size of the balloon in the President's analogy. Charlie suddenly understood that Strengloft would never have thought of this argument, and realized further— instantly thereby understanding several people in his past who had mystified him at the time—that sometimes people known for intelligence were actually quite dim, while people who seemed simple could be very sharp.

"Granted, sir, very good," Charlie conceded. "But think of that CO_2 skin as being a kind of glass that lets in light but traps all the heat inside. It's that kind of barrier. So the thickness isn't as important as the glassiness."

"Then maybe more of it won't make all that much of a difference," the President said kindly. "Look, Charles. Fanciful comparisons are all very well, but the truth is we have to slow the growth of these emissions before we can try to stop them, much less reverse them."

This was exactly what the President had said at a recent press conference, and over at the computer Strengloft beamed and nodded to hear it, perhaps because he had authored the line. The absurdity of taking pride in writing stupid lines for a quick president suddenly struck Charlie as horribly funny. He was glad Anna wasn't there beside him, because in moments like these they could with the slightest shared glance set each other off. Even the thought of her in such a situation almost made him laugh.

So now he banished his wife and her glorious hilarity from his mind, not without a final bizarre tactile image of the back of his neck as one of her breasts, being suckled more and more hungrily by Joe. Very soon it would be time for a bottle.

Charlie persevered nevertheless. "Sir, it's getting kind of urgent now. And there's no downside to taking the lead on this issue. The economic advantages of being in the forefront of climate rectification and bioinfrastructure mitigation are *huge*. It's a growth industry with uncharted potential. It's the future no matter which way you look at it."

Joe clamped down hard on his neck. Charlie shivered. Hungry, no doubt about it. Would be ravenous on waking. Only a bottle of milk or formula would keep him from going ballistic at that point. He could not be roused now without disaster striking. But he was beginning to inflict serious pain. Charlie lost his train of thought. He twitched. A little snort of agony combined with a giggle. He choked it back, disguised it as a smothered cough.

"What's the matter, Charles, is he waking up on you?"

"Oh no sir, still out. Maybe stirring a little—ah! The thing is, if we don't address these issues now, nothing else we're doing will matter. None of it will go well."

"That sounds like alarmist talk to me," the President said, an avuncular twinkle in his eye. "Let's calm down about this. You've got to stick to the common sense idea that sustainable economic growth is the key to environmental progress."

"Sustainable, ah!"

"What's that?"

He clamped down on a giggle. "Sustainable's the point! Sir."

"We need to harness the power of markets," Strengloft said, and nattered on in his usual vein, apparently oblivious to Charlie's problem. The President however eyed him closely. Huge chomp. Charlie's spine went electric. He suppressed the urge to swat his son like a mosquito. His right fingers tingled. Very slowly he lifted a shoulder, trying to dislodge him. Like trying to budge a limpet. Sometimes Anna had to squeeze his nostrils shut to get him to come off. Don't think about that.

The President said, "Charles, we'd be sucking the life out of the economy if we were to go too far with this. You chew on that a while. As it is, we're taking *bites* out of this problem every day. Why, I'm like a dog with a bone on this thing! Those enviro special interests are like pigs at a trough. We're weaning them from all that now, and they don't like it, but they're going to have to learn that if you can't *lick* them, you..."

And Charlie dissolved into gales of helpless laughter.

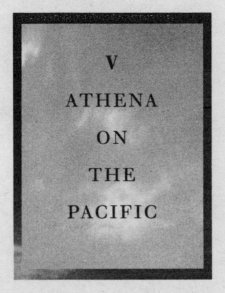

V

ATHENA

ON

THE

PACIFIC

California is a place apart.

Gold chasers went west until the ocean stopped them, and there in that remote and beautiful land, separated from the rest of the world by desert and mountain, prairie and ocean, they saw there could be no more moving on. They would have to stop and make a life there.

Civil society, post-Civil War. A motley of argonauts, infused with Manifest Destiny and gold fever, also with Emerson and Thoreau, Lincoln and Twain, their own John Muir. They said to each other, Here at the end of the road it had better be different, or else world history has all come to naught.

So they did many things, good and bad. In the end it turned out the same as everywhere else, maybe a little more so.

But among the good things, encouraged by Lincoln, was the founding of a public university. Berkeley in 1867, the farm at Davis in 1905, the other campuses after that; in the 1960's new ones sprang up like flowers in a field. The University of California. A power in this world.

An oceanographic institute near La Jolla wanted one of the new campuses of the sixties to be located nearby.

Next door was a U.S. Marine Corps rifle training facility. The oceanographers asked the Marines for the land, and the Marines said yes. Donated land, just like Washington, D.C., but in this case a eucalyptus grove on a sea cliff, high over the Pacific.

The University of California, San Diego.

By then California had become a crossroads, east and west all met together, San Francisco the great city, Hollywood the dream machine. UCSD was the lucky child of all that, Athena leaping out of the tall forehead of the state. Prominent scientists came from everywhere to start it, caught by the siren song of a new start on a Mediterranean edge to the world.

They founded a school and helped to invent a technology: biotech, Athena's gift to humankind. University as teacher and doctor too, owned by the people, no profit skimmed off. A public project in an ever-more-privatized world, tough and determined, benign in intent but very intent. What does it mean to give?

FRANK CONSIDERED adding a postscript to Yann Pierzinski's Form Seven, suggesting that he pursue internal support at Torrey Pines Generique. Then he decided it would be better to work through Derek Gaspar. He could do it in person during the trip he was making to San Diego to prepare for his move back.

A week later he was off. On the first flight west he fell asleep watching a DVD. Transfer at Dallas, a good people-watching airport, then up into the air again, and back to sleep.

He woke when he felt the plane tilt down. They were still over Arizona, its huge baked landforms flowing by underneath. A part of Frank that had been asleep for much longer than the nap began to wake up too: he was returning to home ground. It was amazing the way things changed when you crossed to the dry side of the ten-inches-of-rain-a-year isobar. Frank put his forehead against the inner window of the plane, looked ahead to the next burnt range coming into view. Thought to himself, I'll go surfing.

The pale umber of the Mojave gave way to Southern

California's big scrubby coastal mountains. West of those suburbia hove into view, spilling eastward on filled valleys and shaved hilltops: greater San Diego, bigger all the time. He could see bulldozers busy scraping platforms of flat soil for the newest neighborhood. Freeways glittering with their arterial flow.

Frank's plane slowed and drifted down, past the last peaks and over the city proper. Downtown's cluster of glassy skyscrapers came into view immediately to the left of the plane, seemingly at about the same height. Those buildings had been Frank's workplace for a time when he was young, and he watched them as he would any old home. He knew exactly which buildings he had climbed; they were etched on his mind. That had been a good year. Disgusted with his advisor, he had taken a leave of absence from graduate school, and after a season of climbing in Yosemite and living at Camp Four, he had run out of money and decided to do something for a living that would require his physical skills and not his intellectual ones. A young person's mistake, although at least he had not thought he could make his living as a professional climber. But the same skills were needed for the work of skyscraper window maintenance; not just window washing, which he had also done, but repair and replacement. It had been an odd but wonderful thing, going off the roofs of those buildings and descending their sides to clean windows, re-pair leaking caulk and flashing, replace cracked panes, and so on. The climbing was straightforward, usually involving platforms for convenience; the belays and T-bars and dashboards and other gear had been bombproof. His fellow workers had been a mixed bag, as was always true with climbers—everything from nearly illiterate cowboys to eccentric scholars of Nietzsche or Adam Smith. And the window work itself had been a funny thing, what the Nietzsche scholar had called the apotheosis of kindergarten skills, very satisfying to perform—slicing out old caulk, applying heated caulk, unscrewing and screwing screws and bolts, sticking giant suckers to panes, levering them out and winching them up to the roofs or onto the platforms—and all under the cool onrush of the marine layer, just under clouds all mixed together with bright sun, so that it was warm when it was sunny, cool when it was cloudy, and the whole spread of downtown San Diego there below to entertain him when he wasn't working. Often he had felt surges of happiness, filling him in moments when he stopped to look around: a rare thing in his life.

Eventually the repetition got boring, as it will, and he had moved on, first to go traveling, until the money he had saved was gone; then back into academia again, as a sort of test, in a different lab, with a different advisor, at a different university. Things had gone better there. Eventually he had ended up back at UCSD, back in San Diego—his childhood home, and still the place where he felt most comfortable on this Earth.

He actually noticed that feeling as he left the airport terminal's glassed-in walkway over the street, and hopped down the outdoor escalator to the rental car shuttles. The comfort of a primate on home ground, no doubt—a familiarity in the slant of the light and the shape of the hills, but above all in the air itself, the way it felt on his skin, that combination of temperature, humidity, and salinity that together marked it as particularly San Diegan. It was like putting on familiar old clothes after spending a year in a tux; he was home, and his cells knew it.

He got in his rental car (always the same one, it seemed) and drove out of the lot. North on the freeway, crowded but not impossibly so, people zipping along like starlings, following the flocking rules *keep as far apart from the rest as possible* and *change speeds as little as possible*. The best drivers in the world. Past Mission Bay and Mount Soledad on the left, into the region where every off-ramp had been a major feature of his life at one time or another. Off at Gilman, up the tight canyon of apartments hanging over the freeway, past the one where he had once spent a night with a girl, ah, back in the days when such things had happened to him. Down a hill and onto campus.

UCSD. Home base. The school in the eucalyptus grove. Quick-witted, sophisticated, scarily powerful—even from inside it, Frank remained impressed by the place. Among other things it was a very effective troop of primates, collaborating to further the welfare of its members.

Even after a year in the East Coast's great hardwood forest, there was something appealing about the campus's eucalyptus grove—something charming, even soothing. The trees had been planted as a railroad-tie farm, before it was discovered that the wood was unsuitable. Now they formed a kind of mathematically gridded space, within which the architectural mélange of UCSD's colleges lay scattered, connected by two broad promenades that ran north and south.

Frank had arranged an afternoon of appointments. The department had given him the use of an empty office facing the Revelle Plaza; his own was still occupied by a visiting researcher from Berlin. After getting the key from Rosaria, the department secretary, he sat at a dusty desk by a functioning phone, and discussed dissertation progress with his four remaining graduate students. Forty-five minutes each, and aware the whole time that he really wasn't doing them justice, that it had been their bad luck to get him as their advisor, because of his decision to go to NSF for a year. Well, he would try to make up for it on his return—but not all at once, and certainly not today. The truth was that none of their projects looked that interesting. Sometimes it happened that way.

After that there was an hour and a half to go before his meeting with Derek. Parking at UCSD was a nightmare, but he had gotten a pass to a department slot from Rosaria, and Torrey Pines was only a few hundred yards up the road, so he decided to walk. Then, feeling restless, and even a bit jumpy, it occurred to him to take the climbers' route that he and some friends had devised for a kind of run/climb workout, when they were all living at Revelle; that would nicely occupy the amount of time he had to kill.

It involved walking down La Jolla Shores and turning onto La Jolla Farms Road and heading out onto the bluff of land owned by the university—a squarish plateau between two canyons running down to the beach, ending in a steep three-hundred-and-fifty-foot cliff over the sea. This land had been left in its natural state, more or less—there were some old World War Two bunkers melting away on it—and as they had found seven-thousand-year-old graves on it, likely to stay forever protected in the UC Natural Reserve system. A superb prospect and one of Frank's favorite places on Earth. He had lived on it, sleeping out there every night and using the old gym as his bathroom; he had had romantic encounters out there; and he had often dropped down the steep surfer's trail that descended to the beach right at Blacks Canyon.

When he got to the cliff's edge he found a sign announcing that the route down was closed due to erosion of the cliff, and it was hard to argue, as the old trail was now a kind of gully down the edge of a sandstone buttress. But he still wanted to do it, and he strolled south along the cliff's edge, looking out at the Pacific and feeling the onshore wind blow through him. The view was just as mind-boggling as ever, despite the gray cloud layer; as often happened, the clouds seemed to accentuate the great distances to the horizon, the two plates of ocean and sky converging at such a very slight angle toward each other.

California, the edge of history—it was a stupid idea, and totally untrue in all senses of the word, except for this physical one, and the reach beyond to a metaphorical landscape: it did appear to be the edge of something.

An awesome spot. And the tighter, steeper canyon on the south side of the empty bluff had an alternative trail down that Frank was willing to break the rules and take. No one but a few cronies of his had ever used this one, because the initial drop was a scarily exposed knife-edge of a buttress, the gritty sandstone eroding in the wind to steep gullies on both sides. The drop into the gully to the left was similarly hairy. The trick was to descend fast and boldly and so Frank did that, skidding out as he turned into the gully, and sliding onto his side and down; but against the other wall of the gully he stopped, and was able to hop down after that very quickly and uneventfully.

Down to the salt roar of the beach, the surf louder here because of the tall cliff leaping up from the back of the beach. He walked north down the strand, enjoying yet another familiar place. Blacks Beach, the UCSD surfers' home away from home.

The ascent to Torrey Pines Generique reversed the problems of the descent, in that here all the problems were right down on the beach. A hanging gully dripped over a hard sill some forty feet up, and he had to free climb the grit to the right of the green algal spill; then just scramble up that gully, to the clifftop near the hang-glider port. At the top he discovered a sign that declared this climb too had been illegal.

Oh well. He had loved it. He felt refreshed, awake for the first time in weeks somehow. This was what it meant to be home. He could brush his hands through his slightly sweaty and seaspray-dampened hair, and walk in and see what happened.

Onto the parklike grounds of Torrey Pines Generique, through the newly beefed-up security gates. The place was looking empty, he thought as he entered the main building and walked down its halls to Derek's office. They had definitely let a lot of people go; several labs he passed stood empty and unused.

Frank entered the reception room and greeted Derek's secretary, Susan, who buzzed him in. Derek got up from his broad desk to shake hands.

"Good to see you again, how are you?"

"Fine, and you?"

"Oh, getting by, getting by."

His office looked the same as the last time Frank had visited: window view of the Pacific; framed copy of Derek's cover portrait on a *U.S. News & World Report;* skiing photos.

"So, what's new with the great bureaucrats of science?"

"They call themselves technocrats, actually."

"Oh I'm sure it's a big difference." Derek shook his head. "I never understood why you went out there. I suppose you made good use of your time."

"Yes."

"And now you're almost back."

"Yes. I'm almost done." Frank paused. "But look, like I said to you on the phone, I did see something interesting come in from someone who has worked here."

"Right, I looked into it. We could still hire him full-time, I'm pretty sure. He's on soft money up at Caltech."

"Good. Because I thought it was a very interesting idea."

"So NSF funded it?"

"No, the panel wasn't as impressed as I was. And they might have been right—it was a bit undercooked. But the thing is, if it did work, you could test genes by computer simulation, and identify proteins you wanted, even down to specific ligands, so you could get better attachments to cells in vivo. It would really speed the process. Sharpen it."

Derek regarded him closely. "You know we don't really have any funds for new people."

"Yeah I know. But this guy is a postdoc, right? And a mathematician. He was only asking NSF for some computer time really. You could hire him full-time for a starter salary, and put him on the case, and it would hardly cost you a thing. I mean, if you can't afford that... Anyway, it could be interesting."

"What do you mean, 'interesting'?"

"I just told you. Hire him full-time, and get him to sign the usual contract concerning intellectual property rights and all. Really secure those."

"I get that, but 'interesting' how?"

Frank sighed. "In the sense that it might be the way to solve your targeted delivery problem. If his methods work and you get a patent, then the potential for licensing income might be really considerable. Really."

Derek was silent. He knew that Frank knew the company was nearly on life support. That being the case, Frank would not bother him with trifles, or even with big deals that needed capital and time to get going. He had to be offering a fix of some kind.

"Why did he send this grant proposal to NSF?"

"Beats me. Maybe he was turned down by one of your guys when he was here. Maybe his advisor at Caltech told him to do it. It doesn't matter. But have your people working on the delivery problem take a look at it. After you get this guy hired."

"Why don't you talk to them? Go talk to Leo Mulhouse about this."

"Well..." Frank thought it over. "Okay. I'll go talk to them and see how things are going. You get this Pierzinski back on board. Call him today. We'll see what happens from there."

Derek nodded, still not happy. "You know, Frank, what we really need here is you. Like I said before. Things haven't been the same in the labs since you left. Maybe when you get back here we could rehire you at whatever level UCSD will allow."

"I thought you just said you didn't have any money for hires."

"Well that's true, but for you we could try to work something out, right?"

"Maybe. But let's not talk about that now. I need to get out of NSF first, and see what the blind trust has done with my stock. I used to have some options here."

"You sure did. Hell, we could bury you in those, Frank, I'd love to do that."

Giving people options to buy stock cost a company nothing. They were feel-good gestures, unless everything went right with the company and the market; and with NASDAQ having been in the tank for so long, they were not often seen as real compensation anymore. More a kind of speculation. And in fact Frank expressing interest in them had cheered Derek up, as it was a sign of confidence in the future of Torrey Pines Generique. Also a sign of Frank's interest in taking part in it, on his return.

"Do what you can to get some funding to tide you over a bit longer," Frank suggested as he got up to leave.

"Oh I will. I always am."

Outside, Frank sighed. Torrey Pines was looking like a thin reed. But it was his reed, and anything might happen. Derek was good at keeping things afloat. But Sam Houston was a loss. Derek needed Frank there as scientific advisor. Or consultant, given his UCSD position. And if they had Pierzinski under contract, things might work out. By the end of the year the whole Torrey Pines situation might be turned around. And if it all worked out, the potential was there for it to do very well indeed.

Frank wandered down to Leo's lab. It was noticeably lively compared to the rest of the building—people bustling about, the smell of solvents in the air, machines whirring away. Where there's life there's hope. Or perhaps they were only like the musicians on the *Titanic,* playing on while the ship went down.

This, however, represented an attempt to bail the ship out. Frank felt encouraged. He went in and exchanged pleasantries with Leo and his people, feeling that it was easy to be friendly and encouraging. This was the guts of the machine, after all. He mentioned that Derek had sent him down to talk about their current situation, and Leo nodded noncommittally and gave him a rundown, truncated but functional.

Frank regarded him as he spoke, thinking: Here is a scientist at work in a lab. He is in the optimal scientific space. He has a lab, he has a problem, he's fully absorbed and going full tilt. He should be happy. But he isn't happy. He has a tough problem he's trying to solve, but that's not it; people always have tough problems in the lab.

It was something else. Probably, that he was aware of the company's situation—of course, he had to be. Probably this was the source of his unease. The musicians feeling the tilt in the deck. In which case there really was a kind of heroism in the way they played on, focused to the end.

But for some reason Frank was also faintly annoyed by this. People plugging away in the same old ways, trying to do things according to the plan, even a flawed plan: normal science, in Kuhnian terms, as well as in the more ordinary sense. All so normal, so trusting that the system worked, when obviously the system was both rigged and broken.

How could they persevere? How could they be so blink-
ered, so determined, so dense?

Frank slipped his content in. "Maybe if you had a way
to test the genes in computer simulations, find your proteins in advance."

Leo looked puzzled. "You'd have to have a, what. A
theory of how DNA codes its gene expression functions.
At the least."

"Yes."

"That would be nice, but I'm not aware anyone has
that."

"No, but if you did ... Wasn't George working on something like that, or one of his temporary guys? Pierzinski?"

"Yeah that's right, Yann was trying some really interesting things. But he left."

"I think Derek is trying to bring him back."

"Good idea."

Then Marta walked into the lab. When she saw Frank
she stopped, startled.

"Oh hi Marta."

"Hi Frank. I didn't know you were going to be coming by."

"Neither did I."

"Oh no? Well—" She hesitated, turned. The situation
called for her to say something, he felt, something like
Good to see you, if she was going to leave so quickly. But
she said only, "I'm late, I've got to get to work."

And then she was out the door.

Only later, when reviewing his actions, did Frank see
that he had cut short the talk with Leo—and pretty obviously at that—in order to follow Marta. In the moment
itself he simply found himself walking down the hall,
catching up to her before he even realized what he was
doing.

She turned and saw him. "What," she said sharply, looking at him as if to stop him in his tracks.

"Oh hi I was just wondering how you're doing, I haven't seen you for a while, I wondered. Are you up for, how about going out and having dinner somewhere and catching up?"

She surveyed him. "I don't think so. I don't think that would be a good idea. We might as well not even go there. What would be the point."

"I don't know, I'm interested to know how you're doing I guess is all."

"Yeah I know, I know what you mean. But sometimes there are things you're interested in that you can't really ever get to know anymore, you know?"

"Ah yeah."

He pursed his lips, looked at her. She looked good. She was both the strongest and the wildest woman he had ever met. Somehow things between them had gone wrong anyway.

Now he looked at her and understood what she was saying. He was never going to be able to know what her life was like these days. He was biased, she was biased; the scanty data would be inescapably flawed. Talking for a couple hours would not make any difference. So it was pointless to try. Would only bring up bad things from the past. Maybe in another ten years. Maybe never.

Marta must have seen something of this train of thought in his face, because with an impatient nod she turned and was gone.

A FEW DAYS after Frank dropped by, Leo turned on his computer when he came in to the lab and saw there was an e-mail from Derek. He opened and read it, then the attachment that had come with it. When he was done he printed it all out, and forwarded it to Brian and Marta. When Marta came in about an hour later she had already done some work on it.

"Hey Brian," she called from Leo's door, "come check this out. Derek has sent us a new paper from that Yann Pierzinski who was here. He was funny. It's a new version of the stuff he was working on when he was here. That was interesting I thought. If we could get it to find us better matching ligands, you might not need the hydrodynamic pressures to get them to stick in the body."

Brian had come in while she was telling him this, and she pointed to parts of the diagram on Leo's screen as he caught up. "See what I mean?" Liver cells, endothelial cells—all the cells in the body had receptor ligands that were extremely specific for the ligands on the particular proteins that they needed to obtain from the blood;

together they formed something like lock-and-key arrangements, coded by the genes and embodied in the proteins. In effect they were locksmithing at the microscopic level, working with living cells as their material.

"Well, yeah. It would be great. If it worked. Maybe crunch them through this program over and over, until you see repeats. If you did...then test the ones with the ligands that fit best and look strongest chemically."

"And Pierzinski is back to work on it with us!"

"Is he?"

"Yeah, he's coming back. Derek says in his e-mail that we'll have him at our disposal."

"Cool."

Leo checked this in the company's directory. "Yep, here he is. Rehired just this week. Frank Vanderwal came by and mentioned this guy, he must have told Derek about it I bet. He was asking me about it too. Well, Vanderwal should know, this is his field."

"It's my field too," Marta said sharply.

"Right, of course, I'm just saying Frank might have, you know. Well, let's ask Yann to look at what we've got. If it works..."

Brian said, "Sure. It's worth trying anyway. Pretty interesting." He Googled Yann, and Leo leaned over his shoulder to look at the list.

"Derek obviously wants us to talk to him right away."

"He must have rehired him for us."

"I see that. So let's get him before he gets busy with something else. A lot of labs could use another biomathematician."

"True, but there aren't a lot of labs. I think we'll get him. Look, what do you think Derek means here, 'write up the possibilities right away.'"

"I suppose he wants to get started using the idea to try to secure more funding."

"Shit. Yeah, that's probably right. Unbelievable. Okay, let's pass on that for now, and give Yann a call."

Their talk with Yann Pierzinski was indeed interesting. He breezed into the lab just a few days later, as friendly as ever, and happy to be back at Torrey Pines with a permanent job. He was going to be based in George's math group, he told them, but had already been told by Derek to expect to work a lot with Leo's lab; so he arrived curious and ready to go.

Leo enjoyed seeing him again. Yann still had a tendency to become a speed-talker when excited, and he still canted his head to the side when thinking, as if to flood that half of his brain with blood, in just the kind of "rapid hydrodynamic forcing" that they were trying to get away from in their work (and he tilted it to the right, so was giving the boost to the so-called intuitive side, Leo noted). His algorithm sets were still works in progress, he said, and underdeveloped precisely in the gene grammars that Leo and Marta and Brian needed from him for their work; but all that was okay, because they could help him, and he was there to help them. They could collaborate, and when it came right down to it, Yann was a powerful thinker, and good to have on the case. Leo felt secure in his own lab abilities, devising and running experiments and the like, but when it came to the curious mixture of math, symbolic logic, and computer programming that these biomathematicians dove into—mathematicizing human logic, among other things, and reducing it to mechanical steps that could be scripted into the computers—he was way out of his depth. So Leo was happy to watch Yann sit down and plug his laptop into their desktop.

In the days that followed, they tried his algorithms out on the genes of their HDL factory cells, Yann substituting different procedures in the last steps of his operations, then checking what they got in the computer simulations, and selecting some for their dish trials. Pretty soon they found one version of the operation that was consistently good at predicting proteins that matched well with their target cells—making keys for their locks, in effect. "That's what I've been focusing on for the past *year*," Yann said happily after one such success.

As they worked, Pierzinski told them some of how he had gotten to that point in his work, following aspects of his advisor's work at Caltech and the like. Marta and Brian asked him where he had hoped to take it all, in terms of applications. Yann shrugged; not much of anywhere, he told them. He thought the main interest of the operation was what it revealed about the mathematics of codon function. Just finding out more about the mathematics of how genes became organisms. He had not thought much about the implications for clinical or therapeutic applications, though he freely acknowledged they might be there. "It stands to reason that the more you know about this, the more you'll be able to see what's going on." The rest of it was not his field of interest. It was a classic mathematician thing.

"But Yann, don't you see what the applications of this could be?"

"I guess. I'm not really interested in pharmacology."

Leo and Brian and Marta stood there staring at him. Despite his earlier stint there, they didn't know him very well. He seemed normal enough in most ways, aware of the outside world and so on. To an extent.

Leo said "Look, let us take you out to lunch. I want to tell you more about what all this could help us with."

THE LOBBYING firm of Branson and Ananda occupied offices off Pennsylvania Avenue, near the intersection of Indiana and C Streets, about halfway between the White House and the Capitol, and overlooking the Marketplace. It was a very nice office.

Charlie's friend Sridar met them at the front door. First he took them in to meet old Branson himself, then led them into a meeting room dominated by a long table under a window that gave a view of early summer leaves on gnarly branches. Sridar got the Khembalis seated, then offered them coffee or tea; they all took tea. Charlie stood near the door, flexing his knees and bobbing mildly about, keeping Joe asleep on his back, ready to make a quick escape if he had to.

Drepung spoke for the Khembalis, although Sucandra and Padma also pitched in with questions from time to time. They all consulted with Rudra Cakrin, who asked them a lot of questions in Tibetan. Charlie began to think he had been wrong about the old man understanding

English; it was too cumbersome to be a trick, just as Anna had said.

All the Khembalis stared intently at Sridar or Charlie whenever they spoke. They made for a very attentive audience. They definitely had a presence. It had gotten to the point where Charlie felt that their Calcutta cottons, maroon vests, and sandals were normal, and that it was the room itself that was rather strange, so smooth and spotlessly gray. Suddenly it looked to him like the inside of a Gymboree crawl space.

"So you've been a sovereign country since 1960?" Sridar was saying.

"The relationship with India is a little more... complicated than that. We have had sovereignty in the sense you suggest since about 1993." Drepung rehearsed the history of Khembalung, while Sridar asked questions and took notes.

"So—fifteen feet above sea level at high tide," Sridar said at the end of this recital. "Listen, one thing I have to say at the start—we are not going to be able to promise you anything much in the way of results on this global warming thing. That's been given up on by Congress—" He glanced at Charlie: "Sorry, Charlie. Maybe not so much given up on as swept under the rug."

Charlie glowered despite himself. "Not by Senator Chase or anyone else who's really paying attention to the world. And we're still working on it, we've got a big bill coming up and—"

"Yes yes, of course," Sridar said, holding up a hand to stop him before he got into rant mode. "You're doing what you can. But let's put it this way—there are quite a few members of Congress who think of it as being too late to do anything."

"Better late than never!" Charlie insisted, almost waking Joe.

"We understand," Drepung said to Sridar, after a glance at the old man. "We won't have any unrealistic expectations of you. We only hope to engage help that is experienced in the procedures used, the usual protocols you see. We ourselves will be responsible for the content of our appeals to the reluctant bodies, trusting you to arrange the meetings with them."

Sridar kept his face blank, but Charlie knew what he was thinking. Sridar said, "We do our best to give our clients all the benefits of our expertise. I'm just reminding you that we are not miracle workers."

The Khembalis nodded.

"The miracles will be our department," Drepung said, face as blank as Sridar's.

Charlie thought, these two jokers might get along fine.

Slowly they worked out what they would expect from one another, and Sridar wrote down the details of an agreement. The Khembalis were happy to have him write up what in essence was their request for a proposal. "That sure makes it easier," Sridar remarked. "A clever way to make me write you a fair deal." During this part of the negotiation (for such it was) Joe finished waking up, so Charlie left them to it.

Later that day Sridar gave Charlie a call. Charlie was sitting on a bench in Dupont Circle, feeding Joe a bottle and watching two of the local chess hustlers practice on each other. They played too fast for Charlie to follow the game.

"Look, Charlie, this is a bit ingrown, since you put me in touch with these guys, but really it's your man that the lamas ought to be meeting first, or at least early on. The Foreign Relations Committee is one of the main ones we'll have to work on, so it all begins with Chase. Can you set us up with a good chunk of the senator's quality time?"

"I can with some lead time," Charlie said, glancing at

Phil's master calendar on his wrist screen. "How about next Thursday, he's had a cancellation?"

"Is that late morning, so he's at his best?"

"He's always at his best."

"Yeah right."

"No I'm serious. You don't know Phil."

"I'll take your word for it. Thursday at? . . ."

"Ten to ten-twenty."

"Perfect."

Charlie could have made a good case for the energy of Senator Phil Chase being more or less invariant, and always very high. Here in the latter part of his third term he had fully settled into Washington, and his seniority was such that he had become very powerful, and very busy. He was constantly on the go, with every hour from six A.M. to midnight scheduled in twenty-minute units. It was hard to understand how he could keep his easy demeanor and relaxed ways.

Almost too relaxed. He did not sweat the details on most topics. He was a delegating senator, a hands-off senator. As many of the best of them were. Some senators tried to learn everything, and burned out; others knew almost nothing, and were in effect living campaign posters. Phil was somewhere in the middle. He used his staff well—as an exterior memory bank, if nothing else, but often for much more—for advice, for policy, even occasionally for their accumulated wisdom.

His longevity in office, and the strict code of succession that both parties obeyed, had now landed him the chair of the Foreign Relations Committee, and a seat on Environment and Public Works. These were A-list committees, and the stakes were high. The Democrats had come out of the recent election with a one-vote advantage in the Senate, a two-vote disadvantage in the House, and the President was still a Republican. This was in the ongoing American tradition of electing as close to a perfect gridlock of power in Washington as possible, presumably in the hope that nothing further would happen and history would freeze for good. An impossible quest, like building a card house in a gale, but it made for tight politics and good theater. Inside the Beltway it was considered to be an invigorating thing.

In any case, Phil was now very busy with important matters, and heading toward re-election time himself. His old chief of staff Wade Norton was on the road now, and though Phil valued Wade's advice and kept him on staff as a telecommuting general advisor, Andrea had taken over the executive staff duties, and Charlie the environmental research, though he too was a part-timer, and telecommuting much of the time.

When he did make it in, he found operations in the office fully professional, but with a chaotic edge that he had long ago concluded was mostly engendered by Phil himself. Phil would seize the minutes he had between appointments and wander from room to room, looking to needle people. At first this appeared to be wasting time, but Charlie had come to believe it was a kind of quick polling method, Phil squeezing in impressions and reactions in the little time he had that was not scheduled. "We're surfing the big picture today!" he would exclaim as he wandered the offices, or stood by the refrigerator drinking another ginger ale. Those were the moments when he would start arguments for the hell of it. His staff loved it. Congressional staffers were by definition policy wonks; many had joined their high school debate clubs of their own free will. Talking shop with Phil was right up their alley. And his enthusiasm was infectious, his grin like a double shot of espresso. He had one of those smiles that invariably looked as if he was genuinely delighted. If it was directed at you, you felt a glow inside. In fact Charlie was convinced that it was Phil's smile that had gotten him elected the first time, and maybe every time since. What made it so beautiful was that it wasn't faked. He didn't smile if he didn't feel like it. But he often felt like it. That was very revealing, and so Phil had his effect.

With Wade gone, Charlie was now his chief advisor on global climate issues. Actually Charlie and Wade functioned as a sort of tag-team telecommuting advisor, both of them part-time, Charlie calling in every day, dropping by every week; Wade calling in every week, and dropping by every month. It worked because Phil didn't always need them for help when environmental issues came up. "You guys have educated me," he would tell them. "I can take this on my own. Naturally I'll be doing what you told me to do anyway. So don't worry, stay at the South Pole, stay in Bethesda. I'll let you know how it went."

That would have been fine with Charlie, if only Phil had in fact always done what Charlie and Wade advised. But Phil had other advisors as well, and pressures from many directions; and he had his own opinions. So there were divergences.

He would grin his infectious grin whenever he crossed Charlie. It seemed to give him special pleasure. "There are more things in heaven and earth," he would murmur, only half-listening to Charlie's remonstrances. Like most congresspeople, he thought he knew better than his staff how best to get things done; and because he got to vote and his staff didn't, in effect he was right.

On the following Thursday at ten A.M., when the Khembalis had their twenty minutes head-to-head with Phil, Charlie was very interested to see how it would go, but that morning he had to attend a Washington Press Club appearance by a scientist from the Heritage Foundation who was claiming rapidly rising temperatures would be good for agriculture. Marking such people and assisting in the immediate destruction of their pseudoarguments was important work, which Charlie undertook with a fierce indignation; at some point the manipulation of facts became a kind of vast lie, and this was what Charlie felt when he had to confront people like Strengloft: he was combating liars, people who lied about science for money, thus obscuring the clear signs of the destruction of their present world. So that they would end up passing on to all the children a degraded planet, devoid of animals and forests and coral reefs and all the other aspects of a biological support system and home. Liars, cheating their own children, and the many generations to come: this is what Charlie wanted to shout at them, as vehemently as any street-corner nutcase preacher. So that when he went at them, with his tightly polite questions and pointed remarks, there was a certain edge to him. Opponents tried to deflect it by labeling it as self-righteousness or affluent hypocrisy or whatnot; but the edge could still cut if he hit the right spots.

In any case it was perhaps best that Charlie not be there at Phil's meeting with the Khembalis, so that Phil would not be distracted, or feel that Charlie was somehow coaching the visitors. Phil could form his own impressions, and Sridar would be there to do any shepherding necessary. By now Charlie had seen enough of the Khembalis to trust that Rudra Cakrin and his gang would be up to the task of representing themselves. Phil would experience their weird persuasiveness, and he knew enough of the world not to discount them just because they were not Beltway operators dressed in suit and tie.

So Charlie hustled back from the predictably irritating hearing, and arrived right at 10:20. He hurried up the stairs to Phil's offices on the third floor. These offices had a great view down the Mall—the best any senator had, obtained in a typical Phil coup. The Senate, excessively cramped in the old Russell, Dirksen, and Hart buildings, had finally bitten the bullet and taken by eminent domain the headquarters of the United Brothers of Carpenters and Joiners of America, who had owned a fine building in a spectacular location on the Mall, between the National Gallery and the Capitol itself. The carpenters' union had howled at the takeover, of course—only a Republican House and Senate would have dared to do it, happy as they were to smack a union whenever possible—but it had left a political stink such that very few senators were actually willing to brave the negative PR of moving into the new acquisition once all the legal wrangling was over and the building was theirs. Phil, however, had been quite happy to move in, claiming he would represent the carpenters' and all the other unions so faithfully that it would be as if they had never left the building. "Where better to defend the working people of America?" he had asked, smiling his famous smile. "I'll keep a hammer on the windowsill to remind myself who I'm representing."

At 10:23 A.M., Phil ushered the Khembalis out of his corner office, chatting with them cheerfully. "Yes, thanks, of course, I'd love to—talk to Evelyn about setting up a time."

The Khembalis looked pleased. Sridar looked impassive but faintly amused, as he often did.

Just as he was leaving, Phil spotted Charlie and stopped. "Charlie! Good to see you at last!"

Grinning hugely, he came back and shook his blushing staffer's hand. "So you laughed in the President's face!" He turned to the Khembalis: "This man burst out laughing in the President's face! I've always wanted to do that!"

The Khembalis nodded neutrally.

"So what did it feel like?" Phil asked Charlie. "And how did it go over?"

Charlie, still blushing, said, "Well, it felt involuntary, to tell the truth. Like a sneeze. Joe was really tickling me. And as far as I could tell, it went over okay. The President looked pleased. He was trying to make me laugh, so when I did, he laughed too."

"Yeah I bet, because he had you."

"Well, yes. Anyway he laughed, and then Joe woke up and we had to get a bottle in him before the Secret Service guys did something rash."

Phil laughed, then shook his head, growing more serious. "Well, it's too bad, I guess. But what could you do. You were ambushed. He loves to do that. Hopefully it won't cost us. It might even help. —But look I'm late, I've got to go. You hang in there." And he put a hand to Charlie's arm, said good-bye again to the Khembalis, and hustled out the door.

The Khembalis gathered around Charlie, looking cheerful. "Where is Joe? How is it he is not with you?"

"I really couldn't bring him to this thing I was at, so my friend Asta from Gymboree is looking after him. Actually I have to get back to him soon," checking his watch. "But come on, tell me how it went."

They all followed Charlie into his cubicle by the stairwell, stuffing it with their maroon robes (they had dressed formally for Phil, Charlie noted) and their strong brown faces. They still looked pleased.

"Well?" Charlie said.

"It went very well," Drepung said, and nodded happily. "He asked us many questions about Khembalung. He visited Khembalung seven years ago, and met Padma and others at that time. He was very interested, very...sympathetic. He reminded me of Mr. Clinton in that sense."

Apparently the ex-President had also visited Khemba-lung a few years previously, and had made a big impression.

"And, best of all, he told us he would help us."

"He did? That's great! What did he say, exactly?"

Drepung squinted, remembering: "He said—'I'll see what I can do.'"

Sucandra and Padma nodded, confirming this.

"Those were his exact words?" Charlie asked.

"Yes. 'I'll see what I can do.'"

Charlie and Sridar exchanged a glance. Which one was going to tell them?

Sridar said carefully, "Those were indeed his exact words," thus passing the ball to Charlie.

Charlie sighed.

"What's wrong?" Drepung asked.

"Well..." Charlie glanced at Sridar again.

"Tell them," Sridar said.

Charlie said, "What you have to understand is that no congressperson likes to say no."

"No?"

"No. They don't."

"They never say no," Sridar amplified.

"Never?"

"Never."

"They like to say yes," Charlie explained. "People come to them, asking for things—favors, votes—consideration of one thing or another. When they say yes, people go away happy. Everyone is happy."

"Constituents," Sridar expanded. "Which mean votes, which means their job. They say yes and it means votes. Sometimes one yes can mean fifty thousand votes. So they just keep saying yes."

"That's true," Charlie admitted. "Some say yes no matter what they really mean. Others, like our Senator Chase, are more honest."

"Without, however, ever actually saying no," Sridar added.

"In effect they only answer the questions they can say yes to. The others they avoid in one way or another."

"Right," Drepung said. "But he said..."

"He said, 'I'll see what I can do.'"

Drepung frowned. "So that means no?"

"Well, you know, in circumstances where they can't get out of answering the question in some other way—"

"Yes!" Sridar interrupted. "It means no."

"Well..." Charlie tried to temporize.

"Come on, Charlie." Sridar shook his head. "You know it's true. It's true for all of them. 'Yes' means 'maybe'; 'I'll see what I can do' means 'no.' It means 'not a chance.' It means, 'I can't believe you're asking me this question, but since you are, this is how I will say no.'"

"He will not help us?" Drepung asked.

"He will if he sees a way that will work," Charlie declared. "I'll keep on him about it."

Drepung said, "You'll see what you can do."

"Yes—but I mean that, really."

Sridar smiled sardonically at Charlie's discomfiture. "And Phil's the most environmentally aware senator of all, isn't that right Charlie?"

"Well, yeah. That's definitely true."

The Khembalis pondered this.

VI

THE

CAPITAL

IN

SCIENCE

Robot submarines cruise the depths, doing oceanography. Slocum gliders and other AUVs (autonomous underwater vehicles), like torpedoes with wings, dock in underwater observatories to recharge their batteries and download their data. Finally oceanographers have almost as much data as the meteorologists. Among other things they monitor a deep layer of relatively warm water that flows from the Atlantic into the Arctic. (ALTEX, the Atlantic Layer Tracking Experiment.)

But they are not as good at it as the whales. White beluga whales, living their lives in the open ocean, have been fitted with sensors for recording temperature, salinity and nitrate content, matched with a GPS record and a depth meter. Up and down in the blue world they sport, diving deep into the black realm below, coming back up for air, recording data all the while. Casper the Friendly Ghost, Whitey Ford, The Woman in White, Moby Dick, all the rest: they swim to their own desires, up and down endlessly within their immense territories, fast and supple, continuous and thorough, capable of great depths, pale flickers in the blackest blue, the bluest black. Then back up for air. Our cousins. White whales help us to know this world. The warm layer is attenuating.

THE REST of Frank's stay in San Diego was a troubled time. The encounter with Marta had put him in a black mood that he could not shake.

He tried to look for a place to live when he returned in the fall, and checked out some real estate pages in the paper, but it was discouraging. He saw that he should rent an apartment first, and take the time to look around before trying to buy something. It was going to be hard, maybe impossible, to find a house he both liked and could afford. He had some financial problems. And it took a very considerable income to buy a house in north San Diego these days. He and Marta had bought a perfect couple's bungalow in Cardiff, but they had sold it when they split, adding greatly to the acrimony. Now the region was more expensive than a mere professor could afford. Extra income would be essential.

So he looked at some rentals in North County, and then in the afternoons he went to the empty office on campus, meeting with two postdocs who were still working for him in his absence. He also talked with the department chair about what classes he would teach in the fall. It was all very tiresome.

And worse than that, a letter appeared in his department mailbox from the UCSD Technology Transfer Office, Independent Review Committee. Pulse quickening, he ripped it open and scanned it, then got on the phone to the Tech Transfer Office.

"Hi Delphina, it's Frank Vanderwal here. I've just gotten a letter from the review committee, can you please tell me what this is about?"

"Oh hello, Dr. Vanderwal. Let me see…the oversight committee on faculty outside income wanted to ask you about some income you received from stock in Torrey Pines Generique. Anything over two thousand dollars a year has to be reported, and they didn't hear anything from you."

"I'm at NSF this year, all my stocks are in a blind trust. I don't know anything about it."

"Oh, that's right, isn't it. Maybe…just a second. Here it is. Maybe they knew that. I'm not sure. I'm looking at their memo here…ah. They've been informed you're going to be rejoining Torrey Pines when you get back, and—"

"Wait, what? How the hell could they hear that?"

"I don't know—"

"Because it isn't true! I've been talking to colleagues at Torrey Pines, but all that is private. What could they *possibly* have heard?"

"*I* don't know." Delphina was getting tired of his indignation. No doubt her job put her at the wrong end of a lot of indignation, but that was too bad, because this time he had good cause.

He said, "Come on, Delphina. We went over all this when I helped to start Torrey Pines, and I haven't forgotten. Faculty are allowed to spend up to twenty percent of work time on outside consulting. Whatever I make doing that is mine, it only has to be reported. So even if I did go back to Torrey Pines, what's wrong with that? I wouldn't be joining their board, and I wouldn't use more than twenty percent of my time!"

"That's good—"

"And most of it happens in my head anyway, so even if I *did* spend more time on it, how are you going to know? Are you going to read my mind?"

Delphina sighed. "Of course we can't read your mind. In the end it's an honor system. Obviously. We ask people what's going on when we see things in the financial reports, to remind them what the rules are."

"I don't appreciate the implications of that. Tell the oversight committee what the situation is on my stocks, and ask them to do their research properly before they bother people."

"All right. Sorry about that." She did not seem perturbed.

Frank went out for a walk around the campus. Usually this soothed him, but now he was too upset. Who had told the oversight committee that he was planning to rejoin Torrey Pines? And why? Would somebody at Torrey Pines have made a call? Only Derek knew for sure, and he wouldn't do it.

But others must have heard about it. Or could have deduced his intention after his visit. That had been only a few days before, but enough time had passed for someone to make a call. Sam Houston, maybe, wanting to stay head science advisor?

Or Marta?

Disturbed at the thought, at all these machinations, he found himself wishing he were back in D.C. That was shocking, because when he was in D.C. he was always dying to return to San Diego, biding his time until his return, at which point his real life would recommence. But it was undeniable; here he was in San Diego, and he wanted to be in D.C. Something was wrong.

Part of it must have been the fact that he was not really back in his San Diego life, but only previewing it. He didn't have a home, he was still on leave, his days were not quite full. That left him wandering a bit, as he was now. And that was unlike him.

Okay—what would he do with free time if he lived here?

He would go surfing.

Good idea. His possessions were stowed in a storage unit in the commercial snarl behind Encinitas, so he drove there and got his surfing gear, then returned to the parking lot at Cardiff Reef, at the south end of Cardiff-by-the-Sea. A few minutes' observation while he pulled on his long-john wetsuit (getting too small for him) revealed that an ebb tide and a south swell were combining for some good waves, breaking at the outermost reef. There was a little crowd of surfers and body-boarders out there.

Happy at the sight, Frank walked into the water, which was very cool for midsummer, just as they all said. It never got as warm as it used to. But it felt so good now that he ran out and dove through a broken wave, whooping as he emerged. He sat in the water and floated, pulled on his booties, velcroed the ankle strap of the board cord to him, then took off paddling. The ocean tasted like home.

The whole morning was good. Cardiff Reef was a very familiar break to him, and nothing had changed in all the years he had come here. He had often surfed here with Marta, but that had little to do with it. Although if he did run into her out here, it would be another chance to talk. Anyway the waves were eternal, and Cardiff Reef with its simple point break was like an old friend who always said the same things. He was home. This was what made San Diego his home—not the people or the jobs or the unaffordable houses, but this experience of being in the ocean, which for so many years of his youth had been the central experience of his life, everything else colorless by comparison, all the way up until he had discovered climbing.

As he paddled, caught waves and rode the lefts in long ecstatic seconds, and then worked to get back outside, he wondered again about this strangely powerful feeling of saltwater as home. There must be an evolutionary reason for such joy at being cast forward by a wave. Perhaps there was a part of the brain that predated the split with the aquatic mammals, some deep and fundamental part of mentation that craved the experience. Certainly the cerebellum conserved very ancient brain workings. On the other hand perhaps the moments of weightlessness, and the way one floated, mimicked the uterine months of life, which were then called back to mind when one swam. Or maybe it was a very sophisticated aesthetic response, an encounter with the sublime, as one was constantly falling and yet not dying or even getting hurt, so that the discrepancy in information between the danger signals and the comfort signals was experienced as a kind of triumph over reality.

Whatever; it was a lot of fun. And made him feel vastly better.

Then it was time to go. He took one last ride, and rather than kicking out when the fast part was over, rode the broken wave straight in toward the shore.

He lay in the shallows and let the hissing whitewater shove him around. Back and forth, ebb and flow. For a long time he lolled there. In his childhood and youth he had spent a fair bit of time at the end of every ocean session doing this, "grunioning" he called it; and he had often thought that no matter how much people worked to make more complicated sports in the ocean, grunioning was all you really needed. Now he splayed out and let the water wash him back and forth, feeling the sandy surges lift and push him. Grooming by ocean. As it ran back out to sea the water sifted the fine black flakes in the sand, mixing them into the rounded tan and white grains until they made networks of overlapping black V's. Coursing patterns of nature—

"Are you okay?"

He jerked his head up. It was Marta, on her way out.

"Oh, hi. Yeah I'm okay."

"What's this, stalking me now?"

"No," then realizing it might be a little bit true: *"No!"*

He stared at her, getting angry. She stared back.

"I'm just catching some waves," he said, mouth tight. "You've got no reason to say such a thing to me."

"No? Then why did you ask me out yesterday?"

"A mistake, obviously. I thought it might do some good to talk."

"Last year, maybe. But you didn't want to then. You didn't want to so much that you ran off to NSF instead. Now it's too late. So just leave me alone, Frank."

"I am!"

"Leave me alone."

She turned and ran into the surf, diving onto her board and paddling hard. When she got out far enough she sat up on her board and balanced, looking outward.

Women in wetsuits looked funny, Frank thought as he watched her. Not just the obvious, but also the subtler differences in body morphology were accentuated: the callipygosity, the shorter torso-to-leg ratio, the 0.7 waist-to-hip ratio—whatever it was, it was different, and it drew his eye like a magnet. He could tell the difference from as far away as he could see people at all. Every surfer could.

What did that mean? That he was in thrall to a woman who despised him? That he had messed up the main relationship of his life and his best chance so far for reproductive success? That sexual dimorphism was a powerful driver in the urge to reproduction? That he was a slave to his sperm, and an idiot?

All of the above.

His good mood shattered, he hauled himself to his feet. He stripped off the booties and long john, toweled off at his rental car, drove back up to his storage unit, and dropped off his gear. Returned to his hotel room, showered, checked out, and drove down the coast highway to the airport, feeling like an exile even while he was still here on his own home ground.

Something was deeply wrong.

He checked in the car, robotted through the routines to get him on his plane to Dallas. Sat in a window seat looking down at the view as the plane roared off. Point Loma, the ocean blue from up here, the waves breaking on the coast, perpetually renewing their white tapestry. Bank, turn, Mount Soledad, up through the cloud layer, fly up and east.

He fell asleep. By the time he woke up again they were descending into Dallas. It was strange to watch the process of falling toward the Earth, the buildings and cars like toys at first, quickly growing to real things that sped by. Then standing, disembarking into the big curves of the Dallas airport, on to its rail shuttle, over to another arc, to sit and wait for the plane to D.C.

Grimly he watched America walk by. Who were these people who could live so placidly while the world fell into an acute global environmental crisis? Experts at denial. Experts at filtering their information to hear only what made it seem sensible to behave as they behaved. Many of those walking by went to church on Sundays, believed in God, voted Republican, spent their time shopping and watching TV. Obviously nice people. The world was doomed.

He settled in his next plane seat (on the aisle this time,

because the view didn't matter), feeling more and more disgusted and angry. NSF was part of it; they weren't doing a thing to help. He got out his laptop, turned it on, and called up a new word processing file. He started to write.

Critique of NSF, first draft. Private to Diane Chang.

NSF was established to support basic scientific research, and it is generally given high marks for that. But its budget has never surpassed ten billion dollars a year, in an overall economy of some ten trillion. It is to be feared that as things stand, NSF is simply too small to have any real impact.

Meanwhile humanity is exceeding the planet's carrying capacity for our species, badly damaging the biosphere. Neoclassical economics cannot cope with this situation, and indeed, with its falsely exteriorized costs, was designed in part to disguise it. If the Earth were to suffer a catastrophic anthropogenic extinction event over the next ten years, which it will, American business would continue to focus on its quarterly profit and loss. There is no economic mechanism for dealing with catastrophe. And yet government and the scientific community are not tackling this situation either, indeed both have consented to be run by neoclassical economics, an obvious pseudoscience. We might as well agree to be governed by astrologers.

Everyone at NSF knows this is the situation, and yet no one does anything about it. They don't try to instigate the saving of the biosphere, they don't even call for certain kinds of mitigation projects. They just wait and see what comes in. It is a *ridiculously passive position*.

Why such passivity, you ask? Because NSF is chicken! It's a chicken with its smart little head stuck in the sand like an ostrich! It's a chicken ostrich (fix). It's afraid to take on Congress, it's afraid to take on business, it's afraid to take on the American people. Free market fundamentalists are dragging us back to some dismal feudal eternity and destroying everything in the process, and yet we have the technological means to feed everyone, house everyone, clothe everyone, doctor everyone, educate everyone—the ability to end suffering and want as well as ecological collapse is *right here at hand,* and yet NSF continues to dole out its little grants, fiddling while Rome burns!!!

well whatever nothing to be done about it, I'm sure you're thinking poor Frank Vanderwal has spent a year in the swamp and has gone crazy as a result, and that is true but what I'm saying is still right, the world is in big trouble and NSF is one of the few organizations on Earth that could actually help get it out of trouble, and yet it's not. It should be charting worldwide scientific policy and forcing certain kinds of climate mitigation and biosphere management, *insisting on them* as emergency necessities, it should be working Congress like the fucking NRA to get the budget it deserves, which is a *much bigger budget,* as big as the Pentagon's, really those two budgets should be reversed to get them to their proper level of funding, but none of it is happening or will happen, and that is why I'm not coming back and no one in his right mind would come back either

The plane had started to descend.

Well, it would need a little revision. Mixed metaphors; something was either a chicken or an ostrich, even if in fact it was both. But he could work on it. He had a draft in hand, and he would revise it and then give it to Diane Chang, head of NSF, in the slim hope that it would wake her up.

He hit the SAVE button for the first time in about an hour. The plane turned for its final descent into Ronald Reagan Airport. Soon he would be back in the wasteland of his current life. Back in the swamp.

BACK IN Leo's lab, they got busy running trials of Pierzinski's algorithm, while continuing the ongoing experiments in "rapid hydrodynamic insertion," as it was now called in the emerging literature. Many labs were working on the delivery problem and, crazy as it seemed, this was one of the more promising methods being investigated. A bad sign.

Thus they were so busy on both fronts that they didn't notice at first the results that one of Marta's collaborators was getting with Pierzinski's method. Marta had done her Ph.D. studying the microbiology of certain algae, and she was still coauthoring papers with a postdoc named Eleanor Dufours. Leo had met Eleanor, and then read her papers, and been impressed. Now Marta had introduced Eleanor to a version of Pierzinski's algorithm, and things were going well, Marta said. Leo thought his group might be able to learn some things from their work, so he set up a little brown-bag lunch for Eleanor to give a talk.

"What we've been looking into," Eleanor said that day in her quiet steady voice, very unlike Marta's, "is the algae in certain lichens. DNA histories are making it clear that some lichens are really ancient partnerships of algae and fungus, and we've been genetically altering the algae in one of the oldest, *Cornicularia cornuta.* It grows on trees, and works its way into the trees to a quite suprising degree. We think the lichen is helping the trees it colonizes by taking over the tree's hormone regulation and increasing the tree's ability to absorb lignins through the growing season."

She talked about the possibility of changing their metabolic rates. "Lately we've been trying these algorithms Marta brought over, trying to find symbiotes that speed the lichen's ability to add lignin to the trees."

Evolutionary engineering, Leo thought, shaking his head. His lab was trying to do similar things, of course, but he seldom thought of it that way. He needed to get this outside view to defamiliarize what he did, to see better what was going on.

"Why speed up lignin banking?" Brian wanted to know. "I mean, what use would it be?"

"We've been thinking it might work as a carbon sink."

"How so?"

"Well, you know, people are talking about capturing and sequestering some of the carbon we've put into the atmosphere, in carbon sinks of one kind or other. But no method has looked really good yet. Stimulating plant growth has been one suggestion, but the problem is that most of the plants discussed have been very short-lived, and rotting plant life quickly releases its captured CO_2 back into the atmosphere. So unless you can arrange lots of very deep peat bogs, capturing CO_2 in small plants hasn't looked very effective."

Her listeners nodded.

"So, the thing is, living trees have had hundreds of millions of years of practice in not being eaten and outgassed by bugs. So one possibility would be to grow bigger trees.

That turns out not to be so easy," and with a red marker she sketched a ground and a tree growing out of it on the whiteboard, so that it looked like something a five-year-old would draw. "Sorry. See, most trees are already as tall as they can get, because of physical constraints like soil quali-ties and wind speeds. So, you can make them thicker, or"—drawing more roots under the ground line—"you can make the roots thicker. But trying to do that directly in-volves genetic changes that harm the trees in other ways, and anyway is usually very slow."

"So it won't work," Brian said.

"Right," she said patiently, "but many trees host these lichen, and the lichen regulate lignin production in a way that might be bumped, so the tree would quite quickly cap-ture carbon that would remain sequestered for as long as the tree lived.

"So, given all this, what we've been working on is basi-cally a kind of altered tree lichen. The lichen's photosyn-thesis is accomplished by the algae in it, and we've been using this algorithm of Yann's to find genes that can be al-tered to accelerate that. And now we're getting the lichen to export the excess sugar into its host tree, down in the roots. It seems like we might be able to really accelerate the root growth and girth of the trees that these lichens grow on."

"Capturing like how much carbon?"

"Well, we've calculated different scenarios, with the altered lichen being introduced into forests of different sizes, all the way up to the whole world's temperate forest belt. That one has the amount of CO_2 drawn down in the billions of tons."

"Wow."

"Yes. And pretty quickly too."

"Watch out," Brian joked, "you don't want to be caus-ing an ice age here."

"True. But that would be a problem that came later. And we know how to warm things up, after all. But at this point any carbon capture would be good. There are some really bad effects coming down the pike these days, as you know."

"True."

They all sat and stared at the mess of letters and lines and little tree drawings she had scribbled on the whiteboard.

Leo broke the silence. "Wow, Eleanor. That's very interesting."

"I know it doesn't help you with your delivery problem."

"No, but that's okay, that isn't what you do. This is still very interesting. It's a different problem is all, but that happens. This is great stuff. Have you shown this to the chancellor yet?"

"No." She looked surprised.

"You should. He loves stuff like this, and, you know, he's a working scientist himself. He still keeps his lab going even while he's doing all the chancellor stuff." This gave him credit to burn all over the town's scientific community.

Now Eleanor was nodding. "I'll do that, thanks. He has been very supportive."

"Right. And look, I hope you and Marta keep collaborating. Maybe we can get you here to Torrey Pines. Maybe there's some aspect of hormone regulation you'll spot that we're not seeing."

"Oh I doubt that, but thanks."

Soon after that, Leo got an e-mail from Derek, asking him to attend an appointment with a representative of a venture capital group, to explain the scientific issues. This had happened a few times back when Torrey Pines was a hot new start-up, so Leo knew the drill, and was therefore extremely uncomfortable with the idea of doing it again—especially if it came to a discussion of "rapid hydrodynamic insertion." No way did Leo want to be supporting Derek's unfounded assertions to an outsider.

Derek assured him that he would handle any of this guy's "speculative questions"—exactly the sort of questions a venture capitalist would have to ask.

"And so I'll be there to..."

"You'll be there to answer any technical questions about the method as we're using it now."

Great.

Before the meeting Leo was shown a copy of the executive summary and offering memorandum Derek had sent to Biocal, a venture capital firm that Derek had gotten an investment from in the company's early years. This document was very upbeat about the possibilities of the hydrodynamic delivery method. On finishing it Leo's stomach had contracted to the size of a walnut.

Later that week, on the day of the meeting, Leo drove down from work to Biocal's offices, located in an upscale building in downtown La Jolla, just off Prospect near the point. Their meeting room windows had a great view up the coast. Leo could almost spot their own building, on the cliff across La Jolla Cove.

Their host, Henry Bannet, was a trim man in his forties, relaxed and athletic-looking, friendly in the usual San Diego manner. His firm was a private partnership, doing strategic investing in biotechnologies. A billion dollar fund, Derek had said. And they didn't expect any return on their investments for four to six years, sometimes longer. They could afford to work, or had decided to work, at the pace of medical progress itself. Their game was high-risk, high-return, long-range investment. This was not a kind of investment that banks would make, nor anyone else in the loaning world. The risks were *too* great, the returns *too* distant. Only venture capitalists would do it.

So naturally their help was much in demand from small biotech companies. There were something like three hundred biotechs in the San Diego area alone, and many of them were hanging on by the skin of their teeth, hoping for that first successful cash cow to keep them going or get them bought. Venture capitalists would therefore get to pick and choose what they wanted to invest in; and many of them were pursuing particular interests, or even passions. Naturally in these areas they were very well-informed, expert in combining scientific and financial analysis into what they called "doing due diligence." They spoke of being "value-added investors," of bringing much more than money to the table—expertise, networking, advice.

This guy Bannet looked to Leo to be one of the passionate ones. He was friendly, but intent. A man at work. There was very little chance Derek was going to be able to impress him with smoke and mirrors.

"Thanks for seeing us," Derek said.

Bannet waved a hand. "Always interested to talk to you guys. I've been reading some of your papers, and I went to that symposium in L.A. last year. You're doing some great stuff."

"It's true, and now we're on to something really good, with real potential to revolutionize genetic engineering by getting tailored DNA into people who need it. It could be a method useful to a whole bunch of different therapies, which is one of the reasons we're so excited about it—and trying to ramp up our efforts to speed the process along. So I remembered how much you helped us during the start-up, and how well that's paid off for you, so I thought I'd bring by the current situation and see if you would be interested in doing a PIPE with us."

This sounded weird to Leo, like Indians offering a peace pipe, or college students passing around a bong, but Bannet didn't blink; a PIPE was one of their mechanisms for investment, as Leo quickly learned. "Private Investment in Public Equity." And for once it was a pretty good acronym, because it meant creating a pipeline for money to run directly from their cash-flush fund to Derek's penniless company.

But Bannet was a veteran of all this, alert to all the little strategic opacities that were built into Derek's typical talk to stockholders or potential investors. Something like sixty percent of biotech start-ups failed, so the danger of losing some or all of an investment to bankruptcy was very real. No way Derek could finesse him. They would have to come clean and hope he liked what he saw.

Leo gazed out the window at the foggy Pacific, listening to Derek go on. Unbroken waves wrapped around La Jolla Point and pulsed into the cove. The huge apartment block at the end of La Jolla Point blocked his view west, reminding him that big money could accomplish some unlikely things.

Derek finished leading Bannet through a series of financial spreadsheets on his laptop, unable to disguise their tale of woe. Bad profit and loss; layoffs; sale of some subsidiary contracts, even some patents, their crown jewels; empty coffers.

"We've had to focus on the things that we think are really the most important," Derek admitted. "It's made us more efficient, that's for sure. But it means there really isn't any fat anywhere, no resources we can put to the task, even though it's got such incredible potential. So, it seemed like it was time to ask for some outside funding help, with the idea that the financing now would be so crucial that the returns to the investor could and should be really significant."

"Uh-huh," Bannet said, though it wasn't clear what he was agreeing with. He made thoughtful clucking sounds as he scanned the spreadsheets, murmuring "Um-hmmm, um-hmmm," in a sociable way, but now that he was thinking about the information in the spreadsheets, his face betrayed an almost burning intensity. This guy was definitely one of the passionate ones, Leo saw.

"Tell me about this algorithm," he said finally.

Derek looked to Leo, who said, "Well, the mathematician developing it is a recent hire at Torrey Pines, and he's been collaborating with our lab to test a set of operations he's developed, to see how well they can predict the proteins associated with any given gene, and as you can see"— clicking his own laptop screen to the first of the project report slides—"it's been really good at predicting them in certain situations," pointing to them on the screen's first slide.

"And how would this affect the targeted delivery system you're working on?"

"Well, right now it's helping us to find proteins with ligands that bind better to their receptor ligands in target organ cells. It's also helping us test for proteins that we can more successfully shove across cell walls, using the hydrodynamic methods we've been investigating for the past few months." He clicked ahead to the slide that displayed this work's results, trying to banish Brian's and Marta's names from his mind, he definitely did not want to be calling it the Popping Eyeball Method, the Exploding Mouse Method. "As you can see," pointing to the relevant results, "saturation has been good in certain conditions." This seemed a little weak, and so he added, "The algorithm is also proving to be very successful in guiding work we've been doing with botanists on campus, on algal designs."

"How does that connect with this?"

"Well, it's for plant engineering."

Bannet looked at Derek.

Derek said, "We plan to use it to pursue the improvement of targeted delivery. Clearly the method is robust, and people can use it in a wide variety of applications."

But there was no hiding it, really. Their best results so far were in an area that would not necessarily ever become useful to human medicine. And yet human medicine was what Torrey Pines Generique was organized to do. Biocal also.

"It looks really promising, eh?" Derek said. "It could be that it's an algorithm that is more than just a mathematical exercise, more like a law of nature. The grammar of how genes express themselves. It could mean a whole suite of patents when the applications are all worked out."

"Um-hmmm," Bannet said, looking down again at Derek's laptop, which was still at the financial page. Almost pathetic, really; except it must have been a fairly common story, so that Bannet would not necessarily be shocked or put off. He would simply be considering the investment on a risk-adjusted basis, which would take the present situation into account.

Finally he said, "It looks very interesting. Of course it's always a bit of a sketchy feeling, when you've gotten to the point of having all your eggs in one basket like this. But sometimes one is all you need. The truth is, I don't really know yet."

Derek nodded in reluctant agreement. "Well, you know. We believe very strongly in the importance of therapies for the most serious diseases, and so we concentrated on that, and now we kind of have to, you know, go on from there with our best ideas. That's why we've focused on the HDL upgrade. With this targeted delivery, it could be worth billions."

"And the HDL upgrade..."

"We haven't published yet. We're still looking into the patent situation there."

Leo's stomach tightened, but he kept his face blank.

Bannet was even blanker; still friendly and sympathetic enough, but with that piercing eye. "Send me the rest of your business plan, and all the scientific publications that relate to this. All the data. I'll discuss it with some of my partners here. It seems like the kind of thing that I'd like to get my partners' inputs on. That's not unusual, it's just that it's bigger than what I usually do on my own. And some of my colleagues are into agropharmacy stuff."

"Sure," Derek said, handing over a glossy folder of material he had already prepared. "I understand. We can come back and talk to them too if you like, answer any questions."

"That's good, thanks." Bannet put the folder on the table. With a few more pleasantries and a round of hand-shaking, Derek and Leo were ushered out.

Leo found he had no idea whether the meeting had gone well or poorly. And would that be a good sign or a bad one?

VII

TIT

FOR

TAT

The Earth's atmosphere now contains a percentage of carbon dioxide and other greenhouse gases that is higher than it has been since the end of the Cretaceous. This means more heat from the sun is being trapped in our air, and the high-pressure cells we saw this year are bigger, warmer, and loft higher in the tropical atmosphere. Many common jet-stream patterns have been disrupted, and the storms spiraling out of the Tropics have gained in both frequency and intensity. The hurricane season in the Atlantic ran from April to November, and there were eight hurricanes and six tropical storms. Typhoons in the East Pacific happened all year, twenty-two all told. Mass flooding resulted, but it should be noted that in other regions droughts have been breaking records.

So the effects have been various, but the changes are general and pervasive, and the damage for the year was recently estimated at six hundred billion dollars, with deaths in the thousands. So far the United States has escaped major catastrophe, and attention to the problem has not been one of the administration's central concerns. "In a healthy economy the weather isn't important," the President remarked. But the possibility is there that the added energy in the atmosphere could trigger what climatologists call abrupt climate change. How that might begin, no one can be sure.

A NNA FLEW through the blur of a midweek day. Up and off, Metro to the office; pound the keys, wrestling with some faulty data from an NSF educational outreach program, the spreadsheet work eating up hours like minutes. Stop to pump, then to eat at her desk (it felt a little too weird to eat and pump at the same time), all the while data wrangling. Then a look at an e-mail from Drepung and Sucandra about their grant proposals.

Anna had helped them to write a small raft of proposals, and it had indeed been a pleasure, as they did all the real work—and very well too—while she just added her expertise in grant writing, honed through some tens of thousands of grant evaluations. She definitely knew that world, how to sequence the information, what to emphasize, what language to use, what supporting documents, what arguments—all of it. Every word and punctuation mark of a grant proposal she had a feel for, one way or the other. It had been a pleasure to apply that expertise to the Khembalis' attempts.

Now she was pleased again to find that they had heard

back from three of them, two positively. NSF had awarded them a quick temporary starter grant in the "Tropical Oceans, Global Atmosphere" effort; and the INDOEX countries had agreed informally to expand their Project Asian Brown Cloud (ABC) to include a big new monitoring facility on Khembalung, including researchers. This would cement a partnership with the START units already scattered all over South Asia. Altogether it meant funding streams for several years to come—tens of millions of dollars all told, with infrastructure built, and relationships with neighboring countries established. Allies in the struggle.

"Oh that's *very* nice," Anna said, and hit the PRINT button. She cc'd the news to Charlie, sent congratulations to Drepung, and then got back to work on the spreadsheet.

After a while she remembered about the printouts, and went around the corner to the Department of Unfortunate Statistics to get the hard copies.

She found Frank inside, shaking his head over the latest.

"Have you seen this one?" he said, gesturing with his nose at a taped-up printout of yet another spreadsheet.

"No, I don't think so."

"It's the latest Gini figures, do you know those?"

"No?"

"They're a measurement of income distribution in a population, so an index of the gap between rich and poor. Most industrialized democracies rate at between 2.5 and 3.5, that's where we were in the 1950's, see, but our numbers started to shoot up in the 1980's, and now we're worse than the worst third world countries. 4.0 or greater is considered to be very inequitable, and we're at 5.2 and rising."

Anna looked briefly at the graph, interested in the statistical method. A Lorenz curve, plotting the distance away from perfect equality's straight line tilted at forty-five degrees.

"Interesting... So this is for annual incomes?"

"That's right."

"So if it were for capital holdings—"

"It would be worse, I should think. Sure." Frank shook his head, disgusted. He had come back from San Diego in a permanently foul mood. No doubt anxious to finish and go home.

"Well," Anna said, looking at her printout, "maybe the Khembalis aren't so bad off after all."

"How's that?"

Anna showed him the pages. "They've gotten a couple grants. It'll make them some good contacts."

"Very nice, did you do this?" Frank took the pages.

"I just pointed them at things. They're turning out to be good at following through. And I helped Drepung rewrite the grant proposals. You know how it is, after doing this job for a few years you do know how to write a grant proposal."

"No lie. Nice job." He handed the pages back to her. "Good to see someone doing *something*."

Anna returned to her desk, glancing after him. He was definitely edgy these days. He had always been that way, of course, ever since the day he arrived. Dissatisfied, cynical, sharp-tongued; it was hard not to contrast him to the Khembalis. Here he was, about to go home to one of the best departments in one of the best universities in one of the nicest cities in the world's richest country, and he was unhappy. Meanwhile the Khembalis were essentially multigenerational exiles, occupying a tidal sandbar in near poverty, and they were happy.

Or at least cheerful. She did not mean to downplay their situation, but these days she never saw that unhappy look that had so struck her the first time she had seen Drepung.

No, they were cheerful, which was different than happy; a policy perhaps, rather than a feeling. But that only made it more admirable.

Well, everyone was different. She got back to the tedious grind of changing data. Then Drepung called, and they shared the pleasure of the good news about the grant proposals. They discussed the details, and then Drepung said, "We have you to thank for this, Anna. So thank you."

"You're welcome, but it wasn't really me, it's the Foundation and all the other organizations."

"But you are the one who piloted us through the maze. We owe you big time."

Anna laughed despite herself.

"What?"

"Nothing, it's just that you sound like Charlie. You sound like you've been watching sports on TV."

"I do like watching basketball, I must admit."

"That's fine. Just don't start listening to that rap music okay? I don't think I could handle that."

"I won't. You know me, I like Bollywood. Anyway, you must let us thank you somehow for this. We will have you to dinner."

"That would be nice."

"And maybe you can join us at the zoo when our tigers arrive. Recently a pair of Bengal tigers were rescued off Khembalung after a flood. The papers in India call them the Swimming Tigers, and they are coming for a stay at the National Zoo here. We will have a small ceremony when they arrive."

"That would be great. The boys would love that. And also—" An idea had occurred to her.

"Yes?"

"Maybe you could come upstairs and visit us here, and give one of our lunchtime lectures. That would be a great way to return a favor. We could learn more about your situation, and, you know, your approach to science, or to life, or whatever. Something like that. Do you think Rudra would be interested?"

"I'm sure he would. It would be a great opportunity."

"Well not exactly, it's just a lunchtime series of talks that Aleesha runs, but I do think it would be interesting. We could use some of your attitude here, I think, and you could talk about these programs too, if you wanted."

"I'll talk to the rimpoche about it."

"Okay good. I'll put Aleesha in touch."

After that Anna worked on the stats again, until she saw the time and realized it was her day to visit Nick's class and help them with math hour. "Ah shit." Throw together a bag of work stuff, shut down, heft the shoulder bag of chilled milk bottles, and off she went. Down into the Metro, working as she sat, then standing on the crowded Red Line, Shady Grove train; out and up and into a taxi, of all things, to get to Nick's school on time.

She arrived just a little late, dumped her stuff, and settled down to work with the kids. Nick was in third grade now, but had been put in an advanced math group. In general the class did things in math that Anna found surprising for their age. She liked working with them; there were twenty-eight kids in the class, and Mrs. Wilkins, their teacher, was grateful for the help.

Anna wandered from group to group, helping with multipart problems that involved multiplication, division, and rounding off. When she came to Nick's group she sat down on one of the tiny chairs next to him, and they elbowed each other playfully for room at the round low table. He loved it when she came to his class, which she had tried to do on a semiregular basis every year since he had started school.

"All right Nick quit that, show the gang here how you're going to solve this problem."

"Okay." He furrowed his brow in a way she recognized inside the muscles of her own forehead. "Thirty-nine divided by two, that's . . . nineteen and a half . . . round that up to twenty—"

"No, don't round off in the middle of the process."

"Mom, come on."

"Hey, you shouldn't."

"Mom, you're quibbling again!" Nick exclaimed.

The group cackled at this old joke.

"It's not quibbling," Anna insisted. "It's a very important distinction."

"What, the difference between nineteen and a half and twenty?"

"Yes," over their squeals of laughter, "*because* you should never round off in the middle of an operation, because then the things you do later will exaggerate the inaccuracy! It's an *important principle*!"

"Mrs. Quibler is a quibbler, Mrs. Quibler is a quibbler!"

Anna gave in and gave them The Eye, a squinting, one-eyed glare that she had worked up long ago when playing Lady Bracknell in high school. It never failed to crack them up. She growled, "That's Quibler *with one b*," melting them with laughter, as always, until Mrs. Wilkins came over to join the party and quiet it down.

After school Anna and Nick walked home together. It took about half an hour, and was one of the treasured rituals of their week—the only time they got to spend together just the two of them. Past the big public pool where they would go swimming in the summers, past the grocery store, then down their quiet street. It was hot, of course, but bearable in the shade. They talked about whatever came into their heads.

Then they entered the coolness of their house, and returned to the wilder world of Joe and Charlie. Charlie was bellowing as he cooked in the kitchen, an off-key, wordless aria. Joe was killing dinosaurs in the living room. As they entered he froze, considering how he was going to signify his displeasure at Anna's treasonous absence for the day. When younger this had been a genuine emotion, and sometimes when he saw her come in the door he had simply burst into tears. Now it was calculated, and she was immune.

He smacked himself in the forehead with a compsognathus, then collapsed to the rug face first.

"Oh come on," Anna said. "Give me a break Joe." She started to unbutton her blouse. "You better be nice if you want to nurse."

Joe popped right up and ran over to give her a hug.

"Right," Anna said. "Blackmail will get you everywhere. Hi hon!" she yelled in at Charlie.

"Hi babe." Charlie came out to give her a kiss. For a second all her boys hung on her. Then Joe was latched on, and Charlie and Nick went into the kitchen. From there Charlie shouted out from time to time, but Anna couldn't yell back without making Joe mad enough to bite her, so she waited until he was done and then walked around the corner into the kitchen.

"How was your day?" Charlie said.

"I fixed a data error all day long."

"That's good dear."

She gave him a look. "I swore I wasn't going to do it," she said darkly, "but I just couldn't bring myself to ignore it."

"No, I'm sure you couldn't."

He kept a straight face, but she punched him on the arm anyway. "Smartass. Is there any beer in the fridge?"

"I think so."

She hunted for one. "There was some good news that came in, did you see that? I forwarded it. The Khembalis got a couple of grants."

"Really! That is good news." He was sniffing at a yellow curry bubbling in the frying pan.

"Something new?"

"Yeah, I'm trying something out of the paper."

"You're being careful?"

He grinned. "Yeah, no blackened redfish."

"Blackened redfish?" Nick repeated, alarmed.

"Don't worry, even I wouldn't try it on you."

"He wouldn't want you to catch fire."

"Hey, it was in the recipe. It was right out of the recipe!"

"So? A tablespoon each of black pepper, white pepper, cayenne *and* chili powder?"

"How was I supposed to know?"

"What do you mean, you use pepper. You should have known what a tablespoon of pepper would taste like, and that was the least hot of them."

"I guess I didn't know it would all stick to the fish."

Nick was looking appalled. "I wouldn't eat that."

"You aren't kidding." Anna laughed. "One touch with your tongue and you would spontaneously combust."

"It was in a cookbook."

"Even going in the kitchen the next day was enough to burn your eyes out."

Charlie was giggling at his folly, holding the stirring spoon down to Nick to gross him out, although now he had a very light touch with the spices. The curry would be fine. Anna left him to it and went out to play with Joe.

She sat down on the couch, relaxed. Joe began to pummel her knees with blocks, babbling energetically. At the same time Nick was telling her something about something. She had to interrupt him, almost, to tell him about the coming of the Swimming Tigers. He nodded and took off again with his account. She heaved a great sigh of relief, took a sip of the beer. Another day flown past like a dream.

ANOTHER HEAT wave struck, the worst so far. People had thought it was hot before, but now it was July, and one day the temperature in the metropolitan area climbed to 105 degrees, with the humidity over ninety percent. The combination had all the Indians in town waxing nostalgic about Uttar Pradesh just before the monsoon broke, "Oh very much yes, just like this in Delhi, actually it would be a blessing if it were to be like this in Delhi, it would be a great improvement over what they have now, third year of drought you see, they are needing the monsoon to be coming very badly."

The morning *Post* included an article informing Charlie that a chunk of the Ross Ice Shelf had broken off, a chunk more than half the size of France. The news was buried in the last pages of the international section. So many pieces of Antarctica had fallen off that it wasn't big news anymore.

It wasn't big news, but it was a big iceberg. Researchers joked about moving onto it and declaring it a new nation. It contained more fresh water than all the Great Lakes combined. It had come off near a Roosevelt Island, a low black rock that had been buried under the ice and known only to radar probes, and so was exposed to the air for the first time in either two or fifteen million years, depending on which research team you believed. Although it might not be exposed for long; pouring down toward it, researchers said, was the rapid ice of the West Antarctic Ice Sheet, unimpeded now that the Ross Shelf in that region had embarked, and therefore moving faster than ever.

This accelerated flow of ice toward the sea had big ramifications. The West Antarctic Ice Sheet was much bigger than the Ross Ice Shelf, and had been resting on ground that was below sea level but that held the ice much higher than it would have been if it had been floating freely in the ocean. So when it broke up and sailed away, it would displace more ocean water than it had before.

Charlie read on, feeling somewhat amazed that he was learning this in the back pages of the *Post*. How fast could this happen? The researchers didn't appear to know. As the sheet broke away, they said, seawater was lifting the edges of the ice still resting on the bottom, deeper and deeper at every tide, tugging with every current, and thus beginning to tear the sheet apart in big vertical cracks, and launch it out to sea.

Charlie checked this on the web, and watched one trio of researchers explain on camera that it could become an accelerating process, their words likewise accelerating a bit, as if to illustrate how it would go. Modeling inconclusive because the sea bottom under the grounded ice irregular, they said, with active volcanoes under it, so who knew? But it very well might happen fast.

Charlie heard in their voices the kind of repressed delirium of scientific excitement that he had heard once or twice when listening to Anna talk about some extraordinary thing in statistics that he had not even been able to understand. This, however, he understood. They were saying that the possibility was very real that the whole mass of the West Antarctic Ice Sheet would break apart and float away, each giant piece of it then sinking more deeply into the water, thus displacing more water than it had when grounded in place—so much more that sea level worldwide could rise by an eventual total of about seven meters. "This could happen fast," one glaciologist emphasized, "and I'm not talking geology fast here, I'm talking tide fast. A matter of several years in some simulations." The hard thing to pinpoint was whether it would start to accelerate or not. It depended on variables programmed into the models—on they went, the usual kind of scientist talk.

And yet the *Post* had it at the back of the international section! People were talking about it the same way they did any other disaster. There did not seem to be any way to register a distinction in response between one coming catastrophe and another. They were all bad. If it happened it happened. That seemed to be the way people were processing it. Of course the Khembalis would have to be extremely concerned. The whole League of Drowning Nations, for that matter. Meaning everyone. Charlie had done enough research on the tidal power stuff, and other coastal issues, to give him a sharpened sense that this was serious, and perhaps the tipping point into something worse. All of a sudden it coalesced into a clear vision standing before him, and what he saw frightened him. Twenty percent of humanity lived on the coast. He felt like he had one time driving in winter when he had taken a turn too fast and hit an icy patch he hadn't seen, and the car had detached and he found himself flying forward, free of friction or even gravity, as if sideslipping in reality itself.

But it was time to go downtown. He was going to take Joe with him to the office. He pulled himself together, got out the stroller so they would spare each other their body heat. Life had to go on; what else could he do?

Out they ventured into the steambath of the capital. It really didn't feel that much different than the ordinary summer day. As if the sensation of heat hit an upper limit where it just blurred out. Joe was seatbelted into his stroller like a NASCAR driver, so that he would not launch himself out at inopportune moments. Naturally he did not like this and he objected to the stroller because of it, but Charlie had decorated its front bar as an airplane cockpit dashboard, which placated Joe enough that he did not persist in his howls or attempts to escape. "Resistance is futile!"

They took the elevators in the Metro stations and came up on the Mall, to stroll over to Phil's office in the old carpenters' union. A bad idea, as crossing the Mall was like being blanched in boiling air. Charlie, as always, experienced the climate deviation with a kind of grim "I Told You So" satisfaction. But once again he resolved to quit eating boiled lobsters. It would be a bad way to go.

At Phil's they rolled around the rooms trying to find the best spots in the falls of chilled air pouring from the air-conditioning vents. Everyone was doing this, drifting around like a science museum exercise investigating the Coriolis force.

Charlie parked Joe out with Evelyn, who loved him, and went to work on Phil's revisions to the climate bill. It certainly seemed like a good time to introduce it. More money for CO_2 remediation, new fuel efficiency standards and the money to get Detroit through the transition to hydrogen, new fuels and power sources, carbon capture methods, carbon sink identification and formation, hydrocarbon-to-carbohydrate-to-hydrogen conversion funds and exchange credit programs, deep geothermal, tide power, wave power, money for basic research in climatology, money for the Extreme Global Research in Emergency Salvation

Strategies project (EGRESS), money for the Global Disaster Information Network (GDIN)—and so on and so forth. It was a grab bag of programs, many designed to look like pork to help the bill get the votes, but Charlie had done his best to give the whole thing organization, and a kind of coherent shape, as a narrative of the near future.

There were many in Phil's office who thought it was a mistake to try to pass an omnibus or comprehensive bill like this, rather than get the programs funded one by one, or in smaller related groupings. But the comprehensive had been Phil's chosen strategy, and Charlie felt that at this late point it was better to stick to that plan. He added language to make the revisions Phil wanted, pushing the envelope in each case, as it seemed now, if ever, was the time to strike.

Joe was beginning to get rowdy with Evelyn, he could hear the unmistakable sound of dinosaurs hitting walls. All this language would get chopped up anyway; still, all the more reason to get it precise and smooth, armored against attack, low-keyed and unobjectionable, invisibly effective. Bill language as low-post moves to the basket, subtle, quick, unstoppable.

He rushed to a finish and took the revised bill in to Phil, with Joe leading the way in his stroller. They found the senator sitting with his back directly against an air-conditioning duct.

"Jeez Phil, don't you get *too* cold sitting there?"

"The trick is to set up before you're all sweaty, and then you don't get the evaporative cooling. And I keep my head above it," banging the wall with the back of his noggin, "so I don't catch as many a-c colds. I learned that a long time ago, when I was stationed on Okinawa."

He glanced over Charlie's new revision, and they argued over some of the changes. At one point Phil looked at him: "Something bugging you today?" He glanced over at Joe.

"Joe here seems to be grooving. The President's favorite toddler."

"It's not Joe that's getting to me, it's you. You and the rest of the Senate. This is it, Phil—the current situation *requires* a response that is more than business as usual. And that's worrying me, because you guys are only geared to do business as usual."

"Well..." Phil smiled. "We call that democracy, youth. It's a blessing when you think of it. Some give and take, and then some agreement on how to proceed. How can we do without that? There's a certain accountability to it. So if you have a better way of doing it you tell me. But please, meanwhile, no more 'If I Were King' fantasies. There's no king and it's up to us. So help me get this final draft as tight as we can."

"Okay."

They worked together with the speed and efficiency of old teammates. Sometimes collaboration could be a pleasure, sometimes it really was a matter of only having to do half of it, and the two halves adding up to more than their parts.

Then Joe got restive, and nothing would keep him in his stroller but a quick departure and a tour of the street scene. "I'll finish," Phil said.

So, back out into the stupendous heat. Charlie was knocked out by it faster than Joe. The world melted around them. Charlie gumbied along, leaning on the stroller for support. Down an elevator into the Metro. Air-conditioning again, thank God. Crash into pink seat cushions. As they rode north, slumped and rocking slightly with their train, Charlie drowsily entertained Joe with some of the toys in the stroller, picking them up and fingering them one by one. "See, this turtle is NIH. Your Frankenstein monster is the FDA, look how poorly he's put together. This little mole, that's Mom's NSF. These two guys, they're like the guy on the Monopoly game, they must be the two parts of Congress, yeah, very Tammany Hall. Where the hell did you get those. Your Iron Giant is of course the Pentagon, and this yellow bulldozer is the U.S. Army Corps of Engineers. The magnifying glass is the GAO, and this, what is it, like Barbie? That must be the OMB, those bimbos, or maybe this Pinocchio here. And your cowboy on a horse is the President of course, he's your friend, he's your friend, he's your friend."

They were both falling asleep. Joe batted the toy figures into a pile.

"Careful Joe. Ooh, there's your tiger. That's the press corps, that's a circus tiger, see its collar? Nobody's scared of it. Although sometimes it does get to eat somebody."

In the days that followed, Phil took the climate bill back to the Foreign Relations Committee, and the process of marking it up began in earnest. "To mark up" was a very inadequate verb to express the process: "carving," "rendering," "hacking," "hatcheting," "stomping," any of these would have been more accurate, Charlie thought as he tracked the gradual deconstruction of the language of the bill, the result turned slowly into a kind of sausage of thought.

The bill lost parts as they duked it out. Winston fought every phrase of it, and he had to be given some things or nothing would proceed. No precisely spelled-out fuel efficiencies, no acknowledgment of any measurements like the ecological footprint. Phil gave on these because Winston was promising that he would get the House to agree to this version in conference, and the White House would back him too. And so entire methodologies of analysis were being declared off-limits, something that would drive Anna crazy. Another example of science and capital clashing,

Charlie thought. Science was like Beeker from the Muppets, haplessly struggling with the round top-hatted guy from the Monopoly game. Right now Beeker was getting his butt kicked.

Two mornings later Charlie learned about it in the *Post* (and how irritating was that?):

CLIMATE SUPERBILL SPLIT UP IN COMMITTEE

"Say *what*!" Charlie cried. He hadn't even heard of the possibility of such a maneuver.

He read paragraphs per eye-twitch while he got on the phone and told it to call Roy:

> *...proponents of the new bills claimed compromises would not damage effectiveness...President made it clear he would veto the comprehensive bill...promised to sign specific bills on a case-by-case if and when they came to his desk.*

"Ah shit. *Shit.* God damn it!"

"Charlie, that must be you."

"Roy what is this shit, when did this happen?"

"Last night. Didn't you hear?"

"No I didn't! How could Phil do this!"

"We counted votes, and the biggie wasn't going to get out of committee. And if it did, the House wasn't going to go for it. Winston couldn't deliver, or wouldn't. So Phil decided to support Ellington on Ellington's alternative-fuels bill, and he made sure they put more of Ellington's stuff in the first several shorter bills."

"And Ellington agreed to vote for it on that basis."

"That's right."

"So Phil traded horses."

"The comprehensive was going to lose."

"You don't know that for sure! They had Speck with them and so they could have carried it on party lines! Who cares what kind of fuel we're burning if the world has melted! This was *important,* Roy!"

"It wasn't going to win," Roy said, enunciating each word. "We counted the votes and it lost by one. After that we went for what we could. You know Phil. He likes to get things done."

"As long as they're easy."

"You're still pissed off about this. You should go talk to Phil yourself, maybe it will impact what he does next time. I've got to get to a meeting uptown."

"Okay maybe I'll do that."

And as it was another morning of Joe and Dad on the town, he was free to do so. He sat on the Metro, absorbing Joe's punches and thinking things over, and when he got the stroller out of the elevator on the third floor of the office he drove it straight for Phil, who today was sitting on a desk in the outer conference room, holding court as blithe and bald-faced as a monkey.

Charlie aimed the wadded *Post* like a stick at Phil, who saw him and winced theatrically. "Okay!" he said, palm held out to stop the assault. "Okay kick my ass! Kick my ass right here! But I'll tell you right now that they made me do it."

He was turning it into another office debate, so Charlie went for it full bore. "What do you mean they made you do it? You caved, Phil. You gave away the store!"

Phil shook his head vehemently. "I got more than I gave. They're going to have to reduce carbon emissions anyway, we were never going to get much more from them on that—"

"What do you mean!" Charlie shouted.

Andrea and some of the others came out of their

rooms, and even Evelyn looked in, though mostly to say hi to Joe. It was a regular schtick: Charlie hammering Phil for his compromises, Phil admitting to all and baiting Charlie to ever greater outrage. Charlie, recognizing this, was still determined to make his point, even if it meant he had to play his usual part. Even if he didn't convince Phil himself, if Phil's group here would bear down on him a little harder...

Charlie whacked Phil with the *Post*. "If you would have stuck to your guns we could have sequestered *billions of tons* of carbon. The whole world's with us on this!"

Phil made a face. "I would have stuck to my guns, Charlie, but then the rest of our wonderful party would have shot me in the foot with those guns. The House wasn't there either. This way we got what was possible. We got it out of committee, damn it, and that's not peanuts. We got out with the full roadless forest requirement and the Arctic refuge and the offshore drilling ban, all of those, and the President has promised to sign them already."

"They were always gonna give you those! You would have had to have *died* not to get those. Meanwhile you gave up on the really crucial stuff! They played you like a fish."

"Did not."

"Did too."

"Did not."

"Did too!"

Yes, this was the level of debate in the offices of one of the greatest senators in the land. It always came down to that between them.

But this time Charlie wasn't enjoying it like he usually did. "What *didn't* you give up," he said bitterly.

"Just the forests streams and oil of North America!"

Their little audience laughed. It was still a debating society to them. Phil licked his finger and chalked one up, then smiled at Charlie, a shot of the pure Chase grin, fetching and mischievous.

Charlie was unassuaged. "You'd better fund a bunch of submarines to enjoy all those things."

That too got a laugh. And Phil chalked one up for Charlie, still smiling.

Charlie pushed Joe's stroller out of the building, cursing bitterly. Joe heard his tone of voice and absorbed himself in the passing scene and his dinosaurs. Charlie pushed him along, sweating, feeling more and more discouraged. He knew he was taking it too seriously, he knew that Phil's house style was to treat it as a game, to keep taking shots and not worry too much. But still, given the situation, he couldn't help it. He felt as if he had been kicked in the stomach.

This didn't happen very often. He usually managed to find some way to compensate in his mind for the various reversals of any political day. Bright side, silver lining, eventual revenge, whatever. Some fantasy in which it all came right. So when discouragement did hit him, it struck home with unaccustomed force. It became a global thing for which he had no defense; he couldn't see the forest for the trees, he couldn't see the good in anything. The black clouds had black linings. All bad! Bad bad bad bad bad bad bad.

He pushed into a Metro elevator, descended with Joe into the depths. They got on a car, came to the Bethesda stop. Charlie zombied them out. Bad, bad, bad. Sartrean nausea, induced by a sudden glimpse of reality; horrible that it should be so. That the true nature of reality should be so awful. The blanched air in the elevator was unbreathable. Gravity was too heavy.

Out of the elevator, onto Wisconsin. Bethesda was too dismal. A spew of office and apartment blocks, obviously organized (if that was the word) for the convenience of the cars roaring by. A ridiculous, inhuman autopia. It might as well have been Orange County.

He dragged down the sidewalk home. Walked in the front door. The screen door slapped behind him with its characteristic whack.

From the kitchen: "Hi hon!"

"Hi Dad!"

It was Anna and Nick's day to come home together after school.

"Momma Momma Momma!"

"Hi Joe!"

Refuge. "Hi guys," Charlie said. "We need a rowboat. We'll keep it in the garage."

"Cool!"

Anna heard his tone of voice and came out of the kitchen with a whisk in hand, gave him a hug and a peck on the cheek.

"Hmm," he said, a kind of purr.

"What's wrong babe."

"Oh, everything."

"Poor hon."

He began to feel better. He released Joe from the stroller and they followed Anna into the kitchen. As Anna picked up Joe and held him on her hip while she continued to cook, Charlie began to shape the story of the day in his mind, to be able to tell her about it with all its drama intact.

After he had told the story, and fulminated for a bit, and opened and drunk a beer, Anna said, "What you need is some way to bypass the political process."

"Whoa babe. I'm not sure I want to know what you mean there."

"I don't know anyway."

"Revolution, right?"

"No way."

"A completely nonviolent and successful positive revolution?"

"Good idea."

Nick appeared in the doorway. "Hey Dad, want to play some baseball?"

"Sure. Good idea."

Nick seldom proposed this, it was usually Charlie's idea, and so when Nick did it he was trying to make Charlie feel better, which just by itself worked pretty well. So they left the coolness of the house and played in the steamy backyard, under the blind eyes of the banked apartment windows. Nick stood against the brick back of the house while Charlie pitched wiffle balls at him, and he smacked them with a long plastic bat. Charlie tried to catch them if he could. They had about a dozen balls, and when they were scattered over the downsloping lawn, they re-collected them on Charlie's mound and did it over again, or let Charlie take a turn at bat. The wiffle balls were great; they shot off the bat with a very satisfying plastic *whirr*, and yet it was painless to get hit by one, as Charlie often learned. Back and forth in the livid dusk, sweating and laughing, trying to get a wiffle ball to go straight.

Charlie took off his shirt and sweated into the sweaty air. "Okay here comes the pitch. Sandy Koufax winds up, rainbow curve! Hey why didn't you swing?"

"That was a ball, Dad. It bounced before it got to me."

"Okay here I'll try again. Oh Jesus. Never mind."

"Why do you say Jesus, Dad?"

"It's a long story. Okay here's another one. Hey, why didn't you swing?"

"It was a ball!"

"Not by much. Walks won't get you off de island mon."

"The strike zone is taped here to the house, Dad. Just throw one that would hit inside it and I'll swing."

"That was a bad idea. Okay, here you go. Ooh, very nice. Okay, here you go. Hey come on swing at those!"

"That one was *behind me.*"

"Switch-hitting is a valuable skill."

"Just throw strikes!"

"I'm trying. Okay here it comes, boom! Very nice! Home run, wow. Uh-oh, it got stuck in the tree, see that?"

"We've got enough anyway."

"True, but look, I can get a foot onto this branch... here, give me the bat for a second. Might as well get it while we remember where it is."

Charlie climbed a short distance up the tree, steadied himself, brushed leaves aside, reached in and embraced the trunk for balance, knocked the wiffle ball down with Nick's bat.

"There you go!"

"Hey Dad, what's that vine growing up into the tree? Isn't that poison ivy?"

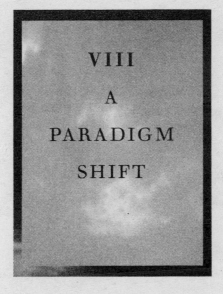

VIII

A

PARADIGM

SHIFT

L et's rehearse what we know about who we are. We are primates, very closely related to chimps and other great apes. Our ancestors speciated from the other apes about five million years ago, and evolved in parallel lines and overlapping subspecies, emerging most clearly as hominids about two million years ago.

East Africa in this period was getting drier and drier. The forest was giving way to grassland savannahs dotted with scattered groves of trees. We evolved to adapt to that landscape: the hairlessness, the upright posture, the sweat glands, and other physical features. They all made us capable of running long distances in the open sun near the equator. We ran for a living and covered broad areas. We used to run game down by following it until it tired out, sometimes days later.

In that basically stable mode of living the generations passed, and during the many millennia that followed, the size of hominid brains evolved from about three hundred cubic millimeters to about nine hundred cubic millimeters. This is a strange fact, because everything else remained relatively stable. The implication is that the way we lived then was tremendously stimulating to the growth of the brain. Almost every aspect of hominid life has been proposed as the main driver of *this growth, everything from the calculation of accurate rock throwing to the ability to dream, but certainly among the most important must have been language and social life. We talked, we got along; it's a difficult process, requiring lots of thought. Because reproduction is crucial to any definition of evolutionary success, getting along with the group and with the opposite sex is fundamentally adaptive, and so it must be a big driver of increasing brain size. We grew so fast we can hardly fit through the birth canal these days. All that growth from trying to understand other people, the other sex, and look where we are.*

ANNA WAS pleased to see Frank back in the office, brusque and grouchy though he was. He made things more interesting. A rant against oversized pickup trucks would morph into an explanation of everything in terms of yes or no, or a discussion of the social intelligence of gibbons, or an algebra of the most efficient division of labor in the lab. It was impossible to predict what he would say next. Sentences would start reasonably and then go strange, or vice versa. Anna liked that.

He did, however, seem overly impressed by game theory. "What if the numbers don't correspond to real life?" she asked him. "What if you don't get five points for defecting when the other person doesn't, what if all those numbers are off, or even backward? Then it's just another computer game, right?"

"Well—" Frank was taken aback. A rare sight. Immediately he was thinking it over. That was another thing Anna liked about him; he would really think about what she said.

Then Anna's phone rang and she picked up.

"Charlie! Oh dovelie, how are you?"

"Screaming agony."

"Oh babe. Did you take your pills?"

"I took them. They're not doing a thing. I'm starting to see things in the corners of my eyes, crawlies you know? I think the itches have gotten into my brain. I'm going nuts."

"Just hold on. It'll take a couple of days for the steroids to have an effect. Keep taking them. Is Joe giving you a break?"

"No. He wants to wrestle."

"Oh God don't let him! I know the doctor said it wasn't transmissible, but still—"

"Don't worry. Not a fucking chance of wrestling."

"You're not touching him?"

"And he's not touching me, that's right. He's getting pretty pissed off about it."

"You're putting on the plastic gloves to change him?"

"Yes yes yes yes, tortures of the damned, when I take them off the skin comes too, blood and yuck, and then I get *so itchy.*"

"Poor babe. Just try not to do anything."

Then he had to chase Joe out of the kitchen. Anna hung up.

Frank looked at her. "Poison ivy?"

"Yep. He climbed into a tree that had it growing up its trunk. He didn't have his shirt on."

"Oh no."

"It got him pretty good. Nick recognized it, and so I took him to urgent care and the doctor put some stuff on him and put him on steroids even before the blistering began, but he's still pretty wiped out."

"Sorry to hear."

"Yeah, well, at least it's something superficial."

Then Frank's phone rang, and he went into his cubicle to answer. Anna couldn't help but hear his end of it, as they had already been talking—and then also, as the call went on, his voice got louder several times. At one point he said "You're kidding" four times in a row, each time sounding more incredulous. After that he only listened for a while, his fingers drumming on the tabletop next to his terminal.

Finally he said, "I don't know what happened, Derek. You're the one who's in the best position to know that.... Yeah, that's right. They must have had their reasons.... Well you'll be okay whatever happens, you were vested right?...Everyone has options they don't exercise, don't think about that, think about the stock you did have.... Hey that's one of the winning endgames. Go under, go public, or get bought. Congratulations.... Yeah it'll be fascinating to see, sure. Sure. Yeah, that is too bad. Okay yeah. Call me back with the whole story when I'm not at work here. Yeah bye."

He hung up. There was a long silence from his cubicle.

Finally he got up from his chair, *squeak-squeak*. Anna swiveled to look, and there he was, standing in her doorway, expecting her to turn.

He made a funny face. "That was Derek Gaspar, out in San Diego. His company Torrey Pines Generique has been bought."

"Oh really! That's the one you helped start?"

"Yeah."

"Well, congratulations then. Who bought it?"

"A bigger biotech called Small Delivery Systems, have you ever heard of it?"

"No."

"I hadn't either. It's not one of the big pharmaceuticals by any means, midsized from what Derek says. Mostly into agropharmacy, he says, but they approached him and made the offer. He doesn't know why."

"They must have said?"

"Well, no. At least he doesn't seem to be clear on why they did it."

"Interesting. So, well—it's still good, right? I mean, I thought this was what start-ups hoped for."

"True…"

"But you're not looking like someone who has just become a millionaire or whatever."

He quickly waved that away, "It's not that, I'm not involved like that. I was only ever a consultant, UCSD only lets you have a small involvement in outside firms. I had to stop even that when I came here. Can't be working for the Feds and someone else too, you know."

"Uh-huh."

"My investments are in a blind trust, so who knows. I didn't have much in Torrey Pines, and the trust may have gotten rid of it. I heard something that made me think they did. I would have if I were them."

"Oh well that's too bad then."

"Yeah yeah," frowning at her. "But that isn't the problem."

He stared out the window, across the atrium into all the other windows. There was a look on his face she had never seen before—chagrined—she couldn't quite read it. Distressed.

"What is then?"

Quietly he said, "I don't know." Then: "The system is messed up."

She said, "You should come to the brown-bag lecture tomorrow. Rudra Cakrin, the Khembali ambassador, is going to be talking about the Buddhist view of science. No, you should. You sound more like them than anyone else, at least sometimes."

He frowned as if this were a criticism.

"No, come on. I want you to."

"Okay. Maybe. If I finish a letter I'm working on."

He went back to his cubicle, sat down heavily. "God damn it," Anna heard him say.

Then he started to type. It was like the sound of thought itself, a rapid-fire plastic tipping and tapping, interrupted by hard *whaps* of his thumb against the space bar. His keyboard really took a pounding sometimes.

He was still typing like a madman when Anna saw her clock and rushed out the door to try to get home on time.

THE NEXT morning Frank drove in with his farewell letter in a manila envelope. He had decided to elaborate on it, make it into a fully substantiated, crushing indictment of NSF, which, if taken seriously, might do some good. He was going to give it directly to Diane Chang. Private letter, one hard copy. That way she could read it, consider it in private, and decide whether she wanted to do something about it. Meanwhile, whatever she did, he would have taken his shot at trying to improve the place, and could go back to real science with a clean conscience. Leave in peace. Leave behind some of the anger in him. Hopefully.

He had heavily revised the draft he had written on the flight back from San Diego. Bulked up the arguments, made the criticisms more specific, made some concrete suggestions for improvements. It was still a pretty devastating indictment when he was done, but this time it was all in the tone of a scientific paper. No getting mad or getting cloquent. Five pages single-spaced, even after he had cut it to the bone. Well, they needed a kick in the pants. This would certainly do that.

He read it through one more time, then sat there in his office chair, tapping the manila envelope against his leg, looking sightlessly out into the atrium. Wondering, among other things, what had happened to Torrey Pines Generique. Wondering if the hire of Yann Pierzinski had anything to do with it.

Suddenly he heaved out of his chair, walked to the elevators with the manila envelope and its contents, took an elevator up to the twelfth floor. Walked around to Diane's office and nodded to Laveta, Diane's secretary. He put the envelope in Diane's in-box.

"She's gone for today," Laveta told him.

"That's all right. Let her know when she comes in tomorrow that it's there, will you? It's personal."

"All right."

Back to the sixth floor. He went to his chair and sat down. It was done.

He heard Anna in her office, typing away. Her door was closed, so presumably she was using her electric breast pump to milk herself while she was working. Frank would have liked to have seen that, not just for prurient reasons, though there were those too, but more for the pleasure of seeing her multitasking like that. She typed with forefingers and thumbs only, like a 1930's reporter in the movies; whether this was an unconscious rejection of all secretarial skills or simply happenstance, he couldn't say. But he bet it made for an attractive sight.

He recalled that this was the day she wanted him to join her at the brown-bag lecture. She had apparently helped to arrange for the Khembali ambassador to give the talk. Frank had seen it listed on a sheet announcing the series, posted next to the elevators:

"Purpose of Science from the Buddhist Perspective."

It didn't sound promising to him. Esoteric at best, and perhaps much worse. That would not be atypical for these lunch talks, they were a very mixed bag. People were burnt out on regular lectures, the last thing they wanted to do at lunch was listen to more of the same, so this series was deliberately geared toward entertainment. Frank remembered seeing titles like "Antarctica as Utopia," or "The Art of Body Imaging," or "Ways Global Warming Can Help Us." Apparently it was a case of the wackier the topic, the bigger the crowd.

This one would no doubt be well-attended.

Anna's door opened and Frank's head jerked up, reflexively seeking the sight of a bare-chested science goddess, something like the French figure of Liberty; but of course not. She was just leaving for the lecture.

"Are you going to come?" she asked.

"Yeah sure."

That pleased her. He accompanied her to the elevators, shaking his head at her, and at himself. Up to the tenth floor, past the spectacular Antarctic underwater photo gallery, into the big conference room. It held about two hundred people. By the time the Khembalis arrived, every seat was occupied.

Frank sat down near the back, pretending to work on his hand pad. Air-conditioned air fell on him like a blessing. People who knew each other were finding each other, sitting down in groups, talking about this and that. The Khembalis stood by the lectern, discussing mike arrangements with Anna and Laveta. The old ambassador, Rudra Cakrin, wore his maroon robes, while the rest of the Khembali contingent were in off-white cotton pants and shirts, as if in India. Rudra Cakrin needed his mike lowered. His young assistant helped him, then adjusted his own. Translation; what a pain. Frank groaned soundlessly.

They tested the mikes, and the noise of talk dampened. The room was impressively full, Frank had to admit, wacky factor or not. These were people still interested enough in ideas to spend a lunch hour listening to a lecture on the philosophy of science. It would be like that in some departments at UCSD, perhaps even on most university campuses, despite the insane pace of life. Surplus time and energy, given over to curiosity: a fundamental hominid behavioral trait. The basic trait that got people into science, that made science in the first place, surviving despite the mind-numbing regimes of its modern-day expression. Here he was himself, after all, and no one could be more burnt out and disenchanted than he was. But still following a tropism helplessly, like a sunflower turning to look at the sun.

The old monk cut quite a figure up at the lectern. Incongruous at best. This might be an admirably curious audience, but it was also a skeptical gang of hardened old technocrats. A tough sell, one would think, for a wizened man in robes, now peering out at them as if from a distant century, looking in fact quite like an early hominid.

And yet there he stood, and here they sat. Something had brought them together, and it wasn't just the air-conditioning. They sat in their chairs, attentive, courteous, open to suggestion. Frank felt a small glimmer of pride. This is how it had all begun, back in those Royal Society meetings in London in the 1660's: polite listening to a lecture by some odd person who was necessarily an autodidact; polite questions; the matter considered reasonably by all in attendance. An agreement to look at things reasonably. This was the start of it.

The old man stared out with a benign gaze. He seemed to mirror their attention, to study them.

"Good morning!" he said, then made a gesture with his hand to indicate that he had exhausted his store of English, except for what followed: "Thank you."

His young assistant then said, "Rimpoche Rudra Cakrin, Khembalung's ambassador to the United States, thanks you for coming to listen to him."

A bit redundant that, but then the old man began to speak in his own language—Tibetan, Anna had said—a low, guttural sequence of sounds. Then he stopped, and the young man, Anna's friend Drepung, began to translate.

"The rimpoche says, Buddhism begins in personal experience. Observation of one's surroundings and one's reactions, and one's thoughts. There is a scientific...foundation to the process. He adds, 'If I truly understand what you mean in the West when you say science.' He says, 'I hope you will tell me if I am wrong about it. But science seems to me to be about what happens that we can all agree on.'"

Now Rudra Cakrin interrupted to ask a question of Drepung, who nodded, then added: "What can be asserted. That if you were to look into it, you would come to agree with the assertion. And everyone else would as well."

A few people in the audience were nodding.

The old man spoke again.

Drepung said, "The things we can agree on are few, and general. And the closer to the time of the Buddha, the more general they are. Now, two thousand and five hundred years have passed, more or less, and we are in the age of the microscope, the telescope, and...the mathematical description of reality. These are realms we cannot experience directly with our senses. And yet we can still agree in what we say about these realms. Because they are linked in long chains of mathematical cause and effect, from what we can see."

Rudra Cakrin smiled briefly, spoke. It began to seem to

Frank that Drepung's translated pronouncements were much longer than the old man's utterances. Could Tibetan be so compact?

"This network is a very great accomplishment," Drepung added.

Rudra Cakrin then sang in a low gravelly voice, like Louis Armstrong's, only an octave lower.

Drepung chanted in English:

> *"He who would understand the meaning of Buddha nature,*
> *Must watch for the season and the causal relations.*
> *Real life is the life of causes."*

Rudra Cakrin followed this with some animated speech. Drepung translated, "This brings up the concept of Buddha nature, rather than nature in itself. What is that difference? Buddha nature is the appropriate... *response* to nature. The reply of the observing mind. Buddhist philosophy ultimately points to seeing reality as it is. And then..."

Rudra Cakrin spoke urgently.

"Then the response, the reply, the human moment— the things we say, and do, and think—that moment arrives. We come back to the realm of the expressible. The nature of reality—as we go deeper, language is left further behind. Even mathematics is no longer germane. But..."

The old man went on for quite some time, until Frank thought he saw Drepung make a gesture or expression with his eyelids, and instantly Rudra Cakrin stopped.

"But, when we come to what we should do, it returns to the simplest of words. Compassion. Right action. Helping others. It always stays that simple. Reduce suffering. There is something... *reassuring* in this. Greatest complexity of what is, greatest simplicity in what we should do. Much preferable to the reverse situation."

Rudra Cakrin spoke in a much calmer voice now.

"Here again," Drepung went on, "the two approaches overlap and are one. Science began as the hunt for food, comfort, health. We learned how things work in order to control them better. In order to reduce our suffering. The methods involved—observation and trial—in our tradition were refined in medical work. That went on for many ages. In the West, your doctors too did this, and in the process, became scientists. In Asia the Buddhist monks were the doctors, and they too worked on refining methods of observation and trial, to see if they could...*reproduce* their successes, when they had them."

Rudra Cakrin nodded, put a hand to Drepung's arm. He spoke briefly. Drepung said, "The two are now parallel studies. On the one hand, science has specialized, through mathematics and technology, on natural observations, finding out what is, and making new tools. On the other, Buddhism has specialized in human observations, to find out—how to become. Behave. What to do. How to go forward. Now, I say, they are like the two eyes in the head. Both necessary to create whole sight. Or rather...there is an old saying: 'Eyes that see, feet that walk.' We could say that science is the eyes, Buddhism the feet."

Frank listened to all this with ever more irritation. Here was a man arguing for a system of thought that had not contributed a single new bit of knowledge to the world for the last twenty-five hundred years, and he had the nerve to put it on an equal basis with science, which was now adding millions of new facts to its accumulated store of knowledge every day. What a farce!

And yet his irritation was filled with uneasiness as well. The young translator kept saying things that weirdly echoed things Frank had thought before, or answered things Frank was wondering at that very moment. Frank thought, for instance, Well, how would all this compute if we were remembering that we are all primates recently off the savan-

nah, foragers with brains that grew to adapt to that particular surrounding—would any of this make sense? And at
that very moment, answering a question from the audience
(they seemed to have shifted into that mode without a formal announcement of it), Drepung said, still translating
the old man:

"We are animals. Animals whose wisdom has extended
so far as to tell us we are mortal creatures. We die. For fifty
thousand years we have known this. Much of our mental
energy is spent avoiding this knowledge. We do not like to
think of it. Then again, we know now that even the cosmos is mortal. Reality is mortal. All things change ceaselessly. Nothing remains the same in time. Nothing can be
held on to. The question then becomes, what do we *do* with
this knowledge? How do we live with it? How do we make
sense of it?"

Well—indeed. Frank leaned forward, piqued, wondering what Drepung would tell them the old man had said
next. That gravelly low voice, growling through its incomprehensible sounds—it was strange to think it was expressing such meanings. Frank suddenly wanted to know what
he was saying.

"One of the scientific terms for compassion," Drepung
said, looking around the ceiling as if for the word, "...you
say, 'altruism.' This is a question in your animal studies.
Does true altruism exist, and is it a good adaptation? Does
compassion work, in other words? You have done studies
that suggest altruism is the best adaptive strategy, if seen
from the group context. This then becomes a kind of...
admonishment. To practice compassion in order to successfully evolve—this, coming from your science, which
claims to be descriptive only! Only describing what has
worked to make us what we are. But in Buddhism we have
always said, if you want to help others, practice compassion; if you want to help yourself, practice compassion.

Now science adds, if you want to help your species, practice compassion."

This got a laugh, and Frank also chuckled. He started to think about it in terms of prisoners' dilemma strategies; it was an invocation for all to make the always generous move, for maximum group return, indeed maximum individual return.... Thus he missed what Drepung said next, absorbed in something more like a feeling than a thought: *If only I could believe in something, no doubt it would be a relief.* All his rationality, all his acid skepticism; suddenly it was hard not to feel that it was really just some kind of disorder.

And at that very moment Rudra Cakrin looked right at him, him alone in all the audience, and Drepung said, "An excess of reason is itself a form of madness."

Frank sat back in his seat. What had the question been? Rerunning his short-term memory, he could not find it.

Now he was lost to the conversation again. His flesh was tingling, as if he were a bell that had been struck.

"The experience of enlightenment can be sudden."

He didn't hear that, not consciously.

"The scattered parts of consciousness occasionally assemble at once into a whole pattern."

He didn't hear that either, as he was lost in thought. All his certainties were trembling. He thought, an excess of reason itself a form of madness—it's the story of my life. And the old man *knew.*

He found himself standing. Everyone else was too. The thing must be over. People were filing out. They were massed in a group at the elevators. Someone said to Frank, "Well, what did you think?" clearly expecting some sharp put-down, something characteristically Frank-ish, and indeed his mouth was forming the words "Not much for twenty-five hundred years of concentrated study." But he said "Not" and stopped, shuddering at his own habits. He could be such an asshole.

The elevator doors opened and rescued him. He flowed in, rubbed his forearms as if to warm them from the conference room's awesome a-c. He said to the inquiring eyes watching him, "Interesting."

There were nods, little smiles. Even that one word, often the highest expression of praise in the scientific tongue, was against type for him. He was making a fool of himself. His group expected him to conform to his persona. That was how group dynamics worked. Surprising people was an unusual thing, faintly unwelcome. Except was it? People certainly paid to be surprised; that was comedy; that was art. It could be proved by analysis. Right now he wasn't sure of anything.

"...paying attention to the real world," someone was saying.

"A weak empiricism."

"How do you mean?"

The elevator door opened; Frank saw it was his floor. He got out and went to his office. He stood there in the doorway looking at all his stuff, scattered about for disposal or for packing to be mailed back west. Piles of books, periodicals, offprints, Xeroxed sheets of stapled or loose paper, folded or rolled graphs and charts and tables and spreadsheets. His exteriorized memory, the paper trail of his life. An excess of reason.

He sat there thinking.

Anna came in. "Hi Frank. How did you like the talk?"

"It was interesting."

She regarded him. "I thought so too. Listen, Charlie and I are having a party for the Khembalis tonight at our place, a little celebration. You should come if you want."

"Thanks," he said. "Maybe I will."

"Good. That would be nice. I've gotta go get ready for it."

"Okay. See you there maybe."

"Okay." With a last curious look, she left.

Sometimes certain images or phrases, ideas or sentences, tunes or snatches of tunes, stick in the head and repeat over and over. For some people this can be a problem, as they get stuck in such loops too often and too long. Most people skip into new ideas or new loops fairly frequently—others at an almost frightening rate of speed, the reverse of the stuck-in-a-loop problem.

Frank had always considered himself to be unstable in this regard, veering strongly either one way or the other. The shift from something like obsessive-compulsive to something like attention-deficit sometimes occurred so quickly that it seemed he might be exhibiting an entirely new kind of bipolarity.

No excess of reason there!

Or maybe that was the base cause of it all. An attempt to gain control. The old monk had looked him right in the eye. An excess of reason is itself a form of madness. Maybe in trying to be reasonable, he had been trying to stay on an even keel. Who could say?

He could see how this might be what Buddhists called a *koan*, a riddle without an answer, which if pondered long enough might cause the thinking mind to balk, and give up thinking. Give up thinking! That was crazy. And yet, in that moment, perhaps the sensory world would come pouring in. Experience of the present, unmediated by language. Unspeakable by definition. Just *felt*. Experienced in mentation of a different sort, languageless, or language-transcendent. Something *other*.

Frank hated that sort of mysticism. Or maybe he loved it; the experience of it, that is. Like anyone who has ever entered a moment of nonlinguistic absorption, he recalled it as a kind of blessing. Like in the old days, hanging there cleaning windows, singing What's my line, I'm happy cleaning windows. Climbing, surfing... you could think far faster than you could verbalize in your mind. No doubt one knew the world by way of a flurry of impressions and thoughts that were far faster than consciousness could track. Consciousness was just a small part of it.

He left the building, went out into the humid afternoon. The sight of the street somehow repelled him. He couldn't drive right now. Instead he walked through the car-dominated, slightly junky commercial district surrounding Ballston, spinning with thoughts and with something more. It seemed to him that he was learning things as he walked that he couldn't have said out loud at that moment, and yet they were real, they were felt; they were quite real.

An excess of reason. Well, but he had always tried to be reasonable. He had tried very hard. That attempt was his mode of being. It had seemed to help him. Dispassionate; sensible; calm; reasonable. A thinking machine. He had loved those stories when he was a boy. That was what a scientist was, and that was why he was such a good scientist. That was the thing that had bothered him about Anna, that she was undeniably a good scientist but she was a passionate scientist too, she threw herself into her work and her ideas, had preferences and took positions and was completely engaged emotionally in her work. She cared which theory was true. That was all wrong, but she was so smart that it worked, for her anyway. If it did. But it wasn't science. To care that much was to introduce biases into the study. It wasn't a matter of emotions. You did science simply because it was the best adaptation strategy in the environment into which they had been born. Science was the gene trying to pass itself along more successfully. Also it was the best way to pass the hours, or to make a living. Everything else was so trivial and grasping. Social primates, trapped in a technocosmos of their own devise; science was definitely the only way to see the terrain well enough to know which way to strike forward, to make something new for all the rest. No passion need be added to that reasoned way forward.

And yet, it occurred to him, why did things live? What got them through it, really? What made them make all these efforts, when death lay in wait at the end for every one of them? This was what these Buddhists had dared to ask.

He was walking toward the Potomac now, along Fairfax Drive, a huge commercial street rumbling with traffic, just a few cars away from gridlock. Long lines of vehicles, with most of the occupants in them talking on phones, talking to some other person somewhere else on the planet. A strange sight when you looked at it!

Reason had never explained the existence of life in this universe. Life was a mystery; reason had tried and failed to explain it, and science could not start it from scratch in a lab. Little localized eddies of antientropy, briefly popping into being and then spinning out, with bits of them carried elsewhere in long invisible chains of code that spun up yet more eddies. A succession of pattern dust devils. A mystery, a kind of miracle—a miracle struggling in harsh inimical conditions, succeeding only where it found water, which gathered in droplets in the universe just as it did on a windowpane, and gave life sustenance. Water of life. A miracle.

He felt the sweat breaking out all over his skin. When hominids went bipedal they lost hair and gained sweat glands, so they could convey away the extra heat caused by all that walking. But it didn't really work in a jungle. Tall trees, many species of trees and bushes; it could have been a botanical garden with a city laid into it, the plants a hundred shades of green. People walking by in small groups. Only runners were alone, and even they usually ran in pairs or larger groups. A social species, like bees or ants, with social rules that were invariant to the point of invisibility, people did not notice them. A species operating on pheromones, lucky in its adaptability, unstable in the environment. Knowledge of the existence of the future, awareness of the future as part of the calculations made in daily life, for daily living. Live for the future. A cosmic history read out of signs so subtle and mathematical that only the effort of a huge transtemporal group of powerful minds could ever have teased it out; but then those who came later could be given the whole story, with its unexplored edges there to take off into. *This* was the human project, *this* was science, this was what science was. This was what life was.

He stood there, thrumming with thought, queasy, anxious, frightened. He was a confused man. Free-floating anxiety, he thought anxiously; except it had clear causes. People said that paradigm shifts only occurred when the old scientists died, that people individually did not have them, they were too stubborn, too set in their ways, it was a more social process, a diachronic matter of successive generations.

Occasionally, however, it must be otherwise. Individual scientists, more open-minded or less certain than most, must have lived through one. Frank almost ran into a woman walking the other direction, almost said, "Sorry ma'am, I'm in the midst of a paradigm shift." He was disoriented. He saw that moving from one paradigm to the next was not like moving from one skyscraper to another, as in the diagrams he had once seen in a philosophy of science book. It was more like being inside a kaleidoscope, where he had gotten used to the pattern, and now the tube was twisting and he was falling and every aspect of what he saw was clicking to something different, click after click: colors, patterns, everything awash. Like dying and being reborn. Altruism, compassion, simple goddamned foolishness, loyalty to people who were not loyal to you, playing the sap for the defectors to take advantage of, competition, adaptation, displaced self-interest—or else something real, a real force in the world, a kind of physical constant, like gravity, or a basic attribute of life, like the drive to propagate one's DNA to subsequent generations. A reason for being. Something beyond DNA. A rage to live, an urge to goodness. Love. A green force, *élan vital,* that was a metaphysics, that was bad, but how else were you going to explain the data?

An excess of reason wasn't going to do it.

Genes, however, were very reasonable. They followed their directive, they reproduced. They were a living algorithm, creatures of four elements. Strings of binaries, codes of enormous length, codes that spoke bodies. It was a kind of reason that did that. Even a kind of monomania—an excess of reason, as the *koan* suggested. So that perhaps they were all mad, not just socially and individually, but genomically too. Molecular obsessive-compulsives. And then up from there, in stacked emergent insanities. Unless it was infused with some other quality that was not rational, some late emergent property like altruism, or compassion, or love—something that was not a code— then it was all for naught.

He felt sick. It could have just been the heat and humidity, the speed of his walking, something he ate, a bug that he had caught or that had bit him. It felt like all those, even though he suspected it was all starting in his mind, a kind of idea infection or moral fever. He needed to talk to someone.

But it had to be with someone he trusted. That made for a very short list. A very, very, very short list. In fact, my God, who exactly would be on that list, now he came to think of it?

Anna. Anna Quibler, his colleague. The passionate scientist. A rock, in fact. A rock in the tide. Who *could* you trust, after all? A good scientist. A scientist willing to take that best scientific attitude toward all of reality. Maybe that's what the old lama had been talking about. If too much reason was a form of madness, then perhaps *passionate reason* was what was called for. Passionate scientist, compassionate scientist, could analysis alone parse out which was which there? It could be a religion, some kind of humanism or biocentrism, philabios, philocosmos. Or simply Buddhism. If he had understood the old man correctly.

Suddenly he remembered that Anna and Charlie were hosting a party, and Anna had invited him. To help celebrate the day's lecture, ironically enough. The Khembalis would be there.

He walked, sweating, looking at street signs, figuring out where he was. Ah. Almost to Washington Boulevard. He could continue to the Clarendon Metro station. He did that, descended the Metro escalator into the ground. A weird action for a hominid to take—a religious experience. Following the shaman into the cave. We've never lost any of that.

He sat zoned in one of the train cars until the change of lines at Metro Center. The interior there looked weirder than ever, like a shopping mall in hell. A Red Line, Shady Grove train pulled in, and he got on and stood with the multitude. It was late in the day, he had wandered a long time. It was near the end of the rush hour.

The travelers at this hour were almost all professionally dressed. They were headed home, out to the prosperous parts of Northwest and Chevy Chase and Bethesda and Rockville and Gaithersburg. At each stop the train got emptier, until he could sit down on one of the garish orange seats.

Sitting there, he began to feel calmer. The coolness of the air, the sassy but soothing orange and pink, the people's faces, all contributed to this feeling. Even the driver of the train contributed, with a stop in each station that was as smooth as any Frank had ever felt, a beautiful touch on the big brakes that most drivers could not help but jerk to one degree or another. This guy eased smoothly in, over and over, station after station. It was like a musical perform-ance. The concrete caves changed their nameplates, other-wise each cave was almost the same.

Across from him sat a woman wearing a black skirt and white blouse. Hair short and curly, glasses, almost invisible touch of makeup. Bra strap showing at her collarbone. A professional of some sort, going home. Face intelligent and friendly-seeming, not pretty but attractive. Legs crossed, one running-shoed foot sticking into the aisle. Her skirt had ridden up her leg and Frank could see the side of one thigh, made slightly convex from her position and the mass of solid quadriceps muscles. No stockings, skin smooth, a few freckles. She looked strong.

Like Frank, she stood to get out at the Bethesda stop. Frank followed her out of the train. It was interesting the way dresses and skirts all were different, and framed or featured the bodies they covered uniquely. Height of bot-tom, width of hips, length and shape of legs, of back and shoulders, proportions of the whole, movement: the compounded variations were infinite, so that no two women looked the same to Frank. And he looked all the time.

This one was businesslike and moved fast. Her legs were just a touch longer than the usual proportion, which discrepancy drew the eye, as always. It was discrepancy from the norm that drew the eye. She looked like she was wearing high heels even though she wasn't. That was attractive; indeed, women wore high heels to look like her. Another savannah judgment, no doubt—the ability to out-run predators as part of the potential reproductive success. Whatever. She looked good. It was like a kind of balm, after what he had gone through. Back to basics.

Frank stood below her as they rose up the first escalator from trackside to the turnstiles, enjoying that view, which exaggerated the length of her legs and the size of her bottom. At that point he was hooked, and would therefore, as was his custom, follow her until their paths diverged, just to prolong the pleasure of watching her walk. This happened to him all the time, it was one of the habits one fell into, living in a city of such beautiful women.

Through the turnstiles, then, and along the tunnel toward the big escalator up and out. Then to his surprise she turned left, into the nook that held the station's elevators.

He followed her without thinking. He never took the Metro system's elevators, they were extremely slow. And yet there he was, standing beside her waiting for this one to arrive, feeling conspicuous but unable to do anything about it now that he was there, except look up at the display lights over the elevator doors. Although he could just walk away.

The light lit. The doors opened on an empty car. Frank followed the woman in and turned and stared at the closing doors, feeling red-faced.

She pushed the street-level button, and with a slight lift

they were off. The elevator hummed and vibrated as they rose. It was hot and humid, and the little room smelled faintly of machine oil, sweat, plastics, perfume, and electricity.

Frank studiously observed the display over the doors. The woman did the same. She had the strap of her armbag hooked under her thumb. Her elbow was pressed into her blouse just over the waistline of her skirt. Her hair was so curly that it was almost frizzy, but not quite; brown, and cut short, so that it curled tight as a cap on her head. A little longer in a fringe at the back of her neck, where two lines of fine blonde hairs curved down toward her deltoid muscles. Wide shoulders. A very impressive animal. Even in his peripheral vision he could see all this.

The elevator whined, then shuddered and stopped. Startled, Frank refocused on the control panel, which still showed them as going up.

"Shit," the woman muttered, and looked at her watch. She glanced at Frank.

"Looks like we're stuck," Frank said, pushing the UP button.

"Yeah. Damn it."

"Unbelievable," Frank agreed.

She grimaced. "What a day."

A moment or two passed. Frank hit the DOWN button: nothing. He gestured at the little black phone console set in the panel above the UP and DOWN buttons.

"I guess we're at the point this is here for."

"I think so."

Frank picked up the receiver, put it to his ear. The phone was ringing already, which was good, as it had no numberpad. What would it have been like to pick up a phone and hear nothing?

But the ringing went on long enough to concern him. Then it stopped, and a woman's voice said, "Hello?"

"Hi? Hey listen, we're in the elevator at the Bethesda Metro stop, and it's stuck."

"Okay. Bethesda did you say? Did you try pushing the CLOSE DOOR button then the UP button?"

"No." Frank pushed these buttons. "I am now, but... nothing. It feels pretty stuck."

"Try the DOWN button too, after the CLOSE DOOR."

"Okay." He tried it.

"Do you know how far up you are?"

"We must be near the top." He glanced at the woman, and she nodded.

"Any smoke?"

"No!"

"Okay. There's people on the way. Just sit tight and stay cool. Are you crowded in there?"

"No, there's just two of us."

"That's okay then. They said they'll be about half an hour to an hour, depending on traffic and the problem with the elevator. They'll call you on your phone when they get there."

"Okay. Thanks."

"No problem. Pick up again if something changes. I'll be watching."

"I will. Thanks again."

The woman had already hung up. Frank did also.

They stood there.

"Well," Frank said, gesturing at the phone.

"I could hear," the woman said. She looked around at the floor. "I guess I'll sit down while we wait. My feet are tired."

"Good idea."

They sat down next to each other, backs to the back wall of the elevator.

"Tired feet?"

"Yeah. I went running today at lunch, and it was mostly on sidewalks."

"You're a runner?"

"No, not really. That's why my feet hurt. I ride with a cycling club, and we're doing a triathlon, so I'm trying to add some running and swimming. I could just do the cycling leg of a team, but I'm seeing if I can get ready to do the whole thing."

"What are the distances?"

"A mile swim, twenty mile bike, ten k run."

"Ouch."

"It's not so bad."

They sat in silence.

"So are you going to be late for something here?"

"No," Frank said. "Well, it depends, but it's just a kind of party."

"Too bad to miss that."

"Maybe. It's a work thing. There was a lunchtime lecture today, and now the organizer is having a thing for the speakers."

"What did they talk about?"

He smiled. "A Buddhist approach to science, actually. They were the Buddhists."

"And you were the scientists."

"Yes."

"That must have been interesting."

"Well, yes. It was. It's given me a lot to think about. More than I thought it would. I don't exactly know what to say to them tonight though."

"Hmm." She appeared to consider it. "Sometimes I think about cycling as a kind of meditation. Lots of times I kind of blank out, and when I come to a lot of miles have passed."

"That must be nice."

"Your science isn't psychology, is it?"

"Microbiology."

"Good. Sorry. Anyway, I like it, yeah. I don't think I could do it by trying for it, though. It just happens, usually late in a ride. Maybe it's low blood sugar. Not enough energy to think."

"Could be," Frank said. "Thinking does burn some sugars."

"There you go."

They sat there burning sugars.

"So what about you, are you going to be late for something?"

"I was going to go for a ride, actually. My legs would be less sore tomorrow if I did. But after this, who knows what I'll feel like . . . maybe I still will. If we get out of here pretty soon."

"We'll see about that."

"Yeah."

The trapped air was stifling. They sat there sweating. There was some quality to it, some combination of comfort and tension, their bodies simply breathing together, resting, almost touching, ever so slightly incandescent to each other . . . it was nice. Two animals resting side by side, one male one female. A lot of talk goes on below the radar. And indeed somehow it had come to pass that as they relaxed their legs had drifted outward and met each other, so that now they were just very slightly touching, at the outsides of the knees, kind of resting against each other in a carefully natural way, her leg bare (her skirt had fallen down into her lap) and his covered by light cotton pants. Touching. Now the talk under the radar was filling Frank's whole bandwidth, and though he continued his part of the conversation, he could not have immediately said what they were talking about.

"So you must ride quite a lot?"

"Yeah, pretty much."

She was in a cycling club, she told him. "It's like any other club." Except this one went out on long bike rides. Weekends, smaller groups more often than that. She too was making talk. "Like a social club really. Like the Elks Club or something, only with bikes."

"Good for you."

"Yes, it's fun. A good workout."

"It makes you strong."

"Well, the legs anyway. It's good for legs."

"Yes," Frank agreed, and took the invitation to glance down at hers. She did as well, tucking her chin and looking as if inspecting something outside of herself. Her skirt had fallen so that the whole side of her left leg was exposed.

She said, "It bulks up the quads."

Frank intended to agree by saying "Uh-huh," but somehow the sound got interrupted, as if he had been tapped lightly on the solar plexus while making it, so that it came out "nnnnn," like a short hum or purr. A little moan of longing, in fact, at the sight of such long strong legs, all that smooth skin, the sweet curve of the underthigh. Her knees stood distinctly higher than his.

He looked up to find her grinning at him. He hunched his shoulders and looked away just a touch, yes, guilty as charged, feeling the corners of his mouth tug up in the helpless smile of someone caught in the act. What could he say, she had great legs.

Now she was watching him with an interrogatory gaze, searching his face for something specific, it seemed, her eyes alight with mischief, amused. It was a look that had a whole person in it.

And she must have liked something about what she saw, because she leaned his way, into his shoulder, and then pressed farther in and stretched her head toward his and kissed him.

"Mmm," he purred, kissing back. He shifted around the

better to face her, his body moving without volition. She was shifting too. She pulled back briefly to look again in his eyes, then she smiled broadly and shifted into his arms. Their kiss grew more and more passionate, they were like teenagers making out. They flew off into that pocket universe of bliss. Time passed, Frank's thoughts scattered, he was absorbed in the feel of her mouth, her lips on his, her tongue, the awkwardness of their embrace. It was very hot. They were both literally dripping with sweat; their kisses tasted salty. Frank slid a hand under her skirt. She hummed and then shifted onto one knee and over onto him, straddling him. They kissed harder than ever.

The elevator phone rang.

She sat up. "Oops," she said, catching her breath. Her face was flushed and she looked gorgeous. She reached up and behind her and grabbed the receiver, staying solidly on him.

"Hello?" she said into the phone. Frank flexed under her and she put a hand to his chest to stop him.

"Oh yeah, we're here," she said. "You guys got here fast." She listened and quickly laughed, "No, I don't suppose you do hear that very often." She glanced down at Frank to share a complicit smile, and it was in that moment that Frank felt the strongest bond of all with her. They were a pair in the world, and no one else knew it but them.

"Yeah sure—we'll be here!"

She rolled off him as she hung up. "They say they've got it fixed and we're on our way up."

"Damn it."

"I know."

They stood. She brushed down her skirt. They felt a few jerks as the elevator started up again.

"Wow, look at us. We are just *dripping*."

"We would have been no matter what. It's hot in here."

"True." She reached up to straighten his hair and then

they were kissing again, banging against the wall in a sudden blaze of passion, stronger than ever. Then she pushed him away, saying breathlessly, "Okay, no more, we're almost there. The door must be about to open."

"True."

Confirming the thought, the elevator began its characteristic slow-motion deceleration. Frank took a deep breath, blew it out, tried to pull himself together. He felt flushed, his skin was tingling. He looked at her. She was almost as tall as he was.

She laughed. "They're gonna bust us for sure."

The elevator stopped. The doors jerked open. They were still a foot below street level, but it was an easy step up and out.

Before them stood three men, two in workers' coveralls, one in a Metro uniform.

The one in the uniform held a clipboard. "Y'all okay?" he said to them.

"Yeah" "We're fine" they said together.

Everyone stood there for a second.

"Must have been hot in there," the uniformed one remarked.

The three black men stared at them curiously.

"It was," Frank said.

"But not much different than out here," his companion quickly added, and they all laughed. It was true, getting out had not made any marked change. It was like stepping from one sauna to another. Their rescuers were also sweating profusely. Yes—the open air of a Washington, D.C., evening was indistinguishable from the inside of an elevator stuck deep underground. This was their world: and so they laughed.

They were on the sidewalk flanking Wisconsin Avenue,

next to the elevator box and the old post office. Passersby glanced at them. The foreman gave the woman his clipboard. "If you'd fill out and sign the report, please. Thanks. Looks like it was about half an hour from your call to when we pulled you."

"Pretty fast," the woman said, reading the text on her form before filling in some blanks and signing. "It didn't even seem that long." She looked at her watch. "All right, well—thanks very much." She faced Frank, extended a hand. "It was nice to meet you."

"Yes, it was," Frank said, shaking her hand, struggling for words, struggling to think. In front of these witnesses nothing came to him, and she turned and walked south on Wisconsin. Frank felt constrained by the gazes of the three men; all would be revealed if he were to run after her and ask for her name, her phone number, and besides now the foreman was holding the clipboard out to him, and it occurred to him that he could read what she had written down there.

But it was a fresh form, and he looked up to see that down the street she was turning right, onto one of the smaller streets west of Wisconsin.

The foreman watched him impassively while the technicians went back to the elevator.

Frank gestured at the clipboard. "Can I get that woman's name, please?"

The man frowned, surprised, and shook his head. "Not allowed to," he said. "It's a law."

Frank felt his stomach sink. There had to be a physiological basis for that feeling, some loosening of the gut as fear or shock prepared the body for fight-or-flight. Flight in this case. "But I need to get in touch with her again," he said.

The man stared at him, stone-faced. He had to have

worked on that look in a mirror, it was like something out of the movies. Samuel L. Jackson perhaps.

"Should have thought of that when you was stuck with her," he said, sensibly enough. He gestured in the direction she had gone. "You could probably still catch her."

Released by these words Frank took off, first walking fast, then, after he turned right on the street she had taken, running. He looked forward down the street for her black skirt, white blouse, short brown hair; there was no sign of her. He began sweating hard again, a kind of panic response. How far could she have gotten? What had she said she was late for? He couldn't remember—horribly, his mind seemed to have blurred on much that she had said before they started kissing. He needed to know all that now! It was like some memory experiment foisted on undergraduates, how much could you remember of the incidents right before a shock? Not much! The experiment had worked like a charm.

But then he found the memory, and realized that it was not blurred at all, that on the contrary it was intensely detailed, at least up until the point when their legs had touched, at which point he could still remember perfectly, but only the feel on the outside of his knee, not their words. He went back before that, rehearsed it, relived it— cyclist, triathlon, one mile twenty mile ten k. Good for the legs, oh my God was it. He had to find her!

There was no sign of her at all. By now he was on Woodson, running left and right, looking down all the little side streets and into shop windows, feeling more and more desperate. She wasn't anywhere to be seen. He had lost her.

It started to rain.

THE DOORBELL rang. Anna went to the door and opened it.

"Frank! Wow, you're soaked."

He must have been caught in the downpour that had begun about half an hour before, and was already mostly finished. It was odd he hadn't taken shelter during the worst of it. He looked like he had dived into a swimming pool with all his clothes on.

"Don't worry," she said as he hesitated on the porch, dripping like a statue in a fountain. "Here, you need a towel for your face." She provided one from the vestibule's coat closet. "The rain really got you."

"Yeah."

She was somewhat surprised to see him. She had thought he was uninterested in the Khembalis, even slightly dismissive of them. And he had sat through the afternoon's lecture wearing one of his signature looks—he had a kind of Jon Gruden face, able to express fifty minute gradations of displeasure, and the one at the lecture had been the one that said "I'm keeping my eyes from rolling in my head only by the greatest of efforts." Not the most pleasant of expressions on anyone's face, and it had only gotten worse as the lecture went on, until eventually he had looked stunned and off in his own world.

On the other hand, he had gone to it. He had left in silence, obviously thinking something over. And now here he was.

So Anna was pleased. If the Khembalis could capture Frank's interest, they should be able to do it with any scientist. Frank was the hardest case she knew.

Now he seemed slightly disoriented by his drenching. He was shaking his head ruefully.

Anna said, "Do you want to change into one of Charlie's shirts?"

"No, I'll be all right. I'll steam dry." Then he lifted his arms and looked down. "Well—maybe a shirt I guess. Will his fit me?"

"Sure, you're only just a bit bigger than he is."

She went upstairs to get one, calling down, "The others should be here any minute. There was flooding on Wisconsin, apparently, and some problems with the Metro."

"I know about those, I got caught in one!"

"You're kidding! What happened?" She came down with one of Charlie's bigger T-shirts.

"The elevator I was in got stuck halfway up."

"Oh no! For how long?"

"About half an hour I guess."

"Jesus. That must have been spooky. Were you by yourself?"

"No, there was someone else, a woman. We got to talking, and so the time passed fast. It was interesting."

"That's nice."

"Yes. It was. Only I didn't get her name, and then when we got out they had forms for us to fill out and, and she took off while I was doing mine, so I never caught what hers was. And then the guy from the Metro wouldn't give it to me from her form, so now I'm kicking myself, because—well. I'd like to talk to her again."

Anna inspected him, startled by this story. He was looking past her abstractedly, perhaps remembering the incident. He noticed her gaze and grinned, and this startled her once again, because it was a real smile. Always before Frank's smile had been a skeptical thing, so ironic and knowing that only one side of his mouth tugged back. Now he was like a stroke victim who had recovered the use of the damaged side of his face.

It was a nice sight, and it had to have been because of this woman he had met. Anna felt a sudden surge of affection for him. They had worked together for quite some time, and that kind of collaboration can take two people into a realm of shared experience that is not like family or marriage but rather some other kind of bond that can be quite deep. A friendship formed in the world of thought. Maybe they were always that way. Anyway he looked happy, and she was happy to see it.

"This woman filled out a form, you say?"

"Yeah."

"So you can find out."

"They wouldn't let me look at it."

"No, but you'll be able to get to it somehow."

"You think so?"

Now she had his complete attention. "Sure. Get a reporter from the *Post* to help you, or an archival detective, or someone from the Metro. Or from Homeland Security for that matter. The fact you were in there with her, that might be the way to get it, I don't know. But as long as it's written down, something will work. That's informatics, right?"

"True." He smiled again, looking quite happy. Then he took Charlie's shirt from her and walked around toward the kitchen while changing into it. He took another towel from her and toweled off his head. "Thanks. Here, can I put this in your dryer? Down in the basement, right?" He stepped over the baby gate, went downstairs. "Thanks Anna," he called back up to her. "I feel better now." When he came back up, the sound of the dryer on behind him, he smiled again. "A lot better."

"You must have liked this woman!"

"I did. It's true, I did. I can't believe I didn't get her name!"

"You will. Want a beer?"

"You bet I do."

"In the door of the fridge. Oops, there's the door again, here come the rest."

Soon the Khembalis and many other friends and acquaintances from NSF filled the Quiblers' little living room and the dining room flanking it, and the kitchen beyond the dining room. Anna rushed back and forth from the yellow kitchen through the dining room to the living room, carrying drinks and trays of food. She enjoyed this, and was doing it more than usual to keep Charlie from doing too much and inflaming his poison ivy. As she hurried around she enjoyed seeing Joe playing with Drepung, and Nick discussing Antarctic dinosaurs with Curt from the office right above hers; he was one of the U.S. Antarctic Program managers. That NSF also ran one of the continents of the world was something she tended to forget, but Curt had come to the talk, and liked it. "These Buddhist guys would go over big in McMurdo," he told Nick. Meanwhile Charlie, skin devastated to a brown crust across wide regions of his neck and face, eyes brilliantly bloodshot with sleep deprivation and steroids, was absorbed in conversation with Sucandra. Then he noticed her running around and joined her in the kitchen to help. "I gave Frank one of your shirts," she told him.

"I saw. He said he got soaked."

"Yes. I think he was chasing around after a woman he met on the Metro."

"*What?*"

She laughed. "I think it's great. Go sit down, babe, don't move your poor torso, you'll make yourself itchy."

"I've transcended itchiness. I'm only itchy for you."

"Come on don't. Go sit down."

Only later in the evening did she see Frank again. He was sitting in the corner of the room, on the floor between the couch and the fireplace, quizzing Drepung about something or other. Drepung looked as if he was struggling to understand him. Anna was curious, and when she got a chance she sat down on the couch just above the two of them.

Frank nodded to her and then continued pressing a point, using one of his catchphrases: "But how does that work?"

"Well," Drepung said, "I know what Rudra Cakrin says in Tibetan, obviously. His import is clear to me. Then I have to think what I know of English. The two languages are different, but so much is the same for all of us."

"Deep grammar," Frank suggested.

"Yes, but also just nouns. Names for things, names for actions, even for meanings. Equivalencies of one degree or another. So, I try to express my understanding of what Rudra said, but in English."

"But how good is the correspondence?"

Drepung raised his eyebrows. "How can I know? I do the best I can."

"You would need some kind of exterior test."

Drepung nodded. "Have other Tibetan translators

listen to the rimpoche, and then compare their English versions to mine. That would be very interesting."

"Yes it would. Good idea."

Drepung smiled at him. "Double blind study, right?"

"Yes I guess so."

"Elementary, my dear Watson," Drepung intoned, reaching out for a cracker with which to dip hummus. "But I expect you would get a certain, what, range. Maybe you would not uncover many surprises with your study. Maybe just that I personally am a bad translator. Although I must say, I have a tough job. When I don't understand the rimpoche, translating him gets harder."

"So you make it up!" Frank laughed. His spirits were still high, Anna saw. "That's what I've been saying all along." He settled back against the side of the couch next to her.

But Drepung shook his head. "Not making things up. Re-creation, maybe."

"Like DNA and phenotypes."

"I don't know."

"A kind of code."

"Well, but language is never just a code."

"No. More like gene expression."

"You must tell me."

"From an instruction sequence, like a gene, to what the instruction creates. Language to thought. Or to meaning, or comprehension. Whatever! To some kind of living thought."

Drepung grinned. "There are about fifty words in Tibetan that I would have to translate to the word 'thinking.'"

"Like Eskimos with 'snow.'"

"Yes. Like Eskimos have snow, we Tibetans have thoughts."

He laughed at the idea and Frank laughed too, shaken by that low giggle which was all he ever gave to laughter, but now emphatic and helpless with it, bubbling over with it. Anna could scarcely believe her eyes. He was as ebullient as if he were drunk, but he was still holding the same beer she had given him on his arrival. And she knew what he was high on anyway.

He pulled himself together, grew intent. "So today, when you said, 'An excess of reason is itself a form of madness,' what did your lama really say?"

"Just that. That's easy, that's an old proverb." He said the sentence in Tibetan. "One word means 'excess' or 'too much,' you know, like that, and *rig-gnas* is 'reason,' or 'science.' Then *zugs* is 'form,' and *zhe sdang* is 'madness,' a version of 'hatred,' from an older word that was like 'angry.' One of the *dug gsum,* the Three Poisons of the Mind."

"And the old man said that?"

"Yes. An old saying. Milarepa, I should think."

"Was he talking about science, though?"

"The whole lecture was on science."

"Yeah yeah. But I found that idea in particular pretty striking."

"A good thought is one you can act on."

"That's what mathematicians say."

"I'm sure."

"So, was the lama saying that NSF is crazy? Or that Western science is crazy? Because it is pretty damned reasonable. I mean, that's the point. That's the method in a nutshell."

"Well, I guess so. To that extent. We are all crazy in some way or other, right? He did not mean to be critical. Nothing alive is ever quite in balance. It might be he was suggesting that science is out of balance. Feet without eyes."

"I thought it was eyes without feet."

Drepung waggled his hand: either way. "You should ask him."

"But you'd be translating, so I might as well just ask you and cut out the middleman!"

"No," laughing, "*I* am the middleman, I assure you."

"But you can tell me what he *would* say," teasing him now. "Cut right to the chase!"

"But he surprises me a lot."

"Like when, give me an example."

"Well. One time last week, he was saying to me…"

But at that point Anna was called away to the front door, and she did not get to hear Drepung's example, but only Frank's distinctive laughter, burbling under the clatter of conversation.

By the time she ran into Frank again he was out in the kitchen with Charlie and Sucandra, washing glasses and cleaning up. Charlie could only stand there and talk. He and Frank were discussing Great Falls, both recommending it very highly to Sucandra. "It's more like Tibet than any other place in town," Charlie said, and Frank giggled again, more so when Anna exclaimed "Oh come on love, they aren't the slightest bit the same!"

"No, yes! I mean they're more alike than anywhere else around here is like Tibet."

"What does that mean?" she demanded.

"Water! Nature!" Then: "*Sky,*" Frank and Charlie both said at the same time.

Sucandra nodded. "I could use some sky. Maybe even a horizon." And all the men were chuckling.

Anna went back out to the living room to see if anyone needed anything. She paused to watch Rudra Cakrin and Joe playing with blocks on the floor again. Joe was filled with happiness to have such company, stacking blocks and babbling. Rudra nodded and handed him more. They had been doing that off and on for much of the evening. It occurred to Anna that they were the only two people at the party who did not speak English.

She went back to the kitchen and took over Frank's spot at the sink, and sent Frank down to the basement to get his shirt out of the dryer. He came back up wearing it, and leaned against the counter, talking.

Charlie saw Anna rest against the counter as well, and got her a beer from the fridge. "Here snooks have a drink."

"Thanks dove."

Sucandra asked about the kitchen's wallpaper, which was an uncomfortably brilliant yellow, overlaid with large white birds caught in various moments of flight. When you actually looked at it it was rather bizarre. "I like it," Charlie said. "It wakes me up. A bit itchy, but basically fine."

Frank said he was going to go home. Anna walked him around the ground floor to the front door.

"You'll be able to catch one of the last trains," she said.

"Yeah I'll be okay."

"Thanks for coming, that was fun."

"Yes it was."

Again Anna saw that whole smile brighten his face.

"So what's she like?"

"Well—I don't know!"

They both laughed.

Anna said, "I guess you'll find out when you find her."

"Yeah," Frank said, and touched her arm briefly, as if to thank her for the thought. Then as he was walking down the sidewalk he looked over his shoulder and called, "I hope she's like you!"

FRANK LEFT Anna and Charlie's and walked through a warm drizzle back toward the Metro, thinking hard. When he came to the fateful elevator's box he stood before it, trying to order his thoughts. It was impossible—especially there. He moved on reluctantly, as if leaving the place would put the experience irrevocably in the past. But it already was. Onward, past the hotel, to the stairs, down to the Metro entry level. He stepped onto the long escalator going down and descended into the earth, thinking.

He recalled Anna and Charlie, in their house with all those people. The way they stood by each other, leaned into each other. The way Anna put a hand on Charlie when she was near him—on this night, avoiding his poisoned patches. The way they shuffled their kids back and forth between them, without actually seeming to notice each other. Their endlessly varying nicknames for each other, a habit Frank had noticed before, even though he would rather have not: not just the usual endearments like hon, honey, dear, sweetheart, or babe, but also more exotic ones that were saccharine or suggestive beyond belief—snooks, snookybear, honeypie, lover, lovey, lovedove, sweetie-pie, angel man, goddessgirl, kitten, it was unbelievable the inwardness of the monogamous bond, the unconscious twin-world narcissism of it—disgusting! And yet Frank craved that very thing, that easy, deep intimacy that one could take for granted, could lose oneself in. ISO-LTR. Primate seeks partner for life. An urge seen in every human culture, and across many species too. It was not crazy of him to want it.

Therefore he was now in a quandary. He wanted to find the woman from the elevator. And Anna had given him hope that it could be done. It might take some time, but as Anna had pointed out, everyone was in the data banks somewhere. In the Department of Homeland Security records, if nowhere else; but of course elsewhere too. Beg or break your way into Metro maintenance records, how hard could that be? There were people breaking into the genome!

But he wasn't going to be able to do it from San Diego. Or rather, maybe he could make the hunt from there—you could Google someone from anywhere—but if he then succeeded in finding her, it wouldn't do him any good. It was a big continent. If he found her, if he wanted that to matter, he would need to be in the D.C. area.

And what would he do if he found her?

He couldn't think about that now. About anything that might happen past the moment of locating her. That would be enough. After that, who knew what she might be like. After all she had jumped him (he shivered at the memory, still there in his flesh), jumped a total stranger in a stuck elevator after twenty minutes of conversation. There was no doubt in his mind that she had initiated the encounter; it simply wouldn't have occurred to him. Maybe that made him an innocent or a dimwit, but there it was. Maybe on the other hand she was some kind of sexual adventuress, the free papers might be right after all, and certainly everyone talked all the time about women being all Buffyed and sexually assertive, though he had seen little personally to confirm it. Though it had been true of Marta too, come to think of it.

Howsoever that might be, he had been there in the elevator, had shared all responsibility for what happened. And happily so—he was pleased at himself, amazed but glowing. He wanted to find her.

But after that—if he could do it—whatever might happen, if anything were to happen—he needed to be in D.C.

Fine. Here he was.

But he had just put his parting shot in Diane's in-box that very day, and tomorrow morning she would come in and read it. A letter that was, now that he thought of it, virulently critical, possibly even contemptuous—and how stupid was *that*, how impolitic, self-indulgent, irrational, maladaptive—what could he have been *thinking*? Well, somehow he had been angry. Something had made him bitter. He had done it to burn his bridges, so that when Diane had read it he would be toast at NSF.

Whereas without that letter, it would have been a relatively simple matter to re-up for another year. Anna had asked him to, and she had been speaking for Diane, Frank was sure. A year more, and after that he would know where things stood, at least.

A Metro train finally came rumbling windily into the station. Sitting in it as it jerked and rolled into the darkness toward the city, he mulled over in jagged quick images of memory and consideration all that had occurred recently, all crushed and scattered into a kind of kaleidoscope or mandala: Pierzinski's algorithm, the panel, Marta, Derek, the Khembalis' lecture; seeing Anna and Charlie, leaning side by side against a kitchen counter. He could make no sense of it really. The parts made sense, but he could not pull a theory out of it. Just part of a more general sense that the world was going smash.

And, in the context of that sort of world, did he want to go back to a single lab anyway? Could he bear to work on a single tiny chip of the giant mosaic of global problems? It was the way he had always worked before, and it might be the only way one could, really; but might he not be better off deploying his efforts in a way that magnified them by using them in this small but potentially strong arm of the government, the National Science Foundation? Was that what his letter's furious critique of NSF had been all about—his frustration that it was doing so little of what it could? If I can't find a lever I won't be able to move the world, isn't that what Archimedes had declared?

In any case his letter was there in Diane's in-box. He had torched his bridge already. It was very stupid to forestall a possible course of action in such a manner. He was a fool. It was hard to admit, but he had to admit it. The evidence was clear.

But he could go to NSF now and take the letter back.

Security would be there, as always. But people went to work late or early, he could explain himself that way. Still, Diane's offices would be locked. Security might let him in to his own office, but the twelfth floor? No.

Perhaps he could get there as the first person arrived on the twelfth floor next morning, and slip in and take it.

But on most mornings the first person to the twelfth floor, famously, was Diane Chang herself. People said she often got there at 4 A.M. So, well ... He could be there when she arrived. Just tell her he needed to take back a letter he had put in her box. She might with reason ask to read it first, or she might hand it back, he couldn't say. But either way, she would know something was wrong with him. And something in him recoiled from that. He didn't want anyone to know any of this, he didn't want to look emotionally overwrought or indecisive, or as if he had something to hide. His few encounters with Diane had given him reason to believe she was not one to suffer fools gladly, and he hated to be thought of as one. It was bad enough having to admit it to himself.

And if he were going to continue at NSF, he wanted to be able to do things there. He needed Diane's respect. It would be so much better if he could take the letter back without her ever knowing he had left it.

Unbidden an old thought leapt to mind. He had often sat in his office cubicle, looking through the window into the central atrium, and thought about climbing the mobile hanging in there. There was a crux in the middle, shifting from one piece of it to another, a stretch of chain that looked to be hard if you were free-climbing it. And a fall would be fatal. But he could come down to it on a rappel from the skylight topping the atrium. He wouldn't even have to descend as far as the mobile. Diane's offices were on the twelfth floor, so it would be a short drop. A matter of using his climbing craft and gear, and his old skyscraper window skills. Come down through the skylight, do a pendulum traverse from above the mobile over to her windows, tip one out, slip in, snatch his letter out of the in-box, and climb back out, sealing the windows as he left. No security cameras pointed upward in the atrium, he had noticed during one of his climbing fantasies; there were no alarms on window framing; all would be well. And the top of the building was accessible by a maintenance ladder bolted permanently to the south wall. He had noticed that once while walking by, and had already worked it into various daydreams of the past year. Occupying his mind with images of physical action, perhaps to model the kind of dexterity needed to solve some abstract problem, biomathematics as a kind of climbing up the walls of reality—or perhaps just to compensate for the boredom of sitting in a chair all day.

Now it was a plan, fully formed and ready to execute. He did not try to pretend to himself that it was the most rational plan he had ever made, but he urgently needed to do something physical, right then and there. He was quivering with the tension of contained action. The operation's set of physical maneuvers were all things he could do, and that being the case, all the other factors of his situation inclined him to do it. In fact he had to, if he was really going to take responsibility for his life at last, and cast it in the direction of his desire. Make a sea change, start anew—make possible whatever follow-up with the woman in the elevator he might later be able to accomplish.

It had to be done.

He got out at the Ballston station, still thinking hard. He walked to the NSF parking garage door by way of the south side of the building, to confirm the exterior ladder's lower height. Bring a box to step on, that's all it would need. He walked to his car and drove west to his apartment over wet empty streets, not seeing a thing.

At the apartment he went to the closet and pawed through his climbing gear. Below it, as in an archaeological dig, were the old tools of a windowman's trade.

When it was all spread out on the floor it looked like he had spent his whole life preparing to do this. For a moment, hefting his caulking gun, he hesitated at the sheer weirdness of what he was contemplating. For one thing the caulking gun was useless without caulk, and he had none. He would have to leave cut seals, and eventually someone would see them.

Then he remembered again the woman in the elevator. He felt her kisses still. Only a few hours had passed, though since then his mind had spun through what seemed like years. If he were to have any chance of seeing her again, he had to act. Cut seals didn't matter. He stuffed all the rest of the gear into his faded red nylon climber's backpack, which was shredded down one side from a rock fall in the Fourth Recess, long ago. He had done crazy things often back then.

He went to his car, threw the bag in, hummed over the dark streets back to Arlington, past the Ballston stop. He parked on a wet street well away from the NSF building. No one was about. There were eight million people in the immediate vicinity, but it was two A.M. and so there was not a person to be seen. Who could deny sociobiology at a moment like that! What a sign of their animal natures, completely diurnal in the technosurround of postmodern society, fast asleep in so many ways, and most certainly at night. Unavoidably fallen into a brain state that was still very poorly understood. Frank felt a little exalted to witness such overwhelming evidence of their animal nature. A whole city of sleeping primates. Somehow it confirmed his feeling that he was doing the right thing. That he himself had woken up for the first time in many years.

On the south side of the NSF building it was the work of a moment to stand a plastic crate on its side and hop up to the lowest rung of the service ladder bolted to the concrete wall, and then quickly to pull himself up and ascend the twelve stories to the roof, using his leg muscles for all the propulsion. As he neared the top of the ladder it felt very high and exposed, and it occurred to him that if it was really true that an excess of reason was a form of madness, he seemed to be cured. Unless of course this truly was the most reasonable thing to do—as he felt it was.

Over the coping, onto the roof, land in a shallow rain puddle against the coping. In the center of a flat roof, the atrium skylight.

It was a muggy night, the low clouds orange with the city's glow. He pulled out his tools. The big central skylight was a low four-sided pyramid of triangular glass window-panes. He went to the one nearest the ladder and cleaned the plate of glass, then affixed a big sucker to it.

Using his old X-Acto knife he cut the sun-damaged polyurethane caulking on the window's three sides. He pulled it away and found the window screws, and zipped them out with his old Grinder screwdriver. When the win-dow was unscrewed he grabbed the handle on the sucker and yanked to free the window, then pulled back gently; out it came, balanced in the bottom frame stripping. He pulled it back until the glass was almost upright, then tied the sling-rope from the handle of the sucker to the lowest rung of the ladder. The open gap near the top of the atrium was more than big enough for him to fit through. Cool air wafted up from some very slight internal pressure.

He laid a towel over the frame, stepped into his climbing harness, and buckled it around his waist. He tied his ropes off on the top rung of the service ladder; that would be bombproof. Now it was just a matter of slipping through the gap and rappelling down the rope to the point where he would begin his pendulum.

He sat carefully on the angled edge of the frame. He could feel the beer from Anna's reception still sloshing in him, impeding his coordination very slightly, but this was climbing, he would be all right. He had done it in worse condition in his youth, fool that he had been. Although it was perhaps the wrong time to be critical of that version of himself.

Turning around and leaning back into the atrium, he tested the figure eight device constricting the line—good friction—so he leaned farther back into the atrium, and immediately plummeted down into it. Desperately he twisted the rappelling device and felt the rope slow; it caught fast and he was bungeeing down on it when he crashed into something—a horrible surprise because it didn't seem that he had had time to fall to the ground, so he was confused for a split second—then he saw that he had struck the top piece of the mobile, and was now hanging over it, head downward, grasping it and the rope both with a desperate prehensile clinging.

And very happy to be there. The brief fall seemed to have affected him like a kind of electrocution. His skin burned everywhere. He tugged experimentally on his rope; it seemed fine, solidly tied to the roof ladder. Perhaps after putting the figure eight on the rope he had forgotten to take all the slack out of the system, he couldn't remember doing it. That would be forgetting a well-nigh instinctual action for any climber, but he couldn't honestly put it past himself on this night. His mind was full or perhaps overfull.

Carefully he reached into his waistbag. He got out two ascenders and carabinered their long loops to his harness, then connected them to the rope above him. Next he whipped the rope below him around his thigh, and had a look around. He would have to use the ascenders to pull himself back up to the proper pendulum point for Diane's window—

The whole mobile was twisting slightly. Frank grabbed it and tried to torque it until it stilled, afraid some security person would walk through the atrium and notice the motion. Suddenly the big space seemed much too well-lit for comfort, even though it was only a dim greenish glow created by a few nightlights in the offices around him.

The mobile's top piece was a bar bent into a big circle, hanging by a chain from a point on its circumference, with two shorter bars extending out from it—one about thirty degrees off from the top, bending to make a staircase shape, the other across the circle and below, its two bends making a single stair down. The crescent bar hung about fifteen feet below the circle. In the dark they appeared to be different shades of gray, though Frank knew they were primary colors. For a second that made it all seem unreal.

Finally the whole contraption came still. Frank ran one ascender up his rope, put his weight on it. Every move had to be delicate, and for a time he was lost to everything else, deep in that climber's space of purely focused concentration.

He placed the other ascender even higher, and carefully shifted his weight to it, and off the first ascender. A very mechanical and straightforward process. He wanted to leave the mobile with no push on it at all.

But the second ascender slipped when he put his weight on it, and instinctively he grabbed the rope with his hand and burned his palm before the other ascender caught him. A totally unnecessary burn.

Now he really began to sweat. A bad ascender was bad news. This one was slipping very slightly and then catching. Looking at it he thought that maybe it had been smacked in the fall onto the top of the mobile, breaking its housing. Ascender housings were often cast, and sometimes bubbles left in the casting caused weaknesses that broke when struck. It had happened to him before, and it was major adrenaline time. No one could climb a rope unaided for long.

But this one kept holding after its little slips, and fiddling with his fingertips he could see that shoving the cam back into place in the housing after he released it helped it to catch sooner. So with a kind of teeth-clenching patience, a holding-the-breath, antigravitational effort, he could use the other one for the big pulls of the ascent, and then set the bad one by hand, to hold him (hopefully) while he moved the good one up above it again.

Eventually he got back up to the height he had wanted

to descend to in the first place, finally ready to go. He was drenched in sweat and his right hand was burning. He tried to estimate how much time he had wasted, but could not. Somewhere between ten minutes and half an hour, he supposed. Ridiculous.

Swinging side to side was easy, and soon he was swaying back and forth, until he could reach out and place a medium sucker against Laveta's office window. He depressed it slightly as he swung in close, and it stuck first try.

Held thus against her window, he could pull a T-bar from his waistbag and reach over, just barely, and fit it into the window washer's channel next to the window. After that he was set, and could reach up and place a dashboard into the slot over the window, and rig a short rope he had brought to tie the sucker handle up to the dashboard, holding open Laveta's window.

All set. Deploy the X-Acto, unscrew the frame, haul up the window toward the dashboard, almost to horizontal, keeping its top edge in the framing. Tie it off. Gap biggest at the bottom corner; slip under there and pull into the office, twisting as agilely as the gibbons at the National Zoo, then kneeling on the carpeted floor, huffing and puffing as quietly as possible.

Clip the line to a chair leg, just to be sure it didn't swing back out into the atrium and leave him stuck. Tiptoe across Laveta's office, over to Diane's in-box where he had left his letter.

Not there.

A quick search of the desktop turned up nothing there either.

He couldn't think of any other high-probability places to look for it. The halls had surveillance cameras, and besides, where would he look? It was supposed to be here,

Diane had been gone when he had left it in her in-box. Laveta had nodded, acknowledging receipt of same. Laveta?

Helplessly he searched the other surfaces and drawers in the office, but the letter was not there. There was nothing else he could do. He went back to the window, unclipped his line. He clipped his ascenders back onto it, making sure the good one was high, and that he had taken all the slack out before putting his weight on it. Faced with the tilted window and the open air, he banished all further consideration of the mystery of the absent letter, with one last thought of Laveta and the look he sometimes thought he saw in her eye; perhaps it was a purloined letter. On the other hand, Diane could have come back. But enough of that for now; it was time to focus. He needed to focus. The dreamlike quality of the descent had vanished, and now it was only a sweaty and poorly illuminated job, awkward, difficult, somewhat dangerous. Getting out, letting down the window, rescrewing the frame, leaving the cut seal to surprise some future window washer...Luckily, despite feeling stunned by the setback, the automatic-pilot skills from hundreds of work hours came through. In the end it was an old expertise, a kid skill, something he could do no matter what.

Which was a good thing, because he wasn't actually focusing very well. On various levels his mind was racing. What could have happened? Who had his letter? Would he be able to find the woman from the elevator?

Thus only the next morning, when he came into the building in the ordinary way, did he look up self-consciously and notice that the mobile now hung at a ninety-degree angle to the position it had always held before. But no one seemed to notice.

IX

TRIGGER

EVENT

Transcript NSF 3957396584

Phones 645d/922a

922a: *Frank are you ready for this?*

645d: *I don't know Kenzo, you tell me.*

922a: *Casper the Friendly Ghost spent last week swimming over the sill between Iceland and Scotland, and she never got a salinity figure over 34.*

645d: *Wow. How deep did she go?*

922a: *Surface water, central water, the top of the deep water. And never over 34. 33.8 on the surface once she got into the Norwegian Sea.*

645d: *Wow. What about temperatures?*

922a: *0.9 on the surface, 0.75 at three hundred meters. Warmer to the east, but not by much.*

645d: *Oh my God. It's not going to sink.*

922a: *That's right.*

645d: *What's going to happen?*

922a: *I don't know. It could be the stall.*

645d: *Someone's got to do something about this.*

922a: *Good luck my friend! I personally think we're in for some fun. A thousand years of fun.*

ANNA WAS working with her door open, and once again she heard Frank's end of a phone conversation. Having eavesdropped once, it seemed to have become easier; and as before, there was a strain in Frank's voice that caught her attention. Not to mention louder sentences like:

"*What?* Why would they do *that?*"

Then silence, except for a squeak of his chair and a brief drumming of fingers.

"Uh-huh, yeah. Well, what can I say. It's too bad. It sucks, sure... Yeah. But, you know. You'll be fine either way. It's your workforce that will be in trouble. —No no, I understand. You did your best. Nothing you can do after you sell. It wasn't your call, Derek.... Yeah I know. They'll find work somewhere else. It's not like there aren't other biotechs out there, it's the biotech capital of the world, right? Yeah, sure. Let me know when you know.... Okay, I do too. Bye."

He hung up hard, cursed under his breath.

Anna looked out her door. "Something wrong?"

"Yeah."

She got up and went to her doorway. He was looking down at the floor, shaking his head disgustedly.

He raised his head and met her gaze. "Small Delivery Systems closed down Torrey Pines Generique and let almost everyone go."

"Really! Didn't they just buy them?"

"Yes. But they didn't want the people." He grimaced. "It was for something Torrey Pines had, like a patent. Or one of the people they kept. There were a few they invited to join the Small Delivery lab in Atlanta. Like that mathematician I told you about. The one who sent us a proposal, did I tell you about him?"

"One of the jackets that got turned down?"

"That's right."

"Your panel wasn't that impressed, as I recall."

"Yeah, that's right. But I'm not so sure they were right." He shrugged. "We'll never know now. They'll get him to sign a contract that gives them the rights to his work, and then they'll have it to patent, or keep as a trade secret, or even bury if it interferes with some other product of theirs. Whatever their legal department thinks will make the most."

Anna watched him brood. Finally she said, "Oh well."

He gave her a look. "A guy like him belongs at NSF."

Anna lifted an eyebrow. She was well aware of Frank's ambivalent or even negative attitude toward NSF, which he had let slip often enough.

Frank understood her look and said, "The thing is, if you had him here then you could, you know, sic him on things. Sic him like a dog."

"I don't think we have a program that does that."

"Well you should, that's what I'm saying."

"You can add that to your talk to the Board this afternoon," Anna said. She considered it herself. A kind of human search engine, hunting math-based solutions . . .

Frank did not look amused. "I'll already be out there far

enough as it is," he muttered. "I wish I knew why Diane asked me to give this talk anyway."

"To get your parting wisdom, right?"

"Yeah right." He looked at a pad of yellow legal-sized paper, scribbled over with notes.

Anna surveyed him, feeling again the slightly irritated fondness for him she had felt on the night of the party for the Khembalis. She would miss him when he was gone. "Want to go down and get a coffee?"

"Sure." He got up slowly, lost in thought, and reached out to close the program on his computer.

"Wow, what did you do to your hand?"

"Oh. Burned it in a little climbing fall. Grabbed the rope."

"My God Frank."

"I was belayed at the time, it was just a reflex thing."

"It looks painful."

"It is when I flex it." They left the offices and went to the elevators. "How is Charlie getting along with his poison ivy?"

"Still moaning and groaning. Most of the blisters are healing, but some of them keep breaking open. I think the worst part now is that it keeps waking him up at night. He hasn't slept much since it happened. Between that and Joe he's kind of going crazy."

In the Starbucks she said, "So are you ready for this talk to the Board?"

"No. Or as much as I can be. Like I said, I don't really know why Diane wants me to do it."

"It must be because you're leaving. She wants to get your parting wisdom. She does that with some of the visiting people. It's a sign she's interested in your take on things."

"But how would she know what that is?"

"I don't know. Not from me. I would only say good things, of course, but she hasn't asked me."

He rubbed a finger gently up and down the burn on his palm.

"Tell me," he said, "have you ever heard of someone getting a report and, you know, just filing it away? Taking no action on it?"

"Happens all the time."

"Really."

"Sure. With some things it's the best way to deal with them."

"Hmm."

They had made their way to the front of the line, and so paused for orders, and the rapid production of their coffees. Frank continued to look thoughtful. It reminded Anna of his manner when he had arrived at her party, soaking wet from the rain, and she said, "Say, did you ever find that woman you were stuck in the elevator with?"

"No. I was going to tell you about it. I did what you suggested and contacted the Metro offices, and asked service and repair to get her name from the report. I said I needed to contact her for my insurance report."

"Oh really! And?"

"And the Metro person read it right off to me, no problem. Read me everything she wrote. But it turns out she wrote down the wrong stuff."

"What do you mean?"

They walked out of the Starbucks and back into the building.

"It was a wrong address she put down. There's no residence there. And she wrote down her name as Jane Smith. I think she made everything up."

"That's strange! I guess they didn't check your IDs."

"No."

"I'd have thought they would."

"People just freed from stuck elevators are not in the mood to be handing over their IDs."

"No, I suppose not." An UP elevator opened and they got in. They had it to themselves. "Like your friend, apparently."

"Yeah."

"I wonder why she would write down the wrong stuff though."

"Me too."

"What about what she told you—something about being in a cycling club, was it?"

"I've tried that. None of the cycling clubs in the area will give out membership lists. I cracked into one in Bethesda, but there wasn't any Jane Smith."

"Wow. You've really been looking into it."

"Yes."

"Maybe she's a spook. Hmm. Maybe you could go to all the cycling club meetings, just once. Or join one and ride with it, and look for her at meets, and show her picture around."

"What picture?"

"Get a portrait program to generate one."

"Good idea, although"—sigh—"it wouldn't look like her."

"No, they never do."

"I'd have to get better at riding a bike."

"At least she wasn't into skydiving."

He laughed. "True. Well, I'll have to think about it. But thanks, Anna."

Later that afternoon they met again, on the way up to one of Diane's meetings with the NSF Board of Directors. They got out on the twelfth floor and walked around the hallways. The outer windows at the turns in the halls revealed that the day had darkened, low black clouds now tearing over themselves in their hurry to reach the Atlantic, sheeting down rain as they went.

In the big conference room Laveta and some others were repositioning a whiteboard and PowerPoint screen according to Diane's instructions. Frank and Anna were the first ones there.

"Come on in," Diane said. She busied herself with the screen and kept her back to Frank.

The rest of the crowd trickled in. NSF's Board of Directors was composed of twenty-four people, although usually there were a couple of vacant positions in the process of being filled. The directors were all powers in their parts of the scientific world, appointed by the President from lists provided by NSF and the National Academy of Science, and serving six-year terms.

Now they were looking wet and windblown, straggling into the room in ones and twos. Some of Anna's fellow division directors came in as well. Eventually fifteen or sixteen people were seated around the big table, including Sophie Harper, their congressional liaison. The light in the room flickered faintly as lightning made itself visible diffusely through the coursing rain on the room's exterior window. The gray world outside pulsed as if it were an aquarium.

Diane welcomed them and moved quickly through the agenda's introductory matter. After that she ran down a list of large projects that had been proposed or discussed in the previous year, getting the briefest of reports from Board members assigned to study the projects. They included climate mitigation proposals, many highly speculative, all extremely expensive. A carbon sink plan included reforestations that would also be useful for flood control; Anna made a note to tell the Khembalis about that one.

But nothing they discussed was going to work on the

global situation, given the massive nature of the problem, and NSF's highly constricted budget and mission. Ten billion dollars; and even the fifty-billion-dollar items on their list of projects only addressed small parts of the global problem.

At moments like these Anna could not help thinking of Charlie playing with Joe's dinosaurs, holding up a little pink mouselike thing, a first mammal, and exclaiming, "Hey it's NSF!"

He had meant it as a compliment to their skill at surviving in a big world, or to the way they represented the coming thing, but unfortunately the comparison was also true in terms of size. Scurrying about trying to survive in a world of dying dinosaurs—worse yet, trying to save the dinosaurs too—where was the mechanism? As Frank would say, How could that work?

She banished these thoughts and made her own quick report about the infrastructure distribution programs that she had been studying. These had been in place for some years, and she could therefore provide some quantitative data, tallying increased scientific output in the participating countries. A lot of infrastructure had been dispersed in the last decade. Anna's concluding suggestion that the programs were a success and should be expanded was received with nods all around, as an obvious thing to do. But also expensive.

There was a pause as people thought this over.

Finally Diane looked at Frank. "Frank, are you ready?"

Frank stood to answer. He did not exhibit his usual ease. He walked over to the whiteboard, took up a red marker, fiddled with it. His face was flushed.

"All the programs described so far focus on gathering data, and the truth is we have enough data already. The world's climate has already changed. The Arctic Ocean ice pack breakup has flooded the surface of the North

Atlantic with fresh water, and the most recent data indicate that that has stopped the surface water from sinking, and stalled the circulation of the big Atlantic current. That's been pretty conclusively identified as a major trigger event in Earth's climactic history, as most of you no doubt know. Abrupt climate change has almost certainly already begun."

Frank stared at the whiteboard, lips pursed. "So. The question becomes, what do we do? Business as usual won't work. For you here, the effort should be toward finding ways that NSF can make a much broader impact than it has up until now."

"Excuse me," one of the Board members said, sounding a bit peeved. He was a man in his sixties, with a gray Lincoln beard; Anna did not recognize him. "How is this any different from what we are always trying to do? I mean, we've talked about trying to do this at every Board meeting I've ever been to. We always ask ourselves, how can NSF get more bang for its buck?"

"Maybe so," said Frank. "But it hasn't worked."

Diane said, "What are you saying, Frank? What should we be doing that we haven't already tried?"

Frank cleared his throat. He and Diane stared at each other for a long moment, locked in some kind of undefined conflict.

Frank shrugged, went to the whiteboard, uncapped his red marker. "Let me make a list."

He wrote a 1 and circled it.

"One. We have to knit it all together." He wrote *Synergies at NSF.*

"I mean by this that you should be stimulating synergistic efforts that range across the disciplines to work on this problem. Then," he wrote and circled a 2, "you should be looking for immediately relevant applications coming out of the basic research funded by the Foundation. These applications should be hunted for by people brought in specifically to do that. You should have a permanent in-house innovation and policy team."

Anna thought, That would be that mathematician he just lost.

She had never seen Frank so serious. His usual manner was gone, and with it the mask of cynicism and self-assurance that he habitually wore, the attitude that it was all a game he condescended to play even though everyone had already lost. Now he was serious, even angry it seemed. Angry at Diane somehow. He wouldn't look at her, or anywhere else but at his scrawled red words on the whiteboard.

"Three, you should commission work that you think needs to be done, rather than waiting for proposals and funding choices given to you by others. You can't afford to be so passive anymore. Four, you should assign up to fifty percent of NSF's budget every year to the biggest outstanding problem you can identify, in this case catastrophic climate change, and direct the scientific community to attack and solve it. Both public and private science, the whole culture. The effort could be organized through something like Germany's Max Planck Institutes, which are funded by the government to go after particular problems. There's about a dozen of them, and they exist while they're needed and get disbanded when they're not. It's a good model.

"Five, you should make more efforts to increase the power of science in policy decisions everywhere. Organize all the scientific bodies on Earth into one larger body, a kind of UN of scientific organizations, which then would work together on the important issues, and would collectively *insist* they be funded, for the sake of all the future generations of humanity."

He stopped, stared at the whiteboard. He shook his

head. "All this may sound, what. Large-scaled. Or interfering. Antidemocratic, or elitist or something—something beyond what science is supposed to be."

The man who had objected before said, "We're in no position to stage a coup."

Frank shook him off. "Think of it in terms of Kuhnian paradigms. The paradigm model Kuhn outlined in *The Structure of Scientific Revolutions.*"

The bearded man nodded, granting this.

"Kuhn postulated that in the usual state of affairs there is general agreement to a group of core beliefs that structure people's theories, that's a paradigm, and the work done within it he called 'normal science.' He was referring to a theoretical understanding of nature, but let's apply the model to science's social behavior. We do normal science. But as Kuhn pointed out, anomalies crop up. Undeniable events occur that we can't cope with inside the old paradigm. At first scientists just fit the anomalies in as best they can. Then when there are enough of them, the paradigm begins to fall apart. In trying to reconcile the irreconcilable, it becomes as weird as Ptolemy's astronomical system.

"That's where we are now. We have our universities, and the Foundation and all the rest, but the system is too complicated, and flying off in all directions. Not capable of coming to grips with the aberrant data."

Frank looked briefly at the man who had objected. "Eventually, a new paradigm is proposed that accounts for the anomalies. It comes to grips with them better. After a period of confusion and debate, people start using it to structure a new normal science."

The old man nodded. "You're suggesting we need a paradigm shift in how science interacts with society."

"Yes I am."

"But what is it? We're still in the period of confusion, as far as I can see."

"Yes. But if we don't have a clear sense of what the next paradigm should be, and I agree we don't, then it's our job now as scientists to force the issue and make it happen, by employing all our resources in an organized way. To get to the other side faster. The money and the institutional power that NSF has assembled ever since it began has to be used like a tool to build this. No more treating our grantees like clients whom we have to satisfy if we want to keep their business. No more going to Congress with hat in hand, begging for change and letting them call the shots as to where the money is spent."

"Whoa now," objected Sophie Harper. "They have the right to allocate federal funds, and they're very jealous of that right, believe you me."

"Sure they are. That's the source of their power. And they're the elected government, I'm not disputing any of that. But we can go to them and say look, the party's over. We need this list of projects funded or civilization will be hammered for decades to come. Tell them they can't give half a trillion dollars a year to the military and leave the rescue and rebuilding of the world to chance and some kind of free-market religion. It isn't working, and science is the only way out of the mess."

"You mean the scientific deployment of human effort in these causes," Diane said.

"Whatever," Frank snapped, then paused, as if recognizing what Diane had said. His face went even redder.

"I don't know," another Board member said. "We've been trying more outreach, more lobbying of Congress, all that. I'm not sure more of that will get the big change you're talking about."

Frank nodded. "I'm not sure they will either. They were the best I could think of, and more needs to be done there."

"In the end, NSF is a small agency," someone else said.

"That's true too. But think of it as an information cascade. If the whole of NSF was focused for a time on this project, then our impact would hopefully be multiplied. It would cascade from there. The math of cascades is fairly probabilistic. You push enough elements at once, and if they're the right elements and the situation is at the angle of repose or past it, boom. Cascade. Paradigm shift. New focus on the big problems we're facing."

The people around the table were thinking it over.

Diane never took her eyes off Frank. "I'm wondering if we are at such an obvious edge-of-the-cliff moment that people will listen to us if we try to start such a cascade."

"I don't know," Frank said. "I think we're past the angle of repose. The Atlantic current has stalled. We're headed for a period of rapid climate change. That means problems that will make normal science impossible to pursue."

Diane smiled tautly. "You're suggesting we have to save the world so science can proceed?"

"Yes, if you want to put it that way. If you're lacking a better reason to do it."

Diane stared at him, offended. He met her gaze unapologetically.

Anna watched this standoff, on the edge of her seat. Something was going on between those two, and she had no idea what it was. To ease the suspense she wrote down on her handpad, *saving the world so science can proceed*. The Frank Principle, as Charlie later dubbed it.

"Well," Diane said, breaking the frozen moment, "what do people think?"

A discussion followed. People threw out ideas: creating a kind of shadow replacement for Congress's Office of Technology Assessment; campaigning to make the President's scientific advisor a cabinet post; even drafting a new amendment to the Constitution that would elevate a body like the National Academy of Science to the level of a branch of government. Then also going international, funding a world body of scientific organizations to push everything that would create a sustainable civilization. These ideas and more were mooted, hesitantly at first, and then with more enthusiasm as people began to realize that they all had harbored various ideas of this kind, visions that were usually too big or strange to broach to other scientists. "Pretty wild notions," as one of them noted.

Frank had been listing them on the whiteboard. "The thing is," he said, "the way we have things organized now, scientists keep themselves out of political policy decisions in the same way that the military keeps itself out of civilian affairs. That comes out of World War Two, when science *was* part of the military. Scientists recused themselves from policy decisions, and a structure was formed that created civilian control of science, so to speak.

"But I say to hell with that! Science isn't like the military. It's the solution, not the problem. And so it has to *insist on itself*. That's what looks wild about these ideas, that scientists should take a stand and become a part of the political decision-making process. If it were the folks in the Pentagon saying that, I would agree there would be reason to worry, although they do it all the time. What I'm saying is that it's a *perfectly legitimate move for us to make,* even a necessary move, because we are not the military, we are already civilians, and we have the only methods there are to deal with these global environmental problems."

The group sat for a moment in silence, thinking that over. Monsoonlike rain coursed down the room's window, in an infinity of shifting delta patterns. Darker clouds rolled over, making the room dimmer still, submerging it until it was a cube of lit neon, hanging in aqueous grayness.

Anna's notepad was covered by squiggles and isolated words. So many problems were tangled together into the one big problem. So many of the suggested solutions were either partial or impractical, or both. No one could pretend they were finding any great strategies to pursue at this point. It looked as if Sophie Harper was about to throw her hands in the air, perhaps taking Frank's talk as a critique of her efforts to date, which Anna supposed was one way of looking at it, although not really Frank's point.

Now Diane made a motion as if to cut the discussion short. "Frank," she said, drawing his name out; "Fraannnnnk—you're the one who's brought this up, as if there is something we could do about it. So maybe you should be the one who heads up a committee tasked with figuring out what these things are. Sharpening up the list of things to try, in effect, and reporting back to this Board. You could proceed with the idea that your committee would be building the way to the next paradigm."

Frank stood there, looking at all the red words he had scribbled so violently on the whiteboard. For a long moment he continued to look at it, his expression grim. Many in the room knew that he was due to go back to San Diego. Many did not. Either way Diane's offer probably struck them as another example of her managerial style, which was direct, public, and often had an element of confrontation or challenge in it. When people felt strongly about taking an action she often said, You do it, then. Take the lead if you feel so strongly.

At last Frank turned and met her eye. "Yeah, sure," he said. "I'd be happy to do that. I'll give it my best shot."

Diane revealed only a momentary gleam of triumph. Once when Anna was young she had seen a chess master play an entire room of opponents, and there had been only one player among them he was having trouble with; when he had checkmated that person, he had moved on to the next board with that very same quick satisfied look.

Now, in this room, Diane was already on to the next item on her agenda.

AFTERWARD, THE bioinformatics group sat in Anna's and Frank's rooms on the sixth floor, sipping cold coffee and looking into the atrium.

Edgardo came in. "So," he said cheerily, "I take it the meeting was a total waste of time."

"No," Anna snapped.

Edgardo laughed. "Diane changed NSF top to bottom?"

"No."

They sat there. Edgardo went and poured himself some coffee.

Anna said to Frank, "It sounded like you were telling Diane you would stay another year."

"Yep."

Edgardo came back in, amazed. "Will wonders never cease! I hope you didn't give up your apartment yet!"

"I did."

"Oh no! Too bad!"

Frank flicked that away with his burned hand. "The guy is coming back anyway."

Anna regarded him. "So you really are changing your mind."

"Well…"

The lights went out, computers too. Power failure.

"Ah shit."

A blackout. No doubt a result of the storm.

Now the atrium was truly dark, all the offices lit only by the dim green glow of the emergency exit signs. EXIT. The shadow of the future.

Then the emergency generator came on, making an audible hum through the building. With a buzz and several computer pings, electricity returned.

Anna went down the hall to look north out the corner window. Arlington was dark to the rain-fuzzed horizon. Many emergency generators had already kicked in, and more did so as she watched, powering glows that in the rain looked like little campfires. The cloud over the Pentagon caught the light from below and gleamed blackly.

Frank came out and looked over her shoulder. "This is what it's going to be like all the time," he predicted gloomily. "We might as well get used to it."

Anna said, "How would that work?"

He smiled briefly. But it was a real smile, a tiny version of the one Anna had seen at her house. "Don't ask me." He stared out the window at the darkened city. The low thrum of rain was cut by the muffled sound of a siren below.

THE HYPERNIÑO that was now into its forty-second month had spun up another tropical system in the East Pacific, north of the equator, and now this big wet storm was barreling northeast toward California. It was the fourth in a series of pineapple-express storms that had tracked along this course of the jet stream, which was holding in an exceptionally fast run directly at the north coast of San Diego County. Ten miles above the surface, winds flew at a hundred and seventy miles an hour, so the air underneath was yanked over the ground at around sixty miles an hour, all roiled, torn, downdrafted and compressed, its rain squeezed out of it the moment it slammed into land. The sea cliffs of La Jolla, Blacks, Torrey Pines, Del Mar, Solana Beach, Cardiff-by-the-Sea, Encinitas, and Leucadia were all taking a beating, and in many places the sandstone, eaten by waves from below and saturated with rain from above, began to fall into the sea.

Leo and Roxanne Mulhouse had a front seat on all this, of course, because of their house's location on the cliff edge in Leucadia. Leo had spent many an hour since being let go sitting before their west window, or even standing out on the porch in the elements, watching the storms come onshore. It was an astonishing thing to see that much weather crashing into a coastline. The clouds and sky appeared to pour up over the southwest horizon together. They flew overhead and yet the cliffs and the houses held, making the wind howl at the impediment, compressed and intensified in this first assault on the land.

This particular morning was the worst yet. Tree branches tossed violently; three eucalyptus trees had been knocked over on Neptune Avenue alone. And Leo had never seen the sea look like this before. All the way out to where rapidly approaching black squalls blocked the view of the horizon, the ocean was a giant sheet of raging surf. Millions of whitecaps rolled toward the land under flying spume and spray, the waves toppling again and again over infinitely wind-rippled gray water. The squalls flew by rapidly, or came straight on in black bursts of rain against the house's west side. Brief patches and shards of sunlight lanced between these squalls, but failed to light the sea surface in their usual way; the water was too shredded. The gray shafts of light appeared to be eaten by spray.

Up and down Neptune Avenue, their cliff was wearing away. It happened irregularly, in sudden slumps of various sizes, some at the cliff top, some at the base, some in the middle.

The erosion was not a new thing. The cliffs of San Diego had been breaking off throughout the period of modern settlement, and presumably for all the centuries before that. But along this level stretch of seaside cliff north and south of Moonlight Beach, the houses had been built close to the edge. Surveyors studying photos had seen little movement in the cliff's edge between 1928 and 1965, when the construction began. They had not known about the storm of October 12, 1889, when 7.58 inches of rain had fallen on Encinitas in eight hours, triggering a flood and bluff collapse so severe that A, B, and C Streets of the new town had disappeared into the sea. They also did not understand that grading the bluffs and adding drainage pipes that led out the cliff face destroyed natural drainage patterns that led inland. So the homes and apartment blocks had been built with their fine views, and then years of efforts had been made to stabilize the cliffs.

Now, among other problems, the cliffs were often unnaturally vertical as a result of all the shoring up they had been given. Concrete and steel barriers, iceplant berms, wooden walls and log beams, plastic sheets and molding, crib walls, boulder walls, concrete abutments—all these efforts had been made in the same period when the beaches were no longer being replenished by sand washing out of the lagoons to the north, because all these had had their watersheds developed and their rivers made much less prone to flooding sand out to sea. So over time the beaches had disappeared, and these days waves stuck directly at the bases of ever-steepening cliffs. The angle of repose was very far exceeded.

Now the ferocity of the Hyperniño was calling all that to account, overwhelming a century's work all at once. The day before, just south of the Mulhouses' property, a section of the cliff a hundred feet long and fifteen feet deep went, burying a concrete berm lying at the bottom of the cliff. Two hours later a hemispheric arc forty feet deep had fallen into the surf just north of them, leaving a raw new gap between two apartment blocks—a gap that quickly turned into a gritty mudslide that slid down into the tormented water, staining it brown for hundreds of yards offshore. The usual current was southerly, but the storm was shoving the ocean as well as the air northward, so that the water offshore was chaotic with drifts, with discharge from suddenly raging river mouths, with backwash from the strikes of the big swells, and with the everpresent wind, slinging spray over all. It was so bad no one was even surfing.

As the dark morning wore on, many of the residents of Neptune Avenue went out to look at their stretch of the bluff. Various authorities were there as well, and interested spectators were filling the little cross streets that ran east to the coast highway, and gathering at public places along the cliff's edge. Many residents had gone the previous evening to hear a team from the U.S. Army Corps of Engineers give a presentation at the town library, explaining their plan to stabilize the cliff at its most vulnerable points with impromptu riprap seawalls made of boulders dumped from above. In some places getting the boulders over the side would damage the iceplant covering. Routes out to some of the cliff top dumping points might also be trashed. Given the situation it was felt the damage was justified for the greater good. Repairs when the crisis had passed were promised. Of course some things could not be fixed; in many places the already narrow beach would be buried, becoming a wall of boulders even at low tide—like the side of a jetty, or a stretch of some very rocky coastline. Some people at the meeting lamented this loss of the area's signature landscape feature, a beach that had been four hundred yards wide in the 1920's, and even in its present narrowed state, the thing that made San Diego what it was. There were people there who felt that was worth more than houses built too close to the edge. Let them go!

But the cliff-edge homeowners had argued that it was not necessarily true that the cliffside line of houses would be the end of the losses. Everyone now knew the story behind the westernmost street in Encinitas being named D Street. The whole town was on the edge of a sandstone cliff, when you got right down to it, a cliff badly fractured and faulted. If massive rapid erosion had happened before, it could happen again. One look at the raging surface of the Pacific roaring in at them was enough to convince people it was possible.

So, later that morning, Leo found himself standing near the edge of the cliff at the south end of Leucadia, his rain jacket and pants plastered to his windward side as he shoved a wheelbarrow over a wide plank path. Roxanne was inland helping at her sister's, and so he was free to pitch in, and happy to have something to do. A county dump truck working with the Army Corps of Engineers was parked on Europa, and men running a small hoist were lifting granite boulders from the truck bed down into wheelbarrows. A lot of amateur help milled about, looking like a volunteer fire company that had never met before. The county and Army people supervised the operations, lining up plankways and directing rocks to the various points on the cliff's edge where they were dumping them over.

Meanwhile scores or even hundreds of people had come out in the storm, to stand on the coast highway or in the viewpoint parking lots, and watch the wheelbarrowed boulders bound down the cliff and crash into the sea. It was already the latest spectator event, like a new extreme sport. Some of the bounding rocks caught really good air, or spun, or held still like knuckleballs, or splashed hugely. The surfers who were not helping (and there were only so many volunteers who could be accommodated at any one time) cheered lustily at the most dramatic falls. Every surfer in the county was there, drawn like moths to flame, entranced, and on some level itching to go out; but it was not possible. The water was crazy everywhere, and when the big broken waves smashed into the bottom of the cliffs, they had nowhere to go. Big surges shoved up, disintegrated into a white smash of foam and spray, hung suspended for a moment—balked masses of water, regathering themselves high against the cliff face—then they fell and muscled back out to sea, bulling into the incoming waves and creating thick tumultuous backwash collisions, until all in the brown shallows was chaos and disorder, and another surge managed to crash in only slightly impeded.

And all the while the wind howled over them, through them, against them. It was basically a warm wind, perhaps sixty or even sixty-five degrees. Leo found it impossible to judge its speed. Even though the cliffs in this area were low compared to those at Torrey Pines—about eighty feet tall rather than three hundred and fifty—that was still enough and more to block the terrific onshore flow and cause the wind to shoot up the cliffs and over them, so that a bit back from the edge it could be almost still, while right at the edge a blasting updraft was spiked by frequent gusts, like uppercuts from an invisible fist. Leo felt as if he could have leaned out over the edge and put out his arms and be held there at an angle—even jump and float down. Young windsurfers would probably be trying it soon, or surfers with their wetsuits altered to make them something like flying squirrels. Not that they would want to be in the water now. The sheer height of the whitewater surge against the cliffside was hard to believe, truly startling; bursts of spray regularly shot up into the wind and were whirled inland onto the already-drenched houses and people.

Leo got his wheelbarrow to the end of the plank road, and let a gang of people grasp his handles with him and help him tilt the stone out at the right place. After that he got out of the way and stood for a moment, watching people work. Restricted access to some of the weakest parts of the cliff meant that this was going to take days. Right now the rocks simply disappeared into the waves. No visible result whatsoever. "It's like dropping rocks in the ocean," he said to no one. The noise of the wind was terrific, a constant howl, like jets warming up for takeoff, interrupted by frequent invisible whacks on the ear. He could talk to himself without fear of being overheard, and did: a running narration of his day. His eyes watered in the wind, but that same wind tore the tears away and cleared his vision again and again.

This was purely a physical reaction to the gale; he was basically very happy to be there. Happy to have the distraction of the storm. A public disaster, a natural world event; it put everyone in the same boat, somehow. In a way it was even inspiring—not just the human response, but the storm itself. Wind as spirit. It felt uplifting. As if the wind had carried him off and out of his life.

Certainly it put things in a very different perspective. Losing a job, so what? How did that signify, really? The world was so vast and powerful. They were tiny things in it, like fleas, their problems the tiniest of flea perturbations.

So he returned to the dump truck and took another rock, and then focused on balancing the broken-edged thing at the front end of the wheelbarrow: turning it, keeping it on the flexing line of planks, shouldering into the blasts. Tipping a rock into the sea. Wonderful, really.

He was running the empty wheelbarrow back to the street when he saw Marta and Brian, getting out of Marta's truck parked down at the end of the street. "Hey!" This was a nice surprise—they were not a couple, or even friends outside the lab, as far as Leo knew, and he had feared that with the lab shut down he would never see either of them again.

"Marta!" he bellowed happily. "Bri-man!"

"LEO!"

They were glad to see him. Marta ran up and gave him a hug. Brian did the same.

"How's it going?" "How's it going?"

They were jacked up by the storm and the chance to do something. No doubt it had been a long couple of weeks for them too, no work to go to, nothing to do. Well, they would have been out in the surf, or otherwise active. But here they were now, and Leo was glad.

Quickly they all got into the flow of the work, trundling rocks out to the cliff. Once Leo found himself following Marta down the plank line, and he watched her broad bunched shoulders and soaking black curls with a sudden blaze of friendship and admiration. She was a surfer gal, slim hips, broad shoulders, raising her head at a blast of the wind to howl back at it. Hooting with glee. He was going to miss her. Brian too. It had been good of them to come by like this; but the nature of things was such that they would surely find other work, and then they would drift apart. It never lasted with old work colleagues, the bond just wasn't strong enough. Work was always a matter of showing up and then enjoying the people who had been hired to work there too. Not only their banter, but also the way they did the work, the experiments they made together. They had been a good lab.

The Army guys were waving them back from the edge of the cliff. It had been a lawn and now it was all torn up, and there was a guy there crouching over a big metal box, USGS on his soaking windbreaker. Brian shouted in their ears: they had found a fracture in the sandstone parallel to the cliff's edge here, and apparently someone had felt the ground slump a little, and the USGS guy's instrumentation was indicating movement. It was going to go. Everyone dumped their rocks where they were and hustled the empty wheelbarrows back to Neptune.

Just in time. With a short dull roar and *whump* that almost could have been the sound of more wind and surf—the impact of a really big wave—the cliff edge slumped.

Then where it had been, they were looking through space at the gray sea hundreds of yards offshore. The cliff top was fifteen feet closer to them.

Very spooky. The crowd let out a collective shout that was audible above the wind. Leo and Brian and Marta drifted forward with the rest, to catch a glimpse of the dirty rage of water below. The break extended about a hundred yards to the south, maybe fifty to the north. A modest loss in the overall scheme of things, but this was the way it was happening, one little break at a time, all up and down this stretch of coast. The USGS guy had told them that there was a whole series of faults in the sandstone here, all parallel to the cliff, so that it was likely to flake off piece by piece as the waves gouged away support from below. That was how A through C Streets had gone in a single night. It could happen all the way inland to the coast highway, he said.

Amazing. Leo could only hope that Roxanne's mother's house had been built on one of the more solid sections of the bluff. It had always seemed that way when he descended the nearby staircase and checked it out; it stood over a kind of buttress of stone. But as he watched the ocean flail, and felt the wind strike them, there was no reason to be sure any section would hold. A whole neighborhood could go. And all up and down the coast they had built close to the edge, so it would be much the same in many other places.

No house had gone over in the slump they had just witnessed, but one at the southern end of it had lost parts of its west wall—been torn open to the wind. Everyone stood around staring, pointing, shouting unheard in the roar of wind. Milling about, running hither and thither, trying to get a view.

There was nothing else to be done at this point. The end of their plank road was gone along with everything else. The Army and county guys were getting out saw-horses and rolls of orange plastic stripping; they were going to cordon off this section of the street, evacuate it, and shift the work efforts to safer platforms.

"Wow," Leo said to the storm, feeling the word ripped out of his mouth and flung to the east. "My Lord, what a wind." He shouted to Marta: "We were standing right out there!"

"Gone!" Marta howled. "That baby is gone! It's as gone as Torrey Pines Generique!"

Brian and Leo shouted their agreement. Into the sea with the damned place!

They retreated to the lee of Marta's little Toyota pickup, sat on the curb behind its slight protection and drank some espressos she had in the cab, already cold in paper cups with plastic tops.

"There'll be more work," Leo told them.

"That's for sure." But they meant boulder work. "I heard the coast highway is cut just south of Cardiff," Brian said. "San Elijo Lagoon is completely full, and now the surf is coming up the river mouth. Restaurant Row is totally gone. The overpass fell in and then the water started ripping both ways at the roadbed."

"Wow!"

"It's going to be a mess. I bet that will happen at the Torrey Pines river mouth too."

"*All* the big lagoons."

"Maybe, yeah."

They sipped their espressos.

"It's good to see you guys!" Leo said. "Thanks for coming by."

"Yeah."

"That's the worst part of this whole thing," Leo said.

"Yeah."

"Too bad they didn't hang on to us—they're putting all their eggs in one basket now."

Marta and Brian regarded Leo. He wondered which part of what he had just said they disagreed with. Now that they weren't working for him, he had no right to grill them about it, or about anything else. On the other hand there was no reason to hold back either.

"What?"

"I just got hired by Small Delivery Systems," Marta said, almost shouting to be heard over the noise. She glanced at Leo uncomfortably. "Eleanor Dufours is working for them now, and she hired me. They want us to work on that algae stuff we've been doing."

"Oh I see! Well good! Good for you."

"Yeah, well. Atlanta."

There was a whistle from the Army guys. A whole gang of Leucadians were trooping behind them down Neptune, south to another dump truck that had just arrived. There was more to be done.

Leo and Marta and Brian followed, went back to work. Some people left, others arrived. Lots of people were documenting events on video cameras and digital cameras. As the day wore on, the volunteers were glad to take heavy-duty work gloves from the Army guys to protect their palms from further blistering.

About two that afternoon the three of them decided to call it quits. Their palms were trashed. Leo's thighs and lower back were getting shaky, and he was hungry. The cliff work would go on, and there would be no shortage of volunteers while the storm lasted. The need was evident, and besides it was fun to be out in the blast, doing something. Working made it seem like a practical contribution to be out there, although many would have been out to watch in any case.

The three of them stood on a point just north of

Swami's, leaning into the storm and marveling at the spectacle. Marta was bouncing a little in place, stuffed with energy still, totally fired up; she seemed both exhilarated and furious, and shouted at the biggest waves when they struck the stubborn little cliff at Pipes. "Wow! Look at that. Outside, outside!" She was soaking wet, as they all were, the rain plastering her curls to her head, the wind plastering her shirt to her torso; she looked like the winner of some kind of extreme-sport wet T-shirt contest, her breasts and belly button and ribs and collarbones and abs all perfectly delineated under the thin wet cloth. She was a power, a San Diego surf goddess, and good for her that she had gotten hired by Small Delivery Systems. Again Leo felt a glow for this wild young colleague of his.

"This is so great," he shouted. "I'd rather do this than work in the lab!"

Brian laughed. "They don't pay you for this, Leo."

"Ah hey. Fuck that. This is still better." And he howled at the storm.

Then Brian and Marta gave him hugs; they were taking off.

"Let's try to stay in touch you guys," Leo said sentimentally. "Let's really do it. Who knows, we may all end up working together again someday anyway."

"Good idea."

"I'll probably be available," Brian said.

Marta shrugged, looking away. "We either will be or we won't."

Then they were off. Leo waved at Marta's receding truck. A sudden pang—would he ever see them again? The reflection of the truck's taillights smeared in two red lines over the street's wet asphalt. Blinking right turn signal—then they were gone.

X

BROADER

IMPACTS

It takes no great skill to decode the world system today. A tiny percentage of the population is immensely wealthy, some are well off, a lot are just getting by, a lot more are suffering. We call it capitalism, but within it lies buried residual patterns of feudalism and older hierarchies, basic injustices framing the way we organize ourselves. Everybody lives in an imaginary relationship to this real situation; and that is our world. We walk with scales on our eyes, and only see what we think.

And all the while on a sidewalk over the abyss. There are islands of time when things seem stable. Nothing much happens but the rounds of the week. Later the islands break apart. When enough time has passed, no one now alive will still be here; everyone will be different. Then it will be the stories that will link the generations, history and DNA, long chains of the simplest bits—guanine, adenine, cytosine, thymine—love, hope, fear, selfishness—all recombining again and again, until a miracle happens

and the organism springs forth!

CHARLIE, AWAKENED by the sound of a loud alarm, leapt to his feet and stood next to his bed, hands thrown out like a nineteenth-century boxer.

"What?" he shouted at the loud noise.

It was not an alarm. It was Joe in the room, wailing. He stared at his father amazed. "Ba."

"Jesus, Joe." The itchiness began to burn across Charlie's chest and arms. He had tossed and turned in misery most of the night, as he had every night since encountering the poison ivy. He had probably fallen asleep only an hour or two before. "What time is it. Joe, it's not even seven! Don't *yell* like that. All you have to do is tap me on the shoulder if I'm asleep, and say, 'Good morning Dad, can you warm up a bottle for me?' "

Joe approached and tapped his leg, staring peacefully at him. "Mo Da. Wa ba."

"Wow Joe. Really good! Say, I'll get your bottle warmed up right away! Very good! Hey listen, have you pooped in your diaper yet? You might want to pull it down and sit on *your own toilet* in the bathroom like a big boy, poop like Nick and then come on down to the kitchen and your bottle will be ready. Doesn't that sound good?"

"Ga Da." Joe trundled off toward the bathroom.

Charlie, amazed, padded after Joe and descended the stairs as gently as he could, hoping not to stimulate his itches. In the kitchen the air was delightfully cool and silky. Nick was there reading a book. Without looking up he said, "I want to go down to the park and play."

"I thought you had homework to do."

"Well, sort of. But I want to play."

"Why don't you do your homework first and then play, that way when you play you'll be able to really enjoy it."

Nick cocked his head. "That's true. Okay, I'll go do my homework first." He slipped out, book under his arm.

"Oh, and take your shoes up to your room while you're on your way."

"Sure Dad."

Charlie stared at his reflection in the side of the stove hood. His eyes were round.

"Hmm," he said. He got Joe's bottle in its pot, stuck an earphone in his left ear. "Phone, give me Phil.... Hello, Phil, look I wanted to catch you while the thought was fresh, I was thinking that if only we tried to introduce the Chinese aerosols bill again, then we could catch the whole air problem at a kind of fulcrum point and either start a process that would finish with the coal plants here on the East Coast, or else it would serve as a stalking horse, see what I mean?"

"So you're saying we go after the Chinese again?"

"Well yeah, but as part of your whole package of efforts."

"And then it either works or it doesn't work, but gives us some leverage we can use elsewhere? Hmm, good idea Charlie, I'd forgotten that bill, but it was a good one. I'll give that a try. Call Roy and tell him to get it ready."

"Sure Phil, consider it done."

Charlie took the bottle out of the pot and dried it. Joe appeared in the door, naked, holding up his diaper for Charlie's inspection.

"Wow Joe, very good! You pooped in your toilet? Very, very good, here's your bottle all ready, what a perfect kind of Pavlovian reward."

Joe snatched the bottle from Charlie's hand and waddled off, a length of toilet paper trailing behind him, one end stuck between the halves of his butt.

Holy shit, Charlie thought. So to speak.

He called up Roy and told him Phil had authorized the reintroduction of the Chinese bill. Roy was incredulous. "What do you mean, we went down big-time on that, it was a joke then and it would be worse now!"

"No not so, it lost bad but that was good, we got lots of credit for it that we deployed elsewhere, and it'll happen the same way when we do it again because it's *right*, Roy, we have right on our side on this."

"Yes of course obviously that's not the point—"

"Not the point, have we gotten so jaded that being right is no longer relevant?"

"No of course not, but that's not the point either, it's like playing a chess game, each move is just a move in the larger game, you know?"

"Yes I do know because that's my analogy, but that's my point, this is a good move, this checks them, they have to give up a queen to stop from being checkmated."

"You really think it's that much leverage? Why?"

"Because Winston has such ties to Chinese industry, and he can't defend that very well to his hard-core constituency, Christian *realpolitik* isn't really a supercoherent philosophy and so it's a *vulnerability* he has don't you see?"

"Well yeah, of course. You said Phil okayed it already?"

"Yes he did."

"Okay, that's good enough for me."

Charlie got off and did a little dance in the kitchen, circling out into the living room, where Joe was sitting on the floor trying to get back into his diaper. Both adhesive tags had torn loose. "Good try Joe, here let me help you."

"Okay Da." Joe held out the diaper.

"Hmm," Charlie said, suddenly suspicious.

He called up Anna and got her. "Hey snooks, how are you, yeah I'm just calling to say I love you and to suggest that we get tickets to fly to Jamaica, we'll find some kind of kid care and go down there just by ourselves, we'll rent a whole beach to ourselves and spend a week down there or maybe two, it would be good for us."

"True."

"It's really inexpensive down there now because of the unrest and all, so we'll have it all to ourselves almost."

"True."

"So I'll just call up the travel agent and have them put it all on my business-expenses card."

"Okay, go for it."

Then there was a kind of cracking sound and Charlie woke up for real.

"Ah shit."

He knew just what had happened, because it had happened before. His dreaming mind had grown skeptical at something in a dream that was going too well or badly—in this case his implausibly powerful persuasiveness—and so he had dreamed up ever-more-unlikely scenarios, in a kind of test-to-destruction, until the dream had popped and he had awakened.

It was almost funny, this relationship to dreams. Except sometimes they crashed at the most inopportune moments. It was perverse to probe the limits of believability rather than just go with the flow, but that was the way Charlie's mind worked, apparently. Nothing he could do about it but groan and laugh, and try to train his sleeping mind into a more wish fulfillment–tolerant response.

It turned out that in the real world it was a work-at-home day for Anna, scheduled to give Charlie a kind of poison ivy vacation from Joe. Charlie was planning to take advantage of that to go down to the office by himself for once, and have a talk with Phil about what to do next. It was crucial to get Phil on line for a set of small bills that would save the best of the comprehensive.

He padded downstairs to find Anna cooking pancakes for the boys. Joe liked to use them as little frisbees. "Morning babe."

"Hi hon." He kissed her on the ear, inhaling the smell of her hair. "I just had the most amazing dream. I could talk anybody into anything."

"How exactly was that a dream?"

"Yeah right! Don't tease me about that, obviously I can't talk anybody into anything. No, this was definitely a dream. In fact I pushed it too far and killed it. I tried to talk you into going off with me to Jamaica, and you said yes."

She laughed merrily at the thought, and he laughed to see her laugh, and at the memory of the dream. And then it seemed like a gift instead of a mockery.

He scanned the kitchen computer screen for the news. *Stormy Monday,* it proclaimed. Big storms were swirling up out of the subtropics, and the freshly minted blue of the Arctic Ocean was dotted by a daisy chain of white patches, all falling south. The highest satellite photos, covering most of the Northern Hemisphere, reminded Charlie of how his skin had looked right after his outbreak of poison ivy. A huge white blister had covered Southern California the day before; another was headed their way from Canada, this one a real bruiser—big, wet, slightly warmer than usual, pouring down on them from Saskatchewan.

The media meteorologists were already in a lather of anticipation and analysis, not only over the arctic blast but also in response to a tropical storm now leaving the Bahamas, even though it had wreaked less damage than had been predicted.

"'Unimpressive,' this guy calls it. My God! Everybody's a critic. Now people are *reviewing the weather*."

"'Tasteful little cirrus clouds,'" Anna quoted from somewhere.

"Yeah. And I heard someone talking about an 'ostentatious thunderhead.'"

"It's the melodrama," Anna guessed. "Climate as bad art, as soap opera. Or some kind of unstaged reality TV."

"Or staged."

"Do you think you should stay home?"

"No it'll be okay. I'll just be at work."

"Okay." This made sense to Anna; it took a lot to keep her from going to work. "But be careful."

"I will. I'll be indoors."

Charlie went back upstairs to get ready. A trip out without Joe! It was like a little adventure.

Although once he was actually walking up Wisconsin, he found he kind of missed his little puppetmaster. He stood at a corner, waiting for the light to change, and when a tall semi rumbled by he said aloud, "Oooh, big truck!" which caused the others waiting for the light to give him a look. Embarrassing; but it was truly hard to remember he was alone. His shoulders kept flexing at the unaccustomed lack of weight. The back of his neck felt the wind on it. It was somehow an awful realization: he would rather have had Joe along. "Jesus, Quibler, what are you coming to."

It was good, however, not to have the straps of the baby backpack cutting across his chest. Even without them the poison ivy damage was prickling at the touch of his shirt and the first sheen of sweat. Since the encounter with the tree he had slept so poorly, spending so much of every night awake in an agony of unscratchable itching, that he felt thoroughly and completely deranged. His doctor had prescribed powerful oral steroids, and given him a shot of them too, so maybe that was part of it. That or simply the itching itself. Putting on clothes was like a kind of skin-deep electrocution.

It had only taken a few days of that to reduce him to a gibbering semi-hallucinatory state. Now, over a week later, it was worse. His eyes were sandy; things had auras around them; noises made him jump. It was like the dregs of a crystal-meth jag, he imagined, or the last hours of an acid trip. A sandpapered brain, spacy and raw, everything leaping in through the senses.

He took the Metro to Dupont Circle, got off there just to take a walk without Joe. He stopped at Kramer's and got an espresso to go, then started around the circle to check the Dupont Second Story, but stopped when he realized he was doing exactly the things he would have done if he had had Joe with him.

He carried on southeastward instead, strolling down Connecticut toward the Mall. As he walked he admired a great spectacle of clouds overhead, vast towers of pearly white lobes blooming upward into a high pale sky.

He stopped at the wonderful map store on Eye Street, and for a while lost himself in the cloud shapes of other countries. Back outside, the clouds were growing in place rather than heaving in from the west or the southeast. Brilliant anvil heads were blossoming sixty thousand feet overhead, forming a hyper-Himalaya that looked as solid as marble.

He pulled out his phone and put it in his left ear. "Phone, call Roy."

After a second: "Roy Anastophoulus."

"Roy, it's Charlie. I'm coming on in."

"I'm not there."

"Ah come on!"

"I know. When was the last time I actually saw you?"

"I don't know."

"You have two kids, right?"

"Oh, didn't you hear?"

"Ha ha ha. I'd like to see that."

"Jesus no."

"What are you going in for?"

"I need to talk to Phil. I had a dream this morning that I could convince anybody of anything, even Joe. I convinced Phil to reintroduce the Chinese aerosols bill, and then I got you to approve it."

"That poison ivy has driven you barking mad."

"Very true. It must be the steroids. I mean, the clouds today are like *pulsing*. They don't know which way to go."

"That's probably right, there's two low-pressure systems colliding here today, didn't you hear?"

"How could I not."

"They say it's going to rain really hard."

"Looks like I'll beat it to the office, though."

"Good. Hey listen, when Phil gets in, don't be too hard on him. He already feels bad enough."

"He does?"

"Well, no. Not really. I mean, when have you ever seen Phil feel bad about anything?"

"Never."

"Right. But, you know. He would feel bad about this if he were to go in for that kind of thing. And you have to remember, he's pretty canny at getting the most he can get from these bills. He sees the limits and then does what he can. It's not a zero-sum game to him. He really doesn't think of it as us-and-them."

"But sometimes it *is* us-and-them."

"True. But he takes the long view. Later some of them will be part of us. And meanwhile, he finds some pretty good tricks. Breaking the superbill into parts might have been the right way to go. We'll get back to a lot of this stuff later."

"Maybe. We never tried the Chinese aerosols again."

"Not yet."

Charlie stopped listening to check the street he was crossing. When he started listening again Roy was saying, "So you dreamed you were Xenophon, eh?"

"How's that?"

"Xenophon. He wrote the *Anabasis,* which tells the story of how he and a bunch of Greek mercenaries got stuck and had to fight all the way across Turkey to get home to Greece. They argue the whole time about what to do, and Xenophon wins every argument, and all his plans always work perfectly. I think of it as the first great political fantasy novel. So who else did you convince?"

"Well, I got Joe to potty train himself, and then I convinced Anna to leave the kids at home and go with me on a vacation to Jamaica."

Roy laughed heartily. "Dreams are so funny."

"Yeah, but bold. So bold. Sometimes I wake up and wonder why I'm not as bold as that all the time. I mean, what have we got to lose?"

"Jamaica, baby. Hey, did you know that some of those hotels on the north shore there are catering to couples who like to have a lot of semipublic sex, out around the pools and the beaches?"

"Talk about fantasy novels."

"Yeah, but don't you think it'd be interesting?"

"You are sounding kind of, I don't want to say desperate here, but deprived maybe?"

"It's true, I am. It's been *weeks*."

"Oh poor guy. It's been weeks since I left my house."

Actually, for Roy a few weeks was quite a long time between amorous encounters. One of the not-so-hidden secrets of Washington, D.C., was that among the ambitious young single people gathered there to run the world, there was a whole lot of collegial sex going on. Now Roy said dolefully, "I guess I'll have to go dancing tonight."

"Oh poor you! I'll be at home not scratching myself."

"You'll be fine. You've already got yours. Hey listen, my food has come."

"So where are you anyway?"

"Bombay Club."

"Ah geez." This was a restaurant run by a pair of Indian-Americans, its decor Raj, its food excellent. A favorite of staffers, lobbyists and other political types. Charlie loved it.

"Tandoori salmon?" he said.

"That's right. It looks and smells fantastic."

"Yesterday my lunch was Gerber's baby spinach."

"No. You don't really eat that stuff."

"Yeah sure. It's not so bad. It could use a little salt."

"Yuck!"

"Yeah, see what I do is I mix a little spinach and a little banana together?"

"Oh come on quit it!"

"Bye."

"Bye."

The light under the thunderheads had gone dim. Rain was soon to arrive. The cloud bottoms were black. Splotches like dropped water balloons starred the sidewalk pavement. Charlie started hurrying, and got to Phil's office just ahead of a downpour.

He looked back out through the glass doors and watched the rain grow in strength, hammering down the length of the Mall. The skies had really opened. The raindrops remained large in the air; it looked like hail the size of baseballs had coalesced in the thunderheads, and then somehow been melted back to rain again before reaching the ground.

Charlie watched the spectacle for a while, then went upstairs. There he found out from Evelyn that Phil's flight in had been delayed, and that he might be driving back from Richmond instead.

Charlie sighed. No conferring with Phil today.

He read reports instead, and made notes for when Phil did arrive. Went down to get his mailbox cleared. Evelyn's office window had a southerly view, with the Capitol looming to the left, and across the Mall the Air and Space Museum. In the rainy light the big buildings took on an eerie cast. They looked like the cottages of giants.

Then it was past noon, and Charlie was hungry. The rain seemed to have eased a bit since its first impact, so he went out to get a sandwich at the Iranian deli on C Street, grabbing an umbrella at the door.

Outside it was raining steadily but lightly. The streets were deserted. Many intersections had flooded to the curbs, and in a few places well over the curbs, onto the sidewalks.

Inside the deli the grill was sizzling, but the place was almost as empty as the streets. Two cooks and the cashier were standing under a TV that hung from a ceiling corner, watching the news. When they recognized Charlie they went back to looking at the TV. The characteristic smell of basmati rice and hummus enfolded him.

"Big storm coming," the cashier said. "Ready to order?"

"Yeah, thanks. I'll have the usual, pastrami sandwich on rye and potato chips."

"Flood too," one of the cooks said.

"Oh yeah?" Charlie replied. "What, more than usual?"

The cashier nodded, still looking at the TV. "Two storms and high tide. Upstream, downstream and middle."

"Oh my."

Charlie wondered what it would mean. Then he stood watching the TV with the rest of them. Satellite weather photos showed a huge sheet of white pouring across New York and Pennsylvania. Meanwhile that tropical storm was spinning past Bermuda. It looked like another perfect storm might be brewing, like the eponymous one of 1991. Not that it took a perfect storm these days to make the Mid-Atlantic states seem like a literal designation. A far less than perfect storm could do it. The TV spoke of eleven-year tide cycles, of the longest and strongest El Niño ever recorded. "It's a fourteen-thousand-square-mile watershed," the TV said.

"It's gonna get wet," Charlie observed.

The Iranians nodded silently. Five years earlier they would probably have been closing the deli, but this was the fourth "perfect storm" synergistic combination in the last three years, and they, like everyone else, were getting jaded. It was Peter crying wolf at this point, even though the previous three storms had all been major disasters at the time, at least in some places. But never in D.C. Now people just made sure their supplies and equipment were okay and then went about their business, umbrella and phone in hand. Charlie was no different, he realized, even though he had been performing the role of Peter for all he was worth when it came to the global situation. But here he was, getting a pastrami sandwich with the intention of going back to work. It seemed like the best way to deal with it.

The Iranians finally finished his order, all the while

watching the TV images: flooding fields, apparently in the upper Potomac watershed, near Harpers Ferry.

"Three meters," the cashier said as she gave him his change, but Charlie wasn't sure what she meant. The cook chopped Charlie's wrapped sandwich in half, put it in a bag. "First one is worst one."

Charlie took it and hurried back through the darkening streets. He passed an occasional lit window, occupied by people working at computer terminals, looking like figures in a Hopper painting.

Now it began to rain hard again, and the wind was roaring in the trees and hooting around the building corners. The curiously low-angle nature of the city made big patches of lowering sky visible through the rain.

Charlie stopped at a street corner and looked around. His skin was on fire. Things looked too wet and underlit to be real; it looked like stage lighting for some moment of ominous portent. Once again he felt that he had crossed over into a space where the real world had taken on all the qualities of a dream, becoming as glossy and surreal, as unlikely and beautiful, as stuffed to a dark sheen with un-graspable meaning. Sometimes just being outdoors in bad weather was all it took.

Back in the office he settled at his desk, and ate while look-ing over his list of things to do. The sandwich was good. The coffee from the office's coffee machine was bad. He wrote an update report to Phil, urging him to follow up on the elements of the bill that seemed to be dropping into the cracks. *We have to do these things.*

The sound of the rain outside made him think of the Khembalis and their low-lying island. What could they possibly do to help their watery home? Thinking about it, he Googled "Khembalung," and when he saw there were

over eight thousand references, Googled "Khembalung +
history." That got him only dozens, and he called up the
first one that looked interesting, a site called "Shambhala
Studies" from an .edu site.

The first paragraph left his mouth hanging open:
Khembalung, a shifting kingdom. Previously Shambhala...
He skimmed down the screen, scrolling slowly:

> ...*when the warriors of Han invade central Tibet, Khem-
> balung's turn will have arrived. A person named Drepung will
> come from the East, a person named Sonam will come from the
> North, a person named Padma will come from the West...*

"Holy shit—"

> ...*the first incarnation of Rudra was born as King of
> Olmolungring, in 16,017 BC.*

> ...*then dishonesty and greed will prevail, an ideology of brutal
> materialism will spread all over the earth. The tyrant will come to
> believe there is no place left to conquer, but the mists will lift and
> reveal Shambhala. Outraged to find he does not rule all, the
> tyrant will attack, but at that point Rudra Cakrin will rise and
> lead a mighty host against the invaders. After a big battle the evil
> will be destroyed (see Plate 4)*

"Holy moly."

Charlie read on, face just inches from the screen, which
was now also the dim room's lamp. *Reappearance of the kingdom... reincarnation of its lamas...* This began a section describing the methods used for locating reincarnated lamas
when they reappeared in a new life. The hairs on Charlie's
forearms suddenly prickled, and a wave of itching rolled
over his body. Toddlers speaking in tongues, recogniz-

ing personal items from the previous incarnation's belongings—

His phone rang and he jumped a foot.

"Hello!"

"Charlie! Are you all right?"

"Hi babe, yeah, you just startled me."

"Sorry, oh good. I was worried, I heard on the news that downtown is flooding, the Mall is flooding."

"The what?"

"Are you at the office?"

"Yeah."

"Is anyone else there with you?"

"Sure."

"Are they just sitting there working?"

Charlie peered out of his carrel door to look. In fact his floor sounded empty. It sounded as if everyone was gathered down in Evelyn's office.

"I'll go check and call you back," he said to Anna.

"Okay call me when you find out what's happening!"

"I will. Thanks for tipping me. Hey before I go, did you know that Khembalung is a kind of reincarnation of Shambhala?"

"What do you mean?"

"Just what I said. Shambhala, the hidden magical city—"

"Yes I know—"

"—well it's a kind of movable feast, apparently. Whenever it's discovered, or the time is right, it moves on to a new spot. They recently found the ruins of the original one in Kashgar, did you know that?"

"No."

"Apparently they did. It was like finding Troy, or the Atlantis place on Santorini. But Shambhala didn't end in Kashgar, it moved. First to Tibet, then to a valley in east Nepal or west Bhutan, a valley called Khembalung. I suppose when the Chinese conquered Tibet they had to move it down to that island."

"How do you know this?"

"I just read it online."

"Charlie that's very nice, but right now go find out what's going on down there in your office! I think you're in the area that may get flooded!"

"Okay, I will. But look"—walking down the hall now—"did Drepung ever talk to you about how they figure out who their reincarnated lamas have been reborn as?"

"No! Go check on your office!"

"Okay I am, but look honey, I want you to talk to him about that. I'm remembering that first dinner when the old man was playing games with Joe and his blocks, and Sucandra didn't like it."

"So?"

"So I just want to be sure that nothing's going on there! This is serious, honey, I'm serious. Those folks looking for the new Panchen Lama got some poor little kid in terrible trouble a few years ago, and I don't want any part of anything like that."

"What? I don't know what you're talking about Charlie, but let's talk about it later. Just find out what's going on there."

"Okay okay, but remember."

"I will!"

"Okay. Call you back in a second."

He went into Evelyn's office and saw people jammed around the south window, with another group around a TV set on a desk.

"Look at this," Andrea said to him, gesturing at the TV screen.

"Is that our door camera?" Charlie exclaimed, recognizing the view down Constitution. "That's our door camera!"

"That's right."

"My God!"

Charlie went to the window and stood on his tiptoes to see past people. The Mall was covered by water. The streets beyond were flooded. Constitution was floored by water that looked to be at least two feet deep, maybe deeper.

"Incredible isn't it."

"Shit!"

"Look at that."

"Will you look at that!"

"Why didn't you guys call me?" Charlie cried, shocked by the view.

"Forgot you were here," someone said. "You're never here."

Andrea added, "It just came up in the last half hour, or even less. It happened all at once, it seemed like. I was watching." Her voice quivered. "It was like a hard downburst, and the raindrops didn't have anywhere to go, they were splashing into a big puddle everywhere, and then it was there, what you see."

"A big puddle everywhere."

Constitution Avenue looked like the Grand Canal in Venice. Beyond it the Mall was like a rainbeaten lake. Water sheeted equally over streets, sidewalks and lawns. Charlie recalled the shock he had felt many years before, leaving the Venice train station and seeing the canal right there outside the door. A city floored with water. Here it was quite shallow, of course. But the front steps of all the buildings came down into an expanse of brown water, and the water was all at one level, as with any other lake or sea. Brownblue, blue-brown, brown-gray, brown, gray, dirty white—drab urban tints all. The rain pocked it into an infinity of rings and bounding droplets, and gusts of wind tore cats' paws across it.

Charlie maneuvered closer to the window as people left it. It seemed to him then that the water in the distance was flowing gently toward them; for a moment it looked (and even felt) as if their building had cast anchor and was steaming westward. Charlie felt a lurch in his stomach, put his hand to the windowsill to keep his balance.

"Shit, I should get home," he said.

"How are you going to do that?"

"We've been advised to stay put," Evelyn said.

"You're kidding."

"No. I mean, take a look. It could be dangerous out there right now. That's nothing to mess with—look at that!" A little electric car floated or rather was dragged down the street, already tipped on its side. "You could get knocked off your feet."

"Jesus."

"Yeah."

Charlie wasn't quite convinced, but he didn't want to argue. The water was definitely a couple of feet deep, and the rain was shattering its surface. If nothing else, it was too weird to go out.

"How extensive is it?" he asked.

Evelyn switched to a local news channel, where a very cheerful woman was saying that a big tidal surge had been predicted, because the tides were at the height of an eleven-year cycle. She went on to say that this tide was cresting higher than it would have normally because Tropical Storm Sandy's surge was now pushing up Chesapeake Bay. The combined tidal and storm surges were moving up the Potomac toward Washington, losing height and momentum all the while, but impeding the outflow of the river, which had a watershed of "fourteen thousand square miles" as Charlie had heard in the Iranian deli—a watershed which had that morning experienced record-shattering rainfall. In the last four hours ten inches of rain had fallen in several widely separated parts of the watershed, and now all that was pouring downstream and encountering the tidal bore, right in the metropolitan area. The four inches of rain that had fallen on Washington during its midday squall, while spectacular in itself, had only added to the larger problem; for the moment, there was nowhere for any of the water to go. All this the reporter explained with a happy smile.

Outside, the rain was falling no more violently than during many a summer evening's shower. But it was coming down steadily, and striking water when it hit.

"Amazing," Andrea said.

"I hope this washes the International Monetary Fund away."

This remark opened the floodgates, so to speak, on a loud listing of all the buildings and agencies the people in the room most wanted to see wiped off the face of the earth. Someone shouted "the Capitol," but of course it was located on its hill to the east of them, high ground that stayed high for a good distance to the east before dipping down to the Anacostia. The people up there probably wouldn't even get stranded, as there should be a strip of high ground running to the east and north.

Unlike them, situated below the Capitol by about forty vertical feet:

"We're here for a while."

"The trains will be stopped for sure."

"What about the Metro? Oh my God."

"I've gotta call home."

Several people said this at once, Charlie among them. People scattered to their desks and their phones. Charlie said, "Phone, get me Anna."

He got a quick reply: "All circuits are busy. Please try again." This was a recording he hadn't heard in many years, and it gave him a bad start. Of course it would happen now if at any time, everyone would be trying to call someone, and lines would be down. But what if it stayed like that for hours—or days? Or even longer? It was a sickening thought; he felt hot, and the itchiness blazed anew across his broken skin. He was almost overcome by something like dizziness, as if some invisible limb were being threatened with immediate amputation—his sixth sense, in effect, which was his link to Anna. All of a sudden he understood how completely he took his state of permanent communication with her for granted. They talked a dozen times a day, and he relied on those talks to know what he was doing, sometimes literally.

Now he was cut off from her. Judging by the voices in the offices, no one's connection was working. They regathered; had anyone gotten an open line? No. Was there an emergency phone system they could tap into? No.

There was, however, e-mail. Everyone sat down at their keyboards to type out messages home, and for a while it was like an office of secretaries or telegraph operators.

After that there was nothing to do but watch screens, or look out windows. They did that, milling about restlessly, saying the same things over and over, trying the phones, typing, looking out the windows or checking out the channels and sites. The usual news channels' helicopter shots and all other overhead views lower than satellite level were impossible in the violence of the storm, but almost every channel had cobbled together or transferred direct images from various cameras around town, and one of the weather stations was flying drone camera balloons and blimps into the storm and showing whatever it was they got, mostly swirling gray clouds, but also astonishing shots of the surrounding countryside as vast tree- or roof-studded lakes. One camera on top of the Washington Monument gave a splendid view of the extent of the flooding around the Mall, truly breathtaking. The Potomac had almost overrun Roosevelt Island, and spilled over its banks until it disappeared into the huge lake it was forming, thus onto the Mall and all the way across it, up to the steps of the White House and the Capitol, both on little knolls, the Capitol's well higher. The entirety of the little Southwest district was floored by water, though its big buildings stood clear; the broad valley of the Anacostia looked like a reservoir. The city south of Pennsylvania Avenue was a building-studded lake.

And not just there. The flood had filled Rock Creek to the top of its deep but narrow ravine, and now water was pouring over at the sharp bends the gorge took while dropping through the city to the Potomac. Cameras on the bridges at M Street caught the awesome sight of the creek roaring around its final turn west, upstream from M Street, and pouring over Francis Junior High School and straight south on 23rd Street into Foggy Bottom, joining the lake covering the Mall.

Then on to a different channel, a different camera. The Watergate Building was indeed a curving water gate, like a remnant portion of a dam. The wave-tossed spate of the Potomac poured around its big bend looking as if it could knock the building down. Likewise the Kennedy Center just south of it. The Lincoln Memorial, despite its pedestal mound, appeared to be flooded up to about Lincoln's feet. Across the Potomac the water was going to inundate the lower levels of Arlington National Cemetery. Reagan Airport was completely gone.

"Unbelievable."

Charlie went back to the view out their window. The water was still there. A voice on the TV was saying something about a million acre-feet of water converging in the metropolitan area, partially blocked in its flow downstream by the high tide. With more rain predicted.

Out the window Charlie saw that people were already taking to the streets around them in small watercraft, despite the wind and drizzle. Zodiacs, kayaks, a waterski boat, canoes, rowboats; he saw examples of them all. Then as the evening wore on, and the dim light left the air below the black clouds, the rain returned with its earlier intensity. It poured down in a way that surely made it dangerous to be on the water. Most of the small craft had appeared to be occupied by men who it did not seem had any good reason to be out there. Out for a lark—thrill-seekers, already!

"It looks like Venice," Andrea said, echoing Charlie's earlier thought. "I wonder what it would be like if it were like this all the time."

"Maybe we'll get to find out."

"How high above sea level are we here?"

No one knew, but Evelyn quickly found and clicked a topographical map to her screen. They jammed around her to look at it, or to get the address to bring it up on their own screens.

"Look at that."

"Ten feet above sea level? Can that be true?"

"That's why they call it the Tidal Basin."

"But isn't the ocean like what, fifty miles away? A hundred?"

"Ninety miles downstream to Chesapeake Bay," Evelyn said.

"I wonder if the Metro has flooded."

"How could it not?"

"True. I suppose it must have in some places."

"And if in some places, wouldn't it spread?"

"Well, there are higher and lower sections. Seems like the lower ones would for sure. And anywhere the entries are flooded."

"Well, yes."

"Wow. What a mess."

"Shit, I got here by Metro."

Charlie said, "Me too."

They thought about that for a while. Taxis weren't going to be running either.

"I wonder how long it takes to walk home."

But then again, Rock Creek ran between the Mall and Bethesda.

Hours passed. Charlie checked his e-mail frequently, and finally there was a note from Anna: *we're fine here glad to hear you're set in the office, be sure to stay there until it's safe, let's talk as soon as the phones will get through love, A and boys*

Charlie took a deep breath, feeling greatly reassured. When the topo map had come up he had checked Bethesda first, and found that the border of the District and Maryland at Wisconsin Avenue was some two hundred and fifty feet above sea level. And Rock Creek was well to the east of it. Little Falls Creek was closer, but far enough to the west not to be a concern, he hoped. Of course Wisconsin Avenue itself was probably a shallow stream of sorts now, running down into Georgetown—and wouldn't it be great if snobbish little Georgetown got some of this, but wouldn't you know it, it was on a rise overlooking the river, in the usual correlation of money and elevation. Higher than the Capitol by a good deal. It was always that way; the poor people lived down in the flats, as witness the part of Southeast in the valley of the Anacostia River, now flooded from one side to the other.

It continued to rain. The phone connections stayed busy and no calls got through. People in Phil's office watched the TV, stretched out on couches, or even lay down to catch some sleep on chair cushions lined on the floor. Outside the wind abated, rose again, dropped. Rain fell all the while. All the TV stations chattered on caffeinistically, talking to the emptied darkened rooms. It was strange to see how they were directly involved in an obviously historical moment, right in the middle of it in fact, and yet they too were watching it on TV.

Charlie could not sleep, but wandered the halls of the big building. He visited with the security team at the front doors, who had been using rolls of Department of Homeland Security gas-attack tape to try to waterproof the bottom halves of all the doors. Nevertheless the ground floor was getting soggy, and the basement even worse, though clearly the seal was fairly good, as the basement was by no means filled to the ceiling. Apparently over in the Smithsonian buildings there were hundreds of people moving stuff upstairs from variously flooding situations. People in their building mostly worked at screens or on laptops, though now some reported that they were having trouble getting online. If the Internet went down they would be completely out of touch.

Finally Charlie got itchy enough from his walking, and tired enough from his already acute lack of sleep, to go back to Phil's office and lie down on a couch and try to sleep.

Gingerly he rested his fiery side on some couch cushions. "Owwwwww." The pain made him want to weep, and all of a sudden he wanted to be home so badly that he couldn't think about it. He moaned to think of Anna and the boys. He needed to be with them; he was not himself here, cut off from them. This was what it felt like to be in an emergency of this particular kind—scarcely able to believe it, but aware nevertheless that bad things could happen. The itching tortured him. He thought it would keep him from getting to sleep; but he was so tired that after a period of weird hypnagogic tossing and turning, during which the memory of the flood kept recurring to him like a bad dream that he was relieved to find was not true, he drifted off.

CROSS THE great river it was different. Frank was at NSF when the storm got bad. He had gotten authorization from Diane to convene a new committee to report to the Board of Directors; his acceptance of the assignment had triggered a whole wave of communications to formalize his return to NSF for another year. His department at UCSD would be fine with it; it was good for them to have people working at NSF.

Now he was sitting at his screen, Googling around, and for some reason he had brought up the website for Small Delivery Systems, just to look. While tapping through its pages he had come upon a list of publications by the company's scientists; this was often the best way to tell what a company was up to. And almost instantly his eye picked out one coauthored by Dr. P. L. Emory, CEO of the company, and Dr. F. Taolini.

Quickly he typed "consultants" into the search engine, and up came the company's page listing them. And there she was: Dr. Francesca Taolini, Massachusetts Institute of Technology, Center for Biocomputational Studies.

"Well I'll be damned."

He sat back, thinking it over. Taolini had liked Pierzinski's proposal; she had rated it "Very Good," and argued in favor of funding it, persuasively enough that at the time it had given him a little scare. She had seen its potential. . . .

Then Kenzo called up, raving about the storm and the flood, and Frank joined everyone else in the building in watching the TV news and the NOAA website, trying to get a sense of how serious things were. It became clear that things were serious indeed when one channel showed Rock Creek overflowing its banks and running deep down the streets toward Foggy Bottom; then the screen shifted the image to Foggy Bottom, waist-deep everywhere, and then came images from the inundated-to-the-rooftops Southwest district, including the classically pillared War College Building at the confluence of the Potomac and the Anacostia, sticking out of the water like a temple of Atlantis.

The Jefferson Memorial was much the same. Rain-lashed rooftop cameras all over the city transmitted more images of the flood, and Frank stared, fascinated; the city was a lake.

The climate guys on the ninth floor were already posting topographical map projections with the flood peaking at various heights. If the surge got to twenty feet above sea level at the confluence of the Potomac and the Anacostia, which Kenzo thought was a reasonable projection given the tidal bore and all, the new shore along this contour line would run roughly from the Capitol up Pennsylvania Avenue to where it crossed Rock Creek. That meant the Capitol on its hill, and the White House on its lower rise, would probably both be spared; but everything to the south and west of them was underwater already, as the videos confirmed.

Upstream monitoring stations showed that the peak of the flood had not yet arrived.

"Everything has combined!" Kenzo exclaimed over the phone. "It's all coming together!" His usual curatorial tone had shifted to that of an impresario—the Master of Disaster—or even to an almost parental pride. He was as excited as Frank had ever heard him.

"Could this be from the Atlantic stall?" Frank asked.

"Oh no, very doubtful. This is separate I think, a collisionary storm. Although the stall might bring more storms like this. Windier and colder. This is what that will be like!"

"Jesus ... Can you tell me what's going on on the Virginia side?" There would be no way to cross the Potomac until the storm was over. "Are people working anywhere around here?"

"They're sandbagging down at Arlington Cemetery," Kenzo said. "There's video on channel 44. It's got a call out for volunteers."

"Really!"

Frank was off. He took the stairs to the basement, to be sure he didn't get caught in an elevator, and drove his car up onto the street. It was awash in places, but only to a depth of a few inches. Possibly this would soon get worse; runoff wouldn't work when the river was flowing back up the drainpipes. But for now he was okay to get to the river.

As he turned right and stopped for the light, he saw the Starbucks people out on the sidewalk, passing out bags of food and cups of coffee to the cars in front of him. Frank opened his window as one of them approached, and the employee passed in a bag of pastries, then handed him a paper cup of coffee.

"Thanks!" Frank shouted. "You guys should take over emergency services!"

"We already did. You go and get yourself out of here." She waved him on.

Frank drove east toward the river, laughing as he downed the pastry. Like everyone else still on the road, he plowed through the water at about five miles an hour. Fire trucks passed through at a faster clip, leaving big wakes.

As he crossed one intersection Frank spotted a trio of men ducking behind a building, carrying something. Could there be looters? Would anyone really do it? How sad to think that there were people so stuck in always defect mode that they couldn't get out of it, even when a chance came for everything to change. What a waste of an opportunity!

Eventually he came to a roadblock and parked, following the directions of a man in an orange vest. It was a moment of hard rain. In the distance he could see people passing sandbags down a line, just to the east of the U.S. Marines' Memorial. He hustled over to join them.

From where he worked he could often see the Potomac, pouring down the Boundary Channel between the mainland and Columbia Island, tearing away the bridges and the marinas and threatening the low-lying parts of Arlington National Cemetery. Hundreds or perhaps even thousands of people were working around him, carrying small sandbags that looked like fifty-pound cement bags, and no doubt were about that heavy. Some big guys were lifting them off truck beds and passing them to people who passed them down lines, or carried them over shoulders, to near or far sections of a sandbag wall under the Virginia end of Memorial Bridge, where firemen were directing construction.

The noise of the river and the rain together made it hard to hear. People shouted to one another, sharing instructions and news. The airport was drowned, old Alexandria flooded, the Anacostia Valley filled for miles. The Mall a lake, of course.

Frank nodded at anything said his way, not bothering to

understand, and worked like a dervish. It was very satisfying. He felt deeply happy, and looking around he could see that everyone else was happy too. That's what happens, he thought, watching people carry limp sandbags like coolies out of an old Chinese painting. It takes something like this to free people to be always generous.

Late in the day he stood on their sandbag wall. It gave him a good view over the flood. The wind had died down, but the rain was falling almost as hard as ever. In some moments it seemed there was more water in the air than air.

His team had been given a break by a sudden end to the supply of sandbags. His back was stiff, and he stretched himself in circles, like the trunks of the trees had been doing all day. The wind had shifted frequently, and had included short hard blasts from the west or north, vicious slaps like microbursting downdrafts. But now there was some kind of aerial truce.

Then the rain too relented. It became a very light drizzle. Over the foamy water in the Boundary Channel he could now see far across the Potomac proper: a swirling brown plate, sheeting as far as he could see to the east. The Washington Monument was a dim obelisk on a watery horizon. The Lincoln Memorial and Kennedy Center were both islands in the stream. Black clouds formed a low ceiling above them, and between the two, water and cloud, he could feel the air being smashed this way and that. Despite the disorderly gusts he was still warm from his exertions, wet but warm, with only his hands and ears slightly nipped by the wind. He stood there flexing his spine, feeling the tired muscles of his lower back.

A powerboat growled slowly up the Boundary Channel below them. Frank watched it pass, wondering how shallow its draft was; it was twenty-five or maybe even thirty feet long, a rescue boat like a sleek cabin cruiser, hull painted a shade of green that made it almost invisible. The illuminated cockpit shed its light on a person standing upright at the stern, looking like one of the weird sisters in the movie *Don't Look Now.*

This person looked over at the sandbag levee, and Frank saw that it was the woman from the elevator in Bethesda. Shocked, he put his hands to his mouth and shouted, "HEY!" as loud as he could, emptying his lungs all at once.

No sign in the roar of flood and rain that she had heard him. Nor did she appear to see him waving. As the boat began to disappear around a bend in the channel, Frank spotted white lettering on its stern—GCX88A—then it was gone. Its wake had already splashed the side of the levee and roiled away.

Frank pulled his phone out of his windbreaker pocket, shoved it in his ear, then tapped the button for NSF's climate office. Luckily it was Kenzo who picked up. "Kenzo, it's Frank—listen, write down this sequence, it's very important, please? GCX88A, have you got that? Read it back. GCX88A. Great. Great. Wow. Okay, listen Kenzo, that's a boat's number, it was on the stern of a powerboat about twenty-six feet long. I couldn't tell if it was public or private, I suspect public, but I need to know whose it is. Can you find that out for me? I'm out in the rain and can't see my phonepad well enough to Google it."

"I can try," Kenzo said. "Here, let me . . . well, it looks like the boat belongs to the marina on Roosevelt Island."

"That would make sense. Is there a phone number for it?"

"Let's see—that should be in the Coast Guard records. Wait, they're not open files. Hold a minute, please."

Kenzo loved these little problems. Frank waited, trying not to hold his breath. Another instinctive act. As he waited he tried to etch the woman's face again on his mind, thinking he might be able to get a portrait program to draw something like what he was remembering. She had looked serious and remote, like one of the Fates.

"Yeah, Frank, here it is. Do you want me to call it and pass you along?"

"Yes please, but write it down for me too."

"Okay, I'll pass you over and get off. I have to get back to it here."

"Thanks Kenzo, thanks a lot."

Frank listened, sticking a finger in his other ear. There was a pause, a ring. The ring had a rapid pulse and an insistent edge, as if it were designed to compete with the sounds of an inboard engine on a boat. Three rings, four, five; if an answering machine message came on, what would he say?

"Hello?"

It was her voice.

"Hello?" she said again.

He had to say something or she would hang up.

"Hi," he said. "Hi, this is me."

There was a static-filled silence.

"We were stuck in that elevator together in Bethesda."

"Oh my God."

Another silence. Frank let her assimilate it. He had no idea what to say. It seemed like the ball was in her court, and yet as the silence went on, a fear grew in him.

"Don't hang up," he said, surprising himself. "I just saw your boat go by, I'm here on the levee at the back of the Davis Highway. I called information and got your boat's number. I know you didn't want— I mean, I tried to find you afterward, but I couldn't, and I could tell that you didn't—that you didn't want to be found. So I figured I would leave it at that, I really did."

He could hear himself lying and added hastily, "I didn't

want to, but I didn't see what else I could do. So when I saw you just now, I called a friend who got me the boat's number. I mean how could I not, when I saw you like that."

"I know," she said.

He breathed in. He felt himself filling up, his back straightening. Something in the way she said "I know" brought it all back again. The way she had made it a bond between them.

After a time he said, "I wanted to find you again. I thought that our time in the elevator, I thought it was..."

"I know."

His skin warmed. It was like a kind of St. Elmo's fire running over him, he'd never felt anything like it.

"But—" she said, and he learned another new feeling; dread clutched him under the ribs. He waited as for a blow to fall.

The silence went on. An isolated freshet of rain pelted down, cleared, and then he could see across the wind-lashed Potomac again. A huge rushing watery world, awesome and dreamlike.

"Give me your number," her voice said in his ear.

"What?"

"Give me your phone number," she said again.

He gave her his number, then added, "My name is Frank Vanderwal."

"Frank Vanderwal," she said, then repeated the number. "That's it."

"Now give me some time," she said. "I don't know how long." And the connection went dead.

THE SECOND day of the storm passed as a kind of suspended moment, everything continuing as it had the day before, everyone in the area living through it, enduring, waiting for conditions to change. The rain was not as torrential, but so much of it had fallen in the previous twenty-four hours that it was still sheeting off the land into the flooded areas and keeping them flooded. The clouds continued to crash together overhead, and the tides were still higher than normal, so that the whole Piedmont region surrounding Chesapeake Bay was inundated. Except for immediate acts of a lifesaving nature, nothing could be done except to endure. All transport was drowned. The phones remained down, and power losses left hundreds of thousands without electricity. Escapes from drowning took precedence even over journalism (almost), and even though reporters from all over the world were converging on the capital to report on this most spectacular story—the capital of the hyperpower, drowned and smashed—most of them could only get as close as the edges of the storm, or the flood; inside that it was an ongoing state of

emergency, and everyone was involved with rescues, relo-
cations, and escapes of various kinds. The National Guard
was out, all helicopters were enlisted into the effort; the
video and digital imagery generated for the world to see
was still incidental to other things; that in itself meant
ordinary law had been suspended, and there was pressure
to bring things back to all-spectacle all-the-time. Part of
the National Guard found itself posted on the roads outside the region, to keep people from flooding the area as
the water had.

Very early on the second morning it became evident
that while most areas had seen high water already, the
flooding of Rock Creek had not yet crested. That night its
headwaters had received the brunt of one of the hardest
downpours of the storm, and the already saturated land
could only shed this new rainfall into the streambed. The
creek's drop to the Tidal Basin was precipitous in some
places, and for most of its length the creek ran at the bottom of a narrow gorge carved into the higher ground of
Northwest District. There was nowhere to hold an excess
flow.

All this meant big trouble for the National Zoo, which
was located on a sort of peninsula created by three turns in
Rock Creek, and therefore directly overlooking the gorge.
After the hard downpour in the night, the staff of the zoo
congregated in the main offices to discuss the situation.

They had some visiting dignitaries on hand, who had
been forced to spend the previous night there; several
members of the embassy of the nation of Khembalung
had come to the zoo the morning before, to take part in a
ceremony welcoming two Bengal tigers brought from their
country to the zoo. The storm had made it impossible for
them to return to Virginia, but they had seemed happy to
spend the night at the zoo, concerned as they were about
their tigers, and the other animals as well.

Now they all watched together as one of the office's computers showed images of Rock Creek's gorge walls being torn away and washed downstream. Floating trees were catching in drifts against bridges over the creek, forming temporary impediments that forced water out into the flanking neighborhoods, until the bridges blew like failed dams, and powerful low walls of debris-laden water tore down the gorge harder than ever, ripping it away even more brutally. The eastern border of the zoo made it obvious how this endangered them: the light brown torrent was ripping around the park, just a few feet below the lowest levels of the zoo grounds. That plus the images on their computers made it ever more clear that the zoo was very likely to be overwhelmed, and soon. It looked like it was going to turn into something like a reversal of Noah's flood, becoming one in which the people mostly survived, but two of every species were drowned.

The Khembali legation urged the National Park staffers to evacuate the zoo as quickly as possible. The time and vehicles necessary for a proper evacuation were completely lacking, of course, as the superintendent quickly pointed out, but the Khembalis replied that by evacuation they meant opening all the cages and letting the animals escape. The zookeepers were skeptical, but the Khembalis turned out to be experts in flood response, well-acquainted with the routines required in such situations. They quickly called up photos of the zookeepers of Prague, weeping by the bodies of their drowned elephants, to show what could happen if drastic measures were not taken. They then called up the Global Disaster Information Network, which had a complete protocol for this very scenario (threatened zoos), along with real-time satellite photos and flood data. It turned out that released animals did not roam far, seldom threatened humans (who were usually locked into buildings anyway), and were easy to re-collect when the waters subsided. And the data showed Rock Creek was certain to rise further.

This prediction was easy to believe, given the roaring brown water bordering most of the zoo, and almost topping the gorge. The animals certainly believed it, and were calling loudly for freedom. Elephants trumpeted, monkeys screamed, the big cats roared and growled. Every living creature, animal and human both, was terrified by this cacophony. The din was terrific, beyond anything any jungle movie had dared. Panic was in the air.

Connecticut Avenue now resembled something like George Washington's canal at Great Falls: a smooth narrow run of water, paralleling a wild torrent. All the side streets were flooded as well. Nowhere was the water very high, however—usually under a foot—and so the superintendent, looking amazed to hear himself, said "Okay let's let them out. Cages first, then the enclosures. Work from the gate down to the lower end of the park. Come on—there's a lot of locks to unlock."

In the dark rainy air, beside the roaring engorged creek, the staff and their visitors ventured out and began unlocking the animals. They drove them toward Connecticut when necessary, though most animals needed no urging at all, but bolted for the gates with a sure sense of the way out. Some however huddled in their enclosures or cages, and could not be coaxed out. There was no time to spare for any particular cage; if the animals refused to leave, the zookeepers moved on and hoped there would be time to return.

The tapirs and deer were easy. They kept the biggest aviaries closed, feeling they would not flood to their tops. Then the zebras, and after them the cheetahs, the Australian creatures, kangaroos bounding with great splashes; the pandas trundling methodically out in a group, as if they had planned this for years. Elephants on parade; giraffes;

hippos and rhinos, beavers and otters; after some consultation, and the coaxing of the biggest cats into their moving trucks, the pumas and smaller cats; then bison, wolves, camels; the seals and sea lions; bears; the gibbons all in a troop, screaming with triumph; the single black jaguar slipping dangerously into the murk; the reptiles, the Amazonian creatures already looking right at home; the prairie dog town, the drawbridge dropped to Monkey Island, causing another stampede of panicked primates; the gorillas and apes following more slowly. Now washes of brown water were spilling over the north end of the park and running swiftly down the zoo's paths, and the lower end of the zoo was submerged by the brown flow. Very few animals continued to stay in their enclosures, and even fewer headed by mistake toward the creek; the roar was simply too frightening, the message too obvious. Every living thing's instincts were clear on where safety lay.

The water lapped higher again. It seemed to be rising in distinct surges. It had taken two full hours of frantic work to unlock all the doors, and as they were finishing, a roar louder than before overwhelmed them, and a dirty debris-filled surge poured over the whole park. Something upstream must have given way all at once. Any animals remaining in the lower section of the park would be swept away or drowned in place. Quickly the humans remaining drove the few big cats and polar bears they had herded into their trucks out the entrance and onto Connecticut Avenue. Now all Northwest was the zoo.

The truck that had delivered the Swimming Tigers of Khembalung headed north on Connecticut, containing the tigers in back and the Khembali delegation piled into its cab. They drove very slowly and cautiously through the empty, dark, watery streets. The looming clouds made it look like it was already evening.

The Swimming Tigers banged around in back as they drove. They sounded scared and angry, perhaps feeling that this had all happened before already. They did not seem to want to be in the back of the truck, and roared in a way that caused the humans in the cab to hunch forward unhappily. It sounded like the tigers were taking it out on each other; big bodies crashed into the walls, and the roars and growls grew angrier.

The Khembali passengers advised the driver and zoo-keeper. They nodded and continued north on Connecticut. Any big dip would make a road impassably flooded, but Connecticut ran steadily uphill to the northwest. Then Bradley Lane allowed the driver to get most of the way west to Wisconsin. When a dip stopped him, he retreated and worked his way farther north, following streets without dips, until they made it to Wisconsin Avenue, now something like a wide smooth stream, flowing hard south, but at a depth of only six inches. They crept along against this flow until they could make an illegal left onto Woodson, and thus around the corner, into the driveway of a small house backed by a big apartment complex.

In the dark air the Khembalis got out, knocked on the kitchen door. A woman appeared, and after a brief conversation, disappeared.

Soon afterward, if anyone in the apartment complex had looked out of their window, they would have seen a curious sight: a group of men, some in maroon robes, others in National Park khakis, coaxing a tiger out of the back of a truck. It was wearing a collar to which three leashes were attached. When it was out the men quickly closed the truck door. The oldest man stood before the tiger, hand upraised. He took up one of the leashes, led the wet beast across the driveway to steps leading down to an open cellar door. Rain fell as the tiger stopped on the steps and looked around. The old man spoke urgently to it. From the house's kitchen window over them, two little faces stared out round-eyed. For a moment nothing seemed to move but the rain. Then the tiger ducked in the door.

SOMETIME DURING that second night the rain stopped, and though dawn of the third morning arrived sodden and gray, the clouds scattered as the day progressed, flying north at speed. By nine the sun blazed down between big puffball clouds onto the flooded city. The air was breezy and unsettled.

Charlie had again spent this second night in the office, and when he woke he looked out the window hoping that conditions would have eased enough for him to be able to attempt getting home. The phones were still down, although e-mails from Anna had kept him informed and reassured—at least until the previous evening's news about the arrival of the Khembalis, which had caused him some alarm, not just because of the tiger in the basement, but because of their interest in Joe. He had not expressed any of this in his e-mail replies, of course. But he most definitely wanted to get home.

Helicopters and blimps had already taken to the air in great numbers. Now all the TV channels in the world could reveal the extent of the flood from on high. Much of downtown Washington, D.C., remained awash. A giant shallow lake occupied precisely the most famous and public parts of the city; it looked like someone had decided to expand the Mall's reflecting pool beyond all reason. The rivers and streams that converged on this larger tidal basin were still in spate, which kept the new lake topped up. In the washed sunlight the flat expanse of water was the color of caffe latte, with foam.

Standing in the lake, of course, were hundreds of buildings-become-islands, and a few real islands, and even some freeway viaducts, now acting as bridges over the Anacostia Valley. The Potomac continued to pour through the west edge of the lake, overspilling its banks both upstream and down, whenever lowlands flanked it. Its surface was studded with floating junk which moved slower the farther downstream it got. Apparently the ebb tides had only begun to draw this vast bolus of water out to sea.

As the morning wore on, more and more boats appeared. The TV shots from the air made it look like some kind of regatta—the Mall as water festival, like something out of Ming China. Many people were out on makeshift craft that did not look at all seaworthy. Police boats on patrol were even beginning to ask people who were not doing rescue work to leave, one report said, though clearly they were not having much of an impact. The situation was still so new that the law had not yet fully asserted itself. Motorboats zipped about, leaving beige wakes behind. Rowers rowed, paddlers paddled, kayakers kayaked, swimmers swam; some people were even out in the blue foot-pedaled boats that had once been confined to the Tidal Basin, pedaling around the Mall in majestic ministeamboat style.

Although these images from the Mall dominated the media, some channels carried other news from around the region. Hospitals were filled. The two days of the storm had killed many people, no one knew how many; and there had been many rescues as well. In the first part of the third morning, the TV helicopters often interrupted their over-views to pluck people from rooftops. Rescues by boat were occurring all through Southwest district and up the Anacostia Basin. Reagan Airport remained drowned, and there was no passable bridge over the Potomac all the way upstream to Harpers Ferry. The Great Falls of the Potomac were no more than a huge turbulence in a nearly unbroken, gorge-topping flow. The President had evacuated to Camp David, and now he declared all of Virginia, Maryland, and Delaware a federal disaster area; the District of Columbia, in his words, "worse than that."

Charlie's phone chirped and he snatched it to him. "Anna?"

"Charlie! Where are you!"

"I'm still at the office! Are you home?"

"Oh good yes! I'm here with the boys, we never left. We've got the Khembalis here with us too, you got my e-mails?"

"Yes, I wrote back."

"Oh that's right. They got caught at the zoo. I've been trying to get you on the phone this whole time!"

"Me you too, except when I fell asleep. I was so glad to get your e-mails."

"Yeah that was good. I'm so glad you're okay. This is crazy! Is your building completely flooded?"

"No no, not at all. So how are the boys?"

"Oh they're fine. They're loving it. It's all I can do to keep them inside."

"Keep them inside."

"Yes yes. So your building isn't flooded? Isn't the Mall flooded?"

"Yes it is, no doubt about that, but not the building

here, not too badly anyway. They're keeping the doors shut, and trying to seal them at the bottoms. It's not working great, but it isn't dangerous. It's just a matter of staying up-stairs."

"Your generators are working?"

"Yes."

"I hear a lot of them are flooded."

"Yeah I can see how that would happen. No one was expecting this."

"No. Generators in basements, it's stupid I suppose."

"That's where ours is."

"I know. But it's on that table, and it's working."

"What about food, how are we set there?" Charlie tried to imagine their cupboards.

"Well, we've got a bit. You know. It's not great. It will get to be a problem soon if we can't get more. I figure we might have a few weeks' worth in a pinch."

"Well, that should be fine. I mean, they'll *have* to get things going again by then."

"I suppose. We need water service too."

"Will the floodwaters drain away very fast?"

"I don't know, how should I know?"

"Well, I don't know—you're a scientist."

"Please."

They listened to each other breathe.

"I sure am glad to be talking to you," Charlie said. "I hated being out of touch like that."

"Me too."

"There are boats all around us now," Charlie said. "I'll try to get a ride home as soon as I can. Once I get ferried to land, I can walk home."

"Not necessarily. The Taft Bridge over Rock Creek is gone. You'd only be able to cross on the Mass. Ave. bridge, from what I can see on the news."

"Yeah, I saw Rock Creek flooding, that was amazing."

"I know. The zoo and everything. Drepung says most of the animals will be recovered, but I wonder about that." Anna would be nearly as upset by the deaths of the zoo's animals as she would be by people. She made little distinction.

Charlie said, "I'll take Mass. Ave. then."

"Or maybe you can get them to drop you off west of Rock Creek, in Georgetown. Anyway, be careful. Don't do anything rash just to get here quick."

"I won't. I'll make sure to stay safe, and I'll call you regularly, at least I hope. That was awful being cut off."

"I know."

"Okay, well . . . I don't really want to hang up, but I guess I should. Let me talk to the boys first."

"Yeah good. Here talk to Joe, he's been pretty upset that you're not here, he keeps asking for you. Demanding you, actually—here," and then suddenly in his ear:

"Dadda?"

"Joe!"

"Da! Da!"

"Yeah Joe, it's Dad! Good to hear you, boy! I'm down at work, I'll be home soon buddy."

"Da! Da!" Then, in a kind of moan: "Wan Daaaaaaaaaaa."

"It's okay Joe," Charlie said, throat clenching. "I'll be home real soon. Don't you worry."

"*Da!*" Shrieking.

Anna got back on. "Sorry, he's throwing a fit. Here, Nick wants to talk too."

"Hey, Nick! Are you taking care of Mom and Joe?"

"Yeah, I was, but Joe is kind of upset right now."

"He'll get over it. So what's it been like up there?"

"Well you see, we got to burn those big candles? And I made a big tower out of the melted wax, it's really cool. And then Drepung and Rudra came and brought their tigers, they've got one in their truck and one in our basement!"

"That's nice, that's very cool. Be sure to keep the door to the basement closed by the way."

Nick laughed. "It's locked Dad. Mom has the key."

"Good. Did you get a lot of rain?"

"I think so. We can see that Wisconsin is kind of flooded, but there are still some cars going in it. Most of the big stuff we've only seen on the TV. Mom was really worried about you. When are you going to get home?"

"Soon as I can."

"Good."

"Yeah. Well, I guess you get a few days off school out of all this. Okay, give me your mom back. Hi babe."

"Listen, you stay put until some really safe way to get home comes."

"I will."

"We love you."

"I love you too. I'll be home soon as I can."

Then Joe began to wail again, and they hung up.

Charlie rejoined the others and told them his news. Others were getting through on their cell phones as well. Everyone was talking. Then there came yells from down the hall.

A police motor launch was at the second-floor windows, facing Constitution, ready to ferry people to dry ground. This one was going west, and yes, would eventually dock in Georgetown, if people wanted off there. It was perfect for Charlie's hope to get west of Rock Creek and then walk home.

And so, when his turn came, he climbed out the window and down into the big boat. A stanza from a Robert Frost poem he had memorized in high school came back to him suddenly:

It went many years, but at last came a knock,
And I thought of the door with no lock to lock . . .
The knock came again, my window was wide;
I climbed on the sill and descended outside.

He laughed as he moved forward in the boat to make room for other refugees. Strange what came back to the mind. How had that poem continued? Something something; he couldn't remember. It didn't matter. The relevant part had come to him, after waiting all these years. And now he was out the window and on his way.

The launch rumbled, glided away from the building, turned in a broad curve west down Constitution Avenue. Then left, out onto the broad expanse of the Mall. They were boating on the Mall.

The National Gallery reminded him of the Taj Mahal; same water reflection, same gorgeous white stone. All the Smithsonian buildings looked amazing. No doubt they had been working inside them all night to get things above flood level. What a mess it was going to be.

Charlie steadied himself against the gunwale, feeling so stunned that it seemed he might lose his balance and fall. That was probably the boat's doing, but he was, in all truth, reeling. The TV images had been one thing, the actual reality another; he could scarcely believe his eyes. White clouds danced overhead in the blue sky, and the flat brown lake was gleaming in the sunlight, reflecting a blue glitter of sky, everything all glossy and compact—real as real, or even more so. None of his visions had ever been as remotely real as this lake was now.

Their pilot maneuvered them farther south. They were going to pass the Washington Monument on its south side. They puttered slowly past it. It towered over them like an obelisk in the Nile's flood, making all the watercraft look correspondingly tiny.

The Smithsonian buildings appeared to be drowned to about ten feet. Upper halves of their big public doors emerged from the water like low boathouse doors. For some of the buildings that would be a catastrophe. Others had steps, or stood higher on their foundations. A mess any way you looked at it.

Their launch growled west at a walking pace. Trees flanking the western half of the Mall looked like water shrubs in the distance. The Vietnam Memorial would of course be submerged. The Lincoln Memorial stood on its own pedestal hill, but it was right on the Potomac, and might be submerged to the height of all its steps; the statue of Lincoln might even be getting his feet wet. Charlie found it hard to tell, through the strangely shortened trees, just how high the water was down there.

Boats of all kinds dotted the long brown lake, headed this way and that. The little blue pedal boats from the Tidal Basin were particularly festive, but all the kayaks and rowboats and inflatables added their dots of neon color, and the little sailboats tacking back and forth flashed their triangular sails. The brilliant sunlight filled the clouds and the blue sky. The festival mood was expressed even by what people wore—Charlie saw Hawaiian shirts, bathing suits, even Carnival masks. There were many more black faces than Charlie was used to seeing on the Mall. It looked as if something like Trinidad's Mardi Gras parade had been disrupted by a night of storms, but was reemerging triumphant in the new day. People were waving to one another, shouting things (the helicopters overhead were loud); standing in boats in unsafe postures, turning in precarious circles to shoot three-sixties with cameras. It would only take a water skier to complete the scene.

Charlie moved to the bow of the launch, and stood there soaking it all in. His mouth hung open like a dog's. The effort of getting out the window had reinflamed his chest and arms; now he stood there on fire, torching in the wind, drinking in the maritime vision. Their boat chugged west like a vaporetto on Venice's broad lagoon. He could not help but laugh.

"Maybe they should keep it this way," someone said.

A Navy river cruiser came growling over the Potomac toward them, throwing up a white bow wave on its upstream side. When it reached the Mall it slipped through a gap in the cherry trees, cut back on its engines, settled down in the water, continued east at a more sedate pace. It was going to pass pretty close by them, and Charlie felt their own launch slow down as well.

Then he spotted a familiar face among the people standing in the bow of the patrol boat. It was Phil Chase, waving to the boats he passed like the grand marshal of a parade, leaning over the front rail to shout greetings. Like a lot of other people on the water that morning, he had the happy look of someone who had already lit out for the territory.

Charlie waved with both arms, leaning over the side of the launch. They were closing on each other. Charlie cupped his hands around his mouth and shouted as loud as he could.

"HEY PHIL! Phil Chase!"

Phil heard him, looked over, saw him.

"Hey Charlie!" He waved cheerily, then cupped his hands around his mouth too. "Good to see you! Is everyone at the office okay?"

"Yes!"

"Good! That's good!" Phil straightened up, gestured broadly at the flood. "Isn't this amazing?"

"Yes! It sure is!" Then the words burst out of Charlie: "So *Phil*! Are you going to do something about global warming *now*?"

Phil grinned his beautiful grin. "I'll see what I can do!"

ACKNOWLEDGMENTS

Many thanks for help from Guy Guthridge, Grant Heidrich, Charles Hess, Tim Higham, Dick Ill, Chris McKay, Oliver Morton, Lisa Nowell, Ann Russell, Mark Schwartz, Sharon Strauss, Jim Shea, and Buck Tilley.

ABOUT THE AUTHOR

Kim Stanley Robinson is a winner of the Hugo, Nebula, and Locus Awards. He is the author of ten previous books, including the bestselling Mars trilogy and *The Years of Rice and Salt*, named one of the best science fiction novels of 2002 by *Book* magazine. He lives in Davis, California.

Be sure not to miss

FIFTY DEGREES BELOW

by

Kim Stanley Robinson

The thrilling sequel to

FORTY SIGNS OF RAIN

Here's how the future unfolds...

On sale November 2005

KIM STANLEY
ROBINSON

FROM THE BESTSELLING AUTHOR OF
FORTY SIGNS OF RAIN

FIFTY
DEGREES
BELOW

FIFTY DEGREES BELOW
On Sale November 2005

Chapter I

IT WAS NOT A GOOD TIME to have to look for a place to live.

And yet this was just what Frank Vanderwal had to do. He had leased his apartment for a year, covering the time he had planned to work for the National Science Foundation; then he had agreed to stay on for a second year. Now, only a month after the flood, his apartment had to be turned over to its owner, a State Department foreign-service person he had never met, returning from a stint in Brazil. So he had to find someplace else.

No doubt the decision to stay another year had been a really bad idea.

This thought had weighed on him as he searched for a new apartment, and as a result he had not persevered as diligently as he ought to have. Very little was available in any case, and everything on offer was prohibitively expensive. Thousands of people had been drawn to D.C. by a flood that had also destroyed thousands of residences, and damaged thousands more beyond immediate repair and reoccupation. It was a real seller's market, and rents shot up accordingly.

Many of the places Frank had looked at were also physically repulsive in the extreme, including some that had been thrashed by the storm and not entirely cleaned up: the bottom of the barrel, still coated with sludge. The low point in this regard came in one semibasement hole in Alexandria, a tiny dark place barred for safety at the door and the single high window, so that it looked like a prison for troglodytes; and two thousand a month. After that Frank's will to hunt was gone.

Now the day of reckoning had come. He had cleared out and cleaned up, the owner was due home that night, and Frank had nowhere to go.

It was a strange sensation. He sat at the kitchen counter in the dusk, strewn with the various sections of the *Post*. The "Apartments for Rent" section was less than a column long, and Frank had learned enough of its code by now to know that it held nothing for him. More interesting had been an article in the day's Metro section about Rock Creek Park. Officially closed due to severe flood damage, it was apparently too large for the overextended National Park Service to be able to enforce the edict. As a result the park had become something of a no-man's land, "a return to wilderness," as the article had put it.

Frank surveyed the apartment. It held no more memories for him than a hotel room, as he had done nothing but sleep there. That was all he had needed out of a home, his life proper having been put on hold until his return to San Diego. Now, well...it was like some kind of premature resuscitation, on a voyage between the stars. Time to wake up, time to leave the deep freeze and find out where he was.

He got up and went down to his car.

———

Out to the Beltway to circle north and then east, past the elongated Mormon temple and the great overpass graffiti referencing it: GO HOME DOROTHY! Get off on Wisconsin, drive in toward the city. There was no particular reason for him to visit this part of town. Of course the Quiblers lived over here, but that couldn't be it.

He kept thinking: Homeless person, homeless person. You are a homeless person. A song from Paul Simon's *Graceland* came to him, the one where one of the South African groups kept singing, *Homeless; homeless, Da da da, da da da da da da . . .* something like, *Midnight come, and then you wanna go home.* Or maybe it was a Zulu phrase. Or maybe, as he seemed to hear now: *Homeless; homeless; he go down to find another home.*

Something like that. He came to the intersection at the Bethesda Metro stop, and suddenly it occurred to him why he might be there. Of course—this was where he had met the woman in the elevator. They had gotten stuck together coming up from the Metro; alone together underground, minute after minute, until after a long talk they had started kissing, much to Frank's surprise. And then when the repair team had arrived and they were let out, the woman had disappeared without Frank learning anything about her, even her name. It made his heart pound just to remember it. Up there on the sidewalk to the right, beyond the red light—there stood the very elevator box they had emerged from. And then she had appeared to him again, on a boat in the Potomac during the height of the great flood. He had called her boat on his cell phone, and she had answered, had said, "I'll call. I don't know when."

The red light turned green. She had not called and yet here he was, driving back to where they had met as if he might catch sight of her. Maybe he had even been thinking that if he found her, he would have a place to stay.

That was silly: an example of magical thinking at its most unrealistic. And he had to admit that in the past couple of weeks he had been looking for apartments in this area. So it was not just an isolated impulse, but a pattern of behavior.

Just past the intersection he turned into the Hyatt driveway. A valet approached and Frank said, "Do you know if there are any rooms available here?"

"Not if you don't got a reservation."

Frank hurried into the lobby to check anyway. A receptionist shook her head: no vacancies. She wasn't aware of the situation at any other hotel. The ones in their chain were full all over the metropolitan area.

Frank got back in his car and drove onto Wisconsin heading south, peering at the elevator kiosk when he passed it. She had given a fake name on the Metro forms they had been asked to fill out. She would not be there now.

Down Wisconsin, past the Quiblers' house a couple of blocks over to the right. That was what had brought him to this part of town, on the night he and the woman got stuck in the elevator. Anna Quibler, one of his colleagues at NSF, had hosted a party for the Khembali ambassador, who had given a lecture at NSF earlier that day. A nice party. An excess of reason is itself a form of madness, the old ambassador had said to Frank. Frank was still pondering what that meant, and if it were true, how he might act on it.

But he couldn't visit Anna and her family now. Showing up unannounced, with no place to go—it would have been pitiful.

He drove on. *Homeless, homeless—he go down to find another home.*

Chevy Chase looked relatively untouched by the flood. There was a giant hotel above Dupont Circle, the Hilton; he drove down Wisconsin and Massachusetts and turned up Florida to it, already feeling like he was wasting his time. There would be no rooms available.

There weren't. "Homeless, homeless. Midnight come, and blah blah blah blah blahhhh."

He drove up Connecticut Avenue, completely without a

plan. Near the entrance to the National Zoo damage from the flood suddenly became obvious, in the form of a mud-based slurry of trash and branches covering the sidewalks and staining the storefronts. Just north of the zoo, traffic stopped to allow the passage of a backhoe. Street repairs by night, in the usual way. Harsh blue spotlights glared on a scene like something out of Soviet cinema, giant machines dwarfing a cityscape.

Impatiently Frank turned right onto a side street. He found an empty parking spot on one of the residential streets east of Connecticut, parked in it.

He got out and walked back to the clean-up scene. It was still about 90 degrees out, and tropically humid. A strong smell of mud and rotting vegetation evoked the tropics, or Atlantis after the flood. Yes, he was feeling a bit apocalyptic. He was in the end time of something, there was no denying it. *Home-less; home-less.*

A Spanish restaurant caught his eye. He went over to look at the menu in the window. Tapas. He went in, sat down and ordered. Excellent food, as always. D.C. could almost always be relied on for that. Surely it must be the great restaurant city of the world.

He finished his meal, left the restaurant and wandered the streets, feeling better. He had been hungry before, and had mistaken that for anxiety. Things were not so bad.

He passed his car but walked on east toward Rock Creek Park, remembering the article in the *Post*. A return to wilderness.

At Broad Branch Road Frank came to the park's boundary. There was no one visible in any direction. It was dark under the trees on the other side of the road; the yellow streetlights behind him illuminated nothing beyond the first wall of leaves.

He crossed the street and walked into the forest.

———

The flood's vegetable stench was strong. Frank proceeded slowly; if there had been any trail here before it was gone now, replaced by windrows of branches and trash, and an uneven deposition of mud. The rootballs of toppled trees splayed up dimly, and snags caught at his feet. As his eyes adjusted to the darkness he came to feel that everything was very slightly illuminated, mostly no doubt by the luminous city cloud that chinked every gap in the black canopy.

He heard a rustle, then a voice. Without thought he slipped behind a large tree and froze there, heart pounding.

Two voices were arguing, one of them drunk.

"Why you buy this shit?"

"Hey you never buy anything. You need to give some, man."

The two passed by and continued down the slope to the east, their voices rasping through the trees. *Home—less, home—less.* Their voices had reminded Frank of the scruffy guys in fatigues who hung out around Dupont Circle.

Frank didn't want to deal with any such people. He was annoyed; he wanted to be out in a pure wilderness, empty in the way his mountains out west were empty. Instead, harsh laughter nicotined through the trees like hatchet strokes. "Ha ha ha harrrrrr." There went the neighborhood.

He slipped off in a different direction, down through windrows of detritus, then over hardened mud between trees. Branches clicked damply underfoot. It got steeper than he thought it would, and he stepped sideways to keep from slipping.

Then he heard another sound, quieter than the voices. A soft rustle and a creak, then a faint crack from the forest below and ahead. Something moving.

Frank froze. The hair on the back of his neck was standing up. Whatever it was, it sounded big. The article in the *Post* had mentioned that many of the animals from the National Zoo had not yet been recaptured. All had been let loose just before the zoo was inundated, to give them a chance of surviving. Some had drowned anyway; most had been recovered afterward; but not all. Frank couldn't remember if any species in particular had been named in the article as being still at large. It was a big park of course. Possibly a jaguar had been mentioned.

He tried to meld into the tree he was leaning against.

Whatever it was below him snapped a branch just a few trees away. It sniffed; almost a snort. It was big, no doubt about it.

Frank could no longer hold his breath, but he found that if he let his mouth hang open, he could breathe without a sound. The tock of his heartbeat in the soft membrane at the back of his throat must surely be more a feeling than a sound. Most animals relied on scent anyway, and there was nothing he could do about his scent. A thought that could reduce one's muscles to jelly.

The creature had paused. It huffed. A musky odor that wafted by was almost like the smell of the flood detritus. His heart tocked like Captain Hook's alarm clock.

A slow scrape, as of shoulder against bark. Another branch click. A distant car horn. The smell now resembled damp fur. Another crunch of leaf and twig, farther down the slope.

When he heard nothing more, and felt that he was alone again, he beat a retreat uphill and west, back to the streets of the city. It was frustrating, because now he was intrigued, and wanted to explore the park further. But he didn't want to end up one of those urban fools who ignored the reality of wild animals and then got chomped. Whatever that had been down there, it was big. Best to be prudent, and return another time.

After the gloom of the park, all Connecticut seemed as garishly illuminated as the work site down the street. Walking back to his car, Frank thought that the neighborhood resembled one of the more handsome Victorian districts of San

Francisco. It was late now, the night finally cooling off. He could drive all night and never find a room.

He stood before his car. The Honda's passenger seat tilted back like a little recliner. The nearest streetlight was down at the corner.

He opened the passenger door, moved the seat all the way back, lowered it, slipped in and sat down. He closed the door, lay back, stretched out. After a while he turned on his side and fell into an uneasy sleep.

For an hour or two. Then passing footsteps woke him. Anyone could see him if they looked. They might tap the window to see if he was okay. He would have to claim to be a visiting reporter, unable to find a room—very close to the truth, like all the best lies. He could claim to be anyone really. Out here he was not bound to his real story.

He lay awake, uncomfortable in the seat, pretty sure he would not be able to fall back asleep; then he was lightly under, dreaming about the woman in the elevator. A part of his mind became aware that this was unusual, and he fought to stay submerged despite that realization. He was speaking to her about something urgent. Her face was so clear, it had imprinted so vividly: passionate and amused in the elevator, grave and distant on the boat in the flood. He wasn't sure he liked what she was telling him. Just call me, he insisted. Give me that call and we can work it out.

Then the noise of a distant siren hauled him up, sweaty and unhappy. He lay there a while longer, thinking about the woman's face. Once in high school he had made out with a girl in a little car like this one, in which the laid-back seat had allowed them somehow to lie on each other. He wanted her. He wanted to find her. From the boat she had said she would call. I don't know how long, she had said. Maybe that meant long. He would just have to wait. Unless he could figure out some new way to hunt for her.

The sky was lightening. Now he definitely wouldn't be able to fall back asleep.

—————

National Science Foundation, Arlington, Virginia, basement parking lot, seven AM. A primate sitting in his car, thinking things over. As one of the editors of *The Journal of Sociobiology,* Frank was very much aware of the origins of their species. The third chimp, as Diamond had put it. Now he thought: chimps sleep outdoors. Bonobos sleep outdoors.

Housing was ultimately an ergonomic problem. What did he really need? His belongings were here in the car, or upstairs in his office, or in boxes at UCSD, or in storage units in Encinitas, California, or down the road in Arlington, Virginia. The fact that stuff was in storage showed how much it really mattered. By and large he was free of worldly things. At age forty-three he no longer needed them. That felt a little strange, actually, but not necessarily bad. Did it feel good? It was hard to tell. It simply felt strange.

He got out of his car and took the elevator to the third floor, where there was a little exercise room, with a men's room off its entryway that included showers. In his shoulder bag he carried his laptop, his cell phone, his bathroom kit, and a change of clothes. The three shower stalls stood behind white curtains, near an area with benches and lockers. Beyond it extended the room containing toilets, urinals, and a counter of sinks under a long mirror.

Frank knew the place, having showered and changed in it many times after runs at lunch with Edgardo and Kenzo and Bob and the others. Now he surveyed it with a new regard. It was as he remembered: an adequate bathroom, public but serviceable.

He undressed and got in one of the showers. A flood of hot water, almost industrial in quantity, washed away some of the stiffness of his uncomfortable night. Of course no one would want to be seen showering there every day. Not that anyone was watching, but some of the morning exercisers would eventually notice.

A membership in some nearby exercise club would provide an alternative bathroom.

What else did one need?

Somewhere to sleep, of course. The Honda would not suffice. If he had a van, and an exercise club membership, and this locker room, and his office upstairs, and the men's rooms up there... As for food, the city had a million restaurants.

What else?

Nothing he could think of. Many people more or less lived in this building, all the NSF hardcores who spent sixty or seventy hours a week here, ate their meals at their desks or in the neighborhood restaurants, only went home to sleep— and these were people with families, with kids, homes, pets, partners!

In a crowd like that it would be hard to stick out.

He got out of the shower, dried off (a stack of fresh white towels was there at hand), shaved, dressed.

He glanced in the mirror over the sink, feeling a bit shy. He didn't look at himself in mirrors anymore, never met his eye when shaving, stayed focused on the skin under the blade. He didn't know why. Maybe it was because he did not resemble his conception of himself, which was vaguely scientific and serious, say Darwinesque; and yet there in the glass getting shaved was always the same old sun-fried jock.

But this time he looked. To his surprise he saw that he looked normal—that was to say, the same as always. Normative. No one would be able to guess by his appearance that he was sleep-deprived, that he had been thinking some pretty abnormal thoughts, or, crucially, that he had spent the previous night in his car because he no longer had a home.

"Hmm," he told his reflection.

He took the elevator up to the tenth floor, still thinking it over. He stood in the doorway of his new office, evaluating the place by these new inhabitory criteria. It was a true room, rather than a carrel in a larger space, so it had a door he could close. It boasted one of the big inner windows looking into the building's central atrium, giving him a direct view of the big colored mobile that filled the atrium's upper half.

There was room for a short couch against one wall, if he moved the bookcase there to the opposite corner. It would then be like a kind of living room, with the computer as entertainment center. There was an ordinary men's room around the corner, a coffee nook down the hall, the showers downstairs. All the necessities. As Sucandra had remarked, at dinner once at the Quiblers', tasting spaghetti sauce with a wooden spoon: Ahhhh—what now is lacking?

Same answer: Nothing.

It had to be admitted that it made him uneasy to be contemplating this idea. Unsettled. It was deranged, in the literal sense of being outside the range. Typically people did not choose to live without a home. No home to go home to; it was perhaps a little crazy.

But in some obscure way, that aspect pleased him too. It was not crazy in the way that breaking into the building through the skylight had been crazy; but it shared that act's commitment to an idea. And was it any crazier than handing well over half of your monthly take-home income to pay for seriously crappy lodging?

Nomadic existence. Life outdoors. So often he had thought about, read about, and written about the biological imperatives in human behavior—about their primate nature, and the evolutionary history that had led to humanity's Paleolithic lifestyle, which was the suite of behaviors that had caused their brains to balloon as rapidly as they had; and about the residual power of all that in modern life. And all the while, through all that thinking, reading, and writing, he had been sitting at a desk. Living like every other professional worker in America, a brain in a bottle, working with his fingertips or his voice or simply his thoughts alone, distracted sometimes by daydreams about the brief bursts of weekend activity that would get him back into his body again.

That was what was crazy, living like that when he held the beliefs he did.

Now he was considering acting in accordance with his beliefs. Something else he had heard the Khembalis say at the Quiblers, this time Drepung: If you don't act on it, it wasn't a true feeling.

He wanted these to be true feelings. Everything had changed for him on that day he had gone to the Khembali ambassador's talk, and then run into the woman in the elevator, and afterward talked to Drepung at the Quiblers' party, and then, yes, broken into the NSF building and tried to recover his resignation. Everything had changed! Or so it had felt; so it felt still. But for it to be a true feeling, he had to act on it.

Meaning also, as part of all these new behaviors, that he had to meet with Diane Chang, and work with her on coordinating NSF's response to the climate situation that was implicated in the great flood and many other things.

This would be awkward. His letter of resignation, which Diane had never directly acknowledged receiving, was now an acute embarrassment to him. It had been an irrational attempt to burn his bridges, and by all rights he should now be back in San Diego with nothing but the stench of smoke behind him. Instead, Diane appeared to have read the letter and then ignored it, or rather, considered how to use it to play him like a fish, and reel him back into NSF for another year of service. Which she had done very skillfully.

So now he found that he had to stifle a certain amount of resentment as he went up to see her. He had to meet her secretary Laveta's steely eye without flinching; pretend, as the impassive black woman waved him in, that all was normal. No way of telling how much she knew about his situation.

Diane sat behind her desk, talking on the phone. She gestured for him to sit down. Graceful hands. Short, Chinese-American, good-looking in an exotic way, businesslike but friendly. A subtly amused expression on her face when she listened to people, as if pleased to hear their news.

As now, with Frank. Although it could be amusement at his resignation letter, and the way she had jujitsued him into staying at NSF. So hard to tell with Diane; and her manner, though friendly, did not invite personal conversation.

"You're into your new office?" she asked.

"My stuff is, anyway. It'll take a while to sort out."

"Sure. Like everything else these days! What a mess it all is. I have Kenzo and some of his group coming this morning to tell us more about the Gulf Stream."

"Good."

Kenzo and a couple of his colleagues in climate duly appeared. They exchanged hellos, got out laptops, and Kenzo started working the Power Point on Diane's wall screen.

All the data, Kenzo explained, indicated stalls in what he called the "thermohaline circulation." At the north ends of the Gulf Stream, where the water on the surface normally cooled and sank to the floor of the Atlantic before heading back south, a particularly fresh layer on the surface had stalled the downwelling. With nowhere to go, the water in the current farther south had slowed to a halt.

What was more, Kenzo said, just such a stall in the thermohaline circulation had been identified as the primary cause of the abrupt climate change that paleoclimatologists had named the Younger Dryas, a bitter little ice age that had begun about eleven thousand years before the present, and lasted for a few thousand years. The hypothesis was that the Gulf Stream's shutdown, after floods of fresh water coming off the melting ice cap over North America, had meant immediately colder temperatures in Europe and the eastern half of North America. This accounted for the almost unbelievably quick beginning of the Younger Dryas, which analysis of the Greenland ice cores revealed had happened in only three years. Three years, for a major global shift from the worldwide pattern that climatologists called warm-wet, to the worldwide pattern called cool-dry-windy. It was such a radical notion that it had forced climatologists to acknowledge that there must be nonlinear tipping points in the global climate, leading to general acceptance of what was really a new concept in climatology: abrupt climate change.

So, Kenzo continued, fresh water, dumped into the North Atlantic all at once, appeared to block the thermohaline cycle. And nowadays, for the last several years, the Arctic Ocean's winter sea ice had been breaking up into great fleets of icebergs, which then sailed south on currents until they encountered the Gulf Stream's warm water, where they melted. The melting zones for these icebergs, as a map on the next slide made clear, were just above the northern ends of the Gulf Stream, the so-called downwelling areas. Meanwhile the Greenland ice cap and glaciers were also melting much faster than had been normal, and running off both sides of that great island.

"How much fresh water in all that?" Diane asked.

Kenzo shrugged. "The Arctic is about ten million square kilometers. The sea ice lately is about five meters thick. Not all of that drifts into the Atlantic, of course. There was a paper that estimated that about twenty thousand cubic kilometers of fresh water had diluted the Arctic over the past thirty years, but it was plus or minus five thousand cubic kilometers."

"Let's get better parameters on that figure, if we can," Diane said.

"Sure."

They stared at the final slide. The implications tended to stall on the surface of the mind, Frank thought, like the water in the north Atlantic, refusing to gyre down. The whole world, ensconced in a global climate mode called warm and wet, and getting warmer and wetter because of global warming caused by anthropogenically released greenhouse gases, could switch to a global pattern that was cold, dry, and windy. And the last time it happened, it had taken three years.